The BOOKS of The SOUTH

Tales of The BLACK COMPANY

TOR BOOKS BY GLEN COOK

An Ill Fate Marshalling
Reap the East Wind
The Swordbearer
The Tower of Fear

THE BLACK COMPANY

The Black Company (The First Chronicle)
Shadows Linger (The Second Chronicle)
The White Rose (The Third Chronicle)
Shadow Games (The First Book of the South)
Dreams of Steel (The Second Book of the South)
The Silver Spike
Bleak Seasons (Book One of Glittering Stone)
She Is the Darkness (Book Two of Glittering Stone)
Water Sleeps (Book Three of Glittering Stone)
Soldiers Live (Book Four of Glittering Stone)
Chronicles of the Black Company
(Comprising *The Black Company,*
Shadows Linger, and *The White Rose*)
The Books of the South
(Comprising *Shadow Games,*
Dreams of Steel, and *The Silver Spike*)

THE INSTRUMENTALITIES OF THE NIGHT

The Tyranny of the Night
Lord of the Silent Kingdom

THE BOOKS of THE SOUTH
Tales of THE BLACK COMPANY

GLEN COOK

TOR®

A TOM DOHERTY ASSOCIATES BOOK / NEW YORK

THE BOOKS OF THE SOUTH: TALES OF THE BLACK COMPANY

Copyright © 2008 by Glen Cook

Shadow Games, copyright © 1989 by Glen Cook
Dreams of Steel, copyright © 1990 by Glen Cook
The Silver Spike, copyright © 1989 by Glen Cook

A Tor Book
Published by Tom Doherty Associates, LLC
175 Fifth Avenue
New York, NY 10010

www.tor-forge.com

Tor® is a registered trademark of Tom Doherty Associates, LLC.

ISBN-13: 978-0-7653-2066-7
ISBN-10: 0-7653-2066-5

Printed in the United States of America

20   19   18   17   16   15   14

Contents

SHADOW
GAMES

Got to be for Harriet McDougal,
whose gentle hands
guided Croaker and the Company
out of the darkness

With Special Thanks to
Lee Childs of North Hollywood,
for historical research
and valued suggestions

The Crossroads

We seven remained at the crossroads, watching the dust from the eastern way. Even irrepressible One-Eye and Goblin were stricken by the finality of the hour. Otto's horse whickered. He closed her nostrils with one hand, patted her neck with the other, quieting her. It was a time for contemplation, the final emotional milemark of an era.

Then there was no more dust. They were gone. Birds began to sing, so still did we remain. I took an old notebook from my saddlebag, settled in the road. In a shaky hand I wrote: *The end has come. The parting is done. Silent, Darling, and the Torque brothers have taken the road to Lords. The Black Company is no more.*

Yet I will continue to keep the Annals, if only because a habit of twenty-five years is so hard to break. And, who knows? Those to whom I am obliged to carry them may find the account interesting. The heart is stilled but the corpse stumbles on. The Company is dead in fact but not in name.

And we, O merciless gods, stand witness to the power of names.

I replaced the book in my saddlebag. "Well, that's that." I swatted the dust off the back of my lap, peered down our own road into tomorrow. A low line of greening hills formed a fencerow over which sheeplike tufts began to bound. "The quest begins. We have time to cover the first dozen miles."

That would leave only seven or eight thousand more.

I surveyed my companions.

One-Eye was the oldest by a century, a wizard, wrinkled and black as a dusty prune. He wore an eyepatch and a floppy, battered black felt hat. That hat seemed to suffer every conceivable misfortune, yet survived every indignity.

Likewise Otto, a very ordinary man. He had been wounded a hundred times and had survived. He almost believed himself favored of the gods.

Otto's sidekick was Hagop, another man with no special color. But another survivor. My glance surprised a tear.

Then there was Goblin. What is there to say of Goblin? The name says it all, and yet nothing? He was another wizard, small, feisty, forever at odds with One-Eye, without whose enmity he would curl up and die. He was the inventor of the frog-faced grin.

We five have been together twenty-some years. We have grown old together. Perhaps we know one another too well. We form limbs of a dying organism. Last of a mighty, magnificent, storied line. I fear we, who look more like bandits than the best soldiers in the world, denigrate the memory of the Black Company.

Two more. Murgen, whom One-Eye sometimes calls Pup, was twenty-eight. The youngest. He joined the Company after our defection from the empire. He was a quiet man of many sorrows, unspoken, with no one and nothing but the Company to call his own, yet an outside and lonely man even here.

As are we all. As are we all.

Lastly, there was Lady, who used to be the Lady. Lost Lady, beautiful Lady, my fantasy, my terror, more silent than Murgen, but from a different cause: despair. Once she had it all. She gave it up. Now she has nothing.

Nothing she knows to be of value.

That dust on the Lords road was gone, scattered by a chilly breeze. Some of my beloved had departed my life forever.

No sense staying around. "Cinch them up," I said, and set an example. I tested the ties on the pack animals. "Mount up. One-Eye, you take the point."

Finally, a hint of spirit as Goblin carped, "I have to eat *his* dust?" If One-Eye had point that meant Goblin had rearguard. As wizards they were no mountain movers, but they were useful. One fore and one aft left me feeling far more comfortable.

"About his turn, don't you think?"

"Things like that don't deserve a turn," Goblin said. He tried to giggle but only managed a smile that was a ghost of his usual toadlike grin.

One-Eye's answering glower was not much pumpkin, either. He rode out without comment.

Murgen followed fifty yards behind, a twelve-foot lance rigidly upright. Once that lance had flaunted our standard. Now it trailed four feet of tattered black cloth. The symbolism lay on several levels.

We knew who we were. It was best that others did not. The Company had too many enemies.

Hagop and Otto followed Murgen, leading pack animals. Then came Lady and I, also with tethers behind. Goblin trailed us by seventy yards. And thus we always traveled for we were at war with the world. Or maybe it was the other way around.

I might have wished for outriders and scouts, but there was a limit to what seven could accomplish. Two wizards were the next best thing.

We bristled with weaponry. I hoped we looked as easy as a hedgehog does to a fox.

The eastbound road dropped out of sight. I was the only one to look back in hopes Silent had found a vacancy in his heart. But that was a vain fantasy. And I knew it.

In emotional terms we had parted ways with Silent and Darling months ago, on the blood-sodden, hate-drenched battleground of the Barrowland.

A world was saved there, and so much else lost. We will live out our lives wondering about the cost.

Different hearts, different roads.

"Looks like rain, Croaker," Lady said.

Her remark startled me. Not that what she said was not true. It did look like rain. But it was the first observation she had volunteered since that dire day in the north.

Maybe she was going to come around.

The Road South

The farther we come, the more it looks like spring," One-Eye observed. He was in a good mood.

I caught the occasional glint of mischief brewing in Goblin's eyes too, lately. Before long those two would find some excuse to revive their ancient feud. The magical sparks would fly. If nothing else, the rest of us would be entertained.

Even Lady's mood improved, though she spoke little more than before.

"Break's over," I said. "Otto, kill the fire. Goblin. Your point." I stared down the road. Another two weeks and we would be near Charm. I had not yet revealed what we had to do there.

I noticed buzzards circling. Something dead ahead, near the road.

I do not like omens. They make me uncomfortable. Those birds made me uncomfortable.

I gestured. Goblin nodded. "I'll go now," he said. "Stretch it out a bit."

"Right."

Murgen gave him an extra fifty yards. Otto and Hagop gave Murgen additional room. But One-Eye kept pressing up behind Lady and I, rising in his stirrups, trying to keep an eye on Goblin. "Got a bad feeling about that, Croaker," he said. "A bad feeling."

Though Goblin raised no alarm, One-Eye was right. Those doombirds did mark a bad thing.

A fancy coach lay overturned beside the road. Two of its team of four had been killed in the traces, probably because of injuries. Two animals were missing.

Around the coach lay the bodies of six uniformed guards and the driver, and that of one riding horse. Within the coach were a man, a woman, and two small children. All murdered.

"Hagop," I said, "see what you can read from the signs. Lady. Do you know these people? Do you recognize their crest?" I indicated fancywork on the coach door.

"The Falcon of Rail. Proconsul of the empire. But he isn't one of those. He's older, and fat. They might be family."

Hagop told us, "They were headed north. The brigands overtook them." He held up a scrap of dirty cloth. "They didn't get off easy themselves." When I did not respond he drew my attention to the scrap.

"Grey boys," I mused. Grey boys were imperial troops of the northern armies. "Bit out of their territory."

"Deserters," Lady said. "The dissolution has begun."

"Likely." I frowned. I had hoped decay would hold off till we got a running start.

Lady mused, "Three months ago travelling the empire was safe for a virgin alone."

She exaggerated. But not much. Before the struggle in the Barrowland consumed them, great powers called the Taken watched over the provinces and requited unlicensed wickedness swiftly and ferociously. Still, in any land or time, there are those brave or fool enough to test the limits, and others eager to follow their example. That process was accelerating in an empire bereft of its cementing horrors.

I hoped their passing had not yet become a general suspicion. My plans depended on the assumption of old guises.

"Shall we start digging?" Otto asked.

"In a minute," I said. "How long ago did it happen, Hagop?"

"Couple of hours."

"And nobody's been along?"

"Oh, yeah. But they just went around."

"Must be a nice bunch of bandits," One-Eye mused. "If they can get away with leaving bodies laying around."

"Maybe they're supposed to be seen," I said. "Could be they're trying to carve out their own barony."

"Likely," Lady said. "Ride carefully, Croaker."

I raised an eyebrow.

"I don't want to lose you."

One-Eye cackled. I reddened. But it was good to see some life in her.

We buried the bodies but left the coach. Civilized obligation fulfilled, we resumed our journey.

Two hours later Goblin came riding back. Murgen stationed himself where he could be seen on a curve. We were in a forest now, but the road was in good repair, with the woods cleared back from its sides. It was a road upgraded for military traffic.

Goblin said, "There's an inn up ahead. I don't like its feel."

Night would be along soon. We had spent the afternoon planting the dead. "It look alive?" The countryside had gotten strange after the burying. We met no one on the road. The farms near the woods were abandoned.

"Teeming. Twenty people in the inn. Five more in the stables. Thirty horses. Another twenty people out in the woods. Forty more horses penned there. A lot of other livestock, too."

The implications seemed obvious enough. Pass by, or meet trouble head-on?

The debate was brisk. Otto and Hagop said straight in. We had One-Eye and Goblin if it got hairy.

One-Eye and Goblin did not like being put on the spot.

I demanded an advisory vote. Murgen and Lady abstained. Otto and Hagop were for stopping. One-Eye and Goblin eyeballed one another, each waiting for the other to jump so he could come down on the opposite side.

"We go straight at it, then," I said. "These clowns are going to split but still make a majority for . . ." Whereupon the wizards ganged up and voted to jump in just to make a liar out of me.

Three minutes later I caught my first glimpse of the ramshackle inn. A hardcase stood in the doorway, studying Goblin. Another sat in a rickety chair, tilted against the wall, chewing a stick or piece of straw. The man in the doorway withdrew.

Grey boys Hagop had called the bandits whose handiwork we encountered on the road. But grey was the color of uniforms in the territories whence we came. In Forsberger, the most common language in the northern forces, I asked the man in the chair, "Place open for business?"

"Yeah." Chair-sitter's eyes narrowed. He wondered.

"One-Eye. Otto. Hagop. See to the animals." Softly, I asked, "You catching anything, Goblin?"

"Somebody just went out the back. They're on their feet inside. But it don't look like trouble right away."

Chair-sitter did not like us whispering. "How long you reckon on staying?" he asked. I noted a tattoo on one wrist, another giveaway betraying him as an immigrant from the north.

"Just tonight."

"We're crowded, but we'll fit you in somehow." He was a cool one.

Trapdoor spiders, these deserters. The inn was their base, the place where they marked out their victims. But they did their dirt on the road.

Silence reigned inside the inn. We examined the men there as we entered, and a few women who looked badly used. They did not ring true. Wayside inns usually are family-run establishments, infested with kids and old folks and all the oddities in between. None of those were evident. Just hard men and bad women.

There was a large table available near the kitchen door. I seated myself with my back to a wall. Lady plopped down beside me. I sensed her anger. She was not accustomed to being looked at the way these men were looking at her.

She remained beautiful despite road dirt and rags.

I rested a hand upon one of hers, a gesture of restraint rather than of possession.

A plump girl of sixteen with haunted bovine eyes came to ask how many we were, our needs in food and quarters, whether bath water should be heated, how long we meant to tarry, what was the color of our coin. She did it listlessly but right, as though beyond hope, filled only with dread of the cost of doing it wrong.

I intuited her as belonging to the family who rightfully operated the inn.

I tossed her a gold piece. We had plenty, having looted certain imperial treasures before departing the Barrowland. The flicker of the spinning coin sparked a sudden glitter in the eyes of men pretending not to be watching.

One-Eye and the others clumped in, dragged up chairs. The little black man whispered, "There's a big stir out in the woods. They have plans for us." A frog-gish grin yanked at the left corner of his mouth. I gathered he might have plans of his own. He likes to let the bad guys ambush themselves.

"There's plans and plans," I said. "If they are bandits, we'll let them hang themselves."

He wanted to know what I meant. My schemes sometimes got more nasty than his. That is because I lose my sense of humor and just go for maximum dirt.

We rose before dawn. One-Eye and Goblin used a favorite spell to put everyone in the inn into a deep sleep. Then they slipped out to repeat their performance in the woods. The rest of us readied our animals and gear. I had a small skirmish with Lady. She wanted me to do something for the women kept captive by the brigands.

"If I try to right every wrong I run into, I'll never get to Khatovar."

She did not respond. We rode out minutes later.

One-Eye said we were near the end of the forest. "This looks as good a place as any," I said. Murgen, Lady, and I turned into the woods west of the road. Hagop, Otto, and Goblin turned east. One-Eye just turned around and waited.

He was doing nothing apparent. Goblin was busy, too.

"What if they don't come?" Murgen asked.

"Then we guessed wrong. They're not bandits. I'll send them an apology on the wind."

Nothing got said for a while. When next I moved forward to check the road One-Eye was no longer alone. A half-dozen horsemen backed him. My heart twisted. His phantoms were all men I had known, old comrades, long dead.

I retreated, more shaken than I had expected. My emotional state did not improve. Sunlight dropped through the forest canopy to dapple the doubles of more dead friends. They waited with shields and weapons ready, silently, as befit ghosts.

They were not ghosts, really, except in my mind. They were illusions crafted by One-Eye. Across the road Goblin was raising his own shadow legion.

Given time to work, those two were quite the artists.

There was no doubt, now, even who Lady was.

"Hoofbeats," I said, needlessly. "They're coming."

My stomach turned over. Had I bet to an inside straight? Taken too long a shot? If they chose to fight . . . If Goblin or One-Eye faltered . . .

"Too late for debate, Croaker."

I looked at Lady, a glowing memory of what she had been. She was smiling. She knew my mind. How many times had she been there herself, albeit on a grander game board?

The brigands pounded down the aisle formed by the road. And reined in in confusion when they saw One-Eye awaiting them.

I started forward. All through the woods ghost horses moved with me. There was harness noise, brush noise. Nice touch, One-Eye. What you call verisimilitude.

There were twenty-five bandits. They wore ghastly expressions. Their faces went paler still when they spied Lady, when they saw the specter-banner on Murgen's lance.

The Black Company was pretty well known.

Two hundred ghost bows bent. Fifty hands tried to find some sky-belly to grab. "I suggest you dismount and disarm," I told their captain. He gulped air a few times, considered the odds, did as directed. "Now clear away from the horses. You naughty boys."

They moved. Lady made a gesture. The horses all turned and trotted toward Goblin, who was their real motivator. He let the animals pass. They would return to the inn, to proclaim the terror ended.

Slick. Oh, slick. Not even a hangnail. That was the way we did it in the old days. Maneuver and trickery. Why get yourself hurt if you can whip them with a shuffle and con?

We got the prisoners into a rope coffle where they could be adequately controlled, then headed south. The brigands were greatly exercised when Goblin and One-Eye relaxed. They didn't think it was fair of us.

Two days later we reached Vest. With One-Eye and Goblin again supporting her grand illusion, Lady remanded the deserters to the justice of the garrison commander. We only had to kill two of them to get them there.

Something of a distraction along the road. Now there was none, and Charm drew closer by the hour. I had to face the fact that trouble beckoned.

The bulk of the Annals, which my companions believed to be in my possession, remained in Imperial hands. They had been captured at Queen's Bridge, an old defeat that still stings. I was promised their return shortly before the crisis in the Barrowland. But that crisis prevented their delivery. Afterward, there was nothing to do but go fetch them myself.

A Tavern in Taglios

Willow scrunched a little more comfortably into his chair. The girls giggled and dared one another to touch his cornsilk hair. The one with the most promising eyes reached, ran her fingers down its length. Willow looked across the room, winked at Cordy Mather.

This was the life—till their fathers and brothers got wise. This was every man's dream—with the same old lethal risks a-sneaking. If it kept on, and did not catch up, he'd soon weigh four hundred pounds and be the happiest slug in Taglios.

Who would have thought it? A simple tavern in a straitlaced burg like this. A hole in the wall like those that graced every other street corner back home, here such a novelty they couldn't help getting rich. If the priests didn't get over their inertia and shove a stick into the spokes.

Of course, it helped them being exotic outlanders that the whole city wanted to see. Even those priests. And their little chickies. Especially their little brown daughters.

A long, insane journey getting here, but worth every dreadful step now.

He folded his hands upon his chest and let the girls take what liberties they wanted. He could handle it. He could put up with it.

He watched Cordy tap another barrel of the bitter, third-rate green beer he'd brewed. These Taglian fools paid three times what it was worth. What kind of a place never ran into beer before? Hell. The kind of place guys with no special talents and itchy feet dream of finding.

Cordy brought a mug over. He said, "Swan, this keeps on, we're going to have to hire somebody to help me brew. We're going to be tapped out in a couple days."

"Why worry? How long can it last? Those priest characters are starting to smolder now. They're going to start looking for some excuse to shut us down. Worry about finding another racket as sweet, not about making more beer faster. What?"

"What do you mean, what?"

"You got a grim look all of a sudden."

"The blackbird of doom just walked in the front door."

Willow twisted so he could see that end of the room. Sure enough, Blade had come home. Tall, lean, ebony, head shaved to a polish, muscles rippling with the slightest movement, he looked like some kind of gleaming statue. He looked around without approval. Then he strode to Willow's table, took a seat. The girls gave him the eye. He was as exotic as Willow Swan.

"Come to collect your share and tell us how lousy we are, corrupting these children?" Willow asked.

Blade shook his head. "That old spook Smoke's having dreams again. The Woman wants you."

"Shit." Swan dropped his feet to the floor. Here was the fly in the ointment. The Woman wouldn't leave them alone. "What is it this time? What's he doing? Hemp?"

"He's a wizard. He don't need to do nothing to get obnoxious."

"Shit," Swan said again. "What do you think, we just do a fade-out here? Sell the rest of Cordy's rat piss and head back up the river?"

A big, slow grin spread across Blade's face. "Too late, boy. You been chosen. You can't run fast enough. That Smoke, he might be a joke if he was to open shop up where you came from, but around here he's the bad boss spook pusher. You try to head out, you're going to find your toes tied in knots."

"That the official word?"

"They didn't say it that way. That's what they meant."

"So what did he dream this time? Why drag us in?"

"Shadowmasters. More Shadowmasters. Been a big meet at Shadowcatch, he says. They're going to stop talking and start doing. He says Moonshadow got the call. Says we'll be seeing them in Taglian territory real soon now."

"Big deal. Been trying to sell us that since the day we got here, practically."

Blade's face lost all its humor. "It was different this time, man. There's scared and scared, you know what I mean? And Smoke and the Woman was the second kind this time. And it ain't just Shadowmasters they got on the brain now. Said to tell you the Black Company is coming. Said you'd know what that means."

Swan grunted as if hit in the stomach. He stood, drained the beer Cordy had brought, looked around as if unable to believe what he saw. "Damnedfoolest thing I ever heard, Blade. The Black Company? Coming here?"

"Said that's what's got the Shadowmasters riled, Willow. Said they're rattled good. This's the last free country north of them, under the river. And you know what's on the other side of Shadowcatch."

"I don't believe it. You know how far they'd have to come?"

"About as far as you and Cordy." Blade had joined Willow and Cordwood Mather two thousand miles into their journey south.

"Yeah. You tell me, Blade. Who in the hell besides you and me and Cordy would be crazy enough to travel that far without any reason?"

"They got a reason. According to Smoke."

"Like what?"

"I don't know. You go up there like the Woman says. Maybe she'll tell you."

"I'll go. We'll all go. Just to stall. And first chance we get we're going to get the hell out of Taglios. If they got the Shadowmasters stirred up down there, and the Black Company coming in, I don't want to be anywhere around."

Blade leaned back so one of the girls could wiggle in closer. His expression was questioning.

Swan said, "I seen what those bastards could do back home. I saw Roses caught between them and . . . Hell. Just take my word for it, Blade. Big mojo, and all bad. If they're coming for real, and we're still around when they show, you might end up wishing we'd let those crocs go ahead and snack on you."

Blade never had been too clear on why he had been thrown to the crocodiles. And Willow was none too clear on why he had talked Cordy into dragging him out and taking him along. Though Blade had been a right enough guy since. He'd paid back the debt.

"I think you ought to help them, Swan," Blade said. "I like this town. I like the people. Only thing wrong with them is they don't have sense enough to burn all the temples down."

"Damnit, Blade, I ain't the guy can help."

"You and Cordy are the only ones around who know anything about soldiering."

"I was in the army for two months. I never even learned how to keep in step. And Cordy don't have the stomach for it anymore. All he wants is to forget that part of his life."

Cordy had overheard most of what had been said. He came over. "I'm not that bad off, Willow. I don't object to soldiering when the cause is right. I just was with the wrong bunch up there. I'm with Blade. I like Taglios. I like the people. I'm willing to do what I can to see they don't get worked over by the Shadowmasters."

"You heard what he said? The Black Company?"

"I heard. I also heard him say they want to talk about it. I think we ought to go find out what's going on before we run our mouths and say what we're not going to do."

"All right. I'm going to change. Hold the fort, and all that, Blade. Keep your mitts off the one in the red. I got first dibs." He stalked off.

Cordy Mather grinned. "You're catching on how to handle Willow, Blade."

"If this's going down the way I think, he don't need handling. He'll be the guy out front when they try to stop the Shadowmasters. You could roast him in coals and he'd never admit it, but he's got a thing for Taglios."

Cordy Mather chuckled. "You're right. He's finally found him a home. And no one is going to move him out. Not the Shadowmasters *or* the Black Company."

"They as bad as he lets on?"

"Worse. Lots worse. You take all the legends you ever heard back home, and everything you heard tell around here, and anything you can imagine, and double it, and maybe you're getting close. They're mean and they're tough and they're good. And maybe the worst thing about them is that they're tricky like you can't imagine tricky. They've been around four, five hundred years, and no outfit lasts that long without being so damned nasty even the gods don't screw with them."

"Mothers, hide your babies," Blade said. "Smoke had him a dream."

Cordy's face darkened. "Yeah. I've heard tell wizards maybe make things come true by dreaming them first. Maybe we ought to cut Smoke's throat."

Willow was back. He said, "Maybe we ought to find out what's going on before we do anything."

Cordy chuckled. Blade grinned. Then they began shooing the marks out of the tavern—each making sure an appointment was understood by one or more of the young ladies.

The Dark Tower

I piddled around another five days before working myself up to a little after-breakfast skull session. I introduced the subject in a golden-tongued blurt: "Our next stopover will be the Tower."

"What?"

"Are you crazy, Croaker?"

"Knew we should have kept an eye on him after the sun went down." Knowing glances Lady's way. She stayed out of it.

"I thought *she* was going with *us*. Not the other way around."

Only Murgen did not snap up a membership in the bitch-of-the-minute club. Good lad, that Murgen.

Lady, of course, already knew a stopover was needed.

"I'm serious, guys," I said.

If I wanted to be serious, One-Eye would be, too. "Why?" he asked.

I sort of shrank. "To pick up the Annals I left behind at Queen's Bridge." We got caught good, there. Only because we were the best, and desperate, and sneaky, had we been able to crack the imperial encirclement. At the cost of half the Company. There were more important concerns at the time than books.

"I thought you already got them."

"I asked for them and was told I could have them. But we were busy at the time. Remember? The Dominator? The Limper? Toadkiller Dog? All that lot? There wasn't any chance to actually lay hands on them."

Lady supported me with a nod. Getting really into the spirit, there.

Goblin pasted on his most ferocious face. Made him look like a saber-toothed toad. "Then you knew about this clean back before we ever left the Barrowland."

I admitted that that was true.

"You goatfu—lover. I bet you've spent all this time concocting some half-assed off-the-wall plan that's guaranteed to get us all killed."

I confessed that that was mostly true, too. "We're going to ride up there like we own the Tower. You're going to make the garrison think Lady is still number one."

One-Eye snorted, stomped off to the horses. Goblin got up and stared down at me. And stared some more. And sneered. "We're just going to strut in and snatch them, eh? Like the Old Man used to say, audacity and more audacity." He did not ask his real question.

Lady answered it for him, anyway. "I gave my word."

Goblin did not mouth the next question, either. No one did. And Lady left it hanging.

It would be easy for her to job us. She could keep her word and have us for breakfast afterward. If she wanted.

My plan (sic), boiled down, depended entirely on my trust in her. It was a trust my comrades did not share.

But they do, however foolishly, trust *me*.

T he Tower at Charm is the largest single construction in the world, a feature-less black cube five hundred feet to the dimension. It was the first project undertaken by the Lady and the Taken after their return from the grave, so many lifetimes ago. From the Tower the Taken had marched forth, and raised their armies, and conquered half the world. Its shadow still fell upon half the earth, for few knew that the heart and blood of the empire had been sacrificed to buy victory over a power older and darker still.

There is but one ground-level entrance to the Tower. The road leading to it runs as straight as a geometrician's dream. It passes through parklike grounds that only someone who had been there could believe was the site of history's bloodiest battle.

I had been there. I remembered.

Goblin and One-Eye and Hagop and Otto remembered, too. Most of all, One-Eye remembered. It was on this plain that he destroyed the monster that had murdered his brother.

I recalled the crash and tumult, the screams and terrors, the horrors wrought by wizards at war, and not for the first time I wondered, "Did they really all die here? They went so easily."

"Who you talking about?" One-Eye demanded. He did not need to concentrate on keeping Lady englamored.

"The Taken. Sometimes I think about how hard it was to get rid of the Limper. Then I wonder how so many Taken could have gone down so easy, a whole bunch in a couple days, almost never where I could see it. So sometimes I get to suspecting there was maybe some faking and two or three are still around somewhere."

Goblin squeaked, "But they had six different plots going, Croaker. They was all backstabbing each other."

"But I only *saw* a couple of them check out. None of you guys *saw* the others go. You heard about it. Maybe there was one more plot behind all the other plots. Maybe . . ."

Lady gave me an odd, almost speculative look, like maybe she had not thought much about it herself and did not like the ideas I stirred now.

"They died dead enough for me, Croaker," One-Eye said. "I saw plenty of bodies. Look over there. Their graves are marked."

"That don't mean there's anybody in them. Raven died on us twice. Turn around and there he was again. On the hoof."

Lady said, "You have my permission to dig them up if you like, Croaker."

A glance showed me she was chiding me gently. Maybe even teasing. "That's all right. Maybe someday when I'm good and bored and got nothing better to do than look at rotten corpses."

"Gah!" Murgen said. "Can't you guys talk about something else?" Which was a mistake.

Otto laughed. Hagop started humming. To his tune Otto sang, "The worms crawl in, the worms crawl out, the ants play the bagpipes on your snout." Goblin and One-Eye joined in. Murgen threatened to ride over and puke on somebody.

We were distracting ourselves from the dark promise looming ahead.

One-Eye stopped singing to say, "None of the Taken were the sort who could lie low all these years, Croaker. If any survived we would have seen the fireworks. Me and Goblin would have heard something, anyway."

"I guess you're right." But I did not feel reassured. Maybe some part of me just did not want the Taken to be all dead.

We were approaching the incline that led up to the doorway into the Tower. For the first time the structure betrayed signs of life. Men clad as brightly as peacocks appeared on the high battlements. A handful came out of the gateway, hastily preparing a ceremonial in greeting to their mistress. One-Eye hooted derisively when he saw their apparel.

He would not have dared last time he was there.

I leaned over and whispered, "Be careful. She designed the uniforms on them guys."

I hoped they wanted to greet the Lady, hoped they had nothing more sinister in mind. That depended on what news they had had from the north. Sometimes evil rumors travel swifter than the wind.

"Audacity, guys," I said. "Always audacity. Be bold. Be arrogant. Keep them reeling." I looked at that dark entrance and reflected aloud, "They know me here."

"That's what scares me," Goblin squeaked. Then he cackled.

The Tower filled more and more of the world. Murgen, who'd never seen it before, surrendered to openmouthed awe. Otto and Hagop pretended that that stone pile did not impress them. Goblin and One-Eye became too busy to pay much attention. Lady could not be impressed. She had built the place when she was someone both greater and smaller than the person she was now.

I became totally involved in creating the persona I wanted to project. I recognized the colonel in charge of the welcoming party. We had crossed paths when my fortunes had led me into the Tower before. Our feelings toward one another were ambiguous at best.

He recognized me, too. And he was baffled. The Lady and I had left the Tower together, most of a year ago.

"How you doing, Colonel?" I asked, putting on a big, friendly grin. "We finally made it back. Mission successful."

He glanced at Lady. I did the same, from the edge of my eye. Now was her chance.

She had on her most arrogant face. I could have sworn she was the devil who haunted this Tower—Well, she was. Once. That person did not die when she lost her powers. Did she?

It looked like she would play my game. I sighed, closed my eyes momentarily, while the Tower Guard welcomed their liege.

I trusted her. But always there are reservations. You cannot predict other people. Especially not the hopeless.

Always there was the chance she might reassume the empire, hiding in her secret part of the Tower, letting her minions believe she was unchanged. There was nothing to stop her trying.

She could go that route even after keeping her promise to return the Annals.

That, my companions believed, was what she would do. And they dreaded her first order as empress of shadow restored.

Chains of Empire

Lady kept her promise. I had the Annals in hand within hours of entering the Tower, while its denizens were still overawed by her return. But . . .

"I want to go on with you, Croaker." This while we watched the sun set from the Tower's battlements the second evening after our arrival.

I, of course, replied with the golden tongue of a horse seller. "Uh . . . Uh . . . But . . ." Like that. Master of the glib and facile remark. Why the hell did she want to do that? She had it all, there in the Tower. A little careful faking and she could spend the rest of her natural life as the most powerful being in the world. Why go riding off with a band of tired old men, who did not know where they were going or why, only that they had to keep moving lest something—their consciences, maybe—caught them up?

"There's nothing here for me anymore," she said. As if that explained anything. "I want . . . I just want to find out what it's like to be ordinary people."

"You wouldn't like it. Not near as much as you like being the Lady."

"But I never liked that very much. Not after I had it and found out what I really had. You won't tell me I can't go, will you?"

Was she kidding? No. I would not. It had been the surface understanding, anyway. But it was an understanding I expected to perish once she reestablished herself in the Tower.

I was disconcerted by the implications.

"Can I go?"

"If that's what you want."

"There's a problem."

Isn't there always if there's a woman involved?

"I can't leave right now. Things have gotten confused here. I need a few days to straighten them out. So I can leave with a clear conscience."

We had not encountered any of the troubles I expected. None of her people dared scrutinize her closely. All the labors of One-Eye and Goblin were wasted effort with that audience. The word was out: the Lady was at the helm again. The Black Company was in the fold once more, under her protection. And that was enough for her people.

Wonderful. But Opal was only a few weeks away. From Opal it was a short passage over the Sea of Torments to ports outside the empire. I thought. I wanted to get out while our luck was holding.

"You understand, don't you, Croaker? It'll only be a few days. Honest. Just long enough to shape things up. The empire is a good machine that works smooth as long as the proconsuls are sure someone is in charge."

"All right. All right. We can last a couple days. As long as you keep people away. And you keep out of the way yourself, most of the time. Don't let them get too good a look at you."

"I don't intend to. Croaker?"

"Yeah?"

"Go teach your grandmother to suck eggs."

Startled, I laughed. She kept getting more human all the time. And more able to laugh at herself.

She had good intentions. But he—or she—who would rule an empire becomes slave to its administrative detail. A few days came and went. And a few more. And a few more still.

I could entertain myself skulking around the Tower's libraries, digging into rare texts from the Domination or before, unravelling the snarled threads of northern history, but for the rest of the guys it was rough. There was nothing for them to do but try to keep out of sight and worry. And bait Goblin and One-Eye, though they did not have much luck with that. To those of us without talent the Tower was just a big dark pile of rock, but to those two it was a great throbbing engine of sorcery, still peopled by numerous practitioners of the dark arts. They lived every moment in dread.

One-Eye handled it better than Goblin. He managed to escape occasionally, going out to the old battlefield to prowl among his memories. Sometimes I joined him, halfway tempted to take up Lady's invitation to open a few old graves.

"Still not comfortable about what happened?" One-Eye asked one afternoon, as I stood leaning on a bowstave over a marker bearing the name and sigil of the Taken who had been called the Faceless Man. One-Eye's tone was as serious as it ever gets.

"Not entirely," I admitted. "I can't pin it down, and it don't matter much now, but when you reflect on what happened here, it don't add up. I mean, it did at the time. It all looked like it was inevitable. A great kill-off that rid the world of a skillion Rebels and most of the Taken, leaving the Lady a free hand and setting her up for the Dominator at the same time. But in the context of later events . . ."

One-Eye had started to stroll, pulling me along in his wake. He came to a place that was not marked at all, except in his memory. A thing called a forvalaka had perished there. A thing that had slaughtered his brother—maybe—way back in the days when we first became involved with Soulcatcher, the Lady's legate to Beryl. The forvalaka was a sort of vampirous wereleopard originally native to One-Eye's own home jungle, somewhere way down south. It had taken One-Eye a year to catch up with and have his revenge upon this one.

"You're thinking about how hard it was to get rid of the Limper," he said. His voice was thoughtful. I knew he was recalling something I thought he had put out of mind.

We were never certain that the forvalaka which killed Tom-Tom was the forvalaka that paid the price. Because in those days the Taken Soulcatcher worked closely with another Taken called Shapeshifter and there was evidence to suggest Shifter might have been in Beryl that night. And using the forvalaka shape to assure the destruction of the ruling family so the empire could take over on the cheap.

If One-Eye had not avenged Tom-Tom on the right creature it was far too late for tears. Shifter was another of the victims of the Battle at Charm.

"I'm thinking about Limper," I admitted. "I killed him at that inn, One-Eye. I killed him good. And if he hadn't turned up again, I'd never have doubted that he was gone."

"And no doubts about these?"

"Some."

"You want to sneak out after dark and dig one of them up?"

"What's the point? There'll be somebody in the grave, and no way to prove it isn't who it's supposed to be."

"They were killed by other Taken and by members of the Circle. That's a little different than getting worked on by a no-talent like you."

He meant no talent for sorcery. "I know. That's what keeps me from getting obsessed with the whole mess. Knowing that those who supposedly killed them really had the power to do them in."

One-Eye stared at the ground where once a cross stood with the forvalaka nailed upon it. After a while he shivered and came back to now. "Well, it doesn't matter now. It was long ago, if not very far away. And far away is where we'll be if we ever get out of here." He pulled his floppy black hat forward to keep the sun out of his eyes, looked up at the Tower. We were being watched.

"Why does she want to go with us? That's the one I keep coming back to. What's in this for her?"

One-Eye looked at me with the oddest expression. He pushed his hat back, put his hands on his hips, cocked his head a moment, then shook it slowly. "Croaker. Sometimes you're too much to be believed. Why are you hanging around here waiting for her instead of heading out, putting miles behind?"

It was a good question and one I shied off anytime I tried to examine it. "Well, I guess I kind of like her and think she deserves a shot at some kind of regular life. She's all right. Really."

I caught a transient smirk as he turned to the unmarked grave. "Life wouldn't be half fun without you in it, Croaker. Watching you bumble through is an education in itself. How soon can we get moving? I don't like this place."

"I don't know. A few more days. There're things she has to wrap up first."

"That's what you said—"

I am afraid I got snappish. "I'll let you know when."

When seemed never to come. Days passed. Lady remained ensnared in the web of the administrative spider.

Then the messages began pouring in from the provinces, in response to edicts from the Tower. Each one demanded immediate attention.

We had been closed up in that dread place for two weeks.

"Get us the hell out of here, Croaker," One-Eye demanded. "My nerves can't take this place anymore."

"Look, there's stuff she's got to do."

"There's stuff we've got to do, according to you. Who says what we got to do has to wait on what she's got to do?"

And Goblin jumped on me. With both feet. "We put up with your infatuation for about twenty years, Croaker," he exaggerated. "Because it was amusing. Something to ride you about when times got boring. But it ain't nothing I mean to get killed over, I absodamnlutely guarantee. Even if she makes us all field marshals."

I warded a flash of anger. It was hard, but Goblin was right. I had no business hanging around there, keeping everyone at maximum risk. The longer we waited, the more certain it was that something would go sour. We were having enough trouble getting along with the Tower Guards, who resented our being so close to their mistress after having fought against her for so many years.

"We ride out in the morning," I said. "My apologies. I was elected to lead the Company, not just Croaker. Forgive me for losing sight of that."

Crafty old Croaker. One-Eye and Goblin looked properly abashed. I grinned. "So go get packed. We're gone with the morning sun."

She wakened me in the night. For a moment I thought . . .
    I saw her face. She had heard.

She begged me to stay just one more day. Or two, at the most. She did not want to be here any more than we did, surrounded and taunted by all that she had lost. She wanted to go away, to go with us, to remain with me, the only friend she'd ever had—

She broke my heart.

It sounds sappy when you write it down in words, but a man has to do what a man has to do. In a way I was proud of me. I did not give an inch.

"There is no end to it," I told her. "There'll always be just one more thing that has to be done. Khatovar gets no closer while I wait. Death does. I value you, too. I don't want to leave . . . Death lurks in every shadow in this place. It writhes in the heart of every man who resents my influence." It was that kind of empire too, and in the past few days a lot of old imperials were given cause to resent me deeply.

"You promised me dinner at the Gardens in Opal."

I promised you a lot more than that, my heart said. Aloud, I replied, "So I did. And the offer still stands. But I have to get my men out of here."

I turned reflective while she turned uncharacteristically nervous. I saw the fires of schemes flickering behind her eyes, being rejected. There were ways she could manipulate me. We both knew that. But she never used the personal to gain political ends. Not with me, anyway.

I guess each of us, at some time, finds one person with whom we are compelled toward absolute honesty, one person whose good opinion of us becomes a substitute for the broader opinion of the world. And that opinion becomes more important than all our sneaky, sleazy schemes of greed, lust, self-aggrandizement, whatever we are up to while lying the world into believing we are just plain nice folks. I was her truth object, and she was mine.

There was only one thing we hid from one another, and that was because we were afraid that if it came into the open it would reshape everything else and maybe shatter that broader honesty.

Are lovers *ever* honest?

"I figure it'll take us three weeks to reach Opal. It'll take another week to find a trustworthy shipmaster and to work One-Eye up to crossing the Sea of Torments. So twenty-five days from today I'll go to the Gardens. I'll have the Camelia Grotto reserved for the evening." I patted the lump next to my heart. That lump was a beautifully tooled leather wallet containing papers commissioning me a general in the imperial armed forces and naming me a diplomatic legate answerable only to the Lady herself.

Precious, precious. And one good reason some longtime imperials had a big hate on for me.

I am not sure just how that came about. Some banter during one of those rare hours when she was not issuing decrees or signing proclamations. Next thing I knew I had been brought to bay by a pack of tailors. They fitted me out with a complete imperial wardrobe. Never will I unravel the significance of all the piping, badges, buttons, medals, doodads, and gewgaws. I felt silly wearing all that clutter.

I didn't need much time to see some possibilities, though, in what at first I interpreted as an elaborate practical joke.

She does have that kind of sense of humor, not always taking this great dreadfully humorless empire of hers seriously.

I am sure she saw the possibilities long before I did.

Anyway, we were talking the Gardens in Opal, and the Camelia Grotto there, the acme of that city's society see-and-be-seen. "I'll take my evening meal there," I told her. "You're welcome to join me."

Hints of hidden things tugged at her face. She said, "All right. If I'm in town."

It was one of those moments in which I become very uncomfortable. One of those times when nothing you say can be right, and almost anything you do say is wrong. I could see no answer but the classic Croaker approach.

I began to back away.

That is how I handle my women. Duck for cover when they get distressed.

I almost made it to the door.

She could move when she wanted. She crossed the gap and put her arms around me, rested a cheek against my chest.

And that is how they handle me, the sentimental fool. The closet romantic. I mean, I don't even have to know them. They can work that one on me. When they really want to drill me they turn on the water.

I held her till she was ready to be let go. We did not look at one another as I turned and went away. So. She hadn't gone for the heavy artillery.

She played fair, mostly. Give her that. Even when she was the Lady. Slick, tricky, but more or less fair.

The job of legate comes with all sorts of rights to subinfeudation and plunder of the treasury. I had drafted that pack of tailors and turned them loose on the men. I handed out commissions. I waved my magic wand and One-Eye and Goblin became colonels. Hagop and Otto turned into captains. I even cast a glamor on Murgen, so that he looked like a lieutenant. I drew us all three months' pay in advance. It all boggled the others. I think one reason One-Eye was anxious to get moving was an eagerness to get off somewhere where he could abuse his newfound privileges. For the time being, though, he mostly bickered with Goblin about whose commission carried the greater seniority. Those two never once questioned our shift in fortunes.

The weirdest part was when she called me in to present my commissions, and insisted on a real name to enter into the record. It took me a while to remember what my name was.

We rode out as threatened. Only we did not do it as the ragged band that rode in.

I travelled in a black iron coach drawn by six raging black stallions, with Murgen driving and Otto and Hagop riding as guards. With a string of saddle horses trailing behind. One-Eye and Goblin, disdaining the coach, rode before and behind upon mounts as fey and magnificent as the beasts which pulled the coach. With twenty-six Horse Guards as escort.

The horses she gave us were of a wild and wonderful breed, hitherto given only to the greatest champions of her empire. I had ridden one once, long ago, during the Battle at Charm, when she and I had chased down Soulcatcher. They could run forever without tiring. They were magical beasts. They constituted a gift precious beyond belief.

How do these weird things happen to me?

A year earlier I was living in a hole in the ground, under that boil on the butt of the world, the Plain of Fear, with fifty other men, constantly afraid we would be discovered by the empire. I had not had new or clean clothing in a decade, and baths and shaves were as rare and dear as diamonds.

Lying opposite me in that coach was a black bow, the first gift she ever gave me, so many years ago, before the Company deserted her. It was precious in its own right.

How the wheel turns.

Opal

Hagop stared as I finished primping. "Gods. You really *look* the part, Croaker."

Otto said, "Amazing what a bath and a shave will do. I believe the word is 'distinguished.'"

"Looks like a supernatural miracle to me, Ott."

"Be sarcastic, you guys."

"I mean it," Otto said. "You do look good. If you had a little rug to cover where your hairline is running back toward your butt . . ."

He did mean it. "Well, then," I mumbled, uncomfortable. I changed the subject. "I meant what I said. Keep those two in line." In town only four days and already I'd bailed Goblin and One-Eye out of trouble twice. There was a limit to what even a legate could cover, hush, and smooth over.

"There's only three of us, Croaker," Hagop protested. "What do you want? They don't want to be kept in line."

"I know you guys. You'll think of something. While you're at it, get this junk packed up. It has to go down to the ship."

"Yes sir, your grand legateship, sir."

I was about to deliver one of my fiery, witty, withering rejoinders when Murgen stuck his head into the room and said, "The coach is ready, Croaker."

And Hagop wondered aloud, "How do we keep them in line when we don't even know where they are? Nobody's seen them since lunchtime."

I went out to the coach hoping I would not get an ulcer before I got out of the empire.

We roared through Opal's streets, my escort of Horse Guards, my black stallions, my ringing black iron coach, and I. Sparks flew around the horses' hooves and the coach's steel wheels. Dramatic, but riding in that metal monster was like being locked inside a steel box that was being enthusiastically pounded by vandalistic giants.

We swept up to the Gardens' understated gate, scattering gawkers. I stepped down, stood more stiffly erect than was my wont, made an effete gesture of dismissal copied from some prince seen somewhere along life's twisted way. I strode through the gate, thrown open in haste.

I marched back to the Camelia Grotto, hoping ancient memory would not betray me. Gardens employees yapped at my heels. I ignored them.

My way took me past a pond so smooth and silvery its surface formed a mirror. I halted, mouth dropping open.

I did, indeed, cut an imposing figure, cleaned up and dressed up. But were my eyes two eggs of fire, and my open mouth a glowing furnace? "I'll strangle those two in their sleep," I murmured.

Worse than the fire, I had a shadow, a barely perceptible specter, behind me. It hinted that the legate was but an illusion cast by something darker.

Damn those two and their practical jokes.

When I resumed moving I noted that the Gardens were packed but silent. The guests all watched me.

I had heard that the Gardens were not as popular as once they had been.

They were there to see me. Of course. The new general. The unknown legate out of the dark tower. The wolves wanted a look at the tiger.

I should have expected it. The escort. They had had four days to tell tales around town.

I turned on all the outward arrogance I could muster. And inside I echoed to the whimper of a kid with stage fright.

I settled in in the Camelia Grotto, out of sight of the crowd. Shadows played about me. The staff came to enquire after my needs. They were revolting in their obsequiousness.

A disgusting little part of me gobbled it up. A part just big enough to show why some men lust after power. But not for me, thank you. I am too lazy. And I am, I fear, the unfortunate victim of a sense of responsibility. Put me in charge and I try to accomplish the ends to which the office was allegedly created. I guess I suffer from an impoverishment of the sociopathic spirit necessary to go big time.

How do you do the show, with the multiple-course meal, when you are accustomed to patronizing places where you take whatever is in the pot or starve? Craft. Take advantage of the covey hovering about, fearful I might devour *them* if not pleased. Ask this, ask that, use a physician's habitual intuition for the hinted and implied, and I had it whipped. I sent them to the kitchens with instructions to be in no haste, for a companion might join me later.

Not that I expected Lady. I was going through the motions. I meant to keep my date without its other half.

Other guests kept finding excuses to pass by and look at the new man. I began to wish I had brought my escort along.

There was a rolling rumble like the sound of distant thunder, then a hammerclap close at hand. A wave of chatter ran through the Gardens, followed by grave-dead silence. Then the silence gave way to the rhythm of steel-tapped heels falling in unison.

I did not believe it. Even as I rose to greet her, I did not believe it.

Tower Guards hove into view, halted, parted. Goblin came hup-two-threeing between them, strutting like a drum major, looking like his namesake freshly scrounged from some especially fiery Hell. He glowed. He trailed a fiery mist which evaporated a few yards behind him. He stepped down into the Grotto and gave the place the fish-eye, and me a wink. He then marched up the farside steps and posted himself facing outward.

What the hell were they up to now? Expanding on their already overburdened practical joke?

Then Lady appeared, as fell and as radiant as fantasy, as beautiful as a dream. I clicked my heels and bowed. She descended to join me. She *was* a vision. She extended a hand. My manners did not desert me, despite all the hard years.

Wouldn't this give Opal fuel for gossip?

One-Eye followed Lady down, wreathed in dark mists through which crawled shadows with eyes. He inspected the Grotto, too.

As he turned to go back the way he had come, I said, "I'm going to incinerate that hat." Tricked out like a lord, he was, but still wearing his ragpicker's hat.

He grinned, assumed his post.

"Have you ordered?" Lady asked.

"Yes. But only for one."

A small horde of staff tumbled past One-Eye, terrified. The master of the Gardens himself drove them. If they had been fawning with me, they were downright disgusting with Lady. *I* have never been that impressed with anyone in any position of power.

It was a long, slow meal, undertaken mostly in silence, with me sending unanswered puzzled glances across the table. A memorable dining experience for me, though Lady hinted that she had known better.

The problem was, we were too much on stage to take any real enjoyment from it. Not only for the crowd, but for one another.

Along the way I admitted I had not expected her to appear, and she said my storming out of the Tower made her realize that if she did not just drop everything and go she would not shake the tentacles of imperial responsibility till someone freed her by murdering her.

"So you just walked? The place will be coming apart."

"No. I left certain safeguards in place. I delegated powers to people whose judgment I trust, in such fashion that the empire will accrete to them gradually, and become theirs solidly before they realize that I've deserted."

"I hope so." I am a charter member of that philosophical school which believes that if anything can go sour, it will.

"It won't matter to us, will it? We'll be well out of range."

"Morally, it matters, if half a continent is thrown into civil war."

"I think I have made sufficient moral sacrifice." A cold wind overswept me. Why can't I keep my big damned mouth shut?

"Sorry," I said. "You're right. I didn't think."

"Apology accepted. I must confess something. I've taken a liberty with your plans."

"Eh?" One of my more intellectual moments.

"I cancelled your passage aboard that merchantman."

"What? Why?"

"It wouldn't be seemly for a legate of the empire to travel aboard a broken-down grain barge. You are too cheap, Croaker. The quinquirireme Soulcatcher built, *The Dark Wings*, is in port. I ordered her readied for the crossing to Beryl."

My gods. The very doomship that brought us north. "We aren't well loved in Beryl."

"Beryl is an imperial province these days. The frontier lies three hundred miles beyond the sea now. Have you forgotten your part in what made that possible?"

I only wanted to. "No. But my attention has been elsewhere the past few decades." If the frontier had drifted that far, then imperial boots tramped the asphalted avenues of my own home city. It never occurred to me that the southern proconsuls might expand the borders beyond the maritime city-states. Only the Jewel Cities themselves were of any strategic value.

"Now who's being bitter?"

"Who? Me? You're right. Let's enjoy the civilized moment. We'll have few enough of them." Our gazes locked. For a moment there were sparks of challenge in hers. I looked away. "How did you manage to enlist those two clowns in your charade?"

"A donative."

I laughed. Of course. Anything for money. "And how soon will *The Dark Wings* be ready to sail?"

"Two days. Three at the most. And no, I won't be handling any imperial business while I'm here."

"Uhm. Good. I'm stuffed to the gills and ripe for roasting. We ought to go walk this off, or something. Is there a reasonably safe place we could go?"

"You probably know Opal better than I do, Croaker. I've never been here before."

I suppose I looked surprised.

"I can't be everywhere. There was a time when I was preoccupied in the north and east. A time when I was preoccupied with putting my husband down. A time when I was preoccupied with catching you. There never was a time when I was free for broadening travel."

"Thank the stars."

"What?"

"Meant to be a compliment. On your youthful figure."

She gave me a calculating look. "I won't say anything to that. You'll stick it all in your Annals."

I grinned. Threads of smoke snaked between my teeth.

I swore I'd get them.

7

Smoke and the Woman

Willow figured you could pick Smoke for what he was in any crowd. He was a wrinkled, skinny little geek that looked like somebody tried to do him in black walnut husk stain, only they missed some spots. There were spatters of pink on the backs of his hands, one arm, and one side of his face. Like maybe somebody threw acid at him and it killed the color where it hit him.

Smoke had not done anything to Willow. Not yet. But Willow did not like him. Blade did not care one way or another. Blade didn't care much about anybody. Cordy Mather said he was reserving judgment. Willow kept his dislike back out of sight, because Smoke was what he was and because he hung out with the Woman.

The Woman was waiting for them, too. She was browner than Smoke and most anyone else in town, as far as Willow knew. She had a mean face that made it hard to look at her. She was about average size for Taglian women, which was not very big by Swan's standards. Except for her attitude of "I am the boss" she would not have stood out much. She did not dress better than old women Willow saw in the streets. Black crows, Cordy called them. Always wrapped up in black, like old peasant women they saw when they were headed down through the territories of the Jewel Cities.

They had not been able to find out who the Woman was, but they knew she was somebody. She had connections in the Prahbrindrah's palace, right up at the top. Smoke worked for her. Fishwives didn't have wizards on the payroll. Anyway, both of them acted like officials trying not to look official. Like they did not know how to be regular people.

The place they met was somebody's house. Somebody important, but Willow had not yet figured who. The class lines and heirarchies did not make sense in Taglios. Everything was always screwed up by religious affiliation.

He entered the room where they waited, helped himself to a chair. Had to show them he wasn't some boy to run and fetch at their beck. Cordy and Blade were more circumspect. Cordy winced as Willow said, "Blade says you guys want to kick it up 'bout Smoke's nightmares. Maybe pipe dreams?"

"You have a very good idea why you interest us, Mr. Swan. Taglios and its dependencies have been pacifistic for centuries. War is a forgotten art. It's been unnecessary. Our neighbors were equally traumatized by the passage—"

Willow asked Smoke, "She talking Taglian?"

"As you wish, Mr. Swan." Willow caught a hint of mischief in the Woman's eye. "When the Free Companies came through they kicked ass so damned bad that for three hundred years anybody who even looked at a sword got so scared he puked his guts up."

"Yeah." Swan chuckled. "That's right. We can talk. Tell us."

"We want help, Mr. Swan."

Willow mused, "Let's see, the way I hear, around seventy-five, a hundred years ago people finally started playing games. Archery shoots, whatnot. But never anything man-to-man. Then here come the Shadowmasters to take over Tragevec and Kiaulune and change the names to Shadowlight and Shadowcatch."

"Kiaulune means Shadow Gate," Smoke said. His voice was like his skin, splotched with oddities. Squeaks, sort of. They made Willow bristle. "Not much change. Yes. They came. And like Kina in the legend they set free the wicked knowledge. In this case, how to make war."

"And right away they started carving them an empire and if they hadn't had that trouble at Shadowcatch and hadn't got so busy fighting each other they would've been here fifteen years ago. I know. I been asking around ever since you guys started hustling us."

"And?"

"So for fifteen years you knew they was coming someday. And for fifteen years you ain't done squat about it. Now when you all of a sudden know the day, you want to grab three guys off the street and con them into thinking they can work some kind of miracle. Sorry, sister. Willow Swan ain't buying. There's your conjure man. Get old Smoke to pull pigeons out of his hat."

"We aren't looking for miracles, Mr. Swan. The miracle has happened. Smoke dreamed it. We're looking for time for the miracle to take effect."

Willow snorted.

"We have a realistic appreciation of how desperate our situation is, Mr. Swan. We have had since the Shadowmasters appeared. We have *not* been playing ostrich. We have been doing what seems most practical, given the cultural context. We have encouraged the masses to accept the notion that it would be a great and glorious thing to repel the onslaught when it comes."

"You sold them that much," Blade said. "They ready to go die."

"And that's all they would do," Swan said. "Die."

"Why?" the Woman asked.

"No organization," said Cordy. The thoughtful one. "But organization wouldn't be possible. No one from any of the major cult families would take orders from somebody from another one."

"Exactly. Religious conflicts make it impossible to raise an army. Three armies, maybe. But then the high priests might be tempted to use them to settle scores here at home."

Blade snorted. "They ought to burn the temples and strangle the priests."

"Sentiments my brother often expresses," the Woman said. "Smoke and I feel they might follow outsiders of proven skill who aren't beholden to any faction."

"What? You going to make me a general?"

Cordy laughed. "Willow, if the gods thought half as much of you as you think of yourself, you'd be king of the world. You figure you're the miracle Smoke saw in his dream? They're not going to make you a general. Not really. Unless maybe for show, while they stall."

"What?"

"Who's the guy keeps saying he only spent two months in the army and never even learned to keep step?"

"Oh." Willow thought for a minute. "I think I see."

"Actually, you will be generals," the Woman said. "And we'll have to rely heavily on Mr. Mather's practical experience. But Smoke will have the final say."

"We have to buy time," the wizard echoed. "A lot of time. Someday soon Moonshadow will send a combined force of five thousand to invade Taglios. We have to keep from being beaten. If there's any way possible, we have to beat the force sent against us."

"Nothing like wishing."

"Are you willing to pay the price?" Cordy asked. Like he thought it could be done.

"The price will be paid," the Woman said. "Whatever it may be."

Willow looked at her till he could no longer keep his teeth clamped on the big question. "Just who the hell are you, lady? Making your promises and plans."

"I am the Radisha Drah, Mr. Swan."

"Holy shit," Swan muttered. "The prince's big sister." The one some people said was the real boss bull in those parts. "I knew you was somebody, but . . ." He was rattled right down to his toenails. But he would not have been Willow Swan if he had not leaned back, folded his hands on his belly, put on a big grin, and asked, "What's in it for us?"

Opal: Crows

Though the empire retained a surface appearance of cohesion, a failure of the old discipline snaked through the deeps beneath. When you wandered the streets of Opal you sensed the laxness. There was flip talk about the new crop of overlords. One-Eye spoke of an increase in black marketeering, a subject on which he had been expert for a century. I overheard talk of crimes committed that were not officially sanctioned.

Lady seemed unconcerned. "The empire is seeking normalcy. The wars are over. There's no need for the strictures of the past."

"You saying it's time to relax?"

"Why not? You'd be the first to scream about what a price we paid for peace."

"Yeah. But the comparative order, the enforcement of public safety laws . . . I admired that part."

"You sweetheart, Croaker. You're saying we weren't all bad."

She knew damned well I'd claimed that all along. "You know I don't believe there's any such thing as pure evil."

"Yes there is. It's festering up north in a silver spike your friends drove into the trunk of a sapling that's the son of a god."

"Even the Dominator may have had some redeeming quality sometime. Maybe he was good to his mother."

"He probably ripped her heart out and ate it. Raw."

I wanted to say something like, you married him, but did not need to give her further excuses to change her mind. She was pressed enough.

But I digress. I was remarking on the changes in the Lady's world. What brought the whole thing home was having a dozen men drop in and ask if they could sign on with the Black Company. They were all veterans. Which meant there were men of military age at loose ends these days. During the war years there had been no extra bodies anywhere. If they were not with the grey boys or that lot they were with the White Rose.

I rejected six guys right away and accepted one, a man with his front teeth done up in gold inlays. Goblin and One-Eye, self-appointed name givers, dubbed him Sparkle.

Of the other five there were three I liked and two I did not and could find no sound reasons for going either way with any of them. I lied and told them they were all in and should report aboard *The Dark Wings* in time for our departure. Then I conferred with Goblin. He said he would make sure that the two I did not like would miss our departure.

I first noticed the crows then, consciously. I attached no special significance, just wondered why everywhere we went there seemed to be crows.

One-Eye wanted a private chat. "You nosed around that place where your girlfriend is staying?"

"Not to speak of." I had given up arguing about whether or not Lady was my girlfriend.

"You ought to."

"It's a little late. I take it you have. What's your beef?"

"It isn't something you can pin down like sticking a nail through a frog, Croaker. Kind of hard to get a good look around there, anyway, what with she brought a whole damned army along. An army that I think she figures on dragging along wherever we go."

"She won't. Maybe she rules this end of the world, but she don't run the Black Company. Nobody runs with this outfit who don't answer to me and only to me."

One-Eye clapped. "That was good, Croaker. I could almost hear the Captain talking. You even got to standing the way he did, like a big old bear about to jump on something."

I was not original, but I didn't think I was that transparent a borrower, either. "So what's your point, One-Eye? Why has she got you spooked?"

"Not spooked, Croaker. Just feeling cautious. It's her baggage. She's dragging along enough stuff to fill a wagon."

"Women get that way."

"Ain't women's stuff. Not unless she wears magical lacies. You'd know that better than me."

"Magical?"

"Whatever that stuff is, it's got a charge on it. A pretty hefty one."

"What am I supposed to do about it?"

He shrugged. "I don't know. I just thought you ought to know."

"If it's magical it's your department. Keep an eye out"—I snickered—"and let me know if you find anything useful."

"Your sense of humor has gone to hell, Croaker."

"I know. Must be the company I keep. My mother warned me about guys like you. Scat. Go help Goblin give those two guys the runs, or something. And stay out of trouble. Or I'll take you across the water in a nice bouncy rowboat we'll pull along behind the ship."

It takes some doing for a black man to get green around the gills. One-Eye managed it.

The threat worked. He even kept Goblin from getting into mischief.

Though not in keeping with the time sequence, I hereby make notation of four new members of the Company. They are: Sparkle, Big Bucket (I don't know why; he came with the name), Red Rudy, and Candles. Candles came with his name, too. There is a long story to tell how he got it. It does not make sense and is not especially interesting. Being the new guys they mostly stayed quiet, stayed out of the way, did the scut work, and worked on learning what we were all about. Lieutenant Murgen was happy to have somebody around he outranked.

Across the Screaming Sea

Our black iron coaches roared through Opal's streets, flooding the dawn with fear and thunder. Goblin outdid himself. This time the black stallions breathed smoke and fire, and flames sprang up where their hooves struck, fading only after we were long gone. Citizens stayed under cover.

One-Eye lolled beside me, restrained by protective cords. Lady sat opposite us, hands folded in her lap. The lurching of the coach bothered her not at all.

Her coach and mine parted ways. Hers headed for the north gate, bound toward the Tower. All the city—we hoped—would believe her to be in that coach. It would disappear somewhere in uninhabited country. The coachmen, handsomely bribed, should head west, to make new lives in the distant cities on the ocean coast. The trail, we hoped, would be a dead one before anyone became concerned.

Lady wore clothing that made her look like a doxy, the legate's momentary fancy.

She travelled like a courtesan. The coach was jammed with her stuff and One-Eye reported that a load had been delivered to *The Dark Wings* already, with a wagon to carry it.

One-Eye was limp because he had been drugged.

Faced by a sea voyage, he became balky. He always does. Old in knowing One-Eye's ways, Goblin had been prepared. Knockout drops in his morning brandy did the trick.

Through wakening streets we thundered, down to the waterfront, amidst the confusion of arriving stevedores. Onto the massive naval dock we rolled, to its very end, and up a broad gangway. Hooves drummed on deck timbers. Finally, we halted.

I stepped down from the coach. The ship's captain met me with all the appropriate honors and dignities—and a furious scowl on behalf of his savaged deck. I looked around. The four new men were there. I nodded. The captain shouted. Hands began casting off. Others began helping my men unharness and unsaddle horses. I noticed a crow perched on the masthead.

Small tugs manned by convict oarsmen pulled *The Dark Wings* off the pier. Her own sweeps came out. Drums pounded the beat. She turned her bows seaward. In an hour we were well down the channel, running with the tide, the ship's great black sail bellied with an offshore breeze. The device thereon was unchanged since our northward journey, though Soulcatcher had been destroyed by the Lady herself soon after the Battle at Charm. The crow kept its perch.

It was the best season for crossing the Sea of Torments. Even One-Eye admitted it was a swift and easy passage. We raised the Beryl light on the third morning and entered the harbor with the afternoon tide.

The advent of *The Dark Wings* had all the impact I expected and feared.

The last time that monster put in at Beryl the city's last free, homegrown tyrant had died. His successor, chosen by Soulcatcher, became an imperial puppet. And *his* successors were imperial governors.

Local imperial functionaries swarmed onto the pier as the quinquirireme warped in. "Termites," Goblin called them. "Tax farmers and pen-pushers. Little things that live under rocks and shy from the light of honest employment."

Somewhere in his background was a cause for a big hatred of tax collectors. I understand in an intellectual sort of way. I mean there is no lower human lifeform—with the possible exception of pimps—than that which revels in its state-derived power to humiliate, extort, and generate misery. I am left with a disgust for my species. But with Goblin it can become a flaming passion, with him trying to work everybody up to go out and treat a few tax people to grotesque excruciations and deaths.

The termites were shaken and distressed. They did not know what to make of this sudden, obviously portentous arrival. The advent of an imperial legate could mean a hundred things, but nothing good for the entrenched bureaucracy.

Elsewhere, all work came to a halt. Even cursing gang leaders paused to stare at the harbinger ship.

One-Eye eyeballed the situation. "Better get us out of town fast, Croaker. Else it will turn into the Tower all over again, this time with too many people asking too damned many questions."

The coach was ready. Lady was inside. The mounts, both great and normal, were saddled. A small, light, closed wagon was brought up and assembled by the Horse Guards and filled with Lady's plunder. We were ready to roll when the ship's captain was ready to let us.

"Mount up," I ordered. "One-Eye, when that gangway goes down you make

like the horns of hell. Otto, take this coach off here like the Limper himself is after you." I turned to the commander of the Horse Guards. "You break trail. Don't
give those people down there a chance to slow us down." I boarded the coach.

"Wise thinking," Lady said. "Get away fast or risk falling into the trap I
barely escaped at the Tower."

"That's what I'm afraid of. I can fake this legate business only if nobody
looks at me too close." Far better to roar through town and leave them thinking
me a foul-tempered, contemptuous, arrogant Taken legate southward bound on
a mission that was no business of the procurators of Beryl.

The gangway slammed down. One-Eye let loose the hell-horn howl I
wanted. My mob surged forward. Gawkers and the privileged alike scattered
before our fire-and-darkness apparition. We thundered through Beryl as we
had thundered through Opal, our passage spreading terror. Behind us, *The
Dark Wings* put out with the evening tide, under orders to proceed to the Garnet Roads and begin an extended patrol against pirates and smugglers. We ex-
ited the Rubbish Gate. Though the normal animals were exhausted, we carried
on till darkness lent us its mask.

Despite our haste to get away from the city, we did not camp far enough out
to escape its attention entirely. When I wakened in the morning I found
Murgen waiting on me with three brothers who wanted to join up. Their names
were Cletus, Longinus, and Loftus. They had been kids when we were in Beryl
before. How they recognized us during our wild ride I do not know. They
claimed to have deserted the Urban Cohorts in order to join us. I did not feel
much like dealing with an extensive interrogation, so took Murgen's word that
they seemed all right. "They're fools enough to want to jump in with us without
knowing what's going on, let them. Give them to Hagop."

I now had two feeble squads, Otto and the four from Opal, and Hagop and
the three from Beryl. Such was the Company's history. Pick up a man here, enlist two there, keep on keeping on.

Southward and southward. Through Rebosa, where the Company had seen
service briefly, and where Otto and Hagop had enlisted. They found their
city changed immensely and yet not at all. They had no trouble leaving it behind. They brought in another man there, a nephew, who quickly earned the
name Smiley because of his consistent sullenness and sarcastic turn of phrase.

Then Padora, and on, to that great crossroads of trade routes where I was
born and where I enlisted just before the Company ended its service there. I
was young and foolish when I did. Yes. But I did get to see the far reaches of the
world.

I ordered a day of rest at the vast caravan camp outside the city wall, along the westward road, while I went into town and indulged myself, walking streets I had run as a kid. Like Otto said about Rebosa, the same and yet dramatically changed. The difference, of course, was inside me.

I stalked through the old neighborhood, past the old tenement. I saw no one I knew—unless a woman glimpsed briefly, who looked like my grandmother, was my sister. I did not confront her, nor ask. To those people I am dead.

A return as imperial legate would not change that.

We stood before the last imperial mile marker. Lady was trying to convince the lieutenant commanding our guards that his mission was complete, that imperial soldiers crossing the frontier might be construed as an unacceptable provocation.

Sometimes her people are too loyal.

A half-dozen border militiamen, equally divided between sides, clad identically and obviously old friends, stood around a short distance away, discussing us in murmurs of awe. The rest of us fidgeted.

It seemed ages since I had been beyond imperial frontiers. I found the prospect vaguely unsettling.

"You know what we're doing, Croaker?" Goblin asked.

"What's that?"

"We're travelling backward in time."

Backward in time. Backward into our own history. A simple enough statement, but an important thought.

"Yeah. Maybe you're right. Let me go stir the pot. Else we'll never get moving."

I joined Lady, who gave me a nasty look. I pasted on my sweetest smile and said, "Look here. I'm over on the other side of the line. You got a problem, Lieutenant?"

He bobbed his head. He was more in awe of my rank and title, unearned though they were, than he was of the woman who was supposed to be his boss. And that was because he believed he owed her certain duties even she could not overrule.

"The Company has openings for a few good men with military experience," I said. "Now that we're out of the empire and don't have to have the imperial permission, we're actively recruiting."

He caught on real fast, skipped across beside me, gave Lady a big grin.

"There is one thing," I said. "You come over here and do it, you're going to have to take the oath to the Company, same as anybody else. Meaning you can't pledge yourself to any higher loyalty."

Lady gave him a nasty-sweet smile. He stepped back across, figuring he'd better do some serious thinking before he committed himself.

I told Lady, "That goes for everybody. I would not presume before. But if you come out of the empire and continue to ride with us it will be under the same conditions accepted by everyone else."

Such a look she gave me. "But I'm just a woman. . . ."

"Not a precedent, friend. It didn't happen often. The world don't have much room for female adventurers. But women have marched with the Company." Turning to the lieutenant, I said, "And if you sign on, your oath will be taken as genuine. First time you get an order and look to her for advice on yes or no, out you go. Alone in a foreign land." It was one of my more assertive days.

Lady muttered some very unladylike sniggen snaggen riddly rodden racklesnatzes under her breath, then told the lieutenant, "Go talk it over with your men." The moment he was out of hearing she demanded, "Does this mean we stop being friends? If I take your damned oath?"

"Do you reckon I stopped being friends with the others when they elected me Captain?"

"I admit I don't hear a lot of 'yes sir,' 'no sir,' 'your worship sir.'"

"But you do see them do what they're told when they know I mean what I say."

"Most of the time."

"Goblin and One-Eye need a little extra convincing once in a while. What's it going to be? You going to be a soldier?"

"Do I have a choice, Croaker? You can be a bastard."

"Of course you have a choice. You can go back with your men and be the Lady."

The lieutenant was talking to his troops and the idea of going on south was proving less popular than he or I had thought it would. Most of the bunch started getting their horses together, facing north, before he finished talking.

He finally came over and presented us with six men who wanted to go on with us. He did not include himself with the group. Evidently his conscience had shown him a way around doing what he considered to be his duty minutes before.

I questioned the men briefly and they did seem interested in going on. So I brought them over the line and swore them all in, making a production of it for Lady's sake. I do not recall doing anything particularly formal for anyone else before.

I gave the six to Otto and Hagop for dividing between them, and kept the one for me, and later entered their names into the Annals when we learned how they wanted to be known.

Lady remained content to be called Lady. It sounded like a name when heard by speakers of any language but one, anyway.

Crows watched the whole show from a nearby tree.

Shadowmasters

Though the sun stared in through a dozen vaulted windows there was darkness in that place where Darkness met.

A pool of molten stone simmered in the center of the vast floor. It cast bloody light upon four seated figures floating a few feet in the air. They faced one another over the pool, forming an equilateral triangle with a couple at its apex. Those two were leagued more often than not. They were allied now.

There had been war among the four for a long time, with nothing gained, one in relation to another. But at the moment there was an armistice.

Shadows slithered and swirled and pranced around them. Nothing could be seen of any of them except vague shapes. All four chose to conceal themselves within robes of black, behind black masks.

The smallest, one of the couple, broke a silence that had reigned an hour. "She has begun moving south. Those who served her and still bear her indelible mark are moving also. They have crossed the sea, and they come bearing mighty talismans. And their road is strewn with those who would join their destinies to that black standard. Including some whose power we would be foolish not to beware."

One angle of the triangle made a sound of contempt. The other asked, "And what of the one in the north?"

"The Great One remains secure. The lesser one who lay in the shade of the prisoning tree does so no longer. It has been resurrected and given new form. It comes south too, but it is so insane and vengeance-starved that it is not to be feared. A child could dispose of it."

"Have we cause to fear that our presence here is known?"

"None. Even in Trogo Taglios only a few are convinced that we exist. Beyond the First Cataract we are but a rumor, and not that above the Second. But he who has made himself master in the great swamps may have sensed us stirring. It is possible he suspects there is more afoot than he knew."

The reporter's companion added, "They come. She comes. But harnessed to the pace of man and animal. We still have a year. Or more."

The one snorted again, then spoke. "The swamps would be a very good place for them to die. Take care of it. You may impress the one who rules them with the majesty and terror of my Name." He began to drift away.

The others stared hard. The anger in the place became palpable.

The other ceased his drift. "You know what sleeps so restlessly upon my southern border. I dare not relax my vigilance."

"Unless to stab another of us in the back. I note that the threat becomes secondary whenever you care to try."

"You have my pledge. Upon my Name. The peace will not be broken by me while those who bring danger from the north survive. You may speak of me as one with you when you extend your hands beyond the shadows. I cannot, I *dare* not, give you more." He resumed his drift.

"So be it, then," said the woman. The triangle rearranged itself so as to exclude him. "He spoke one truth, certainly. The swamps would be a very good place for them to die. If Fate does not take them in hand sooner."

One of the others began to chuckle. The shadows scurried about, frantic, as growing laughter tormented them.

"A very good place for them to die."

A March into Yesteryear

At first the names were echoes from my childhood. Kale. Fratter. Grey. Weeks. Some the Company had served, some had been its foes. The world changed and became warmer and the cities became more scattered. Their names faded to legend and memories from the Annals. Tire. Raxle. Slight. Nab and Nod. We passed beyond any map I had ever seen, to cities known to me only through the Annals and visited only by One-Eye previously. Boros. Teries. Viege. Ha-jah.

And still we headed south, still making the first long leg of our journey. Crows followed. We gathered another four recruits, professional caravan

guards from a nomad tribe called the roi, who deserted to join us. I started a
squad for Murgen. He was not thrilled. He was content being standard-bearer
and had developed hopes of taking over the Annalist's chores from me because
I had so much to do as Captain and medic. I dared not discourage him. The
only alternative substitute was One-Eye. He was not reliable.

And south some more, and still we were not back to One-Eye's origin, the
jungles of D'loc-Aloc.

One-Eye swore that never in his life, outside the Company, had he heard the
name Khatovar. It had to lie far beyond the waist of the world.

There are limits to what frail flesh can endure.

Those long leagues were not easy. The black iron coach and Lady's wagon
drew the eye of bandits and princes and princes who were bandits. Most times
Goblin and One-Eye bluffed us through. The rest of the time we forced them to
back down with a little applied terror. There was one long stretch where the
magic had gone away.

If those two had learned anything during their years with the Company, it
was showmanship. When they conjured an illusion you could smell its bad
breath from seventy feet away.

I wished they would refrain from wasting that flash upon one another.

I decided it was time we laid up for a few days. We needed to regain our
youthful bounce.

One-Eye suggested, "There's a place down the road called the Temple of
Travellers' Repose. They take in wanderers. They have for two thousand years. It
would be a good place to lay up and do some research."

"Research?"

"Two thousand years of travellers' tales makes a hell of a library, Croaker.
And a tale is the only donative they ever require."

He had me. He grinned cockily. The old scoundrel knew me too well. Nothing else could have stilled my determination to reach Khatovar so thoroughly.

I passed the word. And gave One-Eye the fish-eye. "That means you're going to do some honest work."

"What?"

"Who do you think is going to translate?"

He groaned and rolled his eye. "When am I going to learn to keep my big
damned mouth shut?"

The Temple was a lightly fortified monastery sprawled atop a low hill. It
looked golden in the light of a late afternoon sun. The forest beyond and
the fields before were as intense a dark green as ever I have seen. The place
looked restful.

As we entered, a wave of well-being cleansed us. A feeling of *I have come home* washed over us. I looked at Lady. The things I felt glowed in her face, and touched my heart.

I could retire here," I told Lady two days into our stay. Clean for the first time in months, we stalked a garden never disturbed by conflicts more weighty than the squabbles of sparrows.

She gave me a thin smile and did me the courtesy of saying nothing about the delusive nature of dreams.

The place had everything I thought I wanted. Comfort. Quiet. Isolation from the ills of the earth. Purpose. Challenging historical studies to soothe my lust to *know* what had gone on before.

Most of all, it provided a respite from responsibility. Each man added to the Company seemed to double my burden as I worried about keeping them fed, keeping them healthy, and out of trouble.

"Crows," I muttered.

"What?"

"Everywhere we go there're crows. Maybe I only started noticing them the past couple months. But everywhere we go I see crows. And I can't shake the feeling they're watching us."

Lady gave me a puzzled look.

"Look. Right over there in that acacia tree. Two of them squatting there like black omens."

She glanced at the tree, gave me another look. "I see a couple of doves."

"But . . ." One of the crows launched itself, flapped away over the monastery wall. "That wasn't any—"

"Croaker!" One-Eye charged through the garden, scattering the birds and squirrels, ignoring all propriety. "Hey! Croaker! Guess what I found! Copies of the Annals from when we came past here headed north!"

Well. And well. This tired old mind cannot find words adequate. Excitement? Certainly. Ecstasy? You'd better believe. The moment was almost sexually intense. My mind focused the way one's does when an especially desirable woman suddenly seems attainable.

Several older volumes of the Annals had become lost or damaged during the years. There were some I'd never seen, and never had known a hope of seeing.

"Where?" I breathed.

"In the library. One of the monks thought you might be interested. When we were here heading north I don't remember leaving them, but I wasn't much interested in that kind of thing then. Me and Tom-Tom was too busy looking over our shoulders."

"I might be interested," I said. "I might." My manners deserted me. I deserted Lady without so much as an "Excuse me."

Maybe that obsession was not as powerful as I'd worked it up to be.

I felt like an ass when I realized what I had done.

Reading those copies required teamwork. They had been recorded in a language no longer used by anyone but the temple monks. None of them spoke any language I understood. So our reader translated into One-Eye's native tongue, then One-Eye translated for me.

What filtered through was damned interesting.

They had the Book of Choe, which had been destroyed fifty years before I enlisted and only poorly reconstructed. And the Book of Te-Lare, known to me only through a cryptic reference in a later volume. The Book of Skete, previously unknown. They had a half dozen more, equally precious. But no Book of the Company. No First or Second Book of Odrick. Those were the legendary first three volumes of the Annals, containing our origin myths, referenced in later works but not mentioned as having been seen after the first century of the Company's existence.

The Book of Te-Lare tells why.

There was a battle.

Always, there was a battle in any explanation.

Movement; a clash of arms; another punctuation mark in the long tale of the Black Company.

In this one the people who had hired our forebrethren had bolted at the first shock of the enemy's charge. They had broken so fast they were gone before the Company realized what was happening. The outfit beat a fighting retreat into its fortified encampment. During the ensuing siege the enemy penetrated the camp several times. During one such penetration the volumes in question vanished. Both the Annalist and his understudy were slain. The Books could not be reconstructed from memory.

Oh, well. I was ahead of the game.

Books available charted our future almost to the edge of the maps owned by the monks, and those ran all the way to Here There Be Dragons. Another century and a half of a journey into our yesterdays. By the time we retraced our route that far I hoped we would stand at the heart of a map that encompassed our destination.

As soon as it was clear that we had struck gold I obtained writing materials and a virgin volume of the Annals. I could write as fast as One-Eye and the monk could translate.

Time fled. A monk brought candles. Then a hand settled on my shoulder. Lady said, "Do you want to take a break? I could do that for a while."

For half a minute I just sat there turning red. That, after I practically ditched her outside. After I never even thought of her all day.

She told me, "I understand."

Maybe she did. She had read the various Books of Croaker—or, as posterity might recall them, the Books of the North—several times.

With Murgen and Lady spelling me the translation went quickly. The only practical limit was One-Eye's endurance.

It was not all one way. I had to trade my later Annals for their older ones. Lady sweetened the deal with a few hundred anecdotes about the dark empire of the north, but the monks never connected my Lady with the queen of darkness.

One-Eye is a tough old buzzard. He held up. Four days after he made his great discovery the job was done.

I let Murgen into the game but he did all right. And I had to beg/buy four blank journals in order to get everything transcribed.

Lady and I resumed our stroll about where we had broken it, but with me a little down.

"What's the matter?" she chided, and to my astonishment wanted to know if it was a postcoital depression. Just the faintest of digs there, I think.

"No. I've just found out a ton about the Company's history. But I didn't learn anything that's really new."

She understood but she kept quiet and let me articulate my dissatisfaction.

"It's told a hundred ways, poorly and well, according to the skill of the particular Annalist, but, except for the occasional interesting detail, it was the same old march, countermarch, fight, celebrate or run away, record the dead, and, sooner or later, get even with the sponsor for betraying us. Even at that place with the unpronounceable name, where the Company was in service for fifty-six years."

"Gea-Xle." She got her mouth around it like she had had practice.

"Yeah, there. Where the contract lasted so long the Company almost lost its identity, intermarrying with the population and all that, becoming a sort of hereditary bodyguard, with arms handed down from father to son. But as it always will, the essential moral destitution of those would-be princes made itself evident and somebody decided to cheat us. He got his throat cut and the Company moved on."

"You certainly read selectively, Croaker."

I looked at her. She was laughing at me quietly.

"Yeah, well." I'd stated it pretty baldly. A prince did try to cheat our forebrethren and did get his throat cut. But the Company installed a new, friendly, beholden dynasty and did hang around a few years before that Captain got a wild hair and decided to go treasure hunting.

"You have no reservations about commanding a band of hired killers?" she asked.

"Sometimes," I admitted, sliding past the trap nimbly. "But we never cheated a sponsor." Not exactly. "Sooner or later, every sponsor cheated us."

"Including yours truly?"

"One of your satraps beat you to it. But given time we would have become less than indispensable and you would have started looking around for a way to shaft us instead of doing the honorable thing and paying us off and simply terminating our commission."

"That's what I love about you, Croaker. Your unflagging faith in humanity."

"Absolutely. Every ounce of my cynicism is supported by historical precedent," I grumped.

"You really know how to melt a woman, you know that, Croaker?"

"Huh?" I come armed with a whole arsenal of such brilliant repartee.

"I came out here with some feebleminded notion of seducing you. For some reason I'm not in the mood to try anymore."

Well. Some of them you screw up royal.

There was an observation catwalk along some parts of the monastery wall. I went up into the northeast corner, leaned on the adobe and stared back the way we had come. Busy feeling sorry for myself. Every couple hundred years that sort of thing leads to a productive insight.

The damned crows were thicker than ever. Must have been twenty of them now. I cursed them and, I swear, they mocked me. When I threw a loose piece of adobe they all jumped up and fled toward . . .

"Goblin!" I think he was out keeping an eye on me in case I got suicidal.

"Yeah?"

"Get One-Eye and Lady and come up here. Fast." I turned and stared up the slope at the thing that had caught my eye.

It stopped moving but was unmistakably a human figure in robes so black looking at them was like looking at a rent in the fabric of existence. It carried something under its right arm, about the size of a hatbox, held in place by the natural fall of the limb. The crows swarmed around it, twenty or thirty of them, squabbling over the right to perch upon its shoulders. It was a good quarter mile from where I stood but I felt the gaze from its hooded, unseen face beating upon me like the heat from a furnace.

The crowd turned up with Goblin and One-Eye as quarrelsome as ever. Lady asked, "What is it?"

"Take a look out there."

They looked. Goblin squeaked, "So?"

"So? What do you mean, so?"

"What's so interesting about an old tree stump and a flock of birds?"

I looked. Damn! A stump . . . But as I stared there was an instant's shimmer and I saw the black figure again. I shuddered.

"Croaker?" Lady asked. She was still mad at me but concerned even so.

"Nothing. My eyes were playing tricks on me. I thought I saw the damned thing moving. Forget it."

They took me at my word, stomped off to whatever they had been doing. I watched them go and for another moment doubted my own senses.

But then I looked again.

The crows were flying off in a crowd, except for two headed straight toward me. And the stump was hiking off across the hillside as though intent on circling the monastery.

I mumbled a little to myself but it did not do any good.

I tried giving the Temple a few more days to work its magic but the next one hundred fifty years of our journey drummed on in my mind. There was no repose now. I was too itchy to sit. I announced my intention. And I got no kickbacks. Just acquiescent nods. Maybe even relieved nods.

What was this?

I sat up and came out of myself, where I had been spending a lot of time reexamining the familiar old furniture. I had not been paying attention to the others.

They were restless, too.

There was something in the air. Something that told us all it was time to hit the road. Even the monks seemed eager to see us move out. Curious.

Them that stays alive in the soldiering business are them that listens to such feelings even when they make no sense. You feel like you got to move, you move. You stay put and get stomped, it is too late to whine about all that work for nothing.

The Shaggy Hills

To reach One-Eye's jungle we had to pass through several miles of woods, then climb over a range of decidedly odd hills. The hills were very round, very steep, and completely treeless, though not especially high. They were covered with a short brown grass that caught fire easily, so that many bore black scars. From a distance they looked like a herd of giant, tawny, humped beasts sleeping.

I was in a state of high nerves. That sleeping-beast image haunted me. I kept half expecting those hills to waken and shrug us off. I caught up with One-Eye. "Is there something weird about these hills that you accidentally forgot to tell me about on purpose?"

He gave me a funny look. "No. Though the ignorant believe them to be burial mounds from a time when giants walked the earth. But they aren't. They're just hills. All dirt and rock inside."

"Then why do they make me feel funny?"

He glanced back the way we had come, puzzled. "It's not the hills, Croaker. It's something back there. I feel it, too. Like we just dodged an arrow."

I did not ask him what it was. He would have told me if he had known.

As the day wore on I realized the others were as jumpy as I was.

Worrying about it did as much good as worrying ever does.

Next morning we ran into two wizened little men of One-Eye's race. They both looked a hundred years old. One of them kept hacking and coughing like he was about to croak. Goblin cackled. "Must be old Lizard Lips's illegitimate grandchildren."

There was a resemblance. I suppose that was to be expected. We were just accustomed to One-Eye being unique.

One-Eye scowled at Goblin. "Keep it up, Barf Bag. You'll be grocery shopping with the turtles."

What the hell did that mean? Some kind of obscure shop talk? But Goblin was as croggled as the rest of us.

Grinning, One-Eye resumed gabbling with his relatives.

Lady said, "I presume these are the guides the monks sent for?"

They had done us that favor on learning our intentions. We would need guides. We were near the end of any road we could call familiar. Once past One-Eye's jungle we would need somebody to translate for One-Eye, too.

Goblin let out a sudden aggrieved squawk.

"What's your problem?" I demanded.

"He's feeding them a pack of lies!"

So what was new about that? "How do you know? You don't talk that lingo."

"I don't have to. I've known him since before your dad was whelped. Look at him. He's doing his classic mighty-sorcerer-from-a-faraway-land act. In about twenty seconds he's going to . . ." A wicked grin spread his mouth around his face. He muttered something under his breath.

One-Eye raised a hand. A ball of light formed within his curled fingers.

There was a pop like that of a cork coming out of a wine bottle.

One-Eye held a hand full of swamp bottom. It oozed between his fingers and ran down his arm. He lowered his hand and stared in disbelief.

He let out a shriek and whirled.

Innocent Goblin was faking a conversation with Murgen. But Murgen was not up to the deceit. His shifty eyes gave Goblin away.

One-Eye puffed up like a toady frog, ready to explode. Then a miracle occurred. He invented self-restraint. A nasty little smile pranced across his lips and he turned back to the guides.

That was the second time in my experience that he had controlled himself when provoked. But, then, it was one of those rare times when Goblin had initiated the process of provocation. I told Otto, "This could get interesting."

Otto grunted an affirmative. He was not thrilled.

Of One-Eye, I asked, "Have you finished telling them you're the necromancer Voice of the North Wind come to ease the pain in their hearts brought on by worry about their wealth?" He'd actually tried to sell that once, to a tribe of savages coincidentally in possession of an eye-popping cache of emeralds. He found out the hard way that primitive does not mean stupid. They were fixing to burn him at the stake when Goblin decided to bail him out. Against his better judgment, he always insisted afterward.

"It ain't like that this time, Croaker. I wouldn't do it to my own people."

One-Eye does not have an ounce of shame. Nor even the sense not to lie to those who know him well. Of course he would do it to his own people. He would do it to anybody if he thought he could get away with it. And he has so little trouble conning himself on that.

"See that you don't. We're too few and too far from safety to let you indulge yourself in your usual line of shit."

I got enough menace into my voice to make him gulp. His tone was markedly different when he resumed gobbling at our prospective guides.

Even so, I decided I would pick up a smatter of the language. Just to keep an ear on him. His often misplaced self-confidence has a way of asserting itself at the most unpropitious moments.

Straight for a time, One-Eye negotiated a deal that pleased everyone. We had ourselves guides for the passage through the jungle and intermediary interpreters for the land that lay beyond.

Relying on his usual moronic sense of humor, Goblin dubbed them Baldo and Wheezer, for reasons that were self-evident. To my embarrassment, the names stuck. Those two old boys probably deserved better. But then again . . .

We wended our way between the shaggy, hump-backed hills the rest of that day, and as darkness approached we topped the cleavage between the pair that flanked the summit of our passage. From there we could see the sunset, reflecting bloody wounds of a broad river, and the rich green of the jungle beyond. Behind us lay the tawny humps, and beyond them a hazy sprawl of indigo.

My mood was reflective, flat, almost down. It seemed we might have reached a watershed in more than a geographical sense.

Much later, unable to sleep for thoughts that questioned what I was doing here in an alien land, thoughts that replied that I had nothing else to do and nowhere else to go, I left my bedroll and the remaining warmth of our campfire. I headed for one of the flanking hills, moved by some vague notion of going up where I could get a better view of the stars.

Wheezer, who had the watch, gave me a gap-toothed leer before spitting a wad of brown juice into the coals. I heard him start wheezing before I was halfway up the hill.

A lunger I got, yet.

The moon threatened to rise soon. It would be fat and bright. I picked me a spot and stood looking at the horizon, waiting for that fat orange globe to roll over the lip of the world. The faintest of cool, moist breezes stirred my hair. It was so damned peaceful it hurt.

"You couldn't sleep, either?"

I jerked around.

She was a dark glob on the hillside just ten feet away. If I had noted her at all, it was as a rock. I stepped closer. She was seated, her arms wrapped around her knees. Her gaze was fixed on the north.

"Sit down."

I sat. "What are you looking at so hard?"

"The Reaper. The Archer. Vargo's Ship." And yesterdays, no doubt.

Those were constellations. I considered them, too. They were very low, seen from here. This time of year they would be quite high in the sky up north. What she meant began to sink in.

We had come a far piece, indeed. With many a mile to go.

She said, "It's intimidating when you think about it. It's a lot of walking."

It was.

The moon clambered over the horizon, monstrous in size and almost red. She whispered "Wow!" and slipped her hand into mine. She was shivering, so after a minute I slid over and put my arm around her. She leaned her head against my shoulder.

That old moon was working its magic. That sucker can do it to anybody.

Now I knew what made Wheezer grin.

The moment seemed right. I turned my head—and her lips were rising to meet mine. When they touched mine I forgot who and what she had been. Her arms surrounded me, pulled me down. . . .

She shivered in my grasp like a captive mouse. "What is it?" I whispered.

"Shh," she said. And that was the best thing she could have said. But she could not leave it there. She had to add, "I never . . . I never did this. . . ."

Well, shit. She sure knew how to distract a man, and put a thousand reservations into his mind.

That moon climbed the sky. We began to relax with each other. Somehow, there were fewer rags separating us.

She stiffened. The mist went out of her eyes. She lifted her head and stared past me, face slack.

If one of those clowns had sneaked up to watch I was going to break his kneecaps. I turned.

We did not have company. She was watching the flash of a distant storm. "Heat lightning," I said.

"You think so? It doesn't seem much farther off than the Temple. And we never saw a storm the whole time we were crossing that country."

Jagged lightning bolts ripped down like a fall of javelins.

That feeling I had discussed with One-Eye redoubled.

"I don't know, Croaker." She began gathering her clothing. "The pattern seems familiar."

I followed her lead, relieved. I am not sure I would have been able to finish what we started. I was distracted now.

"Another time will be better, I think," she said, still staring at that lightning. "That is too distracting."

We returned to camp to find everyone awake yet totally uninterested in the fact that we had been away together. The view was not as good from below, but flashes could be seen. They did not let up.

"There's sorcery out there, Croaker," One-Eye said.

Goblin nodded. "The heavy stuff. You can feel the screaming edges of it from here."

"How far away?" I asked.

"About two days. Close to that place we stopped."

I shivered. "Can you tell what it's about?"

Goblin said nothing. One-Eye shook his head. "All I can tell you is I'm glad I'm here and not there."

I agreed, even in my ignorance of what was happening.

Murgen blanched. He pointed over the book he was studying, which he held out like a protective fetish. "Did you *see* that?"

I was looking at Lady and brooding about my luck. The others could sweat the little stuff, like some bloody sorcerers' duel fifty miles away. I had troubles of my own.

"What?" I grumbled, knowing he wanted a response.

"It looked like a giant bird. I mean, like one with a twenty-mile wingspan. That you could see through."

I looked up. Goblin nodded. He had seen it, too. I looked to the north. The lightning ended, but some pretty fierce fires had to be burning up there. "One-Eye. Your new buddies there got any idea what's going on?"

The little black man shook his head. He had the brim of his hat pulled forward, cutting his line of sight. That business up there—whatever it was— had him rattled. By his own admission he is the greatest wizard ever produced by his part of the world. With the possible exception of his dead brother, Tom-Tom. Whatever that was out there, it was alien. It did not belong.

"Times change," I suggested.

"Not around here, they don't. And if they did, these guys would know about it." Wheezer nodded vigorous agreement although he could not have understood a word. He hawked and spat a brown glob into the fire.

I had a feeling I was going to have as much fun with him as I did with One-Eye. "What is that crap he's all the time chewing? It's disgusting."

"Qat," One-Eye said. "A mild narcotic. Doesn't do his lungs any good, but when he's chewing it he doesn't care how much they hurt him." He said it lightly, but he meant it.

I nodded uncomfortably, looked away. "Quieting down up there."

No one had anything to say to that.

"We're all awake," I said. "So get packing. I want to move out as soon as we can see to walk."

I did not get a bit of argument. Wheezer nodded and spat. Goblin grunted and started getting his things together. The others followed his example, Murgen putting the book away with a care that I approved. The boy might make an Annalist after all. We all kept sneaking looks at the north when we thought our uneasiness would go unnoticed.

When I was not looking that way, or tormenting myself with glances at Lady, I tried to get an estimate of the reactions of the newer men. We had encountered no sorcery directly yet, but the Company has a way of stumbling into its path. They seemed no more uncomfortable than the old hands.

Glances at Lady. I wondered if what seemed inevitable on the one hand and foredoomed on the other would ever cease crackling between us. So long as it did it would distort everything else in our relationship. Hell. I liked her fine as a friend.

There is nothing so unreasonable and irrational and blind—and just plain silly-looking—as a man who works himself into an obsessive passion.

Women do not look as foolish. They are expected to be weak. But they are also expected to become savage bitches when they are frustrated.

Willow's Last Night Little

Willow, Cordy Mather, and Blade still had their tavern. Mainly because they had the countenance of the Prahbrindrah Drah. Business wasn't good now. The priests found out they couldn't control the foreigners. So they put them off limits. A lot of Taglians did what the priests told them.

"Shows you how much sense people have," Blade said. "They had any, they would take the priests to the river and hold them under an hour to remind them they drone like termites."

Willow said, "Man, you got to be the sourest son of a bitch I ever seen. I bet if we hadn't dragged you out, those crocs would of thrown you back. Too rancid to eat."

Blade just grinned as he went through the door to the back room.

Willow asked Cordy, "You reckon it was priests that throwed him in?"

"Yeah."

"Good house tonight. For once."

"Yeah."

"Tomorrow's the day." Willow took a long drink. Cordy's brew was getting better. Then he stood up and hammered the bar with his empty mug. In Taglian he said, "We who are about to die salute you. Drink and be merry, children. For tomorrow, and so forth. On the house." He sat down.

Cordy said, "You know how to cheer a place up, don't you?"

"You figure we got anything to be cheerful about? They'll screw it up. You know they will. All those priests mucking about in it? I tell you right out, I get my chance there's a couple accidentally ain't going to come back from out there."

Cordy nodded and kept his mouth shut. Willow Swan was a lot more bark than bite.

Swan grumbled, "Up the river if this works out. I'll tell you something, Cordy. These feet get to moving that direction they're just going to keep on shuffling."

"Sure, Willow. Sure."

"You don't believe me, do you?"

"I believe everything you tell me, Willow. If I didn't, would I be here, up to my neck, wallowing in rubies and pearls and gold doubloons?"

"Man, what do you expect of someplace nobody ever heard of six thousand miles past the edge of any map anybody ever seen?"

Blade came back. "Nerves getting you guys?"

"Nerves? What nerves? They didn't put no nerves in when they made Willow Swan."

Through D'loc Aloc

We moved out as soon as there was a ghost of light. It was an easy downhill trail with only a few places where we had trouble with the coach and Lady's wagon. By noon we reached the first trees. An hour later the first contingent were aboard a ferry raft. Before sundown we were inside the jungle of D'loc Aloc, where only ten thousand kinds of bugs tormented our bodies. Worse on our nerves than their buzzing, though, was One-Eye's suddenly inexhaustible store of praises and tales of his homeland.

From my first day in the Company I had been trying to get a fix on him and his country. Every lousy detail had had to be pried out. Now it was everything anyone ever wanted to know, and more. Except specifics of why he and his brother had run away from such a paradise.

From where I sat swatting myself the answer to that seemed self-evident. Only madmen and fools would subject themselves to such continuous torment.

So which was I?

For all there was a route through, we spent almost two months in that jungle. The jungle itself was the biggest problem. It was huge, and getting the coach through was, shall we say politely, a chore. But the people were a problem, too.

Not that they were unfriendly. Too much the opposite. Their ways were much easier than ours in the north. Those sleek, delectable little brown beauties had never seen anything like Murgen and Otto and Hagop and their boys. They all wanted a taste of novelty. The guys were cooperative.

Even Goblin got lucky often enough to keep an ear-to-ear grin on his ugly clock.

Poor hapless, inhibited old Croaker planted himself firmly among the spectators and longed his heart out.

I do not have the hair it takes to pursue a little casual funtime bouncy-bouncy while a more serious proposition is watching from the wings.

My attitude caused no direct verbal comment—those guys have some tact, sometimes—but I caught enough snide sidelongs to know what they were thinking. And them thinking made me think. When I get introspective I can become broody and unfit company for man or beast. And when I know I am being watched a natural shyness or reluctance sets in and I do not do anything, no matter how auspicious the omens.

So I sat around on my hands, getting depressed because I feared something important might be slipping away and I was constitutionally incapable of doing anything about it.

Life sure was less complicated in the old days.

My temper improved after we scaled a last excessively vegetated and overly bug-infested mountain range and broke out of the jungle onto high plateau savannah.

From there one of the more interesting aspects of D'loc-Aloc seemed to be the fact that we had not attracted a single volunteer soldier. It said something about the peace the people had with their environment. And something about One-Eye and his long-gone brother.

What the hell had they *done*? I noticed he made a point of avoiding any talk about his past, his age, or his earlier identity while in the jungle with Baldo and Wheezer. Like anybody would remember something a couple of teenagers had done that long ago.

Baldo and Wheezer planted us as soon as they had us outside the country of their own people. They claimed they had reached the limit of territory they knew. [They promised to round up a couple of trustworthy natives who could take us on.] Baldo announced that he was going to turn back despite his earlier contract. [He claimed Wheezer would do us just fine as intermediary interpreter.]

Something had happened to disenchant Baldo. I did not argue with him. His mind was made up. I just did not pay him the full fee he had been promised.

I was thrilled that Wheezer was going to stay. That guy was a second-rate soul son of One-Eye, full of ridiculous mischief. Maybe there is something in the water in the jungle of D'loc-Aloc. Except that Baldo and everyone else we met was almost normal.

I guess my magnetic personality draws the One-Eye/Wheezer types.

For sure there was fun in the offing. One-Eye had been taking it from Goblin for two months with never a spark in response. When the blowup came it was sure to be a beauty.

"The whole thing is backwards," I said as Lady and I mulled things over. "One-Eye is supposed to pick at scabs while Goblin lays in the weeds waiting like a snake."

"Maybe it's because we've crossed the equator. The seasons are reversed."

I did not understand that remark until I had given it hours of thought. Then I realized that it had no meaning. It was one of her droll, deadpan jokes.

The Savannah

We waited six days at the edge of the savannah. Twice bands of dark-skinned warriors came to look us over. The first time, Wheezer told us, "Don't let them lure you off the road."

He said it to One-Eye, not knowing that I had picked up enough of the chatter to follow what they said. I have a fair gift for tongues.

Most of us old hands do. We have to learn so many.

"What road?" One-Eye demanded. "That cow path?" He indicated a track that meandered into the distance.

"Whatever is between the white stones is the road. The road is holy. As long as you stay on it you'll be safe."

On first pitching camp we were warned not to leave a circle circumscribed by white stones. I guessed the significance of the lines of white stones running southward. Trade would demand sheltered routes. Though little trade seemed to be moving these days. Seldom had we encountered any sizable caravan heading north since leaving the empire. We saw no one headed south. Except perhaps a walking stump.

Wheezer continued, "Beware the plains peoples anyway. They are treacherous. They will employ every blandishment and deceit imaginable to draw you outside. Their women are especially notorious. Remember: They are always watching. To leave the road is death."

Lady was intensely interested in the discussion. She understood, too. And Goblin cracked, "You're dead, Maggot Lips."

"What?" One-Eye squeaked.

"The first set of sweet hips that shakes your way will lead you right off to the cannibals' cookpots."

"They aren't cannibals. . . ." Sudden panic tautened One-Eye's face.

It took him that long to realize that Goblin had understood him while he was talking with Wheezer. He looked at the rest of us. Some of us gave ourselves away.

He looked that much more distraught. He whispered to Wheezer with great animation.

Wheezer cackled. His laugh seemed half chicken cluck, half peacock call. It cost him a coughing fit.

It was a bad one. One-Eye beckoned me. "You're sure you can't do something for this guy, Croaker? He busts a lung and dies, we're hurting."

"Nothing. He shouldn't be traipsing around to begin with. . . ." No point singing that song. Wheezer refused to hear it. "You or Goblin ought to be able to do him more good than I can."

"You can't help a guy who won't let you."

"Ain't it the truth," I said, looking him straight in the eye. "How long before we get us some guides?"

"All I hear is 'soon' when I ask."

Soon indeed. A pair of tall black men came up the road at a steady, hardy trot. They were the sleakest, healthiest specimens I had seen in a long time. Each carried a sheaf of javelins across his back; a short-hafted, long-bladed spear in his right hand; and a shield of some white and black striped hide upon his left arm. Their limbs moved in perfect cadence, as though each man was half of some marvelous, rhythmic machine.

I glanced at Lady. No thoughts were evident on her face. "They would make grand soldiers," she said.

The two trotted straight to Wheezer, feigning a vast indifference to the rest of us. But I felt them studying us sidelong. White people had to be rare this side of the jungle. They barked at Wheezer in an arrogant tongue filled with clicks and stops.

Wheezer did some heavy kowtowing. He responded in the same language, whining like a slave addressing an ill-tempered master.

"Trouble," Lady prophesied.

"Right-o." This contempt for the outsider was not a new experience. I had to get busy and establish who said "Jump!" and who asked "How high?"

I talked to Goblin using the finger speech of the deaf. One-Eye caught it. He cackled. That stirred our new guides' indignation.

It would be touchy. They had to give me what they themselves knew was provocation. Only then would they accept being put in their place.

One-Eye was getting big ideas. I signed him to restrain himself, to prepare some impressive illusion. Aloud, I demanded, "What's all the babble? Get into the middle of that."

He started nagging Wheezer.

Wheezer carried on like a man caught between a rock and a hard place. He told One-Eye that the K'Hlata did not bargain. He said they would go through our things and pick out what they thought was worth their trouble.

"They try that and they'll get their fingers bitten off at the elbow. Tell them that. Politely."

It was too late for polite. Those guys understood the language. But One-Eye's growling threw them. They did not know what to do next.

"Croaker!" Murgen called. "Company."

Company indeed. Some of the boys who had given us the fish-eye earlier.

They were just the specific for the bruised egos of our new friends. The boys jumped up and down and howled and banged their spears against their shields. They hurled taunts. They pranced along the stone-marked boundary. One-Eye trotted after them.

The fish were not biting. But they had a little bait of their own. Something got said.

The two warriors howled and attacked. That caught everyone off guard. Three outsiders went down. The others subdued our guides quickly, though not without further mishap.

Wheezer poised on the boundary, wringing his hands and carping at One-Eye. While crows circled high above.

"Goblin!" I snapped. "One-Eye! Get with it!"

One-Eye cackled, reached up, grabbed his hair, and yanked.

He peeled himself from under that silly hat. And the fanged and fiery thing behind the peeling was ugly enough to turn a buzzard's stomach.

Which was all show, all distraction, while Goblin got on with the meat of it.

Goblin seemed to be surrounded by giant worms. It took me a moment to realize all those squirms were lengths of rope. I shrieked when I saw the state of our gear.

Goblin howled with laughter as a hundred chunks of rope went slithering through grass and air to pester, climb, bind, garrote.

Wheezer pranced around in an absolute apoplectic fit. "Stop! Stop! You're destroying the whole concord."

One-Eye ignored him. He put the mask back over the horror while punishing Goblin with ferocious looks. He resented Goblin's ingenuity.

Goblin was not finished. Having strangled everyone not already carved up or nominally friendly, he had his ropes drag the corpses across the boundary.

"No outside witnesses," One-Eye assured me, blind to those damned crows. He glared at Goblin. "What might the little toad have been up to?"

"Say what?"

"Those ropes. That was no spur-of-the-moment piece of work, Croaker. It would take months to charm that much line. I know who he had in mind, too. No bloody more nice, polite, long-suffering One-Eye. The gloves are off now. I'm going to get my revenge before that little bastard catches me with my back turned."

"Preemptive vengeance?" There was a One-Eye concept for you.

"I told you, he's up to something. I'm not going to stand around and wait. . . ."

"Ask Wheezer what to do about the bodies."

Wheezer said bury them deep and do a prime job of camouflaging.

"Trouble," Lady said. "Any way you look at it."

"The animals are rested. We'll outrun it."

"I hope so. I wish . . ." There was something in her voice that I could not decipher. I did not get it till later. Nostalgia. Homesickness. Longing for something irrevocably lost.

Goblin dubbed our new guides the Geek and the Freak. Despite my displeasure the names clung.

We crossed the savannah in fourteen days, without mishap, though Wheezer and the guides panicked each time they heard distant drums.

The message they dreaded did not come till we had left the savannah for the mountainous desert bounding it on the south. Both guides immediately begged to be allowed to stay with the Company. An extra spear is an extra spear.

One-Eye told me, "The drums said they've been declared outlaws. What they said about us you don't want to hear. You decide to go back north again you'd better think about another way to get there."

Four days later we made camp on some heights overlooking a large city and a broad river that flowed southeast. We had come to Gea-Xle, eight hundred miles below the equator. The mouth of that river, sixteen hundred miles farther south, lay at the edge of the world on the map I had made at the Temple of Travellers' Repose. The last place name marked, with great uncertainty, was Troko Tallio, a ways upriver from the coast.

Once camp was set to my satisfaction I went looking for Lady. I located her among some high rocks. But instead of studying the view she was staring into a tin teacup. For an instant the cup appeared to contain a pinprick spark. Then she sensed my approach. She looked up, smiled.

There was no spark in the cup when I looked again. Must have been my imagination.

"The Company is growing," she said. "You've accumulated twenty men since leaving the Tower."

"Uhm." I sat down, stared at the city. "Gea-Xle."

"Where the Black Company was in service. But where wasn't the Company in service?"

I chuckled. "You're right. We're wading around in our own past. We put the present dynasty in power down there. When we left it was without the usual hard feelings. What would happen if we rode in with Murgen showing our true colors?"

"There's only one way to find out. Let's try it."

Our gazes met and locked. The multiple meaning sparked between us. It had been a long time since that lost moment. We had been evading moments like this, a sort of delayed adolescent shyness and guilt.

The sun settled in a glorious conflagration, the only fire there was that evening.

I just could not get past who she used to be.

She was angry with me. But she hid it well and joined me in watching the city put on its night face. That was a cosmetic job worthy of an aging princess.

She did not need to waste energy getting mad at me. I was doing a fine job being mad at myself. "Strange stars, strange skies," I observed. "The constellations are completely out of whack now. Much more and I'll start feeling like I'm in the wrong world."

She made a snorting sound.

"More than I do already. Hell. I'd better rummage the Annals to see what they say about Gea-Xle. I don't know why, but the place bothers me." Which was true, though I'd only just realized it. That was unusual. People intimidate me, not places.

"Why don't you do that?" I could almost hear her thinking, *Go hide in your books and your yesterdays. I'll sit here staring today and tomorrow in the eye.*

It was one of those times when no matter what you say, it will be the wrong thing. So I did the second worst thing and went away without saying anything at all.

I almost tripped over Goblin going back to camp. Though I was making a racket stumbling through the dark, he was so intent he did not hear me.

He was peeping over a rock, eyeballing the slump of One-Eye's back. He was so obviously up to no good I could not resist. I bent and whispered, "Boo!"

He let out a squawk and jumped about ten feet, stood there giving me the evil eye.

I tramped on into camp and started digging for the book I wanted to read.

"Why don't you mind your own business, Croaker?" One-Eye demanded.

"What?"

"Mind your own business. I was laying for the little toad. If you hadn't stuck your nose in, I'd have had him strung up like an antelope ready for gutting." A rope slithered out of the darkness and curled up in his lap.

"I won't let it happen again."

The Annals did nothing to relieve my apprehension. I got really paranoid, getting that nervous itch between the shoulder blades. I began studying the darkness, trying to see who was watching.

Both Goblin and One-Eye had a big sullen on. I asked, "Can you guys come up for a little serious business?"

Well, yes, they could, but they could not admit that their pouting was not of earthshaking significance, so they just stared at me and waited for me to get on with it. "I've got a bad feeling. Not exactly a premonition, but the same family, and it keeps getting worse."

They stared, stone-faced, refusing comment.

But Murgen volunteered, "I know what you mean, Croaker. I've had the heebie-jeebies since we got here."

I gave the rest a scan. They stopped yakking. The Tonk games came to a halt. Otto and Hagop had small nods to admit that they felt unsettled, too. The rest were too macho to admit anything.

So. Maybe my collywobbles were not imaginary.

"I get a feeling going down there could become a watershed of Company history. Can one of you geniuses tell me why?"

Goblin and One-Eye looked at each other. Neither spoke.

"The only thing the Annals say that's weird is that Gea-Xle was one of those rare places the Company walked away from."

"What does that mean?" That Murgen was a natural shill.

"It means our forebrethren didn't have to fight their way out. They could have renewed their commission. But the Captain heard about a treasure mountain up north where the silver nuggets were supposed to weigh a pound."

There was more to the tale but they did not want to hear it. We were not really the Black Company anymore, just rootless men from nowhere headed the same direction. How much was that my fault? How much the fault of bitter circumstance?

"No comment?" They both looked thoughtful, though. "So. Murgen. Break out the real colors tomorrow. With all the honors."

That jacked up some eyebrows.

"Finish the tea, guys. And tell your bellies to get ready for some real brew. They make the genuine elixir down there."

That sparked some interest.

"You see? The Annals are good for something after all."

I set about doing some writing in the latest of my own volumes, occasionally peeking at one or another of the wizards. They had forgotten their feud, were using their heads for something more than the creation of mischief.

During one of my upward glances I caught a silvery yellow flash. It seemed to come from the rocks where I had been a while back, watching the city lights.

"Lady!"

I barked my shins a dozen times getting there, then felt like a fool when I found her seated on a rock, arms around her legs, chin on her knees, contemplating the night. The light of a newly risen moon fell upon her from behind. She was astonished by my wild stumble to the rescue.

"What happened?" I demanded.

"What?"

"I saw some weird flashes up here."

Her expression, in that light, seemed honestly baffled.

"Must have been a trick of the moonlight. Better turn in pretty soon. I want to get an early start."

"All right," she said in a small, troubled voice.

"Is something wrong?"

"No. I'm just lost." ·

I knew what she meant without her having to explain.

Going back I ran into Goblin and One-Eye moving up carefully. Fireflies of magic danced in their hands and dread smoldered in their eyes.

16

Willow's War

Willow was amazed. It actually went pretty much the way it was supposed to. The Taglians gave up their territories below the Main without a finger raised to resist. The army of the Shadowmasters came over the river and still met no resistance. It dissolved into its four elements. Still meeting no opposition, those forces broke up into companies, the better to plunder. The looting was so good all discipline collapsed.

Taglian marauders began picking off foragers and small raiding parties, suddenly, everywhere. The invaders suffered a thousand casualties before they understood. Cordy Mather engineered that phase, claiming to emulate his military idols, the Black Company. When the invaders responded with larger foraging parties he countered by leading them into traps and ambushes. At his peak he twice suckered entire companies into densely built and specially prepared towns that he burned down around them. The third time he tried that, though, the invaders did not take the bait. His overconfident Taglians got whipped. Wounded, he went back to Taglios to contemplate the fickleness of fate.

Willow, meantime, was marching around the eastern Taglian territories with Smoke and twenty-five hundred volunteers, keeping close to the enemy commander, trying to look like a menace that would become nemesis the moment the invaders made a mistake. Smoke had no intention of fighting, and was so stubborn even Willow was tempted to grumble.

Smoke claimed he was waiting for something to happen. He wouldn't say what.

Blade got stuck down south, in the territories yielded without a fight, along the Main River. He was supposed to get the locals together and keep any messengers from going back and forth. It was an easy job. There were no bridges across the river and only four places where it could be forded. The Shadowmasters must have been preoccupied. Their suspicions were not aroused. Or maybe they just assumed no news was good news.

What Smoke was waiting for happened.

Like Blade said, Taglios was hag-ridden by its priests. Three major religions existed there, not in harmony. Each had its splinters, factions, and subcults that feuded among themselves when they weren't feuding with the others. Taglian culture centered upon religious differences and the efforts of the priests to get ahead of each other. A lot of lower-class people weren't signed up with anybody. Especially out in the country. Likewise the ruling family, who did not dare get religion if they wanted to stay in charge.

Old Smoke was waiting for one of the boss priests to get the idea he could make a name for himself and his tribe by getting out and busting the heads of the invaders nobody else would fight. "Purely a cynical political maneuver," Smoke told Willow. "The Prahbrindrah's waited a long time to show someone what can happen if they don't do things his way."

He showed them.

One of the priests got the bright idea. He conned about fifteen thousand guys into thinking they could handle experienced professionals, heads up. He led the mob out to look for the invaders. They didn't have any trouble finding them. The Shadowmasters' commander thought this was what he was waiting for, too. The Shadowmasters' other conquests had all been settled by one big brawl.

Willow and Smoke and a few others stood on top of a hill where both sides could see them and spent an afternoon watching two thousand men massacre fifteen thousand. The Taglians that got away did so mostly because the invaders were too tired to chase them.

"Now we'll fight," Smoke said. So Willow moved his force up and poked till the invaders got aggravated and came after him. He ran till they stopped. Then he poked again. And ran again. And so forth. He got the notion from a poorly remembered version of a time when the Black Company ran for a thousand miles and led their enemies into a trap where they died almost to a man, thinking they had it won almost to the end.

Maybe these guys heard the same story. Anyway, they didn't want to be led. First time they balked they just camped and wouldn't move. So Willow talked it over with Smoke and Smoke rounded up some volunteers from the countryside and started building a wall around the invaders.

Next time the invaders just turned and marched off toward Taglios, which is what they should have done at the start, instead of trying to get rich. So Willow jumped on them from behind and kept making a nuisance of himself till he convinced the enemy commander that he had to be gotten rid of or there just wouldn't be any rest.

He told Smoke, "I don't know squat about strategy or tactics or anything, but I figure I only got to work on one guy, really. The head guy over there. I get him to do what I want, he brings everybody else with him. And I know how to aggravate a guy till he'll fight me."

Which is what he did.

The Shadowmasters' general finally chased him into a town that had been getting ready all along. It was a bigger version of Cordy's game. Only this time there wasn't going to be a fire. All the people had been got out and about twelve thousand volunteers put in their place. While Willow and Smoke were running the invaders around, those guys were building a wall.

Willow ran into the town and thumbed his nose. He did everything he could to get the enemy chief mad. The man did not get mad fast, though. He surrounded the town, then got every man he had in Taglian territory that could still walk. Then he attacked.

It was a nasty brawl. The invaders had it bad because in the tight streets they could not take advantage of better discipline. They always had guys shooting arrows at them off the rooftops. They always had guys with spears jumping out of doors and alleys. But they were better soldiers. They killed a lot of Taglians before they realized they were in a box, with about six times as many Taglians after them as they expected. By then it was too late for them to get out. But they took a lot of Taglians with them.

When it was over Willow went back to Taglios. Blade came home too, and they opened the tavern back up and celebrated for a couple weeks.

Meantime, the Shadowmasters figured out what happened and got thoroughly pissed. They made all kinds of threats. The prince, the Prahbrindrah Drah, basically thumbed his nose and told them to put it where the sun don't shine.

Willow, Cordy, and Blade got a month off, then it was time for the next part, which was to take a long trip north with the Radisha Drah and Smoke. Willow didn't figure this part was going to be a lot of fun, but nobody could figure a better way to work it.

Gea-Xle

I got them all up and decked out in their second best. Murgen had the standard out. There was a nice breeze to stretch it. Those great black horses stamped and champed, eager to get on down the road. Their passion communicated itself to their lesser cousins.

The gear was packed and loaded. There was no reason to hold movement—except that rattling conviction that the event would be something more than a ride into a city.

"You in a dramatic mood, Croaker?" Goblin asked. "Feel like showing off?"

I did and he knew it. I wanted to spit defiance in the face of my premonition. "What have you got in mind?"

Instead of answering directly, he told One-Eye, "When we get down there and come over that saddleback where they can get their first good look at us, you do a couple of thunders and a Trumpet of Doom. I'll do a Riding Through the Fire. That ought to let them know the Black Company is back in town."

I glanced at Lady. She seemed partly amused, partly patronizing.

For a moment One-Eye looked like he wanted to squabble. He swallowed it and nodded curtly. "Let's do it if we're going to do it, Croaker."

"Move out," I ordered. I did not know what they had in mind, but they could get flashy when they wanted.

They took the point together, Murgen a dozen yards behind with the standard. The rest fell into the usual file, with me and Lady side by side leading our share of pack animals. I recall eyeing the gleaming bare backs of the Geek and the Freak and reflecting that we had us some real infantry now.

The beginning of it was tight twists and turns on a steep, narrow path, but after a mile the way widened till it was almost a road. We passed several cottages evidently belonging to herdsmen, not nearly as poor and primitive as one would suspect.

Up we went into the backside of the saddle Goblin mentioned, and the show started. It was almost exactly what he prescribed.

One-Eye clapped his hands a couple of times and the results were sky-shaking crashes. Then he set them to his cheeks and let fly a trumpet call just as loud. Meantime, Goblin did something that filled the saddleback with a dense black smoke that turned into ferocious-looking but harmless flames. We rode through. I fought down a temptation to order a gallop and tell the wizards to have the horses breathe fire and kick up lightnings. I wanted a showy announcement of the Company's return, but not the appearance of a declaration of war.

"That ought to impress somebody," I said, looking back at the men riding out of the flames, the ordinary horses prancing and shying.

"If it doesn't scare hell out of them. You should be more careful how much you give away, Croaker."

"I feel daring and incautious this morning." Which was maybe the wrong thing to say after my failure of daring and lack of incaution the night before. But she let it pass.

"They're talking about us up there." She indicated the pair of stocky watchtowers flanking the road, three hundred yards ahead. There was no way to avoid riding between them, through a narrow passage filled with the shadow of death. Up top, heliographs chatted tower to tower and presumably with the city as well.

"Hope they're saying something nice, like hurray, the boys are back in town." We were close enough so I could make out the men up there. They did not look like guys getting ready for a fight. A couple sat on the merlons with their legs dangling outside. One that I took to be an officer stood in a crenel with one foot up on a merlon, leaning on his knee, watching casually.

"About the way I'd do it if I had me a really sneaky trap set," I grumped.

"Not everyone in the world has the serpentine sort of mind you do, Croaker."

"Oh yeah? I'm plain simple compared to some I could name."

She gave me one of her sharp old-time Lady-on-fire withering looks.

One-Eye was not there to say it himself, so I said it for him. "That snake's probably got more smarts than you do, Croaker. The only trouble he goes hunting is breakfast."

We were close to the one tower now, with Goblin and One-Eye and Murgen already past. I raised my hat in a friendly salute.

The officer reached down beside him, picked up something, tossed it down. It came tumbling toward me. I snatched it out of the air. "What an athlete! Maybe I'll go for two out of three."

I looked at what I caught.

It was a black stick about an inch and a quarter in diameter and fifteen inches long, carved from some heavy wood, decorated all over with ugly what-is-its. "I'll be damned."

"No doubt. What is it?"

"An officer's baton. I've never seen one before. But they're mentioned all through the Annals, up through the fall of Sham, which was some sort of mysterious lost city up on the plateau we just crossed." I lifted the baton in a second salute to the man above.

"The Company was there?"

"It's where it ended up after it left Gea-Xle. The Captain didn't find his silver mountain. He did find Sham. The Annals are pretty confused. The people of Sham are supposed to have been a lost race of whites. It seems that about three days after the Company found Sham, so did the ancestors of the Geek and the Freak. They got themselves worked up into some kind of religious frenzy and jumped all over the city. The first horde to get there killed damned near everybody, including most of the Company officers, before the Company finished killing them. The guys who survived headed north because there was another mob closing in from the south, keeping them from heading back this way. These batons aren't mentioned after that."

To which her only response was, "They knew you were coming, Croaker."

"Yeah." It was a mystery. I do not like mysteries. But it was only one of a herd and the bellies of most of them would never come floating up where I could give them the eyeball.

There were two guys waiting down the road from the watchtowers, a third of a mile from the city wall. The surrounding countryside was pretty barren for so close to a city. I guess the ground was poor. Farther north and south there was plenty of green. One of the two guys gave Goblin an old Company standard. There was no doubt what it was, though I did not recognize any of the honors. It was damned ragged, as you would expect of something as old as it had to be.

What the hell was going on here?

One-Eye tried talking to those guys but it was like starting a conversation with a stone. They faced their mounts around and got out front. I gave One-Eye a nod when he looked back to see if we should follow.

A twelve-man honor guard presented arms as we passed through the gate. But nobody else greeted us. Silence ran with us as we moved through the streets, people stopping to stare at the pale-faced strangers. Lady got half the attention.

She deserved it. She looked damned good. Very damned good. Black and tight both became her. She had the body to pull it off.

Our guides led us to a barracks and stable. The barracks part had been maintained but not used for a long time. It seemed we were supposed to make ourselves at home. All right.

Our guides did a fade while we were checking the place out.

"Well," Goblin said. "Bring on the dancing girls."

There were no dancing girls. There was not a lot of anything else either, unless you count apparent indifference. I had everybody stick tight the rest of the day, but nothing happened. We had been shelved and forgotten. Next morning I turned loose our two most recent recruits, along with One-Eye and Wheezer, on a mission meant to find a barge that would take us down the river.

"You just sent the fox to get a new latch for the chicken coop," Goblin protested. "You should've sent me along to keep him honest."

Otto busted out laughing.

I grinned but kept the rest inside. "You aren't brown enough to get by out there, little buddy."

"Oh, horse hockey. You bothered to look outside since we got here? There's white folks around, Fearless Leader."

Hagop said, "He's right, Croaker. Ain't a lot of them, but I seen a few."

"Where the hell did they come from?" I muttered, going to the door. Sparkle and Candles got out of my way. They were there to ambush any surprise unwanted guests. I went outside and leaned against the whitewashed wall, chewed a piece of horse sorrel I plucked from the edge of the street.

Yeah. The boys were right. There were a pair of whites, an old man and a twenty-fivish woman, skulking down the way. They made a production of being indifferent to me while everyone else gawked.

"Goblin. Get your tail out here."

He stumped outside, sulky. "Yeah?"

"Take a discreet look down there. You see an old man and a younger woman?"

"White?"

"Yes."

"I see them. So what?"

"Ever seen them before?"

"At my age everybody looks like somebody I've seen before. But we've never been in this part of the world. So maybe they look like somebody we seen somewhere else. She does, anyway."

"Hunh. Other way around for me. Something about the way he moves rings alarms."

Goblin plucked his own horse sorrel. I watched. When I looked back the odd couple were gone. Headed our way were three black guys who looked like trouble on the hoof. "Gods. I didn't know they made them that big."

Goblin muttered, stared past them. He wore a puzzled frown. He cocked his head like he was having trouble hearing.

The three big guys marched up, stopped. One started talking. I did not understand a word. "No spikee, pal. Try another lingo."

He did. I did not get any of that, either. He shrugged and checked his buddies. One of them tried a clicky tongue.

"You lose again, guys."

The biggest broke into a ferocious dance of frustration. His buddies gabbled. And Goblin wandered away on me without a fare-thee-well Croaker. I caught a glimpse of his back as he scooted into a passage between buildings.

Meantime, my new friends decided I was deaf or stupid. They yelled at me, slowly. Which brought Sparkle and Candles outside, followed by the others. The three big guys cussed each other some more and decided to go away.

"What was that all about?" Hagop asked.

"You got me."

Goblin came trooping back wearing a big smug frog grin.

"I'm amazed," I said. "I figured I was going to lose a week while I hunted down the local hoosegow and sold my soul to dig you out."

He put on a show of being hurt. He squeaked, "I thought I saw your girl-friend sneaking off. I just went to check."

"Judging by your smugness, you did see her."

"Sure did. And I saw her meet up with your old man and his fluff."

"Yeah? Let's go inside and give it a think."

I checked around in there just to make sure Goblin was not seeing things. Lady was gone, sure enough.

What the hell?

One-Eye and his crew came strutting in late that afternoon. One-Eye smirked like a cat with feathers in his whiskers. Geek and Freak lugged a big closed basket between them. Wheezer hacked and chewed and smiled like there was big mischief afoot and he maybe had a big hand in it.

Goblin jumped up from a nap with a squawk of protest before One-Eye got started. "You get right on back out that door with that whatever-it-is, Buzzard Breath. Before I turn that spider's nest you call a brain into toys for tumble-bugs."

One-Eye did not give him a look. "Check this out, Croaker. You ain't going to believe what I found."

The boys set the basket down and popped the lid.

"I probably won't," I agreed. I snuck up on that basket, expecting a gross of cobras, or something such. What I saw was a pint-sized ringer for Goblin. . . . Better say demitasse-sized, since Goblin is not much more than a half-pint himself. "What the hell is it? Where'd it come from?"

One-Eye stared at Goblin. "I been asking myself that for years." He had the biggest "Gotcha!" grin I ever saw.

Goblin howled like a leopardess in heat, started making mystical passes. His fingers raked furrows of fire out of the air.

Even I ignored him. "What is it?"

"It's an imp, Croaker. An honest-to-god imp. Don't you know an imp when you see one?"

"No. Where'd it come from?" I was not sure I wanted to know, knowing One-Eye.

"Heading down to the river we come on this little bunch of shops around an outdoor bazaar where they got all kinds of neat stuff for wizards, fortune-tellers, spirit talkers, Ouija workers, and such. And right there in the window of this dinky hole-in-the-wall shop, just begging for a new home, was this little guy. I couldn't resist. Say hello to the Captain, Frogface."

The imp piped, "Hello to the Captain, Frogface." It giggled just like Goblin, in a higher voice.

"Jump on out of there, bitty buddy," One-Eye said. The imp popped into the air as if shot up. One-Eye chortled. He caught it by a foot and stood there with it dangling head down like a toddler with a doll. He eyeballed Goblin, who was positively apoplectic, so fussed he could not go on with the magical funny business he had started.

One-Eye dropped the imp. It flipped and landed on its feet, sped across and stared up at Goblin like a young bastard having a sudden epiphany about the identity of its sire. It did cartwheels back to One-Eye, said, "I'm going to like it here with you guys."

I snagged One-Eye by the collar and lifted him off the floor. "What about the damned boat?" I shook him a little. "I sent you out to hire a goddamned boat, not to buy talking knickknacks." It was one of those flashes of rage that last about three seconds, rare for me but usually strong enough to let me make an ass of myself.

My father had them a lot. When I was little I would hide under the table for the minute or so they took to pass.

I set One-Eye down. Looking amazed, he told me, "I found one, all right? Pulls out day after tomorrow, at first light. I couldn't get an exclusive charter because we couldn't afford anything big enough to haul us and the animals and coaches if that was all the barge would be carrying. I ended up making a deal."

The imp Frogface was behind Wheezer, clinging to and peeking around his leg like a frightened child—though I got the feeling it was laughing at us. "All right. I apologize for blowing up. Tell me about the deal."

"This is only good to what they call the Third Cataract, understand. That's a place eight hundred sixty miles down that a boat can't get past. There's about an eight-mile portage, then you have to hire passage again."

"To the Second Cataract, no doubt."

"Sure. Anyway, we can get the long first leg free, with food and fodder provided, if we serve as guards on this commercial barge."

"Ah. Guards. What do they need guards for? And why so many?"

"Pirates."

"I see. Meaning we'd end up fighting even if we did pay for our passage."

"Probably."

"Did you get a good look at the boat? Is it defensible?"

"Yeah. We could turn it into a floating fort in a couple days. It's the biggest damned barge I ever seen."

A tinkle of alarm began nagging in the back of my thoughts. "We'll give it another look in the morning. All of us. The deal sounds too good to be true, which probably means it is."

"I figured. That was one of the reasons I bought Frogface. I can send him sneaking around to check things out." He grinned and glanced at Goblin, who had gone into a corner to plot and pout. "Also, with Frogface along we don't have to waste no coin on guides and interpreters. He can do all that for us."

That sent my eyebrows up. "Really?"

"That's right. See? I do do something useful once in a while."

"You're threatening to. You say the imp is ready to use?"

"As ready as he can be."

"Come on outside where it's private. I got about ten jobs for it."

The Barge

I took the outfit to the waterfront before the sun got its rump over the hills be-yond the river. The city remained somnolent, except for traffic headed the way we were. The nearer the river the worse it got. And the waterfront was a frenzied hive.

There were crows.

"Looks like they've been at it all night," I said. "Which one is it, One-Eye?"

"That big one over there."

I headed the direction he pointed. The barge was a monster, all right. It was a giant wooden shoe of a thing meant mainly to drift with the current. Travel would be slow on a fat, sluggish river like this. "It looks new."

We moved in an island of silence and stares. I tried to read the faces of the laborers we passed. I saw little but a slight wariness. I noted a few armed men, as big as my visitors of yesterday, boarding some of the lesser barges. I eyed the stevedores marching aboard our craft. "Why the lumber, do you suppose?"

"My idea," One-Eye said. "It's to build mantlets. The only protection from missile fire they had was wicker screens. I'm surprised they listened and went to the bother and expense. Maybe they took me up on all my suggestions. We're set if they did."

"I'm not surprised." I was now sure that not only had our arrival been fore-seen, it had been calculated into the schemes of an entire city. That pirate infes-tation was more than a nuisance. These folks meant to hammer it down using a band of expendable adventurers.

I did not understand why they thought they had to run a game on us. That was our trade. And we had to go down that river anyway.

Maybe it was the way the society worked. Maybe they could not believe the truth.

With Frogface's help it took about six minutes to straighten out the barge-master and the committee of bigwigs waiting with him. I wrangled the promise of a huge fee on top of our passage. "We go to work as soon as we see the money," I told them. Lo. It appeared almost magically.

One-Eye told me, "You could have held them up."

"They're desperate," I agreed. "Must be something they have to get through. Let's get to work."

"Don't you want to know what?"

"It doesn't matter. We're going anyway."

"Maybe. But I'll have Frogface look around."

"Whatever." I toured the main deck. Otto and Hagop tagged along. We talked upgraded defensibility. "We need a better idea of what we're up against. We want to be prepared for pirate tactics. For example, we might set up engines behind the mantlets if they attack from small boats."

I paused along the wharf-side rail. It was obvious a convoy would follow our barge, which as obviously had been constructed to lead the way. Never would they get it back upriver. It had only enough oars to keep it pointed the right direction.

There were crows over the chaos. I ignored them. I had begun to suspect I was obsessed.

Then I spied an island of emptiness against a warehouse wall. People avoided it without noting what they were doing. A vague shape stood in shadow. Crows fluttered up and down.

I felt like someone was staring at me. *Was* it my imagination? No one else saw the damned crows. "Time I found out what the hell is going on. One-Eye! I need to borrow your new pet."

I told Frogface to go over and take a gander. He went. And in a minute he was back, giving me a funny look. "What was I supposed to see, Captain?"

"What did you see?"

"Nothing."

I looked over there. Nothing was what I saw now. But then I spotted the three big guys who had tried to talk to me yesterday. They had a bunch of cousins with them, getting in the way. They were watching our barge. I presumed they were interested in us still. "Got a translating job for you, runt."

The biggest guy's name was Mogaba. Him and his buddies wanted to sign on with the Company. He said there were more at home like them if I would have them. Then he claimed a right. He told me that all the big men I saw wandering around with sharp steel were descendants of the Black Company men who had served Gea-Xle in olden times. They were the Nar, the military caste of the city. I got the impression that to them I was something holy, the real Captain, a demigod.

"What do you think?" I asked One-Eye.

"We could use guys like them. Look at them. Monsters. Take all you can get if they're for real."

"Can Frogface find out?"

"You bet." He instructed the imp, sent him scooting.

C roaker."

I jumped. I had not heard One-Eye coming. "What?"

"Those Nar are the real thing. Tell him, Frogface."

The imp piped away in that high Goblin voice.

The Nar were indeed descendants of our forebrethren. They did form a separate caste, a warrior cult built around the myths the Company left behind. They kept their own set of Annals and observed the ancient traditions better than we did. Then Frogface hit me with the kicker.

Somebody called Eldon the Seer, a famous local wizard, foretold our coming months ago, about the time we were crossing those shaggy-backed hills headed for D'loc-Aloc. The Nar (a word meaning black) had initiated a series of contests and trials to select the best man of each hundred to rejoin the father standard and make the pilgrimage to Khatovar. If we would have them.

Eldon the Seer had deciphered our mission from afar, too.

I do not like it when things are going on that I do not understand. Understand?

Mogaba was chosen commander of the delegation by virtue of being the champion of the caste.

While the Nar prepared for a holy hadj the lords and merchants of Gea-Xle began setting up to use us to break through a pirate blockade that had become impenetrable in recent years.

The great hope from the north. That was us.

"I don't know what to say," I told One-Eye.

"I'll tell you one thing, Croaker. You aren't going to be able to tell those Nar guys no."

I did not have that inclination. These pirates, about whom nobody would say much, sounded increasingly nasty. Somewhere down the line, without it having been stated explicitly, I had come on the notion that they had big magic they could call out when the going got hairy. "Why not?"

"Those guys are serious, Croaker. Religious serious. They'd do something crazy like throw themselves on their swords because the Captain found them inadequate to march with the Company."

"Come on."

"Really. I mean it. It's a religious thing with them. You're always telling about old ways. When the standard was a tutelary deity and whatnot. They've gone the other direction from what we did. The Company that went north turned into your basic gang of cutthroats. The kids they left behind turned them into gods."

"That's scary."

"Better believe."

"They're going to be disappointed in us. I'm the only one left who takes the traditions seriously."

"Horseapples, Croaker. Spit and polish and beating the drum for the olden days ain't all there is to it. I got to go find that little geek Goblin and see if he can stop pouting long enough for us to do a layout on how we work this scow if it gets hit. Hell. The pirates know everything that's going on up here. Maybe our reputation will scare them into letting us slide through."

"Think so?" It sounded like a nice idea.

"No. Frogface! Get over here. Acts like a damned kid, getting into things. Frogface, I want you to stick with Croaker. You do what he tells you just like if he was me. Got it? You don't and I'll paddle your butt."

For all its talents, the imp had the mind of a five-year-old. With an attention span to match. It told One-Eye it would behave and help me, but I did not expect that to be easy.

I went down to the wharf and accepted thirty-two recruits into our brotherhood of arms. Mogaba was so pleased I thought he might hug me.

They were a damned impressive thirty-two men, every one a monster and quick and lithe as a cat. If they were the mongrel children of the men who had served in Gea-Xle, what must those old-timers have been like?

First thing after I swore them in, Mogaba asked if it was all right if his caste brothers did guard duty aboard the other boats. So they could tell their sons that they had followed the hadj as far as the Third Cataract.

"Sure. Why not?" Mogaba and his boys had my head spinning. For the first time since I got stiffed with the job, I really *felt* like I was the Captain.

The gang dispersed to get their gear and to spread the good news.

I noted the master of the barge watching from up forward. He was wearing a big poo-eating grin.

Things were going just dandy for his crowd. They thought they had us by the short hairs and broken to the bridle.

H ey, Croaker. Here comes your prodigal girlfriend."

"You too, Pup? I ought to toss you in the river." If I could run the imp down. He had the energy of a five-year-old, too.

I spotted her by the commotion she caused. Or the lack of it. Where she passed men paused to look and sigh and shake their heads wistfully. It did not occur to them to whistle, catcall, or make crude remarks.

I looked around and picked a victim. "Murgen!"

Murgen ambled over. "What do you need?"

"When Lady gets here show her her quarters. The attached room is for her guests."

"I thought . . ."

"Don't think. Just do."

I made myself scarce. I was not yet ready for the inevitable battle.

The River

Night on the river. A moon splattering the dark mirror of water. A stillness at times almost supernatural, then the cacophony of a festival in hell: crocodiles grunting, fifty kinds of frogs singing, birds hooting and squawking, hippos snorting; the gods only knew what all.

And bugs buzzing. The bugs were almost as bad as they had been in the jungle. They would get worse once we entered the wetlands farther south. The river was said to flow imperceptibly through a swamp ten to eighty miles wide and three hundred miles long. Here the west bank was still tame. The east was three-quarters wild. The people we saw watching from boats in the mouths of sloughs and creeks were as poorly tamed as their land.

I was assured that they, living in the shadow of the city, were harmless. When they came whooping out it was to hawk crocodile hides and parrot-feather cloaks. On impulse I bought one of the cloaks, the biggest and most outrageously colorful one available. It must have weighed sixty pounds. Wearing it I became the very image of a savage chieftain.

Mogaba examined the cloak and pronounced it a wise buy. He told me it would shed darts and arrows better than armor of steel.

Some of the Nar bought croc hides to toughen their shields.

Goblin got a wild hair and bought him a couple of preserved croc heads. One was so big it looked like it had been lopped off a dragon. While I was seated up top contemplating the nighttime river, wondering about crows, he was up forward mounting his monster purchase as a figurehead. I supposed he had some drama up his sleeve.

He came to me with the smaller head. "I want to fit you out to wear this."

"You what?"

"I want to fit you out to wear this. So when the pirates come you can strut around up here in your feather coat breathing fire like some mythological beast."

"That's a great gimmick. I really like it. In fact, I love it. Why don't we see if we can't get some dope like Big Bucket to try it."

"But—"

"You don't think *I'm* going to stand up there and let people snipe at *me*, do you?"

"You'll have plenty of protection from me and One-Eye."

"Yeah? Then my prayers are answered at last. For years I've wanted nothing more than protection from you and One-Eye. 'Preserve me, O sainted fathers of the Company!' I've cried a thousand times. Yea, ten thousand times have I called—"

Sputtering, he cut me off and changed the subject. He squeaked, "Those people your girlfriend brought aboard—"

"Next fool who calls Lady my girlfriend gets to throw a saddle on a croc and see if they can be broken. You get my drift?"

"Yeah. You got your feelings hurt on account of reality is catching up with you."

I kept my mouth shut, but just barely.

"Bad news, those two are, Croaker." He whispered in the no-breath whisper we use when we are creeping past enemy sentries. "There's big mojo brewing down in their cabin."

He was trying to make himself useful. He had been overshadowed since the appearance of Frogface. So I did not tell him I was on to that already and had had me a thought or two about what could be done.

A fish jumped up and skipped across the water to get away from some predator. For his effort he got his reward: some night bird snagged him on the bounce.

I grunted. Should I let Goblin know how much I knew and suspected? Or should I just go on looking dumb while setting the moment up? Building a mystique had become important now that the Company was on the grow. It should work for a while. The old hands should not suspect me of taking as cynical and pragmatic an approach to command as I planned.

I listened to Goblin's outpouring of fact, suspicion, and speculation. Little that he said was new. What *was* new only more thoroughly framed the picture I had. I told him, "I think it's time you came up with the masterpiece of your life, Goblin. Something plain, direct, and powerful, that you can cut loose in a second."

He turned on the famous Goblin grin. "I'm way ahead of you, Croaker. I've got a couple of things in the works that are going to amaze people when I use them."

"Good." I had a feeling One-Eye was in for a shock somewhere down the line.

The journey to the Third Cataract takes a minimum two weeks because the current does not exceed a slow walk. Adding pirate trouble could make the trip last forever.

By the end of our fourth day the barge was as defensible as possible. Timber shields protected the main deck. Their lower ends projected over the water to make boarding from boats difficult. None of the embrasures in that shielding were big enough for a man to weasel through. The guys had put together four ballistae for each side. Thanks to One-Eye's foresight we had the makings for firebombs by the score, and ready bombs in well-protected nests atop the deckhouse. The three brothers from Beryl built us a dolphin, which is a fish-shaped weight attached to a long chain. It is swung out on a boom and dropped through the bottoms of boats. My favorite engine, though, was thought up by Patience, a former caravan guard.

A springboard would slap the base of a cartridge filled with poisonous darts, throwing a hail of missiles. The poison needed only the tiniest cut to cause quick paralysis. The engine's one shortcoming was that it was immobile. You had to wait for your target to cross your aim.

Once construction was finished I treated everyone to a rich diet of my own pet peeves from my days as a follower instead of chieftain. Drills and exercises. And intense language study. I kept One-Eye and his pet in a sweat trying to establish at least one common tongue among the men. There was plenty of grumbling. Only the Nar were impressed favorably.

Lady did not appear. She might not have existed for all we could tell.

We entered the wetlands, mostly cypress swamp, early the sixth morning. Everyone became more alert.

There was no sign of pirates for another two days. When they did come we had plenty of warning from One-Eye and Goblin.

We were passing through a place where the cypress crowded the channel. The attackers, in twenty boats, came at us head-on, around a bend. I could bring only two ballistae to bear. Those stopped just one boat. Arrows from those of us atop the deckhouse—which ran most of the length and width of the barge—did no good. The boats had canopies of crocodile hide.

They rushed in alongside. Grapnels on chains not easily cut caught on the top of the shielding. Pirates began clambering up.

I had them where I wanted them.

The shields were perforated with small holes. Mogaba's Nar stabbed through those at legs. The few pirates reaching the top had to balance on a four-inch width of timber before leaping to the deckhouse roof.

It was a turkey shoot. None survived to make the jump.

Goblin and One-Eye did not lift a sorcerous finger. They amused themselves throwing firebombs. The pirates had not encountered those before. They fled sooner than they would have had the boys not gotten into the game.

My guess is the pirates lost fifty to sixty men. Not a small hurt, but smaller than it could have been, and the good merchants of Gea-Xle hoped we would break the pirates.

The bargemaster appeared out of nowhere, like a ghost, as the pirates hauled ass. Neither he nor his crew had been visible during the skirmish. We had been drifting free, at the whim of the river.

Frogface appeared coincidentally. I used him to give the man nine kinds of hell. My rage took the edge off the complaining he did about us letting so many pirates get away.

"You'll have to fight them again, now. Next time they'll know what to expect."

"The way I heard, the first attack is just a probe. What the hell is going on out there?" The river had begun to foam with underwater excitement. Something began thumping against the barge's hull.

"Needleteeth." The bargemaster shuddered. Even Frogface seemed unsettled. "A fish as long as your arm. Heads for blood in the water. When there's a lot they go mad and attack everything. They can devour a hippo, bones and all, in a minute."

"Is that so?"

The river grew wilder. The dead pirates, and the wounded who had not gotten aboard boats and away, vanished. Broken and burning boats and driftwood went down piscine gullets. At least the needleteeth gave it the heroic try.

Once I was convinced the crew would participate in wreaking their own salvation next time, I went and had me a powwow with my tame wizards.

The second attack came at night. This time those guys were serious. Their earlier asskicking had them feeling no-prisoners mean.

We had plenty of warning, of course. Goblin and One-Eye were on the job.

It was in another narrow place and this time they had a boom across to catch and hold us. I screwed them up by having anchors dropped when Goblin detected the boom. We stopped two hundred yards above the heart of the trap. We waited.

"Goblin? One-Eye? You guys set?" We had our surprises.

"Ready, Mom."

"Cletus. You on the dolphin?"

"Yes sir."

We had not used that before. "Otto. I don't hear that goddamned pump. What the hell is going on back there?"

"I'm looking for the crew guys now, Croaker."

All right. They wanted to chicken out again, eh? Hoped they could buy off the pirates by not resisting? "Murgen, dig that barge boss out of his hiding hole." I knew where he was. "I want him up here. One-Eye. I need your pet."

"Soon as he gets back from scouting."

Frogface showed first. He was telling me that every adult male in the swamp was out there when Murgen brought the bargemaster to me whimpering in a hammerlock. As the first pirate arrows fell I said, "Tell him he goes over the side if his people aren't on the job in two minutes. And that I'll keep throwing guys out till I get what I want." I meant what I said.

The message got through. I heard the pumps begin squeaking and clinking when Murgen and I were getting set to see how far we could throw a man.

The arrow fall picked up. It was ill-directed and did no harm, but its only purpose was to keep our heads down.

There was a big outbreak of cussing and caterwauling yonder when Goblin tested a favorite gimmick from his White Rose days, a spell that started every insect in a small area noshing on the nearest human flesh.

The whoop and holler died quickly. Test fulfilled, question answered. They had somebody capable of undoing trivial witcheries.

One-Eye was supposed to sneak along to spot the guy responsible, if one turned up, so he and Goblin could gang up and nail his hide to the nearest cypress.

The arrow fall stopped. And speak of the devil, here came One-Eye. "Big trouble, Croaker. That guy over there is a heavyweight. I don't know what we can do about him."

"Do what you can. Blindside him. Did you notice? The arrows stopped?" There was a lot of carrying on in the swamp, to cover the sounds of oars.

"Right." One-Eye ran to his place. A point of pink light soared upward. I donned the crocodile head Goblin had fixed. It was time for the show.

Half of winning a battle is showmanship.

The pink point grew up fast and shed light on the river.

There must have been forty boats sneaking toward us. They had extended their croc-hide protection in hopes of shedding firebombs.

I was glowing and breathing fire. Bet I made a hell of a sight from over there.

The nearest boats were ten feet away. I saw the ladder boxes and grinned behind my croc teeth. I had guessed right.

I threw my hands up, then down.

A single firebomb arced out to shatter upon a boat.

"Stop pumping, you goddamned idiots!" I yelled.

The bomb was a dud.

I did my act again.

Second time had the charm. Fire splattered. In seconds the river was aflame except for a narrow strip around the barge.

The trap was almost too good. The fire sucked most of the air away and heated what was left till it was almost unbearable. But the burning did not last long, thanks to the lack of enthusiasm of the oil pumpers.

Fewer than half the attack wave succumbed, but the survivors had no stomach left for combat. Especially after the dolphin and ballistae started knocking their boats apart. They headed for cover. Slowly. Painfully. The ballistae and dart throwers left their sting.

A big, big howl went up over there. It took them a while to get the anger worked out.

A rattle, clank, and slap of oars against water announced a second wave.

I was laying for these guys, too. It was the third wave that would be the bitch, if they did not get it out of their systems right away. The third wave and that unknown quantity that One-Eye had discovered were what worried me.

The pirate boats were a hundred feet from the barge when Goblin gave me the high sign.

He had the needleteeth gathering in baffled thousands.

The lead boats got close enough. I went into my dance.

The dolphin went down, shattering a large wooden swamp boat. Every engine cut loose. Fire bombs and javelins flew.

The idea was to get some wounded pirates into the water with the needleteeth.

Some got.

The river went mad.

Half the pirate boats were hides stretched on wooden frames. Those did not last at all. Wooden boats fared better, but only the heaviest withstood repeated strikes. And even they were at the mercy of the panic of the men aboard.

The smartest and quickest pirates charged the barge. If they could get aboard and take control . . . . But that was the chance I wanted them to see.

They had come prepared with ladders that had planks fixed to their backs. Thrown up on our mantlets and nailed into place the ladder backing would protect pirate arms and legs from the stabbing Nar.

Except that I had had the Nar driving spikes and sharpened wooden slats through the cracks between the mantlet timbers. Those made it hard to put the ladders up. Cletus and his brothers smashed several boats before the pirates discovered what wonderful hand and foot holds the spikes made.

The Nar had instructions to leave them alone as long as they did nothing but hang there. Their presence would discourage sniping by their brothers and fathers and cousins.

It took a while, but silence came to the night and stillness to the river. The wreckage drifted off to pile up against the boom. My men sat down to rest. One-Eye pulled his pink lights out of the sky. He, Goblin, Frogface, my squad leaders, Mogaba, and, lo!, the barge's master, joined me for a powwow. The latter suggested we up anchor and roll.

"How long have we been here?" I asked.

"Two hours," Goblin said.

"We'll let it rest a while." The convoy was supposed to have fallen back till it was an estimated eight hours behind, the theory being that if they overtook us because we were in action, they would arrive with the pirates in a state of exhaustion and would be able to overcome them if we had been wiped out. "One-Eye. What's the situation with the sorcerer over there?"

He did not sound well when he replied, "We could be in big trouble, Croaker. He's even more potent than we guessed at first."

"You tried getting him?"

"Twice. I don't think he even noticed."

"If he's that bad why's he laying off instead of stomping us?"

"We don't know."

"Should we take the initiative? Should we bait him and try to draw him out?"

Murgen asked, "Why don't we just break the boom and go? We got enough of them to keep the swamp in mourning for a year."

"They won't let us, that's why. They can't. One-Eye. Can you find that wizard?"

"Yeah. Why should I? I agree with the kid. Break the boom. They might surprise us."

"They'd surprise us, all right. What the hell do you think the boom is there for, dummy? Why do you think I stopped us up here? Can you put one of your little pink balls in his hair?"

"If I have to. For maybe half a minute."

"You have to. When I tell you." I had been trying to find unusual parameters to the situation and thought I had one. I was set for an interesting, if potentially fatal, experiment. "Hagop. You and Otto get all the ballistae around to the east side. Take forty percent of the tension off them so they can throw firebombs without breaking them in the trough." With Frogface's help I told Mogaba I wanted his archers on the deckhouse roof. "When One-Eye spots our target I want half high-angle, plunging fire, half flat trajectory. And I want firebombs flying like we're trying to burn the swamp down."

A pirate let out a cry of despair as he lost his grip and fell from the shielding. A riot in the water told us the needleteeth knew a good thing and had hung around.

"Let's get at it."

Goblin hung on till the others had gone. "I think I know what you're trying to do, Croaker. I hope you don't regret it."

"You hope? I blow it and we're all dead."

I gave the command. One-Eye's rangefinder squirted across the water. The moment it blossomed everyone cut loose.

For a minute I thought we had the sucker.

Suddenly, Lady materialized on the deckhouse roof. I removed my crocodile head. "Heck of a show there, eh?" Cypress and moss *will* burn, liberally primed.

"What do you think you're doing?"

"You finally deign to report for duty, soldier?"

Her left cheek twitched. My tactic had not been deployed against the pirate sorcerer at all.

An arrow burred between us, not six inches from either of our noses. Lady jumped.

Then the pirates clinging to the shielding finally tried coming on up and over to the deckhouse roof. The half dozen not swept away by the archers just threw themselves into a hedgehog of spears set to receive them.

"I think I've fixed it so there's only one way they can take us." I gave her a moment to think. "They have a sorcerer who's a heavy hitter. So far he's laid low. I've just told him I know he's there and I'm going to get him if I can."

"You don't know what you're doing, Croaker."

"Wrong. I know exactly what I'm doing."

She spat an epithet of disbelief, stamped away.

"Frogface!" I called.

He materialized. "Better put that croc hat back on, chief. The spell won't keep the arrows off if you don't." One whimpered past as he spoke.

I grabbed the head. "You do the job on her stuff?"

"All taken care of, chief. I rolled it over into a place that isn't this place. You'll hear them howling in a minute."

The fires among the cypress winked out like snuffed candles. Several of One-Eye's pink fireflies sailed across and simply vanished. The night began to fill with an oppressive and dreadful sense of presence.

The only light left flickered around me and around the mouth of the croc head mounted on the bow.

Lady came at a run. "Croaker! What did you do?"

"I told you I knew what I was doing."

"But—"

"All gone all your little toys from the Tower? Call it intuition, love. Reaching a conclusion from inadequate and scattered information. Though I think it helped being familiar with the people I'm playing with."

The darkness grew deeper. The stars vanished. But the night had a gleam on, like a polished piece of coal. You could see glimmers though there was no light at all—not even from the figurehead.

"You're going to get us killed."

"That possibility has existed since I was elected Captain. It existed when we left the Barrowland. It existed when we walked away from the Tower. It existed when we sailed from Opal. It existed when you swore your oath to the Black Company. It became highly probable when I accepted this hasty and misrepresented commission from the merchants of Gea-Xle. Nothing new there, friend."

Something like a large, flat black stone came skipping across the water, throwing up sprays of silver. Goblin and One-Eye scuttled it.

"What do you want, Croaker?" Her voice was taut, maybe even edged with fear.

"I want to know who runs the Black Company. I want to know who makes the decisions about who travels with us and who doesn't. I want to know who gives members of the Company permission to wander off for days at a time, and who gives out the right to hide out for a week, shirking all duties. Most of all, I want to know who decides which adventures and intrigues will involve the Company."

The skipping stones kept coming, leaving their sprays and ripples of silver. Each came nearer the barge.

"Who's going to run things, Lady? You or me? Whose game are we going to play? Yours or mine? If not mine, all your treasures stay where you can't get at them. And we go to the needleteeth. Now."

"You're not bluffing, are you?"

"You don't bluff when you're sitting across the table from somebody like you. You bet everything you've got and wait to see if you're called."

She knew me. She had had her looks inside me. She knew I could do it if I had to. She said, "You've changed. Gone hard."

"To be the Captain you have to *be* the Captain, not the Annalist or the Company physician. Though the romantic is still alive back in there somewhere. You might have pulled it off if you'd gone through with it that night on that hill."

One of the skipping stones nudged the barge.

I said, "You had me going for a while."

"You idiot. That night didn't have anything to do with this. Back then I didn't think there was a chance this would work. That was a woman on that hill with a man she cared about and wanted, Croaker. And she thought that was a man who—"

The next stone *whamm*'d home. The barge shuddered. Goblin yelled, "Croaker!"

"Are we going to make a move?" I asked. "Or should I shuck down so I can try to outswim the needleteeth?"

"Damn you! You win."

"Your promise good this time? For them, too?"

"Yes, damnit."

I took a chance. "Frogface. Roll it over. Bring the stuff back."

A stone hit the barge. Timbers groaned. I staggered and Goblin yelled again.

I said, "Your stuff is back, Lady. Get Shifter and his girlfriend up here."

"You knew?"

"I told you. I figured it out. Move."

The old man called Eldron the Seer appeared, but now he wore his true guise. He was the supposedly slain Taken called Shapeshifter, half as tall as a house and half as wide, a monster of a man in scarlet. Wild, stringy hair whipped around his head. His jungle of a beard was matted and filthy. He leaned upon a glowing staff that was an elongated, improbably thin female body, perfect in its detail. It had been among Lady's things and had been the final clue that had convinced me when Frogface reported its presence. He pointed that staff across the river.

A hundred-foot splash of oily fire boiled up amidst the cypress.

The barge reeled at the kiss of another flat stone. Timbers flew. Below, the horses shrieked in panic. Some of the crew sang with them. My companions looked grim in the light of the fires.

Shapeshifter kept laying down splash after splash, till the swamp was immersed in a holocaust that beggared both of mine put together. The screams of the pirates became lost in the roar of the flames.

I won my bet.

And Shifter kept laying it down.

A great howling rose within the fire. It faded into the distance.

Goblin looked at me. I looked at him. "Two of them in ten days," I muttered.

We had heard that howling last during the Battle at Charm. "And not friends anymore. Lady, what would I have found if I *had* opened those graves?"

"I don't know, Croaker. Anymore, I don't. I never expected to see the Howler again. That's for sure." She sounded like a frightened, troubled child.

I believed her.

A shadow passed the light. A night-flying crow? What next?

Shifter's companion saw it, too. Her eyes were tight and intense.

I took Lady's hand. I liked her a lot better now that she had her vulnerability back.

Willow up the Creek

Willow scowled at the boat. "I'm so thrilled I could shit."

"What's wrong?" Cordy asked.

"I don't like boats."

"Why don't you walk? Me and Blade will cheer you on whenever we see you puffing along the riverbank."

"If I had your sense of humor, I'd kill myself and save the world the pain, Cordy. Hell, we got to do it, let's do it." He headed out the wharf. "You seen the Woman and her pup?"

"Smoke was around earlier. I think they're on already. Low profile. On the sneak. They don't want anybody knowing the Radisha is leaving town."

"What about us?"

Blade grinned. "Going to cry because the girls didn't come down to drag him back."

"Going to cry a lot, Blade," Cordy said. "Old Willow can't go anywhere without bitching to keep his feet moving."

The boat wasn't that bad. It was sixty feet long and comfortable for its cargo, which consisted only of the five passengers. Willow got in his gripe about that too, as soon as he discovered that the Radisha hadn't brought a platoon of servants. "I was sort of counting on having somebody take care of me."

"Getting soft, man," Blade said. "Next thing, you be wanting to hire somebody to fight in your place when you get trouble."

"Sounds good to me. We done enough of that for somebody else. Haven't we, Cordy?"

"Some."

The crew poled the boat into the current, which was almost nonexistent that far down the river. They upped a linen sail and swung the bow north. There was a good breeze. They gained on the current about as fast as a man moving at a lazy stroll. Not fast. But no one was in a big hurry.

"I don't see why we got to start now," Willow said. "We ain't going where she wants. I bet you the river's still blockaded above the Third Cataract. There won't be no way we can get past Thresh. That's far enough to suit me, anyway."

"Thought you was going to keep on hiking," Cordy said.

"He remembered they laying for him in Gea-Xle," Blade said. "Moneylenders got no sense of humor."

It took two weeks to reach Catorce, below the First Cataract. They hardly saw Smoke or the Radisha the whole time. They got damned tired of the crew, as humorless a bunch of river rats as ever lived, all of them fathers and sons and brothers and uncles of each other so nobody ever dared loosen up. The Radisha would not let them put in at night. She figured somebody would shoot his mouth off and the whole world would find out who was on the river without benefit of armed guards.

That hurt Willow's feelings from a couple different directions.

The First Cataract was an obstacle to navigation only to traffic coming up the river. The current was too swift for sail or oars and the banks too far and boggy for a towpath. The Radisha had them leave the boat at Catorce, with the crew to wait there for their return, and they made the eighteen-mile journey to Dadiz, above the cataract, on foot.

Willow looked out at river barges coming down, riding the current, and griped.

Blade and Cordy just grinned at him.

The Radisha hired another boat for the passage to the Second Cataract. She and Smoke stopped trying to stay out of sight. She figured they were too far from Taglios for anybody to recognize them. The First Cataract was four hundred eighty miles north of Taglios.

Half a day out of Dadiz Willow joined Cordy and Blade in the bows. He said, "You guys notice some little brown guys back in town? Kind of watching us?"

Cordy nodded. Blade grunted an affirmative. Willow said, "I was afraid it was my imagination. Maybe I'll wish it was. I didn't recognize the type. You guys?"

Cordy shook his head. Blade said, "No."

"You guys don't break a jaw chinning."

"How would they know to be watching us, Willow? Whoever they are? Only one who knows where we're headed is the Prahbrindrah Drah, and even he don't know why."

Willow started to say something, decided he should shut his mouth and think. After a minute, he grunted. "The Shadowmasters. They might know somehow."

"Yeah. They might."

"You think they might give us some trouble?"

"What would you do if you was them?"

"Right. I better go nag on Smoke." Smoke could be the hole card. Smoke claimed the Shadowmasters didn't know about him. Or if they did, they had no good estimate of his competence.

Smoke and the Radisha had made themselves comfortable in the shade of the sail and were watching the river go by. The river was something worth seeing, Willow would admit. Even here it was half a mile wide. "Smoke, old buddy, we maybe got us a problem."

The wizard stopped chewing on something he had had in his mouth all morning. He peered at Willow with narrowed eyes. Willow's style was getting to him.

"Back in Dadiz there was these little brown guys about so high, skinny and wrinkly, that was watching us. I asked Cordy and Blade. They seen them, too."

Smoke looked at the woman. She looked at Willow. "Not someone you made an enemy of coming south?"

Willow laughed. "Hey. I don't have no enemies. No. There's nobody like these guys anywhere between Roses and Taglios. I never saw anybody like them before. I figure that means it's not me they're interested in."

She looked at Smoke. "Did you notice anyone?"

"No. But I wasn't watching. It seemed unnecessary."

"Hey. Smoke. You always watch," Willow said. "This here's your basic unfriendly old world. You better always be on the lookout when you're travelling. There's bad guys out here. Believe it or not, not everybody's as polite as you Taglians."

Swan returned to the bow. "That dolt wizard never even noticed the brownies. The guy's got lard for brains."

Blade took out a knife and whetstone and went to work. "Better sharpen up. Edge might dull down before the old boy wakes up and sees we're under attack."

It was a three-hundred-mile passage to the Second Cataract, where the river scampered nervously between dark and brooding hills, as though too wary to stay in one place long. On the right bank the haunted ruins of Cho'n Delor stared down on the flood, reminding Willow of a heap of old skulls. No traffic had passed along the right bank since the fall of the Paingod. Even animals shunned the area.

On the hilltops beyond the left bank were the ruins of the Triplet Cities, Odd the First, Odd the Second, and Odd the Third. Stories Cordy had heard coming south said they had sacrificed themselves to bring the Paingod down.

Now people lived only along a narrow strip beside the Cataract, in a walled city one street wide and ten miles long, perpetually nervous about ghosts from the wars that were. They called their bizarre city Idon, and had the weirdest bunch of quirks anyone ever saw. Travellers stayed in Idon only as long as absolutely necessary. Likewise, many of the people of Idon themselves.

Passing through, keeping his eyes open while pretending to be gawking at the weirdos, Willow noticed little brown guys skulking everywhere. "Hey. Smoke. You eagle-eyed bastard. You see them now?"

"What?"

"He don't," Blade said. "Better sharpen me a couple more knives."

"Pay attention, old man. They're all over like roaches." Actually, Willow had seen only eight or nine. But that was plenty enough. Especially if they had the Shadowmasters behind them.

They had somebody behind them. They made that clear soon after the Radisha found a boat for the trip to Thresh and the Third Cataract.

They got around a bend in the river, where it flowed through country that looked like it was left over from the war between the Triplet Cities and Cho'n Delor, and here came two fast boats loaded down with little brown guys rowing like the winner of the race got to become immortal.

The crew the Radisha had hired took maybe twenty seconds to decide it wasn't their squabble. They dived overboard and headed for the bank.

"You see them now, Smoke?" Willow asked, starting to ready his weapons. "I hope you're half the wizard you think you are." There were at least twenty brown men in each boat.

Smoke's jaw went high speed as he chomped whatever he chewed all the time. He did nothing till the boats began creeping up to either side. Then he stuck out both hands toward one, closed his eyes and wriggled his fingers.

All the nails and pegs holding the boat together flew around like swarming swallows, pattered into the water. Brown men hollered and gurgled. It didn't look like many of them knew how to swim.

Smoke took a moment to catch his breath, then turned on the other boat. The brown men there were turning already, heading for shore.

Smoke took that boat apart, too. Then he gave Willow one dark look and went back to his seat in the shadow of the sail. He smirked forever afterward whenever he heard Willow bitching about having to work ship.

"At least we know he's the real thing now," Willow grumbled to himself.

The situation in Thresh was exactly what Willow had predicted. The river was closed to the north. Pirates. The Radisha could find no one willing to hazard the long run north to Gea-Xle, which is where she was determined to go, to wait. Nothing she offered would get anybody to risk the journey. Not even her companions, whom she urged to steal a boat.

She was furious. You would have thought the hinges of the world would lock up if she didn't get to Gea-Xle.

She did not get.

For months they hung around Thresh, staying out of the way of little brown guys, hearing rumors that the merchants of Gea-Xle had gotten desperate enough to try doing something about the river pirates. Thresh was a snake's nest of gloom. Without trade upriver it would wither. Any hope that the northerners would break through seemed absurd. Everyone who tried died.

One morning Smoke came to breakfast looking thoughtful. "I had a dream," he announced.

"Oh, wonderful," Willow snapped. "I been sitting around here for months now just praying you'd have another one of your nightmares. What do we do this time? Storm the Shadowlands?"

Smoke ignored him. He had been doing that a lot, communicating through the Radisha. It was the only way he could deal with Swan without getting violent. He told the woman, "They've departed Gea-Xle. A whole convoy."

"Can they break through?"

Smoke shrugged. "There's a power as mighty and cruel as the Shadowmasters in the swamps. Maybe greater than the Shadowmasters. I haven't been able to find it in my dreams."

Willow muttered, "I hope the brownies aren't smoking something, too. They figure we're going to connect up they might get more ambitious."

"They don't know why we're here, Swan. I poked around. I found out that much. They just want you and me and Cordy. Would have done it to us in Taglios if they caught us there." •

"Comes to the same thing. How long before that convoy gets here?"

The Radisha said, "Smoke? How long?"

The wizard responded with all the steely certitude of his breed. He shrugged.

The lead boat was spotted by somebody fishing upriver. The news reached Thresh a few hours before the barge. Willow and his group went down to the piers with half the city to wait for it. People howled and cheered until those aboard began disembarking. Then a deep, dread silence fell.

The Radisha grabbed Smoke's shoulder in a grip obviously painful. "*These are your saviors? Old man, I'm about out of patience with you. . . .*"

Thresh

We broke the boom. We headed for the trading city Thresh, which lies above the Third Cataract. It was a quiet river going down. There might have been no other human beings in the world outside of us on the barge. But the wreckage that kept pace was a screaming reminder that we were not alone, that we belonged to a bleak and bloody-minded species. I was not fit company for man or beast, as they say.

One-Eye joined me where I stood under the battered croc head Goblin had mounted in the bows. "Be there in a little bit, Croaker."

I dipped into my trick bag of repartee and countered with an unenthusiastic grunt.

"Me and the runt been trying to get a feel for the place up ahead."

I cracked him up with another grunt. That was his job.

"Don't got a good feel to it." We watched another small fishing boat hoist anchor and raise sail and skitter south with the news of our coming. "Not a real danger feel. Not an all-bad feel. Just not a right feel. Like there's something going on."

He sounded puzzled around the edges. "You figure it's something that might concern us, send your pet to find out what. That's what you bought him for. Isn't it?"

He smirked.

The current in a lazy turn of the river held us close to the right bank. Two solemn crows watched our progress from a lone dead tree. Gnarled and ugly, the tree made me think of nooses and hanged men.

"Now why didn't I think of that, Croaker? Here I just sent him into town to check on the quiff situation."

Teach your grandmother to suck eggs, Croaker.

The imp came back with a disturbing report. There were people in Thresh waiting for us. Specifically us, the Black Company.

How the hell did everybody know we were coming?

The waterfront was mobbed when we warped in, though nobody really believed we had come from Gea-Xle. I guess they figured we spontaneously generated on the river up around the bend. I kept everyone aboard and mostly out of sight till the rest of the convoy arrived.

It came through untouched. Its guards and crews were simmering with stories of the devastation they had found in our wake. Rejoicing spread through Thresh. The blockade had been strangling the city.

I watched the good citizens from behind a mantlet. Here and there I noted hard-eyed little brown men who seemed less than enchanted with our advent.

"Those the guys you were talking about?" I asked One-Eye.

He gave them the fish-eye, then shook his head. "Ours should be over that way. There they are. Weird."

I saw what he meant. A man with long blond hair. What the hell was he doing down here? "Keep an eye on them."

I collected Mogaba and Goblin and a couple of the guys who looked like they ate babies for breakfast and went into conference with the bosses of the convoy. They surprised me. They not only did not argue about paying the balance of our fee, they tossed in a bonus on account of every barge got through. Then I got my key people together and told them, "Let's get off-loaded and hit the road. This place gives me the creeps."

Goblin and One-Eye complained. Naturally. They wanted to stay and party.

They came around when the iron coach and the great black horses and the Company standard hit the wharfside road. The joy went out of the grand celebration almost immediately. I'd figured it would.

Blank faces watched the unforgotten standard pass.

Thresh had been on the other side when the Company was in service in Goes. Our forebrethren had kicked their butts good. So good they recalled the Company this long after the fact, though Goes itself no longer existed.

We paused in an open market toward the south edge of Thresh. Mogaba had a couple of his lieutenants dicker for supplies. Goblin went stomping around in a squeaking rage because One-Eye had set Frogface to following him, aping his every word and move. The imp was trudging behind him at the moment, looking deep in thought. Otto and Hagop and Candles were trying to thrash out the details of a pool that would pay off big to the guy who guessed closest to when Goblin would come up with a definitive counterstroke. The trouble was a definition of what could be considered definitive.

One-Eye observed proceedings with a benign, smug smile, certain he had attained ascendancy at last. The Nar stood around looking grimly military and still a little baffled because the rest of us had less rigid, absolute standards. They had not been disappointed in us on the river.

One-Eye ambled over. "Them people are giving us the eye again. Got them all picked out now. Four men and a woman."

"Round them up and bring them over. We'll see what's on their minds. Where's Wheezer?"

One-Eye pointed, then did a fade. As I approached Wheezer I noted that a dozen of my men had disappeared. One-Eye wasn't going to take any chances.

I told Wheezer to tell Mogaba we weren't stocking up for a six-month campaign. We just wanted enough stuff for a meal or two getting past the Cataract. We yakked it back and forth, Mogaba struggling with the Jewel Cities dialect he had begun to pick up already. He was a sharp, smart man. I liked him. He was flexible enough to understand that our two versions of the Company could have arisen easily over two hundred years. He worked at being nonjudgmental.

So did I.

"Hey, Croaker. Here you go." Here came One-Eye, grinning like a possum, bringing in his catch. The three younger men, two of whom were whites, seemed baffled. The woman looked angry. The old man looked like he was daydreaming.

I eyeballed the white men, again wondering how the hell they had gotten here. "They got anything to say for themselves?"

Mogaba drifted over. He looked at the black man thoughtfully.

About then the woman had plenty to say. The darker haired white man wilted slightly but the other just grinned. I said, "Let's check them on languages. Between us we've got most of them they speak up north."

Frogface popped up. "Try them out on Rosean, chief. I got a hunch." Then he rattled something at the old man. The guy jumped about a foot off the ground. Frogface chortled. The old man stared like he was seeing a ghost.

Before I could ask what verbal stunt he'd pulled, the blond man asked, "You the captain of this outfit?" He spoke Rosean. I understood him, but my Rosean was rusty. I hadn't used it in a long time.

"Yeah. You got any other languages you use?"

He had. He tried a couple. His Forsberger was not good, but my Rosean was worse. He asked, "What the hell happened to you guys?" He regretted saying it immediately.

I looked at One-Eye. He shrugged. I asked, "What do you mean?"

"Uh . . . coming down the river. You done the impossible. Ain't nobody gotten through in a couple years. Me and Cordy and Blade, we were about the last ones."

"Just lucky."

He frowned. He had heard the stories spread by the boatmen.

Mogaba said something to one of his lieutenants. They looked the black man, Blade, over good. The Geek and the Freak, who had confessed to being brothers and having the real names Claw-of-the-Lion and Heart-of-the-Lion, also moved in to look him over. He wasn't pleased. I asked Heart, "Is there something special about that guy?"

"Maybe, Captain. Maybe. Tell you later."

"Right." Back to Forsberger. "You've been watching us. We want to know why."

He had an answer all ready. "My buddies and me, we been hired to take the broad and the old boy down the river. We was kind of hoping we could hook on with you guys as far as Taglios. For the extra protection, you know what I mean?" He looked at Murgen and the standard. "I seen that somewhere before."

"Roses. Who are you?" How stupid did I look? Maybe I needed to check a mirror.

"Oh. Yeah. Sorry. I'm Swan. Willow Swan." He stuck out a hand. I didn't take it. "This here's my buddy Cordy Mather. Cordwood. Don't ask. Even he don't know why. And this's Blade. We been doing what you might call freelancing, up and down the river. Taking advantage of being exotic. You know how it is. You guys been about everywhere."

He was rattled. You couldn't have tortured it out of him, maybe, but he was scared half to death. He kept looking at the standard and the coach and the horses and the Nar and shuddering.

He was a lot of things, maybe, that he was not going to admit. A liar was the biggest. I thought it might be interesting, even entertaining, to have him and his bunch along. So I gave him what he wanted. "All right. Tag along. As long as you pull your weight and remember who's in charge."

He broke out in smiles. "Great. You got it, chief." He started chattering at his pals. The old man said something sharp that shut him up.

I asked Frogface, "He give anything away there?"

"Nah. He just said, 'I did it!,' chief. And went to bragging on his golden tongue."

"Swan. Where the hell is this Taglios? I don't have a Taglios on my maps."

"Let me see."

Half an hour later I knew his Taglios was a place my best map named Troko Tallios. "Trogo Taglios," Swan told me. "There's this monster city, Taglios, that surrounds an older one that was called Trogo. The official name is Trogo Taglios but nobody ever calls it anything but Taglios anymore. It's a nice place. You'll like it."

"I hope so."

One-Eye said, "He's going to try to sell you something, Croaker."

I grinned. "We'll have some fun with him while he tries. Watch them. Be friendly with them. Find out whatever you can. Where's Lady gotten off to now?"

I was too fussed. She wasn't far off. She was standing aside, inspecting our new acquisitions from another angle. I beckoned her. "What do you think?" I asked when she joined me. Swan's eyes popped when he got a good look at her. He was in love.

"Not much. Watch the woman. She's in charge. And she's used to getting her own way."

"Aren't you all?"

"Cynic."

"That's me. To the bone. And you're the one made me that way, love."

She gave me a funny look, forced a smile.

I wondered if we'd ever recover that moment on that hillside so many miles to the north.

We were just coming back to the river, after having walked past the Third Cataract, when Willow joined me as I walked my horse. He eyed the big black nervously and got around where I would be between it and him. He asked, "Are you guys *really* the Black Company?"

"The one and only. The evil, mean, rude, crude, nasty, and sometimes even unpleasant Black Company. You never spent any time in the military, did you?"

"As little as I could. Man, last I heard there was a thousand of you guys. What happened?"

"Times got hard up north. A year ago we were down to seven men. How long ago did you leave the empire?"

"Way back. Me and Cordy bugged out of Roses maybe a year after you guys were in there after that Rebel general, Raker. I wasn't much more than a kid. We sort of drifted from one thing to another, headed south. First thing you know, we was across the Sea of Torments. Then we got into some trouble with the imperials, so we had to get out of the empire. Then we just kept drifting, a little bit this year, a little bit that. We hooked up with Blade. Next thing you know, here we are down here. What're you guys doing here?"

"Going home." That was all I needed to tell him.

He knew plenty about us if he had come to us knowing Taglios was on our itinerary but not our final destination.

I said, "In a military outfit it's not acceptable behavior for just anybody to walk up and start shooting the shit with the commander any time they feel like it. I try to keep this outfit looking military. It intimidates the yokels."

"Yeah. Gotcha. Channels, and all that. Right." He went away.

His Taglios was a long way off. I figured we had time to sort his bunch out. So why press?

22

Taglios

We returned to the river and sailed down to the Second Cataract. Faster traffic had carried the word that the boys were back. Idon, a bizarre strip of a town, was a ghost city. We saw not a dozen souls there. Once again we had come to a place where the Black Company was remembered. That made me uncomfortable.

What had our forebrethren done down here? The Annals went on about the Pastel Wars but did not recall the sort of excesses that would terrify the descendants of the survivors forever.

Below Idon, while we waited to find a bargemaster with guts enough to take us south, I had Murgen plant the standard. Mogaba, as serious as ever, got a ditch dug and our encampment lightly fortified. I swiped a boat and crossed the river and climbed the hills to the ruins of Cho'n Delor. I spent a day roaming that haunted memorial to a dead god, alone except for crows, always wondering about the sort of men who had gone before me.

I suspected and feared that they had been men very much like me. Men caught in the rhythm and motion and pace, unable to wriggle free.

The Annalist who recorded the epic struggle that took place while the Company was in service to the Paingod had written a lot of words, sometimes

going into too great a detail about daily minutiae, but he had had very little to
say about the men with whom he had served. Most had left their mark only
when he recorded their passing.

I have been accused of the same. It has been said that too often when I
bother to mention someone in particular it is only as a name of the slain. And
maybe there's truth in that. Or maybe that's getting it backward. There is always
pain in writing about those who have perished before me. Even when I mention
them only in passing. These are my brethren, my family. Now, almost, my children. These Annals are their memorial. And my catharsis. But even as a child I
was a master at damping and concealing my emotions.

But I was speaking of ruins, the spoor of battle.

The Pastel Wars must have been a struggle as bitter as that we had endured
in the north, confined to a smaller territory. The scars were still grim. They
might take a thousand years to heal.

Twice during that outing I thought I glimpsed the mobile stump I had seen
from the wall of the Temple of Travellers' Repose. I tried getting closer, for a
better look, but it always disappeared on me.

It was never more than a glimpse from the corner of my eye, anyway.
Maybe I was imagining it.

I did not get to explore as thoroughly as I wanted. I was tempted to hang
around but the old animal down inside told me I did not want to be stranded in
those ruins after dark. It told me wicked things stalked Cho'n Delor's night. I
listened. I went back over the river. Mogaba met me at the shore. He wanted to
know what I had found. He was as interested in the Company's past as I was.

I liked and respected the big black man more with every hour. That evening
I formalized his hitherto *de facto* status as commander of the Company infantry. And I resolved to take Murgen's Annalist training more seriously.

Maybe it was just a hunch. Whatever, I decided that it was time I got the
Company's internal workings whipped into order.

All these natives, lately, were afraid of us. They carried old grudges. Maybe
farther down the river there was somebody with less fear and a bigger grudge.

We were on the brink of lands where the Company's adventures were recalled in the early lost volumes of the Annals. The earliest extant picked up our
tale in cities north of Trogo Taglios—cities that no longer exist. I wished there
was some way I could dig details of the past out of the locals. But they were not
talking to us.

While I moped around Cho'n Delor One-Eye found a southern bargemaster willing to carry us all the way to Trogo Taglios. The man's fee was exorbi-
tant, but Willow Swan assured me I was unlikely to get a better offer. We were
haunted by our historical legacy.

I got no help from Swan or his companions unearthing that.

My notion for unmasking Swan and his gang gradually made very little headway. The woman forced them to stay to themselves, which did not please Cordy Mather. He was hungry for news from the empire. I did find out that the old man was called Smoke, but never got a hint of the woman's name. Even with Frogface on the job.

They were cautious people.

Meantime, they watched us so closely I felt they were taking notes whenever I bellied up to the rail to increase the flow in the river.

Other concerns plagued me, too. Crows. Always, crows. And Lady, who hardly spoke these days. She pulled her turns at duty with the rest of the Company but stayed out of the way otherwise.

Shifter and his girlfriend were not to be seen. They had disappeared while we unloaded at Thresh—though I held the disturbing certainty that they were still around, close enough to be watching.

What with the crows and all our arrivals anticipated I had the feeling I was being watched all the time. It was not hard to get a little paranoid.

We rode the rapids of the First Cataract and swept on down the great river, into the dawn of Company history.

My maps called it Troko Tallios. Locally they called it Trogo Taglios, though those who lived there used the shorter Taglios, mostly. As Swan said, the Trogo part refers to an older city that has been enveloped by the younger, more energetic Taglios.

It was the biggest city I had ever seen, a vast sprawl without a protective wall, still growing rapidly, horizontally instead of vertically. Northern cities grow upward because no one wants to build outside the wall.

Taglios lay on the southeast bank of the great river, actually inland a little, straddling a tributary that snakes between a half-dozen low hills. We debarked in a place that was really a satellite of the greater city, a riverport town called Maheranga. Soon Maheranga would share the fate of Trogo.

Trogo retained its identity only because it was the seat of the lords of the greater principiate, its governmental and religious center.

The Taglian people seemed friendly, peaceable, and overly god-ridden, much as Swan and Mather had described in brief exchanges during our journey. But underneath that they seemed to be frightened. And Swan had told us nothing about that.

And it was not the Company that was their terror. They treated us with respect and courtesy.

Swan and party vanished as soon as we tied up. I did not have to tell One-Eye to keep an eye on them.

The maps showed the sea only forty miles from Taglios, but that was along a straight line to the nearest coast, west across the river. Down the river's mean-der and delta it was two hundred miles to salt water. On the map the delta looked like a many-fingered, spidery hand clawing at the belly of the sea.

It is useful to know a little about Taglios because the Company ended up spending a lot more time there than any of us planned. Maybe even more than the Taglians themselves hoped.

Once I was convinced we would be secure doing so I ordered a break at Taglios. The rest was overdue. And I needed to do some heavy research. We were near the edge of the maps in my possession.

I discovered that I had come to count on Swan and Mather to show me around. Without them I was forced to rely on One-Eye's pet devil. And that I did not like. For no reason I could finger, I did not entirely trust the imp. Maybe it was because his sense of humor so closely reflected his owner's. The only time you trusted One-Eye was when your life was at stake.

I hoped we were now far enough south that I could chart the rest of our course to Khatovar before we resumed travelling.

Lady had been the perfect soldier since the encounter on the river, though not much of a companion otherwise. She was shaken badly by the Howler's re-turn and enmity. He had been a staunch supporter in the old days.

She was still caught in the purgatory zone between the old Lady and the new that had to be, and the heart was not bound in the same direction as the head. She could not find her way out and, much as I ached for her, I did not know how to take her hand and show her.

I figured she deserved a distraction. I had Frogface shop for a local equiva-lent of Opal's Gardens and he astonished me by finding one. I asked Lady if she would be interested in a real social evening out.

She was amenable, if not excited after so many months of neglect. Not thrilled. Just, "I don't have anything better to do, so why not."

She never was the social sort. And both my maneuver on the river and my evasions through attention to duty had not left her pleased with me.

We did it decked out, with drama, though without as much uproar as we had raised in Opal. I did not want the local lords taking offense. One-Eye and Goblin behaved. Frogface was the only clear evidence of sorcery. None of that nastiness we had shown in Opal. Frogface went along in his capacity as universal translator.

One-Eye decked his pet out in a costume as flamboyant as his own, one that mocked Goblin's dress subtly. It seemed to state that this was how nice Goblin could look if he would get over being a slob.

Taglios's elite went to see and be seen in an olive grove past its prime bearing years. The grove bestrode a hill near old Trogo. A hot spring fed a score of private baths. It cost a bundle to get in when you were not known, most of that in bribes. Even so, it was two days after I asked before room could be found for us.

We went in the coach with Goblin and One-Eye up top and squads of four Nar each marching before and behind. Murgen drove. He took the coach away after he delivered us. The others accompanied us into the grove. I wore my legate's costume. Lady was dressed for the kill, but in black. All the time with the black. It looked good on her, but times were I wished she would try another color.

She said, "Our presence has stirred more interest than you expected." Our advent had caused very little stir in the streets of Taglios.

She was right. Unless the grove was a major *in* place to spend an evening a lot of class folks had come out just to give us the eye. It looked like everyone who might be anyone was there. "Wonder why?"

"There's something going on here, Croaker."

I am not blind. I knew. I knew after a few minutes with Willow Swan way back upriver. But I could not find out what. Even Frogface was no help. If they did any scheming they did it when he was not around.

Except for the Nar, who had lived with ceremony in Gea-Xle, we were all uncomfortable under the pressure of so many eyes. I admitted, "This might not have been one of my brighter ideas."

"On the contrary. It confirms our suspicions that there's a greater interest in us than should be for simple travellers. They mean to use us." She was disturbed.

"Welcome to life in the Black Company, sweetheart," I said. "Now you know why I'm cynical about lords and such. Now you know one of the feelings I've been trying to get across."

"Maybe I get it. A little. I feel demeaned. Like I'm not human at all but an object that might be useful."

"Like I said, welcome to the Black Company."

That was not all her problem. I harken back to the rogue Taken Howler, the dead unexpectedly alive and inimical. No amount of tall talking would convince me his appearance on the river was chance. He had been there to do us hurt.

Moreover, there had been an odd and unusual interest in us at least since Opal. I looked for crows.

There were crows in the olive trees, quiet and still. Watching. Always watching.

Shapeshifter's presence in Gea-Xle, the dead again living, waiting for Lady. There were hidden schemes brewing. Too much had happened to let me believe otherwise.

I had not pressed her. Yet. She was being a good soldier. Maybe waiting . . .

For what?

I had learned long ago that I can find out more around her sort by watching and listening and thinking than I ever do by asking. They lie and mislead even when there is no need. More, except in her own case, I did not think she had any better idea what was stirring than I did.

The grove staff showed us to a private bower with its own hot mineral bath. The Nar spread out. Goblin and One-Eye found themselves inconspicuous posts. Frogface stayed close, to interpret.

We settled.

"How is your research coming?" Lady asked. She toyed with some plump purple grapes.

"Strangely is the only way to describe it. I think we're right up next to the place where you come to the end of the earth and fall off the edge."

"What? Oh. Your sense of humor."

"Taglios is infested with chartmakers. They do good work. But I can't find one map that will get me where I want to go."

"Maybe you haven't been able to make them understand what you need."

"It wasn't that. They understood. That's the problem. You tell them what you need and they go deaf. New maps only run to the southern borders of Taglian territory. When you can find an old one, it fades to blank eight hundred miles southeast of the city. It's the same even with maps so good they show damned near every tree and cottage."

"They're hiding something?"

"A whole city? Don't seem likely. But it does look like there's no other explanation."

"You asked the appropriate questions?"

"With the silver-tongued cunning of a snake. When the blank space comes up translation problems develop."

"What will you do?"

Dusk had come. Lamplighters were at work. I watched a moment. "Maybe use Frogface somehow. I'm not sure. We're far enough back that the Annals are almost useless. But the indicators are that we head straight for that blank space. You have any thoughts about it?"

"Me?"

"You. Things are happening around the Company. I don't think that's because *I* strut so pretty."

"Phooey."

"I haven't pressed, Lady. For all there's reason. And I won't—unless I have to. But it *would* be nice to know why we've got one dead Taken hanging around watching us out of the bushes and another one that used to be your buddy trying to kill us back in those swamps. Might be interesting to know if he knew you were aboard that barge, or if he was working on a grudge against Shifter, or if he just wanted to keep traffic from moving down the river. Might be interesting to know if we're likely to run into him again. Or somebody else who didn't die on time."

I tried to keep my tone gentle and neutral but some of my anger got through.

The first food arrived, bits of iced melon soaked in brandy. While we nibbled, some thoughtful soul gave our guardians food as well. Less elegant fare, perhaps, but food nevertheless.

Lady sucked a melon ball and looked thoughtful. Then her whole stance changed. She shouted, "Don't eat that stuff!" She used the tongue of the Jewel Cities, which by now even the most thick-witted of the Nar understood.

Silence grabbed the grove. The Nar dropped their platters.

I rose. "What is it?"

"Someone has tampered with their food."

"Poison?"

"Drugged, I'd guess. I'd have to check more closely."

I went and got the nearest's platter. He looked grim behind his Nar mask of indifference. He wanted to hurt somebody.

He got his chance when I turned back with my plunder.

A quick shuffle of feet. A *thwack!* of wood against flesh. A cry of pain that was little more than a whimper. I turned. The Nar had his spearpoint resting on the throat of a man sprawled before him. I recognized one of the lamplighters.

A long knife lay not far from his outflung hand.

I surveyed our surroundings. Bland faces watched from every direction.

"One-Eye. Frogface. Come here." They came. "I want something low-key. Something that won't disturb anybody's dinner. But something that will have him in a mood to talk when I'm ready. Can do?"

One-Eye snickered. "I know just the thing." He rubbed his hands in wicked glee while Goblin, left out, pouted. "I know just the thing. Go enjoy your dinner and sweet nothings. Old One-Eye will take care of everything. I'll have him ready to sing like a canary."

He gestured. An invisible force snagged the lamplighter's heels. Up he went, wriggling like a fish on a line, mouth stretched to scream but nothing coming out.

I settled opposite Lady. A jerk of my head. "One-Eye's idea of low-key. Don't let the victim scream." I popped a melon ball into my mouth.

One-Eye stopped lifting the lamplighter when his nose was twenty feet off the ground.

Lady began poking through the Nar's food.

The expedient of turning my back on One-Eye did not let me attain the mood I'd had in mind when arranging the evening. And Lady remained troubled.

I glanced over my shoulder occasionally.

The captive shed bits of clothing like dead leaves peeling away. The flesh beneath, betrayed, crawled with tiny lime and lemon glowing worms. When two of different hues butted heads they sparked and the failed assassin tried to shriek. When the mood took him, One-Eye let the man fall till his nose was a foot off the ground. Frogface whispered into his ear till One-Eye hoisted him up again.

Real low-key. What the hell would he have done if I'd asked for a show?

Goblin caught my eye. I raised an eyebrow. He used deaf sign to tell me, "Company coming. Looks like big stuff."

I pretended no greater interest than my meal while watching Lady intently. She seemed possessed of no special awareness.

There were two of them, well dressed and courteous. One was a native, walnut brown but not of negroid stock. The people of Taglios were dark but not negroid. The negroid peoples we had seen there were all visitors from up the river. The other one we knew already, Willow Swan, with the hair as yellow as maize.

Swan spoke to the Nar nearest him while his companion appraised One-Eye's efforts. I nodded to Goblin, who went to see if he could get any sense from Swan.

He came back looking thoughtful. "Swan says the guy with him is the boss wog around here. His choice of words, not mine."

"I guess it was bound to come." I exchanged glances with Lady. She had on her empress's face, readable as a rock. I wanted to shake her, to hug her, to do *something* to free up the passion that had appeared so briefly before going underground. She shrugged.

I said, "Invite them to join us. And tell One-Eye to send the imp over. I want him to check on Swan's translations."

The serving staff got down on their faces as our guests approached. It was the first time I had seen that kind of behavior in Taglios. Swan's prince was the real thing.

Swan got right to it. "This here's the Prahbrindrah Drah, the head guy around here."

"And you work for him."

He smiled. "In a left-hand sort of way. Drafted. He wants to know if you're looking for a commission."

"You know we're not."

"I told him. But he wanted to check it out personal."

"We're on a quest." I thought that sounded dramatic enough.

"A mission from the gods?"

"A what?"

"These Taglians are superstitious. You ought to know that by now. That would be the way to get the quest idea across. Mission from the gods. Sure you couldn't stick around for a while? Take a break from the road. I know how rough it is, travelling and travelling. And my man needs somebody to do his dirty work. You guys got a rep for handling that stuff."

"What do you really know about us, Swan?"

He shrugged. "Stories."

"Stories. Hunh."

The Prahbrindrah Drah said something.

"He wants to know why that guy is hanging up in the air."

"Because he tried to stab me in the back. After somebody tried to poison my guards. After a while I'm going to ask him why."

Swan and the Prahbrindrah chattered. The Prahbrindrah looked irked. He glanced at One-Eye's pet, chattered some more.

"He wants to know about your quest."

"You heard it all coming down the river. You told him already."

"Man, he's trying to be polite."

I shrugged. "How come so much interest in a few people just passing through?"

Swan started looking nervous. We were starting to move in toward it. The Prahbrindrah said several sentences.

Swan said, "The Prahbrindrah says you've talked about where you've been—and he would like to hear more about your adventures because far peoples and places intrigue him—and your quest, but you haven't really said where you're going." He sounded like he was trying to translate very accurately. Frogface gave me a shallow nod.

We had told Swan's bunch little during the passage south from the Third Cataract. We had hidden from them as much as they from us. I decided to pronounce the name maybe better kept to myself. "Khatovar."

Willow did not bother translating.

The Prahbrindrah chattered.

"He says you shouldn't do that."

"Too late to stop, Swan."

"Then you got troubles you can't even imagine, Captain." Swan translated. The Prince replied. He got excited.

"Boss says it's your neck and you can shave with an axe if you want, but no sane man says that name. Death could strike you down before you finished." He shrugged and smirked as he spoke. "Though it's likely more mundane forces will slaughter you if you insist on chasing that chimera. There's bad territory between here and there." Swan looked at the Prince and rolled his eyes. "We hear tales of monsters and sorcery."

"Hey, really." I plucked a morsel from a small bird, chewed, swallowed. "Swan, I brought this outfit here all the way from the Barrowland. You remember the Barrowland. Monsters and sorcery? Seven thousand miles. I never lost a man. You remember the river? Folks who got in my way didn't live to be sorry. Listen close. I'm trying to say a couple of things here. I'm eight hundred miles from the edge of the map. I won't stop now. I can't." It was one of the longest speeches I've ever made, outside reading to the men from the Annals.

"Your problem is those eight hundred miles, Cap. The other seven thousand were a stroll in the country."

The Prahbrindrah said something short. Swan nodded but did not translate. I looked at Frogface. He told me, "Glittering stone."

"What?"

"That's what he said, chief. Glittering stone. I don't know what he meant."

"Swan?"

"It's a local expression. 'The walking dead' is the closest way to say it in Rosean. It has something to do with old times and something called the Free Companies of Khatovar, which was bad medicine back when."

I raised an eyebrow. "The Black Company is the last of the Free Companies of Khatovar, Swan."

He gave me a sharp look. Then he translated.

The Prince chattered back. He stared at One-Eye's victim as he did.

"Cap, he says he supposes anything is possible. But a returning company ain't been spotted since his granddaddy's granddaddy was a pup. He wonders, though. Says maybe you're real. Your coming was foretold." Quick glance at Frogface, with a scowl, like the imp was a traitor. "And the Shadowmasters have warned him against dealing with you. Though that would be the natural inclination, considering the devastation and despair spread by the fanatics of old."

I glanced at Frogface. He nodded. Swan was striving for exactitude.

Lady said, "He's playing games, Croaker. He wants something. Tell him to get to the point."

"That would be nice, Swan."

He continued translating, "But yesterday's terror means nothing today. You are not those fanatics. That was seen on the river. And Trogo Taglios will bow the neck to no one. If the pestilence in the south fears a band of freebooters, he is willing to forget the ancient scores and tend to those of his own time. If you too can forget."

I didn't have the foggiest what the hell he was talking about.

"Croaker!" Lady snapped, catching the scent of what was in the back of my mind almost before I did. "We don't have time for you to indulge your curiosity about the past. There's something going on here. Tend to it before we get our butts in a sling."

She was turning into one of the guys for sure.

"You getting the idea where we stand, Swan? You don't really figure we think running into you and the woman up there was by chance, do you? Talk me some plain talk."

Some not so very plain talk took a while. Darkness came and the moon rose. It climbed the sky. The operators of the grove became exasperated but were too polite to ask their ruling prince to bug off. And while we stayed, so did the scores who had come out to look at us.

"Definitely something going on," I whispered to Lady. "But how do I dig it out of him?"

The Prahbrindrah played down everything he said, but the presence of the city fathers shrieked that Taglios was approaching a perilous crossroads. An undercurrent in what I heard told me the Prince wanted to spit in the face of calamity.

Willow tried to explain. "A while back—and nobody's sure exactly when because nobody was looking for it—what you might call a darkness turned up in a place called Pityus, which is like four hundred miles southeast of Taglios. Nobody worried about it. Then it spread to Tragevec and Kiaulune, which are pretty important, and Six and Fred, and all of a sudden everybody was worried but it was too late. You had this huge chunk of country ruled by these four sorcerers that refugees called Shadowmasters. They had a thing about shadows. Changed Tragevec's name to Shadowlight and Kiaulune to Shadowcatch and nowadays most everybody calls their empire the Shadowlands."

"You're going to get around to telling me what this's got to do with us, aren't you?"

"Within a year after the Shadowmasters took over they had those cities—which hadn't practiced war since the terror of Khatovar—armed and playing imperial games. In the years since, the Shadowmasters have conquered most of the territories between Taglios's southern frontiers and the edge of the map."

"I'm starting to smell it, Croaker," Lady said. She had grown grim as she listened.

"I am, too. Go on, Swan."

"Well, before they got to us . . . Before they went to work on Taglios they had some kind of falling out down there. Started feuding. The refugees talk about the whole big show. Intrigues, betrayals, subversions, assassinations, alliances shifting all over. Whenever it looked like one of them was starting to get ahead the others would gang up. Was like that for fifteen, eighteen years. So Taglios wasn't threatened."

"But now they are?"

"Now they're all looking this way. They made a move last year but it didn't work out for them." He looked smug. "What they got here in this berg is all the guts anybody could ask—and not a bat in broad daylight's notion what the hell to do with them. Me and Cordy and Blade, we kind of got drafted last year. But I wasn't never much of a soldier and neither was they. As generals we're like tits on a boar hog."

"So this isn't about bodyguarding and dirty-tricking for your Prince at all. Is it? He wants to drag us into his fight. Did he think he could get us on the cheap or something? Didn't you make a report about our trip down here?"

"He's the kind of guy who's got to check things for himself. Maybe he figured to see if you rated yourself cheap. I told him all the stories I ever heard about you guys. He still wanted to see for himself. He's a pretty good old boy. First prince I ever seen that tries to do what a prince is supposed to do."

"Rarer than frog hair, then. I'm sure. But you said it, Swan. We're on a mission from the gods. We don't have time to mess in local disputes. Maybe when we're on our way back."

Swan laughed.

"What's so funny?"

"You really don't got no choice."

"No?" I tried to read him. I couldn't. Lady shrugged when I looked at her. "Well? Why not?"

"To get where you want to go you got to head right through the Shadowlands. Seven, eight hundred miles of them. I don't think even you guys can make it. Neither does he."

"You said they were four hundred miles away."

"Four hundred miles to Pityus, Cap. Where it started. They got everything from the border south now. Seven, eight hundred to Shadowcatch. And like I said, they started on us last year. Took everything south of the Main."

I knew the Main to be a broad river south of Taglios, a natural frontier and barrier.

Swan continued, "Their troops are only eighty miles from Taglios some places. And we know they're planning a push as soon as the rivers go down. And we don't figure they're gonna be polite. All four Shadowmasters said they would get mean if the Prahbrindrah had anything to do with you guys."

I looked at Lady. "Damned awful lot of folks know more about what I'm doing and where I'm going than I do."

She ignored me. She asked, "Why didn't he run us off, Swan? Why did he send you to meet us?"

"Oh, he never sent us. He didn't know about that part till we got back. He just figures if the Shadowmasters are scared of you guys then he ought to be friends with you."

It wasn't me who frightened them, but why give that away? Swan and his buddies and boss didn't need to know who Lady had been. "He's got guts."

"They all got guts. Out the yang-yang. Pity is, they don't know what to do with them. And I can't show them. Like he says, the Shadowmasters would come sooner or later anyway, so why appease them? Why let them pick their time?"

"What's in this for Willow Swan? You come on pretty strong for a guy just passing through."

"Cordy ain't here to hear me, so I'll tell it straight. I'm not on the run no more. I've found my place. I don't want to lose it. Good enough?"

Maybe. "I couldn't give him an answer here, now. You know that if you know anything about the Black Company at all. I don't think there's much chance. It isn't what we want to do. But I'll give the situation a fair look. Tell him I want a week and the cooperation of his people." I planned to spend another eleven days resting and refitting. I was out nothing making that promise. Nothing but some of my share of the rest.

"That's it?" Swan asked.

"What else is there? You expect me to jump in just because you're a sweet guy? Swan, I'm headed for Khatovar. I'll do what I have to do to get there. You made your pitch. Now's the time to back off and let the customer think."

He babbled to his prince. The more the evening went on, the more I was tempted to issue a flat rejection. Croaker was getting old and cranky and not thrilled with the idea of learning yet another language.

The Prahbrindrah Drah nodded to Swan. He agreed with me. They rose. I did likewise, and gave the Prince a shallow bow. He and Swan walked away, pausing here and there to speak to other midnight diners. No telling what he said. Maybe what they wanted to hear. The faces I could see were smiling.

I got myself comfortable, leaned back to watch One-Eye at play. He had a swarm of bugs zipping around his victim's head. I asked Lady, "What do you think?"

"It's not my place to think."

"Where would you be inclined to stand?"

"I'm a soldier of the Black Company. As you're inclined to remind me."

"So was Raven. So long as it suited his convenience. Don't play games with me. Talk to me straight. Do you know these Shadowmasters? Are they Taken you sent down here to start building you a new empire?"

"No! I salvaged Shifter and sent him south, just in case, when the fury of the war and Stormbringer's enmity were enough to explain his disappearance. That's all."

"But Howler . . ."

"Had his own escape planned. Knows of my condition and nurtures ambitions of his own. Obviously. But the Shadowmasters . . . I know nothing. Nothing. You should've asked more about them."

"I will. If they're not Taken they sound close enough as makes no difference. So I want to know. Where do you stand?"

"I'm a soldier of the Black Company. They've already declared themselves my enemies."

"That's not a definitive answer."

"It's the best you're going to get."

"I figured. What about Shifter and his sidekick?" I hadn't seen them since Thresh, but had the feeling they were just around the corner. "If it's as bad as it looks we'll need all the resources we can muster."

"Shifter will do what I tell him."

Not the most reassuring answer, but I did not press. Again, it was the best I was going to get.

"Eat your dinner and stop pestering me, Croaker."

I looked down at food now so old it was no longer palatable.

Smirking, Frogface ambled off to help his master soften the will of an assassin.

One-Eye overdid it. He has that way when he has an audience. He gets too exuberant. Our prisoner expired from sheer terror. We gained nothing from him but notoriety.

As though we needed that.

23

Willow, Bats, and Things

It was late. Willow yawned as he tumbled into his chair. Blade, Cordy, and the Woman looked at him expectantly. Like the Prahbrindrah couldn't talk for himself. "We talked."

"And?" the Radisha demanded.

"You maybe expected him to jump up and down and yell, 'Oh, goodie!'"

"What did he say?"

"He said he'd check it out. Which is about the best you could expect."

"I should have gone myself."

The Prahbrindrah said, "Sister, the man wouldn't have listened at all had not someone just tried to kill him."

She was astonished.

Willow said, "Those guys aren't stupid. They knew we was up to something way back when they let us hook up with them at the Third Cataract. They been watching us as close as we been watching them."

Smoke drifted in with all the racket of his namesake. It was a big room in the cellar of a friend of the Radisha, near the olive grove. It smelled moldy although it was open to the night in places. Smoke came a few steps into the light cast by three oil lamps. His face puckered into a frown. He looked around.

"What's the matter?" Cordy asked. He shivered visibly. Swan got a creepy feeling, too.

"I'm not sure. For a moment . . . like something was staring at me."

The Radisha exchanged looks with her brother, then with Willow. "Willow. Those two odd little men. One-Eye and Goblin. Fact or fraud?"

"Six of one and half a dozen of the other. Right, Blade? Cordy?"

Cordy nodded. Blade said, "The little one. Like a child. Frogface. That's dangerous."

"What is it?" the Woman asked. "The oddest child I've ever seen. There were times when it acted a hundred years old."

"Maybe ten thousand," Smoke said. "An imp. I dared not investigate lest it recognize me as more than a silly old man. I don't know its capacities. But definitely a supernatural entity of great efficacy. My question is how an adept of a capacity as limited as the One-Eye creature obtained control. I'm superior to him in talent, skill, and training, but I can neither summon nor control such a thing."

Sudden squeaks and flutters came from the darkness. Startled, everyone turned. Bats hurtled into the light, peeping, diving, dodging. A sudden larger shape flashed through, dark as a chunk of night. It ripped a bat on the fly. Another shape flung through a second later, dropping another bat. The others got away through a barred but otherwise unclosed ground-level window.

"What the hell?" Willow squawked. "What's going on?"

Blade said, "Couple of crows. Killing bats." He sounded perfectly calm. As if crows killing bats in a basement at midnight, around his head, was something that happened all the time.

The crows did not reappear.

"I don't like it, Willow," Cordy said. "Crows don't fly at night. Something's going on."

Everyone looked at everyone else and waited for somebody to say something. Nobody noticed the pantherine shadow settle outside the window, one eye peeking inside. Nor did anybody realize that a child-sized figure lounged atop an old crate beyond the light, grinning. But Smoke began to shiver and turn in slow circles, again with that feeling of being watched.

The Prahbrindrah said, "I recall saying it wouldn't be a good idea to meet this close to the grove. I recall suggesting we get together in the palace, in a room that Smoke has sealed against prying. I don't know what just happened, but it wasn't natural and I don't want to talk here. Let's go. The delay can't hurt. Can it, Smoke?"

The old man shuddered violently, said, "It might be most wise, my Prince. Most wise. There is more here than meets the eye. . . . Henceforth we must assume we are under surveillance."

The Radisha was irked. "By who, old man?"

"I don't know. Does it matter, Radisha? There are those who are interested. The High Priests. These soldiers you wish to use. The Shadowmasters. Perhaps forces of which we are unaware."

They all looked at him. "Explain that," the Woman ordered.

"I cannot. Except to remind you that those men successfully fought their way through river pirates who have held the river closed for some time. None of them would say much about it, but a word here and a word there added together suggested that there was sorcery of the highest order involved, on both sides. And theirs was sufficient to force the blockade. But, except for the imp, there was nothing of that sort evident when we joined them. If they had it, where did it go? Could it be that well hidden? Maybe, but I doubt it. Maybe it travels with them without being with them, if you see what I mean."

"No. You're up to your old tricks. Being deliberately vague."

"I'm vague because I have no answers, Radisha. Only questions. I wonder, more and more, if the band we see isn't an illusion cast for our benefit. A handful of men, hard and tough and skilled in their murderous ways, to be sure, but nothing that should terrify the Shadowmasters. There aren't enough of them to make a difference. So why are the Shadowmasters concerned? Either they know more than we do or they see better than we do. Remember the history of the Free Companies. They weren't just bands of killers. And these men are determined to reach Khatovar. Their captain has tried everything short of violence to unearth information about the way."

"Hey, Smoke! You said go someplace else and talk," Blade said. "So how about we go?"

Swan agreed. "Yeah. This dump gives me the creeps. I don't get you guys, Radisha. You and the Prince claim you run Taglios, but you go around hiding out in holes like this."

"Our seats aren't secure." She started moving. "We rule with the consent of the priests, really. And we don't want them knowing everything we're doing."

"Every damned lord and priest who was anybody was up in that grove tonight. They know."

"They know what we told them. Which is only part of the truth."

Cordy eased in close to Willow. "Keep it down, man. Can't you see what's up? They're playing for a lot more than just turning back the Shadowmasters."

"Uhm."

Behind them, something resembling a panther padded from one pool of darkness to another, silent as death itself. Crows glided from one point of vantage to another. A childlike figure tagged along behind, apparently openly but remaining unseen. But no bats darted overhead.

Willow understood, with that one admonition. The Woman and her brother thought the struggle with the Shadowmasters would preoccupy the priests and cults. While they were distracted they would gather all the reins of the state. . . .

He did not begrudge them. He had little use for priests. He thought maybe Blade was on to something. Here, sure. They ought all to be drowned so Taglios could be put out of its misery.

Each dozen or so paces he turned, looked back. The street was always empty behind him. Yet he was sure something was watching.

"Creepy," he muttered. And wondered how he'd gotten himself into this mess.

24

Taglios: A Princely Pressure

That Prahbrindrah Drah might have been one of the good guys but he was as slick as any villain. Two days after our visit I couldn't go out without being hailed Guardian, Protector, and Deliverer. "What the hell is going on?" I asked One-Eye.

"Trying to lock you in." He glared at Frogface. The imp had not been much good since that night. He couldn't get near anybody—except Swan and his buddies, in a dive they owned. And they didn't talk business there. "You sure you want to go to this library?"

"I'm sure." Somehow the Taglians had gotten the idea I was a big healer as well as some kind of messianic general. "What the hell is wrong with them? I can see the Prince trying to sell them the load of sheep shit, but why are they buying it?"

"They want to."

Mothers thrust their babies at me to be touched and blessed. Young men clashed anything metal and roared songs with a martial beat. Maidens threw flowers on my path. And sometimes themselves.

"That's nice, Croaker," One-Eye said, as I disentangled myself from a day-dream about sixteen years old. "You don't want her, toss her my way."

"Take it easy. Before you give in to your baser instincts think about what's going on."

He was reserved to an extreme that baffled me. I think he saw it all as illusion. Or at least as a honeytrap. One-Eye is silly but he isn't stupid. Sometimes.

One-Eye chuckled. "Surrender to temptation. Lady can't look over your shoulder all the time."

"I might. I just might. It *is* my duty not to disappoint these people when they're trying so hard to hustle us. Isn't it?"

"There you go." But he did not sound like he believed himself. He was uncomfortable with his good fortune.

We went into the library. I found nothing. So much nothing I got even more suspicious than I was. Frogface wasn't much use, but he could eavesdrop. The conversations he reported contributed to my concern.

It was a good time for the men. Even the supreme discipline of the Nar was not proof against some temptations. Mogaba did not hold them on too tight a leash. As Goblin howled one morning, "Heaven's on fire, Croaker!"

Always there was this feeling of something happening just out of the corner of my eye.

The geopolitical situation was clear. It was just as Swan had described. Meaning that to reach Khatovar we would have to slice through seven hundred miles of country ruled by the Shadowmasters. If Shadowmasters there were.

I had some slight doubts. Everyone I talked to, through Frogface, believed they existed, but nobody provided any concrete evidence.

"Nobody has ever seen the gods, either," a priest told me. "But we all believe in them, don't we? We see their handiwork. . . ." He realized that I had scowled at his suggestion that everyone believed in gods. His eyes narrowed. He scurried away. For the first time I had found me somebody less than thrilled with my presence in Taglios. I told One-Eye it might be more profitable if we started spying on the High Priests instead of the Prince and Swan, who knew when to keep their mouths shut.

That we were being manipulated into going up against some heavyweight sorcerers did not intimidate me. Much. We had been up against the best for twenty years. What troubled me was my ignorance.

I did not know the language. I did not know the Taglian people. Their history was a mystery and Swan's bunch were no help tossing light into the shadows. And, of course, I knew nothing about the Shadowmasters or the peoples they ruled. Nothing but what I had been told, which could be worse than nothing. Worst of all, I was not acquainted with the ground where any struggle would take place. And I had too little time to learn all the answers.

Sundown of the third day. We moved to quarters farther south in the city, provided by the state. I gathered everyone but the half-dozen men on guard duty. While most of the guys ate supper—cooked and served by people provided by the Prahbrindrah—the folks at my long table got their heads together. The rest had orders to keep the Taglians hopping. I doubted they could understand us, but you don't take chances.

I sat at the head of the table, Lady to my left and Mogaba to my right, he with his two leading men next to him. Goblin and One-Eye were beyond Lady on her side, tonight with Goblin in the seat nearer the head. I had to make them trade off each meal. Beyond them were Murgen and Hagop and Otto, with

Murgen at the foot of the table, in his capacity as apprentice Annalist. I made like I was telling a story as we ate. The paterfamilias entertaining his children.

"I'm taking the imperial horses out tonight. Lady, Goblin, Hagop, Otto, you'll come. One of the roi. One of your lieutenants, Mogaba, and one of your men. Men who can ride."

One-Eye drew a breath to complain. So did Murgen. But Mogaba slid in ahead of both. "A sneak?"

"I want to scout to the south. These people could be selling us a pig in a poke."

I didn't think they were, but why take a man's word when you can see for yourself? Especially when he's trying to use you?

"One-Eye, you stay here because I want you working your pet. Day and night. Murgen, write down whatever he tells you. Mogaba, cover for us. If they've been telling it straight we won't be gone long."

"You told the Prahbrindrah you'd give him an answer in a week. You have four days left."

"We'll be back in time. We'll go after next watch change, after Goblin and One-Eye knock out anybody who might see us."

Mogaba nodded. I glanced at Lady. She didn't contribute much anymore. If I wanted to be the boss, I was going to be the boss and she would keep her opinion to herself.

Mogaba said, "Several of my men have approached me on a matter of some delicacy. I think we need a policy."

This was something unexpected. "A policy? About what?"

"To what extent the men can use violence to defend themselves. Several have been attacked. They want to know how much restraint they have to show, for political reasons. Or if they have permission to make examples."

"Gah! When did this start?"

"I received the first report this afternoon."

"All today, then?"

"Yes sir."

"Let's see the men involved."

He brought them to the table. They were Nar. There were five of them. It did not seem likely that such things would happen to the Nar alone. I sent Murgen around. He returned. "Three incidents. They took care of it themselves. Said they didn't figure it was something worth reporting."

Discipline. Something to be said for it.

It took half a minute to decide the attackers were not, apparently, Taglians. "Wrinkly little brown guys? We saw those on the river. I asked Swan. He said he didn't know where they came from. But they gave him the collywobbles. If they're not Taglians, don't take no shit. Ace them unless you can take a couple prisoners. One-Eye. If you could snag a couple and give them the works. . . ."

We did all this amidst the comings and goings of our Taglian servitors. At that point several came to collect empty plates, forestalling One-Eye from poormouthing about how he was so grossly overworked. He did not squawk fast enough when they cleared away, either.

Murgen got the first word in. "I got a problem, Croaker." Mogaba winced. Flexible man, Mogaba, but he could not get used to me letting anybody call me anything but Captain.

"What's that?"

"Bats."

Goblin snickered.

"Can it, runt. Bats? What about bats?"

"Guys keep finding dead bats around."

I noted, from the corner of my eye, that Lady had grown more attentive. "I don't follow you."

"The men have been finding dead bats every morning since we got here. Bats all torn up, not just dropped over dead. And they're only around where we are. Not all over town."

I looked at One-Eye. He looked at me. He said, "I know. I know. One more job for good old One-Eye. How's this outfit ever going to get along without me when I go?"

I don't know if the others bought it or not.

There were things One-Eye and I hadn't shared with everyone.

"Any other problems?"

Nobody had a problem, but Murgen had a question. "All right if we work on Swan a little? I checked out that place he owns. It's the kind of place some of our guys would hang out. We might find out something interesting there."

"At least you'd keep him nervous. Good idea. Have some of the Nar hang out there, too. To work on that Blade character."

"He's a spooky one," Otto said.

"The most dangerous too, I'd bet. One of those guys like Raven. Kill you without batting an eye and not even remember it five minutes later."

Mogaba said, "You must tell me more of this Raven. Each time I hear of him he sounds more intriguing."

Lady paused with fork half lifted to mouth. "It's all in the Annals, Lieutenant." The gentlest of admonitions. For all his devotion to things Company, Mogaba had yet to make a serious attempt to explore those Annals set down after the Company had departed Gea-Xle.

"Of course," he replied, voice perfectly even, but eyes hard as steel. There was a distinct coolness between them. I had sensed it before, mildly. Negative chemistry. Neither had any reason to dislike the other. Or maybe they did. I spent more time with Mogaba these days than I did with Lady.

"That's that, then," I said. "Out of here after the next watch change. Be ready."

Mostly nods as they pushed back from the table, but Goblin stayed put, scowling, for several seconds before he rose.

He suspected that he was being drafted mainly to keep him out of mischief while I was gone.

He was sixty percent right.

Taglios: Scouting Southward

Try sneaking someplace on a plowhorse sometime. You'll get half the idea of the trouble we had sliding out of town unnoticed on those monsters Lady had given us. We wore poor Goblin down to the nubs, covering up. By the time we cleared town I was thinking maybe we would have done as well to have taken the coach.

Getting out unnoticed was a relative notion, anyway. There were crows on watch. Seemed one of those damned birds was perched on every tree and roof we passed.

Though we hurried through it, and it could not be seen well in the dark, the countryside immediately south of Taglios seemed rich and intensively cultivated. It had to be to support an urban area so large—though there appeared to be garden areas inside the city, especially in the well-to-do neighborhoods. Surprisingly, Taglians did not eat much meat though it was food that could be walked to market.

Two of the three great religious families banned the eating of flesh.

Along with everything else, our great steeds could see in the dark. It did not bother them to canter when I could not see my hand in front of my face. Dawn caught us forty miles south of Taglios, thoroughly saddle sore.

Opened-mouth peasants watched us flash by.

Swan had told me about the Shadowmasters' invasion of the previous summer. Twice we crossed the path of that struggle, coming upon gutted villages. In
each the villagers had rebuilt, but not on the same site.

We paused near the second. A hetman came to look us over while we ate.
We had no words in common. When he saw he wasn't going to get anywhere he
just grinned, shook my hand, and walked away.

Goblin said, "He knew who we are. And figures us the same as the people in
the city."

"For dopes?"

"Nobody thinks we're stupid, Croaker," Lady said. "And maybe that's the
problem. Maybe we aren't as smart as they think we are."

"Say what?" I threw a stone at a crow. I missed. She gave me a funny look.

"I think you're right when you say there's a conspiracy of silence. But maybe
they aren't hiding as much as you think. Maybe they just think we know more
than we know."

Sindawe, Mogaba's lieutenant and third, offered, "I feel this to be the heart
of it, Captain. I have spent much time on the streets. I have seen this in the eyes
of all who look upon me. They think I am much more than what I am."

"Hey. They don't just look at me. I go out they start hailing me everything
but emperor. It's embarrassing."

"But they won't talk," Goblin said, starting to pack up. "They'll bow and
grin and kiss your backside and give you anything but their virgin daughters,
but they won't say squat if you go after a concrete answer."

"Truth is a deadly weapon," Lady said.

"Which is why priests and princes dread it," I said. "If we're more than we
seem, what do they think we are?"

Lady said, "What the Company was when it came through heading north."

Sindawe agreed. "The answer would be in the missing Annals."

"Of course. And they're missing." If I had had my own along I would have
paused to review what I had learned at the Temple of Traveller's Repose. Those
first few books had been lost down here somewhere.

None of the names on my maps rang any bells. None of what I remembered
contained any echoes. Cho'n Delor had been the end of history, so to speak.
The beginning of unknown country, though there was much in the Annals
from before the Pastel Wars.

Could they have changed all the names?

"Oh, my aching ass," Goblin complained as he clambered into the saddle. A
sight to behold, a runt like him getting up the side of one of those horses. Every
time Otto had a crack about getting him a ladder. "Croaker, I got an idea."

"That sounds dangerous."

He ignored that. "How about we retire? We're not young enough for this crap anymore."

Hagop said, "Those guys we ran into on the road down from Oar probably had the right idea. Only they were small-time. We ought to find a town and take over. Or sign on with somebody permanent like."

"That's been tried fifty times. Never lasts. Only place it worked was Gea-Xle. And there the guys got itchy feet after a while."

"Bet that wasn't the same guys who rode in."

"We're all old and tired, Hagop."

"Speak for yourself, Granddad," Lady said.

I threw a rock and mounted up. That was an invitation to banter. I did not take it up. I felt old and tired that way, too. She shrugged, mounted up herself. I rode out wondering where we were at, she and I. Probably nowhere. Maybe the spark had been neglected too long. Maybe propinquity was counterproductive.

As we moved farther south we noted a phenomenon. Post riders in numbers like we had seen nowhere else. In every village we were recognized. It was the same old salute and cheer that started in Taglios. Where they had them the young men came out with weapons.

I'm not much for morality. But I felt morally reprehensible when I saw them, as if I were somehow responsible for transmuting a pacific people into fire-eyed militarists.

Otto was of the opinion the weapons had been taken from last year's invaders. Maybe. Some. But most looked so old and rusted and brittle I would wish them only on my enemies.

The commission looked more improbable by the hour.

Nowhere did we encounter evidence that Taglians were anything but a pleasant, friendly, industrious people blessed with a land where survival was not a day-to-day struggle. But even these country folk seemed to devote most of their leisure time, whence culture springs, to their bewildering battalions of gods.

"One signal victory," I told Lady when we were about eighty miles south of the city, "and these people will be psyched up to take any hardships the Shadowmasters can dish out."

"And if we take the commission and lose the first battle it won't matter anyway. We won't be around to have to suffer the consequences."

"That's my girl. Always thinking positive."

"Are you really going to take the commission?"

"Not if I can help it. That's why we're out here. But I've got a bad feeling that what I want won't have much to do with what I'll have to do."

Goblin snorted and grumbled something about being dragged around on the claws of fate. He was right. And my only notion for breaking loose was to find a way to keep heading south, Shadowmasters be damned.

We did not press hard, and paused for lunch before our breakfasts were really settled. Our bodies were not up to the continuous abuse of a sustained ride. Getting old.

Otto and Hagop wanted to lay on a fire and fix a real meal. I told them go ahead. Sore and tired, I settled down nearby, head pillowed on a rock, and stared at clouds trudging across alien skies that by day looked no different than those whence I had come.

Things were happening too fast and too strange to wring any sense out of them. I was plagued by a dread that I was the wrong man in the wrong place and wrong time for the Company. I did not feel competent to handle the situation Taglios threatened. Could *I* presume to lead a nation to war? I did not think so. Even if every Taglian man, woman, and child proclaimed me savior.

I tried comforting myself with the thought that I was not the first Captain with doubts, and far from the first to get embroiled in a local situation armed only with a glimmer of the true problems and stakes. Maybe I was luckier than some. I had Lady, for whom the waters of intrigue were home. If I could tap her talent. I had Mogaba, who, despite those cultural and language barriers that still existed between us, had begun to look like the best pure soldier I'd ever known. I had Goblin and One-Eye and Frogface and—maybe—Shifter. And I had four hundred years of Company shenanigans in my trick bag. But none of that appeased my conscience or stilled my doubts.

What *had* we gotten into on our simple ride back into the Company's origins?

Was that half the trouble? That we were in unknown territory so far as the Annals were concerned? That I was trying to work without a historical chart?

There *were* questions about our forebrethren and this country. I'd had little opportunity to ferret out information. The hints I had gathered suggested that those old boys had not been nice fellows. I got the impression that the diaspora of the original Free Companies had been a nut religious thing. The moving doctrine, a vestige of which survived among the Nar, must have been terrible. The name of the Company still struck fear and stirred intense emotion.

The exhaustion caught up. I fell asleep, though I did not realize it till the conversation of crows awakened me.

I bounced up. The others looked at me oddly. They did not hear it. They were about finished with their meal. Otto was keeping the pot hot for me.

I looked into a lone nearby tree and saw several crows, their ugly heads all cocked so they could look at me. They started chattering. I had a definite feeling they wanted my attention.

I ambled toward them.

Two flew when I was halfway to the tree, gaining altitude in that clumsy way crows have, gliding to the southeast toward an isolated stand of trees maybe a mile away. A good fifty crows circled above those trees.

The remaining crow left the lone tree when he was satisfied I had seen that. I turned to lunch in a thoughtful mood. Halfway through a bad stew I concluded that I had to assume I had been given a warning. The road passed within yards of those trees.

As we mounted up, I said, "People, we ride with weapons bare. Goblin. See those trees yonder? Keep an eye on them. Like your life depends on it."

"What's up, Croaker?"

"I don't know. Just a hunch. Probably wrong, but it don't cost nothing to be careful."

"If you say so." He gave me a funny look, like he was wondering about my stability.

Lady gave me an even funnier look when, as we approached the woods, Goblin squeaked, "The place is infested!"

That's all he got to say. The infestation broke cover. Those little brown guys. About a hundred of them. Real military geniuses, too. Men on foot just don't go jumping people on horseback even if they do outnumber them.

Goblin said, "Gleep!" And then he said something else. The swarm of brown men became surrounded by a fog of insects.

They should have shot us down with arrows.

Otto and Hagop chose what I considered the stupider course. They charged. Their momentum carried them through the mob. My choice seemed the wiser. The others agreed. We just turned away and trotted ahead of the brown guys, leaving them to Goblin's mercies.

My beast stumbled. Master horseman that I am, I promptly fell off. Before I could get to my feet the brown guys were all around me, trying to lay hands on. But Goblin was on the job. I don't know what he did, but it worked. After they knocked me around a little, leaving me a fine crop of bruises, they decided to keep after those who had had sense enough to stay on their horses.

Otto and Hagop thundered past, making a rear attack. I staggered to my feet, looked for my mount. He was a hundred yards away, looking at me in a bemused sort of way. I limped toward him.

Those little guys had some kind of petty magic of their own going, and no sense at all. They just kept on. They dropped like flies, but when they outnumber you a dozen to one you got to worry about more than just a favorable kill ratio.

I did not see it well, busy as I was. And when I did manage to drag my abused flesh aboard my animal's back the whole brouhaha had swept out of sight down a narrow, shallow valley.

I have no idea how, but somehow I managed to get disoriented. Or something. When I got organized and started after my bunch I could not find them. Though I never got much chance to look. Fate intervened in the form of five little brown guys on horses that would have been amusing if they hadn't been waving swords and lances and rushing at me with intent to be obnoxious.

On another day I might have stayed forty yards ahead and plinked at them with my bow. But I wasn't in the mood. I just wanted to be left alone and to get back together with the others.

I galloped off. Up and down and around a few hills and I lost them easily. But in the process I lost myself. During all the fun the sky clouded over. It started to drizzle. Just to make me that much more enchanted with my chosen way of life. I set out to find the road, hoping I would find traces of my companions there.

I topped a hill and spied that damned crow-surrounded figure that had been haunting me since the Temple of Travellers' Repose. It was striding along in the distance, directly away from me. I forgot about the others. I kicked my mount into a gallop. The figure paused and looked back. I felt the weight of its stare but did not slow. I would unravel this mystery now.

I charged down a shallow hill, leapt a wash in which muddy water gurgled. The figure was out of sight for a moment. Up the other side. When I reached the crest there was nothing to be seen but a few random crows circling no particular point. I used language that would have distressed my mother immensely.

I did not slow but continued my career till I reached the approximate point where I had seen the thing last. I reined in, swung down, began stomping around looking for a sign. A mighty tracker, me. But, moist as the ground was already, there had to be traces. Unless I was crazy and seeing things.

I found traces, sure enough. And I felt the continued pressure of that stare. But I did not see the thing I sought. I was baffled. Even considering the probability that there was sorcery involved, how could it have vanished so completely? There was no cover anywhere around.

I spotted some crows starting to circle about a quarter mile away. "All right, you son of a bitch. We'll see how fast you can run."

There was nothing there when I got there.

The cycle repeated itself three times. I got no closer. The last time I halted I did so atop a low crest that, from a quarter mile, overlooked a hundred-acre wood. I dismounted and stood beside my horse. We stared. "You, too?" I asked. His breathing was as uneven as mine. And those monster beasts never got winded.

That was a sight, down there. Never have I seen so many crows except maybe on a recent battlefield.

In a lifetime of travel and study I have come upon half a hundred tales about haunted forests. The woods are always described as dark and dense and old or the trees are mostly dead, skeleton hands reaching for the sky. This wood fit none of the particulars except for density. Yet it sure felt haunted.

I tossed my reins across the horse's neck, strapped on a buckler, drew my sword from its saddle scabbard, and started forward. The horse came along behind me, maybe eight feet back, head down so his nostrils were almost to the ground, like a hound on the track.

The crows were most numerous over the center of the wood. I did not trust my eyes but thought I detected some squat dark structure among the trees there. The closer I got the slower I moved, meaning maybe a part of me was still infected with common sense. The part that kept telling me that I was not cut out for this sort of thing. I wasn't some lone brawling swordsman who stalked evil into its lair.

I am a dope cursed with an unhealthy portion of curiosity. Curiosity had me by the chin whiskers and kept right on dragging me along.

There was one lone tree that approximated the stereotype, a bony old thing about half dead, as big around as me, standing like a sentinel thirty feet from the rest of the wood. Scrub and saplings clustered around its feet, rising waist high. I paused to lean against it while I talked myself into or out of something. The horse came up till his nose bumped my shoulder. I turned my head to look at him.

Snake hiss. *Thump!*

I gawked at the arrow quivering in the tree three inches from my fingers and only started to get myself down when it struck me that the shaft had not been meant to stick me in the brisket.

Head, shaft, and fletching, that bolt was as black as a priest's heart. The shaft itself had an enameled look. An inch behind the head was a wrap of white. I levered the arrow out of the tree and held the message close enough to read.

It is not yet time, Croaker.

The language and alphabet were those of the Jewel Cities.

Interesting. "Right. Not yet time." I peeled the paper off, crumpled it into a ball, tossed it at the wood. I looked for some sign of the archer. There was none. Of course.

I shoved the arrow into my quiver, swung onto my saddle, turned the horse and rode about a step. A shadow ran past, of a crow flying up to have a look at the seven little brown men waiting for me atop the hill. "You guys never give up, do you?"

I got back down, behind the horse, took out my bow, strung it, drew an arrow—the arrow just collected—and started angling across the hillside, staying behind my mount. The little brown guys turned their toy horses and moved with me.

When I had a nice range I jumped out and let fly at the nearest. He saw it coming and tried to dodge, only he did himself more harm than good. I meant to put the shaft into his pony's neck. It slammed in through his knee, getting him and the animal both. The pony threw him and took off, dragging him from a stirrup.

I mounted up fast, took off through the gap. Those little horses did not move fast enough to close it.

So we were off, them pounding after me at a pace to kill their animals in an hour, my beast barely cantering and, I think, having a good time. I can't recall any other horse I've ridden looking back to check the pursuit and adjusting its pace to remain tantalizingly close.

I had no idea who the brown guys were but there had to be a bunch of them the way they kept turning up. I considered working on this bunch, taking them out one by one, decided discretion was the better part. If need be I could bring the Company down and forage for them.

I wondered what became of Lady and Goblin and the others. I doubted they had come to any harm, what with our advantage in mounts, but . . .

We were separated and there was no point spending the remaining daylight looking for them. I would get back to the road, turn north, find a town and someplace dry.

The drizzle irritated me more than the fact that I was being hunted.

But that stretch of forest bothered me more than the rain. That was a mystery that scared the crap out of me.

The crows and walking stump were real. No doubt of that anymore. And the stump knew me by name.

Maybe I ought to bring the Company down and go after whatever hid there.

The road was one of those wonders that turns to mud hip deep if somebody spits on it. There were no fences in this part of the world, so I just rode beside it. I came to a village almost immediately.

Call it a stroke of fate, or timing. Timing. My life runs on weird timing. There were riders coming into town from the north. They looked even more bedraggled than I felt. They were not little brown men but I gave them the suspicious eye anyway and looked for places to duck. They were carrying more lethal hardware than I was, and I had enough to outfit a platoon.

"Yo! Croaker!"

Hell. That was Murgen. I got a little closer and saw that the other three were Willow Swan, Cordy Mather, and Blade.

What the hell were they doing down here?

26

Overlook

The one who had withdrawn everything but moral support did not give up his right to complain and criticize.

The gathering of the Shadowmasters took place in the heights of a soaring tower in that one's new capitol fortress, Overlook, which lay two miles south of Shadowcatch. It was a strange, dark fortress, more vast than some cities. It had thick walls a hundred feet high. Every vertical surface was sheathed in plates of burnished brass or iron. Ugly silver lettering in an alphabet known only to a few damascened those plates, proclaiming fearful banes.

The Shadowmasters assembled in a room not at all in keeping with their penchant for darkness. The sun burned through a skylight and through walls of crystal. The three shrank from the glare, though they were clad in their darkest apparel. Their host floated near the southern wall, seldom withdrawing his gaze from the distance. His preoccupation was obsessive.

Out there, many miles away but visible from that great height, lay a vast flat expanse. It shimmered. It was as white as the corpse of an old dead sea. The visitors thought his fear and fixation dangerously obsessive. If it was not feigned. If it was not the fulcrum of an obscure and deadly strategem. But it was impossible not to be impressed by the magnitude of the defenses he had raised.

The fortress had been seventeen years in the building and was not yet more than two-thirds completed.

The small one, the female, asked, "It's quiet out there now?" She spoke the language that was emblazoned upon the fortress walls.

"It's always quiet during the day. But come the night . . . Come the night . . ." Fear and hatred blackened the air.

He blamed *them* for his dire circumstances. *They* had mined the shadows and had awakened the terror, then they had left him to face the consequences alone.

He turned. "You have failed. You have failed and failed and failed. The Radisha went north without inconvenience. *They* sailed through the swamps like vengeance itself, so easily *she* never had to lift a finger. They go where they will and do what they will, without peril, so blithely sure they don't even notice your meddling. And now they and she are on your marches, conjuring mischief there. So you come to me."

"Who could have suspected they would have a Great One as companion? That one was supposed to have perished."

"Fool! Was he not a master of change and illusion? You should have known he was there waiting for them. How could such a one hide?"

"Did you know he was there and fail to inform us?" the female mocked.

He whirled back to the window. He did not answer. He said, "They are on your marches now. Will you deal with them this time?"

"They are but fifty mortal men."

"With her. And the Great One."

"And we are four. And we have armies. Soon the rivers will go down. Ten thousand men will cross the Main and obliterate the very Name of the Black Company."

A sound came from the one at the window, a hissing that grew up to become cold, mocking laughter. "They will? That has been tried numberless times. Numberless. But they endure. For four hundred years they have endured. Ten thousand men? You joke. A million might not suffice. The empire in the north could not exterminate them."

The three exchanged glances. Here was madness. Obsession and madness. When the threat from the north was expunged perhaps this one ought to follow it.

"Come here," he said. "Look down there. Where that ghost of an old road winds through the valley up toward the brilliance." Something turned and coiled there, a blackness deeper than that of their apparel. "You see that?"

"What is it?"

"My shadow trap. They come through the gateway you breached, the great old strong ones. Not the toys you drew into your services, these. I could loose them. I might if you fail again."

The three stirred. He had to go for certain.

He laughed, reading their thoughts. "And the key to that trap is my Name, my brethren. If *I* perish the trap collapses and the gateway stands open to the world." He laughed again.

The male who spoke the least when they gathered spat angrily and made to depart. After hesitating the other two followed. There was nothing more to be said.

Mad laughter pursued them down the endless spiral of the stairs.

The woman observed, "Maybe he can't be conquered. But while he persists in facing south he offers us no peril. Let us ignore him henceforth."

"Three against two, then," her companion grumbled. The other, in the lead, grunted.

"But there is one in the swamps, whose debt of anger might be manipulated if we grow desperate. And we have gold. Always there are tools to be found in the ranks of the enemy when gold is allowed to speak. Not so?" She laughed. Her laughter was almost as crazy as that peeling out above.

27

Night Strife

I gave Murgen my dirtiest look as he rode up. He understood it. We would talk later. For the moment he said, "You told me to keep an eye on them."

Swan reached me a moment later. "Gods, you guys move fast. I'm shot." He made an obscene gesture at the sky. "We leave five minutes after you and find out you had time to take a couple of breaks and still stay ahead of us." He shook his head. "Bunch of iron men. Told you I wasn't cut out for this crap, Cordy."

"Where is everybody?" Murgen asked.

"I don't know. We got ambushed. We got separated."

Mather, Swan, and Blade exchanged glances. Swan asked, "Little brown guys? All wrinkly?"

"You know them?"

"We had a run-in with them when we were headed north. Man, I got me a brainstorm. We going to jaw, let's do it out of the rain. My lumbago is killing me."

"Lumbago?" Mather asked. "When did you come up with lumbago?"

"When I forgot my hat and it started raining on my head. Blade, you was in this place last year. They got like an inn, or something?"

Blade didn't say anything, just turned his horse and headed out. He was an odd one for sure. But Swan thought he was an all-right guy, and I liked Swan as much as I could like anybody who worked for somebody who was trying to play games with me.

I was about to follow up last, with Murgen, when Murgen said, "Hold up. Somebody's coming." He pointed.

I looked into the drizzle to the south and saw three shapes, riders coming in. Their mounts were tall enough that they could be nothing but Lady's gifts. Swan cursed the delay but we waited.

The three were Hagop, Otto, and the roi Shadid. Shadid looked ragged. And Hagop and Otto were wounded. "Damn you two. Can't you take a crap without getting hurt?" In the thirty or so years I had known them it seemed they had come up wounded about three times a year. And survived everything. I'd begun to suspect they were immortal and the blood was the price they paid.

"They piled an ambush on top of the ambush, Croaker," Hagop said. "They ran us down that valley right into another gang on horseback."

My stomach tightened. "And?"

He put on a feeble grin. "I figure they're sorry they did. We cut them up bad."

"Where are the others?"

"I don't know. We scattered. Lady said for Shadid to ride back up here with us and wait. She led them off."

"All right. Blade. Why don't you show us where to roost?"

Murgen looked at me with a question unspoken. I told him, "Yeah. We'll get them settled. Then we'll go."

The place Blade took us wasn't really an inn, just a big house where the owner made a bit taking in travellers. He was not thrilled to see us, though like everybody else in this end of the world he seemed to know who we were. The color of our coin brightened his day and livened his smile. Still, I think he let us in mainly because he thought we would get rowdy if he didn't.

I got Otto and Hagop sewed up and bandaged and generally settled into a routine they knew all too well. Meanwhile, the householder brought food, for which Swan expressed our sincere gratitude.

Murgen said, "It's going to be getting dark, Croaker."

"I know. Swan, we're going out to find the others. Got a spare horse if you want to ride along."

"You kidding? Go out in that muck when I don't have to? Hell. All right. I guess." He started levering himself out of his chair.

"Sit down, Willow," Mather said. "I'll go. I'm in better shape than you are."

Swan said, "You talked me into it, you smooth-talking son of a bitch. I don't know how you do it, you golden-tongued bastard. You can get anything you want out of me. Be careful."

"Ready?" Mather asked me. He stifled a small smile.

"Yeah."

We went out and climbed onto the horses, who were beginning to look a little put-upon. I led out, but Shadid soon slipped past, suggesting he lead since he knew whence they had come. The day was getting on. The light was feeble. It was about as dreary as it could get. More to distract myself than because I cared, I told Murgen, "Better explain what's going on."

"Cordy can tell you better than me. I just stuck with them."

The roi was not setting a blistering pace. I fought down the growls breeding in my gut. It kept telling me she was a big girl and she'd been taking care of herself since before I was born. But the man in me kept saying that's your woman, you got to take care of her.

Sure.

"Cordy? I know you guys don't work for me and you got your own priorities, but . . ."

"Nothing to cover up, Captain. Word came that some of you guys was going to ride out. That boggled the Woman. She figured you all to make a break for the Main in a mob and learn about the Shadowmasters the hard way. Instead, you went to scout it. She didn't think you were that smart."

"We're talking about the old broad you guys brought down the river, right. The Radisha?"

"Yeah. We call her the Woman. Blade hung it on her before we knew who she was."

"And she knew we were heading out before we went. Interesting. This is a wondrous time of my life, Mr. Mather. For the last year everybody in the world has known what I was going to do before I did. It's enough to make a guy nervous."

We passed some trees. In one I spied this incredibly bedraggled crow. I laughed, and hoped aloud he was as miserable as me. The others eyed me uncertainly. I wondered if I shouldn't start cultivating a new image. Work it up slowly. All the world dreads a madman. If I played it right . . .

"Hey, Cordy, old travelling buddy. You sure you don't know anything about those little brown guys?"

"All I know is they tried to ice us when we was headed north. Nobody ever saw anybody like them before. They figure to be out of the Shadowlands."

"Why are the Shadowmasters paranoid about us?" I did not expect an answer. I did not get one. "Cordy, you guys really serious about winning it for the Prahbrindrah?"

"I am. For Taglios. I found something there I never found anywhere else. Willow too, though you could roast him and never get it out of him. I don't know about Blade. I guess he's in because we're in. He's got one and a half friends in the world and nothing else to live for. He's just going on."

"One and a half?"

"Willow he's got. I'm the half. We pulled him out when somebody threw him to the crocodiles. He stuck because he owed us a life. After what we've been through since then if you was keeping accounts you couldn't figure who owes who what anymore. I can't tell you about the real Blade. He never lets you see that."

"What are we into? Or is that something you figure you shouldn't tell me?"

"What?"

"There's more going on than your Woman and the Prahbrindrah trying to get us to keep the Shadowmasters out. Otherwise they'd make a straight deal instead of trying to con us."

We travelled a mile while he thought. He finally said, "I don't know for sure. I think they're doing the way they are because of the way the Black Company did Taglios before."

"I thought so. And we don't know what our forebrethren did. And no one will tell us. It's like one giant conspiracy where everybody in Taglios won't tell us anything. In a city that big you'd think I'd find one guy with an axe to grind."

"You'd find platoons if you looked in the right place. All them priests spend their lives looking to cut each others' throats."

He had given me something there. I wasn't sure what. "I'll keep it in mind. I don't know if I can handle priests, though."

"They're like any other guys if you get your bluff in."

The gloom closed in tighter as the day advanced. I was so soaked I no longer paid that much attention. We hit a stretch where we had to go single file. Cordy and Murgen dropped back. "I picked up a few things I'll tell you about later," Murgen said before he went.

I moved up behind the roi to ask how much farther. It was just the misery of the day, but I felt like I'd been travelling for weeks.

Something whipped across our path so suddenly that that unflappable mount of Shadid's reared and whinnied. He shouted, "What the hell was that?" in his native tongue. I understood because I'd learned a few words when I was a kid.

I caught only a glimpse. It looked like a monster grey wolf with a deformed pup clinging to its back. It vanished before my eye could track it.

Do wolves do that? Carry their young on their backs?

I laughed almost hysterically. Why worry about that when I ought to be wondering if there was such a thing as a wolf the size of a pony?

Murgen and Cordy caught up and wanted to know what had happened. I said I didn't know because I was no longer sure I had seen what I had seen.

But the wonder lay back there in the shadows of my mind, ripening.

Shadid stopped two miles past the place where we'd been ambushed originally. It was getting hard to see. He peered around, trying to read landmarks. He grunted, moved out to his left, off the road. I spied signs suggesting this was the way he had come with Otto and Hagop.

After another half mile the ground dropped into a small valley where a narrow creek ran. Rocks stuck up seemingly at random. Likewise, trees grew in scatters. It was now so dark I could not see more than twenty feet.

We started finding bodies.

A lot of little brown men had died for their cause. Whatever that was.

Shadid stopped again. "We led them in from the other direction. Here's where we split. We went up that way. The others held on to give us a head start." He dismounted, began snooping around. The light was almost gone before he found the track out of the valley. It was full dark before we covered a mile.

Murgen said, "Maybe we ought to go back and wait. We can't accomplish much stumbling around in the dark."

"You go back if you want," I snapped, with a savagery that surprised me. "I'm staying till I find . . ."

I could not see him, but I suspected he was grinning through his misery. He said, "Maybe we shouldn't split up. That much more trouble getting everybody back together."

Riding through the night in unfamiliar territory is not one of the smarter things I've done. Especially with a horde out there that wanted to do me harm. But the gods take care of fools, I guess.

Our mounts stopped. Their ears pricked. After a moment mine made a sound. A moment later still that sound was repeated from our left quarter. Without being urged the animals turned that way.

We found Sindawe and the man he'd brought in a crude bough shelter, their mounts hanging around outside. Both were injured, Sindawe the worst. We talked briefly while I did some stitching and patching and bandaging. Lady had ordered them to disappear. Goblin had covered for them while the pursuit went on off to the southeast. They had planned to head north in the morning.

I told them where to meet up, then got back into my saddle.

I was dead on my butt, barely able to stay upright, but something made me go on. Something I did not want to examine too closely lest I have to mock myself for my sentiment.

I got no arguments, though I think Mather was getting a little unsure of my sanity. I heard him whispering with Murgen, and Murgen telling him to can it.

I took the lead and gave my horse his head, telling him to find Lady's mount. I'd never determined how intelligent the beasts were, but it seemed worth a try. And the animal went walking, though his pace was a little slow to suit me.

I don't know how long the ride went on. There was no way to estimate time. After a while I began drifting off and coming awake with a start, then drifting off again. Near as I could tell, the others were doing the same thing. I could have raised hell with them and me both, but that would have been unreasonable. Reasonable men would have been in a warm room, back at that village, snoring.

I was about half awake when the crest of a hill half a mile ahead burst into flames. It was like an explosion. One moment darkness, the next several acres ablaze and men and animals scattering, burning, too. The smell of sorcery was so strong I could detect it.

"Go, horse!"

There was light enough for it to risk a trot.

A minute later I was moving over ground dotted by smoldering, twitching bodies. Little brown men. One hell of a lot of little brown men.

The flaming trees illuminated a racing silhouette, a gigantic wolf with a smaller wolf astride, clinging with paws and claws. "What the hell is that?" Mather demanded.

Murgen guessed, "That Shifter, Croaker?"

"Maybe. Probably. We know he's around somewhere. Lady!" I yelled it at the burning trees. The fire was dying in the drizzle.

A sound that might have been an answer slithered through the crackling.

"Where are you?"

"Here."

Something moved amidst an outcrop of small rocks. I jumped down. "Goblin! Where the hell are you?"

No Goblin. Just Lady. And now not enough light to see how badly she was hurt. And hurt she was, no doubt about that. A fool damned thing to do, and me a physician who ought to know better, but I sat down and pulled her into my lap and held her, rocking her like a baby.

The mind goes.

From the minute you sign on with the Company you're doing things that make no sense, drills and practices and rehearsals, so that when the crunch comes you'll do the right thing automatically, without thought. The mind goes. I was without thought of anything but loss. I did not do the right thing.

I was lucky. I had companions whose brains had not turned to mud.

They got together enough burnable wood to get a fire started, got me my gear, and with a little judicious yelling got me to stop fussing and start doing.

She wasn't as bad off as she'd seemed in the dark. A few cuts, a lot of bruises, maybe a concussion to account for her grogginess. The old battlefield reflexes took over. I became a military physician. Again.

Murgen joined me after a while. "I found her horse. No sign of Goblin, though. How is she?"

"Better than she looks. Banged around some but nothing critical. She'll hurt all over for a while."

About then her eyelids fluttered, she looked up at me, and recognized me. She threw herself at me, wrapped her arms around me, and started crying.

Shadid said something. Murgen chuckled. "Yeah. Let's see if we can find Goblin." Cordy Mather was a beat slow, but he got it and went away, too.

She settled down quickly. She was who she was, and was not in the habit of yielding to her emotions. She peeled herself off me. "Excuse me, Croaker."

"Nothing to excuse. You had a close call."

"What happened?"

"I was going to ask you."

"They had me. They had me dead, Croaker. I thought we'd given them the slip, but they knew right where we were. They split us apart and ran me up here, and there must have been a dozen of them sneaking around, jumping in on me and jumping away. They were trying to capture me, not kill me. Guess I should be glad. Otherwise, I'd be dead. But there's some time missing. I don't remember you showing up and running them off."

"I didn't. Near as I can tell, Shifter saved you." I told her about the sudden fire and the wolf.

"Maybe. I didn't know he was around."

"Where's Goblin?"

"I don't know. We split about a mile from here. He tried to baffle them with illusions. We must have killed a hundred of those men today, Croaker. I never saw anybody so inept. But they never stopped coming. When we tried to outrun them there were always more in ambush no matter which way we went. If we tried to fight they always outnumbered us and two more turned up for every one we killed. It was a nightmare. They always knew where we were." She snuggled in close again. "There had to be some kind of sorcery involved. I was never so scared."

"It's all right now. It's over." It was the best I could think to say. Now that my nerves were settled I was intensely aware of her as a woman.

What appeared to be lightning flashed to the east, several miles away. But there had been no lightning running with this petty drizzle. I heard Shadid and Murgen and Mather yelling at each other, then the sounds of their mounts moving away. "That's got to be Goblin," I said, and started to get up.

She tightened her grip, held me down. "They can handle it, Croaker."

I looked down. It did not take much light to show me what was in her face. "Yeah. I guess they can." After a moment's hesitation, I did what she wanted.

As the breathing got heavier I broke away and said, "You're not in any shape for—"

"Shut up, Croaker."

I shut up, and paid attention to business.

Back to Scouting

The pinhead gods had other ideas.

I am not a swift worker, and Lady had her natural reluctances—and all of a sudden the sky opened up like somebody chopped open the bellies of the clouds. The downpour was heavy and cold and came with just a breath or two of chill wind for warning. I'd have thought I was already wet enough not to mind more, but . . .

We'd hardly stopped scrambling around trying to find some shelter when Murgen and the others came out of the night. Murgen said, "It was Goblin, all right, but he was gone when we got there." He assumed I knew what he was talking about. "Croaker, I know us Black Company types is tough he-men and neither rain nor snow nor little brown geeks is supposed to stop us from doing any damned thing we want, but I'm burned out on this rain. I guess I got what you call conditioned at the Barrowland. I can't handle too much of it. I get the collywobbles."

I was burned out on it, too. Especially now it was coming down serious. But . . . "What about Goblin?"

"What about him? I'll make you a bet, Croaker. That little dork is all right. Goddamned well better off than we are. Eh?"

This is where command really gets you. When you make a choice that feels like you're taking the easy way out. When you think you are taking convenience over obligation. "Right, then. Let's see if we can't find our way back to town." I let go Lady's hand. We got ourselves in better array. Those guys pretended not to notice. I supposed the troops back in Taglios would know before sunrise, somehow. Rumor works that way.

Damn, I wished I was guilty as suspected.

We reached the village as the world began to turn grey. Even those fabulous mounts of ours were worn out. We boothorned them into a stable meant for half a dozen normal animals and went clumping inside. I was sure the owner would be thrilled to death to see his clientele expanded again and looking like they'd just spent the night rolling around in the mud.

The old boy wasn't around. Instead, a pudgy little woman appeared from the kitchen, looked at us like she thought the barbarians had invaded, then saw Lady.

Lady looked just as rough as the rest of us. Just as mean. But there was no mistaking her for a guy. The old gal rushed her and babbled in Taglian and reached up to pat her back and I didn't need Cordy to tell me she was doing an "Oh, you poor dear" routine. We followed them back into the kitchen.

And there was friend Goblin, leaning back with his feet up on a log in front of a fire, sipping something from a huge mug.

"Get the little bastard!" Murgen said, and started after him.

Goblin bounced up and squeaked, "Croaker!"

"Where you been, runt? Sitting here drinking toddies while we're out stomping in the mud trying to save your butt from the baddies, eh?"

Murgen got him cornered. "Hey! No! I just got here myself."

"Where's your horse? The stable was one short when we put ours in."

"It's pretty miserable out there. I left it out back and came straight inside."

"It's not miserable for a horse? Murgen, throw him out and don't let him back inside till he takes care of his horse."

Not that we had done all that decent a job ourselves. But we'd at least gotten them in out of the wet.

"Cordy, when the old gal finishes fussing over Lady ask her how far it is to the Main."

"The Main? You're not still—"

"I'm still. As soon as I get some chow inside me and a couple hours of sleep. It's what I came down for and it's what I'm going to do. Your pals have been running a game on us, whatever their reasons, and I don't like it. If I can take the Company on without getting drafted into somebody's fight, I'm going to do it."

He sort of smiled. "All right. If you have to see for yourself, see for yourself. But be careful."

Goblin came in, looking sheepish and conciliatory and wet. "Where are you going now, Croaker?"

"Where we were going in the first place. The river."

"Maybe I can save you the trouble."

"I doubt it. But let's hear it. You find out something while you were adventuring on your own?"

His eyes narrowed.

"Sorry. It wasn't one of my all-time best nights."

"You're having a lot of not-so-good times in recent years, Croaker. Being Captain gives you a sour stomach."

"Yeah."

We exchanged stares. I won the lookdown. He said, "After Lady and I split up I only got about half a mile before I realized them brown guys weren't being fooled. I knew I did a good job with the illusion. If they didn't all come after me, then they had some mojo of their own somewhere. I already suspected they did on account of how they stuck all the time even when we outran them. So I figured if I couldn't get back to Lady I'd do the next best thing and go after whoever was controlling and guiding them. When I started sniffing around for it it was damned easy to find. And they gave me no trouble. I guess they figured if I would go away from Lady they'd leave me alone. Only a few stuck with me. I turned on them and uncorked a few specials I was saving for the next time One-Eye got out of line, and after they all stopped kicking I buzzed over there and sneaked up and there was this hilltop that had been sort of hollowed out, like a bowl, and down in the bowl there was these six guys all facing a little fire. Only there was something weird. You couldn't see them right. It was like you was looking at them through a fog. Only the fog was black. Sort of. Lots of little shadows, I'd guess you'd call them. Some of them no bigger than a mouse's shadow. All buzzing around like bees."

He was talking as fast as his mouth would go, yet I knew he was having trouble telling what he had seen. That words for what he wanted to convey did not exist, at least in any languages us mundanes would understand.

"I *think* they were seeing what we were doing in the flames, then sending those shadows out to tell their boys what to do to us and how to get into our way."

"Hunh?"

"Maybe you were lucky, not dealing with them so much in the daytime."

"Right." I figured I'd had troubles enough chasing a walking tree stump around the countryside. "See any crows while you were at it?"

He looked at me funny. "Yeah. As a matter of fact. See, I was laying there in the mud looking at these guys, trying to figure what I had in the trick bag that I could smack them with, and all of a sudden there's about twenty crows swooping around. The whole thing blew up like it was raining naptha instead of water. Cooked those brown guys good. Only those crows maybe weren't crows. You know what I mean?"

"Not till you tell me."

"I only saw them for a second, but it seemed like I could see right through them."

"You always do," I muttered, and he looked at me weird again. "So you figure any of the brown guys who're still out there are wandering around lost now? Like puppies without their masters?"

"I wouldn't say that. I figure they're as smart as you or me. Well, as smart as you, anyway. They just don't have their advantage anymore."

The old woman was still fussing over Lady. She had taken her somewhere to get bathed and patched up. As if she needed patching.

"How does this save me a trip to the Main?"

"I'm not finished yet, Your Grand Impatience. Right after the blowup here came one of the guys I thought I'd finished, tracking me down, all on his lonesome, and he's stumbling around holding his head like something got ripped out. I grabbed him. And I grabbed a couple loose shadows that were hanging around and I slapped one of them around a little and sent it off to tell One-Eye I needed to borrow his little beast. I taught another shadow how to make a guy talk and when the little monster showed up we asked the brown guy a few hundred questions."

"Frogface is here?"

"He went back. Mogaba's got them working their butts off up there."

"Good for him. You asked questions. You got answers?"

"Not that made much sense. These little brown guys come from a berg called Shadowcatch. Specifically, out of some kind of superfortress called Overlook. Their boss is one of the Shadowmasters. Longshadow, they call him. He gave the shadows to the six guys that was in the bowl place. These were just wimpy little shadows not good for much but carrying messages. They supposedly got bad ones they can turn loose, too."

"We're having some fun now, aren't we? You find out what's going on?"

"This Longshadow is up to something. He's in with the whole bunch trying to keep the Company away—the brown guys didn't know why they're worried—but he's running a game on his own, too. The impression I got was he wanted them to capture you and Lady and have you dragged down to his castle, where he was going to make some kind of deal, maybe. And that's about it."

I had five hundred questions and I started asking them, but Goblin didn't have the answers. The man he had interrogated hadn't had them. Most of the questions had occurred to him.

He asked, "So, are you going down to the Main?"

"You haven't changed my mind. Neither have those brown runts. If they don't have their mojo men anymore, they won't give me much trouble. Will they?"

Goblin groaned. "Probably not."

"So what's the matter?"

"You think I'm going to let you ride out there without some kind of cover? I'm groaning about the state of my butt." He grinned his big frog grin. I grinned back.

According to our hosts it was a four-hour ride to the Ghoja ford, the nearest and best crossing over the Main. Swan said there were four along an eighty-mile stretch of the Main: Theri, Numa, Ghoja, and Vehdna-Bota. Theri being the farthest upriver. Above Theri the Main coursed through rugged canyons too steep and bleak for military operations—though Goblin said our little brown friends had come that way, to evade the attention of the other Shadowmasters. They had lost a third of their number making the journey.

Vehdna-Bota lay nearest the sea and was useful only during the driest months of the year. The eighty miles of river between Vehdna-Bota and the sea were always impassable. Both Vehdna-Bota and Theri fords took their names from Taglian villages that had been abandoned when the Shadowmasters had invaded last year. They remained empty.

Numa and Ghoja were villages below the Main, formerly Taglian, now occupied. Ghoja appeared to be the critical crossing, and Swan, Mather, and Blade had all seen it. They told me what they could. I asked about the other fords and made an amusing discovery. Each was unfamiliar with at least one. Ha!

"Me and Goblin will scout the Ghoja crossing. Murgen, you and Cordy check out Vehdna-Bota. Shadid, you and Swan go to Numa. Sindawe, you and Blade check out Theri." I was sending each of the three into strange country.

Cordy laughed. Swan scowled. And Blade . . . Well, I wonder if you could get a reaction out of Blade by sticking his feet in a fire.

We split up. Lady, Otto, Hagop, and Sindawe's man all stayed behind to recuperate. Goblin rode beside me but did not say much after he hoped the weather would not go sour again. He did not sound like he expected the drizzle to hold off.

Swan said he had heard the Shadowmasters were fortifying the south bank of the Ghoja ford. Another indication the enemy would put his main force over there. I hoped it would come out that way. On the maps the terrain looked very favorable.

Two hours after we split the drizzle resumed. Perfect weather for the dreary thoughts tramping my brain.

Despite my adventure yesterday it seemed forever since I had been alone long enough to think a thought through. So with Goblin still as the grave I expected to do some serious brooding about where Lady and I were going. But she hardly crossed my mind. Instead, I mulled over what I'd gotten me and the Company into.

I was in charge but not in control. As far back as that monastery things had been happening that I could not control and could not unravel into sense. Gea-Xle and the river worsened matters. Now I felt like driftwood tumbling through a rapid. I had only the slightest idea who was doing what to whom, and why, but I was locked into the middle of it. Unless this last frantic gesture showed me an out.

For all I knew if I let the Prahbrindrah suck me in I would be enlisting on the "wrong" side. Now I knew how the Captain felt when Soulcatcher dragged us into the Lady's service. We were fighting in the Forsberg campaigns before the rest of us began to suspect we'd made a mistake.

It is not necessary for mercenary soldiers to know what is going on. It is sufficient for them to do the job for which they have taken the gold. That had been drummed into me from the moment I enlisted. There is neither right nor wrong, neither good nor evil, only our side and theirs. The honor of the Company lies within, directed one brother toward another. Without, honor lies only in keeping faith with the sponsor.

Nothing I knew of the Company's experiences resembled our present circumstance. For the first time—mainly by my doing—we were fighting for ourselves first. Our contract, if we accepted it, would be coincidental to our own desires. A tool. If I kept my head and perspective as I should, Taglios and all Taglians would become instruments of our desires.

Yet I doubted. I liked what I had seen of the Taglian people and especially liked their spirit. After the wounds they had taken keeping their independence they were still fired up for the Shadowmasters. And I had a good notion I wouldn't like those folks if I got to know them. So before it was fairly begun I'd broken the prime rule and become emotionally involved. Fool that I am.

That damned rain had a personal grudge. It got no heavier but it never let up. Yet to east and west I saw light that indicated clear skies in those directions. The gods, if such existed, were laying on the misery especially for me.

The last tenanted place we passed lay six miles from the Ghoja ford. Beyond, the countryside had been abandoned. It had been empty for months. It was not bad land, either. The locals must have had a big fear on to uproot and flee. A change of overlords usually isn't that traumatic for peasants. The five thousand who had come north and not returned must have had a real way about them.

The country was not rugged. It was mostly cleared land that rolled gently, and the road was not awful, considering, though it had not been built to carry military traffic. Nowhere did I see any fortifications, man-made or natural. I'd seen none of the former anywhere in Taglian territory. There would be no place to run and few places to hide in the event of disaster. I became a bit more respectful of Swan and his buddies, daring what they had.

The ground, when soaked, became a clayey, clinging mud that exercised the strength and patience even of my tireless steed. Note to the chief of staff. Plan our battles for clear, dry days.

Right. And while we're at it, let's order up only blind enemies.

You have to take what is handed you in this trade.

"You're damned broody today, Croaker," Goblin said, after a long while.

"Me? You been chattering like a stone yourself."

"I'm troubled about all this."

He was troubled. That was a very un-Goblin-like remark. It meant he was worried right down to his toenails. "You don't think we can handle it if we have to take the commission?"

He shook his head. "I don't know. Maybe. You always grab something out of the trick bag. But we're getting worn out, Croaker. There's no zest in it anymore. What if we did pull it off, and broke through, and got to Khatovar, and ended up with a big nothing?"

"That's been the risk since we started. I never claimed anything for this trip. It's just something I thought had to be done because I pledged to do it. And when I turn the Annals over to Murgen I'll extract the same oath from him."

"I guess we don't have anything better to do."

"To the end of the world and back again. It's an accomplishment of sorts."

"I wonder about the first purpose."

"So do I, old friend. It got lost somewhere between here and Gea-Xle. And I think these Taglians know something about it. But they're not talking. Going to have to try some old-fashioned Company double shuffle on them sometime."

The drizzle had its good side, I suppose. It lessened visibility. We were over the last crest and headed down toward the Main and Ghoja ford before I realized we had come that far. Sentries on the south bank would have spotted us immediately in better weather.

Goblin sensed it first. "We're there, Croaker. The river's right down there."

We reined in. I asked, "You feel anything on the other side?"

"People. Not alert. But there's a couple poor fools on sentry duty."

"What kind of outfit does it feel like?"

"Sloppy. Third-rate. I could get a better look if I had a little time."

"Take some time. I'm going to roam around and look it over."

The site was what I had been told it would be. The road wandered down a long, bare slope to the ford, which lay just above an elbow in the river. Below the elbow a creek ran into the river from my side, though I had to go make sure because it lay behind higher ground. The creek had a beard of the usual growth along both banks. There was also a slight rise in the other direction, so that the road to the ford ran down the center of a slight concavity. Above the ford the river arched southward in a slow, lazy curve. On my side its bank was anywhere from two to eight feet high and overgrown with trees and brush everywhere but at the crossing itself.

I examined all that very carefully, on foot, while my mount waited with Goblin beyond the ridge. I sneaked down to the edge of the ford itself and spent a half hour sitting in the wet bushes staring at the fortifications on the other side.

We were not going to get across here. Not easily.

Were they worried about us coming to them? Why?

I used the old triangulation trick to figure out that the watchtower of the fortress stood about seventy feet high, then withdrew and tried to calculate what could be seen from its parapet. Most of the light was gone when I finished.

"Find out what you need to know?" Goblin asked when I rejoined him.

"I think so. Not what I wanted, either. Unless you can cheer me up. Could we force a crossing?"

"Against what's in there now? Probably. With the water down. If we tried in the dead of the night and caught them napping."

"And when the water does go down they'll have ten thousand men hanging around over there."

"Don't look good, does it?"

"No. Let's find a place to get out of the rain."

"I can stand to ride back if you can."

"Let's try. We'll sleep dry if we make it. What do you think of the men over there? Professionals?"

"My guess is they're just a little better than men disguised as soldiers."

"They looked pretty sloppy to me, too. But maybe they don't have to be any better in these parts."

I had seen and watched four men while I was crouching near the ford. They had not impressed me. Neither had the design or construction of the fortifications. Clearly, these Shadowmasters had brought in no professionals to train their forces and they had not developed a good edge on what they did have.

" 'Course, maybe we saw what we were supposed to see."

"There's always that." An interesting thought, maybe worth some consideration, because at that moment I noticed a couple of bedraggled crows watching us from a dead branch on an elm tree. I started to look around for the stump, thought the hell with it. I would handle that when the time came.

"You remember Shifter's woman, Goblin?"

"Yeah. So?"

"You said you thought she seemed familiar back in Gea-Xle. Now it's all of a sudden coming on me that maybe you were right. I'm sure we ran into her somewhere before. But I can't for the life of me think where or when."

"Does it matter?"

"Probably not. Just one of those things that nag at you. Let's cut off to the left here."

"What the hell for?"

"There's a town on the map, called Vejagedhya, that I want to look at."

"I thought we were going back—"

"It'll only take a few minutes extra."

"Right." Grumble, grumble, ragglesnatz.

"Looks like we might have to fight. I need to know the country."

Fraggin snigglebark.

We ate cold food as we rode. It is not often that I do so, but at such moments I sometimes envy the man with a cottage and wife.

Everything costs something. It was ghost country we rode, spooky country. The hand of man was evident everywhere, even in darkness. Some of the homes we inspected looked like they had been closed up only yesterday. But not once did we encounter another human being. "I'm surprised thieves haven't been working all this."

"Don't tell One-Eye."

I forced a chuckle. "I guess they were smart enough to take their valuables with them."

"These people do seem determined to pay whatever price they have to, don't they?" He sounded impressed.

Grudgingly, I was developing a case of respect. "And it looks like the Company is going to be their one toss of the bones with fate."

"If you let them."

There was the town, Vejagedhya. It might once have been home to as many as a thousand people. Now it was even more spooky than the abandoned farms. Out there, at least, we had encountered wildlife. In the town I saw nothing but a few crows fluttering from roof to roof.

The townsfolk had not locked their doors. We checked maybe two dozen buildings. "It would do for a headquarters," I told Goblin.

He grunted. After a while, he asked, "You making up your mind?"

"Beginning to look made up for me. Right? But we'll see what the others have to say."

We headed north. Goblin did not have much to say after that. That gave me time to dwell on and invent deeper meanings to my roles as Captain and potential warlord.

If there was no choice but to fight, and to lead a nation, I was going to make demands. I was not going to let the Taglians put me in a position where they could second-guess and override my every decision. I had watched my predecessors get half crazy dealing with that. If the Taglians hooked me, I was going to hook them right back.

We might call it something prettier, but by damn I was going to be a military dictator.

Me. Croaker. The itinerant military physician and amateur historian. Able to indulge in all the abuses I'd damned in princes for so long. It was a sobering notion.

If we bought it, and took the commission, and I got what I would demand, I might have Wheezer follow me around and remind me that I'm mortal. He wasn't good for much else.

The rain let up as we were riding into town.

Now I knew the gods loved me.

29

Smoke's Hideout

Smoke was perched on a tall stool, bent over a huge old book. The room was filled with books. It looked like a wave of books had swept in and left tidal pools behind. Not only were there shelves dripping books, there were books stacked hip-high on the floor, books on tables and chairs, even books piled on the sill of the room's one small, high window. Smoke read by the light of a single candle. The room was sealed so tight the smoke had begun to irritate his nose and eyes.

From time to time he grunted, made a note on a piece of paper to his left. He was left-handed.

In all the Palace that room was the best protected from spying eyes. Smoke had woven webs and walls of spells to secure it. No one was supposed to know about it. It did not show on any plan of the Palace.

Smoke felt something touch the outermost of the protective spells, something as light as a mosquito's weight as it lands. Before he could swing his attention to it it was gone and he was not sure he had not imagined it. Since the incident of the crows and bats he had been almost paranoid.

Intuition told him he had reason. There were forces at work that were way beyond him. His best weapon was the fact that no one knew he existed.

He hoped.

He was a very frightened man these days. Terror lurked in every shadow.

He jumped and squeaked when the door opened.

"Smoke?"

"You startled me, Radisha."

"Where are they, Smoke? There's been no word from Swan. Have they gotten away?"

"Leaving most of their people behind? Radisha, be patient."

"I have no patience left. Even my brother is becoming unsettled. We have only weeks left before the rivers fall."

"I'm aware of that, madam. Concentrate on what you *can* do, not what you wish you could do. Every force possible is being bent upon them. But we cannot compel them to help."

The Radisha kicked over a pile of books. "I've never felt so powerless. I don't like the feeling."

Smoke shrugged. "Welcome to the world where the rest of us live."

In a high corner of the room a point no bigger than a pinprick oozed something like a black smoke. The smoke slowly filled out the shape of a small crow. "What are the rest of them doing?"

"Making preparations for war. In case."

"I wonder. That black officer. Mogaba. Could he be the real captain?"

"No. Why?"

"He's doing the things I want them to do. He's acting like they're going to serve us."

"It makes sense, Radisha. If their captain comes back convinced they can't sneak away, they'll be that much farther ahead."

"Has he made preparations to run back north?"

"Of course."

The Radisha looked vexed.

Smoke smiled. "Have you considered being forthright with them?"

She gave him a look to chill the bones.

"I thought not. Not the way of princes. Too simple. Too direct. Too logical. Too honest."

"You grow too daring, Smoke."

"Perhaps I do. Though as I recall my mandate from your brother is to remind you occasionally—"

"Enough."

"They are what they pretend to be, you know. Wholly ignorant of their past."

"I'm aware of that. It makes no difference. They could become what they were if we let them. Sooner bend the knee to the Shadowmasters than endure that again."

Smoke shrugged. "As you will. Maybe." He smiled slyly. "And as the Shadowmasters will, perhaps."

"You know something?"

"I am constrained by my need to remain unnoticed. But I've been able to catch glimpses of our northern friends. They have fallen afoul of more of our little friends from the river. Ferocious things are happening down near the Main."

"Sorcery?"

"High magnitude. Recalling that which manifested during their passage through the pirate swamps. I no longer dare intrude."

"Damn! Damn-damn-damn! Are they all right? Have we lost them?"

"I no longer dare intrude. Time will tell."

The Radisha kicked another pile of books. Smoke's bland expression cracked, became one of intense irritation. She apologized. "It's frustration."

"We're all frustrated. Perhaps *you* would be less so if you adjusted your ambitions."

"What do you mean?"

"Perhaps if you followed the course your brother has charted and aimed to climb but one mountain at a time—"

"Bah! Am I, a woman, the only rooster around here?"

"You, a woman, will not be required to pay the price of failure. That will come out of your brother's purse."

"Damn you, Smoke! Why are you always right?"

"That is my commission. Go to your brother. Talk. Recalculate. Concentrate on the enemy of the moment. The Shadowmasters must be turned now. The priests will be here forever. Unless you want shut of them badly enough to let the Shadowmasters win, of course."

"If I could frame just one High Priest for treason . . . All right. I know. The Shadowmasters have shown they know what to do with clerics. Nobody would believe it. I'm going. If you dare, find out what's happening down there. If we've lost them we'll have to move quickly. That damned Swan had to go after them, didn't he?"

"You sent him."

"Why does everybody do what I tell them? Some of the things I say are stupid. . . . Get that grin off your face."

Smoke failed. "Kick over another stack of books."

The Radisha huffed out of the room.

Smoke sighed. Then he returned to his reading. The book's author lingered lovingly over impalements and flayings and tortures visited on a generation unlucky enough to have lived when the Free Companies of Khatovar marched out of that strange corner of the world that spawned them.

The books in that room had been confiscated so they would not fall into the hands of the Black Company. Smoke did not believe their being there would keep secrets forever. But maybe long enough for him to find a way to prevent the sort of bloodshed that had occurred in olden times. Maybe.

The best hope, though, lay in the probability that the Company had mutated with time. That it was not wearing a mask. That it had indeed forgotten its grim origins and its search for its past was more a reflex than the determined return that other Companies, come back earlier, had made.

In the back of Smoke's mind, always, was the temptation to take his own advice, to bring the Company's captain in and turn him loose on the books, if only to see how he responded to the truth.

Taglios Aroused

We approached Taglios with the dawn, days late, all of us at the brink of collapse, Swan and his buddies maybe worse off than the rest. Their mundane mounts were wiped out. I asked Swan, "You figure the Prahbrindrah will be overly pissed because I didn't keep my appointment?"

Swan still had a little pepper left. "What the hell can he do? Put a bug down your shirt? He'll swallow it and smile. You worry about the Woman. She's the one who'll give you trouble. If anybody does. She don't always think right."

"Priests," Blade said.

"Yeah. Watch out for the priests. They sprung this whole thing on them the day you guys landed. They couldn't do anything but go along. But they been thinking about it, you can bet your butt, and when they find them an angle they're going to start messing."

"What's Blade's thing with priests?"

"I don't know. I don't want to know. But I been down here long enough to start thinking he's maybe right. The world might be better off if we drowned some of them."

One thing that made the military situation wonderfully impossible was the absence of fortifications. Taglios itself sprawled everywhere, without a thought to defense.

A people with centuries of pacifism behind them. An enemy with experienced armies and high-power sorcerers to support them. And me with maybe a month to figure out how to help the former whip the latter.

Impossible. When those rivers went down so troops could cross the massacre would be on.

Swan asked, "You make up your mind what you're going to do?"

"Yeah. The Prahbrindrah isn't going to like it, either."

That surprised him. I did not explain. Let them worry. I took my bunch in to the barracks and sent Swan off to announce our return. As we dismounted, with half the Company hanging around waiting to hear something, Murgen said, "I guess Goblin's made up his mind."

Something had been preying on the little wizard. He had been broody and curt all the way home. Now he was grinning. He gave special attention to his saddlebags.

Mogaba joined me. "We've made major progress while you were gone, Captain. I'll report when you feel up to it." His question remained unspoken.

I saw no need to leave it hanging. "We can't sneak through. They've got us. It's fight or turn back."

"Then there is no option, is there?"

"I guess there never was. But I had to see for myself."

He nodded his understanding.

Before business I tended wounds. Lady was coming back fast. Her bruises, though, did nothing to make her more attractive. I felt odd examining her. She had had little to say since our night in the rain. She was doing a lot of thinking again.

Mogaba had a lot to tell me about discussions with Taglios's religious leaders and his ideas for putting together the pretense of an army. I could find nothing in his suggestions I disapproved. He said, "There's one other thing. A priest named Jahamaraj Jah, number two man in the Shadar cult. He has a daughter he thinks is dying. It looks like a chance to make a friend."

"Or get somebody thoroughly pissed." Never underestimate the power of human ingratitude.

"One-Eye saw her."

I looked at the little witch doctor. He said, "Looked like her appendix to me, Croaker. Not that far gone yet, either. But these clowns around here don't have the foggiest. They're trying to exorcise demons."

"I haven't opened anybody up in years. How long before it bursts?"

"Another day at least, unless she's unlucky. I did what I could for the pain."

"I'll check it on the way back from the Palace. Make me a map. . . . No.

You'd better tag along. You might be useful." Mogaba and I were getting dressed for a court appearance now. Lady was supposed to be doing the same.

Swan, not at all improved in appearance, showed up to take us to the Prince. I did not feel like doing anything but take a nap. I sure did not feel up to the games of politicians. But I went.

The people of Trogo Taglios had heard that the moment of decision had come. They were in the streets to watch us. They remained eerily silent.

I saw dread in all those watching eyes, but hope, too. They were aware of the risks, and maybe even of the odds against them. A pity they did not realize that a battlefield is not a wrestling ring.

Once a child cried. I shivered, hoping it was not an omen. As we neared the Trogo an old man stepped out of the crowd and pressed something into my hand. He bowed himself away.

It was a Company badge from olden times. An officer's badge, perhaps booty from some forgotten battle. I fixed it near the badge I wore already, the fire-breathing death's-head of Soulcatcher, which we had retained though we no longer served the Taken or the empire.

Lady and I had outfitted ourselves in our finest, meaning I wore my legate's duds and she her imperial rig. We impressed the mob. Beside us Mogaba looked drab. One-Eye looked like a derelict scraped off the bottom of the worst dive in the worst slum. That damned hat. He was as happy as a snail.

"Showmanship," Lady had told me. An old maxim of my own, albeit directed somewhat differently. "In politics and battle our big weapon will have to be showmanship."

She was coming to life. I think those brown guys pissed her off.

She was right. Showmanship and craft, even more than traditionally, would have to be our tools. If we were to meet and beat the veteran armies commanded by the Shadowmasters we would have to gain our triumphs inside the imaginations of enemy soldiers. It takes ages to create a force with the self-confidence to go slug it out despite the odds.

Despite our being late the Prahbrindrah Drah was a gracious host. He treated us to a dinner the likes of which I have no hope of seeing again. Afterward, he laid on the entertainment. Dancing girls, sword swallowers, illusionists, musicians whose work my ear found too alien to appreciate. He was in no hurry to get to an answer of which he was confident. During the afternoon Swan introduced me to several score of Taglios's leading men, including Jahamaraj Jah. I told Jah I would look at his daughter as soon as I could. The gratitude in the man's face was embarrassing.

Otherwise, I paid no attention to those men. I had no intention of dealing with or through them.

The time came. We were invited out of the crowd into a private chamber. Because I had brought two of my lieutenants the Prahbrindrah did the same. One was that codger Smoke, whom the Prince introduced by title. That translated out as Lord of the Guardians of Public Safety. And that turned out to mean he was boss of the city fire brigade.

Only One-Eye failed to keep a straight face.

The Prahbrindrah's other lieutenant was his enigmatic sister. Put them together and it was obvious she was older and probably tougher than he. Even dressed up she looked like she had been ridden hard and put away wet.

When the Prahbrindrah asked about my companions I introduced Mogaba as my commander of infantry and Lady as my chief of staff. The idea of a woman soldier amazed him. I wondered how much more amazed he would be if he knew her history.

She concealed surprise at the designation. As much for her benefit as the Prahbrindrah's, I said, "There's nobody in the Company more qualified. With the possible exception of the Captain, each post is filled on merit."

Swan was doing the translating. He skirted the edge of the Prahbrindrah's reply, which, I think, actually suggested limited agreement. His sister seemed to be his brain trust.

"To the point," I told Swan. "Time is too tight if we're going to stop an invasion."

Swan smiled. "Then you're going to accept the commission?"

You never doubted it for a second, you jackal. "Don't get your hopes too high, man. I'm going to make a counteroffer. Its terms won't be negotiable."

Swan's smile vanished. "I don't understand."

"I've looked at the land. I've talked with my people. Despite the lay, most of them want to go on. We know what we have to do to get to Khatovar. Meaning we'll consider doing the job your prince wants done. But we won't try it except on our terms. Tell him that, then I'll give him the sad news."

Swan translated. The Prahbrindrah did not look happy. His sister looked like she wanted a fight. Swan faced me. "Let's have it."

"If I'm supposed to run an army that I'll have to build from scratch, I want to have the power to do it. I want to be the boss. No interference from anybody. No political crap. No cult feuding. Even the will of the Prince will have to yield for the duration. I don't know if there's a Taglian word for what I want. I can't think of a Rosean word, either. In the Jewel Cities the man in the job I want is called 'dictator.' They elect him for a year at a time. Tell him that."

Was the Prahbrindrah happy? Sure he was. About as happy as any prince in that fix. He started lawyering, trying to bury me in ifs, ands, and buts. I smiled a lot.

"I said I wouldn't negotiate, Swan. I meant it. The only chance I see is for us to do what needs doing when it's got to be done, not six weeks later, after the ruffled feathers have been smoothed, the special interests have had their say, and the graft has been got out."

Mogaba had on the biggest smile I'd ever seen from him. He was having fun listening. Maybe he'd always wanted to talk that way to his bosses in Gea-Xle.

I said, "The way I hear it, in about five weeks the rivers will be down enough that the Shadowmasters can put their troops across the Main. They won't have internal problems slowing them down. They'll have every advantage but the Black Company on their side. So if the Prahbrindrah wants even a prayer of winning, he has to give me the tools I need. If he doesn't, I walk. I find some other way. I won't commit suicide."

Swan translated. We sat around looking tough and professional and stubborn. Lady and Mogaba did fine. I thought I might blow it by being nervous, but I did not. The Prahbrindrah never tried to call my bluff. He argued, but never so hard I might lose my temper and stomp out. I never gave an inch. I honestly believed that the only chance, and that a ghost of a hope, lay in an absolute military dictatorship. And I had a little inside word, thanks to Frogface.

"Hey, Swan. Are these people in even bigger trouble than they've admitted?"

"What?" He cast a nervous glance at the imp.

"Your boss isn't trying to talk me out of anything. He's lawyering. Politicking. Wasting time. I get the feeling that down deep he's scared to death. He agrees with me. Only he don't want to *have* to make the choice between evils. Because then he has to live with his choice."

"Yeah. Maybe. The Shadowmasters are going to be coming mean after what we did last summer. Going to make an example of us, maybe."

"I'll want the veterans of that business. We'll turn them into squad leaders. Assuming I get to be boss soldier around here."

"There is an archaic Taglian word meaning warlord. You'll get your way. It's been argued out in council. The High Priests don't like it, but they don't have any choice. Priests were the first people the Shadowmasters rubbed out wherever they took over. He can make any deal he has to. They're scared, man. After you win is when you got to start worrying."

All I had to do was go on sitting tight. But I had come into the meeting with that assurance from Frogface.

The damned imp grinned and winked at me.

The day rolled on into night and we had to have another meal, but we sealed our pact.

For the first time since Juniper the Company had a real commission.

Or vice versa.

The Prahbrindrah wanted to know my plans. He was not dumb. He knew Mogaba had been putting in twenty-hour days.

"Put together a big flashy show for the gang that comes across the Main, mostly. But we'll recruit and train for harder times down the line too, assuming we handle that first bunch. While we're at it, we'll get an idea of what resources are available and how best to employ them. We'll root out enemy agents here and try to establish our own over there. We'll learn the terrain where the fighting may take place. Swan. I keep hearing about how little time we have till the rivers go down. How long will they stay down? How long till the next grace period?"

He translated, then said, "There'll be six to seven months when there won't be enough rain to close the fords. Even after the rainy season starts there'll be two or three months when they're passable part of the time."

"Wonderful. We got here in the middle of the safe season."

"Just about. We could get more than five weeks. That's a worst estimate."

"We can count on it, then. Tell him we'll need a lot of help from the state. We have to have weapons, armor, mounts, rations, drays, drayage, equipment. We need a census of all males between sixteen and forty-five, with their skills and occupations. I want to know who to conscript if I don't get volunteers. A census of animals would be helpful. Likewise, a census of weapons and equipment available. And a census of fortifications and places that could be used as fortresses. You should know a lot of this from last summer. Do you write the lingo here, Swan?"

He translated, then said, "No. I can't figure out the alphabet. 'Course, I never learned to read or write Rosean, neither." He grinned. "Not Cordy, neither."

"Blade?"

"You kidding?"

"Wonderful. Find me somebody who can. It's all right if he's one of the Radisha's spies. Two birds with one stone. I'll want you and him both attached to me at the hip till I learn the language. All right. What I need right now is for him to get out the word that volunteers should assemble in the Chandri Square an hour after dawn tomorrow." The Chandri Square was near our barracks and one of the biggest in Taglios. "They should bring any weapons or equipment they have. We'll pick twenty-five hundred to start training immediately and enroll the rest for later."

"You may be too optimistic."

"I thought these people were eager to get into it."

"They are. But tomorrow is a holy day for the Gunni cults. That takes in four-tenths of the lower classes. When they sit down nobody else can do anything, either."

"There aren't any holidays in a war. They better get used to that right now. They don't show up, that's tough. They get left behind. Tell the Prince to spread the word that the guys who volunteer earliest are the guys who're going to get the best deal. But everybody starts at the bottom. Even him, if he enlists. I don't know the class structures here and I don't care. I'll make a prince carry a spear and have a farm boy command a legion if that's what the man can do best."

"That attitude's going to cause problems, Cap. And even if they elect you god you're going to have to walk careful around the priests."

"I'll deal with them when I have to. The politics I can probably handle. I can twist arms and smooth fur if I have to, though mainly I just won't put up with it. Tell the Prince he should hang around my headquarters some. Things will go smoother if people think he's part of what's happening."

Swan and the Prince chattered. The Radisha gave me a searching look, then a smile that said she knew what I was up to. The devil in me made me wink. Her smile broadened.

I decided I should know more about her. Not because I was attracted to her but because I suspected I would like the way she thought. I like a person with a sound cynical attitude.

Old Smoke, the so-called fire chief, did nothing all evening but nod off and start awake. Being a cynic, I approved of him as a public official. The best kind are those who stay the hell out of the way and don't mess with things. Except for me, of course.

"One thing left for tonight," I told Swan. "Financing. The Black Company don't come cheap. Neither does creating, arming, training, and maintaining an army."

Swan grinned. "They got you covered, Cap. Back when they first heard the prophecies of your coming they started raising money. It won't be a problem."

"It's always a problem."

He smiled. "You won't be able to spend like there ain't no bottom to the bucket. The Woman hangs on to the purse strings around here. And she's famous for being tight."

"Good enough. Ask the Prince if there's anything else he needs now. I've got a ton of stuff to do."

There was another hour of talk, none of it important, all of it the Prahbrindrah and Radisha trying to get an idea what I was planning, trying to get a clearer picture of my character and competence. Giving a stranger life-and-death power over their state was one long bet for them. I figured I'd do a little something to help their underground scheme.

I became impatience itself, but was proud of me. I controlled it.

Walking home after dark, without crowds, I asked Lady, "Can we count on Shifter's help?"

"He'll do what I tell him."

"You're sure?"

"Not absolutely. It looks that way, though."

"Could he do some scouting over Shadowmaster country? Shifting into something that flies?"

"Maybe." She smiled. "But he wouldn't have strength enough to carry you. And I know you. You wouldn't trust a report from anybody but you."

"Well . . ."

"You'll have to take your chances. Trust him as much as you dare. He'll serve me if I command him. But he isn't my slave. He has his own goals now. They may not be your goals."

I thought it might be a good time to sneak up on something I'd been sliding around since I'd caught her playing with fire in a cup overlooking Gea-Xle. "And your own restored talent?"

She was not fazed. "You're kidding. I might bother Goblin if I sneaked up on him and hit him with a hammer. Otherwise, I'm useless. Even small talents have to be exercised to be any good. There's no time for exercise."

"I guess we'll all just do what we can."

Mogaba said, "I have several ideas for disarming problems arising from religious friction. At least temporarily."

"Speaking of which. I need to carve on that priest's kid. One-Eye, I'll need you to back me up. Go ahead, Mogaba."

His notion was straightforward. We would raise our own army without regard to religion and use it to meet the Shadowmasters' main thrust. We would encourage the cults to raise their own forces and use them to meet threats that appeared at the secondary fords. But we would not surrender our claim to supreme command.

I laughed. "I have a feeling you're looking for a repeat of the debacle of last summer when—"

"Nothing should disarm them more thoroughly than failures and displays of incompetence. I thought we ought to give them their chances."

"Sounds good to me. Work up a couple of questions for recruits so we can get the drift of their religious commitment and tolerance when we sign them up. You want to tell me how to find this guy Jahamaraj Jah?"

Taglios: a Boot-Camp City

It had been years since I hazarded internal surgery. Before I started I was shaky and filled with doubts, but habit took hold in the crunch. My hand was steady. One-Eye restrained his natural exuberance and used his talents judiciously to control bleeding and deaden pain.

As I washed my hands I said, "I can't believe it went that well. I haven't done one of those since I was a kid, practically."

"She going to pull through?" One-Eye asked.

"Should. Unless there're complications. I want you to check back every day to make sure she's doing all right."

"Hey, Croaker. I got me an idea. Why don't you buy me a broom?"

"What?"

"When I wasn't busy doing anything else I could be sweeping up."

"I'll get myself one, too." I spoke to the child's parents briefly, through Frog-face, clueing them in on what had to be done. Their gratitude was stifling. I doubted it would last. People are that way. But as we were about to leave I told the father, "I'll collect on this."

"Anything."

"It won't be trivial. When the time comes."

He understood. He looked grim as he nodded.

We were about to step into the street when One-Eye said, "Hold up." He pointed.

I looked down at three dead bats arranged in a neat equilateral triangle. "Maybe the boys aren't imagining things." The bat cadavers were not neat.

A crow cawed somewhere nearby.

I muttered, "I'll take my help where I can get it." Louder, "Could you make a bat spy on people?"

One-Eye thought about it. "I couldn't. But it might be possible. Though they aren't long on brains."

"That's all I needed to know." Except for who was running the bats. The Shadowmasters, I presumed.

The twenty-hour days started. When I was not preoccupied with anything else I tried to learn the language. After you have learned enough they come easy. Or easier, anyway.

We went at it trying to keep things simple. All the evidence indicated that the Shadowmasters would use the Ghoja ford for their main crossing. I abdicated the defense of the others to the cult leaders and concentrated on what I thought I'd need to stop that main force in its tracks. If it got across the river and started rolling north, I feared we would have a repeat of Swan's campaign. Any victory at all would be at a price too dear.

I started by forming the cadres of two legions based on the model used by the Jewel Cities in early times, when their armies were citizens with little field experience. The command structure was the simplest possible. The organization was pure infantry. Mogaba was overall commander of the foot and boss of the first legion. His lieutenant Ochiba got the second legion. Each got to keep ten Nar for NCOs and each of those ten picked a hundred candidates from among the Taglian volunteers. That gave each legion a thousand-man base which would be expanded about as fast as the Nar could teach them to march in a straight line. Mogaba got Wheezer, Lion, and Heart for staff work. I did not know what else to do with those three. They were willing but had little practical value.

Sindawe and the remaining Nar were to form a third, training and reserve legion that I expected to employ only in desperation.

Otto, Hagop, the Guards, and the roi I charged with putting together a cavalry force.

Sparkle, Candles, Cletus, and the rest from Opal and Beryl got stuck with the fun stuff, quartermastering and engineering. Hagop's nephew ended up with him. He was another one who was useless.

The ideas were mostly Mogaba's recommendations, which he had worked out while I was scouting southward. I did not agree with all of them, but it seemed a sin to waste the work he had done. And we had to move in some direction. Now.

He had it all figured. Sindawe's legion would both produce new people for the leading two units and would develop as a force itself more slowly. He did not believe we could manage a force larger than three legions till we developed a lot of local talent.

Lady, Goblin, One-Eye, and I were left to handle everything else. The important, exciting stuff, like dealing with the Prahbrindrah and his sister. Like setting up an intelligence operation, finding out if there were any local wizards we could use. Charting strategy. Coming up with gimmicks. Good old Mogaba was willing to leave me the staff work and strategy.

Actually, about the way it should be. The man embarrassed me with his competence.

"Goblin, I guess you should take counterintelligence," I said.

"Har!" One-Eye said. "That fits him perfectly."

"Borrow Frogface whenever you need him." The imp moaned. He got no pleasure out of having to work.

Goblin put on a smug look. "I don't need that thing, Croaker."

I did not like that. The runt was up to something. Ever since we came back from the country he had had that smugness about him. It meant trouble. He and One-Eye could get so involved in their feud they forgot the rest of the world.

Time would tell what was up.

"Whatever you say," I told Goblin. "As long as you get the job done. Dangerous agents of the Shadowmasters I want you to take out. Small-timers set up so we can feed them false information. We've also got to keep one eye on the big priests. They're bound to give us grief as soon as they figure out how. Human nature."

Lady I put in charge of showmanship and planning. I had decided where I wanted to meet the enemy already, before I had anything to meet him with. I told her to work out the details. She was a better tactician than I. She had managed the armies of an empire with astonishing success.

I was learning that part of a captain's job is to delegate. Maybe genius lies in choosing the right person for the right task.

We had maybe five weeks. And the time was counting down. And down. And down.

I did not think we had a prayer.

Nobody got much sleep. Everybody got testy. But that is the way it is in our business. You learn to adjust to it, to understand. Mogaba kept telling me it was going great on his end, but I never got time to review his outfits. Hagop and Otto were less pleased with their progress. Their recruits were of classes that saw discipline as something imposed only upon their inferiors. Otto and Hagop had to resort to asskicking to get their people in line. They came up with a couple of interesting ideas, like adding elephants to the cavalry. The Prahbrindrah's census of animals had turned up a few hundred work elephants.

I spent my time rushing around in confusion, more often a politician than a commander. I avoided recourse to dictate when I could, preferring persuasion, but two of the High Priests gave me no choice most of the time. If I said black they said white just to let me know they considered themselves Taglios's real bosses.

If I'd had time I'd have gotten vexed with them. I didn't, so I didn't play their games. I got them and their chief boys together, with the Prahbrindrah and his sister chaperoning, and told them I didn't care for their attitude, that I would not tolerate it, and the schedule from here on in was do it Croaker's way or die. If they didn't like that, they were welcome to take their best crack at me. Then I would roast them over a slow fire in one of the public squares.

I did not make myself popular.

I was bluffing, sort of. I would do what had to be done, but did not expect to have to do it. My apparently violent nature should cow them while I got on with the job. I would worry about them after I'd turned the Shadowmasters.

Thinking positive all the time. That's me.

I'd have starved if I'd gotten a pound of bread for every minute I really believed we had a chance.

Several people made sure news of the face-off got out. I heard rumors that some temples closed their doors for lack of business. Others had to turn away angry crowds.

Great.

But how long would it last? These peoples' passion for supernatural nonsense was far older and more ingrained than their passion for militarism.

"What the hell happened?" I asked Swan, first chance I got. I was getting the language, but not fast enough to grasp religious subtleties.

"I think Blade happened." He seemed bemused.

"Say what?"

"Ever since we've been here Blade's been spreading seditious nonsense about priests should stick to taking care of souls and karma and keep their noses out of politics. Been selling that down to our place. And when he heard about your confab with the High Priests he got himself out in the streets to spread what he called 'the true story.' These people are all for their gods, you better remember that, but they ain't so hot on some of their priests. Especially the kind that grab them by the purse and squeeze."

I laughed. Then I said, "You tell him to back off. I've got troubles enough without a religious revolution."

"Right. I don't think you got to worry about that."

I had to worry about everything. Taglian society was under extreme stress, though it took an outsider to see it. Too many changes too fast in a traditionalist, restrictive society. No way for conventional mechanisms to adjust. Saving Taglios would be like riding the whirlwind. I would have to stay light on my feet to keep the frustration and fear directed against the Shadowmasters.

One-Eye wakened me in the middle of one of my four-hour snoozes. "Jahamaraj Jah is here. Says he's got to see you right now."

"His kid take a turn for the worse?"

"She's fine. He thinks he's going to pay you off."

"Bring him in."

The priest slipped in looking furtive. He bowed and scraped like a street dweller. He plied me with every title the Taglian people had been able to imagine, including Healer. Appendectomy was a piece of surgery unknown in those parts. He looked around as though expecting ears growing out of the walls. Maybe that was an occupational hazard. He did not like the sight of Frogface at all.

That suggested some people knew what the imp was. I should keep that in mind.

"Is it safe to talk?" he asked. I followed that without translation.

"Yes."

"I must not stay long. They will be watching me, knowing I owe you a great debt, Healer."

Then get on with it, I thought. "Yes?"

"The High Priest of the Shadar, my superior, Ghojarindi Ghoj, whose patron is Hada, one of whose avatars is Death. You distressed him the other night. He has told the Children of Hada that Hada thirsts for your ka."

Frogface translated, and added commentary. "Hada is the Shadar goddess of Death, Destruction, and Corruption, Cap. The Children of Hada are a sub-cult who dedicate themselves by way of murder and torture. Doctrine says that should be random and senseless. The way it works out, though, is that those who die have got onto the boss priest's shitlist."

"I see." I smiled slightly. "And who is your patron, Jahamaraj Jah?"

He smiled back. "Khadi."

"All Sweetness and Light, I take it."

"Hell no, chief. She's Hada's twin sister. Just as damned nasty. Got her fingers into plague, famine, disease, fun stuff like that. One of the big things the Shadar and Gunni cults squabble about is whether Hada and Khadi are separate deities or just one with two faces."

"I love it. I bet people get killed over it. And priests look at me weird when I say I can't take them seriously. One-Eye. You figure I'm guessing right when I think our buddy here is helping himself by trying to weasel out of a debt?"

One-Eye chuckled. "I figure he plans to be the next Shadar boss."

I had Frogface go straight at him. He did not blush. He admitted he was the most likely successor to Ghojarindi Ghoj.

"In that case I don't figure he's done anything but make the vig. Tell him thanks but I figure he still owes me. Tell him that if he all of a sudden finds himself boss priest of the Shadar I'd be real proud if he'd make his people mind and not get too ambitious himself for a year or two."

Frogface told him. His grin went away. His lips tightened into a wrinkly little nut. But he bobbed his head.

"Get him on the road, One-Eye. Wouldn't want him getting in trouble with his boss."

I went and wakened Goblin. "We got priest problems. Character named Ghojarindi Ghoj is siccing assassins on me. Take Murgen, go over to Swan's dive, dig out his resident priest hater, have him finger the guy. He needs promoting to a higher plane. It don't have to be spectacular, just unpleasant. Like having him shit himself to death."

Grumbling, Goblin went to find Murgen.

One-Eye and Frogface got to watch for would-be assassins.

They were professionals but they were not up to getting past Frogface. There were six of them. I had some of the Nar, who favored that sort of thing, take them to a public square and impale them.

Ghojarindi Ghoj went west a day later. He perished of a sudden, dramatic surfeit of boils. The lesson was not lost on anyone.

The lesson was, of course, don't get caught.

Nobody seemed upset or displeased. The attitude was, Ghoj had placed his bets and taken his chances. But the Radisha did give me some thoughtful looks while we fussed over whether I needed another thousand swords and especially if I needed the hundred tons of charcoal I had requisitioned.

Actually, we were to the games-playing stage already. I asked for a hundred tons knowing I wanted ten, figuring to groan and gripe and give in and get more of the arms.

The recruits were providing their own kit. The arms I most wanted financed by the state were pieces that could not be well explained to a civilian. I was having trouble enough convincing Mogaba that wheeled light artillery might be of value.

I was not sure it would myself. That depended on what the enemy did. If they behaved as they had before, artillery would be wasted. But the model was the Jewel Cities legion. Those guys dragged light engines along to knock holes in enemy formations.

Oh, fuss. Some things you just settle by saying I'm the boss and you'll do it my way.

Mogaba did not mind.

Seventeen days to go, estimated. Lady visited me. I asked her, "Will you be ready?"

"I'm almost ready now."

"One positive report amongst the hundreds. You brighten my life."

She gave me a funny look. "I've seen Shifter. He's been across the river." One-Eye and Goblin, in their capacities as spymasters, had had little luck, mostly because the Main was just plain uncrossable. They had no lack of volunteers.

As for cleaning up the Shadowmasters' agents in Taglios, that had not taken them ten days. A bunch of little brown guys had bitten the dust. A few native Taglians remained. We were feeding them plenty of truth, and just enough bull to tempt their masters into making their major crossing effort where I wanted it.

"Ah. And did he learn anything we want to hear?"

She grinned. "He did. You get your wish. They'll bring their main force over at the Ghoja ford. And they won't be with their armies. They don't trust each other enough to leave home base unguarded."

"Beautiful. Suddenly, I feel like we've got a chance. Maybe only one in ten, but a chance."

"And now for the bad news."

"I guess it had to be. What is it?"

"They're sending an extra five thousand men. Ten thousand in the Ghoja force. A thousand each at Theri and Vehdna-Bota. The rest come across at Numa. They tell me Numa is crossable two days earlier than the Ghoja ford is."

"That's bad. They could have three thousand guys behind us when it hits."

"They will unless they're morons."

I closed my eyes and looked at the map. Numa was where I had told Jahamaraj Jah his Shadar people could make their mark. He had raised twenty-five hundred cultists only by straining. Most Shadars wanted to wait and get into our ecumenical force. Three thousand veterans would roll right over him.

"Cavalry?" I asked. "Have Jah meet them at the water's edge and do what he can, and fall back, and have our cavalry hit them from the flank as they're about to break out?"

"I was considering sneaking Mogaba's legion down, smash them, then rout march to Ghoja. But you're right. Cavalry would be more efficient. Do you trust Otto and Hagop to handle it?"

I did not. They were having their problems taking charge. Without the bloodyminded roi to kick ass where that was needed, their force would have been a travelling circus. "You want it? You done a field command?"

She looked at me hard. "Where have you been?"

Right. I'd been there often enough.

"You want it?"

"If you want me to take it."

"Singe me to a crisp in the fire of your enthusiasm. All right. But we won't tell anybody till it's time. And Jahamaraj Jah not at all. He'll try harder if he don't know help is coming."

"All right."

"Any other news from our seldom-seen friend?"

"No."

"Who is that woman he's dragging around?"

She hesitated a moment too long. "I don't know."

"Odd. Seems like I've seen her somewhere before. But I can't place her."

She shrugged. "After a while everybody gets to look like somebody you've seen before."

"Who do I look like?"

She didn't miss a beat. "Gastrar Telsar of Novok Debraken. The voice is different, but the heart could be the same. He moralized and debated with himself, too."

How could I argue? I'd never heard of the guy.

"He moralized once too often. My husband had him flayed."

"You think I moralized about Ghoj?"

"Yes. I think you put yourself through hell after the fact. A net gain. You've gotten smart enough to get them first and cry later."

"I don't think I want to play this game."

"No. You wouldn't. I need some of your time for tailors to take your measurements."

"Say what? I got me a flashy uniform already."

"Not like this one. This one is for boggling the minions of the Shadowmasters. Part of the showmanship."

"Right. Whenever. I can work while I'm being measured. Is Shifter going to be there for the show at Ghoja?"

"We'll find out the hard way. He didn't say. I told you, he has his own agenda."

"Wouldn't mind having a peek at that. He give you one?"

"No. Mogaba is staging a mock battle between legions today. You going?"

"No. I'm going to be sucking up to the Radisha for more transport. I got the charcoal. Now I got to get it down there."

She snorted. "Things were different in my time."

"You had more power."

"That's true. I'll send the tailors and fitters."

I wondered what she had in mind. . . . What? Did I see that? What was that? Did she shake her tail as she was going out? Damn me. My eyes must be starting to go.

Weekly assessment session. I asked Murgen, "How's the bat situation?"

"What?" I had caught him from the blind side.

"You brought the bat problem up. I thought you were keeping track."

"I haven't seen any for a while."

"Good. That means Goblin and One-Eye got the right people out of the way. From where I sit everything looks like it's going smooth. Probably faster than we had reason to expect." I'd had no individual complaints for a while. Lady had found time to help Otto and Hagop put the fear into their snooty horsemen. "Mogaba?"

"Twelve days left on the worst-case estimate. It's time to put teams out to watch the river stages. Worst case might not be absolutely worst."

"The Radisha is ahead of you. I talked to her yesterday. She'd just grabbed off half the post riders for that. Right now the river is running higher than expected. That may not mean anything. We'll have plenty of weather yet."

"Every day we get is another hundred men I can take into each legion."

"Where are you at now?"

"Thirty-three hundred each. I'll stop at four thousand. Be time to move out then, anyway."

"Think five days is enough to get down there? That's twenty miles a day for guys who aren't used to it."

"They'll be used to it. They do ten a day with field pack now."

"I'll get out to look them over this week. Promise. I've got the political end pretty well whipped. Hagop. You guys going to be ready?"

"It's coming together, Croaker. They've started to realize we mean it when we say we're trying to show them how to stay alive."

"It's getting close enough that they have to think about it as more than a game. Big Bucket. How about you guys?"

"Get us fifty more wagons and we can roll tomorrow, Captain."

"You look at the sketches of that town?"

"Yes sir."

"How long to set it up?"

"Depends on materials. For the palisade. And manpower. Lot of trenching. The rest, no problem."

"You'll have the manpower. Sindawe's bunch. They'll go down with you and move on later, as our reserve. I'll tell you, though, the resource situation is bleak. You'll end up depending on the trench more than the palisade. Cletus. What about artillery?"

Cletus and his brothers grinned. They looked proud of themselves. "We got it. Six mobile engines for each legion, already built. We're working the crews on them now."

"Great. I want you to go down with the quartermasters and engineers and get a look at that town. Put some of the engines in there. Big Bucket, you guys better head out as soon as you can. The roads are going to be miserable. If you really need more wagons mooch them from the citizens. Be quicker than me trying to gouge them out of the Radisha. So. Can't anybody come up with anything I can fuss myself about? You know I'm not happy unless I'm worrying."

They looked at me blankly. Finally, Murgen blurted out, "We're going to meet their ten thousand with our eight? Isn't that worry enough? Sir?"

"Ten thousand?"

"That's the rumor. That the Shadowmasters increased the invasion force."

I glanced at Lady. She shrugged. I said, "We have unreliable intelligence to that effect. But we'll be more than eight thousand with the cavalry. With Sindawe we'll actually outnumber them. We'll have the field position. And I have a trick or two up my sleeve."

"That charcoal?" Mogaba asked.

"Among other things."

"You won't tell us?"

"Nope. Word has a way of getting around. If nobody but me knows I can't blame anybody but me if the other side finds out."

Mogaba smiled. He understood me too well. I just wanted to keep it for myself.

We commanders are that way, sometimes.

My predecessors never told anybody anything till it was time to jump.

Afterward, I asked Lady, "What do you think?"

"I think they're going to know they were in a fight. I still have grave doubts about winning, but maybe you're a better captain than you want to admit. You put every man where he can do the most good."

"Or least harm." Wheezer and Hagop's nephew still had not shown me they were good for anything.

Seven days till deadline. The quartermasters and engineers and Sindawe's reserve legion were two days gone. Incoming post riders reported their progress as disappointing. The roads were hopeless. But they were getting help from people along the way. In places the troops and locals backpacked the freight while the teams dragged the empty wagons through the mud.

We were going to get some grace. We were still getting drizzle when that should have ended a week ago. Reports had the fords way too high to cross. The watchers guessed we had at least five extra days.

I told Mogaba, who needed time more than anyone else. He grumbled that his main accomplishment to date was that he had taught his troops to march in straight lines.

I thought that was the critical lesson. If they could maintain order on the battlefield . . .

I was not comfortable with the gift of time. As each day perished in turn, and I had more reports of the trouble the advance party was having, I grew ever more antsy.

Two days before our originally planned departure I summoned Mogaba. "Have you relaxed any because of the extra time?"

"No."

"Not easing up at all?"

"No. If we leave five days later, they'll be five days more prepared."

"Good." I leaned back in my chair.

"You're troubled."

"That mud. I had Frogface go scout. Sindawe is still twenty miles from Ve-jagedhya. What'll it be like for the mob we'll take down?"

He nodded. "You're thinking of leaving early?"

"I'm seriously considering leaving when we originally planned. Just to make sure. If we're there early we can get rested and maybe a little more trained under field conditions."

He nodded again. Then took me by surprise. "You play hunches sometimes, don't you?"

I lifted an eyebrow.

"I've watched you since Gea-Xle. I'm beginning to understand how your mind works, I think. And sometimes I think you don't understand yourself well enough. You've been troubled all week. That is a sign you have a hunch trying to come through." He left his chair. "I'll proceed on the assumption that you'll leave early."

He left. I thought about him knowing how my mind works. Should I feel flattered or threatened?

I went to a window, opened it, looked at the night sky. I saw stars between racing clouds. Maybe the cycle of daily drizzle was over. Or maybe it was just another pause.

I went back to work. My current project, taken catch-as-catch-can, was one I was working on with Frogface. We were trying to figure out what had become of the books missing from all the libraries around town. I had an idea that a certain anonymous official had them squirreled away in the Prahbrindrah's palace. The question was, how to get to them? Invoke my powers as dictator?

"Ignore the river."

"Say what?" I looked around. "What the hell?"

"Ignore the river."

A crow stood on the windowsill. Another settled beside it. It delivered the same message.

Crows are smart. But only for bird brains. I asked what they were talking about. They told me to ignore the river. I could put them on the rack and they would not tell me more. "All right. I got it. Ignore the river. Shoo."

Crows. All the time with the damned crows. They were trying to tell me something, sure. What? They had warned me before. Were they saying I should pay no attention to the river stages?

That was my inclination anyway, because of the mud.

I went to the door and yelled, "One-Eye! Goblin! I need you."

They mustered in looking surly, standing well away from one another. Not a good sign. They were feuding again. Or working up to it. It had been so long since they had eased the pressure that it might be a major blowup.

"Tonight's the night, guys. Take out the rest of the Shadowmasters' agents."

"I thought we had some extra time," One-Eye carped.

"We might have. And we might not. I want it done now. Take care of it."

Under his breath Goblin muttered, "Yessir your dictatorship, sir." I gave him a dirty look. He moved out. I went to the window and stared out at that clearing sky.

"I had a feeling things were going too good."

32

Shadowlight

The Shadowmasters met in a haste that left them exhausted. The meet had been set days earlier but as they travelled a cry had gone out saying it was too late for lazy, comfortable movements.

They were in the place of the pool and uncertain dimensions and shadows. The woman bobbed restlessly. Her companion was agitated. The one who spoke seldom spoke first. "What is the panic?"

"Our resources in Taglios have been exterminated. All but the newest. As suddenly as that." She snapped her fingers.

Her companion said, "They are about to march."

The woman: "They knew who our resources were. Which means everything we learned through them is suspect."

Her companion: "We have to move sooner than we planned. We cannot give them a minute more than we must."

The quiet one asked, "Have we been found out?"

The woman: "No. We have the one resource close to the heart, still undetected if mostly ineffective. It hasn't reported a hint of a suspicion."

"We should join the troops. We should leave nothing to the hazard of battle."

"We've argued this out already. No. We will not risk ourselves. There is no cause to think they will have any chance against our veterans. I have added five thousand men to the invasion force. That is enough."

"There was another thing. The thing you called us here to present."

"Yes. Our comrade of Shadowcatch and Overlook is not as southward obsessed as he would have us think. He infiltrated some of his people into Taglian territory the past year. They attacked the leaders of the Black Company. And failed abysmally. Their efforts served only one purpose—beyond betraying his thinking. They gave me a chance to insinuate our one surviving resource into the enemy fold."

"Then when next we meet him we can mock him in turn."

"Perhaps. If it seems appropriate. One piece of news comes out of his effort. Dorotea Senjak is with them."

A long stillness followed. Finally, the one who spoke so seldom observed, "That alone explains why our friend would send men north secretly. How dearly he would love to own her."

The female replied, "For more reasons than the obvious. There appears to be a relationship with the Company's Captain. She would be a valuable resource if that relationship is strong enough to be manipulated."

"She must be killed as soon as possible."

"No! We must capture her. If he can use her, so can we. Think what she knows. What she was. She might hold the key to ridding the world of him and of closing the gateway. She may be powerless but she has not lost her memory."

The one who spoke seldom began to laugh. His laughter was as insane as that heard in Overlook. He was thinking anyone could use the memories of Dorotea Senjak. Anyone!

The female recognized that laugh, understood what was happening in his mind, knew she and her companion would have to proceed very carefully. But she pretended not to see. She asked her companion, "Have you contacted the one in the swamps?"

"He wants nothing to do with us or our troubles. He is content with his fetid, humid little empire. But he will come around."

"Good. We're agreed? We advance the schedule?"

Heads nodded.

"I will send the orders immediately."

33

Taglios: Drunken Wizards

It had not been a good day. It got no better because the sun went down. The high had been Frogface reporting Sindawe reaching Vejagedhya. The low followed immediately. There was no material to fortify the town. A ditch would be it.

But the ground was so sodden the walls of a ditch would keep collapsing.

Oh, well. If the gods were out to get us they were out to get us. All our wriggling on the hook wouldn't change a thing.

I was ready to collapse into bed when Murgen burst in. I was so tired I was seeing double. Two of him did not improve the state of the universe. "What now?" I snapped.

"Maybe big trouble. Goblin and One-Eye are down at Swan's place, drunk on their asses, and they've started in. I don't like the smell of it."

I got up, resigned to another sleepless night. It had been a long time brewing. It might get out of hand. "What are they doing?"

"Just the usual, so far. But there's no fun in it this time. There's an undercurrent of viciousness. Anyway, it stinks like somebody could get hurt."

"Horses ready?"

"I sent word."

I grabbed up the officer's baton some Nar had tossed me as we had approached Gea-Xle. No special reason other than that it was the nearest thing handy for thumping heads.

The barracks was quiet as we passed through. The men sensed something afoot. By the time I reached the stables Mogaba and Lady had joined the parade. Murgen explained while they cursed our Taglian stablehands into readying two more horses.

That the feud had gotten out of hand was obvious from blocks away. Fires illuminated the night. Taglians were coming out to see what was happening.

The wizards had squared off in the street outside Swan's place. That had been gutted. Fires flickered up and down the street, none major, just patches gnawing the faces of buildings, evidence of the errant aim of a couple of drunken sorcerers.

Those troublesome little shits were having difficulty standing, let alone shooting straight. So maybe the gods do watch out for fools and drunks. Had they been sober they would have murdered each other.

Unconscious bodies lay scattered around. Swan and Mather and Blade and several guys from the Company were among them. They had tried to break it up and gotten creamed for their trouble.

One-Eye and Goblin were escalating. One-Eye had a pained-looking Frog-face sicced on Goblin. Goblin had something that looked like a black snake of smoke growing out of his belt pouch. It was trying to get past Frogface. When the things grappled a shower of light washed the street, revealing Taglians crouched, watching from relative safety.

I halted before they noticed me. "Lady. What's that thing Goblin's got?"

"Can't tell from here. Something he shouldn't. A match for Frogface, which I would have thought was out of One-Eye's class." She sounded vaguely troubled.

There were times I'd had that notion myself. It did not seem reasonable that you could walk into a shop and buy a Frogface off the shelf. But it hadn't bothered One-Eye, and he was the expert.

Frogface and the snake came to grips midway between their masters. They started grunting and straining and screaming and thumping around. I wondered aloud, "Is that what Goblin brought back from the country?"

"What?"

"From the first time I saw him after his set-to with the brown guys directing the shadows he had this smugness about him. Like he finally had him some way to whip the world."

Lady thought. "If he picked it up from the Shadowmasters' men it could be a plant. Shifter could tell us for sure."

"He ain't here. Let's make the assumption."

The last fire burned itself out. Goblin and One-Eye were totally preoccupied. One-Eye stumbled over his own bootlace. For a moment it looked like Goblin would get the upper hand. Frogface barely turned the snake's strike.

"Enough. We can't do without them, much as I'd like to bury them both and have done with their crap." I spurred my horse. Goblin was nearest me. He barely started to turn. I leaned down and thumped his head. I did not see the result. I was on One-Eye already. I whacked him upside the head, too.

I turned for a second charge but Lady, Mogaba, and Murgen had them wrapped up. The battle between Frogface and the snake died out. But they did not. They eyed one another across ten feet of pavement.

I swung down. "Frogface. Can you talk? Or are you as crazy as your boss?"

"He's crazy, Cap, not me. But I got an indenture. I got to do what he says."

"Yeah? Tell me this. What's that thing growing out of Goblin's pouch?"

"A kind of imp. In another form. Where'd he come up with it, Cap?"

"I wonder myself. Murgen, check these other guys out. See if we've got any real casualties. Mogaba, drag that little shit over here. I'm going to knock some heads together."

We plunked them down side by side with Lady and Mogaba holding them sitting from behind. They began to come around. Murgen came to tell me none of the unconscious men were injured.

That was something.

One-Eye and Goblin looked up at me. I paced back and forth, smacking the baton into my hand. My dictator's stalk. I whirled on them. "Next time this happens I'm going to tie you two into a sack, face-to-face, and drop you in the river. I don't have the patience for it. Tomorrow, while your hangovers are still killing you, you're going to get up and come down here and make good the damage. The expense will come out of your pockets. Do you understand?"

Goblin looked a little sheepish. He managed a feeble nod. One-Eye did not respond.

"One-Eye? You want another whack upside the head?"

He nodded. Sullenly.

"Good. Now. Goblin. That thing you brought back from the country. Chances are it belongs to the Shadowmasters. A plant. Before you go to bed I want it stuffed in a bottle or something and buried. Deep."

His eyes bugged. "Croaker . . ."

"You heard me."

An angry, almost roaring hiss filled the street. The snake thing came up off the paving and struck at me.

Frogface flung in from the side, deflecting it.

In a sudden, drunken, bug-eyed panic Goblin and One-Eye both tried to get it under control. I backed off. It was a wild three minutes before Goblin got it squished into his pouch. He stumbled into Swan's place. A minute later he came out carrying a closed wine jar. He looked at me funny. "I'll bury it, Croaker." He sounded embarrassed.

One-Eye was getting himself together, too. He took a deep breath. "I'll give him a hand."

"Right. Try not to talk too much. Don't get started again."

He had the grace to look embarrassed, too. He gave Frogface a thoughtful look. I noted that he did not take the imp along to do the heavy work.

"What now?" Mogaba asked.

"Pains me all to hell, but now we count on their consciences to keep them in line. For a while. If I didn't need them so much I'd make it a night they'd remember the rest of their lives. I don't need this shit. What're you grinning about?"

Lady did not stop. "It's smaller scale, but this is what it was like trying to keep a rein on the Ten Who Were Taken."

"Yeah? Maybe so. Murgen, you were out here boozing anyway, you finish picking up the pieces. I'm going to get some sleep."

To Ghoja

It was worse than I thought it would be. The mud seemed bottomless. The first day out of Taglios, after a cheering parade, we made twelve miles. I did not feel desperate. But the road was better nearer the city. After that it got worse. Eleven miles the next day, nine each of the three days following. We made that good a time only because we had the elephants along.

The day I wanted to reach the Ghoja ford I was still thirty miles away.

Then Shifter came, wearing his wolf shape, prancing in out of the wilds.

The rains had ended but the sky remained overcast, so the ground did not dry. The sun was no ally.

Shifter came with a smaller companion. It looked as though his understudy had caught on to shifting.

He spent an hour with Lady before we moved out. Then he galloped away again.

Lady did not look cheerful.

"Bad news?"

"The worst. They've put one over on us, maybe."

I did not betray the sudden tightness in my innards. "What?"

"Recall the map of the Main. Between Numa and Ghoja there's that low area that floods."

I pictured it. For twelve miles the river ran through an area flanked by plains that flooded whenever the river rose more than a few feet. At its highest stage it could be fourteen miles wide there, with most of the flooding on the southern side. That plain became a huge reservoir, and was the reason the Numa ford became crossable before the Ghoja. But the last I'd heard it was mostly drained.

"I know it. What about it?"

"Ever since they took the south bank the Shadowmasters have been building a levee, from the downriver end, right along the normal bank. It's something that's been talked about for ages. The Prahbrindrah wanted to do it, to claim the plain for farming. But he couldn't afford the labor. The Shadowmasters don't have that problem. They have fifty thousand prisoners on it, Taglians who didn't get across the river last year and enemies from their old territories. No one's paid any attention because the project is one of those things that anyone who could would do."

"But?"

"But. They've gotten the levee run out eight miles to the east. That's not as huge a deal as it sounds because it only needs to be about ten feet tall. Every half mile they put in a larger filled area, maybe a hundred fifty yards to a side, like towers along a wall. They keep the prisoners camped there and use the platforms for materials dumps."

"I don't see where you're going."

"Shifter noticed that they'd stopped extending the levee but they were still stockpiling materials. Then he figured it out. They're going to dam the river, partially. Just enough to divert water into the flood plain so they can drop the level at the Ghoja ford sooner than we expect."

I thought about it. It was a cunning bit of business, and entirely practical. The Company had done a trick or two with rivers in its time. All it had to do was give them a day. If they got across unchallenged we were sunk. "The sneaky bastards. Can we get there in time?"

"Maybe. Even probably, considering you didn't wait to leave Taglios. But at the rate we're going it'll be just barely in time and we'll be worn out from fighting the mud."

"Have they started damming yet?"

"They start that this morning, Shifter says. It should take them two days to get the fill in and one more to divert enough water."

"Will it affect Numa?"

"Not for a week. The water will keep dropping there for now. Shifter's guess is they'll cross at Numa the day before they do at Ghoja."

We looked at each other. She saw what I saw. The Shadowmasters had robbed us of what we had in mind for the night before Ghoja. "Damn them!"

"I know. This mud being what it is, I'll have to leave today to get there in time. I probably won't get back to Ghoja. Use Sindawe in our place. That town is a waste, anyway."

"I'll have to move faster, somehow."

"Abandon the wagons."

"But . . ."

"Leave the engineers and quartermasters behind. Let them make the best time they can. I'll leave them the elephants. They're no good to me anyway. Have each man carry a little extra. Whatever is most practical. Even the wagons might get there in time if they skip stopping at Vejagehdya."

"You're right. Let's get at it." I gathered my people and explained what we were going to do. An hour later I watched Lady and the cavalry file away to the southeast. Mogaba's grumbling infantrymen, each carrying an extra fifteen pounds, started slogging toward Ghoja.

Even the old warlord carried a load.

I was glad I had had the luck or foresight to send out the bulk of the stuff several days early.

I walked with the rest of them. My horse was carrying two hundred pounds of junk and looking humiliated by the experience. One-Eye grumbled along beside me. He had Frogface out scouting for lines of advance where the earth would least resist our passage.

I kept one eye on Lady. I felt hollow, empty. We'd both come to think of the night before the Ghoja battle as *the* night. And now that would not be.

I suspected it would never be. There would always be something to stand in the way. Maybe there were gods who frowned on our admitting and consummating what we felt inside.

A pox on them and all their illegitimate children.

Someday, damnit. Someday.

But what then? Then we would have to give up a lot of pretense. Then we'd have to face some things, decide some things, examine the possibilities and implications of some commitments.

I did not spend a lot of time thinking about saving Taglios that day.

Before Ghoja

Take some ground and sog it real good, all the way down to the earth's core. Bake it under a warm sun a few days. What do you get?

Bugs.

They rose in clouds as I slithered to the crest overlooking the Ghoja ford. The mosquitoes wanted to feed. The smaller guys just wanted to pitch camp in my nose.

The grass had grown since last time. It was two feet tall now. I slid my sword forward and parted it. Mogaba, Sindawe, Ochiba, Goblin, and One-Eye did the same. "*Big* mob over there," One-Eye said.

We had known that beforehand. We could smell their campfires. My own troops were eating cold. If those guys over there didn't know we were here yet, I wasn't going to yell and let them in on it.

Mob was an operative word. That bunch was undisciplined and disorderly, camped in a sprawl that began at the fortress gate and stretched back south along the road.

"What you think, Mogaba?"

"Unless that's show to fool us we have a chance. If we keep them that side of the crest." He inched forward, looked at the ground. "You're sure you want me on the left?"

"I'm assuming your legion is more ready. Put Ochiba's on the right up the steeper ground. The natural tendency of an attack would be to push the direction that looks easiest."

Mogaba grunted.

"If they push either one of you much without pushing the other, they open themselves up to heavier enfilading and quartering fire. If the artillery gets here, I'm going to plant some here and the rest down on that little hump there. Have them going both ways. Long as the hinge holds." The join between legions would be at the road that split the field. "Should be good hunting for archers and javelins, too."

Mogaba grumbled, "Plans are mayflies when the steel begins to sing."

I rolled onto my side, looked at him directly. "Will the Nar stand fast?"

His cheek twitched. He knew what I meant.

Except for the thing on the river, which was a whole different show, Mogaba's men had seen no real combat. I hadn't found out till recently. Their ancestors had gotten Gea-Xle and its neighbors so tamed they just had to make noises to keep things in line. These Nar still believed they were the best that ever was, but that had not been proven on a field of blood.

"They will stand," Mogaba said. "Can they do anything else? If terror turns their spines to water? They have made their brags."

"Right." Men will do damnfool things just because they said they would.

What about the rest of my mob? Most were veterans though few had been into this kind of thing. They had handled themselves on the river. But you can't be sure what a man will do till he does it. I was not sure of myself. I have been in and out of battles all my life, but I have seen old veterans crack.

And I'd never been a general. Never had to make decisions sure to cost lives. Did I have the inner toughness it takes to send men to sure death to achieve greater goals?

I was as new to my role as the greenest Taglian soldier.

Ochiba grunted. I parted the grass.

A dozen men approached the ford on the south side. Well-dressed men. The enemy captains? "One-Eye. Time for Frogface to do a little eavesdropping."

"Check." He slithered away.

Goblin gave me a bland look that concealed intense irritation. One-Eye got to keep his toy and he didn't. I was playing favorites. Children. What difference that that snake had damned near killed me?

Frogface came back.

They were coming in the morning. Early. They expected no resistance. They were gloating about what they were going to do to Taglios.

I had the word spread.

Wasn't nobody going to get much sleep tonight.

Was my little army overprepared? I saw plenty of the anxiety that comes before the hour of blood, but also an eagerness unusual in virgins. Those Taglians knew the odds were long. So how come they were confident in the face of probable disaster?

I realized I did not understand their culture well enough.

Dip into the old trick bag, Croaker. Play the captain game. I went walking through the camp, attended by crows as always, speaking to a man here, a man there, listening to an anecdote about a favorite wife or toddler. It was the first time many had seen me up close.

I tried not to think about Lady. So naturally she would not get out of my mind.

They were coming tomorrow at Ghoja. That meant they had crossed at Numa today. She might be fighting right now. Or it might be over. She might be dead. Three thousand enemy soldiers might be racing to get behind me.

Late that afternoon the wagons began arriving. Sindawe came in from Vejagedhya. My spirits rose. I would get to try my little trick after all.

Stragglers kept coming in all night.

If we lost the fight the train was gone. There would be no getting it out in all that mud.

One-Eye kept Frogface flitting across the river. To little purpose. The enemy strategy was: cross that river. Nothing beyond it. Don't worry about the mules, just load that wagon.

After nightfall I went up and sat in the damp grass and watched the fires burn on the other side. Maybe I dozed some, off and on. Whenever I glanced up I noticed that the stars had wheeled along. . . .

I wakened to a presence. A coldness. A dread. I heard nothing, saw nothing, smelled nothing. But I knew it was there. I whispered, "Shifter?"

A great bulk settled beside me. I amazed myself. I was not afraid. This was one of the two greatest surviving sorcerers in the world, one of the Ten Who Were Taken who had made the Lady's empire all but invincible, a monster terrible and mad. But I was not afraid.

I even noticed that he did not smell as bad as he used to. Must be in love.

He said, "They come with the light."

"I know."

"They have no sorcery at all. Only the strength of arms. You might conquer."

"I was sort of hoping I would. You going to chip in?"

Silence for some time. Then, "I will contribute only in small ways. I do not wish to be noticed by the Shadowmasters. Yet."

I thought about what little things he could do that might mean a lot.

We had started to get some traffic nearby, Taglians lugging fifty-pound sacks of charcoal to the foreslope.

Of course. "How are you with fog? Can you conjure me up a little?"

"Weather is not my strength. Maybe a small patch if there's reason. Explain."

"Be real handy to have a chunk that would lie along the river and reach maybe two hundred feet up this slope. Bottled this side of the creek over there. Just so those guys would have to come through it." I told him about my trick.

He liked it. He chuckled, a small sound that wanted to roar like a volcano. "Man, you were always sneaky, cold-blooded, cruel bastards, smarter than you looked. I like it. I'll try. It should draw no attention and the results may be amusing."

"Thank you."

I was speaking to the air. Or maybe a nearby crow. Shifter had gone without a sound.

I sat there and tormented myself, trying to think of something more I might have done, trying not to think of Lady, trying to excuse myself the dying. The soldiers crossing the ridge made very little noise.

Later, I became aware of a few tendrils of mist forming. Good.

There was a bit of rose in the east. Stars were dying. Behind me, Mogaba and the Nar were wakening the men. Across the river, enemy sergeants did the same. A little more light and I could see the artillery batteries ready to be wheeled into position. They had arrived, but so far only one wagon loaded with missiles.

Shifter had managed a mist, though not all I wanted. Fifteen feet deep at the ford, two hundred fifty yards toward me, not quite reaching the band of charcoal, ten feet wide, that the men had laid out in the night, on an arc from the riverbank in the east around to the bank of the creek.

Time to go give the final pep talk. I slithered off the crest, turned. . . . And there was Lady.

She looked like hell but she was grinning.

"You made it."

"Just got here." She grabbed my hand in hers.

"You won."

"Barely." She sat down and told me. "The Shadar did good. Pushed them back across twice. But not the third try. It broke up into a brawl and chase before we could get into it. When we did, the Shadowmasters' men formed up and held out almost all day."

"Any survivors?"

"A few. But they didn't get back across. I put some men over right away, caught them off guard, and took their fortress. Afterward I sent Jah on across." She smiled. "I gave him a hundred men to scout and told him your orders were to circle around behind them here. He could be in position this afternoon if he pushes."

"He take heavy losses?"

"Eight hundred to a thousand."

"He's dead if we blow it here."

She smiled. "That would be terrible, wouldn't it? Politically speaking."

I lifted an eyebrow. I still had trouble thinking that way.

She said, "I sent a messenger to Theri telling the Gunni to seize the crossing. Another is headed for Vehdna-Bota."

"You have the mercy of a spider."

"Yes. It's almost time. You'd better get dressed."

"Dressed?"

"Showmanship. Remember?"

We headed for camp. I asked, "You bring any of your men with you?"

"Some. More will straggle in."

"Good. I won't have to use Sindawe."

Ghoja

I felt like a fool in the getup Lady put on me. A real Ten Who Were Taken costume, baroque black armor with little threads of bloody light slithering over it. Made me look about nine feet tall when I was up on one of those black stallions. The helmet was the worst. It had big black wings on the side, a tall gismo with fluffy black feathers on the crown, and what looked like fire burning behind the visor.

One-Eye thought it would look intimidating as hell from a distance. Goblin figured my enemies would laugh themselves to death.

Lady got into an outfit just as outrageous, black, grotesque helmet, fires.

I sat there on my horse feeling weird. My people were ready. One-Eye sent Frogface to watch the enemy. Lady's helpers brought shields and lances and swords. The shields had grim symbols on them, the lances matching pennons. She said, "I've created two nasties. With luck we can turn them into something with an image like the Taken. Their names are Widowmaker and Lifetaker. Which one do you want to be?"

I closed my visor. "Widowmaker."

She fish-eyed me a good ten seconds before she told somebody to hand me my stuff. I took all my old familiar hardware along, too.

Frogface popped up. "Get ready, chief. They're about to hit the water."

"Right. Spread the word."

I glanced right. I glanced left. Everyone and everything was ready. I had done all I could. It was in the hands of the gods or the jaws of fate.

Frogface was down in the mist when the enemy hit the water. He popped back. I gave a signal. A hundred drums started pounding. Lady and I crossed the ridgeline. I guess we made a good show. Over in the fortress people scurried around and pointed.

I drew the sword Lady had given me, gestured for them to turn back. They did not. I would not have in their place. But I'll bet they were damned uneasy. I advanced down the hill and touched that burning blade to the charcoal strip.

Flame ripped across the slope. It burned out in twenty seconds but left the charcoal glowing. I got back quickly. The fumes were powerful.

Frogface popped up. "They're pouring across now, chief."

I could not yet see them through the mists. "Tell them to stop the drums."

Instant silence. Then the clangor of troops in the mist. And their cursing and coughing in the sulphur-laden air. Frogface returned. I told him, "Tell Mogaba to bring them over."

The drums started talking again. "March them in a straight line," I muttered. "That's all I ask, Mogaba. March them in a straight line."

They came. I dared not look to see how they were doing. But they passed me soon enough. And they were holding formation.

They assumed positions across the slope from the creek, then down to the river on the left, with the hinge between legions at the road. Perfection.

The enemy began coming out of the mist, swirling it, staggering, disordered, coughing furiously, cursing. They encountered the barrier of charcoal and did not know what to do.

I gestured with my sword.

Missiles flew.

It looked like pure unreasoning panic had seized the fortress. The enemy captains saw they had walked into it and did not know how to respond. They chased their tails and fussed and did not do anything.

Their soldiers just kept coming, not knowing what they were walking into until they came out of the mist and found themselves stopped by the charcoal.

The mist began to drift off downriver. Shifter could not hold it any longer. But a little had been enough.

They had some competent sergeants on the other side. They began bringing up water and cutting paths through the coals with trenching tools. They began getting their men into ragged formations, behind their shields, safer from arrows and javelins. I signalled again. The wheeled ballistae opened up.

Daring the enemy's worst, Mogaba and Ochiba rode back and forth in front of their men, exhorting them to stand fast, to maintain the integrity of their line.

My role was cruel, now. I could do nothing but sit there with the breeze playing around me, being symbolic.

They got aisles cleared through the charcoal and rushed through. A lot got dead for their trouble. The ballistae ran out of missiles and withdrew, but arrows and javelins continued to rain on those coming up from the ford, taking a terrible toll.

More and more pressure all along the line. But the legions did not bend, and gave as good as they got. Their lungs were not burned raw by sulphur gasses.

Over half the enemy had crossed the river. A third of those had fallen. The captains in the fortress remained indecisive.

The Shadowmasters' troops kept coming across. A furious desperation began to animate them. Eighty percent over. Ninety percent. The Taglians began to give a step here and there. I remained frozen, an iron symbol. "Frogface," I muttered into my helmet, "I need you now."

The imp materialized, perched on my mount's neck. "What you need, chief?" I filled him up with orders I wanted relayed to Murgen, to Otto and Hagop, to Sindawe, to damned near everybody I could think of. Some ordered next steps of the plan, some involved innovations.

The morning had been remarkably crow-free. Now that changed. Two monsters, damned near as big as chickens, settled on my shoulders. They were nobody's imagination. I felt their weight. Others saw them. Lady turned to look at them.

A flock passed over the battlefield, circled the fortress, settled into the trees along the riverbank.

The enemy infantry was across. Their train was getting organized to follow.

Thousands of the Shadowmasters' men were down. I doubted they had the advantage of numbers anymore. But experience had begun to tell. My Taglians were giving ground. I felt the first flutters of panic nipping at their formations.

Frogface materialized. "Couple wagons with ballista shafts came in, chief."

"Get them up to the engines. Then tell Otto and Hagop it's time."

Maybe seven hundred horsemen had straggled in from Numa by then. They were dead tired. But they were in place and ready.

They did what they were supposed to do. They stumbled up out of the cover of the creek. They sliced through the chaos behind the enemy line like the fabled hot knife through butter. Soft butter. Then they came back across the hillside, cutting at the back of the enemy line. Like scythes felling wheat.

Murgen came over the hill behind me, displaying the Black Company standard boldly. Sindawe's bunch were behind him. Murgen halted between Lady and me, a few steps back.

The artillery began feeling for the range to the fortress.

Goblin and One-Eye and maybe even Shifter had been at work, using little charms to decompose the mortar between stones.

"It's going to work," I muttered. "I think we're going to do it."

The cavalry sortie did it. They did not get sorted out for another charge before men began running for the ford. The second charge bogged down in the sheer mass of fleeing men.

Mogaba, I love you.

The men he had trained did not break formation and charge. He and Ochiba hustled up and down their lines, getting the ranks dressed and the injured out of the way.

Ballista shafts were knocking stones out of the fortress wall. The captains up top gawked. A few of feeble courage abandoned the battlements.

I raised my sword and pointed. The drums started. I began walking my mount forward. Lady kept pace, as did Murgen and the standard. One-Eye and Goblin worked up a more terrible glamor around us. My two crows shrieked. They could be heard above the tumult.

The enemy train was all crowded up the other side of the ford. Now the teamsters fled, leaving them blocking the retreat of their comrades.

We had them in a bottle, the cork was in, and most of them had their backs to us.

The grim work began.

I continued my slow advance. People stayed away from me and Lady and the standard. Archers on the battlements tried dropping me, but somebody had put some pretty good spells on my armor. Nothing got through, though for a while it was like being in a barrel somebody was whacking with a hammer.

Enemy soldiers began jumping in the river and swimming for it.

The ballistae had a good range, all their shafts striking in a small area. The watchtower creaked and grumbled. Then rumbled. A big chunk fell out, and soon the whole tower collapsed, taking parts of the fortress wall with it.

I pushed into the river, across the ford, and on up between wagons. The standard and Sindawe's men followed. The only enemies I saw were heeling and toeing it south.

Amazing. I never struck a blow myself.

It was almost workaday stuff for Sindawe's bunch to begin clearing the wagons, for some to worm through behind Murgen and cover him while he planted the standard on the fortress wall.

Fighting continued on the north bank but the thing had been decided. It was over and won and I did not believe it. It had been close to being too easy. I had not used all the arrows in my quiver.

Though chaos continued around me I took out my map case to check out what lay to the south.

37

Shadowlight: Coal-Dark Tears

Rage and panic contended in the fountained hall at Shadowlight. Moon-shadow mewled dire prophecies. Stormshadow raged. One maintained a silence as deep as that within a buried coffin. And one was not there at all, though a Voice spoke for him, dark and mocking.

"I said a million men might not be enough."

"Silence, worm!" Stormshadow snarled.

"They have obliterated your invincible armies, children. They have forced bridgeheads everywhere. What will you do now, whimpering dogs? Your provinces are a prostrate and naked woman. A two-hundred-mile jaunt behind the Lance of Passion and they will be hammering at the gates of Stormgard. What will you do, what will you do, what will you do? Oh, woe, what hast befallen thee?" Insane laughter rolled out of that black absence in the air.

Stormshadow snarled, "You haven't been a whole hell of a lot of help, have you? You and your games. Trying to catch Dorotea Senjak? How well did you do? Eh? What would you have done with their Captain? Did you have a bargain in mind? Some deal to trade us for the power they bring? Did you think you could use them to close the Gate? If you did you're the greatest fool of all."

"Whine, children. Moan and wail. They are upon you. Maybe if you beg I'll save you yet again."

Moonshadow snapped, "Bold chatter from one without the ability to save himself. Yes. In the traditions of their Company they caught us off balance. They did what is for them old routine: the impossible. But the fighting along the Main was just one move in the game. Only a pawn has vanished from the board. If they come south, every step will carry them a step nearer their dooms."

Laughter.

The silent one broke his fast of words. "There are three of us, in the fullness of our power. But two great ones dog the path of the Black Company. And they have little interest in furthering its goals. And *she* is a cripple, feeble as a mouse."

More laughter. "Once upon a time someone named the true name of Dorotea Senjak. So now she is the Lady no more. She has no more powers than a talented child. But do you believe she lost her memory when she lost those powers? You do not. Or you would not accuse me as you have. Perhaps she will grow frightened enough or desperate enough to confide in the great one who changes."

No retort. That was the dread that haunted them all.

Moonshadow said, "The reports are confused. Still, a great disaster has befallen our army. But we are dealing with the Black Company. The chance has always existed. We have prepared for it. We will regain our composure. We will deal with them. But there is a mystery from the fighting at Ghoja. Two dire figures were seen there, great dark beings on giant steeds that breathed fire. Beings immune to the bite of darts. The names Widowmaker and Lifetaker have been breathed by those who stood with the Black Company."

This was news to the others. Stormshadow said, "We must learn more about this. It may explain their luck."

The hole in the air: "You must act if you do not want to be devoured. I suggest you put aside terror, eschew squabbling, and cease the dispensation of accusation. I suggest you think of a way to go for the jugular."

No one replied.

"Perhaps I will contribute myself when next fate tries to take its cut."

"Well," Stormshadow mused. "The fear has at last penetrated as far as Overlook."

The bickering resumed, but without heart. Four minds rotated toward thwarting that doom from the north.

38

Invaders of the Shadowlands

Tired is not quite so important when you have just beaten the odds. You've got energy to celebrate.

I did not want a celebration. Enemy soldiers were still trying to get away. I wanted my men to get on with what we had to do while they still thought they were supermen. I had my staff together before the chaos started sorting itself out.

"Otto. Hagop. Come morning you head east along the river and break up the force guarding the prisoners building this levee system. Big Bucket, Candles, you guys get this side of the ford cleaned up. Look through these wagons and see what we've got. Mogaba, get the battlefield cleaned up. Collect weapons. One-Eye, get our casualties moved back to Vejagedhya. I'll help when I get time. Don't let those Taglian butchers do anything stupid." We had a dozen volunteer physicians along. Their ideas of medicine were pretty primitive.

"Lady. What do we know about this Dejagore?" Dejagore was the nearest big city south of the Main, two hundred miles down the road. "Besides the fact that it's a walled city?"

"A Shadowmaster makes his headquarters there."

"Which one?"

"Moonshadow, I think. No. Stormshadow."

"That's it?"

"If you'd take prisoners you might find out something from them."

I raised an eyebrow. She prodding me about excesses? "Keep that in mind, Otto. Bring those prisoners when you catch up."

"All fifty thousand?"

"As many as don't run away. I'm hoping some will be mad enough to help us out. The rest we can use for labor."

Mogaba asked, "You're going to invade the Shadowlands?"

He knew I was. He wanted a formal declaration. "Yes. They supposedly only have fifty thousand men under arms. We just creamed a third. I don't think they can get another mob as big together in time if we go at them as hard as we can, as fast as we can."

"Audacity," he said.

"Yeah. Keep hitting them and don't give them a chance to get their feet under them again."

Lady chided, "They're sorcerers, Croaker. What happens when they come out themselves?"

"Then Shifter will have to kick in. Don't worry about the mules, just load the wagons. We've worked on sorcerers before."

Nobody argued. Maybe they should have. But we all felt that fate had handed us an opportunity and we would be idiots to waste it. I figured too that since we had not expected to survive the first contest, we were out nothing by pressing onward.

"I wonder how beloved these Shadowmasters are to their subjects. Can we expect local support?"

No comment. We would find out the hard way.

Talk went on and on. Eventually I left it to help with the medical work, patching and sewing while issuing orders through a procession of messengers. I got me two hours sleep that night.

The cavalry was heading out east and Mogaba's legion had begun its southward advance when Lady joined me. "Shifter has been scouting. He says you can detect an almost visible change as news of the battle spreads. The mass of people are excited. Those who collaborate with the Shadowmasters are confused and frightened. They'll probably panic and run when they hear we're coming."

"Good. Even great." In ten days we would find out for sure how much impact Ghoja had had. I meant to advance on Dejagore at twenty miles a day. The roads south of the Main were dry. How lovely that must have been for them.

Jahamaraj Jah had gotten his survivors into position in time and set a series of clever ambushes. His mob scrubbed two thousand fugitives from Ghoja.

He was not pleased with my invasion plans. He was even less pleased when I drafted his followers and distributed them as replacements for men we had lost. But he did not argue much.

We encountered no resistance. In territories formerly belonging to Taglios we received warm welcomes in villages still occupied by their original inhabitants. The natives were cooler farther south but not inimical. They thought we were too good to be true.

We encountered our first enemy patrols six days south of Ghoja. They avoided contact. I told everybody to look professional and mean.

Otto and Hagop caught up, dragging along thirty thousand people from the levee project. I looked them over. They had not been treated well. There were some very angry, bitter men among them. Hagop said they were all willing to help defeat the Shadowmasters.

"Damn me," I said. "A year and a half ago there were seven of us. Now we're a horde. Pick out the ones in the best shape. Arm them with captured weapons. Add them to the legions so every fourth man in Mogaba's and Ochiba's is a new one. That would mean trained men left over, so move them over to Sindawe. Give him one in four, too. Should bring him up to strength. Anybody else we arm we can use as auxiliaries, and garrisons for some of these smaller cities."

The countryside was not heavily populated between the river and here, but nearer Dejagore that would change. "The rest can tag along. We'll use them somehow."

But how would I feed them? We'd used up our own supplies and had started on those captured at Ghoja.

Dejagore looked less promising now. Some of the rescued prisoners hailed from that city. They said the walls were forty feet high. The resident Shadowmaster was a demon for keeping them up.

"What will be will be," I thought.

The bloom was off the rose. We'd all had time to think. Still, morale was better than it had been moving toward Ghoja.

There were skirmishes the next few days but nothing serious. Mostly Otto and Hagop's boys overhauling enemy troops not hurrying fast enough to get away. The cavalry had begun to behave professionally at last.

I allowed foraging under strict rules, looting only where people had fled. It worked, mostly. Trouble came only where I expected it, from One-Eye, whose motto is that anything not nailed down is his and anything he can pry loose isn't nailed down.

We knocked over some towns and small cities with no trouble. The last few I left to the freed prisoners, cynically letting them vent their wrath while saving my better troops.

The nearer Dejagore we got—official name Stormgard, according to the Shadowmasters—the more tamed the country became. We made the last day's march through rolling hills that had been terraced and strewn with irrigation canals. So it was startling to come out of the hills and see the city itself.

Stormgard was surrounded by a plain as flat as a tabletop extending a mile in all directions, with the exception of several small mounds maybe ten feet tall. The plain looked like a manicured lawn. "I don't like the looks of that," I told Mogaba. "Too contrived. Lady. Remind you of anything?"

She gave me a blank look.

"The approach to the Tower."

"I see that. But here there's room for maneuver."

"We got some daylight left. Let's get down there and get set up."

Mogaba asked, "How will you fortify the camp?" We had seen little timber lately.

"Turn the wagons on their sides."

Nothing moved on the plain. Only haze over the city indicated life there. "I want a closer look at that. Lady, when we get down there dig out the costumes."

My horde flooded onto the plain. Still no sign anyone in Stormgard was interested. I sent for Murgen and the standard. The way people thought about the Company here in the south, maybe Stormgard would surrender without a fight.

Lady looked terrible in her Lifetaker rig. I supposed I looked as grim. They were effective outfits. They would have scared me had I seen them coming at me.

Mogaba, Ochiba, and Sindawe invited themselves along. They had dolled up in stuff they'd worn in Gea-Xle. They looked pretty fierce themselves. Mogaba told me, "I want to see those walls, too."

"Sure."

Then here came Goblin and One-Eye. In an instant I saw that Goblin had had the idea and One-Eye had decided to go lest Goblin somehow get ahead on points. "No clowning, you guys. Understand?"

Goblin grinned his big frog grin. "Sure, Croaker. Sure. You know me."

"That's the trouble. I know you both."

Goblin faked bruised feelings.

"You guys make these costumes look good. Hear?"

"You'll strike terror to the roots of their souls," One-Eye promised. "They'll flee from the walls screaming."

"Sure they will. Everybody ready?"

They were. "Around it from the right," I told Murgen. "At the canter. As close as you dare."

He rode out. Lady and I followed twenty yards behind. As I got started two monster crows plopped down on my shoulders. A flock came out of the hills and raced ahead, circling the city.

We got close enough to see the scramble on the walls. And impressive walls they were, at least forty feet high. What nobody had bothered to mention was that the city was built upon a mound that raised it another forty feet above the plain.

This was going to be a bitch.

A few arrows wobbled out and fell short.

Finesse. Cunning. Trickery. Only a dip would go up against those walls, Croaker.

I had had liberated prisoners work up maps. I had a good idea of the city's layout.

Four gates. Four paved roads approached from the points of the compass rose, like spokes of a wheel. Nasty barbicans and towers protected the gates. More towers along the wall for laying enfilading fire along its face. Not pleasant.

It was very quiet up on those walls. They had one eye on us and one on the horde still pouring out of the hills, wondering where the hell we all came from.

We got us a little surprise south of Stormgard.

There was a military camp there. A big one set maybe four hundred yards from the city wall. "Oh, shit," I said, and yelled at Murgen.

He misunderstood. On purpose, probably, though I'll never prove it. He kicked his mount into a gallop and headed for the gap between.

Arrows rose from the wall and camp. Miraculously, they fell without doing any harm. I glanced back as we entered the throat of the gap.

That little shit Goblin was standing on his saddle. He was bent over with his pants down, telling the world what he thought of the Shadowmasters and their boys.

Naturally, those folks took exception. As they say in the *chansons*, the sky darkened with arrows.

I was certain fate would take its cut now. But we had moved far and fast enough. The arrowstorm fell behind us. Goblin howled mockingly.

That irritated somebody bigger.

A bolt of lightning from nowhere struck ahead, ripping a steaming hole in the turf. Murgen leapt it. So did I, with my stomach creeping toward my throat. I was sure the next shot would fry somebody in his boots.

Goblin went right on mooning Stormgard. Horsemen began pouring out of the camp. They were no problem. We could outrun them. I tried to concentrate on the wall. Just in case I got out of this alive.

A second bolt seared the backs of my eyeballs. But it too went astray— though I think it shifted course just before it hit.

When my sight cleared I spied a giant wolf racing in from our right, covering ground in strides that beggared those of our black stallions. My old pal Shifter. Right on time.

Another two bolts missed. The gardener was going to be pissed about all the divots knocked out of his lawn. We completed our circuit and headed for camp. Our pursuers gave up.

As we dismounted Mogaba said, "We've drawn fire. Now we know what we're up against."

"One of the Shadowmasters is in there."

"There may be another in that camp," Lady said. "I felt something. . . ."

"Where'd Shifter get to?" He had disappeared again. Everybody shrugged. "I hoped he'd sit in on a brainstorming session. Goblin, that was a dumb stunt."

"It sure was. Made me feel forty years younger."

"Wish I'd thought of it," One-Eye grumbled.

"Well, they know we're here and they know we're bad, but I don't see them making a run for it. Guess we'll have to figure out how to kick their butts."

Mogaba said, "Evidently they mean to fight outside the walls. Otherwise that encampment would not be there."

"Yeah." Things skipped through my mind. Stunts, tricks, strategies. As though I'd been born to come up with them by the hundred. "We'll leave them alone tonight. We'll form up and offer battle in the morning but let them come to us. Where are those city maps? I got a notion."

We talked for hours while the chaos of a camp still settling raged around us. After dark I sent men out to rig a few tricks and plant stakes on which the legions could form and guide their advance. I said, "We shouldn't bother ourselves too much. I don't think they'll fight us unless we get in close to the walls. Get some sleep. We'll see what happens in the morning."

Many pairs of eyes looked at me all at once, then, in cadence, shifted to Lady. A swarm of smiles came and went. Then everyone went away behind their smiles, leaving us alone.

Big Bucket and those guys don't fool around. They had gone into the hills and diverted one of the irrigation canals to bring water to the camp. I figured it in my head. To give every man in the mob one cup we needed about 2,500 gallons. With the animals run it to 3,500. But man and beast need more than a cup to get by. I don't know what the flow was on the canal but not a lot of water was getting wasted.

Not much manpower was going to waste, either. The boys from Opal had dug some holding ponds. One they set aside for bathing. Being the boss wazoo I crowded the line.

Still soggy, I made sure Mogaba had done all the things I didn't really have to check. Sentries out. Barricade manned. Night orders posted. One-Eye working Frogface on scouting missions instead of loafing. What have you.

I was stalling.

This was The Night.

I ran out of busybodying so finally went to my tent. I got out my map of Stormgard, studied it again, then got to work transcribing these Annals. They have grown more spare than I like but that has been the price of keeping up. Maybe Murgen will get me to let go . . . I did three pages and some lines and began to relax, thinking she would not come after all, but then she came in.

She had bathed, too. Her hair was damp. A ghost of lavender or lilac or something hung around her. She was a little pale and a little shaky and not quite able to meet my eye, at a loss what to do or say now that she was here. She buttoned the tent flap.

I closed this book. It went into a brass-bound chest. I closed my ink and cleaned my pen. I could think of nothing to say, either.

The whole shy routine was dumb. We had been playing around like this, and getting older, for over a year. Hell. We were grown-up people. I was old enough to be a grandfather. Might even be one, for all I knew. And she was old enough to be everybody's grandmother.

Somebody had to take the bull by the horns. We couldn't go on forever both of us waiting for the other one to make a move.

So why didn't she do something?

You the guy, Croaker.

Yeah.

I killed the candles, went and took her hand. It was not that dark in there. Plenty of firelight leaked through the fabric of the tent.

She shivered like a captive mouse at first, but it did not take her long to reach a point of no turning back. And for goddamned once nothing happened to interrupt.

The old general amazed himself. The woman amazed him even more.

Sometime in the wee hours the exhausted boss general promised, "Tomorrow night again. Within the walls of Stormgard. Maybe in Stormshadow's own bed."

She wanted to know the basis for his confidence. As time labored on she just got more awake and lively. But the old man fell asleep on her.

39

Stormgard (formerly Dejagore)

Even I grumbled about the time of day I got everybody up. We all ate hurriedly, my valiant commanders in a clique so they could pester me about my plans. A crow perched on the tent pole at the front of my tent, one eye cocked my way, or maybe Lady's. The bastard was leering, I thought. Really! Weren't we getting enough of that from the others?

I felt great. Lady, though, seemed to be having trouble moving with her usual fluid grace. And everybody knew what that meant, the smirking freaks.

"I don't understand you, Captain," Mogaba protested. "Why won't you lay it all out?"

"What only I know inside my head only I can betray. Just assemble up on the stakes I had put out and offer battle. If they accept, we'll see how it goes. If they don't kick our butts, we'll worry about the next step."

Mogaba's lips tightened into a prune. He did not like me much right then. Thought I didn't trust him. He glanced over to where Cletus and his bunch were trying to assemble shovels and baskets and bags in numbers enough for an army. They had a thousand men out scouring the hill farms for tools and more baskets and buckets and had men sewing bags cut from the canvas coverings from the wagons.

They knew only that I had told them to get ready for some major, massive earthmoving.

Another thousand men were out trying to forage timber. You need a lot of timber to invest a city.

"Patience, my friend. Patience. All will be clear in due time." I chuckled.

One-Eye muttered, "He learned his trade from our old Captain. Don't tell nobody nothing till you find some gink trying to shove a spear up your butt."

They could not get to me this morning. He and Goblin could have had them a fuss as bad as back in Taglios and I'd have just grinned. I used a wad of bread to finish soaking up the grease on my plate. "All right, let's get dressed and go kick some ass."

Two things to be observed about being the only guy in forty thousand to get some the night before. Thirty-nine thousand nine hundred ninety-nine guys are so envious they hate your guts. But you're in such a positive mood it becomes infectious.

And you can always tell them their share is behind those walls over there.

Scouts reported while I was getting into my Widowmaker rig. They said the enemy was coming out of the camp and the city both. And there were a lot of the bastards. At least ten thousand in the camp, and maybe every man from the city who could be armed.

That bunch would not be thrilled to be headed into a fight. And they weren't likely to be experienced.

I arrayed Mogaba's legion on the left, Ochiba's on the right, and put Sindawe's new outfit in the middle. Behind them I put all the former prisoners we'd been able to arm and hoped they did not look too much like a rabble. The front formations looked good in their white, organized and professional and ready.

Intimidation games.

I had each legion arrayed by hundreds, with aisles between the companies. I hoped the other side would not be smart enough to jump on that right away.

Lady grabbed my hand before she mounted up, squeezed. "Tonight in Stormgard."

"Right." I kissed her cheek.

She whispered, "I don't think I can stand to sit on this saddle. I'm sore."

"Curse of being a woman."

I mounted up.

Two big black crows dropped onto my shoulders immediately, their sudden weight startling me. Everybody gawked. I scanned the hills but saw no sign of my walking stump. But we were making some kind of headway here. This was the second time everybody else saw the crows.

I donned my helmet. One-Eye stoked the fires of illusion. I assumed my post in front of Mogaba's legion. Lady moved out in front of Ochiba's bunch. Murgen planted the standard in front of Sindawe's legion, ten paces in front of everyone else.

I was tempted to charge right then. The other side was having a fire drill trying to get organized. But I gave them a while. From the looks of them most of the ones out of Stormgard did not want to be there. Let them look at us, all in neat array, all in white, all ready to carve them up. Let them think about how nice it would be to get back inside those incredible walls.

I signalled Murgen. He trotted forward, galloped along the face of the enemy showing the standard. Arrows flew and missed. He shouted mockeries. They were not terrified into running for it.

My two crows flapped after him, and were joined by thousands more who came from the gods knew where. The brotherhood of death, winging it over the doomed. Nice touch, old stump. But not enough to make anybody run away.

My two crows returned to my shoulders. I felt like a monument. I hoped crows had better manners than pigeons.

Murgen did not get enough of a rise first pass so he rode back the other direction, yelling louder.

I noted a disturbance in the enemy formation, moving forward. Someone or something seated in the lotus position, all in black, floating five feet off the ground, drifted to a halt a dozen yards in front of the other army. Shadowmaster? Had to be. I got a creepy feeling just looking at it. Me there in my spiffy but fake outfit.

Murgen's taunts got somebody's goat. A handful of horsemen, then a bunch, lit out after him. He turned in the saddle and shouted at them. There was no way they could catch him, of course. Not when he was on that horse.

I grumbled. The indiscipline was not as general as I wanted.

Murgen dawdled, letting them come closer and closer—then took off when they were only a dozen yards away. They chased him right into the maze of trip-wires I'd had woven into the grass during the night.

Men and horses sprawled. More horses tripped on animals already down. My archers lofted arrows that fell straight down and slaughtered most of the men and horses.

I drew my sword, which smoked and smoldered, and signalled the advance. The drums beat the slow cadence. The men in the front rank slashed the trip-wires, finished the wounded. Otto and Hagop, on the flanks, had trumpets sounded but did not charge. Not yet.

My boys could march in a straight line. On that nice flat ground they kept their dress all across their front. That had to be an impressive sight from across the way, where they still had guys who hadn't found their places in ranks.

We passed the first of the several low mounds that spotted the plain. The artillery was supposed to get up on that one and mass fire wherever it seemed appropriate. I hoped Cletus and the boys had sense enough to harass the Shadowmaster.

That critter was the big unknown quantity here.

I hoped Shifter was around somewhere. This whole thing could go to hell if he wasn't and that bastard over there cut loose.

Two hundred yards away. Their archers lofted poorly aimed shafts at Lady and me. I halted, gave another signal. The legions halted, too. Very good. The Nar were paying attention.

Gods, there were a lot of them over there.

And that Shadowmaster, just floating there, maybe waiting for me to stick my foot in it. Seemed like I was staring up his nostrils.

But he did not do anything.

The ground shuddered. The enemy ranks stirred. They saw it coming and it was too late for them to do anything.

The elephants thundered up the aisles through the legions, gaining momentum. When those monsters passed me the guys over there were already yelling and looking for somewhere to run.

A salvo of twelve ballistae shafts ripped overhead and spattered around the Shadowmaster. They were well aimed. Four actually struck him. They encountered protective sorceries but battered him around. Very sluggish, the Shadowmaster. Keeping himself alive seemed to be his limit.

A second salvo hit him an instant before the elephants reached his men. The ballistae had been laid even more carefully.

I gave the signal that sent my front four thousand men, and the cavalry, howling forward.

The remainder of the men formed a normal front, then advanced.

The carnage was incredible.

We drove them back and back and back, but there were so damned many of them we never really broke them. When they did flee the majority made it into the camp. None got back into Stormgard. The city had closed its gates on them. They dragged their Shadowmaster champion with them. I would not have bothered. He had been useless as tits on a boar hog.

Of course, one of the second flight of ballistae shafts had gotten through his protection. I suppose that distracted him.

His ineffectuality had to be Shifter's doing.

They left maybe five thousand men behind. The warlord side of me was disappointed. I'd hoped to do more damage. I was not going to storm the camp to do it, though. I backed the men off, set men to police up our casualties, placed cavalry to meet anyone coming out of camp or city, then got on with business.

I planted my right wing yards from the road we had followed down to Stormgard, just out of bowshot of the barbican at the gate it entered. My line ran at right angles to the road. I let the men relax.

My levee builders got to work putting their training to use. On the far side of the road they began digging a trench. It started a bowshot from the wall and ran to the foot of the hills. It would be wide and deep and would shield my flank.

The workers carried the earth to the road and began building a ramp. Others began building mantlets to protect the ramp builders as they approached the wall.

That many men can move a lot of earth. The defenders saw we would have a ramp right up to the wall in just a few days. They were not pleased. But they had no means to stop us.

Men scurried like ants. The former prisoners had scores to even and went at it like they wanted blood by sundown.

By mid-afternoon they were taking the city end of the trench downward, deep, and toward the wall, not hiding the fact that they were mining, aiming to go under as well as over. And they had begun breaking ground for a trench on my left flank as well.

In three days my army would be protected by a pair of deep trenches that would funnel my attack up the ramp and over the wall. There would be no stopping us.

They had to do something in there.

I hoped to do something to them before they thought of something to do to me.

Late afternoon. The sky began clouding over. Lightning frolicked behind the hills to the south. Not a good sign. A storm would be tougher on my guys than on theirs.

Even so, despite the cold wind and scattered sprinkles moving in, the

builders only broke for a spartan supper before setting out lanterns and building bonfires so they could continue after dark. I posted pickets so there would
be no surprises, began rotating my troops out of position for food and rest.

Some day. All I'd had to do was sit in one place and look elegant and give
orders I'd already worked out in my head.

And think about what last night had meant, in its highly anticlimactic fashion.

It had been a night of nights of nights, but it had not lived up to the anticipation. Had even been, in a well-we've-finally-gotten-around-to-it way, something of a disappointment.

Not that I would trade it in or take it back. Never.

Someday, when I'm old and retired and have nothing better to do than phi-
losophize, I'm going to sit down for a year and figure out why it's always better
in the anticipation than in the consummation.

I sent Frogface flitting around checking the enemy's mood. That was black.
They wanted no more fighting after duking it out with elephants.

Stormgard's walls were not heavily patrolled. Most of the male population
had marched out in the morning and not made it back. But Frogface reported
no great distress around the central citadel, where another Shadowmaster was
in residence. In fact, he thought he sensed confidence in the eventual outcome.

The storm marched north. And it was a bitch kitty. I gathered my captains.
"We got a mean storm coming. Might make what we're going to try tricky, but
we're going to do it anyway. Be even less expected. Goblin. One-Eye. Get the
dust off your old reliable snooze spell."

They eyed me suspiciously. Goblin muttered, "Here it comes. Some damnfool reason for not getting any sleep again tonight."

One-Eye told him, "I'm going to use that spell on him one of these first
days." Louder, "Right, Croaker. What's up?"

"Us. Up and over those walls and open the gate after you put the sentries to
sleep."

Even Lady was surprised. "You're going to waste all that work on that ramp?"

"I never intended to use it. I wanted them convinced I was committed to
a certain course."

Mogaba smiled. I suspected he'd figured it out ahead of time.

"It won't work," Goblin muttered.

I gave him a look. "The men working the trenches at the city end are armed.
I promised them first crack at getting even. We get the gates open all we have to
do is lean back and watch."

"Won't work. You're forgetting that Shadowmaster in there. You think
you're going to sneak up on him?"

"Yes. Our guardian angel will make sure."

"Shifter? I'd trust him as far as I can throw a pregnant elephant."

"I say anything about trusting him? He wants us for a stalking horse for some scheme. He's got to keep us healthy. Right?"

"Your mind is going, Croaker," One-Eye said. "You been hanging around Lady too long."

She kept a blank face on. That might not have been a compliment.

"Mogaba, I'll need a dozen of the Nar. After Goblin and One-Eye put the sentries to sleep Frogface will climb the wall with a rope and anchor it. Your boys will go up and take the barbican from the rear and open the gate."

He nodded. "How soon?"

"Anytime. One-Eye. Send Frogface scouting. I want to know what that Shadowmaster is doing. If he's watching us we won't go."

We moved an hour later. It went like operations go in textbooks. Like it was ordained by the gods. In another hour every one of the freed prisoners, except those we had enrolled in the legions, was inside the city. They reached the citadel and broke in before resistance developed.

They raged through Stormgard, ignoring the rain and thunder and lightning, venting a lot of rage, probably mostly in directions askew.

Me in my Widowmaker suit stalked through the open gates fifteen minutes after the mob rush. Lifetaker rode beside me. The locals cowered away from us, though some seemed to be welcoming their liberators. Halfway to the citadel Lady said, "You even fooled me this time. When you said tonight in Stormgard. . . ."

A gust and ferocious fusillade of rain silenced her. Lightning cut loose in a sudden vicious duel. By the flashes I witnessed the passage of a pair of panthers that I would have missed otherwise. Chills not of the rain crawled my spine. I had seen that bigger one before, in another embattled city, when I was young.

They were headed toward the citadel, too.

I asked, "What are they up to?" My confidence was less than complete. There were no crows out in this storm. I realized I had come to count them my good luck.

"I don't know."

"Better check it." I increased my pace.

There were a lot of dead men around the entrance to the citadel. Most were my laborers. Sounds of fighting still echoed inside. Grinning guards saluted me clumsily. I asked, "Where's the Shadowmaster?"

"I hear she's in the big tower. Up high. Her men are fighting like crazy. But she isn't helping them."

Thunder and lightning went mad for a full minute. Bolts smashed at the city. Had the god of thunder gone crazy? But for the torrential rainfall a hundred fires might have started.

I pitied the legions, out there on guard. Maybe Mogaba would bring them in out of it.

The storm died into an almost normal rain after that last insane fit, with only a few lightweight flashes.

I looked up the one tower that loomed over the rest of the citadel—and, *déjà vu,* in a flash spied a cat shape scaling its face.

"Damn me!"

The thunder had left me unable to hear the horses coming. I looked back. One-Eye, Goblin, and Murgen, still flaunting the Company standard. One-Eye was staring up at the tower. His face was not pleasant to behold.

He was flashing on the same memory. "Forvalaka, Croaker."

"Shifter."

"I know. I'm wondering if it was him last time."

"What're you talking about?" Lady asked.

I said, "Murgen, let's plant that standard up where the world can see it when the sun comes up."

"Right."

We stalked into the citadel, Lady trying to find out what had passed between me and One-Eye. I developed a hearing problem. One-Eye took the lead. We climbed dark stairs where the footing was treacherous because of blood and bodies. There was no more fighting going on above us.

Ominous.

The last fighters of both sides were in a chamber a couple stories from the top. All dead. "Sorcery here," Goblin muttered.

"We go up," One-Eye snapped.

"I know."

Total agreement between them. For once.

I drew my sword. There was no flame in it, and no color to my costume now. Goblin and One-Eye had other things on their minds.

We caught up with Shifter and the Shadowmaster in the parapet of the tower. Shifter had assumed human form. He had the Shadowmaster at bay. It was a tiny thing in black, almost impossible to take seriously as a danger. There was no sign of Shifter's sidekick. I told Goblin, "There's one missing. Keep an eye out."

"Got you." He knew what was going on. He was as serious as ever I've seen him.

Shifter started moving in on the Shadowmaster. It had nowhere to retreat. I gestured Lady to move out to his right. I went left. I'm not sure what One-Eye was doing.

I glanced toward the camp south of the city. The rain had stopped while we were inside the tower. The camp was plainly visible by its own lights. I got the impression they knew something was wrong over here but they were not about to come find out what.

They were nice and close. Put artillery on the wall and life could get miserable for them.

The Shadowmaster backed up against the merlons edging the parapet, apparently able to do nothing. Why were they impotent? This one was who? Stormshadow?

Shifter was close enough to touch, now. One hand darted out and ripped the black robing off the Shadowmaster.

I gawked. I heard Lady's gasp from fifteen feet away.

One-Eye said it. "I'll go to hell. Stormbringer! But she's supposed to be dead."

Stormbringer. Another of the original Ten Who Were Taken. Another one who was supposed to have perished in the Battle at Charm, after murdering the Hanged Man and . . . and Shifter!

Aha! I said to me, said I. Aha! A settlement of scores. Shifter knew all the time. Shifter had been out to get Stormbringer from the start.

And where one mysteriously surviving Taken was in business for herself, might there not be more? Like about three more?

"What the hell? They all still around but the Hanged Man, Limper, and Soulcatcher?" I'd seen those three go down myself.

Lady stood there shaking her head.

Were even those three gone? I had killed Limper myself once, and he had come back. . . .

Chills got me again.

When they were Shadowmasters they were anonymous creeps who had only standard-issue cause to do me grief. But the Taken . . . Some of them had very special and personal cause to hate the Company.

This moment of revelation had turned it into a whole different kind of war.

I have no idea what passed between Shifter and Bringer, but it left the air crackling with electric hatred.

Stormbringer seemed powerless. Why? A few minutes ago she had been bringing in that monster of a storm to whip on us. Shifter was no greater power than she. Unless, somehow, he had come upon that bane of all the Taken, a True Name.

I looked at Lady.

She knew it. She knew all their True Names. She had not lost her knowledge when she had lost her powers.

Power. I had not thought about what I'd had here, almost under my thumb, all this time. What she knew was worth the ransoms of a hundred princes. The secrets locked in her head could enslave or deliver empires.

If you knew she had them.

Some folks knew.

She had a lot more guts than I'd realized, coming out of the Tower and empire with me.

I had to do some rethinking and strategic reorientation. These Shadowmasters, Shifter, the Howler, they all knew what I'd just realized. She was damned lucky she hadn't been snatched already and squeezed dry.

Shifter laid his huge ugly hands on Stormbringer. And only then did she begin to resist. With sudden, startling violence she did something that hurled Shifter all the way across the parapet. He lay there for a moment, eyes glassy.

Bringer made a break.

I came around with a swordstroke I brought in from the moon, right into her belly. It did not mark her but it stopped her in her tracks. Lady hacked at her overhand. She rolled away from the stroke. I whacked her again. But she got up and started heading out again. And her fingers were dancing. Sparks played between them.

Oh, shit.

One-Eye tripped her. Lady and I hacked at her again, without much effect. Then Murgen let her have it with the spearhead on the lance that bore the Company standard.

She howled like one of the damned.

What the hell?

She started moving again. But now Shifter was back. He had taken the form of the forvalaka, the black were-leopard almost impossible to kill or injure. He jumped on Stormbringer and started tearing her apart.

She gave damned near as good as she got. We backed away, stayed away, gave them room.

I don't know what Shifter did or when. Or if he did anything at all. One-Eye might have imagined it all. But sometime during the thing the little black man sidled up and whispered, "He did it, Croaker. It was him that killed Tom-Tom."

That was a long time ago. I had almost no feelings about it anymore. But One-Eye had not forgotten nor forgiven. That was his brother. . . .

"What you going to do?"

"I don't know. Something. I got to do something."

"What'll that do to the rest of us? We won't have an angel anymore."

"Ain't gonna have one anyway, Croaker. He's done got what he wanted right there. Shifter or no Shifter you're on your own soon as he finishes her off."

He was right. And chances were damned good Shifter would stop being Lady's faithful old dog, too. If there was any getting him, this was the time.

The combatants went on for maybe fifteen minutes, shredding each other. I got the impression things were not going as easy as Shifter had hoped. Bringer was putting up a damned good fight.

But he won. Sort of. She stopped resisting. He lay panting, unable to move. She'd locked her limbs around him. He bled from a hundred small wounds. He cursed softly, and I thought I heard him damning someone for helping her, heard him threatening to get someone next.

"You got any special use for him now?" I asked Lady. "I don't know how much you knew. I don't care now. But you better think about what he's going to have on his mind now he don't need you and me for a stalking horse anymore."

She shook her head slowly.

Something slid over the edge of the parapet behind her. Another, smaller forvalaka. I thought we were in big trouble, but Shifter's apprentice made a tactical error. She began to shift forms. She finished just in time to shriek "No!" at One-Eye.

One-Eye had made him a club out of something, and with two quick and heroic swings he bashed Stormbringer and Shapeshifter into complete unconsciousness. They had weakened one another that much.

Shifter's companion flew at him.

Murgen tripped her by tangling her feet with the head of the lance he carried. He cut her. Blood got all over the standard. She screamed like she was trapped in Hell's agony.

I recognized her, then. She had done a lot of yelling the last time I'd seen her, so long ago.

Sometime during the excitement a whole herd of crows had gathered on the merlons, out of the way. They started laughing.

Everybody jumped on the woman before she could do anything. Goblin did some kind of swift magical bind that left her unable to do anything but wiggle her eyes.

One-Eye looked at me and said, "You got any suture with you, Croaker? I got a needle but I don't think I got enough thread."

What? "Some." I always carried some medical odds and ends.

"Gimme."

I gave him.

He whacked Shifter and Bringer again. "Just to make sure they're out. They don't got no special powers when they're out."

He squatted down and started sewing their mouths shut. He finished Shifter, said, "Get him stripped. Whack him if he stirs."

What the hell?

It got gruesome, then more gruesome. "What the hell you doing?" I demanded.

The crows were having a party.

"Sewing all the holes shut. So the devils don't get out."

"What?" Maybe it made sense to him. It didn't to me.

"Old trick for getting rid of evil witch doctors back home." When he finished with the orifices he sewed fingers and toes together. "Put them in a sack with a hundred pounds of rocks and throw them in the river."

Lady said, "You'll have to burn them. And grind what's left into powder and scatter the powder on the wind."

One-Eye looked at her for ten seconds. "You mean I done all this work for nothing?"

"No. It'll help. You don't want them getting excited while you're roasting them."

I gave her a startled look. That was not like her. I turned to Murgen. "You want to get that standard up?"

One-Eye stirred Shifter's apprentice with a toe. "What about this one? Think I should take care of her, too?"

"She hasn't done anything." I squatted beside her. "I remember you now, darling. It took me a while because we didn't see that much of you in Juniper. You weren't very nice to my buddy Marron Shed." I looked at Lady. "What were you figuring on making out of her?"

She did not answer.

"Be that way. We'll talk later." I looked at the apprentice. "Lisa Daela Bowalk. You hear me name your name, the way these others did?" Crows chuckled to one another. "I'm going to give you a break. That you probably don't deserve. Murgen, find some place to lock this one up. We'll turn her loose when we're ready to move out. Goblin, you help One-Eye with whatever he's got to do." I looked at the Company standard, bloodstained once again, flying defiantly again. "You"—pointing at One-Eye—"take care of it right. Unless you want two more of them after us the way Limper was."

He gulped air. "Yeah."

"Lady, I told you. Tonight in Stormgard. Let's go find someplace."

Something was wrong with me. I felt mildly depressed, vaguely let down, once again victim of an anticlimax, of a hollow victory. Why? Two great wickednesses were about to be removed from the face of the earth. Luck had marched with the Company once more. We had added more impossible triumphs to our roll of victories.

We were two hundred miles nearer our destination than we'd had any right to hope. There was no obvious reason to expect much trouble from those troops locked up in that camp south of the city. Their Shadowmaster captain was wounded. The people of Stormgard, for the most part, were accepting us as liberators.

What was to be bothered about?

40

Dejagore (formerly Stormgard)

Tonight in Stormgard.

Tonight in Stormgard was something, though somehow tainted with that lack of satisfaction that haunted me increasingly. I slept well past dawn. A bugle wakened me. The first thing I saw when I cracked my lids was a big black bastard of a crow eyeballing Lady and me. I threw something at it.

Another bugle call. I stumbled to a window. Then streaked to another. "Lady. Get up. We got trouble."

Trouble snaked out of the southern hills in the form of another enemy army. Mogaba had our boys getting into formation already. Over on the south wall Cletus and his brothers had the artillery harassing the encampment, but their engines could not keep that mob from getting ready for a fight. The people of the city poured from their houses, headed for the walls to watch.

Crows were everywhere.

Lady took a look, snapped, "Let's get dressed," and started helping me with my costume. I helped with hers.

I said of mine, "This thing is starting to smell."

"You may not have to wear it much longer."

"Eh?"

"That bunch coming out of the hills has to be just about everybody they've got left under arms. Break them and the war is over."

"Sure. Except for three Shadowmasters who might not see it that way."

I stepped to the window, shaded my eyes. I thought I could detect a black dot floating among the soldiers. "We don't have anybody on our side now. Maybe I shouldn't have been so hasty with Shifter."

"You did the right thing. He'd fulfilled his agenda. He might even have joined the others against us. He had no grudge against them."

"Did you know who they were?"

"I never suspected. Honest. Not till a day or two ago. Then it seemed too unlikely to mention."

"Let's get at it."

She kissed me, and it was a kiss with oomph behind it. We'd come a long way. . . . She put her helmet on and turned into the grim dark thing called Life-taker. I did my magic trick and turned into Widowmaker. The scurrying rats who people Stormgard—I guessed we should change the name back when the dust settled—stared at us in fear and awe as we strode through the streets.

Mogaba met us. He'd brought our horses. We mounted up. I asked, "How bad does it look?"

"Can't tell yet. With two battles under our belts and two victories I'd say we're the more tempered force. But there'll be a lot of them and I don't think you have any more tricks up your sleeves."

"You're right about that. This is the last thing I expected. If this Shadow-master uses his power . . ."

"Don't mention it to the men. They've been warned we might encounter unusual circumstances. They've been told to ignore them and get on with their jobs. You want to use the elephants again?"

"Everything. Every damned thing we've got. This one could be the whole war. Win it, we've got them off Taglios's back and we've opened the road all the way south. They won't have an army left to field."

He grunted. The same went for us.

We got out onto the field. In moments I had messengers flying everywhere, most of them trying to dig my armed laborers out of the city. We were going to need every sword.

Mogaba had sent the cavalry off to scout and harass already. Good man, Mogaba.

The crows seemed to be having a great time watching the show take shape.

The Shadowmaster out there was in no hurry. He got his men out of the hills and into formation despite my cavalry, then had his horsemen chase mine off. Otto and Hagop might have whipped them, but I'd sent instructions not to try. They just came back, leading the enemy, pelting him with arrows from their saddle bows. I wanted them to rest their animals before the main event. We did not have enough remounts to carry a proper cavalry campaign.

I detailed a few men to assemble the former prisoners as they showed and send them off to get in the way of anybody who sallied from the camp. With weapons captured yesterday and during the night more than half were now armed. They were not trained and were not skilled, but they were determined.

I sent word for Cletus and his brothers to move the artillery over where he could give us support and could bombard the encampment gate.

I looked across at the new army. "Mogaba. Any ideas?" At a guess there were fifteen thousand of them. They looked at least as competent as those we'd met at the Ghoja ford. Limited, but not amateurs.

"No."

"Don't look like they're in a hurry to get at it."

"Would you be?"

"Not if I had a Shadowmaster. And had hopes we'd come to them. Anybody else got any ideas?"

Goblin shook his head. One-Eye said, "The Shadowmasters are the key. You take them out or you don't got a chance."

"Teach your grandmother to suck eggs. Messenger. Come here." I had one idea. I sent him to draft one of the Nar and have him head into town, round up a thousand armed prisoners, and go to the city's west gate. When the fighting started he was to hit the camp from behind.

It was something.

Lady said, "One-Eye is right." I think it pained her to have to say that. "And the one to concentrate on is the healthy one. This is a time for illusion." She outlined an idea.

Ten minutes later I ordered the cavalry forward, to nip at the enemy and try to draw their cavalry out, to see what the Shadowmaster would or would not do himself.

I really wished I could count on the prisoners to hold off the men in that camp.

In the half hour it took the Shadowmaster to lose patience with being harassed, One-Eye and Goblin put together the grand illusion of their careers.

They began by re-creating the ghost of the Company they had used in that forest up north, where we captured the bandits, I think both for sentimental reasons and because it was easier to do something they had done before. They brought them out in front of the army, behind me and Lady and the standard. Then I ordered the elephants brought forward and spread them on a broad front, each supported by ten of our best and most bloodthirsty soldiers. It looked like we had a horde of the beasts because their numbers had been tripled by illusion. I assumed the Shadowmaster would see through the illusions. But so what? His men would not, and it was them I wanted to panic. By the time they knew the truth it would be too late.

Cross your fingers, Croaker.

"Ready?" I asked.

"Ready," Lady said.

The cavalry withdrew, and just in time. The Shadowmaster had begun to express his ire. I gripped Lady's hand a moment. We leaned together and whispered those three words that everybody gets embarrassed saying in public. Silly old fart me, I felt weird saying them to an audience of one. Elegies for youth lost, when I could say them to anyone and mean it with all my heart and soul for an hour.

"All right, Murgen. Let's do it." Lady and I raised our flaming swords. The legions began to chant, "Taglios! Taglios!" And my phantom brigade began its advance.

Showmanship. All those elephants would have scared the crap out of me if I'd been over on the other side.

Where the hell did I ever get the idea a general was supposed to lead from the front? Fewer than a thousand of us going to whip up on fifteen thousand of them? . . .

Arrows came to greet us. They did no harm to the illusions. They slid off the real elephants. They bounced off Murgen, Goblin, One-Eye, Lady, and me because we were sheltered by protective spells. Hopefully, our opponents would be unsettled by our invulnerability.

I signalled for an increase in speed. The enemy front began to shudder in anticipation of the impact of all those elephants. Formations started to dissolve.

About time for the Shadowmaster to do something.

I slowed down. The elephants rumbled past, trumpeting, gaining speed, and in a moment all swerving to rush straight at the Shadowmaster.

A hell of an investment just to take out one guy.

He realized the object of the assault while the elephants were still a hundred yards from him. They were going to converge and trample right over him.

He cut loose with every spell he had ready. For ten seconds it seemed like the skies were collapsing and the earth being racked. Elephants and parts of elephants flew around like children's toys.

The whole enemy front was in disarray now. I heard the signals ordering the cavalry forward again, ordering the infantry to advance.

The surviving elephants rolled over the spot where the Shadowmaster floated.

A trunk seized him and tossed him thirty feet into the air, flailing and tumbling. He fell between massive grey flanks, screamed, flew upward again, possibly under his own power. A flock of arrows darted at him as the soldiers following the elephants used him for target practice. Some got through to him. He kept spinning off spells like a fireworks show, but they seemed purely reflex.

I laughed and closed in. We had the bastard and all his children. My record as a general was going to stay unblemished.

Murgen was there when the Shadowmaster flipped into the sky for the third time. He skewered the sonofabitch with his lance when he came down.

The Shadowmaster screamed. Gods, did he scream. He flailed around like a bug impaled on a needle. His weight carried him down the shaft of the lance till he hung up on the crosspiece that supports the standard.

Murgen struggled to keep the lance upright and get out of the press. Our boys were his worst enemies. Everybody with a bow kept sniping away at the Shadowmaster.

I spurred my mount forward, got beside Murgen and helped him carry our trophy away.

That bastard wasn't spinning off any spells now.

The advancing legions roared their Taglios chant twice as loud.

Otto and Hagop smashed into the confusion in front of Mogaba's legion. There wasn't quite as much confusion as I'd hoped. The enemy soldiers had realized they'd been snookered, though they had not yet gotten into formation again.

They absorbed the elephant charge and the cavalry charge both, taking heavy casualties, but they seemed to have given up the idea of running. Hagop and Otto pulled away before the legions arrived, but the elephants continued to be mixed in with the foe. Just as well. They were beyond control. They had been pricked by enough darts and spearheads and swords to go mad with pain. They no longer cared who they stomped.

I yelled at Murgen, "Let's get this over on that mound where everybody can see that we got him." One of the mounds that dot the plain was about a hundred yards away.

We struggled through the oncoming infantry, climbed the mound, faced the fighting. It took both of us to keep the standard upright, what with all the kicking and screaming and carrying on the Shadowmaster was doing.

It was a good move tactically, carrying him up there. His boys could see they'd lost their big weapon at a time when they were getting their asses kicked already, and mine could see they didn't have to worry about him anymore. They went to work figuring on getting it over with in time for lunch break. Hagop and Otto took the bit in their mouth and circled around the enemy right to get at them from behind.

I cursed them. I did not want them so far away. But the thing was beyond control now.

Strategically, our move was not the best. The boys in the encampment got a whiff of onrushing disaster and decided they'd damned well better do *something*.

Out they came in a mob, their own gimp Shadowmaster floating in front, slipping and sliding around drunkenly but getting off a couple of killer spells that rattled the armed prisoners.

Cletus and his brothers opened fire from the wall and pounded Shadowmaster number two around, cut him a little, and got him so pissed he stopped everything and turned on them with a spell that blew them and all their engines right off the wall. Then he led his mob on out, looking to cause the rest of us just as much grief.

His bunch never did get into a formation, and neither did the prisoners, really, so that turned into a sort of barroom brawl with swords real quick.

The boys at the west gate slid out and hit the camp from behind and got over the wall easily. They went to work on the wounded and camp guards and whoever else got in their way, but their success did not affect the bigger show. The men from the camp just kept after the rest of us.

I had to do something.

"Let's get this thing planted somehow," I told Murgen. I looked out across the chaos before I dismounted. I could not see Lady anywhere. My heart crawled into my throat.

The earth of that mound was soft and moist. Grunting and straining, the two of us were able to force the butt of the lance in deep enough that it would stand by itself, rocking whenever the Shadowmaster had a wriggling, screaming fit.

The attack from the flank made progress against the prisoners. Some of the fainthearted ran for the nearest city gate, joining fellows who had not bothered to come out. Ochiba tried to extend and rotate part of his line to face the onslaught, with limited success. Sindawe's less disciplined outfit had begun to disintegrate in their eagerness to hasten the demise of the enemies they faced. They were unaware of the threat from the right. Only Mogaba had maintained discipline and unit integrity. If I'd had half a brain, I'd have flip-flopped his legion with Ochiba's before we started this. Out where he was now he wasn't much use. Killing off the entire enemy right wing, sure, but not keeping everything else from falling apart.

I had a bad feeling it was going sour.

"I don't know what to do, Murgen."

"I don't think there's anything you *can* do now, Croaker. Except cross your fingers and play it out."

Fireworks spewed over in Ochiba's area. For a while they were so ferocious I thought they might halt the coming collapse there. Goblin and One-Eye were on the job. But the crippled Shadowmaster managed to quiet them down.

What could I throw at him? What could I do? Nothing. I didn't have anything else to send in.

I did not want to watch.

A solitary crow settled onto the writhing Shadowmaster impaled on the standard lance. It looked at him, at me, at the fighting, and made a sound like an amused chuckle. Then it began pecking at the Shadowmaster's mask, trying to get at his eyes.

I ignored the bird.

Men began to scurry past. They were from Sindawe's legion, mostly prisoners who had been enrolled the past few days. I yelled at them and cursed them and called them cowards and ordered them to turn around and form up. Mostly, they did.

Hagop and Otto attacked the men facing Ochiba, probably hoping to ease the pressure so he could go ahead and deal with the threat from the camp. But the attack from behind impelled the enemy forward. While Otto and Hagop's bunch were having a great time the men they were butchering cracked Ochiba's line and ran into the armed prisoners from the side.

Ochiba's legion tried to hold, even so, but they looked like they were in bad trouble. Sindawe's men thought they were about to run and decided to beat them in a footrace. Or something. They collapsed.

Mogaba had begun rotating his axis of attack to support Sindawe from the flank. But when he finished there was nothing to support.

In moments his legion was the only island of order in a sea of chaos. The enemy were no more organized than my people were. The thing was a grand mess, the world's largest brawl.

More of my people ran for the city gates. Some just ran. I stood there under the standard, cussing and yelling and waving my sword and shedding a couple of quarts of tears. And, gods help me, some of the fools heard and listened and started trying to form up with the men I'd organized already, facing around, pushing back into it in tight little detachments.

Guts. From the beginning they had told me those Taglians had guts.

More and more, me and Murgen built us a human wall around the standard. More and more, the enemy concentrated on Mogaba, whose legion refused to break. The Shadowmasters' men heaped their dead around him. He did not see us, it seemed. Despite all resistance he moved toward the city.

I guess Murgen and I got three thousand men together before fate decided it was time to take another bite.

A big mob of the enemy rushed us. I assumed my pose, with my sword up, beside the standard. I did not have much show left me. If Goblin and One-Eye were alive at all they were too busy covering their own asses.

It looked like we would drive them off easily. Our line was locked together solidly. They were just a howling mob.

Then the arrow came out of nowhere and hit me square in the chest and knocked me right off my horse.

Lady

It wasn't always best to be old and wise in the ways of battlefields, Lady thought. She saw what was coming, clearly, long before anybody else did. Briefly, after Murgen skewered the Shadowmaster, she had hopes it would turn, but the advent of the troops from the encampment caused a shift in momentum that could not be reversed.

Croaker should not have attacked. He should have waited as long as it took, made them come to him, not been so concerned about the Shadowmasters. If he had allowed the new army from the south to come forward and get in the way of the men from the encampment, he could have then hurled his elephants in without risk to his right. But it was too late to weep about might-have-beens. It was time to try rooting out a miracle.

One Shadowmaster was out and the other was crippled. If only she had a tenth, even a hundredth, of the power she had lost. If only she'd had time to nurture and channel the little bit that had begun coming back to her.

If only. If only. All life was if only.

Where was that damned imp of One-Eye's? It could turn this around. There was nobody on the other side to keep it from going through those men like a scythe, at least for long enough.

But Frogface was nowhere to be seen. One-Eye and Goblin were working as a team, doing their little bit to stem the tide. Frogface was not with them. They seemed too busy to be curious about that.

The imp's absence was too important to be accident or oversight. *Why?* at this critical juncture?

No time. No time to brood about it and slither down through all the shadows and try to find the meaning of the imp's presences and absences, which had been bothering her so long. Only time to realize, with certainty, that the creature had been planted upon One-Eye and wasn't his to command at all.

By whom?

Not the Shadowmasters. The Shadowmasters would have used the imp directly. Not Shifter. He'd had no need. Not the Howler. He would have gotten his revenge.

What else was loose in the world?

A crow flapped past. It cawed in a way that made her think it was laughing.

Croaker and his crows. He had been muttering about crows for a year. And then they had started turning up around him any time anything big happened.

She glanced at the mound where Croaker and Murgen had set the standard. Croaker had a pair of crows perched on his shoulders. A flock circled above him. He made a dramatic figure there in his Widowmaker disguise, with the doombirds wheeling around him, waving his fiery sword, trying to rally his crumbling legions.

While the mind pursued one clatch of enemies the body dealt with another. She wielded her weapons with a dancer's grace and the deadliness of a demigoddess. At first there had been an exhilaration, realizing she was approaching a state she had not achieved in ages, except by the path of its tantric cousin, last night. And then she went over into the perfect calm, the mystic separation of Self and flesh that actually melded into a greater, more illuminated and deadly whole.

There was no fear in that state, nor any other emotion. It was like being in the deepest meditation, where the Self wandered a field of glimmering insights, yet the flesh performed its deadly tasks with a precision and perfection that left the dead mounded about her and her terrible mount.

The enemy wrestled with one another to stay away from her. Her allies fought to get into the safety of the vacuum surrounding her. Though the right wing had begun to collapse, one stubborn rock formed.

The Self reflected on memories of illuminations won during the night from a pair of bodies, sweating, straining together, on her absolute amazement during and after. Her life had been one of absolute self-control. Yet time and again the flesh had gone beyond any hope of control. At her age.

And she looked at Croaker again, now harried by his enemies.

And the shadow crept into the killing perfection and showed her why she had denied herself for so long.

She thought of loss.

And loss mattered.

Mattering intruded upon the Self, distracting it. It wanted to take control of the flesh, to force things to transpire according to its desires.

She started forcing her way toward Croaker, the knot of men around her moving with her. But the enemy could sense that she was no longer the terrible thing she had been, that she was now vulnerable. They pressed in. One by one, her companions fell.

Then she saw the arrow strike Croaker and drop him at the foot of the standard. She shrieked and spurred her mount over friend and foe alike.

Her pain, and her rage, only carried her into a mass of enemies who attacked from every direction. She cut some, but others dragged her off her rearing steed and harried the beast away. She fought with skill and desperation against poorly trained opponents, but the ineptness of her enemies was not enough. She heaped bodies, but they drove her down to her knees. . . .

A wave of chaos swept over that fight within the battle, men fleeing, men pursuing, and when it passed all that could be seen of her was one arm protruding from a pile of corpses.

That Stump

Lying mostly on my back, clinging to the haft of the lance with my left hand, the standard flapping and the Shadowmaster flopping overhead. I don't think the arrow hit anything vital. But the son of a bitch went through my breastplate and me, too. I think there are a couple inches sticking out in back.

What the hell happened to the spells protecting me?

I never been hit this bad before.

Coupla crows up with the Shadowmaster. Amusing themselves, trying to get his eyes. Four or five prowling around down here, not bothering me. Act like they're standing guard.

Bunch showed up a while ago, when some enemy troops came after the standard. Piled all over them till they went away.

Ah, that damned arrow hurts! Can I get a hand around there and break the shaft? Pull the sucker back out after the head is gone?

Better not. The shaft might be keeping the bleeding from getting too bad inside. Seen that happen.

What's going on? Can't move enough to look around. Hurts too much. All I can see from here is the plain, covered with bodies. Elephants, horses, some men in white, a lot more not. I think we took a lot of them with us. I think if the formations had just held up we'd have kicked their asses.

Can't hear. Total silence. Me? What was that? Silence of stone? Where did I hear that?

Tired. So damned tired. Want to lay down and sleep. Can't. The arrow. Probably be too weak soon, though. Thirsty. But not thirsty like with a belly wound, thank the gods. Never wanted to die with a gut wound. Ha. Never wanted to die.

Keep thinking about sepsis. What if the bowman put garlic or feces on his arrowheads? Blood poisoning. Gangrene. Smell like you're six days dead when you're still breathing. Can't amputate my chest.

Shame and guilt. Brought the Company to this. Didn't want to be the last Captain. Guess none of them did. Shouldn't have fought today. Sure shouldn't have charged. Thought the illusions and elephants would be enough, though. Came close, too.

Know what I should have done, now. Stayed up in the hills where they couldn't see me and let them come to me. Could have sneaked around and used the old Company trickery on them there. Show the standard in one direction and attack from another. But I had to come down here after them.

Feel like a fool lying here in my underwear and a breastplate. Wonder if it did any damn good for Murgen to put that Widowmaker suit on and go try to turn the tide? Mogaba will have his cojones for abandoning the standard.

But I'm here. Still holding the sucker up.

Maybe somebody will come before I pass out. Getting so even somebody from the other side would look good. Damned arrow. Finish it off. Get it over.

Something moving. . . . Just my damned horse. Having lunch. Turning grass into horse hockey. Just another day in the life for him. Go fetch me a bucket of beer, you bastard. You're supposed to be so damned intelligent, why can't you get a dying man a last beer?

How can the world be so damned quiet and bright and cheerful-looking when so many men just died here? Look at that mess. Right down there, fifty dead guys in a patch of wildflowers. Going to smell the stink for forty miles in a couple days.

How come this is taking so long? Am I going to be one of those guys who makes a career out of croaking?

Something out there. Something moving. Way out. Crows circling. . . . My old friend the stump, crossing the plain of the dead on a holiday stroll. Stepping light, though. In a good mood. What was that before? Not yet time? Crows?

This critter Death? I been looking my own death in the eye all the way down here?

Carrying something. Yeah, a box. About a foot by a foot by a foot. Remember noticing that before but not paying much attention. Never heard of Death carrying a box. Usually a sword or a scythe.

Whatever the hell it is, it's here to see me. Headed straight for me. Hang in there, Croaker. Maybe there's new hope for the dead.

Geek up on the lance getting all bent out of shape. I don't think he's happy about developments.

Getting closer now. Definitely no walking stump. A people, or something walking on two legs, very short. Funny. Always looked bigger from a distance. Close enough now we ought to be eyeball to eyeball, if I could see any eyes inside that hood. It's like there's nothing in there at all.

Kneeling. Empty hood, yes, inches away. Damned box right beside me.

Voice like a very slight breath of a breeze in spring willows, soft, gentle, and merry. "*Now* it's time, Croaker." Half a titter, half a chuckle. A glance up at the critter skewered on the lance. "And it's time for you too, you old bastard."

Completely different voice. Not just a different tone or a different inflexion, but an entirely different voice.

I guess all the other dead ones being alive set me up for it. I recognized her instantly. Almost as if something inside me had been expecting her. I gasped, "You! That can't be!" I tried to get up. "Soulcatcher!" I don't know what the hell I thought I was going to do. Run away? How? Where to?

The pain ripped through me. I sagged.

"Yes, my love. Me. You went away without finishing it." Laughter that was a young girl's giggle. "I have waited a long time, Croaker. But she finally exchanged the magic words with you. Now I avenge myself by taking from her what is more precious than life itself." Again the giggle, like she was talking about some simple practical joke with no malice in it.

I had no strength to argue.

She made a lifting gesture with one gloved hand. "Come along, my sweet."

I floated up off the ground. A crow landed on my chest and stared off in the direction I began to move, as though it were in charge of navigation.

There was a good side. The pain faded.

I did not see the lance and its burden move, but sensed that it too was in motion. My captor led the way, floating, too. We moved very fast.

We must have been a sight for anyone watching.

Darkness nibbled around the edge of consciousness. I fought it, fearing it was the final darkness. I lost.

Overlook

Mad laughter rolled out of that high crystal room on top of that tower at Overlook. Somebody was tickled silly about the way things were going up north.

"That's three of them down, half a job done. And the hard half at that. Get the other three and it's all mine."

More insane mirth.

The Shadowmaster gazed out at the brilliant expanse of whiteness. "Is it time to release you from your prison, my beauties of the night? Time to let you run free in the world again? No, no. Not just this moment. Not till this island of safety is invulnerable."

Glittering Stone

The plain is filled with the silence of stone. Nothing lives there. But in the deep hours of the night shadows flutter among the pillars and perch atop the columns with darkness wrapped about them like cloaks of concealment.

Such nights are not for the unwary stranger. Such nights the silence of stone is sometimes broken by screams. Then the shadows feast, though never do they sate the raging hunger.

For the shadows the hunt is ever poorer. Sometimes months pass before an unwise adventurer stumbles into the place of glittering stone. The hunger worsens with the years and the shadows eye the forbidden lands beyond. But they cannot go, and they cannot starve to death, much as they might wish to die. They cannot die, for they are the undead, bound by the silence of stone.

It is immortality of a sort.

DREAMS of STEEL

For Keith, because I like his style

Many months have passed. Much has happened and much has slipped from my memory. Insignificant details have stuck with me while important things have gotten away. Some things I know only from third parties and more I can only guess. How often have my witnesses perjured themselves?

It did not occur to me, till this time of enforced inactivity befell me, that an important tradition was being overlooked, that no one was recording the deeds of the Company. I dithered then. It seemed a presumption for me to take up the pen. I have no training. I am no historian nor even much of a writer. Certainly I don't have Croaker's eye or ear or wit.

So I shall confine myself to reporting facts as I recall them. I hope the tale is not too much colored by my own presence within it, nor by what it has done to me.

With that apologia, herewith, this addition to the Annals of the Black Company, in the tradition of Annalists before me, the Book of Lady.

—Lady, Annalist, Captain

2

The elevation was not good. The distance was extreme. But Willow Swan knew what he was seeing. "They're getting their butts kicked."

Armies contended before the city Dejagore, at the center of a circular, hill-encompassed plain. Swan and three companions watched.

Blade grunted agreement. Cordy Mather, Swan's oldest friend, said nothing. He just tried to kick the stuffing out of a rock.

The army they favored was losing.

Swan and Mather were whites, blond and brunette, hailing from Roses, a city seven thousand miles north of the killing ground. Blade was a black giant of uncertain origins, a dangerous man with little to say. Swan and Mather had rescued him from crocodiles a few years earlier. He had stuck. The three were a team.

Swan cursed softly, steadily, as the battle situation worsened.

The fourth man did not belong. The team would not have had him if he volunteered. People called him Smoke. Officially, he was the fire marshall of Taglios, the city-nation whose army was losing. In reality he was the Taglian court wizard. He was a nut-brown little man whose very existence annoyed Swan.

"That's your army out there, Smoke," Willow growled. "It goes down, you go down. Bet the Shadowmasters would love to lay hands on you." Sorceries yowled and barked on the battlefield. "Maybe make marmalade out of you. Unless you've cut a deal already."

"Ease up, Willow," Mather said. "He's doing something."

Swan looked at the butternut-colored runt. "Sure enough. But what?"

Smoke had his eyes closed. He mumbled and muttered. Sometimes his voice crackled and sizzled like bacon in an overheated pan.

"He ain't doing nothing to help the Black Company. You quit talking to yourself, you old buzzard. We got a problem. Our guys are getting whipped. You want to try to turn that around? Before I turn you over my knee?"

The old man opened his eyes. He stared across the plain. His expression was not pleasant. Swan doubted that the little geek's eyes were good enough to make out details. But you never knew with Smoke. With him everything was mask and pretense.

"Don't be a moron, Swan. I'm one man, too little and too old. There are Shadowmasters down there. They can stomp me like a roach."

Swan fussed and grumbled. People he knew were dying.

Smoke snapped, "All I can do—all any of us can do—is attract attention. Do you really want the Shadowmasters to notice you?"

"They're just the Black Company, eh? They took their pay, they take their chances? Even if forty thousand Taglians go down with them?"

Smoke's lips shrank into a mean little prune.

On the plain a human tide washed around a mound where the Black Company standard had been planted for a last stand. The tide swept on toward the hills.

"You wouldn't be happy about the way things are going, would you?" Swan's voice was dangerous, no longer carping. Smoke was a political animal, worse than a crocodile. Crocs might eat their young but their treacheries were predictable.

Though irked, Smoke replied in a voice almost tender. "They *have* accomplished more than we dreamed."

The plain was dense with the dead and dying, man and beast. Mad war elephants careened around, respecting no allegiance. Only one Taglian legion had maintained its integrity. It had fought its way to a city gate and was covering the flight of other Taglians. Flames rose beyond the city from a military encampment. The Company had scored that much success against the apparent victors.

Smoke said, "They've lost a battle but they saved Taglios. They slew one of the Shadowmasters. They've made it impossible for the others to attack Taglios. Those will spend their remaining troops recapturing Dejagore."

Swan sneered. "Just pardon me if I don't dance for joy. I liked those guys. I didn't like the way you planned to shaft them."

Smoke's temper was strained. "They weren't fighting for Taglios, Swan. They wanted to use us to hammer through the Shadowlands to Khatovar. Which could be worse than a Shadowmasters' conquest."

Swan knew rationalization when he stepped in it. "And because they wouldn't lick your boots, even if they were willing to save your asses from the Shadowmasters, you figure it's handy, them getting caught here. A pity, say I. Would've been some swell show, watching your footwork if they'd come up winners and you had to deliver your end of the bargain."

"Ease up, Willow," Mather said.

Swan ignored him. "Call me a cynic, Smoke. But I'd bet about anything you and the Radisha had it scoped out to screw them from the start. Eh? Wouldn't do to have them slice through the Shadowlands. But why the hell not? I never did get that part."

"It ain't over yet, Swan," Blade said. "Wait. Smoke going to get his turn to cry."

The others gawked at Blade. He spoke so seldom that when he did they knew it meant something. What did he know?

Swan asked, "You see something I missed?"

Cordy snapped, "Damn it, will you calm down?"

"Why the hell should I? The whole damned world is swamped by conniving old farts like Smoke. They been screwing the rest of us since the gods started keeping time. Look at this little poof. Keeps whining about how he's got to lay low and not let the Shadowmasters find out about him. *I* think that means he's got no balls. That Lady . . . You know who *she* used to be? *She* had balls enough to face them. You give that half a think you'll realize how she laid more on the line than this old freak ever could."

"Calm down, Willow."

"Calm down, hell. It ain't right. Somebody's got to tell old farts like this to go suck rocks."

Blade grunted agreement. But Blade didn't like anyone in authority.

Swan, not as upset as he put on, noted that Blade was in position to whack the wizard if he got obnoxious.

Smoke smiled. "Swan, once upon a time all us old farts were young loud-mouths like you."

Mather stepped between them. "Enough! Instead of squabbling, how about we get out of here before that mess catches up with us?" Remnants of the battle swirled around the toes of the foothills. "We can gather the garrisons from the towns north of here and collect everybody at Ghoja."

Swan agreed. Sourly. "Yeah. Maybe some of the Company made it." He glowered at Smoke.

The old man shrugged. "If some get out they can train a real army. They'd have time enough now."

"Yeah. And if the Prahbrindrah Drah and the Radisha was to get off their butts they might even line up a few real allies. Maybe come up with a wizard with a hair on his ass. One who wouldn't spend his whole life hiding out in the weeds."

Mather started down the back of the hill. "Come on, Blade. Let them bicker."

After several seconds Smoke confessed, "He's right, Swan. Let's get on with it."

Willow tossed his long golden hair, looked at Blade. Blade jerked his head toward the horses below the hill. "All right." Swan took a last look at the city and plain where the Black Company had died. "But what's right is right and what's wrong is wrong."

"And what's practical is practical and what's needful is necessary. Let's go."

Swan walked. He would remember that remark. He was determined to have the last word. "Bullshit, Smoke. That's bullshit. I seen a new side of you today. I don't like it and I don't trust it. I'm going to watch you like your conscience."

They mounted up and headed north.

In those days the Company was in service to the Prahbrindrah Drah of Taglios. That prince was too easygoing to master a numerous, factious people like the Taglians. But his natural optimism and forgiving nature were offset by his sister, the Radisha Drah. A small, dark, hard woman, the Radisha had a will of sword steel and the conscience of a hurtling stone.

While the Black Company and the Shadowmasters contested possession of Dejagore, or Stormgard, the Prahbrindrah Drah held an audience three hundred miles to the north.

The prince stood five and a half feet tall. Though dark, his features were caucasic. He glowered at the priests and engineers before him. He wanted to throw them out. But in god-ridden Taglios no one offended the priesthoods.

He spied his sister signalling from the shadowed rear of the chamber. "Excuse me." He walked out. Bad manners they would tolerate. He joined the Radisha. "What is it?"

"Not here."

"Bad news?"

"Not now." The Radisha strode off. "Majarindi looked unhappy."

"He got his hand caught in a monkey trap. He insisted we build a wall because Shaza has been having holy visions. But once the others demanded a share he sang a different song. I asked if Shaza had begun having un-visions. He wasn't amused."

"Good."

The Radisha led her brother through tortuous passages. The palace was ancient. Additions were cobbled on during every reign. No one knew the labyrinth whole except Smoke.

The Radisha went to one of the wizard's secret places, a room sheltered from eavesdroppers by the old man's finest spells. The Prahbrindrah Drah shut the door. "Well?"

"A pigeon brought a message. From Smoke."

"Bad news?"

"Our mercenaries have been defeated at Stormgard." The Shadowmasters called Dejagore Stormgard.

"Badly?"

"Is there any other . . . ?"

"Yes." Before the appearance of the Shadowmasters Taglios had been a pacifist state. But when that danger first beckoned the Prahbrindrah had exhumed the ancient strategikons. "Were they annihilated? Routed? How badly did they hurt the Shadowmasters? Is Taglios in danger?"

"They shouldn't have crossed the Main."

"They had to harry the survivors from Ghoja ford. They're the professionals, Sis. We said we wouldn't second-guess or interfere. We didn't believe they could win at Ghoja, so we're way ahead. Give me details."

"A pigeon isn't a condor." The Radisha made a face. "They marched down with a mob of liberated slaves, took Dejagore by stealth, destroyed Stormshadow and wounded Shadowspinner. But today Moonshadow appeared with a fresh army. Casualties were heavy on both sides. Moonshadow may have been killed. But we lost. Some of the troops retreated into the city. The rest scattered. Most of the mercenaries, including the captain and his woman, were killed."

"Lady is dead? That's a pity. She was exquisite."

"You're a lustful ape."

"I am, aren't I? But she did stop hearts wherever she went."

"And never noticed. The only man she saw was her captain. That Croaker character."

"Are you miffed because he only had eyes for her?"

She gave him a savage look.

"What's Smoke doing?"

"Fleeing north. Blade, Swan, and Mather will try to rally the survivors at Ghoja."

"I don't like that. Smoke should've stayed down there. Rallied them there, to support the men in the city. You don't give away ground you've gained."

"Smoke is scared the Shadowmasters will find out about him."

"They don't know? That would surprise me." The Prahbrindrah shrugged. "What's he saving himself for? I'm going down there."

She laughed.

"What?"

"You can't. Those idiot priests would steal everything but your eyes. Stay. Keep them occupied with their idiot wall. I'll go. And I'll kick Smoke's butt till he gets off it and does something."

The prince sighed. "You're right. But go quietly. They behave better when they think you're watching."

"They didn't miss me last time."

"Don't leave me twisting in the wind. They're hard to deal with when they know more than I do."

"I'll keep them off balance." She patted his arm. "Go shock them with your turnaround. Work them into a wall-building frenzy. Get benevolent toward whichever cult shows the most productivity. Get them cutting each other's throats."

The Prahbrindrah grinned boyishly. That was the game he loved. That was the way to accumulate power. Get the priests to disarm themselves.

It was a bizarre little parade. At its head was a black thing that could not decide if it was a tree stump or someone weirdly built carrying a box under one arm. Behind that a man floated a yard off the ground, feet foremost, inelegantly sprawled. An arrow had pierced his chest. It still protruded from his back. He was alive, but barely.

Behind the floating man was another with a lance through him. He drifted a dozen feet up, alive and in pain, sometimes writhing like an animal with a broken spine. Two riderless horses followed him, both black stallions bigger than any war charger.

Crows by the hundred circled above, coming and going like scouts.

The parade climbed the hills east of Stormgard, moving in twilight. Once it paused, remained motionless twenty minutes while a scatter of Taglian fugitives passed. They saw nothing. There was magic at work there.

The column continued moving by night. The crows continued flying, formed a rearguard, watched for something. Several times they cawed at shifting shadows, but settled down quickly. False alarms?

The party halted ten miles from the beleaguered city. The thing leading spent hours collecting brush and deadwood, piled it in a deep crack in a granitic hillside. Then it seized the floating lance, dragged its victim off, stripped him down.

A bitter, remote, whispering voice exclaimed, "This isn't one of the Taken!" when the man's mask came off.

The crows became raucous. Discussing? Arguing? The leader asked, "Who are you? What are you? Where did you come from?"

The injured man did not respond. Maybe he was beyond communication. Maybe he did not speak that language. Maybe he was stubborn.

Torture produced no answers.

The inquisitor tossed the man into the woodpile, waved a hand. The pile burst into flame. The stump thing used the lance to keep its victim from escaping. The burning man had a bottomless well of energy.

There was sorcery at work here.

The burning man was the Shadowmaster Moonshadow. His army had triumphed outside Stormgard but his own fortune had been inglorious.

The party did not move on till the Shadowmaster was consumed, the fire burned to ashes and the ashes cooled. The stump thing gathered the ashes. As it travelled it disposed of those pinch by pinch.

The man with the arrow in him bobbed in the stump thing's wake. The stallions brought up the rear.

The crows maintained their patrols. Once a large catlike thing came too near and they went into paroxysms. The stump did something mystical. The black leopard wandered away, absent of mind.

A slight figure in ornate black armor strained savagely. A corpse toppled off the heap of corpses piled upon the figure. The shift in weight made it possible to wriggle out of the heap. Free, the figure lay motionless for several minutes, panting inside a grotesque helmet. Then it pulled itself into a sitting position.

After another minute the figure struggled out of its gauntlets, revealed delicate hands. Slim fingers plucked at the fastenings holding its helmet. That came away, too.

Long black hair fell free around a face to stun a man. Inside all that ugly black steel was a woman.

I have to report those moments that way because I don't recall them at all. I remember a dark dream. A nightmare featuring a black woman with fangs like a vampire. Nothing else. My first clear recollection is of sitting beside the heap of corpses with my helmet in my lap. I was panting, only vaguely aware that I had gotten out of the pile somehow.

The stench of a thousand cruel gut wounds filled the air like the stink of the largest, rawest sewer in the world. It was the smell of battlefields. How many times had I smelled it? A thousand. And still I wasn't used to it.

I gagged. Nothing came up. I had emptied my stomach into my helmet while I was under the pile. I had a vague recollection of being terrified that I would drown in my own vomit.

I started shaking. Tears rolled, stinging, hot tears of relief. I had survived! I had lived ages beyond the measure of most mortals but I had lost none of my desire for life.

As I caught my breath I tried to put together where I was, what I was doing there. Besides surviving.

My last clear memories weren't pleasant. I remembered *knowing* that I was about to die.

I couldn't see much in the dark but I didn't need to see to know we had lost. Had the Company turned the tide Croaker would have found me long ago.

Why hadn't the victors?

There *were* men moving on the battlefield. I heard low voices arguing. Moving my way slowly. I had to get out of there.

I got up, managed to stumble four steps before I fell on my face, too weak to move another inch. Thirst was a demon devouring me from the inside out. My throat was so dry I couldn't whine.

I'd made noise. The looters were quiet now.

They were sneaking toward me, after one more victim. Where was my sword?

I was going to die now. No weapon and no strength to use one if I found one before they found me.

I could see them now, three men backlighted by a faint glow from Dejagore. Small men, like most of the Shadowmasters' soldiers. Neither strong nor particularly skilled, but in my case they needed neither strength nor skill.

Could I play dead? No. They wouldn't be deceived. Corpses would be cool now.

Damn them!

Before they killed me they would do more than just rob me.

They wouldn't kill me. They would recognize the armor. The Shadowmasters weren't fools. They knew who I'd been. They knew what I carried inside my head, treasures they dreamed about getting out. There would be rewards for my capture.

Maybe there are gods. A racket broke out behind the looters. Sounded like a sally from Dejagore, some kind of spoiling raid. Mogaba wasn't sitting on his hands waiting for the Shadowmasters to come to him.

One of the looters said something in a normal voice. Someone told him to shut up. The third man entered his opinion. An argument ensued. The first man didn't want to investigate the uproar. He'd had enough fighting.

The others overruled him.

The fates were kind. Two responsible soldiers handed me a life.

I lay where I'd fallen, resting for several minutes before I got onto hands and knees and crawled back to the mound of bodies. I found my sword, an ancient and consecrated blade created by Carqui in the younger days of the Domination. A storied blade, but no one, not even Croaker, had heard its tale.

I crawled toward the hummock where, when I'd seen him last, my love had been making his final stand, just him and Murgen and the Company standard, trying to stem the rout. It seemed an all-night trek. I found a dead soldier with water in his canteen. I drained it and went on. My strength grew as I crept. By the time I reached the hummock I could totter along upright.

I found nothing there. Just dead men. Croaker was not among them. The Company standard was gone. I felt hollow. Had the Shadowmasters taken him? They would want him badly for crushing their army at Ghoja, for taking Dejagore, for killing Stormshadow.

I could not believe they had him. It had taken me too long to find him. No god, no fate, could be so cruel.

I cried.

The night grew quiet. The sortie had withdrawn. The looters would return now.

I started moving, stumbled into a dead elephant and almost shrieked, thinking I had walked right into a monster.

The elephants had carried all kinds of clutter. Some might be useful. I scrounged a few pounds of dried food, a skin of water, a small jar of poison for arrowheads, a few coins, whatever caught my fancy. Then I walked northward, determined to reach the hills before sunrise. I discarded half my plunder before I got there.

I hurried. Enemy patrols would be out looking for important bodies come first light.

What could I do now, besides survive? I was the last of the Black Company. There was nothing left. . . . Something came into me like a lost memory resurfacing. I could turn back time. I could become what I had been.

Trying not to think did not help. I remembered. And the more I remembered the more angry I became. Anger shaped me till all my thoughts were of revenge.

As I started into the hills I surrendered. Those monsters who had raped my dreams had written their own decrees of doom. I would do whatever it took to requite them.

Longshadow paced a room ablaze with light so brilliant he seemed a dark spirit trapped in the mouth of the sun. He clung to that one crystal-walled, mirrored chamber where no shadow ever formed unless called forth by dire exigency. His fear of shadows was pathological.

The chamber was the highest in the tallest tower of the fortress Overlook, south of Shadowcatch, a city on the southern edge of the world. South of Over-look lay a plateau of glittering stone where isolated pillars stood like forgotten supports for the sky. Though construction had been underway for seventeen years, Overlook was incomplete. If Longshadow did finish it, no force material or supernatural would be able to penetrate it.

Strange, deadly, terrifying things hungered for him, lusted for freedom from the plain of glittering stone. They were shadow things that could catch up with a man as suddenly as death if he didn't cling to the light.

Longshadow's sorcery had shown him the battle at Stormgard, four hun-dred miles north of Shadowcatch. He was pleased. His rivals Moonshadow and Stormshadow had perished. Shadowspinner had been injured. A touch here, a touch there, subtly, would keep Shadowspinner weak.

But he couldn't be killed. Oh, no. Not yet. Dangerous forces were at work. Shadowspinner would have to be the breakwater against which the storm spent its energies.

Those mercenaries in Stormgard should be given every chance to sap Spin-ner's troop strength. He was far too strong now that he had possession of all three northern Shadow armies.

Subtlety. Subtlety. Each move had to be made with care. Spinner wasn't stu-pid. He knew who his most dangerous enemy was. If he rid himself of the Taglians and their Free Company leaders he'd turn on Overlook immediately.

And *she* was out there somewhere, shuffling counters in her own game, not in the ripeness of her power but deadly as a krite even so. And there was the woman whose knowledge could be invaluable, alone, a treasure to be harvested by any adventurer.

He needed a catspaw. He couldn't leave Overlook. The shadows were out there waiting, infinitely patient.

He caught a flicker of darkness from the corner of his eye. He squealed and flung himself away.

It was a crow, just a damned curious crow fluttering around outside.

A catspaw. There was a power in the swamps north of that miserable Taglios. It festered with grievances real and imagined. It could be seduced.

It was time he lured that power into the game.

But how, without leaving Overlook?

Something stirred on the plain of glittering stone.

The shadows were watching, waiting. They sensed the rising intensity of the game.

7

I slept in a tangle of brush in a hollow. I'd fled through olive groves and precariously perched hillside paddies, running out of hope, till I'd stumbled onto that pocket wilderness in a ravine. I was so far gone I'd just crawled in, hoping fate would be kind.

A crow's call wakened me from another terrible dream. I opened my eyes. The sun reached in through the brush. It dappled me with spots of light. I'd hoped nobody could see me in there but that proved a false hope.

Someone was moving around the edge of the bushes. I glimpsed one, then another. Damn! The Shadowmasters' men. They moved back a little and whispered.

I saw them for just a moment but they seemed troubled, less like hunters than the hunted. Curious.

They'd spotted me, I knew. Otherwise they wouldn't be back there behind me, murmuring too low for me to catch what they said.

I couldn't turn toward them without showing them I knew they were there. I didn't want to startle them. They might do something I'd regret. The crow called again. I started turning my head slowly.

I froze.

There was another player here, a dirty little brown man in a filthy loincloth and tattered turban. He squatted behind the brush. He looked like one of the slaves Croaker had freed after our victory at Ghoja. Did the soldiers know he was there?

Did it matter? He wasn't likely to be any help.

I was lying on my right side, on my arm. My fingers tingled. My arm was asleep but the sensation reminded me that my talent had shown signs of freshening since we'd come down past the waist of the world. I hadn't had a chance to test it for weeks.

I had to do something. Or they would. My sword lay inches from my hand. . . .

Golden Hammer.

It was a child's spell, an exercise, not a weapon at all, just as a butcher knife isn't. Once it would have been no more work than dropping a rock. Now it was as hard as plain speech for a stroke victim. I tried shaping the spell in my mind. The frustration! The screaming frustration of knowing what to do and being unable to do it.

But it clicked. Almost the way it had back when. Amazed, pleased, I whispered the words of power, moved my fingers. The muscles remembered!

The Golden Hammer formed in my left hand.

I jumped up, flipped it, raised my sword. The glowing hammer flew true. The soldier made a stabbed-pig sound and tried to fend it off. It branded its shape on his chest.

It was an ecstatic moment. Success with that silly child's spell was a major triumph over my handicap.

My body wouldn't respond to my will. Too stiff, too battered and bruised for flight, I tried to charge the second soldier. Mostly I stumbled toward him. He gaped, then he ran. I was astonished.

I heard a sound like the cough of a tiger behind me.

A man came out of nowhere down the ravine. He threw something. The fleeing soldier pitched onto his face and didn't move.

I got out of the brush and placed myself so I could watch the killer and the dirty slave who had made the tiger cough. The killer was a huge man. He wore tatters of Taglian legionnaire's garb.

The little man came around the brush slowly, considered my victim. He was impressed. He said something apologetic in Taglian, then something excited, rapidly in dialect I found unfamiliar, to the big man, who had begun searching his victim. I caught a phrase here and there, all with a cultish sound but uncertain in this context. I couldn't tell if he was talking about me or praising one of his gods. I heard "the Foretold" and "Daughter of Night" and "the Bride" and "Year of the Skulls." I'd heard a "Daughter of Shadow" and a "Year of the Skulls" before somewhere, in the religious chatter of god-ridden Taglians, but I didn't know their significance.

The big man grunted. He wasn't impressed. He just cursed the dead soldier, kicked him. "Nothing."

The little man fawned. "Your pardon, Lady. We've been killing these dogs all morning, trying to raise a stake. But they're poorer than I was as a slave."

"You know me?"

"Oh, yes, Mistress. The Captain's Lady." He emphasized those last two words, separately and heavily. He bowed three times. Each time his right thumb and forefinger brushed a triangle of black cloth that peeped over the top of his loincloth. "We stood guard while you slept. We should have realized *you* would need no protection. Forgive us our presumption."

Gods, did he smell. "Have you seen anyone else?"

"Yes, Mistress. A few, from afar. Running, most of them."

"And the Shadowmasters' soldiers?"

"They search, but with no enthusiasm. Their masters didn't send many. A thousand like these pigs." He indicated the man I had dropped. His partner was searching the body. "And a few hundred horsemen. They must be busy with the city."

"Mogaba will give them hell if he can, buying time for others to get clear."

The big man said, "Nothing on this toad either, *jamadar*."

The little man grunted.

Jamadar? It's the Taglian word for captain. The little man had used it earlier, with a different intonation, when he'd called me the Captain's Lady.

I asked, "Have you seen the Captain?"

The pair exchanged looks. The little man stared at the ground. "The Captain is dead, Mistress. He died trying to rally the men to the standard. Ram saw it. An arrow through the heart."

I sat down on the ground. There was nothing to say. I'd known it. I'd seen it happen, too. But I hadn't wanted to believe it. Till that instant, I realized, I'd been carrying some small hope that I'd been wrong.

Impossible that I could feel such loss and pain. Damn him, Croaker was just a man! How did I get so involved? I never meant it to get complicated.

This wasn't accomplishing anything. I got up. "We lost a battle but the war goes on. The Shadowmasters will rue the day they decided to bully Taglios. What are your names?"

The little man said, "I'm Narayan, Lady." He grinned. I'd get thoroughly sick of that grin. "A joke on me. It's a Shadar name." He was Gunni, obviously. "Do I look it?" He jerked his head at the other man, who was Shadar. Shadar men tend to be tall and massive and hairy. This one had a head like a ball of kinky wire with eyes peering out. "I was a vegetable peddler till the Shadowmasters came to Gondowar and enslaved everyone who survived the fight for the town."

That would have been before we'd come to Taglios, last year, when Swan and Mather had been doing their inept best to stem the first invasion.

"My friend is Ram. Ram was a carter in Taglios before he joined the legions."

"Why did he call you jamadar?"

Narayan glanced at Ram, flashed a grin filled with bad teeth, leaned close to me, whispered, "Ram isn't very bright. Strong as an ox he is, and tireless, but slow."

I nodded but wasn't satisfied. They were two odd birds. Shadar and Gunni didn't run together. Shadar consider themselves superior to everyone. Hanging around with a Gunni would constitute a defilement of spirit. And Narayan was low-caste Gunni. Yet Ram showed him deference.

Neither harbored any obviously wicked designs toward me. At the moment any companion was an improvement on travelling alone. I told them, "We ought to get moving. More of them could show up. . . . *What* is he doing?"

Ram had a ten-pound rock. He was smashing the leg bones of the man he'd killed. Narayan said, "Ram. That's enough. We're leaving."

Ram looked puzzled. He thought. Then he shrugged and discarded the rock. Narayan didn't explain his actions. He told me, "We saw one fair-sized group this morning, maybe twenty men. Maybe we can catch up."

"That would be a start." I realized I was starving. I hadn't eaten since before the battle. I shared out what I'd taken off the dead elephant. It didn't help much. Ram went at it like it was a feast, now completely indifferent to the dead.

Narayan grinned. "You see? An ox. Come. Ram, carry her armor."

Two hours later we found twenty-three fugitives on a hilltop. They were beaten men, apathetic, so down they didn't care if they got away. Few still had their weapons. I didn't recognize any of them. Not surprising. We'd gone into battle with forty thousand.

They knew me. Their manners and attitude improved instantly. It pleased me to see hope blossom among them. They rose and lowered their heads respectfully.

I could see the city and plain from that hilltop. The Shadowmasters' troops were leaving the hills, evidently recalled. Good. We'd have a little time before they picked it up again.

I looked at the men more closely.

They had accepted me already. Good again.

Narayan had begun speaking to them individually. Some seemed frightened of him. Why? What was it? Something was odd about that little man.

"Ram, build us a fire. I want a lot of smoke."

He grunted, drafted four men, headed downhill to collect firewood.

Narayan trotted over, grinning that grin, followed by a man of amazing width. Most Taglians are lean to the point of emaciation. This one had no fat on him. He was built like a bear. "This is Sindhu, Mistress, that I know by reputation." Sindhu bowed slightly. He looked a humorless sort. Narayan added, "He'll be a good man to help out."

I noted a red cloth triangle at Sindhu's waist. He was Gunni. "Your help will be appreciated, Sindhu. You two get this bunch sorted out. See what resources we have."

Narayan grinned, made a small bow, hustled off with his new friend.

I settled cross-legged, separate from the rest, faced the city, closed out the world. The Golden Hammer had come easily. I'd try again.

I opened to what little talent I retained. A peppercorn of fire formed in the bowl of my hands. It *was* coming back.

There is no way to express my pleasure.

I concentrated on horses.

Half an hour later a giant black stallion appeared, trotted straight to me. The men were impressed.

I was impressed. I hadn't expected success. And that beast was only the first of four to respond. By the time the fourth arrived so had another hundred men. The hilltop was crowded.

I assembled them. "We've lost a battle, men. Some of you have lost heart, too. That's understandable. You weren't raised in a warrior tradition. But this war hasn't been lost. And it won't end while one Shadowmaster lives. If you don't have the stomach to stick it out, stay away from me. You'd better go now. I won't let you go later."

They exchanged worried glances but nobody volunteered to travel alone.

"We're going to head north. We'll gather food, weapons, and men. We'll train. We're coming back someday. When we do, the Shadowmasters will think the gates of hell have opened." Still nobody deserted. "We march at first light tomorrow. If you're with me then, you're with me forever." I tried to project a certainty that we could terrify the world.

When I settled for the night Ram posted himself nearby, my bodyguard whether or not I wanted one.

I drifted off wondering what had become of four black stallions that had not responded. We had brought eight south. They had been specially bred in the early days of the empire I had abandoned. One could be more valuable than a hundred men.

I listened to whispers, heard repeats of the terms Narayan had used. They troubled most of the men.

I noticed that Ram had his bit of folded cloth, too. His was saffron. He didn't keep it as fastidiously as did Narayan or Sindhu. Three men from two religions, each with a colored cloth. What was the significance?

Narayan kept the fire burning. He posted sentries. He imposed a modest discipline. He seemed altogether too organized for a vegetable dealer and former slave.

The dark dream, the same as those before, was particularly vivid, though when day came I retained only an impression of a voice calling my name. Unsettling, but I thought it just a trick of my mind.

Somewhere, somehow, the night rewarded Narayan with bounty enough to provide everyone a meager breakfast.

I led the mob out at first light, as promised, amidst reports that enemy cavalry were approaching the hills. Discipline was a pleasant surprise, considering.

8

Dejagore is surrounded by a ring of hills. The plain is lower than the land beyond the hills. Only a dry climate keeps that basin from becoming a lake. Portions of two rivers have been diverted to supply irrigation to the hill farms and water for the city. I kept the band near one of the canals.

The Shadowmasters were preoccupied with Dejagore. While they weren't pressing me I wasn't interested in covering a lot of ground. The future I'd chosen would be no easy conquest. The chance that the enemy might appear encouraged discipline. I hoped to keep that possibility alive till I instilled a few positive habits.

"Narayan, I need your advice."

"Mistress?"

"We'll have trouble holding them together once they feel safe." I always talked as though he, Ram, and Sindhu were extensions of myself. They never protested.

"I know, Mistress. They want to go home. The adventure is over." He grinned his grin. I was sick of it already. "We're trying to convince them they're part of something fated. But they have a lot to unlearn."

That they did. Taglian culture was a religious confusion I hadn't begun to fathom, tangled in caste systems which made no sense. I asked questions but no one understood. Things were as they were. It was the way they'd always been. I was tempted to declare the mess obsolete. But I didn't have the power. I hadn't had that much power in the north. Some things can't be swept away by dictate.

I continued asking questions. If I understood it even a little I could manipulate the system.

"I need a reliable cadre, Narayan. Men I can count on no matter what. I want you to find those men."

"As you say, Mistress, so shall it be." He grinned. That might have been a defensive reflex learned as a slave. Still . . . The more I saw of Narayan the more sinister he seemed.

Yet why? He was essentially Taglian, low caste. A vegetable vendor with a wife and children and a couple of grandchildren already, last he had heard. One of those backbone of the nation sorts, quiet, who just kept plugging away at life. Half the time he acted like I was his favorite daughter. What was sinister in that?

Ram had more to recommend him as strange. He was twenty-three and a widower. His marriage had been a love match, rare in Taglios where marriages are always arranged. His wife had died in childbirth, bearing a stillborn infant. That had left him bitter and depressed. I suspect he joined the legions looking for death.

I didn't find out anything about Sindhu. He wouldn't talk until you forced him and he was creepier than Narayan. Still, he did what he was told, did it well, and asked no questions.

I've spent my entire life in the company of sinister characters. For centuries I was wed to the Dominator, the most sinister ever. I could cope with these small men.

None of the three were particularly religious, which was curious. Religion pervades Taglios. Every minute of every day of every life is a part of the religious experience, is ruled by religion and its obligations. I was troubled till I noted a generally reduced level of religious fervor. I picked a man and quizzed him.

His answer was elementary. "There ain't no priests here."

That made sense. No society consists entirely of committed true believers. And what these men had seen had been enough to displace the foundations of faith. They'd been pulled out of their safe, familiar ruts and had been thrown hard against facts the traditional answers didn't explain. They'd never be the same. Once they took their experiences home Taglios wouldn't be the same.

The band trebled in size. I had better than six hundred followers hailing from all three major religions and a few splinter cults. I had more than a hundred former slaves who weren't Taglian at all. They could make good soldiers once they gained some confidence. They had no homes to run to. The band would be their home.

The problem with the mix was that every day was a holy day for somebody. If we'd had priests along there would have been trouble.

They began to feel safe. That left them free to indulge old prejudices, to grow lax in discipline, to forget the war and, most irritating, to remember that I was a woman.

In law and custom Taglian women are less favored than cattle. Cattle are less easily replaced. Women who gain status or power do so in the shadows, through men they can influence or manipulate.

One more hurdle I'd have to leap. Maybe the biggest.

I summoned Narayan one morning. "We're a hundred miles from Dejagore." I wasn't in a good mood. I'd had the dream again. It had left my nerves raw. "We're safe for the moment." The confidence of the men in their safety showed as they started their day. "I'm going to make some major changes. How many men are reliable?"

He preened. Smug little rat. "A third. Maybe more if put to the test."

"That many? Really?" I was surprised. It wasn't evident to me.

"You see only the other sort. Some men learned discipline and tolerance in the legions. The slaves came out of bondage filled with hatred. They want revenge. They know no Taglian can lead them against the Shadowmasters. Some even sincerely believe in you for yourself."

Thank you for that, little man. "But most will have trouble following me?"

"Maybe." That fawning grin. Hint of cunning. "We Taglians don't deal well with upheavals in the natural order."

"The natural order is that the strong rule and the rest follow. I'm strong, Narayan. I'm like nothing Taglios has ever seen. I haven't yet shown myself to Taglios. I hope Taglios never sees me angry. I'd rather spend my wrath on the Shadowmasters."

He bowed several times, suddenly frightened.

"Our ultimate destination remains Ghoja. You may pass that word. We'll collect survivors there, winnow them and rebuild. But I don't intend to get there till we have this force whipped into shape."

"Yes, Mistress."

"Collect whatever weapons are available. Take no arguments. Redistribute them to the men you think reliable. Assign those men to march in the left-hand file. The men to their right are to be religiously mixed. They are to be separated from those they knew before Dejagore."

"That may cause trouble."

"Good. I want to pinpoint its sources. I'll give it back with interest. Go on. Get them disarmed before they understand what's happening. Ram. Give him a hand."

"But . . ."

"I can look out for myself, Ram." His protection was a nuisance.

Narayan did move fast. Only a few men had to be separated from their weapons by force.

Organized according to my orders, we marched all day, till they were too exhausted to complain. I halted them in the evening and had Narayan form them for review, with the reliables in the rear. I donned my armor, mounted one of the black stallions, rode out to review them with little witchfires prancing about me There wasn't much to those. I hadn't made large strides recapturing my talent.

The armor, horse, and fires formed the visible aspect of a character called

Lifetaker, whom I had created before the Company moved to the Main to face the Shadowmasters at Ghoja. In concert with Croaker's Widowmaker she was supposed to intimidate the enemy by being something larger than life, archetypally deadly. My own men could use a little intimidation now. In a land where sorcery was little more than a rumor the witchfires could be enough.

I passed the formation slowly, studying the soldiers. They understood the situation. I was looking for that which I would not tolerate, the man disinclined to do things my way.

I rode past again. After centuries of watching people it wasn't difficult to spot potential troublemakers. "Ram." I pointed out six men. "Send them away. With the nothing they had when they joined us." I spoke so my voice carried. "Next winnowing, those chosen will taste the lash. And the third winnowing will be a celebration of death."

A stir passed through the ranks. They heard the message.

The chosen six went sullenly. I shouted at the others, "Soldiers! Look at the man to your right! Now look at the man to your left! Look at me! You see soldiers, not Gunni, not Shadar, not Vehdna. Soldiers! We're fighting a war against an implacable and united enemy. In the line of battle it won't be your gods at your left and your right, it will be men like those standing there now. Serve your gods in your heart if you must, but in this world, in the camp, on the march, on the field of battle, you won't set your gods before me. You'll own no higher master. Till the last Shadowmaster falls, no reward or retribution of god or prince will find you more swiftly or surely than mine."

I suspected that was maybe pushing too hard too soon. But there wasn't much time to create my cadre.

I rode off while they digested it. I dismounted, told Ram, "Dismiss them. Make camp. Send me Narayan."

I unsaddled my mount, settled on the saddle. A crow landed nearby, cocked its head. Several more circled above. Those black devils were everywhere. You couldn't get away.

Croaker had been paranoid about them. He'd believed they were following him, spying on him, even talking to him. I thought it was the pressure. But their omnipresence did get irritating.

No time for Croaker. He was gone. I was walking a sword's edge. Neither tears nor self-pity would bring him back.

During the journey north I'd realized that I'd done more than lose my talent at the Barrowland. I'd given up. So I'd lost my edge during the year-plus since.

Croaker's fault. His weakness. He'd been too understanding, too tolerant, too willing to give second chances. He'd been too optimistic about people. He couldn't believe there is an essential darkness shadowing the human soul. For all his cynicism about motives he'd believed that in every evil person there was good trying to surface.

I owe my life to his belief but that doesn't validate it.

Narayan came, sneaky as a cat. He gave me his grin.

"We've gained ground, Narayan. They took that well enough. But we have a long way to go."

"The religion problem, Mistress?"

"Some. But that's not the worst hurdle. I've overcome such before." I smiled at his surprise. "I see doubts. But you don't know me. You know only what you've heard. A woman who abandoned a throne to follow the Captain? Eh? But I wasn't the spoiled, heartless child you imagine. Not a brat with a pinch of talent who fell heir to some petty crown she didn't want. Not a dunce who ran off with the first adventurer who'd have her."

"Little is known except that you were the Captain's Lady," he admitted. "Some think as you suggest. Your companions scarcely hinted at your antecedents. I think you're much more, but how much more I dare not guess."

"I'll give you a hint." I was amused. For all Narayan seemed to want me to be something untraditional he was startled whenever I didn't behave like a Taglian woman. "Sit, Narayan. It's time you understood where you're placing your bets."

He looked me askance but settled. The crow watched him. His fingers teased at that fold of black cloth.

"Narayan, the throne I gave up was the seat of an empire so broad you couldn't have walked it east to west in a year. It spanned two thousand miles from north to south. I built it from a beginning as humble as this. I started before your grandfather's grandfather was born. And it wasn't the first empire I created."

He grinned uneasily. He thought I was lying.

"Narayan, the Shadowmasters were my slaves. Powerful as they are. They disappeared during a great battle twenty years ago. I believed them dead till we unmasked the one we killed in Dejagore.

"I'm weakened now. Two years ago there was a great battle in the northernmost region of my empire. The Captain and I put down a wakening evil left over from the first empire I created. To succeed, to prevent that evil from breaking loose, I had to allow my powers to be neutralized. Now I'm winning them back, slowly and painfully."

Narayan couldn't believe. He was the son of his culture. I was a woman. But he wanted to believe. He said, "But you're so young."

"In some ways. I never loved before the Captain. This shell is a mask, Narayan. I entered this world before the Black Company passed this way the first time. I'm old, Narayan. Old and wicked. I've done things no one would be-lieve. I know evil, intrigue, and war like they're my children. I nurtured them for centuries.

"Even as the Captain's lover I was more than a paramour. I was the Lieu-tenant, his chief of staff.

"I'm the Captain now, Narayan. While I survive the Company survives. And goes on. And finds new life. I'm going to rebuild, Narayan. It may wear another name for a while but behind the domino it will *be* the Black Company. *And* it will be the instrument of my will."

Narayan grinned that grin. "You may be Her indeed."

"I may be who?"

"Soon, Mistress. Soon. It's not yet time. Suffice it to say that not everyone greeted the return of the Black Company with despair." His eyes went shifty.

"Say that, then." I decided not to press him. I needed him pliable. "For the moment. We're building an army. We're woefully beggared of an army's most precious resource, veteran sergeants. We have no one who can teach.

"Tonight, before they eat, sort the men by religion. Organize them in squads of ten, three from each cult plus one non-Taglian. Assign each squad a permanent place in the camp and the order of march. I want no intercourse be-tween squads till each can elect a leader and his second. They'd better work out how to get along. They'll be stuck in those squads."

Another risk. The men were not in the best temper. But they were isolated from the priesthoods and culture which reinforced their prejudices. Their priests had done their thinking for them all their lives. Out here they had no-body but me to tell them what to do.

"I won't approach Ghoja before the squads pick leaders. Fighting amongst squad members should be punished. Set up whipping posts before you make the assignments. Send the squads to supper as you form them. Learning to cook together will help." I waved him away.

He rose. "If they can eat together they can do anything together, Mistress."

"I know." Each cult sustained an absurd tangle of dietary laws. Thus, this approach. It should undermine prejudice at its most basic level.

These men would not rid themselves of ingrained hatred but would set it aside around those with whom they served. It's easier to hate those you don't know than those you do. When you march with someone and have to trust him with your life it's hard to keep hating irrationally.

I tried to keep the band preoccupied with training. Those who had been through it with the hastily raised legions helped, mainly by getting the others to march in straight lines. Sometimes I despaired. There was just so much I could do. There was only one of me.

I needed a firm power base before I dared the political lists.

Fugitives joined us. Some went away again. Some didn't survive the disciplinary demands. The rest strove to become soldiers.

I was free with punishments and freer with rewards. I tried to nurture pride and, subtly, the conviction that they were better men than any who didn't belong to the band, the conviction that they could trust no one who wasn't of the band.

I didn't spare myself. I slept so little I had no time to dream, or didn't remember that I'd dreamed. Every free moment I spent nagging my talent. I'd need it soon.

It *was* coming back slowly. Too slowly.

It was like having to learn to walk again after a prolonged illness.

Though I wasn't trying to move quickly I outdistanced most of the survivors. For loners and small groups, foraging outweighed speed. Once I slowed to avoid reaching Ghoja, though, more and more caught up. Not many decided to enlist.

Already the band was recognizably alien. It scared outsiders.

I guessed maybe ten thousand men had escaped the debacle. How many would survive to reach Ghoja? If Taglios was fortunate, maybe half. The land had turned hostile.

Forty miles from Ghoja and the Main, just inside territory historically Taglian, I ordered a real camp built with a surrounding ditch. I chose a meadow on the north bank of a clean brook. The south bank was forested. The site was pleasant. I planned to stay, rest, train, till my foragers exhausted the countryside.

For days incoming fugitives had reported enemy light cavalry hunting behind them. An hour after we began making camp I got a report of smoke south of the wood. I walked the mile to the far side, saw a cloud rising from a village six miles down the road. They were that close.

Trouble? It had to be considered.

An opportunity? Unlikely at this stage.

Narayan came running through the dusk. "Mistress. The Shadowmasters' men. They're making camp on the south side of the woods. They'll catch us tomorrow." His optimism had deserted him.

I thought about it. "Do the men know?"

"The news is spreading."

"Damn. All right. Station reliable men along the ditch. Kill anybody who tries to leave. Put Ram in charge, then come back."

"Yes, Mistress." Narayan scampered off. At times he seemed a mouse. He returned. "They're grumbling."

"Let them. As long as they don't run. Do the Shadowmasters' men know we're this close?"

Narayan shrugged.

"I want to *know*. Put out a picket line a quarter mile into the wood. Twenty good men. They're not to interfere with scouts coming north but they're to ambush them headed back." They wouldn't be expecting trouble going away. "Use men who aren't good for anything else to raise an embankment along the creek. Drive stakes into its face. Sharpen them. Find vines. Sink them in the water. There's no room to maneuver on the south bank. They'll have to come straight at us, hard. Once you've got that started, come back." Best get everybody busy and distract them from their fears. I snapped, "Narayan, wait! Find out if any of the men can handle horses."

Other than my mounts there were just a half dozen animals with the band, all strays we'd captured. I'd had to teach Ram to care for mine. Riding amongst Taglians was restricted to high-caste Gunni and rich Shadar. Bullock and buffalo were the native work animals.

It was the tenth hour when Narayan returned. In the interim I prowled. I was pleased. I saw no panic, no outright terror, just a healthy ration of fear tempered by the certainty that chances of surviving were better here than on the run. They feared my displeasure more than they feared an enemy not yet seen. Perfect.

I made a suggestion about the angle of the stakes on the face of the embankment, then went to talk with Narayan.

I told him, "We'll scout their camp now."

"Just us?" His grin was forced.

"You and me."

"Yes, Mistress. Though I'd feel more comfortable if Sindhu accompanied us."

"Can he move quietly?" I couldn't picture that bulk sneaking anywhere.

"Like a mouse, Mistress."

"Get him. Don't waste time. We'll need all the darkness we've got."

Narayan gave me an odd look, took off.

We left a password, crossed the creek. Narayan and Sindhu stole through the woods as though to stealth born. Quieter than mice. They took our pickets by surprise. Those had seen nothing of the enemy.

"Awfully sure of themselves," Sindhu grumbled, the first I'd heard him volunteer an opinion.

"Maybe they're plain stupid." The Shadowmasters' soldiers hadn't impressed me with anything but their numbers.

We spied their campfires before I expected them.

They'd camped among the trees. I hadn't foreseen that possibility. Damned inconsiderate of them.

Narayan touched my arm diffidently. Mouth to ear, he breathed, "Sentries. Wait here." He stole forward like a ghost, returned like one. "Two of them. Sound asleep. Walk carefully."

So we just strolled in to where I could see what I wanted. I studied the layout for several minutes. Satisfied, I said, "Let's go."

One of the sentries had wakened. He started up as Sindhu drifted past, firelight glistening off his broad, naked back.

Narayan's hand darted to his waist. His arm whipped, his wrist snapped, a serpent of black cloth looped around the sentry's neck. Narayan strangled him so efficiently his companion didn't waken.

Sindhu took the other with a strip of scarlet cloth.

Now I knew what peeked from their loincloths. Their weapons.

They rearranged their victims so they looked like they were sleeping with their tongues out, all the while whispering cant that sounded ritualistic. I said, "Sindhu, stay and keep watch. Warn us if they discover the bodies. Narayan. Come with me."

I hurried as much as darkness allowed. Once we reached camp I told Narayan, "That was neatly done. I want to learn that trick with the cloth."

The notion surprised him. He didn't say anything.

"Collect the ten best squads. Arm them. Also the twenty men you think best able to handle horses. Ram!"

Ram arrived as I began readying my armor. He grew troubled. "What's the matter now?" Then I saw what he'd done to my helmet. "What the hell is this? I told you clean it, not destroy it."

He was like a shy boy as he said, "This apes one aspect of the goddess Kina, Mistress. One of her names is Lifetaker. You see? In that avatar her aspect is very like this armor."

"Next time, ask. Help me into this."

Ten minutes later I stood at the center of the group I'd had Narayan assemble.

"We're going to attack them. The point isn't glory or victory. We just want to discourage them from attacking us. We're going in, we're doing a little damage, then we're getting out."

I described the encampment, gave assignments, drawing in the dirt beside a fire. "In and out. Don't waste time trying to kill them. Just hurt somebody. A dead man can be left where he falls but a wounded man becomes a burden to his comrades. Whatever happens, don't go beyond the far edge of their camp. We'll retreat when they start getting organized. Grab any weapon you can. Ram, capture every horse you can. Everybody. If you can't grab weapons grab food or tools. Nobody risk anybody's life trying to grab just one more thing. And, lastly, be quiet. We're all dead if they hear us coming."

Narayan reported the dead sentries still undiscovered. I sent him forward to eliminate as many more as he and Sindhu could manage. I had the main party cover the last two hundred yards in driblets. A hundred twenty men moving at once, no matter how they try, make noise.

I looked into the camp. Men were stirring. Looked like it was near time to change the guard.

Ram's bunch joined us. I donned my helmet, turned my back on my men, walked toward the only shelter in the camp. It would belong to the commander. I set the witchfires playing over me, unsheathed my sword.

Fires ran out its blade.

It *was* coming back.

The few southerners awake gawked.

The men poured into the camp, stabbed the sleeping, overwhelmed those who were awake. I struck a man down, reached the tent, hacked it apart as the man within reacted to the uproar. I wound up two-handed and struck off his head, grabbed it by the hair, held it high, turned to check the progress of the raid.

The southerners were making no effort to defend themselves. Two hundred must have died already. The rest were trying to get away. Could I have routed them so easily?

Sindhu and Narayan came running, prostrated themselves, banged their heads on the ground and gobbled at me in that cant they used. Crows fluttered through the trees, raucous. My men hurtled around hacking and slashing, spending the wealth of fear they'd carried through the night.

"Narayan. See what the survivors are doing. Quickly. Before they mount a counterattack. Sindhu. Help me control these men."

Narayan ran off. He came back in a few minutes. "They've started gathering a quarter mile down the road. They think a demon attacked them. They don't want to come back. Their officers are telling them they can't survive if they don't recover their camp and animals."

That was true. Maybe another glimpse of the demon would encourage them to stay away.

I got the men into a ragged line, advanced to the edge of the wood. Narayan and Sindhu sneaked ahead. I wanted warning if the southerners were inclined to fight. I'd back off.

They fled again. Narayan said they killed those officers who tried to rally them.

"Fortune smiles," I recall murmuring. I'd have to take a closer look at this demon Kina. She must have some reputation. I wondered why I'd never heard of her.

I withdrew to the captured encampment. We'd come into a lot of useful material. "Ram, get the rest of the band. Have them bring the stakes from the embankment. Narayan, think about which men are least deserving of receiving arms." There would be enough to go around now, almost.

Arms would be a trust and honor to be earned.

The change was dramatic. You'd have thought it was another Ghoja triumph. Even those who hadn't participated gained confidence. I saw it everywhere. These men had a new feeling of self-worth. They were proud to be part of a desperate enterprise and they gave me my due place in it. I walked through the camp dropping hints that soon they would be part of something with power.

That had to be nurtured, and continually fertilized with suspicion and distrust of everyone outside the band.

It takes time to forge a hammer. More time than I would get, probably. It takes years, even decades, to create a force like the Black Company, which had been carried forward on the crest of a wave of tradition.

Here I was trying to magic up a Golden Hammer, something gaudy but with no real substance, deadly only to the ignorant and unprepared.

It was time for a ceremony alienating them from the rest of the world. Time for a blood rite that would bind them to one another and me.

I had the stakes from the embankment planted along the road south of the wood. Then I had all the dead southerners decapitated and their heads placed atop the stakes, facing southward, ostensibly warning travellers who shared their ambitions.

Narayan and Sindhu were delighted. They hacked off heads with great enthusiasm. No horror touched them.

None touched me, either. I'd seen everything in my time.

10

Swan lay in the shade on the bank of the Main, lazily watching his bobber float on a still, deep pool. The air was warm, the shade was cool, the bugs were too lazy to bother him. He was half asleep. What more could a man ask?

Blade sat down. "Catch anything?"

"Nope. Don't know what I'd do if I did. What's up?"

"The Woman wants us." He meant the Radisha, whom they had found waiting when they'd reached Ghoja—much to Smoke's dismay. "She's got a job for us."

"Don't she always? You tell her to stick it in her ear?"

"Thought I'd save you that pleasure."

"I'd rather you'd saved me the walk. I'm comfortable."

"She wants us to drag Smoke somewhere he don't want to go."

"Why didn't you say so?" Swan pulled his line out of the water. There was no bait on his hook. "And I thought there weren't any fish in that crick." He left his pole against a tree, a statement of sorts. "Where's Cordy?"

"Probably there waiting. He was watching Jah. I told him already."

Swan looked across the river. "I'd kill for a pint of beer." They'd been in the brewery business in Taglios before the excitement swept them up.

Blade snorted, headed for the fortress overlooking Ghoja ford.

The fort stood on the south bank of the Main. It had been built by the Shadowmasters after their invasion of Taglios had been repulsed, to defend their conquests south of the river. The fortress had been overwhelmed by the Black Company after the victory north of the river. Taglian artisans were reinforcing it and beginning a companion fortress on the north bank.

Swan scanned the scabrous encampment west of the fortress. Eight hundred men lived there. Some were construction workers. Most were fugitives from the south. One large group particularly irked him. "Think Jah has figured out that the Woman is here?"

Jahamaraj Jah was a power-hungry Shadar priest. He had commanded the mounted auxiliaries during the southern expedition. His flight north had been so precipitous he'd beaten Swan's party to the ford by several days.

"I think he's guessed. He tried to sneak a messenger across last night." The Radisha, through Swan, had forbidden anyone to cross the river. She didn't want news of the disaster reaching Taglios before its dimensions were known.

"Uhm?"

"Messenger drowned. Cordy says Jah thinks he made it." Blade chuckled wickedly. He hated priests. Baiting them was his favorite sport. All priests, of whatever faith.

"Good. That'll keep him out of our hair till we figure out what to do with him."

"I know what to do."

"Political consequences," Swam cautioned. "That your solution to everything? Cut somebody's throat?"

"Always slows them down."

The guards at the fortress gate saluted. They were favorites of the Radisha and, though neither Blade nor Swan nor Mather wanted it, they commanded Taglios's defenses now.

Swan said, "I got to learn to think in the long term, Blade. Never thought we'd be back at this after the Black Company showed."

"You got a lot to learn, Willow."

Cordy and Smoke waited outside the room where the Radisha holed up. Smoke looked like he had a bad stomach. Like he'd make a run for it if he got a chance.

Swan said, "You're looking grim, Cordy."

"Just tired. Mostly of playing with the runt."

Swan raised an eyebrow. Cordy was the calm one, the patient guy, the one who poured oil on the waters. Smoke must have provoked him good. "She ready?"

"Whenever."

"Let's do it. I got a river full of fish waiting."

"Better figure on them getting grey hair before you get back." Mather knocked, pushed the wizard ahead of him.

The Radisha entered the room from the side as Swan closed the door. Here, in private, with men not from her own culture, she didn't pretend to a traditional sex role. "Did you tell them, Cordy?"

Willow exchanged glances with Blade. Their old buddy on a nickname basis with the Woman? Interesting. What did he call her? She didn't look like a Cuddles.

"Not yet."

"What's up?" Swan asked.

The Radisha said, "I've had my men mixing with the soldiers. They've heard rumors that the woman who was the Lieutenant of the Black Company survived. She's trying to pull the survivors together south of here."

"Best news I've heard in a while," Swan said. He winked at Blade.

"Is it?"

"I thought it was a crying shame to lose such a resource."

"I'll bet. You have a low mind, Swan."

"Guilty. Hard not to once you've had a gander at her. So she made it. Great. Gets us three off the hook. Gives you a professional to carry on."

"That remains to be seen. There'll be difficulties. Cordy. Tell them."

"Twenty-some men from the Second just came in. They'd stayed off the road to avoid the Shadowmasters' patrols. About seventy miles south of here they took a couple prisoners. The night before our guys grabbed them Kina and a ghost army supposedly attacked their camp and killed most of them."

Swan looked at Blade, at the Radisha, at Cordy again. "I missed something. Who's Kina? And what's got into Smoke?" The wizard was shaking like somebody had dunked him in ice water.

Mather and Blade shrugged. They didn't know.

The Radisha sat down. "Get comfortable." She chewed her lip. "This will be difficult to tell."

"Then just go straight at it," Swan said.

"Yes. I suppose." The Radisha collected herself. "Kina is the fourth side of the Taglian religious triangle. She belongs to none of the pantheons but terrifies everybody. She isn't named lest naming invoke her. She's very unpleasant. Fortunately, her cult is small. And proscribed. Membership is punishable by death. The penalty is deserved. The cult's rites always involve torture and murder. Even so, it persists, its members awaiting someone called the Foretold and the Year of the Skulls. It's an old, dark religion that knows no national or ethnic bounds. Its members hide behind masks of respectability. They sometimes call themselves the Deceivers. They live normal lives among the rest of the community. Anyone could belong. Few of the common people know they exist anymore."

Swan didn't get it and said so. "Don't sound much different from the Shadar Hada or Khadi avatars."

The Radisha smiled grimly. "Those are ghosts of the reality." Hada and Khadi were two aspects of the Shadar death god. "Jah could show you a thousand ways Khadi is a kitten compared to Kina." Jahamaraj Jah was a devotee of Khadi.

Swan shrugged, doubting he could tell the difference if they drew pictures.

He'd given up trying to understand the welter of Taglian gods, each with his or her ten or twenty different aspects and avatars. He indicated Smoke. "What's with him? He shakes any more we'll have to change his diaper."

"Smoke predicted a Year of Skulls—a time of chaos and bloodshed—if we employed the Black Company. He didn't believe it would come. He just wanted to scare my brother out of doing something that scared him. But he's on record as having predicted it. Now there's a chance it might come."

"Sure. Come on." Swan frowned, still lost. "Let me get this straight. There's a death cult around that makes Jah and his Khadi freaks look like a bunch of nancy boys? That scares the guano out of anybody who knows who they are?"

"Yes."

"And they worship a goddess named Kina?"

"That is the most common of many names."

"Why aren't I surprised? Is there any god down here without more aliases than a two-hundred-year-old con man?"

"Kina is the name given her by the Gunni. She has been called Patwa, Kompara, Bhomahna, and other names. The Gunni, the Shadar, the Vehdna, all find ways to accept her into their belief systems. Many Shadar who become her followers, for example, take her to be the true form of Hada or Khadi, who is just one of her Deceits."

"Gah. All right. I'll bite. There's a bad-ass in the weeds called Kina. So how come me and Cordy and Blade never heard of her before?"

The Radisha appeared mildly embarrassed. "You were shielded. You're outsiders. From the north."

"Maybe so." What did the north have to do with it? "But why the panic? One garbled thing about this Kina from a prisoner who's got no reason to tell the truth? And Smoke goes to wetting his pants? And you start foaming at the mouth? I got a little trouble taking you serious."

"Point taken. You shouldn't have been shielded. I'm sending you to check out the story."

Swan grinned. He had a lever. "Not without you stop jacking us around. Tell us the whole story. Bad enough you messed with the Black Company. You think you're going to mess us around because we weren't born in Taglios. . . ."

"Enough, Swan." The Radisha wasn't pleased.

Smoke made a whining noise. He shook his head.

"What's with him?" Willow demanded. Much more of that weirdness and he was going to strangle the old guy.

"Smoke sees a ghost in every shadow. In your case he's afraid you're spies sent ahead by the Black Company."

"Sure. Moron! That's another thing. How come everybody is so damned twitchy about those guys? They maybe kicked ass around here heading north but that was back at the dawn of time, practically. Four hundred years ago."

The Radisha ignored that. "Kina's antecedents are uncertain. She's a foreign goddess. The legends say a prince of Shadow tricked the most handsome of the Lords of Light out of his physical aspect for a year. While he wore that he seduced Mahi, Goddess of Love, and sired Kina on her. Kina grew up more beautiful than her mother but empty, without a soul, without love or compassion, but hungry to possess them. Her hunger couldn't be satisfied. She preyed upon men and gods alike, Shadow and Light. Among her names are Eater of Souls and Vampire Goddess. She so weakened the Lords of Light that the Shadows thought to conquer them and sent a horde of demons against them. The Lords of Light were so pressed they begged Kina for help. She did help, though *why* she did isn't explained. She met the demons in battle, overthrew them, and devoured them and all their wickedness."

The Radisha paused a moment. Then, "Kina became much worse than she had been, gaining the names Devourer, Destroyer, Destructor. She became a force beyond the gods, outside the balance of Light and Shadow, enemy of all. She became a terror so great Light and Shadow joined forces against her. Her father himself tricked her into falling into an enchanted sleep."

Blade muttered, "Makes as much sense as the story of any other god. Meaning it don't."

Squeaking, Smoke said, "Kina is a personification of that force some call entropy." To the Radisha, "Correct me if I'm wrong."

The Radisha ignored him. "Before Kina fell asleep she realized she'd been tricked. She took a huge breath, exhaled a minute fraction of her soul-essence, no more than a ghost of a ghost. That specter wanders the world in search of living vessels it can possess and use to bring on the Year of the Skulls. If that avatar can free enough souls and cause enough pain, Kina can be wakened."

Swan chuckled like an old woman scolding. "You believe any of that stuff?"

"What I believe doesn't matter, Swan. The Deceivers believe. If the rumor spreads that Kina has been seen, and there's *any* evidence to support it, they'll preach a crusade of murder and torture. Wait!" She raised a hand. "The Taglian people are ripe for an outburst of violence. By damming the normal discharge for generations they've created a reservoir of potential violence. The Deceivers would like that to explode, to bring on the Year of the Skulls. My brother and I would prefer to harness and direct that ferocity."

Blade grumbled about the absurdities of the theological imagination and why didn't people have sense enough to smother would-be priests in their cradles?

The Radisha said, "We don't think the Deceivers have a formal, hierarchical priesthood. They seem to form loose bands, or companies, under an elected captain. The captain appoints a priest, an omen reader, and so forth. His authority is limited. He has little influence outside his band unless he's done something to gain a reputation."

Blade said, "They don't sound so bad to me."

The Radisha scowled. "The main qualification of a priest seems to be education and probity toward his own kind. The bands indulge in crimes of all sorts. Once a year they share out their spoils according to the priest's estimation of the members' contributions toward the glory of Kina. To support his decisions, in the event of dispute, the priest keeps a detailed chronicle of the band's activities."

"Fine and dandy," Swan said. "But how about we get to what you want us to do? We supposed to drag Smoke around to see if we can sniff out what really happened to the Shadowmasters' soldiers?"

"Yes."

"Why bother?"

"I thought I just explained . . ." The Radisha controlled herself. "If that was a true apparition of Kina we have bigger troubles than we thought. The Shadowmasters may be the lesser half."

"I warned you!" Smoke squealed. "I warned you a hundred times. But you wouldn't listen. You had to bargain with devils."

"Shut up." The Radisha glared. "I'm as tired of you as Swan is. Go find out what happened. And learn what you can about the woman Lady, too."

"I can handle that," Swan said, grinning. "Come on, old buddy." He grabbed Smoke's shoulder. He asked the Radisha, "Think you can manage Jahamaraj Jah without us?"

"I can manage him."

Mounted, ready to ride, waiting for Blade and Smoke, Swan asked, "Cordy, you get the feeling you're out in the woods in the middle of the night and everybody's doing their damnedest to hide the light?"

"Uhm." Mather was more the thinker than Willow or Blade. "They're afraid if we know the whole story we'll desert. They're desperate. They've lost the Black Company. We're all that's left."

"Like the old days."

"Uhm."

The old days. Before the coming of the professionals. When their adopted homeland had made them reluctant captains because the feuding cults couldn't tolerate taking orders from native nonbelievers. A year in the field, playing blind lead the blind, overcoming political shenanigans daily, had convinced Swan that Blade had a point, that it wouldn't hurt the world a bit if you rid it of a few hundred thousand selected priests.

"You buy that Kina stuff?"

"I don't think she told any lies. She just forgot to tell the whole truth."

"Maybe when we get Smoke out there forty miles from nowhere we can squeeze it out of him."

"Maybe. As long as we don't forget what he is. We scare him too much and he's liable to show us what kind of wizard he is. Button it. They're coming."

Smoke looked like he was headed for the gallows. Blade looked as unhappy as ever. But Swan knew he was pleased. Blade figured he was going to get a chance to kick some deserving asses.

The wounded man thought he was trapped in a drug dream. He'd been a physician. He knew drugs did strange things to the mind. Dreams were strange enough. . . . He couldn't wake up.

Some fractured shard of rationality lodged in a corner of his brain watched, sensed, wondered vaguely as he drifted eternally a few feet above a landscape he seldom saw. Sometimes branches passed overhead. Sometimes there were hills in the corners of his eyes. Once he wakened while drifting through tall grass. Once he felt he was passing over a broad expanse of water.

Occasionally a huge black horse looked down at him. He thought he knew the beast but couldn't assemble the pieces in his mind.

Sometimes a figure in shapeless robing bestrode the beast, stared down out of an empty cowl.

These things were all real, he suspected. But they fell into no meaningful pattern. Only the horse seemed familiar.

Hell. He couldn't recall who *he* was. His thoughts wouldn't sequence. Probable pasts kept intruding on the apparent now, often as real.

Those intrusions were shards of battle, uncertain on the jagged edges, bright as blood in the center. Great slaughters, all. Sometimes names attached themselves. Lords. Charm. Beryl. Roses. Horse. Dejagore. Juniper. The Barrowland. Queen's Bridge. Dejagore again. Dejagore often.

Infrequently he recalled a face. The woman had marvellous blue eyes, long black hair, and always wore black. She must have been important to him. Yes. The only woman . . . Whenever she appeared she vanished again in moments, replaced by the faces of men. Unlike the bloodlettings, he could put no names to them. Yet he had known them. He felt they were ghosts, waiting to welcome him among them.

Occasionally pain consumed his chest. He was his most alert when it was most intense. The world almost made sense then. But the creature in black would come and he would tumble back amongst the dreams.

Was the black companion Death? Was this his passage to the nether realm? His mind wouldn't function well enough to examine the proposition.

He hadn't been religious. He'd believed that death was it. When you died you were dead, like a squished bug or drowned rat, and your immortality was in the minds of those you left behind.

He slept far more than he was awake. Thus time eluded him.

He experienced a moment of profound *déjà vu* as he passed beneath a solitary half-dead tree, shortly before entering a dark wood. That tree had been important somehow, sometime.

He drifted through the wood, out, across a clearing, in through the entrance of a building. It was dark inside.

A lamp found life at the edge of his vision. He descended. A flat surface pressed against his back.

The figure in black came, bent over him. A hand concealed in a black glove touched him. Consciousness fled.

He awakened ravenous. A lance of agony bored through his chest, throbbed. He was drenched in his own sweat. His head ached, felt as though it was stuffed with sodden cotton. He was running a fever. His mind worked well enough to catalog symptoms and conclude that he had been wounded and was suffering from a severe cold. That could be a lethal combination.

Memories came tumbling back like a rowdy litter of kittens, all over one another, not making much sense.

He'd led forty thousand men into battle outside Dejagore. It hadn't gone well. He'd been trying to rally the troops. An arrow out of nowhere had driven through his breastplate and chest, miraculously finding nothing vital. He'd fallen. His standard-bearer had donned his armor, trying to turn the tide with a valiant fiction.

Obviously Murgen had failed.

He made a strangling sound through a desert throat.

The figure in black appeared.

Now he remembered. It had dogged the Black Company down the length of the world, accompanied by a horde of crows. He tried to sit up.

The pain was too much for him. He was too weak.

He knew this dread thing!

It came out of nowhere, a lightning bolt, but it was conviction.

Soulcatcher!

The impossible. The dead walking . . .

Soulcatcher. One-time mentor. One-time mistress of the Black Company. More recently a deadly enemy, but still long ago. Supposedly dead for a decade and a half.

He'd been there. He'd seen her slain. He'd helped hunt her down. . . .

He tried to rise again, some vague force driving him to fight the unfightable.

A gloved hand stayed him. A gentle voice told him, "Don't strain yourself. You aren't healing well. You haven't been eating or taking enough fluids. Are you awake? Are you sensible?"

He managed a feeble nod.

"Good. I'm going to prop you up in a slightly elevated position. I'm going to feed you broth. Don't waste energy. Let your strength come back."

She propped him, had him sip through a reed. He downed a pint of broth. And kept it down. Soon a glimmer of strength trickled through his flesh.

"That's enough for now. Now we'll get you cleaned up."

He was a disgusting mess. "How long?" he croaked.

She placed a pot of water in his hands, inserted another reed. "Sip. Don't talk." She started cutting his clothing off him.

"It's been seven days since you were hit, Croaker." Her voice had become another voice entirely. It changed every time she paused. This voice was masculine, mocking, though he wasn't the mockery's object. "Your comrades still control Dejagore, to the embarrassment of the Shadowmasters. Your Mogaba is in command. He's stubborn but he could be embarrassed himself. And however stubborn he is, he can't hold out forever. The powers ranged against him are too great."

He tried to ask a question. She forestalled him. The mocking voice asked, "Her?" Wicked chuckle. "Yes. She survived. There'd be no point to this if she hadn't."

A new voice, female but as hard as a diamond arrowpoint, snarled, "She tried to kill me! Ha-ha! Yes. You were there, my love. You helped. But I don't hold a grudge. You were under her spell. You didn't know what you were doing. You'll redeem yourself by helping me take my revenge."

The man didn't respond.

She bathed him. She was free with the water.

He'd been diminished by his wound but he was still a big man, four inches over six feet tall. He was about forty-five years old. His hair was an average, unnoteworthy brown. He'd begun to go bald in front. His eyes were hard, humorless, icy blue, narrow and deeply set. He had a ragged, greying beard surrounding a thin-lipped mouth that seldom smiled. His face bore scattered reminders of a childhood pox and more than a few memories of acne. He might have been moderately good-looking once. Time had been unkind. Even in repose his face looked hard and a little off center.

He didn't look like what he had been all his adult life, the Black Company's historian and physician. His appearance was more suited to the role he had inherited, that of Captain.

He'd described himself as looking like a child molester waiting for a chance to strike. He wasn't comfortable with his appearance.

Soulcatcher scrubbed him with a vigor that recalled his mother's. "Don't take the skin off."

"Your wound is healing slowly. You'll have to tell me what I did wrong." She'd never been a healer. She was a destroyer.

Croaker was puzzled by her interest. He wasn't valuable. What was he? Just a dinged-up old mercenary, alive well beyond the expectations of his kind. He squeaked a question.

She laughed, voice filled with childlike delight. "Vengeance, dear. A simple, gentle, guileful vengeance. And I won't lay a hand on her. I'll let her do it to herself." She patted his cheek, drew a finger along the line of his jaw.

"It took a while but I knew the moment was inevitable. Fated. The consummation, the exchange of the magic, deadly three words. Fated. I sensed it before you met." Again the childlike laughter. "She was an age finding something so precious. My vengeance will be to take it away."

Croaker closed his eyes. He could not yet reason closely. He understood only that he was in no immediate danger. The plot was easily voided. He would become a tool of no value, broken.

He put it out of mind. First he had to heal. Time enough later to do what had to be done.

More laughter. This from a woman adult and knowing. "Remember when we campaigned together, Croaker? The trick we played on Raker? The fun we had tormenting Limper?"

He grunted. He remembered. Everything but the fun.

"Remember how you always thought I could read your mind?"

He remembered that. And the terror it had inspired. That old fear crept back.

"You *do* remember." She laughed again. "I'm so glad. We're going to have such fun. The whole world thinks we're dead. You can get away with anything when you're dead." Her laugh gained an edge of madness. "We'll haunt them, Croaker. That's what we'll do."

He'd regained enough strength to walk. With help. His captor made him walk, forced him to gain strength. But still he slept most of the time. And dreamed terrible dreams when he did.

The place anchored the dreams. He didn't know that. His dreams told him it wasn't a good place, that the very trees and earth and stone remembered evils done there.

He felt they were true dreams but found no supporting evidence while he was awake. Unless he counted the ominous crows. Always there were the crows, tens and hundreds and thousands of crows.

Standing in the doorway to their shelter—a half-ruined stone structure, buried in vegetation, in the heart of a dark wood—he asked, "What is this place? The wood where I chased you a few months ago?"

"Yes. It's the holy grove of those who worship Kina. If we cleared the creepers you could see carved representations. Once it was important to the Black Company, who took it from the Shadar. The ground is filled with bones."

He turned slowly, looked into her empty cowl. He wouldn't look at the box she carried. He knew what must be in it. "The Black Company?"

"They made sacrifices here. One hundred thousand prisoners of war."

Croaker blanched. That wasn't something he wanted to hear. He had a long romance with the history of the Company. There was no place in that for a wicked past. "Truth?"

"Truth, my love. I've seen the books the wizard Smoke concealed from you in Taglios. They include the missing volumes of your Annals. Your forebears were cruel men. Their mission required the sacrifice of a million souls."

His stomach knotted. "To what? To whom? Why?"

She hesitated. He knew she wasn't being honest when she said, "That wasn't clear. Your lieutenant Mogaba might know, though."

It wasn't what she said but the way she said it, the voice she used. He shuddered. And he believed. Mogaba had been strange and secretive throughout his association with the Company. What was he doing to the Company's traditions now?

"Kina's disciples come here twice a year. Their Festival of Lights comes in a month. We have to finish before then."

Troubled, Croaker asked, "Why *are* we here?"

"We're recovering our health." She laughed. "Where we won't be bothered.

Everyone shuns this place. Once I've nursed you back you're going to help me."
Still amused, she pushed back her cowl.

She had no head.

She lifted that box she always carried, a battered thing a foot to a side,
opened a little door. A face looked out. It was a beautiful face, like the face of his
lover, though less careworn and lacking life's animation.

Impossible.

His stomach knotted again. He recalled the day that head had been struck
from its body, to lie in the dust staring up at him and Lady. Her sister. It had
been a blow well-earned. Soulcatcher had betrayed the Lady. Soulcatcher had
meant to supplant her sister as ruler of the empire.

"I can't do anything like that."

"Of course you can. And you will. Because it will keep both of you alive. We
all want to live, don't we? I want her to live because I want her to hurt. I want to
live because I want to watch her hurt. You want to live because of her, because
you revere the Company, because . . ." Gentle laughter. "Because where there's
life there's hope."

Thunder stampeded. Silver lightning lashed the wine-dark clouds, cracked the
umber sky. A mold-grey horde howled across a basalt plain, toward the
golden chariots of the gods.

A figure stepped from the line, ten feet tall, polished ebony, naked, lifting each
foot knee-high to the side, then swinging the leg forward and stamping down. The
earth shook.

The figure was female, perfection but hairless, wore a girdle of children's
skulls. Her face was protean, one moment radiant dark beauty, the next a nightmare of burning eyes and vampire fangs.

The figure seized a demon and devoured him, rending, tearing, flinging entrails. Demon blood spurted and sprayed. It burned holes in the face of the plain.

The figure's jaws distended. She swallowed the demon's head whole. A lump ran down her neck like a mouse bulging a snake's throat.

The horde beset her. And could do her no harm. She devoured another screaming devil, then another and another. With each she grew and waxed more terrible.

I am here, Daughter. Open to me. I am your dream. I am power."

The voice floated like gossamer in golden caverns where old men sat beside the way, frozen in time, immortal, unable to move an eyelid. Mad, some covered by fairy webs of ice, as though a thousand spiders had spun with threads of frozen water. Above, an enchanted forest of icicles hung from the cavern roof.

"Come. I am what you seek. You are my child."

But the footing was treacherous, making it impossible to advance or retreat.

The voice called, summoned, with infinite patience.

This time I remembered both dreams when I wakened. I still shivered with the chill of those caverns. The dream was different every time, I thought, and yet was the same. A summoning.

I'm not stupid. I've seen enough incredibilities to know the dreams were more than nightmares. Something had singled me out. Something was trying to recruit me, to what cause I couldn't yet guess. The method was ancient. I've used it a thousand times. Offer power, wealth, whatever the desire is, dangling the lure till the fish bites, never revealing the cost.

Did this thing know me? Unlikely. I was receptive so it was trying to pull me.

I wouldn't accept it as a god, though it might want to be thought one. I've met only one god, Old Father Tree, master of the Plain of Fear. And he's no god in the accepted sense, only a being of immense longevity and power.

This world has shown me just two beings stronger than I. My husband, the Dominator, whom I cast into oblivion. In a thousand years he may be remembered as a dark god.

And Father Tree, greater than ever I could have been, who has roots anchoring him. He can project his power outside the Plain of Fear only through his servants.

Croaker told me about a third power that lies buried under Father Tree, imprisoned while the tree survives. The tree is immortal by human standards.

Where there are three great powers there could be more. The world is old. Yesterday is shrouded. Those who become great in one age often do so by mining the secrets of ages past. Who knows how many great evils lie beneath this haunted earth?

Who knows but what the gods of all men in all ages are but echoes of those who followed a path like mine and have, nevertheless, fallen victim to implacable time?

Not a thought to soothe the soul. Time is the enemy whose patience can't be exhausted.

Mistress? Are you troubled?" Narayan's grin was absent. He showed genuine concern.

"Oh." He'd come up quietly. "No. A bad dream that lingered. Nightmares are the coin we pay for doing what we have to do."

He looked at me oddly.

"Do you have nightmares, Narayan?" I'd begun to press him quietly, to weigh his answers to questions probing his flanks.

"Never, Mistress. I sleep like a baby." He turned slowly, surveyed the camp. The countryside was shrouded in mist. "What's the agenda today?"

"Do we have practice weapons enough for a mock combat? One battalion against the other?" I had enough men to field two battalions of four hundred men, with a few hundred left to carry out camp duties and provide one inept cavalry troop.

"Barely. You want that?"

"I'd like to. But how can we reward the victors?" Training involved competitions now, with rewards for winning and for effort. Superior effort, even in losing, deserves recognition. Recognition encourages soldiers to give their best.

"There's relief from fatigues, foraging, and sentry duty."

"That's a possibility." I was also considering letting individuals send for their wives after we moved to Ghoja.

Ram brought me a breakfast bowl. We weren't eating well but we were getting bulk enough, so far. Narayan asked, "How much longer can you stall here?"

"Not long." Time was turning against us. The existence of the band had to be known up north. Potential political enemies would be digging in.

"Instead of mock combat we'll have a review. Spread a rumor that I'm thinking of moving out if what I see pleases me." That ought to motivate them.

"Yes, Mistress." Narayan retreated. He gathered his cronies, a dozen men who showed snips of colored cloth at their waists.

An interesting group. They sprang from all three major religions, two minor cults, and from among the liberated foreign slaves. They pretty much ran the camp though only Narayan and Ram had official standing. They kept the peace. The men weren't quite sure how to take them, but responded seriously because of that aura of the sinister that I'd noted myself.

Narayan admitted nothing. He handled my probes deftly. There was no doubt he directed the dozen, though several sprang from higher castes.

I kept an eye on him. Time would betray him—if he didn't open up, as he hinted he might.

For the moment he was too useful to press.

I nodded approval. "They almost look like soldiers." We'd have to get them uniform dress.

Narayan nodded. He seemed smug, as though his genius had produced our triumph and sparked a renascent spirit.

"How're the riding lessons coming?" Just making talk. I knew. Abysmally. None of these clowns belonged to a caste that got closer to a horse than to trail along behind cleaning up. But, damn, it would be a sin to waste those mounts.

"Poorly. Though a few men show promise. Not including myself or Ram. We were born to walk."

"Show promise" had become his favorite expression. In reference to everything. As he taught me to use the strangler's kerchief, or *rumel*, at my insistence, he said I showed promise.

I suspected he was surprised at how easily I picked it up. Its manipulation came as naturally as breathing, as though it was a skill I'd had all along. Maybe it came of centuries of practice at the quick, subtle gestures needed to manipulate sorceries.

"You were saying you were going to move?" Narayan asked. "Mistress." The honorific was becoming an afterthought. Narayan remained Taglian. He was beginning to take me for granted.

"Our foragers are having to range pretty far."

Narayan didn't reply but seemed reluctant to go.

I had a feeling I was being watched. At first I credited it to the crows. They kept me uncomfortable. Now I understood Croaker's reaction better. They didn't behave the way crows ought. I'd mentioned them to Narayan. He'd grinned and called them a good omen.

Meaning they were a bad omen for someone else.

I scanned our surroundings. The crows were there, in their scores, but . . . "Narayan, collect the dozen best horsemen. I'm taking a patrol out."

"But . . . Do you think . . . ?"

How could I get through? "I'm no garden rose. I'm taking a patrol out."

"As you command, Mistress, so shall it be."

It had better, Narayan. It had better.

13

Swan glanced at Blade. The black man's attitude toward Smoke had grown from disdain into contempt. The wizard had no more spine than a worm. He shook like a leaf.

Cordy said, "That's her."

Swan nodded. He grinned but kept his thoughts to himself. "She's putting something together. That gang is more organized than any I've seen down here."

They backed off the knoll from which they'd been watching the camp. Blade said, "We going to drop in?" He had hold of the wizard's sleeve like he expected the runt to run.

"Not yet. I want to circle around, check it out down south. Shouldn't be that far to where they hit the Shadowmasters' men. I want to see the place. If we can find it."

Cordy asked, "Think they know we're here?"

"What?" The idea startled Swan.

"You said they're organized. Nobody ever accused the Lady of not being efficient. She should have pickets out."

Swan thought. No one had entered or left the camp, but Mather had a point. If they wanted to remain unnoticed they'd better move on. "You're right. Let's go. Blade, you were down here before. Know how to cross that creek somewhere that's not too far out of the way?"

Blade nodded. In those desperate days before the Black Company picked up the reins he'd led guerrillas behind the Shadowmasters' main forces.

"Lead on. Smoke, old buddy, I wish I could get a peek inside your head. I never seen anybody so ready to drizzle down his leg."

The wizard said nothing.

Blade found a game ford three miles east of the south road, led the way through woods narrower than Swan expected. When they reached the southern side, Blade said, "Road's two miles that way."

"I figured." The sky was dark with buzzards. "That's where we'll find our dead men."

That was the place.

The air was still. The stench hung like a poisonous miasma. Neither Swan nor Mather had a stomach strong enough to let them take a close look. Blade, though, seemed to have no sense of smell.

He returned. Swan said, "You look green around the gills."

"Not much but bones left. Been a while. Two hundred, three hundred men. Hard to tell now. Animals been at them. One thing. No heads."

"Eh?"

"No heads. Somebody cut them off."

Smoke moaned, then chucked his breakfast. His mount shied.

"No heads?" Swan asked. "I don't get it."

Mather said, "I've got an idea. Come on." He rode south, toward where crows circled, dipped, and squabbled.

They found the heads.

Blade asked, "Want to get a count?" He chuckled.

"No. Let's drop in on our friends."

Smoke made protesting noises.

Cordy asked, "You still hot to trot with your proud beauty?"

Swan couldn't think of a flip answer. "Maybe I'm starting to see Smoke's viewpoint. Don't let me get on her bad side."

Blade said, "Only a mile to their camp straight up the road."

Swan snorted. "We'll go around, thank you."

After they crossed the game ford, Mather suggested, "Suppose we go up the road a ways and come down like we don't know nothing about back there? See what they say if they think we just rode in."

"Stop whining, Smoke," Swan said. "Go with it. You got no choice. You're right, Cordy. It'll give us a clue if she's going to play games."

They rode north till they were behind a rise, turned west to the road, then turned south. They were almost back to the crest when Mather, in the lead, yelled, "Yo! Look out!"

14

We crossed the creek into the wood, walking our mounts behind Sindhu, who had scouted till he knew every leaf and twig of the surrounding terrain. He led us along a meandering game trail which paralleled the creek going westward. I wondered what had become of the game. We hadn't seen anything bigger than a squirrel. A few native deer might have eased the food problem, though neither Gunni nor Shadar touch meat.

It was a long walk. My companions grumbled and bickered.

The watching presence centered on a grove on a knoll whence it would be possible to observe events in our camp. I'd lapsed. I'd been thinking too far ahead. If I'd had the sense of a goose I'd have had a squad posted there. The outlying pickets were too scattered to spot everything moving in the area, even if people weren't sneaking around. Fugitives slipped through all the time. They left their traces.

I had a good idea what I'd find on that knoll. Somebody from up north who'd heard rumors and had gotten worried that I might be trouble. I meant to be a lot, for the Shadowmasters and anybody who got between us.

We crossed the creek a few miles downstream, out of sight of the knoll, moved back to the east, and discovered that there was no way to approach the grove unseen the last third of a mile. I told the men, "All we can do is ride straight at it. Let's do it without getting in a hurry. Maybe they won't run till we're so close they can't get away."

I didn't know if they could control themselves. The excitement had them again. They were pumped up, scared and eager.

"Let's go."

We'd covered half the open ground when the watchers flushed like quail. "Shadar," somebody noted.

Yes. Mounted Shadar, in uniform, cavalry equipped. "Jahamaraj Jah's men!" I snapped.

The men cursed. Even those who were Shadar.

Jah was the leading Shadar priest in Taglios. Croaker's doing. Jah's concession to his debt hadn't lasted through the fighting at Dejagore. He and his cavalry had abandoned the field while the outcome was in question. Most of the men had seen them run, or had heard. I'd been pushing the idea that the battle would've been ours had Jah stood his ground.

It could be true. Jah had contributed nothing when a feather's weight might have tilted the balance.

I thought he'd run because he'd suffered an opportunistic flash. He'd intuited that the battle would go poorly and had decided to beat everybody home. He'd play a strong hand there because he'd be the only man with a military force—however inept—to back him up.

He deserved some special thought now.

I didn't have to order a chase. There were five Shadar. Their flight was proof they were blackhearts. The men rode with blood in their eyes. Unfortunately, the Shadar were better riders.

I did want to talk to them. I urged my stallion to his best pace and closed up fast.

No everyday mount stood a chance against him.

The Shadar hit the north road. As I nosed up on the most laggardly the leaders swept over the crest. And collided with riders headed south.

Horses shied. Men yelled. Riders came unhorsed. I circled a Shadar who regained his feet and tried to run. He'd lost his helmet. I grabbed him by the hair, ran him fifty yards before turning to examine the victims of the collision.

Well. Swan, Mather, and Blade. And that sneaking twit of a hedge wizard, Smoke. What now?

Mather, Smoke, and Blade had kept their seats. Swan was on the ground, groaning and swearing. He got up, swore some more, kicked a fallen Shadar, looked around for his horse.

Smoke was rattled right down to his ankles. He had no color left, was whispering some sort of prayer.

Mather and Blade ignored Swan's histrionics. I presumed that meant he wasn't hurt.

My captive tried to get away. I ran him a few yards, let him loose when the horse was moving faster than he could keep up. He flung forward, slid on his face, stopped at Swan's feet. Swan sat down on him. I asked Mather, "What are you doing here?" He was the only one of the bunch who made straight sense.

"The Radisha sent us. Wants to know what's happening down here. There have been rumors. Some say you're alive, some say dead."

"I'm not yet. Not quite."

My men arrived. "Ghopal. Hakim. Take these two somewhere and ask them why they were snooping." They were Narayan's cronies, the only two who could ride. He'd probably sent them along to keep an eye on things.

Swan got up and leaned against Mather's leg. "You don't have to twist no arms to find that out. Been some wild rumors lately. You've got Jah jumpy as a cat in a kennel."

"Oh?"

"Things were going his way. He got back from Dejagore before anybody else. Only bad luck put the Radisha at Ghoja before him. She closed the ford. He still figured he had the world by the oysters, then here comes word somebody's kicked the feathers off a gang of the Shadowmasters' boys. Right behind comes a rumor that it was you. You not being dead don't look so good for Jah's ambitions. The Company picked up a lot of respect putting it together so fast. Made all those priests look like conniving, selfish jerks."

Blade chuckled.

Mather said, "You collected some of that respect, being a woman and having everybody know how much you had to do with it falling together." He looked me in the eye. "But being a woman is going to be a handicap now."

"I've been on my own before, Mather." And I hadn't been happy a moment. But happiness is a fleeting creature. It's no birthright. Not anything I expect but something I accept when I stumble into it. Meantime, power will do nicely. "And Jah has liabilities. He's vulnerable. I have a thousand men over there. Every one will tell you Jah ran out on us at Dejagore. We would've won if it wasn't for him."

Swan surprised me. "We watched the battle. We saw. So did a lot of men who've come in. Even some of Jah's own men admit it."

"A liability," Mather said. "But it's not going to undo him."

Ghopal reminded me that three Shadar had escaped. True. And they would fly straight to their master, who was sure to make a move. But I doubted he'd do it right away. He was a vacillator. He'd worry a while before committing himself.

"Back to camp. Swan. Come. Ghopal. Bring the prisoners." I rode ahead as hard as the stallion could carry me.

"Sound the alarm and the recall," I told the soldiers at the north gate. "Narayan! Ram!"

They came running. Narayan gasped, "What is it, Mistress?"

"We're pulling out. Right now. Forced march. Get the men ready. Let the horses carry most of the load. Make sure each man carries food. We won't stop for meals. Move."

They scooted.

It was midafternoon. Ghoja was forty miles away, a ten-hour jaunt if everyone kept the pace. If the night wasn't too dark. It shouldn't be if the sky stayed clear. There'd be a quarter moon rising an hour after sunset. Not a lot of light, but maybe enough.

The horns that we'd taken from the Shadowmasters' cavalry kept sounding recall. The pickets came running. The gang I'd left up the road arrived. Swan and Mather were impressed by the chaos.

Mather said, "You've taught well."

"I think so."

"What're you fixing to do?" Swan asked.

"Take charge at Ghoja before Jah can react."

He groaned.

"You have a problem with that?"

"Only that we just got finished riding down here. Forty more miles and I won't have a spine left."

"So walk. Sindhu! Come here." I took the wide man aside, gave him instructions. He left smiling, gathered two dozen men with strong stomachs, mostly his cronies, and crossed the creek. I sent another man to round up the poles we used for practice pikes and spears.

Swan asked, "You mind if we get something to eat?"

"Help yourself. Then find me. I want to talk to you."

Idiot. He gave me a big, nervous smile. I didn't need to be a mind-reader to get what was going on in the back of his head.

The troops got it together faster than I expected. They had the word. Ghoja. Straight through.

I still had a serious problem, lack of a command structure. I had solid squads and the squad leaders by tens had picked company commanders, but none of those had had more than a few days' practice. And neither of my formally organized battalions had anyone in charge.

"Mather."

He set his food aside. "Ma'am?"

"You strike me as a responsible man. Also, you have field experience and a reputation. I have two battalions of four hundred men but no commanders. My man Narayan can muddle through with one if I keep him out of trouble. I need somebody to handle the other. A known hero would be perfect—if I thought he wouldn't work against me."

Mather looked me in the eye for several seconds. "I work for the Radisha. I couldn't."

"I could."

I turned. That was Blade.

Smoke had a squeaking fit.

Blade grinned, the first I'd seen him do so. "I don't owe you anything, little man." He turned to Swan. "What did I say? Ain't over yet."

Something flickered across Swan's face. He wasn't happy. "You're putting us in a bad spot, Blade."

"You putting yourself there, Swan. You said it, what kind of people they are.

Soon as they got what they want they going to stick it in you. That right, wizard? Like you done the Black Company?"

Smoke staggered. He would've been dead if he'd had a bad heart. He looked like he expected me to roast him. I smiled. I'd let him stew a little first. "I'll accept your offer, Blade. Come meet your hundred-leaders."

Once we were out of earshot of the others I asked, "What did you mean by that remark?"

"Less than it sounded. The wizard, the Radisha, the Prahbrindrah, they hurt you more by deceit than treachery. They withheld information. I can't tell you what. I don't know. They thought we were spies you sent ahead. But I can tell you they never meant to keep their agreement. For some reason they don't want you to get to Khatovar."

Khatovar. Croaker's mystery destination, the place the Black Company had originated. For four hundred years the Company moved northward slowly, in the service of various princes, till it came into mine, then of my enemies, and was reduced to a handful of men. After the battle in the Barrowland, Croaker turned back south with fewer followers than my squad leaders had today.

We'd gathered a man here, a man there, and when we'd reached Taglios we'd discovered we couldn't cross the last four hundred miles because the principalities of the Shadowmasters lay between us and Khatovar. There was only one way to cover those final miles. Take Taglios, already pressed by the Shadowmasters, with its pacifist history, and win an impossible war.

The agreement with the Prahbrindrah had been that the Company would train and lead a Taglian army. Once the war had been won that army would support the Company's quest for Khatovar.

"Interesting," I told Blade. "But not a surprise. Sindhu!" He was back. He'd moved fast. Whatever he was, he could do a job. I told him, "I want you to stick to our guests." I indicated Swan, Mather, and Smoke. "Show the little one your rumel if they abuse our hospitality."

He nodded.

"They're to walk like everyone else."

He nodded again, went back to mounting skulls on poles.

Blade watched for a moment but said nothing, though I'm sure he had thoughts.

We marched out an hour after I decided to move. I was pleased.

15

We didn't reach Ghoja in ten hours but I hadn't expected to make four miles an hour in the dark. We did get in before dawn and, with Blade's connivance, we chose a campsite which both shouldered the road and almost nudged Jahamaraj Jah's encampment. We were there an hour before anyone noticed. Sloppy. Deadly sloppy. If we'd been the Shadowmasters' cavalry we could have cleaned the area.

We used the skulls and poles to mark the bounds of the camp. I had the interior laid out in a checkerboard cross with the center square for the headquarters group, the four squares on its points for four battalions with the squares between as drill grounds. The men grumbled about having to set up for twice their number—especially since certain favored individuals, who had been performing well, only had to stand around holding poles with skulls atop them.

Croaker had been fond of showmanship. He'd said you should adjust the minds of observers to think what you wanted them to think. That was never my style, but in the past I'd had brute force to waste. Here, let everyone think I believed I'd soon have men enough for four battalions and the battalions would expand.

Tired as they were, the men were content to work and grumble. I saw no shirking. No one deserted.

People came out of the fortress and other camps to watch. The men Narayan sent to gather firewood and timber and stone ignored their undisciplined cousins. Skulls looking down moved the curious to keep their distance. Sindhu babysat Swan, Mather, and Smoke. Blade took his appointment seriously. The men in his battalion accepted him. He was one of the heroes of the desperate hours before the coming of the Company.

It was almost too sweet.

But nothing crept up. I watched the watchers.

The camp was three-quarters complete, including a ditch and embankment and the rudiments of a palisade faced with locust thorns and wild rose canes. Jahamaraj Jah rode out of his camp, watched for fifteen minutes. He didn't look pleased by our industry.

I summoned Narayan. "You see Jah?" He was hard to miss. He was as gaudy as a prince. He'd carried all that with him on campaign?

"Yes, Mistress."

"I'll be on the other side of camp for a while. If some of your men—especially Shadar—suffered a lapse of discipline and called him coward and deserter I doubt their punishments would be onerous."

He grinned, started to dart away.

"Hold it."

"Mistress?"

"You seem to have friends everywhere. I wouldn't be averse to knowing what's going on around here if you found contacts. Maybe Ghopal and Hakim and a few others could desert when you weren't looking. Or otherwise get out and poke around."

"Consider it done."

"I do. I trust you that far. I know you'll do what needs to be done."

His grin faded. He caught the warning edge.

From Narayan I went to Swan. "How are you doing?"

"Dying of boredom. Are we prisoners?"

"No. Guests with limited mobility. Now free to go. Or stay. I could use your cachet."

Smoke shook his head vigorously, as though he feared Swan would desert the Radisha. I told him, "You're awfully anxious to hang onto a Black Company spy."

He looked at me and went through some internal change, as though he'd decided to abandon ineffectual tactics. It wasn't a dramatic shift, though. The role he'd been in couldn't have been that far from the real Smoke.

He never said a word.

Swan grinned and winked. "I'm gone. But I got a feeling I'll be back."

The racket started up in Narayan's sector as I watched Swan go. I wondered how Jah was taking it.

Swan was back within the hour. "She wants to see you."

"Why am I not surprised? Ram, get Narayan and Blade. Sindhu, too."

I took Narayan and Blade with me. Sindhu I left in charge, hinting that I'd be pleased if the camp was finished when I got back.

I paused at the gate of the Ghoja fortress, glanced back. It was an hour short of noon. We had been here six hours. Already my camp was the most complete, best protected, most military.

Professionalism and preparedness are relative, I suppose.

16

Croaker hobbled to the temple door, looked out. Soulcatcher was nowhere around. He hadn't seen her for days. He wondered if he'd been abandoned. He doubted it. She'd just waited till he was able to care for himself, then had hurried off on some arcane business.

He thought of making a run for it. He knew the surrounding country. There was a village he could reach in a few hours, even at the pace he could make. But that escape would be no escape.

Soulcatcher was away but the crows had stayed to watch. They would stay with him. They would lead her to him. She had the horses. Those beasts could run forever without tiring. She could spot him a week's lead and catch him.

Still . . .

This place was like an island outside the world. It was dark and depressing.

He started walking, going nowhere, moving for the sake of movement. The crows nagged at him. He ignored them, ignored the ache thumping in his chest. He strolled through the woods, to the countryside beyond, emerging near the half-dead tree.

He recalled it now. Before Dejagore and Ghoja he had come south to scout the terrain, had spied Soulcatcher watching, had chased her into these woods. He'd stood by that tree trying to decide what to do next—and an arrow had hit it, nearly taking off his nose. It had carried a message, telling him it wasn't time for him to catch whomever he was chasing.

Then the Shadowmasters' men had come after him and he'd been too busy running to give the place any more thought.

He walked up to the tree. Crows burdened its branches. He fingered the hole where the arrow had hit. She'd been watching over him then, hadn't she? Not interfering but there just in case, maybe laying on a nudge or two to make sure he was around for her revenge.

A long, lazy hill lay before. He decided to ignore the crows. He kept walking.

The pain in his chest became insistent. He wasn't ready for so much exercise. He couldn't have gone far even without the crows keeping track.

As he paused to rest he wondered how much Soulcatcher had intruded on his affairs. Could she have had some hand in the outcome at Dejagore?

Destroying Stormbringer, who had worn the alias Stormshadow, had been easier than he'd expected. And getting Shapeshifter had been a breeze, too— though there'd been a little treachery to that, since Shifter had been helping Lady. Which reminded him. That girl. Shifter's apprentice. She'd gotten away. She could be thinking of evening scores. Did Soulcatcher know about her? Better mention her next chance he got.

His heartbeat had fallen off toward normal. The pain had waned. He resumed walking. He reached the ridgeline and stood leaning against a gnarly grey piece of exposed rock, panting while crows circled and nattered. "Oh, shut up! I'm not going anywhere."

Another outcrop nearby vaguely suggested a chair. He shuffled over and sat, surveyed his kingdom.

All Taglios could have been his if he'd won at Dejagore, had that been his ambition.

A flight of three crows arrowed in from the north, coming like racing pigeons, swirled into the flock, cawed some. The whole mob scattered. Odd.

He leaned back, thought about the battle's aftermath. Mogaba was alive and holding the city against besieging Shadowmasters, according to Soulcatcher. Maybe a third of the army had managed to get inside the walls. Fine. A stubborn defense would keep them away from Taglios. But he didn't care that much about Taglios. Nice people, but anybody who was anybody was thoroughly treacherous.

He was concerned about the few friends he'd left down south. Had any survived? Had they salvaged the Annals, those precious histories that were the time link cementing the Company? What had become of Murgen and the standard and his Widowmaker armor? Legend said the standard had been with the Company since the day it had marched from Khatovar.

What were those damned crows up to? Moments ago there had been a thousand of them. Now he couldn't see a dozen. Those all glided at high altitude, drifting back and forth over something up the valley.

Had Khatovar become a hopeless dream? Had the last page of the Annals been written just four hundred miles from home?

Sudden memory from the first hours of their journey away from Dejagore. Just an image, of a man floating, writhing upon a lance. Moonshadow? Yes. And Moonshadow had been skewered upon that lance during the fighting. Skewered on the lance that supported the standard.

It wasn't lost! That heirloom more important than the Annals themselves was down there in the temple somewhere. He hadn't seen it. She must have hidden it.

He glanced at a sky where cumulus marched across a turquoise field. The crows were closer, those few still aloft. He jerked, startled. One was headed his way like a winged missile.

It flapped, fluttered, very nearly suicided, making a landing on a rock pinnacle inches from his left hand. The bird said, "Don't move!" in a perfectly intelligible voice.

He didn't move, though instantly he had a dozen questions. It took no genius to understand that something significant was happening. The birds didn't speak to him otherwise. In fact, they had only once before, bringing the warning that had allowed him to move in time to whip the Shadowmasters at Ghoja ford.

The crow hunkered down and became part of the rock. Croaker eased down a little himself, so he'd present no obviously human form against the skyline, then froze. Moments later he spied movement in the shallow valley before him.

It darted from cover to cover. Then there was more movement, and more. His heart hammered as he remembered the shadows the minions of the Shadowmasters had brought north.

These were no shadows. They were small brown men, but not of the race of the small brown men who had managed the shadows. Those had been cousins of the Taglians. Something familiar about these. But they were so far away.

It didn't occur to them to look up where he was seated. Or if they did they couldn't see him. They moved on down the valley.

Then there were more of them, maybe twenty-five, not sneaking like the others, who must have been scouts. He saw this bunch well enough to recall where he'd seen their kind before. On the great river that ran from the heart of the continent down past Taglios to the sea. He had fought them a year ago, two thousand miles north of here. They had blockaded the river against all commerce. The Company had opened the way, crushing them in a wild nighttime battle where sorceries flashed and howled.

The Howler!

The main party was in sight. Eight men carried a ninth on a sedan of sorts. The ninth was a small figure so covered with clothing it looked like a pile of rags. As it came abreast of Croaker it let out a prolonged moan.

The Howler. One of the Ten Who Were Taken who had been servants of the Lady in her northern empire, a terrible wizard, thought slain in battle till that night on the river when he'd tried to even old scores against his former empress. Only the intercession of Shifter had driven him off.

Another moan escaped the sorcerer. It was a feeble shadow of the Howler's usual wails. Probably trying to control his cries to avoid attracting attention.

Croaker sat so still his heart almost stopped. There was little in the world he wanted less than to attract attention now. His concentration was so intense he felt no discomfort from rock or chill breeze.

The party passed on, with more small brown men trailing behind, in rearguard. It was an hour before Croaker was confident that he had seen the last of them.

He had counted one hundred twenty-eight swamp warriors, plus the sorcerer. The warriors wouldn't be much use so far out of their element. This terrain was alien to them. But the Howler . . . Terrain and climate and whatnot meant nothing to him.

Where was he headed? Didn't take much to guess. Down to the Shadowlands. Why was more of a mystery, but probably not so great a one.

The Howler had been one of the Taken. Some of the Shadowmasters had been fugitive Taken, too. It seemed likely the survivors had made contact with their former comrade and had negotiated some compact whereby he would replace the Shadowmasters who had fallen.

Lady was alive and at Ghoja, if Soulcatcher hadn't lied. Not forty miles away. He wished he could make that journey. He wished there was some way he could get a message to her. She needed to know about this.

"Crow, I don't know if you know what we just saw, but you'd better get word to your boss. We got trouble." He got up and walked back to the temple, where he amused himself by trying to find the hidden Company standard.

The everyday business of sorcery is as much stage magic as it is witchcraft. It's misdirection, deceit, what-have-you. I kept an eye on Smoke, expecting him to pass information to the Radisha in some subtle fashion. But if he did he was too crafty for me. Which I doubt.

When you encounter the Radisha you know you're in the presence of a powerful will. It was a shame she was trapped in her culture and had to pretend to be her brother's creature. She might have done interesting things.

"Good afternoon," she said. "We're pleased that you survived."

Was she? Maybe, because there were still Shadowmasters to be conquered. "So am I."

She noted that Blade stood with me instead of his friends. She noted Narayan, of obvious low caste and no cleaner than the day we'd met—though I had no room to criticize. A shadow crossed her brow. "My battalion commanders," I said. "Blade you know. Narayan, who has been helpful pulling the men together."

She looked at Narayan intently, maybe because of his unusual name and the fact that I'd added no other. I didn't know any other name for him. Narayan was a patronym. We had six more Narayans among the Shadar troops. Every one of them carried the personal name Singh, which means Lion.

She caught something with that closer look, started slightly, glanced at Smoke. The wizard replied with a tiny nod. She looked at Blade. "You choose to leave me?"

"I'm going with somebody who can get something done besides talk."

That was a long speech for Blade and one that won him no sympathy. The Radisha glared.

"He's got a point," Swan said. "You and your brother just keep fiddling."

"We're more exposed." People in positions like theirs do have to act within constraints or get pulled down. But try to explain that to men who have never been anything but momentary captains and didn't want that power when they had it.

The Radisha rose. "Come," she told us. As we walked, she told me, "I *am* pleased that you survived. Though you may find it difficult to continue doing so."

That didn't sound like a threat, exactly. "What?"

"You're in a difficult position because your Captain didn't survive." She led us up a spiral stair to the parapet of the fortress's tallest tower. My companions were as puzzled as I. The Radisha pointed.

Beyond the trees and construction across the river there was a large, ragtag encampment. The Radisha said, "Some fugitives crossed elsewhere and carried word north. People started arriving the day after Swan rode south. There are about two thousand already. There'll be thousands more."

"Who are they?" Swan asked.

"Families of legionnaires. Families of men the Shadowmasters enslaved. They've come to find out what happened to their menfolk." She pointed upstream.

Scores of women were stacking wood. I asked, "What are they doing?"

"Building ghats." Narayan sounded nonplussed. "I should have considered that."

"What are ghats?"

"Funeral pyres," Mather said. "The Gunni burn their dead instead of burying them." He looked a little green.

I didn't follow. "There aren't any dead here. Unless somebody makes some." A symbolic gesture? Funerals in absentia?

"The practice is called suttee," Smoke said. I looked at him. He stood straight up and wore a slimy grin. "When a man dies his wife joins him on his ghat. If he dies away from home she joins him in death when she learns of it."

Oh? "Those women are building pyres where they can commit suicide if their husbands have been killed?"

"Yes."

"A damnfool thing to do."

Smoke's smile grew. "It's a custom as old as Taglios. With the force of law."

I didn't like the way he was getting happy. He thought he had a tool to use against me.

"A waste. Who takes care of the children? Never mind. I don't care." The concept was so alien I discounted it. I'm not sure I even believed him.

The Radisha said, "The custom is revered by everyone, even those who aren't Gunni."

"There are crazies everywhere. It's a hideous practice. It should be abolished. But I'm not here to change any social sillinesses. We're at war. We've suffered a setback. A lot of our men are trapped in Dejagore. It's not likely we can save them. More are in flight. We *can* save some of those. And we have to raise new levies so we can cling to what we've gained."

Swan said, "Sweetie, you're missing the point."

"I got the point, Swan. It's irrelevant."

The Radisha said, "You're a woman. You have no friends. Every man of any substance in every priesthood is going to make a point of your relationship with your Captain. A large point of your failure to commit suttee. That will weigh heavily with a large portion of the population."

"It may be the custom. It's an idiot custom and I'll bet it's not universal. I shan't dignify the suggestion—unless I decide that for bringing it up the suggester will be delivered to his suggestion."

Smoke's grin faded.

His eyes narrowed and clouded. His jaw dropped for a second. He was staring at my hand. I realized I'd picked up Narayan's tic, was fingering the bit of yellow cloth peeping from my waist.

Smoke's color turned ghastly.

I said, "Radisha, ask these two about my background." I indicated Swan and Mather. They'd emigrated from my empire while I was at the pinnacle of my power. "Some of the Company have fallen but our contract remains in force. I intend to execute the undertaking."

"Admirable. But you'll find that a lot of people won't want to let you do that."

I shrugged. "What they want doesn't matter. The contract has been made. Better understand that. You people think you know more about us than we do. You must know we don't let anybody back out on a contract."

The Radisha looked at me intently, unafraid, curious about my confident attitude here alone in a sea of enemies.

I said, "I'll present a list of needs tomorrow. Manpower, drayage, animals, weapons, equipment." Half of confidence is the appearance of confidence.

Somebody shouted from the stairwell. The Radisha signalled Mather, who checked it. He came back, said, "Jah's kicking up a fuss. Wants to see you. Guess that means he knows you're here."

I said, "Might as well meet him head on."

"Tell them to bring him, Mather."

Mather passed the word. We waited. The Radisha and I eyed one another like she-leopards. I asked, "Why are you afraid of the Company?"

She didn't bat an eye. "You know quite well."

"I do? I've studied the history of the Company in detail. I don't recall anything that would explain your attitude."

Smoke whispered something. I think he accused me of lying. I was developing an intense dislike for him.

Jahamaraj Jah swept in like a king.

I was curious to see how the Radisha handled the handicap of her sex.

In a moment I was curious to see how Jah handled *his* handicap. He had made his entrance dramatically. He had looked us over. We hadn't responded to the gloriousness of his size, his wealthy apparel, the power he represented. Now he didn't know what to do next.

He was a fool. Croaker hadn't quite erred in ridding the Shadar of his predecessor. That man had been our enemy. But Jah wasn't much of an improvement. He was all appearance without substance.

He was impressive for a Taglian, six feet and two hundred pounds, half a foot taller than average and much more massive. His skin was fairer than most—a desirable trait from the Taglian perspective. Wealthy women often spent their entire lives hiding from the sun. He was handsome even by northern standards. But his mouth was petulant and his eyes gave the impression he was a moment short of breaking into tears because he wasn't getting his own way.

The Radisha gave him ten seconds, snapped, "You have something to say?"

Indecision. He was surrounded by people who had no use for him. Several would have cut his throat happily. Even Smoke found the nerve to look at him like he was a slug.

I said, "Caught by a jury of your enemies. I'd thought you were better at the game."

"What game?" He wasn't good at concealing his feelings. What he thought of me came through.

"Intrigue. That was a poor move, running at Dejagore. Everybody will blame you."

"Hardly. The battle was lost. I made sure a force survived."

"You ran out before it was decided. Your own men say so," the Radisha snapped. "If you give us any grief we'll remind the families of those men who aren't coming home."

Pure hatred. Jah wasn't used to being thwarted. "I'm not accustomed to being threatened. I don't tolerate it from anyone."

I asked, "Do you recall how you came to power? People might be interested in the details."

Among them, everyone there. The others stared, wondering. "You'd be wise to go quietly, abandon the pursuit of arms and power, and content yourself with what you have."

He glared daggers.

"You're vulnerable. You can't erase that. You've made too many poor choices. Keep it up and you'll destroy yourself."

He looked at us, found no sympathy anywhere. His only weapon was bluster. He knew what that was worth. "This round to you." He headed downstairs.

Blade laughed.

He did it knowing Jah couldn't tolerate being mocked.

Blade *wanted* trouble.

I sent him a warning look. He stared back impassively. He wasn't intimidated by anyone.

Jah was gone. I said, "I have work to do. We aren't accomplishing anything. We know where we stand. I expect to finish the Company's work. You intend to let that go only as far as it conveniences you, then you plan to backstab me. I don't plan to let you. Blade. You coming or staying?"

"Coming. There's nothing here for me."

Swan and Mather looked croggled, Smoke pained, and the Radisha exasperated.

As soon as we left the fortress, Blade said, "Jah could try something desperate now."

"I'll handle it. He'll vacillate till it's too late. Check on your battalion." Once he was out of hearing, I told Narayan, "He's right. Do we wait for Jah? Or do we move first?"

He didn't respond, just waited for me to answer myself.

"We'll do something when we know he's planning something himself."

I surveyed the camp. The outer enclosure was complete. It would do for the moment. I'd keep making improvements, mainly to keep the men occupied. A wall can never be too high or a ditch too deep.

"I want the Shadar to know I need cavalrymen. Their response will show us what support Jah has. Pass the word amongst all the fugitives that those who join voluntarily will get preferential treatment. We need volunteers from the provinces, too. We need to spread our story before these idiots unleash the hounds of factionalism."

"There are ways to get word out," Narayan admitted. "But we'll have to send some of my friends across the river."

"Do what you have to. Starting now. We don't mark time. We don't let them catch their balance. Go."

I climbed a platform that had been erected near what would become the camp's north gate, surveyed the countryside. My men were as busy as ants.

Their industry hadn't communicated itself to anyone else. Only the builders across the river, and the Gunni women, were doing much.

Smoke curled up from one of the ghats. When the flames were roaring a woman threw herself in.

I had to believe it now.

I retired to the shelter Ram had built, settled to stretch the limits of my talent. I'd be needing it soon.

18

The dreams worsened. They were dreams of death.

We all have nightmares but I'd never recalled so many so clearly after I wakened. Some force, some power, was summoning me. Was trying to enlist or subject me.

Those dreams were the creations of a sick mind. If they were supposed to appeal to me, that power didn't know me.

Landscapes of despair and death under skies of lead, fields where bodies rotted and stunted vegetation melted down like slow, soft candlewax. Slime covered everything, hung in strands like the architecture of drunken spiders.

Mad. Mad. Mad. And not a touch of color anywhere.

Mad. And yet with its taint of perverse appeal. For amongst the dead I'd see faces I wished amongst the dead. I strode that land unharmed, vitally alive, its ruler. The ghouls that ran with me were extensions of my will.

It was a dream straight out of the fantasies of my dead husband. It was a world he could have made home.

Always, in the late hours, there'd be a dawn in that land of nightmare, a splash of color on a poorly defined horizon. Always in front of me, it seemed the dawn of hope.

Simple and direct, the architect of my dreams.

There was one dream, less common, that did without the death and corruption, yet was as chilling in its way. Black and white too, it placed me upon a plain of stone where deadly shadows lurked behind countless obelisks. I didn't understand it at all but it frightened me.

I couldn't control the dreams. But I refused to let them influence my waking hours, refused to let them wear me down.

I've sent word out, Mistress," Narayan said, responding to my question about recruits. We fenced whenever the subject of his brotherhood arose. He wasn't yet ready to talk.

Blade suggested, "Someone ought to be watching things at Dejagore." I understood, though sometimes his brevity caused problems.

Narayan said, "Ghopal and Hakim can take a party down. Twenty men should have no trouble. It'll be quiet now."

I said, "You had them spying on our neighbors."

"They're done. They've made their contacts. Sindhu can take over. He has a higher reputation."

Another of those little oddities about Narayan and his cronies. They had their own hidden caste system. Based on what, I couldn't tell. Narayan was the man of most respect here. Broad, stolid Sindhu ran a close second.

"Send them. If we have spies everywhere why haven't I gotten any information?"

"There's nothing to report that isn't common knowledge. Except that there's a lot of disaffection among Jah's men. A third might defect if you offered to enlist them. Jah's been doing some talking about you ignoring your duties as a wife because you won't commit suttee or go into isolation, as befits a Shadar woman. He's working on a dozen schemes but none of our friends are in his closest councils."

"Kill him," Blade said. And Sindhu nodded.

"Why?" A political victory would be better, long range.

"You don't let the serpent strike if you know where he lies in wait. You destroy him."

A simplistic solution with a certain appeal. It could have a big impact if we took him out where he seemed least vulnerable. And at the moment I didn't feel patient enough to spin out a long game. "Agreed. But with finesse. Do we have good enough friends over there to let us sneak into camp?"

"Close enough," Narayan admitted. "There'd be a question of timing. So the friends would be on duty."

"Set it up. What about other enemies? Jah is just the most obvious because he's right here. There'll be more in the north."

"It'll be handled," Narayan promised. "When there are men and time. We have too much work and too few hands."

Right. But I felt good about my prospects. No one else was doing as much or pushing as hard. I asked, "Can we get any closer to the Radisha and her pet wizard? Smoke? Are Swan and Mather devoted allies of the Radisha's?"

"Devoted?" Blade said. "No. But they've given their word, more or less. They won't turn unless the Woman turns on them first."

Something to consider. Maybe they could be misdirected, though that would work against me if they found me out.

Offered places in my camp and safety from reprisals, two hundred of Jahamaraj Jah's men defected. Another fifty just deserted and disappeared. Several hundred of the other fugitives enlisted the same day the Shadar came over. I got the impression the Radisha wasn't pleased.

Nearly a hundred Gunni women walked into fire the same day. I heard my name cursed from that side of the river.

I went over and spoke to a few women. We had no basis for communication.

Smoke was at the fortress gate when I recrossed the ford. He smirked as I passed. I wondered how much the Radisha would miss him.

There are times when you wonder about the self hidden from yourself. I certainly did as Narayan, Sindhu, and I stole toward the Shadar cavalry camp.

I was excited. I was eager. I was drawn as a moth to flame. I told myself I was doing this because I had to, not because I wanted it. It wasn't a pleasure. Jah's malice had called this down upon him.

Narayan's friends had confirmed that Jah planned to grab the Radisha and me and make it look like I'd carried her off. How he figured he could get to me I don't know. I guessed his plan included me murdering the Radisha—thus eliminating her brother's spine—then being a good girl who committed suttee. With assistance.

So I was moving first, earlier than I'd wanted.

Narayan exchanged whispered passwords with a friendly sentry who turned blind as we stole past. The camp beyond was a pesthole. Ordinarily Shadar set great store by cleanliness. Morale was abysmal.

We stole like shadows. I was proud of myself. I moved as silently as those two. They were surprised a woman could do it. We approached Jah's own tent.

It was oversized and guarded well. The man knew he wasn't popular. A fire burned on each of the tent's four sides. A guard stood near each fire.

Narayan cursed, said something in cant. Sindhu grunted. Narayan whispered, "No way to get any closer. Those guards will be men he trusts. And they'll know who we are."

I nodded, pulled them back, said, "Let me think."

They whispered while I thought. They didn't expect anything from me.

There was a small spell which could be used to blind the unaware briefly. Perfect, if I could manage it. I recalled it all right. One of those children's things that used to be as easy as blinking. I hadn't tried it in ages. There'd be no way to tell if it was working, unless I messed it up so badly the sentry sensed me and gave the alarm.

Nothing to lose but my life.

I went into that spellcasting as though it was the most dangerous demon-summoning I'd ever done. I did it three times to make sure it had a chance to take, but when I finished I didn't know if I'd succeeded or failed. The guard didn't look changed.

Sindhu and Narayan still had their heads together. I said, "Come on," and returned to the edge of the light. No one was in sight but that guard.

Time to test it or chicken.

I walked straight toward the sentry.

Narayan and Sindhu both cursed and tried to call me back. I summoned them with a gesture. The guard couldn't see me.

He didn't see me!

My heart leaped as it had when I'd summoned the horses. I beckoned Narayan and Sindhu, indicating they should stay out of the guard's direct line of vision. He might remember someone he saw head on. And he *would* be questioned later.

They slunk past like dogs, unable to believe he couldn't see them. They desperately wanted to know what I'd done, how I'd done it, if they could learn to do it, too, but they dared not say a word.

I parted the tent flap an inch, saw no one on the other side. The interior was compartmented by hangings. I slipped into what must have been the audience area. It constituted the majority of the interior. It was well appointed, further evidence that Jah had put his own comfort before the welfare of his men and the safety of his homeland.

I had learned better as a child. You win more loyalty and respect if you share the hardships.

Eyes still big, Narayan gestured, reminding me of the layout as he had it from his spies. I nodded. This late Jah should be asleep. We moved toward his sleeping area. I moved the hanging with a dagger. Narayan and Sindhu got their rumels out.

I know I made no noise. I'm sure they didn't. But as we went in Jah boiled up off his cushions, flung himself between Narayan and Sindhu, bowling them aside. He charged me. There was a lamp burning. He saw us well enough to recognize us.

Ever a fool, Jahamaraj Jah. He never yelled. He just tried to get away.

My hand dipped to the triangle of saffron at my waist, yanked, flipped. My rumel moved as if alive, snaked around his throat. I seized the flying end, yanked the loop tight, rolled my wrists and held on.

Luck, fate, or unconscious skill, none of that would have mattered had I been alone. Jah was a powerful man. He could have carried me outside. He could have shaken me off.

But Narayan and Sindhu grabbed his arms and held them extended, twisted them, forced him down. Sindhu's bull strength counted most. Narayan concentrated on keeping Jah's arms extended.

I got my knees into Jah's back and concentrated on keeping him from breathing.

It takes a while for a man to strangle. The skilled strangler is supposed to move so quickly and decisively that the victim's neck breaks and death comes instantly. I did not yet have the wrist roll perfected. So I had to hang on while Jah went the hard way. My arms and shoulders ached before he shuddered his last.

Narayan lifted me away. I was shaking with the intensity of it, the almost orgasmic elation that coursed through me. I'd never done anything like that, with my own two hands, without steel or sorcery. He grinned. He knew what I was feeling. He and Sindhu seemed unnaturally calm. Sindhu was listening, trying to judge if we'd made too much noise. It had seemed a ferocious uproar to me, there in the middle of it, but evidently we'd made less racket than I'd thought. Nobody came. Nobody asked questions.

Sindhu muttered something in cant. Narayan thought a moment, glanced at me, grinned again. He nodded.

Sindhu pawed through Jah's clutter, looking for the ground. He cleared a small area, looked around some more.

While I watched him, trying to figure out what he was doing, Narayan produced an odd tool he'd carried under the dark robe he'd donned for the adventure. The tool had a head that was half hammer, half pick, that weighed at least two pounds. Maybe more if it was the silver and gold it appeared to be. Its handle was ebony inlaid with ivory and a few rubies that caught the lamplight and gleamed like fresh blood. He began pounding the earth with the pick side, but quietly, unrhythmically.

That wasn't a tool that would be used that way ordinarily. I know a cult object when I see one, even if it's unfamiliar.

Narayan broke up the earth. Sindhu used a tin pan to scoop it onto a carpet he'd turned face down, careful not to scatter any. I had no idea what they intended. They were too intent on what they were doing to explain. A litany of sorts, in cant, passed between them. I heard something about auspices and the promise of the crows, more about the Daughter of Night and those people—or whatever they were.

All I could do was keep watch.

Time passed. I had a tense few minutes when the guard changed outside. But those men had little to say to one another. The new men didn't check inside the tent.

I heard a meaty whack and muted crunch, turned to see what they were doing now.

They'd gotten a hole dug. It was barely three feet deep and not that far across. I couldn't guess what they meant to do with it.

They showed me.

Narayan used the hammer face of his tool to break Jah's bones. Just as Ram had been doing with a rock that morning in that draw. He whispered, "It's been a long time but I still have the touch."

It's amazing how small a bundle a big man makes once you pulverize his joints and fold him up.

They cut open Jah's belly and deposited him in the hole. Narayan's final stroke buried the pick in the corpse's skull. He cleaned the tool, then they filled the hole around the remains, tamping the earth as they went. Half an hour later you couldn't tell where they'd dug.

They put the carpets back, bundled up the excess dirt, looked at me for the first time since they'd begun.

They were surprised to find me impassive. They wanted me to be outraged or disgusted. Or something. Anything that betrayed a feminine weakness.

"I've seen men mutilated before."

Narayan nodded. Maybe he was pleased. Hard to tell. "We still have to get out."

The firelight outside betrayed the positions of the guards. They were where they were supposed to be. If my spell worked a second time we'd only need a little luck to get out unseen.

Narayan and Sindhu scattered dirt as we walked toward our camp. "Good rumel work, Mistress," Narayan said. And something more, in cant, to Sindhu, who agreed reluctantly.

I asked, "Why did you bury him? No one will know what happened to him. I wanted him to become an object lesson."

"Leaving him lie would have told everyone who was responsible. Innuendo is more frightening than fact. Better you're guilty in rumor."

Maybe. "Why did you break him up and cut him open?"

"A smaller grave is harder to find. We cut him open so he wouldn't bloat. If you don't they sometimes bloat so much they come up out of the ground. Or they explode and loose off enough gas so the grave can be found by the smell. Especially by jackals, who dig them up and scatter them all over."

Practical. Logical. Obvious, once he explained it. I'd never had occasion to conceal a body before. I'd surrounded myself with very practical—and clearly very experienced—murderers.

"We have to talk soon, Narayan."

He grinned that grin. He'd tell me some truth when we did.

We slipped back into camp and parted company.

I slept well. There were dreams but they weren't filled with gloom and doom. In one a beautiful black woman came and held me and caressed me and called me her daughter and told me I'd done well. I wakened feeling refreshed and as vigorous as if I'd had a full night's sleep. It was a beautiful morning. The world seemed painted in especially vivid colors.

My exercises with my talent went very well.

The disappearance, without trace, of the high priest Jahamaraj Jah, so trivial an opponent that I recall him only as a faded caricature of a man, stunned the thousands cluttering the region around the Ghoja ford. A whisper went around saying he had schemed against the Radisha and myself and that had sealed his fate. I wasn't responsible for the rumor. Narayan denied having said anything to anybody. Two days after we buried Jah everybody was convinced I'd eliminated him. Nobody knew how.

They were scared.

The possibility had a big impact on Blade. I got the feeling he thought I'd gone through some rite of passage and he could now devote himself to my cause. I was pleased but had to wonder about a man so devoutly antagonistic toward priests.

I had Narayan spread word that I still needed recruits, especially skilled horsemen. Another two hundred Shadar enlisted. Likewise nearly five hundred survivors of the Dejagore battle, though many just wanted regular meals or the comfort of a known place in the hierarchy. Taglian caste systems encourage dependence upon hierarchy. The chaos at the ford provided none of the benefits of social rigidity, only the handicaps.

I told Narayan to think about expanding the camp. Soon we'd be overcrowded. I told Blade to look for likely leaders. We'd never have enough of those.

The Taglians continued to amaze me. They remained pacifistic in their thinking, yet admired what they thought was the direct and casual way I disposed of enemies. The bigger the violence, the more they would applaud. As long as they were not threatened personally.

The Radisha sent for me the third morning after Jah's death. It was a brief interview, of no consequence except that I left convinced that Smoke was more than a fakir. He'd penetrated the veil of time well enough to assure himself that I'd had a hand in Jah's disappearance. He was more frazzled than ever. For the first time the Radisha was rattled.

She saw her control slipping.

That night she and Smoke and a few followers slipped over the Main and headed north. She left Swan and Mather to pretend she was secluded in the fortress. That deceit was useless. Narayan told me what was happening before the Radisha hit the water.

The day was noteworthy, too, because we enlisted our first nonveterans. There were just three of them. Two were friends of Narayan's friends. But their arrival was a sign that word was spreading and there were Taglians willing to join the cause.

Drills and training continued, as intense as I could make them, always designed to strip each man of all loyalties but those to his comrades and commander.

Former slaves had become the most plentiful volunteers—and best students. They had nothing else. The Shadowmasters had destroyed their world. I thought it might be a good idea to send trusted men to roam the lands below the Main in search of more men without strong ties to Taglios.

Narayan and Sindhu told me the Radisha was doing her sneak. I listened, then said, "Sit. The time has come."

They understood. They didn't look as distressed as I'd expected. They had talked it over and had agreed to open up. "Who are you? What are you doing?"

Narayan took a deep breath. He did not look me in the eye. "Mistress, we are Deceivers. Followers of the goddess Kina, who has many names and many guises but whose only truth is death." He went into a long-winded explanation about the goddess and how she related to the gods of Taglios and its neighbors. It was an improbable mishmash like that surrounding the genesis and attributes of most dark gods. Narayan plainly had not thought much about the doctrine. His explanation didn't tell me much except that he and Sindhu were devoted to their goddess.

It took some pressure but they admitted they worshipped Kina, in part, by committing murder.

Sindhu volunteered, "Narayan, jamadar of the Changlor band, is famous among us, Mistress." Evidently he broke the silence because it wasn't good form for a man to brag about his own accomplishments. "He has given the gift of paradise to more than a hundred souls."

"One hundred fifty-three," Narayan said. That, apparently, was not considered braggery.

"Paradise? You want to explain that?"

"Those whose lives are taken for the goddess are freed from the Wheel of Life and ascend to paradise immediately."

The Wheel of Life was a Gunni concept. You kept going around and around, rebirth after rebirth, till the good you did sufficiently outweighed the evil. Then you were allowed escape. But not to paradise. Paradise was not a Gunni concept. The Gunni who escaped the Wheel became one with the generative force that had created the Lords of Light, the gods, who were its champions in the endless struggle with Shadow, which would be defeated only when the generative force had absorbed so many good souls it filled the universe. Shadow, of course, fought back by leading men to evil.

Paradise is a Vehdna notion, something originally imagined by adolescent males and dirty old men. It is stocked with all the comforts a male from a hard world could lust after. In particular it is infested with eager virgins of both sexes so the elevated will have something with which to while away eternity.

The Vehdna paradise gives no gate passes to women. The Vehdna say women have no souls. The gods created them to bear children, serve the lusts of men, and work themselves into early graves.

The Vehdna doctrine is the most perniciously anti-female of Taglios' cults but the most flexible as well. They have their female saints and heroines, and the Vehdna amongst my soldiers adapted to my command more easily than did the Shadar or Gunni. They just cast me in the role of their warrior saints Esmalla (three of the same name, from the same lineage, scattered over a century about eight hundred years back) and concentrated on doing their jobs.

The religions in my end of the world had not made more sense. I did not criticize Taglian beliefs. But I did ask questions. Understanding is an important tool.

Narayan insisted his beliefs were not derivative. He claimed Kina worship antedated all other religions. What I saw were echoes of its primal influence. "Mistress, it is said the Books record the histories of the Children of Kina back to the most ancient times, when men first received the gift of letters. It is said some are in tongues no man has spoken in ten thousand years."

"What books are these? Where are they?"

"The Books of the Dead, they're sometimes called. They are lost now, I think. There was a very bad time for the Children of Kina a long time ago. A great warlord, Rhadreynak, forged a vast empire. He insulted Kina. She visited vengeance upon his house, but by chance he was spared. He launched a crusade without mercy. The keepers of the Books fled into a hidden place. All who knew where they had gone were devoured by Rhadreynak's wrath before the sainted Mahtnahan dan Jakel broke his neck with the silver rumel."

Sindhu said something in cant, softly, the way men of other paths would say "Praise God" or "Blessed be His Name."

"What's that?" I asked.

"Mahtnahan was the only silver rumel man ever to have lived. The only Deceiver ever to have sent more than a thousand souls to paradise."

Sindhu said, still softly, "Every man, when he plies his rumel for the first time and knows the ecstasy of Kina for the first time, aspires to the heights attained by Mahtnahan."

Narayan brightened, grinned his grin. "And to his luck. Mahtnahan not only freed us of our greatest persecutor, he survived the killing. He lived another forty years."

I led them on through legends and oral histories, interested in the way Croaker would have been interested, intrigued by the dark history. Over and over, Narayan insisted there were true written records somewhere and that it was the great dream of every jamadar in every generation to recover them. "This is a feeble world today, Mistress. The greatest powers afoot are these Shadowmasters and they don't really know what they're doing. The Books . . . Ah, the secrets said to lie within their pages. The lost arts."

We talked about those Books again. I did not swallow their story whole. I'd heard similar legends about books filled with earth-shaking secrets before. But Narayan did startle me with a description of the place where they had been hidden.

It could have been the caverns I visited in my dreams. As they might have been recalled after a thousand years of oral history.

The history of Kina's cult might deserve some study someday. After I secured myself in today's world.

I had not spent all my time just waiting for Narayan to decide the time was ripe to let me in on a few secrets. Over the weeks I had done my listening among the men, had dropped a question here and there, to hundreds of individuals, and had put together a fair picture of the Kina cult as it was seen from outside.

Every living Taglian had heard Kina's name and believed she existed. Every Taglian had heard of the Stranglers. They thought of them more as bandits and gangsters than as religious fanatics. And not one in a hundred believed the Stranglers existed today. They were something from the past, eradicated during the last century.

I mentioned that to Narayan. He smiled.

"That is our greatest tool, Mistress. No one believes we exist. You have seen how Sindhu and I make little effort to hide from the men. We go among them and say we are the feared and famous Stranglers and they had better not displease us. And they don't believe us. But they fear us even so, because they know stories and think we might try imitating the Deceivers of old."

"There are some who believe." I suspected those included Smoke, the Radisha, and some others in high places.

"Always. Just enough."

He *was* a sinister little man. And probably really a vegetable peddler honored in his community as a good Gunni, good father, good grandfather. But during the dry season, when large portions of the Taglian population were on the move for reasons of trade, he would be, too. With his band, pretending to be travellers like other travellers, murdering those others when the opportunity arose. He was good at that, obviously. That was why Sindhu thought so highly of him.

Now I understood their caste system. It was based on number of successful murders.

Narayan was, likely, secretly, a wealthy man. The followers of Kina always robbed their victims.

They were more egalitarian than other cults. Narayan, of low caste and cursed with a Shadar name, had become jamadar of his band. Because he was a brilliant tactician and favored of Kina—meaning he was lucky, I assumed—according to Sindhu. He was famous among the Stranglers. A living legend.

"He doesn't need arm-holders," Sindhu said. "Only the best black cloths kill so quickly and efficiently that they don't need arm-holders."

A living legend, and my lieutenant. Interesting. "Arm-holders?" He used the word as a title more than as a job description.

"A band consists of many specialists, Mistress. The newest members begin as grave-diggers and bone-breakers. Many never advance beyond that level, for they develop no skill with the rumel. The yellow rumel men are the lowest

ranked Stranglers. Apprentices. They seldom have a chance to kill, being mostly
assigned as arm-holders for red rumel men and as scouts and victim-finders.
Red rumel men do most of the strangling. Few win the black rumel. Those almost always become jamadars or priests. The priests do the divining and take
omens, intercede with Kina, and keep the chronicles and accounts of the company. When it becomes necessary they act as judges."

"I was never a priest," Narayan said. "A priest has to be educated."

Never a priest but once a slave. He'd managed to keep his rumel throughout
his captivity. I wondered if he had fought back, dealing silent death.

"Sometimes. When the moment was propitious," he admitted. "But Kina
teaches us not to slay indiscriminately, nor in anger, but only for her glory. We
do not slay for political reasons—except for the safety of the brotherhood."

Interesting. "How many followers do you suppose Kina claims?"

"There is no way to tell, Mistress." Narayan seemed almost relieved by this
line of questioning. "We are outlawed. We come under sentence of death the
moment we take our oath to Kina. A jamadar will know how many there are in
his band and will have contacts with a few other jamadars but he'll have no idea
how many bands there are or how strong they might be. There are ways we have
to recognize one another, ways we communicate, but seldom do we dare gather
in large numbers. The risks are too great."

Sindhu said, "The Festival of Lights is our great gathering, when each band
sends men to the rites at the Grove of Doom."

Narayan silenced him with a gesture. "A great holy day but little different
than the Shadar festival of the same name. Many of the band captains come but
bring few of their followers. The priests attend, of course. Decisions are made
and cases judged but I would guess that not one in twenty believers attends. I
would guess that there are between one and two thousand of us today, more
than half living in Taglian territory."

Not many at all, then. And only a minority of those truly skilled murderers.
But what a force to unleash in the darkness if I could make it my instrument.

"And now the true question, Narayan. The heart of the thing. Where do
I fit? Why have you chosen me? And for what?"

20

Crowing and clatter wakened Croaker. He rose and went to the temple entrance. Ghostly dawn light permeated the misty wood.

Soulcatcher had returned. The black stallions were lathered. They had run long and hard. The sorceress was besieged by squawking crows. She cursed them and beat them back, beckoned him. He went out, asked, "Where have you been? Things have been happening."

"So I gather. I went for your armor." She indicated the horse she hadn't ridden.

"You went all the way to Dejagore? For that? Why?"

"We'll need it. Tell me what happened."

"How were they? My men."

"Holding out. Better than I expected. They may hang on for quite a while. Shadowspinner isn't at his best." The voice she chose rasped with irritation. When she continued, though, it had become that of a cajoling child. "Tell me. It'll take forever to get it out of them. They all try to tell me at once."

"The Howler came past yesterday."

She raised that wooden box to eye level, though she didn't make him look at the face inside. "The Howler? Tell me."

He did.

"The game grows more interesting. How did Longshadow lure him out of his swamp?"

"I don't know."

"I was speaking rhetorically, Croaker. Go inside. I'm tired. I was in a bad mood already."

He went. He didn't want to test her temper. Outside, she chattered with a flock of crows so dense she disappeared among them. Somehow she brought confusion out of chaos. Minutes later the temple vibrated to the beat of countless wings. A black cloud flew away south.

Soulcatcher came inside. Croaker kept his distance, kept his mouth shut. Not much intimidated him but he wasn't one to stick his hand in a cobra's mouth.

* * *

Morning came. Croaker wakened. Soulcatcher appeared to be sleeping soundly. He resisted temptation. It was less than a flutter of a thought, anyway. He wouldn't catch her off guard that easily. Chances were she wasn't asleep at all. Resting, yes. Maybe testing him. He couldn't recall ever having seen her sleep.

He made himself breakfast.

Soulcatcher wakened while he cooked. He didn't notice. A dramatic pink flash startled him. He whirled. Pinkish smoke swirled beyond the sorceress. A child-sized creature pranced out, flipped the woman a salute, sauntered over to him. "How they hanging, chief? Long time, no see."

"Want an honest answer or one that will please you, Frogface?"

"Hey! You ain't surprised to see me."

"No. I figured you were a plant. One-Eye doesn't have what it takes to manage a demon."

"Hey! Hey! Let's watch our tongue, eh, Cap? I ain't no demon. I'm an imp."

"Sorry about the ethnic slur. You did fool me, some. I thought you belonged to Shapeshifter."

"That lump? What could he offer?"

Croaker shrugged. "You been in Dejagore?" He contained an old anger. The imp, supposedly helping the Black Company, had been absent in the final debacle there. "What's the news?"

The imp stood only two feet tall though he had the proportions of an adult. He glanced at Soulcatcher, received some intangible permission. "That Mogaba is one bad actor, chief. He's giving the Shadowmasters' boys all the trouble they ever wanted. Making them look like fools. Eating them up a nibble at a time. 'Course, it can't last. He keeps getting into it with your old buddies One-Eye, Goblin, and Murgen. They don't like the way he operates. He don't like them all the time telling him about it. You get a split there, or Shadowspinner breaks loose, you got a whole new game."

Croaker settled with his meal. "Shadowspinner breaks loose?"

"Yeah. He got hurt in the fight, you know. His old buddy from down south, Longshadow, got a whammy in on him while he was down. Keeps him from using his talents. Them Shadowmasters was a lovely bunch, all the time trying to slide around behind each other even when they was up to their asses in alligators. Longshadow, he's got a notion he can play Shadowspinner just loose enough to let him wipe Dejagore, then squish the clown and make himself king of the world."

In a voice little more than a whisper the sorceress said, "He has the Howler to consider, now. And me."

The imp's grin faded. "You ain't as secret as you think, boss. They know you're down here. They all did, from the beginning."

"Damn!" She paced. "I thought I'd been more careful."

"Hey! Not to worry. None of them got the faintest where you are now. And maybe when we get done with them they'll wish they was nicer to you in the old days. Eh? Eh?" He laughed, childlike.

Croaker had encountered Frogface first in Gea-Xle, far to the north. One-Eye, one of the Company wizards, had bought him there. Everyone but One-Eye had doubted the imp's provenance and loyalty, though Frogface *had* made himself useful.

Croaker asked Soulcatcher, "You have something planned?"

"Yes. Stand up." He did. She rested one gloved hand against his chest. "Uhm. You've healed enough. And I'm running out of time."

Nervous excitement flooded him. He knew what she wanted and did not want to do it. "I thought that was why he was here. Do you trust him enough to have him watch me?"

"Hey, chief," the imp said, "you hurt my feelings. Sure she does. I done hitched my star."

"One word from me and he spends eternity in torment." Her voice was a merry little girl's. She could be chilling in her choices.

"That too," the imp said, all of a sudden surly. "It's a hard life, Cap. Nobody don't never trust me. Don't never give me no slack. One teensy slip-up and it's roast forever. Or worse. You mortals got it made, man."

Croaker snorted. "What do you think one slip-up will get me?"

"It only hurts for a little while for you."

Soulcatcher said, "Enough banter. Croaker, calm yourself. Get yourself ready for surgery. The imp and I will ready everything else."

Nude and headless, the sorceress floated four feet off the floor, shoulders elevated. Her unboxed head sat on a stone table nearby, eyes alert. Croaker scanned the body. It was perfect though pale and waxy. He'd seen only one to compare. Her sister's.

He glanced at the imp, perched on the head of a stone monster that protruded from the wall. The imp winked. "Show us what you got, Cap." Croaker was not reassured.

He glanced at his hands. They were steady, a legacy of surgeries performed on a dozen battlefields under terrifying conditions.

He stepped to the table. The sorceress had gathered the best surgical instruments the world had to offer. "This will take a while, imp. If I tell you to do something, you do it now. Understood?"

"Sure, chief. Might help if I knew what you were going to do."

"I'll start by removing the scar tissue. That'll be delicate. You'll have to help control bleeding." He didn't know if there would be bleeding or not. He'd never carved on somebody who should have been dead fifteen years ago. He could not believe this operation was possible. But Catcher being alive was impossible.

How much control would she have? How much would she participate? His would be the least part here, physical preparation for the mating of head and neck. The rest, tying nerve to nerve and blood vessel to blood vessel, would be up to her.

It wouldn't work. It couldn't.

He went to work. Soon he was concentrating enough to forget the price of failure.

Longshadow watched the upper limb of the sun slide below the horizon. He barked an order. A wrinkly little brown man whispered, "Yes, my lord." He scurried out of the crystal room. Longshadow remained motionless, watched the day fade.

"Welcome the enemy hours." It was summertime. Longshadow preferred summers. The nights were shorter.

He was less troubled, less fearful, now. Those nights after the Stormgard debacle had included a crisis of confidence now past. He was not cocky but was sure of himself now. Everything he touched was turning to gold, unfolding to perfection. The Howler was on his way from the swamps, undetected. The siege of Stormgard continued to enervate Shadowspinner's armies. Spinner remained impotent. *She* seemed to have faded, content to avenge herself on Dorotea Senjak. Senjak was playing her own game unaware that she was playing his. Soon, now, she would stumble. He had just one move to make. And it was time.

Each seventy feet along Overlook's wall stood a tower topped by crystal. Inside each cylinder was a large curved mirror. Fires came to life within those towers. The flames burned brightly. The mirrors hurled light onto the old road descending from the plain of glittering stone. No shadow could move there unseen.

His confidence was back. He could leave the night watch to others. He had other business to conduct. There were reports to receive, orders to send, communiques to issue. He turned his back on the outside world, approached a crystal sphere on a pedestal at the heart of the chamber.

The sphere was four feet in diameter. Channels wormholed through it to a hollow at the heart. Shimmers of light rippled over its surface. Snakes of light wriggled through the channels inside. Longshadow rested withered hands on the sphere. Surface light absorbed them. His hands sank into the globe slowly, as though melting through ice. He grasped serpents of light, manipulated them.

A port opened where the sphere rested on the pedestal, unsealing one channel. Darkness oozed in. It came reluctantly, compelled, fighting every inch. It hated the light as the Shadowmaster hated darkness. It filled the heart of the sphere.

Longshadow spoke to it. The light on the sphere rippled, crept up his arms. The sphere vibrated. A sound weaker than a whisper came off it. Longshadow listened. Then he sent the shadow away and summoned another.

To the fourth such shadow he said, "Take this message to Taglios: 'Create the agent.'"

As the shadow oozed away, fleeing the light, the Shadowmaster suddenly felt that he was no longer alone. Frightened, he tried to turn to look at the road from the plain.

Nothing moved there. The shadowtraps were holding. What, then?

Something inky, glossy, flashed through the nearest beam. "Huh?" No shadow, that. A crow! A lot of crows. What were crows doing here?

It was night. Crows didn't fly at night.

It came, then.

There had been crows around Overlook for weeks, seldom behaving as crows should. "Hers!" He cursed, stamped angrily, childishly. She'd been watching all along. She knew everything!

Fear fled before rage. He'd never had much self-control. He tried to yank his arms free, forgetting there should be no quick movement in the sphere. The crows seemed to laugh at him.

Hell. They swarmed over the surrounding walls, cawing mockingly.

He ripped a hand out of the sphere. Bloody sparks crackled between his fingers. There would be an end to those cackling devils! She wouldn't spy on him again!

He hurled a bolt. A dozen crows exploded. Blood and feathers splattered the tower. The survivors cawed uproariously.

Sense penetrated rage. Something was wrong. They *wanted* him to attack them.

Diversion?

The sphere!

A gap remained where he'd freed his hand. The hole penetrated to the core. A darkness was slithering through already.

He screamed.

He clamped down on his fear, removed his other hand slowly. He closed the deadly gap carefully, but not before the shadow escaped.

It darted through the doorway, out of the chamber, down into the bowels of Overlook, fleeing the light.

There was a shadow loose in the fortress!

Somewhere, a scream. The shadow was hunting.

Longshadow forced an icy calm. It was one lone shadow, small, controllable. Outside, the crows made merry.

He stifled rage. They would not provoke him again. "Your hour will come," he promised. "Fly to the bitch. Report your failure. I live. I still live!"

When the watchful eye lapses those who are watched invariably sense the instant of freedom.

A prodigious wail escaped the little thing called the Howler. It gobbled at the men carrying it. They raced forward, carried it into the camp of the Shadowmaster Shadowspinner while the watcher in the south was diverted.

The Howler remained just long enough to make contact, speak briefly, exchange views, reach an understanding by which he stood to evade the inevitable treachery of Longshadow, sure to surface the instant the threat from Taglios evaporated.

He was long gone when Longshadow's seekers found him again. The only evidence of his visit was an improvement in Shadowspinner's condition. Spinner kept that well hidden.

23

The breeze had shifted. It came from the northeast now, carrying smoke from across the river. I asked Narayan, "Could we confiscate their wood?" There had been suicides all morning.

"Unwise, Mistress. Interfering might start a rebellion. Your grip isn't that tight."

And likely would never be, unpleasant as I found that truth. "Just wishful thinking. Tinkering with customs isn't my mission."

Nor his. I had not pressed Narayan about that. I could guess, though. It was implicit in his beliefs. He wanted to bring on the Year of the Skulls. He wanted Kina free. He wanted to become immortal, a Deceiver saint.

"It's all far away, Mistress. What do we do today?"

"We're approaching that point where assembling an army begins snowballing."

"Snowballing?"

I'd used Forsberger for "snowballing," not thinking. I did not know the Taglian for snow. It did not snow here. Narayan had never seen snow. "It starts growing of its own momentum. In another week, ten days, I'd guess, we'll begin getting more recruits than we can handle."

"Even with the Radisha against us?" He was convinced the woman was an enemy.

"That could work for us if we appeal to resentment of the powers that be."

Narayan understood. Such resentments brought recruits to the Deceivers. "There's less of that than you hope. This isn't your land. My people are very fatalistic."

They were. But they had their handles. There would not be two thousand men under my standard now otherwise. "They'll respond to the right spark. True?"

"We all will, Mistress."

"Absolutely. I've provided that spark for you and your friends, haven't I? But how about a spark to fire the masses? One that will make them forget their fear of the Black Company and their objections to a woman commander?" I understood why the Company was feared now. For his sake maybe it was best Croaker had gone before he figured it out. It would have broken his heart.

Narayan had no suggestions.

I said, "We need an electrifying rumor to hand your brotherhood, to whisper everywhere."

"Word should have reached all the jamadars now, Mistress."

"Wonderful, Narayan. So every band captain has heard that your Strangler messiah is come. Assume they all believe because the news came from you, famous and honored master Strangler." My tone was getting sarcastic. "How many men will that bring to a standard that needs thousands? I'd rather have your friends stay where they are, as our hands and knives in hiding. Are there other legends I can exploit? Are there other fears?"

"The Shadowmasters are scary enough, at least in the country, where they remember last year."

True. We were getting volunteers from across the river already, men who'd had no chance to enlist before we marched on Dejagore. The men we had taken down had come from the city or were slaves we had liberated after overrunning Ghoja. The country folk, intimate with the terror of the Shadowmasters, should prove a rich source of manpower. And would be hardier than city folk. But I might have to gather my harvest quickly.

Around here power emanated from the palace and the temples of Trogo Taglios. A few frightened men there could issue bulls and dictates forbidding the faithful from joining me.

"Do you have friends in the city?"

"Not many. None that I know personally. Sindhu may know some."

"Ram came from the city."

"Yes. And a few others. What're you thinking?"

"It might be wise to get established there now, before the Radisha, and especially that whimpering runt Smoke, can swing opinion against us." I said we and us always but meant I and me. Narayan was not fooled much.

"We can't leave Ghoja. Thousands more men will come here. We have to collect them."

I smiled. "Suppose we split what we have? You take half, stay here, do the gathering, and I take half to the city?"

He reacted the way I expected. Almost panicky. He didn't want me out of his sight.

"Or I could leave Blade. Blade is a man of respect, with a strong reputation down here."

"Excellent idea, Mistress."

I wondered who was manipulating whom. "Do you suppose Sindhu is a man of enough respect to leave with him?"

"More than enough, Mistress."

"Good. Blade will have to know something about him. Something about your brotherhood."

"Mistress?"

"If you're going to use a tool you should know its capabilities. Only a priest demands we take things on faith."

"Priests and functionaries," Narayan corrected. "You're right. Blade will take nothing on faith."

He was the last man alive who would. That might come between us someday.

"Are any of your brotherhood cynical enough to be hiding inside other priesthoods?"

"Mistress?" He sounded hurt.

"I have few sources of information. If we had friends within the priesthoods . . ."

"I don't know about Taglios, Mistress. It seems unlikely."

I did miss the old days, when I'd had the unbridled use of my powers, when I could summon a hundred demons to spy for me, when I could recall the memories of a mouse that had been in the wall of a room where my enemies had congregated.

I'd told Narayan that I'd built an empire from beginnings as humble as ours. That was true, but I'd had more weapons. This time I often felt disarmed.

The weapons were coming back, but far too slowly.

"Send Blade to me."

I took Blade for a walk up the river, east of the fortress. He was content to wait on me. He spoke only once, cryptically, as we approached a bankside tree where a fishing pole leaned. "Looks like Swan never got back."

I had him explain. It didn't mean much. I looked at the fortress. Swan and Mather were in there, nominal commanders of all Taglian forces below the river. I wondered how seriously they took that. They hadn't been out much. I wondered if Blade was in touch. He'd hardly had time. He'd been working hours longer than mine, teaching himself as he taught his men. I wondered why he made the effort. I sensed a deep reservoir of irrational hatred inside him.

I suspected he was a man who wanted to change the world.

Such men are easy to manipulate, easier than the Swans, who mostly just want to be left alone.

"I'm thinking of promoting you," I told him.

He responded sardonically. "To what? Unless you're promoting yourself, too."

"Of course. You become legate of the Ghoja legion. I become general of the army."

"You're going north."

He didn't waste words and didn't need many to extract a lot of information. "I should be in Taglios now. To guard my interests."

"It's a bad spot. In the crocodile's jaws."

"I don't follow."

"You need to be here to gather soldiers, to gain power. You need to be there to control the priests who can keep recruits away."

"Yes."

"You need trustworthy lieutenants. But you're alone."

"Am I?"

"Maybe not. Maybe I misinterpret the interest of Narayan and Sindhu."

"Probably not. Their goals aren't mine. What do you know about them?"

"Nothing. They aren't what they pretend."

I thought about that, decided he meant they weren't what they pretended to be to the world. "Have you heard of the Deceivers, Blade? Sometimes called the Stranglers?"

"Death cult. Legendary, probably. The Radisha mentioned them and their goddess. The wizard is terrified of them. The soldiers say they are extinct. That isn't true, is it?"

"No. A few still exist. For their own reasons they're backing me. I won't bore you with their dogma. It's repulsive and I'm not sure it was related to me truthfully."

He grunted. I wondered what went on inside his head. He hid himself well. I'd met others like him. I will be stunned the day I meet someone entirely new.

"Go north without fear. I'll manage Ghoja."

I believed him.

I turned back. We walked toward camp. I tried to ignore the stench from across the river. "What do you want, Blade? Why are you doing this?"

He shrugged, an uncharacteristic action. "There are many evils in the world. I guess I've chosen one for my personal crusade."

"Why such a hatred for priests?"

He didn't shrug. He didn't give me a straight answer, either. "If each man picks an evil and attacks it relentlessly, how long can evil persist?"

That was an easy one. Forever. More evil gets done in the name of righteousness than any other way. Few villains think they are villains. But I left him his illusion. If he had one. I doubted he did. No more than a sword's blade does.

At first I'd thought him moved as Swan so obviously was when he looked at me. But he hadn't so much as hinted that he considered me anything but a fellow soldier.

He confused me.

He asked, "Will you talk to Willow and Cordy? Or shall I?"

"What do you think?"

"Depends. What you want to discuss? How? You wiggle some, you can lead Swan anywhere."

"Not interested."

"I'll talk to them, then. You go ahead. Do what you have to do."

Sunrise next morning I was on the road north with two incompetent and incomplete battalions, Narayan and Ram, and all the trophies I had claimed from the Shadowmasters' horsemen.

The Radisha waited impatiently while Smoke bustled around making sure his spells were proof against eavesdroppers. The Prahbrindrah Drah lounged in a chair, looking indolent and unconcerned. But he spoke first when the wizard signalled satisfaction with his precautions. "More bad news, Sis?"

"Bad? I don't know. Not pleasant. Dejagore was a disaster. Though experts tell me it hurt the Shadowmasters so badly they can't bother us this year. The woman you lust after did survive, though."

The Prahbrindrah grinned. "Is that the good news or the bad?"

"Subject to interpretation. For once, though, I think Smoke might be right."

"Ah?"

"She insists the defeat neither destroyed the Black Company nor terminated our contract. She gave me a requisition for more men, equipment, and materials."

"She's serious?"

"Deadly. She reminded me of the Company's history and what becomes of those who renege on contracts."

The Prahbrindrah chuckled. "Bold wench. All by herself?"

Smoke squeaked something.

The Radisha said, "She's already recruited a force two thousand strong. She's training them. She's dangerous, dear. You'd better take her seriously."

Smoke squeaked again, apparently unable to articulate what he wanted to say.

"Yes. She killed Jahamaraj Jah. Jah tried giving her some trouble. Poof! She made him disappear."

The prince took a deep breath, blew it out between puffed cheeks. "Can't fault her taste. But that's no way to make friends with priests."

Smoke gobbled again.

The Radisha said, "She doesn't intend to try. She got Blade to defect. He's her number two man, now. You know his attitude. Dammit, Smoke! One thing at a time."

"Swan and Mather?"

"They stuck. I think. But Swan is taken with her, too. I really don't know what you see in her."

The Prahbrindrah chuckled. "She's exotic. And gorgeous. Where are they now?"

"I left them in charge. Supposedly. It's meaningless. She considers herself the Captain and free to do whatever she pleases. With those two there I'll have eyes on the scene. They can keep us informed. All right, Smoke. All right."

"What's he lathered about?"

"He thinks she's made an alliance with the Stranglers."

"The Stranglers?"

"Kina worshippers. Like Smoke's been whining all along."

"Oh."

"First time she visited me she brought two of them with her. Or men who appeared to be Stranglers."

Smoke managed a clear statement. "She carried a strangling cloth herself. I believe she slew Jah personally. I believe she disposed of his corpse in a Deceivers' rite."

"Let me think." The prince steepled his fingers before his lips. Finally, he asked, "Were they men she'd recruited? Or did she make an alliance with the whole cult?"

Smoke gobbled. The Radisha contradicted him. "I don't know. Who knows how that cult works?"

"It's not monolithic."

Smoke said, "She carried a rumel herself. She posed as Kina during the fight with the Shadowmasters' cavalry."

The Radisha had to explain that.

The prince observed, "So we assume the worst? No matter how unlikely?"

"Even if she has access to only a few Stranglers, dear, she's acquired an unholy power. They have no fear of death. If they're told to kill, they'll kill. Disregarding any cost to themselves. And we have no way of knowing who might be one of them."

"The Year of the Skulls," Smoke piped. "It's coming."

"Let's don't get carried away. You talked to her, Sis. What does she want?"

"To continue the war. To fulfill the Black Company's commission, then see us meet our end of the agreement."

"Then we're in no immediate danger. Why not let her have her head?"

"Kill her now," Smoke said. "Before she grows any stronger. Destroy her! Or she will destroy Taglios."

"He seems to be overreacting. Don't you think, Sis?"

"I'm not so sure anymore."

"But . . ."

"You didn't talk to her, her with all the confidence of a tidal wave. She's turned damned scary."

"And the Shadowmasters? Who'll handle them?"

"We have a year."

"You think *we* could build an army?"

"I don't know. I think we made a lethal mistake dealing with the Black Company the way we did. Quiet, Smoke. We wove webs of deception. That will come back on us because we're in too deep to retreat. Swan, Blade, and Mather were convinced we were treacherous in our promises. I'm sure Blade shared his opinions with the woman."

"We'll step carefully, then." The Prahbrindrah reflected. "But right now I don't see the threat. If she wants to get the Shadowmasters, I say let her go after them."

Smoke had a fit. He ranted. He cursed. He issued dire prophecies. Every sentence included the words, "The Year of the Skulls."

His histrionics were so craven they drove the Radisha toward her brother's position.

Brother and sister left him to his humors. As they moved toward their part of the palace, the Prahbrindrah asked, "What's gotten into him? He's lost his nerve completely."

"He never had much."

"No. But he's gone from a mouse to a jellyfish. First it was fear of getting found out by the Shadowmasters. Now it's the Stranglers."

"They scare *me*."

The prince snorted. "We have more power than you suspect, Sis. We have the power to manipulate three priesthoods."

The Radisha sneered. She knew what that was worth. So did Jahamaraj Jah, now.

25

Eight men sat around the fire in the room without a roof. That room was on the top floor of a four-storey tenement in Taglios' worst slum. The landlord would have suffered apoplexy had he seen what they had done.

They had been there only a few days. They were wrinkled little brown men unlike any Taglian native. But Taglios lay beside a great river. Strangers came and went. Unusual people seldom drew a second glance.

They had opened the room to the elements and now some regretted it.

A summer shower had come down the river. It was not a heavy rain but the clouds had stalled over the city. They shed a steady drizzle. Taglios' people were pleased. Rain cleared the air and carried away the trash in the streets. Tomorrow, though, the air would be muggy and everyone would complain.

Seven of the eight brown men did nothing but stare into the flames. The eighth occasionally added a bit of fuel or a pinch of something that sent sparks flying and filled the air with aromatic smoke. They were patient. They did this for two hours each night.

Suddenly, shadows rippled in over the tops of the walls, danced behind and among the men. They did not move, did nothing to admit they sensed the new presence. The one added another pinch of aromatic, then rested his hands in his lap. Shadows gathered around him. Shadows whispered. He replied, "I understand." The language he spoke was not Taglian. It was spoken nowhere within six hundred miles of Taglios.

The shadows went away.

The men did not move till the fire died. The rain became a blessing then. It quenched the flames quickly.

The one who had fed the fire spoke briefly. The others nodded. They had their orders. Discussion was unnecessary. In minutes they were out in the Taglian streets.

Smoke muttered curses as he stepped into the rain. "Story of my life. Nothing goes right anymore." He scuttled along, head down. "What am I doing out here?" He ought to be inside trying to make the Radisha see sense so she could make her brother see sense. They were going to ruin everything. All they had worked toward was going to fly away if they didn't do something about that woman.

They were going to destroy Taglios by default. Why couldn't they see that?

Sometimes a walk helped clear the mind. He needed to be out, away, alone, free. Some new avenue would present itself. There was a way to get through, he was sure. There had to be.

A bat zipped past so close he felt the air stirred by its wings. A bat? On a night like this?

He recalled a time, before the legions marched, when bats had been everywhere. And someone had made a considerable effort to eliminate them. Someone like maybe those wizards who had travelled with the Black Company.

He halted, suddenly nervous. Bats in weather when bats should not fly? Not a good omen.

He had not come far. One minute and he'd be safely in the palace.

Another bat whipped past. He turned to run.

Three men blocked his path.

He whirled.

More men. Everywhere, men. He was surrounded. For half a minute they seemed a horde. But there were only six. In very bad Taglian one said, "A man want see you. You come."

He looked around wildly. There was no escape.

The paradox of being Smoke, Smoke thought. Terrified when the danger was insubstantial, calm now with it concrete, he moved through streets dark and wet, surrounded by men no bigger than he. His mind worked perfectly. He could break away whenever he willed. One small spell and he could be gone, safe.

But something was afoot. It might be crucial to know what. That spell could be loosed later as well as now.

He pretended to be as rattled and craven as ever.

They took him to the worst part of the city, to a tenement that looked like it could collapse any second. He was more frightened of it than of them. They led him up four creaky flights. One man tapped a code on a door.

The door opened. They went inside. Smoke eyed the man waiting. He looked just like the six who had brought him. Nor did the man who had opened the door seem any different. All hatched in the same nest. But the man who waited spoke passable Taglian.

He asked, "You are the one called Smoke? The fire marshall? I cannot recall the full title."

The wizard supposed they knew who and what he was, else he would not be here. "I am. You have me at a disadvantage."

"I have no name. I can be called One Who Leads Eight Who Serve." Ghost of a smile. "Unwieldy, yes? It is of no importance. I am the only one here who can speak your language. You won't confuse me with anyone else."

"Why did you interrupt my stroll?" Keep it cool, casual, he thought.

"Because we have a common interest in dealing with a peril so great it could devour the world. The Year of the Skulls."

Now Smoke knew who they were.

He controlled himself but his mind went wild. His efforts to maintain his anonymity had gone for naught. The Shadowmasters knew him.

Maybe Swan was right. Maybe he was just a coward . . . He was. He had known that always. But he was no puling craven. He could manage his fear if he had to.

Still . . . It rankled that Swan could be right about anything. Willow Swan was an animal that walked on its hind legs and made noises like a man.

"The Year of the Skulls?" he asked. "What do you mean?"

The man smiled thinly. "It will save time if we don't pretend. You know Kina is stirring. And when she stirs, ripples go out and waken other things best left undisturbed. The first whisper of Kina passes over the world. Soon the woman who is her avatar will become aware of what she is."

"Do you think me simple?" Smoke demanded. "Do you believe I can be weaned from my loyalty so easily? Do you believe an appeal to my fears will subvert me?"

"No. Subversion is not the point. He who sent me is to you as you are to a mouse. *He* is afraid. He has cast the bones of time. He has seen what may be. That woman can bring on the true Year of the Skulls. What she was once she can become again, filled with the breath of Kina. Before that terror all else pales. The contention of armies becomes the squabbling of children. But he who sent me has no power to reach out where the danger abides. She has surrounded herself with Kina's Children. She grows stronger by the hour. And he who sent me must remain where he is, holding back the tide of darkness that laps at Shadowcatch. He can do nothing but register his appeal for help and offer his friendship, which you may test as you will and call upon as you see fit."

A scheme. A tortuous scheme, surely. But he dared not reject it out of hand. There was sorcery in this place. He hadn't time to take its measure. If he turned them down flatly he might not get out alive.

"Which Shadowmaster do you call lord?" He thought he knew. The man had mentioned Shadowcatch.

The brown man smiled. "You call him Longshadow. He has other names."

Longshadow, master of Shadowcatch. The Shadowmaster whose demesne was farthest from Taglios, who was the least known of the four, rumored to be insane. He hadn't been much involved in the attacks upon Taglios.

The foreigner said, "He who sent me has not been involved in this war. He opposed it from the beginning. He has refused to participate. There are more pressing dangers, more deadly concerns, which preoccupy him."

"Men much like you have attacked Taglians several times."

"Stipulated. On the river. In the southern Taglian territories. Can you guess the common denominator, wizard?"

"The woman."

"The woman. Kina's fulcrum. He who sent me cast the bones of time. And as she becomes a greater danger he becomes more pressed elsewhere, less able to fight. He needs allies. He is desperate with fear. He will give more than he takes. The weed of doom has taken root in Taglios and he can do so little. It must be expunged by Taglians."

"There's a war on. Taglians didn't initiate it."

"Neither did he. But that war can be ended. He has that power. Of the three who wanted war, two are dead. Stormshadow and Moonshadow are gone. Shadowspinner lingers. He controls their combined armies but he is injured. He can be compelled to accept peace. He can be expunged, if that is the price of peace. Peace *can* be restored. Taglios *can* be as it was before the madness began. But he who sent me will *not* invest resources in making these things come true if there is nothing to be gained by letting some of his attention be diverted."

"From what?"

"Glittering stone. Khatovar. You are no unlettered peasant. You have read the ancients. You know the Shadar Khadi is but a pale shade of Kina, though Khadi's priests deny it. You know Khatovar, in the old tongue, means Khadi's Throne and is supposed to be the place where Khadi fell to earth. He who sent me believes the legend of Khatovar is an echo of an older, truer tale of Kina."

Smoke controlled his emotions and fears. He forced a smile. "You've given me a great deal to digest. A veritable feast."

"Only a first course. Truly, he who sent me is desperate. He needs a friend, an ally, who has influence here, who has some chance to cut the weed before it flowers. He will do what he has to do to demonstrate his good faith. He has told me to tell you he will even bring you to him so you can judge his honesty for yourself if that is your wish. If you are able to feel safe doing so. He'll agree to whatever safeguards you feel you need if you wish to speak to him directly."

"A lot to digest," Smoke said again, just wanting to get out of there before somebody turned vicious.

"I expect so. Enough to overturn your world. And more to come. And you have been gone a long time now. We wouldn't want your absence to become an object of concern. Go. Think. Make decisions."

"How should I get in touch?"

The brown man smiled. "We will find you. We will move from this place after you leave, lest you suffer some shortsighted inspiration to make yourself a hero. A bat will find you when it is time. Place yourself where you cannot be watched and these others will meet you."

"All right. You're right. I'd better get back." He eased toward the door, still not sure where he stood. But no one interfered with his departure.

He had a lot to mull over. And the interview had been productive if for no other reason than that it proved the Shadowmasters had put new agents into the city after the Black Company's wizards rooted out those that had been there before.

The little brown man who spoke bad Taglian asked his leader, "Will he take the bait?"

The leader shrugged. "The appeal was broad enough to touch him somewhere. His fears. His ego. His ambitions. He's been handed the chance to destroy what he fears and hates. He's been offered the chance to make himself big as a peacemaker. He's been offered the opportunity to fatten his own power with potent friends. If he has any need to become a traitor we've touched it."

The man smiled. His companions did, too. Then all eight began packing. The leader was sure the wizard's conscience would move him to report this initial approach.

He hoped the wizard would not take long seducing himself. The Shadowmaster was concerned about wasting time. He was not pleasant when he was worried.

26

The Radisha had only a day's start on us. Though a thousand men should find it harder to stop and start than a smaller party, we gained ground. Narayan had supplied us with the most efficient and motivated men. We were only two hours behind when the Radisha reached the city.

I marched in boldly, trophies displayed, and went straight to the barracks the Company had used when we were training the legions. The barracks were occupied by men we had left behind, men who had been injured in the battle at the Ghoja ford, and men who had volunteered after our departure. Most were commuting from their homes for daytime self-training but the barracks were still crowded. Enrollment exceeded four thousand.

"Get them under control," I told Narayan as soon as I grasped the situation. "Make them ours. Isolate them as much as possible. Work on them." Bold words, but how practical?

"Word of our arrival is spreading," he said. "The whole city will know soon."

"No avoiding it. I've been thinking. Between them the men ought to have some notion what happened to almost everybody who didn't come home. A lot of Taglians will want to know what happened to their men. We could make a few friends telling them."

"We'd be swamped." He was forgetting to offer an honorific more and more often. *He* thought he was a partner in my enterprise.

"Maybe. But let it out that we welcome inquiries. And push news that a lot of Taglians are trapped in Dejagore and I could get them out if I could get a little help."

Narayan looked at me oddly. "No chance, Mistress. Those men are dead. Even if they're still breathing."

"We know it. But the world doesn't. Anybody asks, to get them out we just put together enough men and arms quick enough. That will fix anybody who wants to interfere with me. Someone opens his mouth, he says he doesn't care about those men. Blade says the people here all think their priests are thieves. They might get real upset if the priests start playing with their sons' and brothers' and husbands' lives. We take advantage of religious friction. If a Gunni priest gets on me, we just appeal to the Shadar and Vehdna laity. And never stop mentioning that I'm the only professional soldier around."

Narayan grinned that repulsive grin. "You've given this a lot of thought."

"Wasn't much else to do on the way here. Get moving. We have to take control before anybody wonders if we really ought to. Before troublemakers think up ways to give us grief. Get feelers out to members of your brotherhood. We need information."

Narayan had some organizational skills though he was no charismatic leader. He could rise in a small group by demonstrated ability but he'd never get a large gang to follow him just because he cut a bold figure.

Thinking that made me think of Croaker. Croaker hadn't been charismatic. He'd been a workaday sort of commander. He'd identified the task to be accomplished, had considered his options, had put the best-suited men to work. He usually guessed right and got the job done. Except for that last time, at Dejagore, when his weakness became obvious.

He didn't think fast on his feet. He didn't intuit well.

Past tense, woman. He's gone.

I didn't want to think about him. It still hurt too much.

There was plenty of work to occupy me.

I began looking at the manpower resources that had fallen into my lap.

Not promising. Plenty of spear carriers, determined young men, but hardly anyone who stood out as an immediate leader. Damn, I missed the military engine I'd had back home.

I started wondering what I was doing here, why I had come. Pointless, woman. I could not go back. That empire had moved on. It had no place for me now.

I missed more than my armies. I had no intelligence machine. No way to ferret out secrets.

Ram remained my shadow, as much as he could. Determined to protect me, Ram was. Probably under the most dire orders of jamadar Narayan. "Ram, do you know the country around Taglios?"

"No, Mistress. I never went out till I enlisted."

"I need men who do know. Find them, please."

"Mistress?"

"This place is indefensible. Most of the men are drilling out of their homes." Why was I explaining? "We need to get away from distractions and vulnerabilities." Ideally on a hill near the south road, water, and a large wood.

"I'll ask around, Mistress." He was reluctant to leave me but no longer had to be ordered away. He was learning. Give him another year.

Narayan materialized before Ram returned. "It's going all right. A lot of excitement. The men who were there—there must be at least six hundred of them now—are telling inflated stories about how we beat those cavalrymen. There's talk about relieving Dejagore before the rainy season. I didn't have to start it."

During the rainy season the Main became impassable. For five or six months it was Taglios' wall against the Shadowmasters. And theirs against Taglios.

What would happen if I got caught south of the river when the rains came? That would give me time to get the army whipped into shape.

On the other hand, it would not leave me anywhere to run.

"Narayan, get me . . ."

"Mistress?"

"I forget you haven't been with me forever. I was going to send you after something we compiled before we went south."

One of our great enterprises had been a census of men, materials, animals, skills, and other resources an army needs. The results should be around somewhere still.

There was a way around the high water dilemma if the right men and materials were available.

"Mistress?" Narayan asked again.

"Sorry. Just wondering what I'm doing here. I have these moments."

He took me literally. He started in on revenge and rebuilding the Company.

"I know, Narayan. It's just fatigue."

"Rest, then. You'll have to be at your best later."

"Oh?"

"Those who want to know about their men are gathering already. Surely the news of our arrival has reached all the false priests and even the palace. Men will come to see how they can take advantage of you."

"You're right."

Ram returned with a half dozen men and some maps. None were men who had come north with me. They were nervous. They showed me three sites they thought might suit my purpose. I dismissed one immediately. It had a hamlet there already. Neither of the others had much to recommend it either way. Which meant I had to go look for myself.

Something to kill time.

I was getting as sarky as Croaker in my old age.

I thanked everybody and sent them away. A few minutes' rest would be useful. Like Narayan said, the siege would begin soon. We might have problems with men who could not wait to see their loved ones.

I dragged my things into the quarters I had occupied last time, one small room I refused to share. I plopped on the cot. It had not changed while I was gone. Still a rock within a mask of linen.

I'd just relax for a few minutes.

Hours fled. I dreamed. I was confused when Narayan wakened me. He came while I was visiting the caverns of the ancients. The voice calling me was louder, clearer, more insistent, more pressed.

I got hold of myself. "What is it?"

"The crowds of relatives. I was having them visit the gate one by one, but they've started pushing and shoving. There must be four thousand people out there and more arriving all the time."

"It's dark. Why did you let me sleep?"

"You needed it. It's raining, too. That may be a blessing."

"It'll keep some people home." But this would cost time however we handled it. "There's a public square where we paraded before we went south. I don't recall the name. Find out. Tell those people to assemble there. Tell the men to prepare for a short march in the weather. Tell Ram to ready my armor but forget the helmet."

*   *   *

There were five thousand people in the square. I managed to intimidate them into keeping quiet. I faced them on my stallion, looking at a sea of lamps and lanterns and torches while the soldiers formed up behind me.

I said, "You have a right to know what happened to your loved ones. But the soldiers and I have a great work before us yet. If you'll cooperate we'll handle this quickly. If you don't remain orderly we'll never get it done." My Taglian had improved dramatically. No one had trouble understanding me.

"When I point you out name the man you want to know about in a clear, loud voice. If one of the soldiers knew him he'll speak up. Go to that soldier. Talk quickly and quietly. If the news is bad, contain yourself. There are others who want news, too. They have to be able to hear."

I doubted it would go smoothly for long but it was just a gesture meant to get me mentioned kindly outside the corridors of power.

It worked well for longer than I expected, but Taglians are pliable people, used to doing what they're told. When disorder did develop I just announced that we would leave if it did not stop.

Some of my men were the objects of queries. I had Narayan moving through the formation. Those he knew were industrious, cooperative, hard-working, and loyal he could grant a short leave. He was supposed to remind the less diligent why they would remain on duty. Carrot and stick.

It held up. Even the greenest behaved. It took all night but we satisfied half the crowd. I reminded everyone frequently that Mogaba's legion and who knew how many more men were trapped in Dejagore, thanks to the desertion of Jahamaraj Jah. I made it sound like everyone not accounted for was among the besieged.

Most were probably dead.

Whips and carrots and emotional manipulations. I'd been at it so long I could do it in my sleep.

A messenger came. There were priests at the barracks to see me. "Took them long enough," I muttered. Were they late because they were off balance or because they waited till they were ready for a confrontation? No matter. They would wait till we finished.

The rain stopped. It was never much more than a drizzling nuisance.

Once we cleared the square I dismounted and walked with Narayan. We were seventy fewer now. He had let that many go. I asked, "Did you notice the bats?"

"A few, Mistress." He was puzzled.

"Are they special among the omens of Kina?"

"I don't think so. But I was never a priest."

"They're significant to me."

"Eh?"

"They tell me, plain as a shout, that the Shadowmasters have spies here. General order to the men. Kill all bats. If they can, find out where they're roosting. Watch out for foreigners. Pass the word to the populace, too. There are spies among us again and I want to lay hands on a few."

We'd probably end up swamped with useless reports about harmless people, but . . . A few wouldn't be harmless. And those needed their teeth pulled.

The men waiting included delegations from all three religious hierarchies. They were not pleased that I had kept them waiting. I did not apologize. I was not in a good humor and did not mind a confrontation.

They'd had to wait in the mess hall because there was nowhere else to put them. Even there they had to crowd up because they had to get out of the way of men who had nowhere else to spread their blankets.

Before I went in I told Narayan, "First score to my credit. They came to me."

"Probably because none of them want you making a private deal with the others."

"Probably." I put on my best scowl, laid on a light glamor, clanked into the mess hall. "Good morning. I'm honored but I'm also pressed for time. If you have something to discuss please get to the point. I'm an hour behind schedule and didn't budget time for socializing."

They didn't know how to take me. A woman talking hard was something new.

Somebody shot an obnoxious question from the back.

"All right. A position statement. That should save time. My religious attitude is indifference. I'll stay indifferent as long as religion ignores me. My position on social issues is the same. I'm a soldier, one of the Black Company, which contracted with the Prahbrindrah Drah to rid Taglios of the Shadowmasters. My Captain fell. I replaced him. I will fulfill the contract. If that statement doesn't answer your questions then you probably have questions you have no right to ask.

"My predecessor was a patient man. He worried about offending people. I don't share those qualities. I'm direct and unpleasant when aroused. Questions?"

They had them. Of course. They yammered. I picked a man I recognized, one who was offensive and was not loved by his peers. He was a bald Gunni in scarlet. "Tal. You're being unpleasant. Stop it. You have no legitimate business here. None of you have, really. I said I have no interest in religion. You have little cause to be interested in things military. Let's leave each other to our own competences."

Beautiful Tal played his part as though rehearsed. His response was more than offensive, it was a direct challenge predicated upon my sex, speaking to my failure to commit suttee.

I tossed him a Golden Hammer, not to the heart but to the right shoulder. It spun him around and knocked him down. He screamed for more than a minute before he passed out.

It got real quiet. Everyone, including poor fuddled Narayan, stared at me wide-eyed.

"You see? I'm not my predecessor. He would have remained polite. He would have clung to persuasion and diplomacy long past the point where a demonstration is a more effective way to communicate. Go tend to priestly matters. I'll tend to making war and to wartime discipline."

That should not be hard for them to figure out. The Company's contract made the Captain virtual military dictator for a year. Croaker had not used the power. I did not expect to. But it was there if needed.

"Go. I have work to do."

They went. Quietly. Thoughtfully.

"Well," Narayan said after they left. "Well."

"Now they know I'm no fainter. Now they know I'm mission-oriented and don't care who I stomp if they get in the way."

"They're bad men to make enemies."

"They make the choice. Yes! I know. But they're confused. It'll take them a while to decide what to do. Then they'll all get in each other's ways. I've bought time. I need intelligence sources, Narayan. Find Ram. Tell him I want those men he brought to me earlier. It's time to look at those sites." Before he could argue, I added, "And tell him if he plans to keep on being my shadow he'd better learn to ride. I expect to be moving around a lot, now."

"Yes, Mistress." He hurried off, paused just before he left, looked back, frowned. He was wondering who was using who and who had the upper hand. Good. Let him. While he was wondering I'd get my foundations set solidly.

The men in the mess hall all stared at me with varying degrees of awe. Few met my gaze. "Rest while you can, soldiers. The sands are running through the glass."

I went to my quarters to wait for Ram.

Croaker stared into the drizzly night, fingers nervously twisting strands of grass. One of the horses made a sound out there. He thought about walking over there, mounting up bareback, riding away. He would stand a fifty-fifty chance of staying ahead.

Except that things had changed. Now Catcher did not have to catch up physically.

He held up the figure he had made, a man shape two inches tall. The grass gave off a garlic odor. He shrugged, flipped it out into the rain, took more strands of grass from a pocket. He had made hundreds now. Grass figures had become a sort of measure of time.

A steady banging came from behind him. He turned away from the night, walked slowly toward the woman. She had produced a set of armorer's tools from somewhere. This was the second day running she had spent building something. Obviously black armor, but why?

She glanced at the horse figure he was twisting. "I may get you some paper and ink."

"Would you?" There was a lot he wanted to set down. He had grown used to keeping a journal.

"I may. That's no pastime for a grown man."

He shrugged, put the horse aside. "Take a break. Time to check you over."

She no longer wore robes. She was outfitted as she had been when first he had met her, in tight black leather that somehow left her sex ambiguous. Her Soulcatcher costume, she called it. She hadn't bothered with the helmet yet.

She set her tools aside, looked at him with mischief in her eyes. "You sound depressed." The voice she chose was merry.

"I am depressed. Stand up." She did. He peeled away the leather around her neck. "It's healing quickly. I'll remove the sutures tomorrow, maybe."

"Will there be much scarring?"

"I don't know. Depends on how well your healing spells work. I didn't know you were vain."

"I'm human. I'm a woman. I want to look nice." Same voice but less merry.

"You do look nice." He did not think before he spoke. Just making a statement of fact. She looked nice in the sense that she was a beautiful woman. Like her sister. He had become very conscious of that since she had changed her style of dress. That left him nagged by low-grade guilt.

She laughed. "I'm reading your mind, Croaker."

She was not, literally. She would not be pleased with him if she was. But she had been around a long time and had studied people. She could read books from a few physical clues.

He grunted. He was getting used to it. There was no point trying hard to hide from it. "What are you making?"

"Armor. We'll be healed enough to go soon. We'll have great fun."

"I'll bet." He felt a twinge in his chest. He *was* almost healed. There had been none of the complications he had expected. He had begun taking forced exercise.

"We're the gadflies here, love. The chaos factor. My beloved sister and the Taglians know nothing about us. Those clubfooted Shadowmasters know I'm here but they don't know about you. They don't know what you've accomplished. They think I'm a nuisance floating around in the dark. I doubt they've entertained the notion that I could be restored."

She rested a hand on his cheek. "I'm more basic than you think."

"Oh?"

Change of voice, businesslike, masculine, at odds with the invitation. "I have eyes everywhere. I know every word spoken by anyone who interests me. A while back I arranged for Longshadow to be diverted while Howler visited Spinner and cut Longshadow's webs of control."

"Damn! He'll hit Dejagore with everything."

"He'll lie low and pretend he's unchanged. The siege costs him nothing. He'll be more interested in improving his position in relation to Longshadow. He knows Longshadow will destroy him when he's no longer useful. We'll have fun. We'll poke around and make them chase their tails. When the dust settles, maybe there'll be no Longshadow, no Shadowspinner, no Howler, just you and me and an empire of our own. Or maybe the spirit will move me some other direction. I don't know. I'm just having fun with it."

He shook his head slightly. Hard to believe, but it sounded true. Her schemes could kill thousands, could distress millions, and to her it was play.

"I'll never understand you."

She giggled the giggle of a girl with nothing between the ears. She was neither young nor empty-headed. "I don't understand myself. But I gave up trying a long time ago. It's distracting."

Games. From the first she had been involved in tortuous maneuvers and manipulations, to no obvious end. Her great pleasure was to watch a scheme flower and devour its victim. Her only plot to fail had been the one meant to displace her sister. And she had not failed completely then because she had survived, somehow.

She said, "Soon Kina's followers will start arriving. We'll have to be somewhere else. So let's go down to Dejagore and cause some confusion. We ought to get there about the time Spinner figures he's ready to make an independent move. Be interesting to see how it goes."

Croaker did not understand but did not ask. He was used to her talking in riddles. She let him know what she wanted him to know when she was ready to tell him. No point pressing her. He could do little but bide his time and hope.

"It's late," she said. "We've done enough for today. Let's turn in."

He grunted, not eager. The place gave him the creeps when he thought about it, which meant every night as he fell asleep. Which meant at least one potent nightmare. He would be glad to get out.

Maybe out there he could vanish—if he could think of a way to hide from the crows.

Fifteen minutes after the lamp went out Soulcatcher asked, "Are you awake?"

"Yeah."

"It's cold in here."

"Uhm." It always was. Most nights he fell asleep shivering.

"Why don't you come over here?"

The shivering worsened. "I don't think so."

She laughed. "Some other time."

He fell asleep worrying about how she always got her way instead of about the temple. His dreams were more troubling than nightmares.

Once he wakened momentarily. The lamp was alive again. Soulcatcher was murmuring with a clatch of crows. The subject seemed to be events in Taglios. She appeared pleased. He drifted off without understanding what it was about.

29

Neither potential campsite was perfect. One had been fortified before, in ancient times. For centuries people had carried the stone off for use elsewhere. I chose that site.

"Nobody remembers the name," I told Ram as we rode toward town. "Makes you think."

"Huh? About what?"

"The fleeting nature of things. Taglios' entire history could have been influenced by what happened there and now nobody remembers the name."

He looked at me oddly, straining for understanding. He wanted to understand but he didn't have the capacity. The past was last week, the future tomorrow. There was no reality in anything that happened before he was born.

He was not stupid. He seemed big and dull and slow but possessed an average intellect. He just had not learned to employ it.

"Never mind. It doesn't matter. I'm just being moody." He understood moody. He expected it. His wife and mother had been "moody."

He did not have time now to think, anyway. He was too busy staying on his horse.

We returned to the barracks. There was another crowd looking for their loved ones. Narayan was handling them efficiently. They eyed me curiously. Not at all the way they had looked at Croaker. Him they had hailed Liberator everywhere. Me, I was a freak without the sense to know she was not a man.

I would grow on them. Just a matter of creating a legend.

Narayan caught up with me. "There was a messenger from the palace. The prince wants you to dine with him tonight. Someplace called the grove."

"Oh?" That was where I had met him first. Croaker had taken me. The grove was an outdoor place frequented by the rich and influential. "Request or order?"

"Invitation. Will you do me the honor of, like that."

"Did you accept?"

"No. How could I guess what you'd want to do?"

"Good. Send a message. I accept. What time?"

"He wasn't specific."

It would slow me down but I might accomplish something that would save fussing and feuding later. At least I'd learn how much grief I could expect from the state. "I'm going to sketch out the camp I want built. We'll send one company plus five hundred recruits to start. Pick whoever you think we should get out of the city. That mess outside. How's it going?"

"Well enough, Mistress."

"Any volunteers showing?"

"A few."

"And intelligence? Have you gotten anything started?"

"Lot of people want to tell us things. Mostly about foreigners. Nothing really interesting."

"Keep at it. Let me do those sketches. After that I'll make a list to give the Prahbrindrah. After that I'll make myself presentable." Around here somewhere would be my imperial getup, that I'd worn last time, and my coach, that we had brought down from the north and had left here when we had marched on Ghoja.

"Ram, before we went south I had several men help me make special armor. I need to find them again."

I went to work sketching and estimating.

The coach was not as impressive with a four-horse team but people did gawk. I had enough skill to make hooves strike fire and to set a glamor running the coach's exterior. The fire-breathing skull of the Company blazed on both doors. The steel-rimmed wheels and pounding hooves rumbled thunderously.

I was satisfied.

I reached the grove an hour before sunset, entered, looked around. Just like last time, the cream of Taglian society had come out to rubberneck. Ram and a red rumel man named Abda, of Vehdna background, were my bodyguards. I did not know Abda. He was with me because Narayan said he was good.

They had spruced up. Ram cleaned up nicely when you held a knife to his kidneys. Bathed, hair and beard trimmed, in new clothes, he cut a handsome figure. But Abda did not improve much. He was a shifty-eyed little villain who looked like a villain no matter what.

I wished I had brought a Gunni bodyguard, too, to make a symbolic statement. You can't think of everything when you're rushed.

The Prahbrindrah rose as I strode up to him. He smiled. "You found me. I was concerned. I wasn't specific about where we'd meet."

"It seemed logical I'd find you where we met before."

He eyed Ram and Abda. He had come alone. A measure of his confidence in his people's reverence? Misplaced confidence, maybe.

"Make yourself comfortable," he invited. "I've tried to order things I think you'll like." He glanced at Ram and Abda again, perplexed. He did not know what to do about them.

I said, "Last time I was here somebody tried to kill Croaker. Forget them. I trust their discretion." I had no idea whether I could trust Abda or not. Didn't seem smart to make a point of it, though.

Servitors started with refreshments and appetizers. From the state of the grove you could not tell Taglios was a nation threatened with extinction.

"You look radiant this evening."

"I don't feel it. I feel worn out."

"You should relax more. Take life easier."

"Have the Shadowmasters decided to take a holiday?"

He sampled something that looked like shrimp. Where had shrimp come from, here? Well, the sea was not that far away.

Which sparked a germ of an idea. I set it aside for later examination.

The prince swallowed, dabbed his lips with a napkin. "You seem determined to make my life difficult."

"Oh?"

"You roar ahead like the whirlwind, giving no one time to think. You rush headlong. Everyone else has to concentrate on keeping their balance."

I smiled. "If I give anyone time to do anything but run along behind me I'll be up to my ears in grief. None of you seem to understand the magnitude of your enemy. You all have your priorities inverted. Everybody wants to dance around and get the angle on everybody else. Meantime, the Shadowmasters are planning to exterminate all of you."

He nibbled and pretended to think. "You're right. But people are human. Nobody here has ever had to think in terms of external enemies. Or really deadly enemies."

"The Shadowmasters count on that, too."

"No doubt."

A new course arrived, more substantial. Some kind of bird. I was surprised. The prince's background was Gunni. The Gunni were determined vegetarians.

Watching my surroundings I spied two things I did not like. There were dozens of crows among the trees. And that priest Tal I had embarrassed earlier, with several of his cronies, was watching us.

The Prahbrindrah said, "I'm under a lot of pressure because of you. Some from close quarters. It puts me in a delicate position."

Where was his sister? Were she and Smoke riding him? Probably. I shrugged and ate.

The prince said, "It would help if I knew your plans."

I told him.

"Suppose some important people don't approve or don't feel you're the right champion?"

"It wouldn't matter. There's a contract in force. It will be fulfilled. And I don't distinguish between enemies foreign or domestic."

He understood.

Nothing got said during the next course. Then he blurted, "Did you kill Jahamaraj Jah?"

"Yes."

"My gods! Why?"

"His existence offended me."

He gulped some air.

"He deserted at Dejagore. That cost us the battle. That was reason enough. But he also planned to kill your sister and blame me. He had a wife. If Shadar women are foolish enough to kill themselves over men, you can tell her to fire her ghat. Any priest's wife who has a husband like Jah had better start collecting firewood. She'll need it."

He winced. "You'll start a civil war."

"Not if everybody behaves and minds his own business."

"You don't understand. Priests consider everything their business."

"How many men are we talking about? A few thousand? You ever watch a gardener prune? He snips a twig here, a branch there, and the plant grows stronger. I'll prune if I have to."

"But . . . There's only you. You can't take on . . ."

"I can. I will. I'm going to fulfill the contract. And so are you."

"What?"

"I've heard that you and your sister didn't negotiate in good faith. Not smart, my friend. Nobody cheats the Company."

He did not respond.

"I'm not really good at games. I'm not subtle. My solutions are forthright and final."

"Forthright and final begets forthright and final. You kill a Jah, the other Jahs will get the idea their only option is to kill you."

"Only if they ignore the option of minding their own business. And where's my risk? I have nothing to lose. That's the fate planned for me once I'm used up, anyway. Why cooperate in my own destruction?"

"You can't just keep killing people who don't agree with you."

"I won't. Only people who disagree and try to force their ideas on me. Here in Taglios, now, there's no legitimate cause for conflict."

The prince seemed surprised. "I don't follow."

"Taglios must be preserved from the Shadowmasters. The Company contracted to do that. Where's the problem? We do what we agreed, you pay up as agreed, we go away. That ought to make everyone happy."

The prince looked at me like he wondered how I could be so naive. "I'm starting to think we have no basis for communication. This dinner may have been a mistake."

"No. It's been productive. It'll keep on being productive if you *listen* to me. I'm not beating around the bush. I'm telling you how it is and how it's going to be. Without me the Shadowmasters will eat you alive. You think they'll be impressed by which cult got a leg up on what with a boondoggle wall construction grant? I know how those people think. If they reach Taglios they'll slaughter everybody who could possibly make trouble ever. You should understand that. You saw what they did elsewhere."

"It's impossible to argue with you."

"Because you know I'm right. I have a list of things I need right away. I have to build an encampment and prepare a training ground immediately."

This could lead to a quick confrontation. The resources would have to come from that absurd wall project. The city was too big to surround effectively. The project could not be justified. It was a tool for transferring the wealth of the state to a few individuals.

I said, "The men and resources devoted to the wall can be more profitably employed."

He understood. I was asking for trouble. He grunted.

I said, "Why don't we just enjoy our meal?"

We tried but it never turned into a festive evening.

A few courses along, with the conversation darting between his younger years and mine, I took the offensive again. "One more thing I want. The books Smoke hid."

His eyes got big.

"I want to know why you're afraid of the past."

He smiled weakly. "I think you know. Smoke is sure you do. He believes it was the point of your coming."

"Give me a clue."

"The Year of the Skulls."

I was not entirely surprised. I feigned bewilderment. "Year of the Skulls? What's that?"

He glanced at Ram and Abda. Doubt appeared. I recalled toying with my rumel while talking to his sister. He would not doubt long.

"If you don't know you should find out. But I'm not the best authority. Talk it over with your friends."

"I have no friends if I don't have the Prahbrindrah Drah."

"A pity."

"Do you have?"

That baffled him again. He forced a smile. "Perhaps I don't. Perhaps I ought to try to make some." The smile changed.

"We all need a few. Sometimes our enemies won't let us find them. I should be getting back. My number two is inexperienced and handicapped by his place in your caste system."

A hint of disappointment? He had wanted more than a discussion of princes and warlords.

"Thank you for the dinner, Prahbrindrah. I'll treat you in kind, soon. Ram. Abda." They stepped close. Ram offered a hand up. They had stayed behind me, unseen. I was pleased that they were alert. Ram would have been if only because of where we were. A man of his station had no hope of visiting the grove ordinarily. "Have a pleasant evening, Prince. I expect to hand you the heads of Taglios' enemies within the year."

He wore a sort of sad, yearning look as he watched us go. I knew what he was feeling. I had felt it often while I was empress in the north. But I had hidden it better.

Ram waited till he was confident we were out of earshot. "Something is going to happen, Mistress."

"Trouble?"

"We were watched by sneaking Gunni priests all the time. They acted like they were up to no good."

"Ah." I did not question his estimate. He did not have too rich an imagination. I snapped fingers at a nearby servitor. "Fetch Master Gupta."

Master Gupta ran the grove, a benign dictator. He was attentive to his guests—especially those who were close to the Prahbrindrah Drah. He appeared almost instantly.

Bowing like a coolie, he asked, "What could the great lady want of this lowly worm?"

"How about a sword?" Dressed as a woman and empress I had not come heavily armed. I had one short dagger.

His eyes got huge. "A sword? What would I do with a sword, Mistress?"

"I haven't the faintest. But I want to borrow one if you can provide it."

Eyes even bigger, he bowed several times. "I'll see what can be found." He scooted off, throwing uncertain looks over his shoulder.

"Ram, help me shed some of this showpiece."

He was scandalized. He refused.

"Ram, you're pushing for the opportunity to spend your army time digging latrine trenches."

He took my word for it, accepted the disapproval of several dozen watchers as he helped me shed my most cumbersome garments. He was embarrassed.

Abda, not asked to participate, pretended blindness.

Gupta materialized. He had a sword. It was someone's show toy. "I borrowed this from a gentleman who was gracious enough to permit me to carry it to you." He was blind, too. I expect he had seen everything over the years. The grove was a place where lovers managed clever assignations.

"I shall harbor kind thoughts toward you forever, Gupta. Am I correct in assuming the staff sent for my coach when they saw me getting ready to leave?"

"The men responsible will be seeking employment elsewhere if it isn't there when you arrive, Lady."

"Thank you. I'll send this toy back shortly."

Ram again waited till he thought no one could hear, grunted a question. I replied, "If there's to be trouble it'll come just inside the gate. If we reach the coach we'll be safe."

"You have a plan, Mistress?"

"Spring the trap. If there is one. We wipe them out or take them prisoner and carry them off, never to be seen again. How many might there be?"

Ram shrugged. He did not waste time looking at me now. He had eyes for trouble only.

Abda said, "Eight. And the one you embarrassed. But he'll avoid getting too close. He might have to explain if someone saw him."

"Oh?"

"I was involved in two similar schemes when I was an acolyte."

I had no idea what he meant. It did not seem like the best time to fill myself in on his past. We were approaching a brushy area that crowded the path to the exit.

I say brushy but I'm no devotee of formal gardening. The area consisted of heavy vegetation four to eight feet high. Every single leaf was tended and considered daily. Its function was to mask the grove from the world so Taglios' lords would not be defiled by common eyes.

I started a spell as soon as we left Gupta. I was ready when we reached the shrubbery. It was another child's plaything but my most ambitious effort yet. I spoke the initiator and threw the resulting fireball into the growth to my left.

By the time the ball went ten feet it was hot enough to melt steel. It broke into fragments that broke into smaller fragments.

Someone screamed.

Someone else screamed. A man plunged out of the growth pounding his side.

I got another ball ready, threw it the other way.

"Wait," I said. "Let them come out. We'll push them down the path to the gate." There were three men on that path now, wild-eyed. Then three more came out like spooked cattle. The brush was burning. "That's long enough. Let's move."

We hustled forward. The baffled would-be assassins retreated. They piled up against the closed gate. The gatemen stared at the flames, stunned, unsure what to do.

"Ram. Bang them over the head. Put them in the coach." A guard recognized me, did his job by rote as Ram waded into the six.

"Mistress."

Abda was behind me. I turned. A man afire was charging us with an upraised tulwar, a weapon I had not seen here before. It looked like an antique.

Abda ducked, darted, had his rumel around the man's neck in a blink. I did not get to use my borrowed blade. The assassin's impetus broke his neck.

That was it. Ram tossed bodies into the coach. I told the least rattled gate guard, "Thank master Gupta for the loan." I gave him the sword. "And extend my apologies for the damages. The priest Chandra Chan Tal should be happy to make them good. Ready, Ram?"

"Yes, Mistress."

"Abda, get that carrion loaded." I walked to the coach, climbed up beside my driver, looked around, spotted Tal. He and two other priests in red were standing streetside eighty feet away, bug-eyed. I saluted them.

"Loaded, Mistress," Abda called up.

I got some amusement from him and Ram. They did not want me up there, exposed, but did not want me inside with the dead and captive, either. "Shall I run along behind like a good Taglian woman, Ram?"

Embarrassed, he shook his head.

"Climb aboard."

We rolled right past Tal and his cronies. I called down, "Get what pleasure you can from the hours you have left."

Tal blanched. The other two were made of sterner or stupider stuff.

31

It was a gorgeous day. A few clouds above to break up the sky, a gentle breeze, the air unseasonably cool. If you stayed in the shade you could remain sweat-free. It was midafternoon. Work on the camp had begun at dawn. Four thousand men made progress obvious.

First we would provide shelter, mess halls, stables, storage. I had planned ambitiously, for a garrison of ten thousand. Even Narayan was worried that I wanted to grab too much too soon.

I had spent the morning administering oaths to the soldiers in small groups, by cult, having them pledge everything in the sacred defense of Taglios. Wormed into the oath was a line about unquestioning obedience to commanders.

Narayan's cleverer cronies weeded out the priests and religious fanatics beforehand. The dross we isolated in what was supposed to be a special unit. There were about three hundred such men. They were on the field below the hill, being given "accelerated" training. As soon as I found a good one I would send them off on a bold and dramatic mission somewhere far away. I sat in the shade of an old tree observing and directing. Ram hovered.

I spied Narayan approaching. I had left him in the city. I rose, asked, "Well?"

"It's done. The last one was found an hour before I left."

"Good." Tal had been easy but his companions had been hard to trace. Narayan's friends had disposed of them. "That's good. Has it caused excitement?"

"Hard to tell yet, though a Gunni emissary did show up just before I left."

"Oh?"

"He wanted to arrange the release of the men from the grove."

"And?"

"I told him they'd been released. He'll figure it out."

"Excellent. Any word on the Shadowmasters' spies?"

"No. But people have seen the wrinkled little brown men you mentioned. So they must be here."

"They're here. I'd give a couple of teeth to know what they're up to. Anything else?"

"Not yet. Except a rumor that the Prahbrindrah Drah called in the big men in the wall project and told them they have to build you a fortress instead. I've located a friend who works in the palace occasionally, when their normal resources are taxed. Our prince doesn't maintain a household in keeping with his station. He won't get much if the prince doesn't entertain, and probably not much then."

"Look into the possibility of arranging for your friend to become employed full time. Have there been many more volunteers?"

"Only a few. It's still too early. People want to see how you manage with the powers that be."

"Understandable. Nobody wants to sign on with a loser."

Be interesting to know what they said about me at that meeting. A pity I did not command the resources I once had.

I was not going to get them back loafing. "I'll ride back with you. I have things to do." I had recalled one thing my husband had done to secure his rule. A version here just might make everyone forget politics for a while.

I would need a suitable theater. I had to start looking. As we rode, I asked Narayan, "Do we have many archers?" I knew we did not but what I lacked he had a knack for finding.

"No, Mistress. Archery wasn't a skill much encouraged. A hobby for Marhans, that's all." He meant the top-dog caste.

"We had a few, though. Find them. Have them teach the most reliable men."

"You have something in mind?"

"A new twist on an old story. Maybe. I may never need them but if I do I want to know they're there."

"As always, we shall endeavor to provide." He grinned that grin I wished I could scrub off his face forever.

"To create a body of archers you'll need bows and arrows and all the ancillary paraphernalia." That would keep his mind occupied. I did not feel like talking. I did not feel ready to wrestle lions today. Had not for several days, in fact. I supposed it was lack of sleep, bad dreams, and the fact that I had been driving myself to the limit.

The dreams persisted. They were bad but I just shoved them aside in my mind, took the unpleasantness, and got on with getting on. There was just so much I could do in the time available. I would deal with the dreams when I finished with more immediate concerns.

For a while I thought about my one-time husband, the Dominator, and his empire-building techniques, then about my own plight. Lack of leaders continued to plague me. Every day men were handed tasks beyond their training, based on my or Narayan's gut feelings. Some worked out, some folded under the pressure. That was heavier now that we meant to digest a horde with no idea what was happening.

As we neared the city, approaching scaffolding where wall construction had started, Narayan observed, "Mistress, it's less than a month till the Festival of Lights."

He lost me for a moment. Then I recalled the festival as the big holy day of his cult. And remembered him hinting around that I should be there if I wanted the support of the Stranglers. I had to go convince the other jamadars that I was the Daughter of Night and could bring on the Year of the Skulls.

I had to learn more about the cult. To find out what Narayan might be hiding.

There was no time to do everything that had to be done.

We had gotten our first message from the men watching Dejagore last night. Mogaba was holding out. Stubborn Mogaba. I did not look forward to seeing him again. Sparks would fly. He would claim the Captaincy, too. I knew that as sure as I knew the sun rose and set.

One step at a time. One step at a time.

The meeting with the priests had not gone well. The Radisha was in a blistering rage. Her brother looked grim. Smoke squeaked, "Something has to be done about that woman."

They were in a shielded room but something had installed itself amongst clutter on a high shelf. Those below did not notice the one yellow crow eye watching.

"I'm not so sure," the Prahbrindrah Drah replied. "We talked extensively. I think she was truthful. My gut feeling is that we should give her her head."

"Gods!" Smoke swore. "No!"

The Radisha remained neutral. For the moment. "We were inches from getting thrown out tonight. We couldn't drive a wedge between them. The fact that we might be able to point her in their direction was all that saved us. We can't get rid of her, Smoke."

The Prahbrindrah Drah said, "We've got the tiger by the tail. Can't let go. I feel like I'm in a big bowl and all around the rim are people who want to roll boulders down on me."

"She will devour us," Smoke said. He kept his tone reasonable. Panicky talk had worked against him before. The Prahbrindrah Drah and Radisha had to be convinced intellectually. "She traffics with Stranglers."

"Of whom there are maybe only a few hundred in the whole world," the Radisha observed. "How many men are there in the Shadowlands? How many shadows? There're more backstabbing priests here in the city than there are Stranglers anywhere."

"Read those old chronicles again," Smoke suggested. "How numerous were the Black Company when they came here before? Yet before they were driven out our ancestors very nearly witnessed the Year of the Skulls. You can't traffic with this darkness. It wakens the devil in everyone. You can't invite the tiger into your house to keep the wolf away. There are no greys. There is no tightrope to walk. No one can hope to play this off against other darknesses. This is the deep and ultimate evil beyond all evils. Consider what the woman did last night."

The Prahbrindrah Drah said, "I was put out by the damage done. Master Gupta and his predecessors worked on that for a century."

"Not the damned plants!" Smoke almost lost control. "A man is dead, killed by sorcery. Seven more were carried off to who knows what fate? Tal and his cronies were slain in their very temples. Strangled!"

"They asked for it," the Radisha said. "They did something stupid. They paid for it. You notice the other Gunni priests weren't put out."

"Ghapor's bunch? They probably encouraged Tal and didn't mind when he came out on the short end."

"Probably."

"Don't you see what she's done? A year ago no priest would have considered murder. Now it's accepted. Nobody is distressed.

"Tal is gone. You say he was stupid and asked for it and you're right. But he was one of the most important men in Taglios. So was Jahamaraj Jah. He asked for it, too. When she picks off the next one, well, maybe everybody will say the same thing again. He asked for it. And the next one and the next and then it's you and the Prahbrindrah Drah and after that the deluge. Never mind professionalism as a soldier. She might be the best that ever was. Maybe she can ruin the Shadowmasters in her sleep. But even if they never cross the Main again, if they never come north of Dejagore, if they never win another skirmish, if she's in charge, Taglios will lose as certainly as if we hadn't resisted at all."

The Prahbrindrah Drah started to speak. The Radisha jumped in first. "He has a point. Taglios won't ever be the same."

"Oh?"

"If we give the woman a free hand she'll make Taglios over into the image of the Shadowlands because that's what it will take to win. Smoke, I see that. Even if you're obsessive about the Stranglers and the Year of the Skulls. I've watched the woman. I doubt if anyone but that man Croaker ever had any influence on her. Brother, he's right. She'll turn us into what we fear in order to save us."

"Then we're damned if we do and damned if we don't. We let her go on, we're done. We don't, the Shadowmasters eat us."

Smoke said, "There's another way. . . ." But he could not tell them. He had not told them everything when he had reported the approach by Longshadow's agents. Too late now. If he brought up overlooked details they would no longer trust him. They might even think his opposition to the woman had been ordered by Taglios' enemies.

That wrinkled little man had foreseen this. Damn him.

"Well?" the Radisha demanded.

"I had a thought. It was impractical. Emotion guiding the mind. Forget it. Kina is stirring. The Daughter of Night walks among us. We must silence her."

The Prahbrindrah Drah said, "We can talk about this all night. None of us will change our minds. We'd better concentrate on staying a step ahead of the priests till we do agree."

Smoke shook his head. That would not do. The woman would keep everyone confused and divided; then it would be too late. That was the way of darkness. Deceit. Endless deceit.

No point talking anymore. There was only one choice left.

They would hate him if they caught him. They would brand him traitor. But there was no other answer.

He had to pray for courage and a clear head. The Shadowmasters were masters of deceit themselves. They would use him if they could. But if he played the game carefully he could serve Taglios better than any dozen armies.

He started trying to cut the conversation short.

As brother and sister were leaving, the prince said, "Smoke, I meant to ask. Why would she put a bounty on bats all of a sudden?"

"A what?"

"The Shadar Singh mentioned it. He heard it on his way here. She put out word that any children who wanted could pick up a few coppers by bringing her dead bats. Every poor family in town will start hunting them. And the treasury will have to pay for them. Why?"

"I have no idea," Smoke lied. His heart was in his throat. She *knew*. That business about reporting strangers . . . It wasn't a propaganda ploy. She knew. "A few exotic spells use bat parts powdered. Fur, claws, livers. But they're the kind that make your neighbor's cattle sterile or his hens stop laying. Nothing of use to her."

But live bats were useful to the Shadowmasters.

He barely waited till the prince and his sister turned a corner down the hall. Then he headed for the world outside, before there were no bats left to find him.

Croaker sat on a rock in the wood, leaning against a tree, twisting an animal figure. He finished it and tossed it at a stump. Crows watched. He paid them no heed. He was thinking about Soulcatcher.

She was not great company. She had spent ages turned inward. She could be amiable and animated for brief periods but did not know how to keep it up. Neither did he. Sometimes it seemed they were moving in parallel rather than together. But she would not let him go just because they weren't soulmates. She had uses for him.

She had been bustling around the temple all day. He did not know why. He felt no urge to find out. He was depressed. He came to this spot when his mood was at low ebb.

The imp Frogface materialized. "Why the long face, Cap?"

"Why not?"

"You got me there."

"What's happening in Dejagore?"

"Got me there, too. I've been busy."

"Doing what?"

"Can't say." The imp aped his morose stance. "Last time I was there your boys was doing fine. Maybe fussing and feuding a little more than before. Old One-Eye and his sidekick don't get along with that Mogaba, not even a little. They been talking about doing a fade and letting him go to hell his own way."

"He'd get wiped out if they did."

"He don't appreciate them enough, that's sure."

"She says we're going down there."

"Well. Then you can look for yourself."

"I don't think that's what she's got in mind. She call you in?"

"Came to report. Interesting things happening. You could ask. She might tell you."

"What's she doing?"

"Fixing the place up so it don't look like somebody's been living there. That Festival thing is coming up. Them weirdos will be getting here real soon."

Croaker doubted he would get a straight answer but he asked anyway. "How's Lady?"

"Fine. Keeps on, she'll be running the whole show in six months. Got every poobah in Taglios so confused she's doing any damned thing she pleases."

"She's in Taglios?" He hadn't known that. Catcher hadn't told him. He hadn't asked.

"Has been for weeks. Left that Blade character in charge at Ghoja and went up to the city and started taking over."

"She would. She isn't the kind to wait for things to happen."

"Tell me about it. Whoa! I hear the boss calling. Better get on over there. Pack up your things."

"What things?" He did not have much but the clothes he wore. And those were rags.

"Whatever you have to take with you. She's leaving in an hour."

He did not argue. That was as futile as arguing with a stone. His wants and interests did not count. He had less freedom than a slave.

"Take it easy, Cap," the imp said. And vanished.

They rode till Croaker collapsed. They rested, then rode again. Soulcatcher ignored such niceties as restricting travel to daylight hours. She permitted a third halt only after they entered the hills northwest of Dejagore. She spoke seldom except to her crows, and to Frogface briefly after they arrived, while Croaker was sleeping.

She wakened him as the sun rose. "We reenter the world today, my love. Sorry I haven't been as attentive as I should." He could tell nothing from her choice of voices. This one he thought was her own, much like her sister's, always neutral. "I've had a lot on my mind. I should bring you up to date."

"That would be nice."

"Your flair for sarcasm hasn't disappeared."

"It keeps me going."

"Maybe. This is how things stand. Last week Spinner attacked Dejagore in force. He was thrown back. He would have succeeded if he'd used all his skills. But he couldn't without Longshadow finding out he's not as feeble as he pretends. He'll try again tonight. He could succeed. Your One-Eye and Goblin have broken with their commander.

"My beloved sister has obtained a strong position in and around Taglios. She has five or six thousand men, none of them worth a damn.

"She left the man Blade at Ghoja when she headed north. He has the same problems and none of her expertise but some of the men he has have legionary experience. He's decided to let them learn the hard way. He's begun occupying surrounding territories, especially southward along the road to Dejagore."

"Makes it easier to feed his men, probably."

"Yes. He has a force exceeding three thousand men now. His scouts have skirmished with Shadowspinner's patrols.

"And the big news, of course, is that the wizard Smoke has been seduced by Longshadow."

"Say what? That little bastard. I never did trust him."

"Longshadow appealed to his idealism. And to his fear of my sister and the Black Company. Offered him assurances he couldn't help but believe, made him think he could become a hero by saving Taglios from its supposed saviors while he made peace with the Shadowlands."

"That man is a fool. I thought you had to be smart to be a wizard."

"Smart doesn't mean sensible, Croaker. And he isn't a complete fool. He didn't trust Longshadow. He used every device he could to make Longshadow keep his word. His real mistake was going to visit Longshadow at Shadow-catch."

"What?"

"The Howler and Longshadow combined their talents to create a flying carpet like those we had back when, before they were destroyed. It's a puny one but good enough for Howler to fly the wizard to Shadowcatch and to drop spies into Taglios. Smoke is down there now. Frogface is watching him. Longshadow is trying to do a poor man's Taking of Smoke. He'll go back to Taglios as Longshadow's creature."

Croaker did not like the sums he came up with. Three major wizards against Taglios now, and Taglios' only magical defender was a creature of the enemy. Lady might be doing well but could not be doing as well as she must to manage both the Shadowmasters and her enemies behind her.

Doom would be stalking Taglios long before anyone expected it.

Khatovar was farther away than ever.

He could not manage that mission on his own. Taking the Annals back . . . He did not have them. They were trapped inside Dejagore. He could not get to them.

Was Murgen keeping them up? He'd better be.

"You haven't said anything about our part in all this."

"But I have. Often. We're just going to have fun with it. We're going to kick the props out from under people. Tonight we'll have this whole end of the world wondering what's going on and who's doing what to who."

He began to understand soon after she told him to start getting ready. "Ready how?"

"Get your armor on. It's time to scare the shit out of Spinner's men and save Dejagore."

He just stood there, puzzled. She asked, "Would you rather let them be wiped out?"

"No." The Annals were in the city. They had to be preserved. He unpacked the armor they had lugged all the way from the temple. "I can't get this on by myself."

"I know. You'll have to help me with mine, too."

With hers? He had assumed she would use her old Soulcatcher guise. He began to see her subtlety.

The armor she had made at the temple was a copy of Lady's Lifetaker rig. Their appearance would leave all the principals completely confused. His Widowmaker was supposed to be dead. Lady's Lifetaker was supposed to be in Taglios. Neither was supposed to amount to anything in sorcerous terms. The besieged would be stunned. Spinner's men would be dismayed. Longshadow might suspect the truth but would not be sure. Smoke and the Taglian prince and his sister would be baffled. Even Lady would be confused.

He was sure she believed him dead.

"Damn you," he said as he settled her helmet over her head. "Damn you to hell." He could not refuse to cooperate. Dejagore would fall and its defenders would be massacred if he and she did not intercede.

"Relax, my love. Relax. Put emotion aside. Have fun with it. Look. The lance." She pointed.

It was the lance that had carried the Company standard for centuries. He had searched in vain for it at the temple. He had not seen it coming down. Now it stood beyond the fire they had lighted for illumination. It glowed gently. A banner hung from it but he could not make it out.

"How did you . . . ?" To hell with her. Sorcery. He would play her game only as far as he had to. He would give her no pleasure.

"Get it, Croaker. Mount up. It's time." She'd even conjured the armor that went with the stallions, baroque and beginning to show highlights of witch-fire.

He did as he was told. And was startled. Her armor had a subtly different look from that which Lady had created for her Lifetaker character. This was more intimidating. It radiated menace. It had the feel of an archetypal doom.

Two huge black crows settled on his shoulders. Their eyes burned red. More crows circled Catcher. Frogface materialized on the neck of her horse, chattered briefly, vanished. "Come. We should arrive just in time to save the day." The voice she used was that of a happy kid contemplating a prank.

Mather stuck his head into the room. "He's on his way, Willow."

Swan grunted, opened shutters for more light. He looked out at Blade's camp and its satellites. The gods themselves were on Blade's team. Recruits had been arriving in droves. None of them wanted to enlist in the Radisha's guard. He'd had high hopes when he had invented that. But the Radisha's name carried less weight here than Blade's. And, damn him, he was as stubborn about sticking with Lady as Cordy was about the Radisha.

"Cordy, Cordy, why the hell don't we just go home?" he muttered to himself.

Blade came in, escorted by Mather. That human stump Sindu was right behind them. He was like Blade's shadow, anymore. Swan did not like the man. He was creepy.

Blade said, "Cordy says you have something."

"Yeah. We finally got one up on you." He had begun fielding patrols of his

own after Blade started expanding southward. "Our boys grabbed some prisoners."

"I know."

Of course he did. There was no hiding from each other here. They did not
try. They remained friends, however much they disagreed. Blade did most of
his planning in that room, on the map table there. Anything Swan wanted to
know he could see right there.

"There was a big dust-up at Dejagore the other night. Shadowspinner hit
the burg with everything he had. He grabbed our friends by the short hairs.
Then what should pop up but two giant fire-breathing riders in black armor
flinging thunderbolts around and kicking ass wholesale. When the smoke
cleared away it was the Shadowlanders that got whupped. One of the prisoners
saw it with his own eyes. He said Shadowspinner had to yank everything out of
his trick bag to hold those two off. Here's the way they say it went down."

Swan kept a close eye on Blade while he chattered. There was some emotion
showing through that bland facade.

He finished his tale. "What you think, old buddy? Those two miracle visitors sound like anybody we know?"

"Lady and Croaker. In their costume armor."

"Bingo! But?"

"He's dead and she's in Taglios."

"Two in a row. Give the man a prize. I think. So what the hell really went
down? Sindhu. What you grinning about, man?"

"Kina."

The others looked hard at the broad man. Mather said, "Descriptions again,
Willow."

Swan repeated.

Mather said, "Kina. The way she's described by people who know her."

"Not her," Sindhu said. "Kina sleeps. The Daughter is bound in flesh."
Sindhu's association with the Deceivers was an open secret. But he was not much
help. Usually it was like this. He would say one thing, then contradict himself.

Swan said, "I'm not going to try to figure that out, buddy. Somebody fits the
description went in and tore them new buttholes down there. Kina or not-
Kina, I don't care. Somebody wanted people to think Kina. Right?"

Sindhu nodded.

"So who was that with her? That fit anywhere?"

Sindhu shook his head. "This confuses me."

Mather hoisted himself to a seat in the window. Swan shuddered. Cordy
had a forty-foot drop behind him. He said, "Be quiet. Let me think."

Swan echoed, "Quiet. Let him." Cordy was a genius when he took the trouble.

They waited. Swan paced. Blade studied the map. He let no time waste. Sindhu remained impassive and still, yet seemed shaken.

Mather said, "There's another force in the field."

"Say what?" Swan chirped.

"Only way it adds up, Willow. The Shadowmasters are out to get each other but they wouldn't go that far. Helps us too much. Our side doesn't have anybody who could pull off the sorcery angle. So somebody else did it."

"What the hell for?"

"To confuse things?"

"They did that. Why?"

"I couldn't guess."

"Then who?"

"I don't know. Just like everyone else won't know, and will be chasing their tails trying to figure it out."

Was Blade listening? Didn't seem like it. He asked, "How bad were the Shadowlanders hurt?"

"Huh?"

"Shadowspinner's armies. How bad off are they?"

"Bad enough they can't take a crack at Dejagore again till they get replacements. But not so bad our guys have a crack at breaking out."

"Just enough interference to keep the balance, then."

"Our guys got cut up bad, way the prisoners talked. As many as half of them killed. Meaning the Shadowmasters' men really got mauled."

"But they could still send out patrols for you to catch?"

"Shadowspinner is scared we'll move on him. He doesn't want any more surprises."

Blade paced. He returned to the map, tapped out the garrisons and posts he had established as much as a hundred fifty miles south. He paced. He asked Mather, "Is it true? Or is it something they want us to believe? Bait for a trap?"

Swan said, "The prisoners believed it."

Blade said, "Sindhu, why haven't we heard from Hakim? Why did this news reach us this way?"

"I don't know."

"Find out. Go talk to your friends right now. If this is true we should have known before their patrol got here with the prisoners."

Sindhu departed, disturbed.

Swan said, "Now you got rid of him, what's on your mind?"

"Is the story true? That's what's on my mind. Sindhu has people babysitting Dejagore. They should've had a messenger moving the minute the dust-up started. Another should've brought a complete report when it was over. One might not have gotten through but two wouldn't have failed. We made that road safe. We enlisted most of the bandits and feistier peasants."

"You think the prisoners are plants?"

Blade paced. "I don't know. If they are, why on you? Mather?"

Cordy thought. "If they're a plant we shouldn't have been the captors. Unless their purpose is to cause confusion. Or they don't know the difference. It could be they're telling the truth but we're not supposed to believe it because you haven't heard from your scouts. It could be a device to buy time."

"Illusion," Swan said. "You remember what Croaker used to say? That his favorite weapon was illusion?"

"That's not quite what he said, Willow," Mather corrected. "But close enough. Somebody wants us to see something that isn't there. Or to ignore something that is."

Blade said, "I'm moving."

Swan squawked. "What do you mean, moving?"

"I'm heading down there."

"Hey! Man! What are you, crazy? You're getting a little carried away, chasing that tail."

Blade walked out.

Willow spun on Mather. "What do we do, Cordy?"

Mather shook his head. "I don't know about friend Blade anymore. He's looking to get killed. Maybe we shouldn't have taken him away from those crocs."

"Yeah. Maybe. But what do we do now?"

"Send a message north. Then go with him."

"But . . ."

"We're in charge. We can do whatever we want." Mather hustled out.

"They're both crazy," Swan muttered. He looked at the map a minute, went to the window, watched the excitement in Blade's camp, eyed the ford and the swarming engineers setting wooden pylons for Lady's temporary bridge. "Everybody's gone crazy." He laid a finger between his lips and wiggled it furiously while saying, "Why the hell should I be any different?"

35

That's it," I said. "I've had it." I'd just gotten word that a Vehdna priest, Iman ul Habn Adr, had ordered Vehdna construction workers to abandon my camp and report for work on that absurd city wall. It was the second defection of the day. The Gunni contingent had walked an hour after starting time. "The Shadar won't show tomorrow. They've finally decided to test me, Narayan. Assemble the archers. Ram, send those messages I had the scribes prepare."

Narayan's eyes got big. He could not get himself moving. He did not believe I would do it. "Mistress?"

"Move."

They went.

I prowled, trying to walk off my anger. I had no reason to be mad. This was no surprise. The cults had given me no grief since I had taken care of Tal. That meant they were working things out between them before they tested me again.

I took advantage of the respite, recruiting two hundred men a day. I got the camp established in temporary form. The stonework of the fortress, meant to replace it, was well started. I'd gotten some of the men through the first stages of their training. I had cajoled or extorted weapons and animals and money and materials from the Prahbrindrah Drah. In that area I had more than I needed.

I had stretched my talent considerably. I was still no threat even to Smoke but my progress excited me.

The big negatives were the dreams and an incessant mild nausea I could not shake. It might be the water at the campsite though it persisted when I returned to the city. Probably it was mostly reaction to lack of sleep.

I refused to yield to the dreams. I refused to pay attention. I made them something to be suffered through, like boils. Someday I would have the chance to do something about them. Then balances would be redressed.

I watched my messengers trot toward town. Too late to back down now.

Succeed or fail, I would get their attention.

* * *

Ram helped me don my armor. A hundred men watched. The barracks remained as overcrowded as ever, though I had moved five thousand men to the campsite. "More volunteers than I know what to do with, Ram."

He grunted. "Lift your arm, Mistress."

I raised both. And spied Narayan pushing through the press. He looked like he had seen a ghost. "What is it?"

"The Prahbrindrah Drah is here. By himself. He wants to see you." He tried to whisper but men heard. Word spread.

"Quiet! All of you. Here? Where?"

"I told Abda to bring him around the long way."

"That was thoughtful, Narayan. Keep working, Ram."

Narayan fled before Abda brought the prince. I started in on the appropriate public courtesies. He said, "Forget that. Can you clear this out some? I'd like a little privacy."

"Fire drill. Something. You men, outside. Abda, see to it."

The crowd started moving reluctantly. The prince eyed Ram. I said, "Ram stays. I can't get dressed without him."

"Surprised to see me?"

"Yes."

"Good. It's time somebody surprised you."

I just looked at him.

He demanded, "What's all this bull about you quitting?"

"Quitting what?"

"Resigning. Going away. Leaving us to the Shadowmasters."

That had been the implication but not the substance of the messages I'd had delivered. "I don't know what you mean. I'm going to make a speech to some priests. Just to straighten them out. Where did you get the idea I was deserting?"

"That's the talk. They're all excited. They think they've beaten you. That they just stood up to you, stopped letting you walk over them, and you're going to say good-bye."

Exactly what I wanted them to think. What *they* wanted to think. "Then they're going to be disappointed."

He smiled. "I've had nothing but trouble from them all my life. I've got to see this."

"I wouldn't recommend it."

"Why not?"

I could not tell him. "Trust me. If you're there you'll regret it."

"I doubt it. They couldn't give me much more trouble than they have already. I want to see them when you disappoint them."

"You do, you'll never forget. Don't go."

"I insist."

"I warned you." Him being there would not do him any good but it would be good for me. I told myself I'd done my best. My conscience was clear.

Ram finished dressing me. I told him, "I need Narayan. Abda! Would you look after the prince? If you'll excuse me?"

I got Narayan into a corner where we could whisper. I told him what had happened. He grinned that damned grin of his till I was ready to rip it off his face. But he jumped to another subject. "The Festival is almost upon us, Mistress. We have to make travel plans soon."

"I know. The jamadars want to look me over. But I have too much on my mind now. Let's get through tonight first."

"Of course, Mistress. Of course. I didn't mean to press."

"The hell you didn't. Is everything set?"

"Yes, Mistress. Since early this afternoon."

"Will they do it? When it comes to the moment of decision, will they?"

"You never know what a man will do till he's faced with a decision, Mistress. But the men are all former slaves. Very few of them Taglian."

"Excellent. Go. We'll be leaving in a few minutes."

The square was called Aiku Rukhadi, Khadi Junction. It had been a crossroads long ago, before the city swamped the countryside. It was Shadar then but Vehdna now. It was not a big square, being a hundred twenty feet in its greatest dimension. It had a public fountain in its center, water for the neighborhood. It was crowded with priests.

The cult leaders had come and had brought all the friends they wanted to witness the humiliation of the female upstart. They had dressed for the occasion. The Shadar wore white, simple shirts and pantaloons. The Vehdna wore kaftans and glamorous turbans. The most numerous contingent, the Gunni crowd, was subdivided by sect. Some wore scarlet robes, some saffron, some indigo, some aquamarine. Jahamaraj Jah's successors wore black. I guessed the crowd at between eight hundred and a thousand. The square was packed.

"Every priest who's anybody is here," the prince told me. We entered the square behind a half dozen incompetent drummers. They were my only bodyguards. Even Ram was absent. The drummers cleared a space against a wall.

I told the prince, "That's the way I wanted it." I hoped I looked sufficiently impressive in costume. Atop my great black stallion I loomed over the Prahbrindrah, whose chestnut was no dwarf. The priests noticed him and started whispering. Eight hundred men whispering make as much noise as a swarm of locusts.

I positioned us with the wall behind and the drummers in front.

Would it work?

It had, wonderfully, for my husband, so long ago.

"Soul lords of Taglios." Silence fell. I had that spell right. My voice carried well. "Thank you for coming. Taglios faces a severe test. The Shadowmasters are a threat that cannot be exaggerated. The tales out of the Shadowlands are ghosts of the truth. This city and nation has one hope: turn a single face toward the enemy. In faction lies defeat." They listened. I was pleased.

"In faction, defeat. Some of you feel I'm not the champion for Taglios' cause. More of you have been seduced by lust for power. By factionalism. Rather than let that worsen and distract Taglios from its grand mission I've decided to eliminate the cause of factionalism. Taglios will present one face after tonight."

I donned my helmet while they were waiting for me to announce my abdication. I set the witchfires free.

They began to suspect then. Someone shouted, "Kina!"

I drew my sword.

The arrows began to fall.

While I was talking Narayan's picked men had placed barricades in the narrow streets entering the square. When I drew my sword, soldiers inside the surrounding houses let fly. Priests screamed. They tried to flee. They found the barricades too high. They tried to turn on me. My talent was enough to hold them off, beyond my terrified drummers. The arrows continued to fall.

They surged this way and that. They fell. They begged for mercy.

The arrowfall continued till I lowered my sword.

I dismounted. The Prahbrindrah Drah looked down, face bloodless. He tried to say something, could not speak. "I warned you."

Narayan and his friends joined me. I asked, "Did you send for the wagons?" It would take dozens to haul the bodies to an unhallowed mass grave.

He nodded, no more able to speak than the prince. I told him, "This is nothing, Narayan. I've done lots worse. I'll do worse again. Check them out. See if anybody important is missing." I walked across the killing ground to tell the bowmen they could release the people who lived in the houses.

The Prahbrindrah never moved. He just sat there and stared, painfully aware that his presence made it seem he approved.

Ram found me there. "Mistress," he gasped. He had run all the way from the barracks.

"What are you doing here?"

"There is a messenger from Ghoja. From Blade. He rode night and day. Come immediately." He was not affected by the mass of bodies. He might have been watching the neighborhood women at the well instead of Narayan's cronies finishing the wounded.

I went. I spoke with the messenger. For a minute I was furious with Blade. Then I saw the silver lining.

Blade's actions gave me an excuse to move the troops out before they got wind of what had happened here tonight.

The Prahbrindrah Drah sat there an hour, staring at his bedchamber wall. He would not respond to his sister's questions. She was shaken. What had happened?

He looked at her at last.

"Did she go through with it? Did you hope she wouldn't? I told you not to go."

"She didn't resign. No. She didn't." He laughed squeakily. "Not by a long shot." His tone was spooky.

"What happened?"

"She resolved our problems with the priests. Not permanently, but it'll be a long time before . . ." His voice trailed off. "I'm as guilty as she is."

"What happened, dammit! Tell me!"

"She killed them. Every last one of them. She lured them there by making them think they were going to humiliate her. She had archers cut them down. A thousand priests. And I was there. I watched her walk among them afterward, cutting the throats of the wounded."

For a moment the Radisha thought it was some grisly joke. *That* was impossible.

He said, "She made her point. Did she ever make her point. Smoke was right."

The Radisha began pacing, lending only half an ear to his self-flagellation. It was grotesque. It was an atrocity surpassing comprehension. Things like that did not happen in Taglios. They couldn't.

But what an opportunity! The religious hierarchies would be in disarray for

years. Atrocity or not, this was a chance to achieve all they had worked for. It
could mean the return of the primacy of the state.

He heard a sound. She whirled, startled, gawked.

The woman was there, having penetrated the palace who knew how. She
still wore her bizarre armor, covered with blood. "He's told you."

"Yes."

"The Shadowmasters attacked Dejagore. They were repelled with heavy
losses. Blade is moving south to relieve the city before they gather reinforcements. I'm going to join him. I have no one to leave here to continue my work.
You two will have to handle it. Send the construction crews back to the fortress.
Continue enrolling volunteers. There's a slim chance we may get past the worst
in the coming few weeks, leaving no one but Longshadow to deal with. But it's
more likely we'll face a prolonged struggle that will require every man and resource available."

The Radisha could not speak. The woman had the blood of a thousand
priests on her hands. How could you argue with someone like that?

"I've handed you an opportunity you always wanted. Grab it."

The Radisha willed herself to speak. Still nothing came out. Never had she
been so terrified.

The woman said, "I have no ambitions here. You have no need to fear me—
so long as you don't interfere with me. I *will* destroy the Shadowmasters. I *will*
fulfill the Company's undertaking. And I *will* collect its reward."

The Radisha nodded as though a hand had grabbed her hair and forced her
to move her head.

The woman said, "I'll come back after I've seen what's happening at Dejagore." She moved to the Prahbrindrah, rested a hand on his shoulder. "Don't
take it on yourself. They wrote their own destinies. You're a prince. A prince
must be stern. Be stern now. Don't let chaos claim Taglios. I'll leave you a small
garrison. Their reputation should be enough to enforce your will."

She strode out.

The Radisha and her brother stared at one another. "What have we done?"
he asked.

"Too late to cry about it. Let's do what we can with it."

"Where's Smoke?"

"I don't know. I haven't seen him for days."

"Was he right? Is she really the Daughter of Night?"

"I don't know. I just don't know. But we're on the tiger's back now. We can't
let go."

37

I moved out before dawn. I took every man I could round up—except those who had helped despatch the priests. Those I left as a garrison, with orders to remain in the city a week, then to move to the remote Vehdna-Bota ford across the Main. I did not want them talking to the other men, who did not yet know about the massacre.

There were six thousand men in the force. They were scarcely more than an armed rabble. They were enthusiastic, though. They wanted to relieve Dejagore.

I tried to teach them on the march.

Narayan did not like the move. He brooded. He came to me late the third day of the march. We were twenty miles from Ghoja. "Mistress?"

"You've finally decided to talk about it?"

He pretended not to be surprised. He tried to accept everything about me. On the surface. Did he regret his snap decision that I was his Strangler messiah? I am sure he wanted more control. He did not want his Daughter of Night to be independent of his own ambitions and wishful thinking.

"Yes, Mistress. Tomorrow is Etsataya, first day of the Festival. We're only a few miles from the Holy Grove. It is *important* that you present yourself to the jamadars."

I guided him out of the human stream. "I haven't been trying to duck it. I've been preoccupied. You said the first day. I thought this was a one-day holy festival."

"It's three days, Mistress. The middle day is the actual high holy day."

"I can't afford a three-day delay, Narayan."

"I know, Mistress." Funny how the honorifics showed up so much more often when he wanted something. "But we do have men capable of keeping the mob moving. All they have to do is follow the road. With your horses we can overtake them quickly."

I masked my feelings. This was something I had to do but not something I wanted to do. Narayan's cult had not been much use yet.

But Narayan himself was a valuable aide. I had to keep him happy. "All

right. Get this mob pointed in the right direction and going on its own momentum. I'll want Ram and my gear."

"Yes, Mistress."

We left the column half an hour later.

It was dark when we reached the Stranglers' holy grove. I did not see much of
it but I felt it. Seldom had I encountered a place with a darker aura. Some of
Narayan's brotherhood were there already. We joined them. They watched me
sidelong, afraid to look at me directly.

There was nothing to do. I went to sleep early.

The dreams were worse than ever before, unrelenting, continuous. I did not
escape till the sun rose, probed through the mist and dark trees. Ten thousand
crows bickered and squawked overhead. Narayan and his cronies thought that
a hugely favorable omen. The crow was Kina's favorite bird, her messenger and
spy.

Was there a connection with the crows that had followed the Company so
long? According to Croaker they had picked us up before we had crossed the
Sea of Torments. The Sea lies seven thousand miles north of the grove.

As soon as I wakened I was sick. I vomited as I tried to sit up. Men bustled
around, solicitous, unable to do anything helpful. Narayan looked scared to
death. He had a lot invested in me. He would be a nothing if he lost me now.
"Mistress! Mistress! What's the matter?"

"I'm puking my guts up!" I snarled. "Get me something."

There was nothing anyone could do.

The worst passed. After that it was just nausea that worsened drastically if I
moved suddenly. I passed on breakfast. After an hour I was able to get up and
around without too much discomfort—if I took it slowly.

Being sick was new to me. I had not been, ever before. I did not like it.

There were a hundred men in the grove already, maybe more. They all came
for a glimpse at their ragged messiah. I don't think they were impressed. I
would not have been, in their shoes. Nobody could measure up to an anticipation of millennia. Ragged as I was I had to be a double dose of disappointment.

Narayan did a fair job of arguing his case. They did not cut my throat.

They were a mixed bag, all religions, all castes, and as many of them foreigners as Taglians, all sinister in that grove. It reeked of darkness and old
blood.

Nobody seemed festive. They seemed to be waiting for something to happen. I isolated Narayan and asked.

"Nothing much happens before nightfall," he said. "Most of the men will
arrive today. Those who are here already will make preparation. There will be a
ceremony tonight, to open the festival and let Kina know that tomorrow is her

day. The ceremonies tomorrow are meant to invoke her. Candidates will be presented to her, to accept or reject. After the ceremonies the feast will begin. All during Festival the priests will judge petitions presented. There aren't many this year. An old dispute between the Ineld and Twana bands is up for judgment, though. That will attract a lot of attention."

I frowned.

"Bands sometimes come into conflict. The Ineld band is of Vehdna stock, the Twana of Shadar. Each accuses the other of heresy and poaching. It's an old dispute that grew much worse after the Shadowmasters invaded. In parts of their territories the bands are the only law, which makes for bigger stakes."

It was a long story, not pretty, too human, serving to illustrate that the Deceivers were more than a lot of deadly fanatics. In some areas they ruled the underworld. The bands in question hailed from populous Hatchpur State, where the Deceivers were relatively strong. Their true feud was a contest of criminal gangs over territories.

"Anyway," Narayan said, "Iluk of the Ineld band stunned everyone by insisting the conflict be handed to the justice of Kina."

The way he said it was ominous. Kina's must be a very final justice. "That's unusual?"

"Everyone thinks it's a bluff. Iluk expects Kowran, jamadar of the Twana band, to refuse. That would leave the judgment to the priests, who would take his refusal into account."

"And if he doesn't back down?"

"There's no appeal from the judgment of Kina."

"I thought so."

"Are you feeling better?"

"Some. I'm still nauseous but I've got it under control."

"Can you eat? You should."

"A little rice, maybe. Nothing heavily spiced." They liked their spices in Taglios. Cooking odors could be overwhelming in the city.

He handed me over to Ram. Ram hovered. I kept my composure. Well I did. While I nibbled, letting each bite settle, Narayan brought a parade of priests and jamadars for formal introduction. I memorized names and faces carefully. I noted that few of the jamadars boasted the black rumel. I met only four men who did. I mentioned that to Ram.

"Very few are honored, Mistress. And jamadar Narayan is foremost among those. He's a living legend. No other man would have dared bring you here."

Was he warning me? Maybe I had best watch myself. There could be politics here, too. Some band captains might resist me simply because I was associated with Narayan.

Narayan. The living legend.

How had our paths come to cross? I'm no believer in fate or gods, in the accepted senses, but there are powers that move the world. That I know well. Once I was one.

The sender of my dreams arranged it, no doubt. She, or it, had been interested in me long before I became aware of that interest.

Could it have been she who had struck Croaker down? To rid me of an inconvenient emotional entanglement?

Maybe. Maybe when the Shadowmasters fell I might turn to another target.

The anger rose in me. I controlled it and rode it, let Ram finish feeding me, went exploring the grove. I went to its heart and examined the temple for the first time.

It barely passed muster. It was so buried in creepers it was barely recognizable. Nobody challenged my presence outside. I did not press my luck by climbing the steps. Instead, I rambled around.

I found a man willing to get Narayan for me. I did not want to enter the holy place uninvited. He came out looking irritated. "Take a walk with me. I have a few questions. First, will anyone get upset if I go inside?"

He thought. "I don't think so."

"Anybody saying I can't be what you claim? Do you have the kind of enemies who will oppose you on everything?"

"No. But there *are* doubts."

"I'm sure. I don't look the part."

He shrugged.

I'd led him to the area where I wanted him. I suggested, "You'd need a fair hand at woodcraft to survive your summer travels, wouldn't you?"

"Yes."

"Look around."

He did. He came back perplexed. "Someone kept horses here."

"Anyone else come on horseback?"

"A few. High-caste Deceivers from afar. Yesterday and today."

"That's not fresh. Is there a regular guard?"

"No one comes here but us. No one dares."

"Somebody did. And it looks like they stayed awhile. That's a lot of manure for a casual visit."

"I have to tell the others. This will mean purification rites if the temple was profaned." As we ascended the steps to the temple, he said, "You noticing will be a point in your favor. No one else did."

"You don't see what you don't expect to see."

The temple was poorly lighted inside. Just as well. It was ugly in there. The architects had dreamed some of my dreams, then had re-created them in stone.

Narayan collected several jamadars, told them what I had found. They fussed and cussed and grumbled, spread out to see if the infidels had defiled their temple.

I wandered.

They found where the invaders had done their cooking. The place had been cleaned but smoke stains are hard to erase. The stains suggested that someone had camped there for a long time.

Narayan sidled up, gave me his grin. "Now would be a good time to impress them, Mistress."

"Like how?"

"By using your talent to find out something about whoever was here."

"Sure. Just like that. I've maybe got enough skill to find their latrine and garbage pit."

He eyed me, wondering how I could know they had had one, then reasoned it out. There was no garbage or human waste around. "That could tell us a lot."

One of the jamadars told us that now they were looking they had found plenty of evidence of an extended occupation. "One man and one woman. The woman slept near the fire. The man stayed near the altar. They don't appear to have bothered that. Mistress? Would you look?"

"An honor." I did not immediately understand how they knew a woman had slept near the fire. Then one produced a few strands of long black hair. "Can you tell anything from this, Mistress?"

"Yes. She didn't have naturally curly hair. If it was a she." Some Gunni men let their hair grow long. Shadar and Vehdna tended toward curls. Vehdna men wore their hair short. But everyone at this end of the earth had black hair, or very dark brown when it was clean.

Swan was a real curiosity with his golden locks.

My sarcasm did not escape my companions. I said, "Don't expect me to see the past or future. Yet. Kina comes to me only in dreams."

That even startled Narayan.

"Let's see the other place."

They showed me where the man had slept. Again, they had determined sex by length of hair. They had found one strand three inches long, fine, a medium brown. "Hang onto those hairs, Narayan. They could be useful someday."

Deceivers scurried around seeking more signs. Narayan suggested, "Let's find that pit."

We went out. We wandered. I located the place. Some lowlife candidates to the cult got to open it. I wandered while I waited.

"Mistress. I just found this." A jamadar offered me a small animal figure someone had made by bending and braiding and twisting strands of grass, the kind of time-killing thing people do when they have nothing to do. But the man looked disturbed.

"It's just something somebody did for the hell of it. It has no power. But if there are more around I'd like to see them. They might tell us something about whoever made them."

Less than a minute passed before another turned up. "It was hanging from a twig, Mistress. I guess it's supposed to be a monkey."

I had a brainstorm. "Don't move anything. I want to see them right where they are."

Over the next few hours we found scores of those things, some made of grass, some twisted from strips of bark. Someone had had a lot of time and nothing to do. I knew a man once who did that with paper and never realized he was doing it.

Most of those things were stick figures, monkeys hanging from twigs, four-legged beasts that could have been anything. But a few of the four-leggers carried riders. The riders always carried twig swords or spears.

I must have made a noise. Narayan said, "Mistress?"

I whispered, "There's something important about those things. But I'll be damned if I understand what."

Someone found a whole mob of figures where someone had sat on a rock leaning against a tree making them and maybe daydreaming. It was a little clearing about ten feet across. A stump stood in the middle.

I knew I was onto something the instant I arrived. But what? Whatever, it stayed way down below consciousness. I told Narayan, "If there's anything to be learned, it's here." I whispered again. "Get everybody back to what they're supposed to be doing." I perched on the rock. I pulled some grass and started twisting a figure. The men went away. I let my mind drift into the twilight state. Wonder of wonders, dreams did not intrude.

Minutes passed. More and more crows dropped into the trees. My interest must have been too obvious.

Were they watching to see if I found out something? Like maybe something about those who had been staying here? Ah! The birds had more to do with them than with the Deceivers. They were not omens—in the sense the Stranglers hoped. They were messengers and spies.

Crows. Everywhere and always, crows, seldom behaving the way crows should. Tools. Their sudden interest suggested they feared I would learn something I ought not. Which meant there *was* something.

My mind leaped from stone to stone across a brook of ignorance. If I did discover something I had best not be obvious.

Realization.

The clearing felt familiar because it recalled a place I had lived. If that stump represented the Tower, whence I had ruled my empire, then the scatter of stones might represent the badlands I had created so the Tower could be approached along just one narrow, deadly path.

Patterns emerged. They were almost imperceptible, as though put there by someone who knew he was watched. Someone surrounded by crows? If I let my imagination loose, that scatter of rocks, debris, and twisted figures did make a fair representation of the Tower's surroundings. In fact, a couple of sticks and a scatter and a boot scuff and a little soil pushed into a mound described a situation that had existed only once in the history of the Tower.

I had trouble pretending calm and indolence.

If the rocks and twigs and such were significant, so must be the creatures of grass and bark. I stood up for a better view.

One thing jumped right out.

A leaf lay at the foot of the stump. A tiny figure sat upon it. A lot of care had gone into creating that figure. More than enough to make the message clear.

The Howler, my then master of the flying carpet, was supposed to have been killed by a fall from the heights of the Tower. I had known that was not true for some time now. The message had to be that the Howler was somehow involved in current events.

Whoever set this up knew me and expected me to visit the grove. That should mean that someone knew what I was doing. That someone must have access to what the crows reported but was not their master. Else there was no reason for such an elaborate and iffy means of passing a message.

There was more.

Many great sorcerers had been involved in the battle where the Howler was supposed to have died. Most of them were supposed to have been killed. Since then I have discovered that several had fled after faking their deaths. I checked the figures again. Some were identifiable as representing some of those sorcerers. Three had been crushed underfoot. Those known to have been destroyed?

I gave it all the time it needed and still nearly missed the critical message. It was almost dark when I spied the clever little figure carrying what appeared to be a head under its arm. It took a while after that to understand the significance of the figure.

I had told Narayan that we do not see what we do not expect to see.

A lot of things fell into place once I realized that the impossible was not impossible at all. My sister was alive. I saw a whole new picture of what was going on. And I was frightened.

And, frightened, I missed the most important message of all.

38

Narayan was not in a pleasant mood. "The whole temple has to be purified. Everything has been defiled. At least they committed no willful sacrilege, no desecration. The idol and relics remain undisturbed."

I had no idea what he was talking about. All the men had long faces. I looked at Narayan over our cookfire. He took my look for a question.

"Any unbeliever who found the holy relics or the idol would have plundered them."

"Maybe they were afraid of the curse."

His eyes got big. He glanced around, made a gesture urging silence. He whispered, "How did you know that?"

"These things always have curses. Part of their rustic charm." Pardon my sarcasm. I did not feel good. I did not want to spend any more time hanging around the grove. It was not a pleasant place. A lot of people had died there, none of them of old age. The earth was rich with their blood and bones and screams. It had a smell, psychic and physical, probably pleasing to Kina.

"How much longer, Narayan? I'm trying to cooperate. But I'm not going to hang around here the rest of my life."

"Oh. Mistress. There will be no Festival now. The purification will take weeks. The priests are distraught. The ceremonies have been moved to Nadam. It's only a minor holiday usually, when the bands break up for the off-season, and the priests remind them to invoke the Daughter of Night in their prayers. The priests always say the reason she hasn't come yet is we haven't prayed hard enough."

Was he going to dole it out in driblets forever? I guess no one of any religion would have spent much time explaining holidays and saints and such, though. "Why are we still here, then? Why aren't we headed south?"

"We came for more than the Festival."

We had indeed. But how was I supposed to convince these men I was their messiah? Narayan kept the specifications to himself. How could the actress act without being told her role?

There was the trouble. Narayan *believed* I was the Daughter of Night. He wanted me to be. Which meant that he would not coach me if I asked. He expected me to know instinctively.

And I did not have a clue.

The jamadars seemed disappointed and Narayan nervous. I was not living up to expectations and hopes, even if I *had* discovered that their temple had been profaned.

In a whisper, I asked, "Am I expected to do holy deeds in a place no longer holy?"

"I don't know, Mistress. We have no guideposts. It's all in the hands of Kina. She will send an omen."

Omens. Wonderful. I had had no chance to bone up on omens the cult considered significant. Crows were important, of course. Those men thought it wonderful that Taglian territory was infested by carrion birds. They thought that presaged the Year of the Skulls. But what else was significant?

"Are comets important to you?" I asked. "In the north, last year, and once earlier, there were great comets. Did you see them down here?"

"No. Comets are bad omens."

"They were for me."

"They have been called Sword of Sheda, or Tongue of Sheda, Sheda-linca, that shed the light of Sheda upon the world."

Sheda was an archaic form of the name of the chief Gunni god, one of whose titles was Lord of Lords of Light. I suspected the Deceiver cult's beliefs had taken a left turn off the trunk of Gunni beliefs a few thousand years ago.

He said, "The priests say Kina is weakest when a comet is in the sky, for then light rules heaven day and night."

"But the moon . . ."

"The moon is the light of darkness. The moon belongs to Shadow, put up so Shadow's creatures may hunt."

He rambled off into incomprehensibility. Local religion had its light and dark, right and left, good and evil. But Kina, despite her trappings of darkness, was supposed to be outside and beyond that eternal struggle, enemy of both Light and Shadow, ally of each in some circumstances. Just to confuse me, maybe, nobody seemed to know how things really lay in the eyes of their gods. Vehdna, Shadar, and Gunni all respected one another's gods. Within the majority Gunni cult the various deities, whether identified with Light or Shadow, got equal deference. They all had their temples and cults and priests. Some, like Jahamaraj Jah's Shadar Khadi cult, were tainted by the doctrines of Kina.

As Narayan clarified by making the waters murkier he got shifty-eyed, then would not look at me at all. He fixed his gaze on the cookfire, talked, grew morose. He was good at hiding it. No one else noticed. But I had had more practice reading people. I noted tension in some of the jamadars, too.

Something was about to happen. A test? With this crowd that was not likely to be gentle.

My fingers drifted to the yellow triangle at my belt. I had not practiced much lately. There had been little time. I realized what I had done, wondered why. That was hardly the weapon to get me out of trouble.

There *was* danger. I felt it now. The jamadars were nervous and excited. I let my psychic sense sharpen despite the aura of the grove. It was like taking a deep breath in a hot room where a corpse had been rotting for a week. I persevered. If I could take the dreams without bending I could take this.

I asked Narayan a question that sent him off on another ramble. I concentrated on form and pattern in my psychic surroundings.

I spotted it.

I was ready when it happened.

He was a black rumel man, a jamadar with a reputation nearly rivalling Narayan's, Moma Sharra-el, Vehdna. When we'd been introduced I'd had the feeling he was a man who killed for himself, not for his goddess. His rumel moved like black lightning.

I grabbed the weighted end on the fly. I took it away before he recovered his balance, snapped it around his neck. It seemed I'd played this game always, or as though another hand guided my own. I did cheat a little, using a silent spell to strike at his heart. I wasted no mercy. I sensed that that would be an error as deadly as not reacting at all.

I would have had no chance had I not sensed the wrongness gathering around me.

No one cried out. No one said a word. They were shaken, even Narayan. Nobody looked at me. For no reason apparent at the moment, I said, "Mother is not pleased."

That got me a few startled looks. I folded Moma's rumel as Narayan had taught me, discarded my yellow cloth and took the black. No one argued with my self-promotion.

How to reach these men without hearts? They were impressed now, but not indelibly, not permanently. "Ram."

Ram came out of the darkness. He did not speak for fear of betraying his feelings. I think he might have stepped in if Moma's attack had succeeded, though that would have been the end of him. I gave him instructions.

He got a rope and looped one end around the dead man's left ankle, tossed the rope over a branch, hauled the corpse up so it hung head down over the fire. "Excellent, Ram. Excellent. Everyone gather round."

They came reluctantly as the summons spread. Once they were all there I cut Moma's jugular.

The blood did not come fast but it came. A small spell made each drop flash when it reached the fire. I seized Narayan's right arm, forced him to put his hand out and let a few drops fall on his palm. Then I turned him loose. "All of you," I said.

Kina's followers do not like spilled blood. There is a complex and irrational explanation having to do with the legend of the devoured demons. Narayan told me later. It has a bearing only because it made the evening more memorable for those men once they had the blood of their fellow on their hands.

They did not look at me while they endured my little ceremony. I used the opportunity to hazard a spell that, to my surprise, came off without a hitch. It turned the stains on their hands as indelible as tattoos. Unless I took it back they would go through life with one hand marked scarlet.

The jamadars and priests were mine, like it or not. They were branded. The world would not forgive them that brand if its meaning became known. Men with red palms would not be able to deny that they had been present at the debut of the Daughter of Night.

Nowhere did I see any doubts, now, that I was what Narayan claimed.

The dreams were powerful that night but not grim. I floated in the warmth of the approval of that other who wanted to make me her creature.

Ram wakened me before there was light enough to see. He and Narayan and I rode out before the sun rose. Narayan did not speak all day. He remained in shock.

His dreams were coming true. He did not know if that was what he wanted anymore. He was scared.

So was I.

Longshadow had fallen into a permanent rage. The wizard Smoke, a trivial little nothing, was stubborn. He was determined not to be enslaved. He might die first.

A howl echoed through Overlook. The Shadowmaster glanced up, imagined mockery in the cry. That bastard Howler. He had pulled a fast one somehow. No one else could have freed Shadowspinner. Treachery. Always treachery. He would pay. How he would pay. His agony would go on for years.

Later. There was damage to be undone. There was that damnable little wizard to be broken.

What *had* happened at Stormgard?

The obvious assumption was that the Lifetaker character had been *her*. Dorotea Senjak had been in Taglios. Of that there was no doubt. But *she* did not have the powers to battle Shadowspinner to a draw while ensuring the defeat of his armies.

Who had that been with her, bearing the Lance? The real power?

A flicker of fear. He dropped his work, climbed to his crystal chamber, looked out on the plain of glittering stone. Forces were moving. Not even he could grasp them all. Maybe that had not been *her*. Maybe she was gone. The tamed shadows had seen no sign of her for some time. Maybe she had gone north again after taking her revenge. She'd always wanted to rule her sister's empire.

Was there an unknown player in the game? Were Lifetaker and Widowmaker more than phantoms conjured by Senjak? The shadows thought some power was guiding her. Suppose Lifetaker and Widowmaker were real beings? Suppose they had put the notion into her head to create imitations so everyone would believe them unreal, actors, till it was too late?

Grim presentiments. Grim questions. And no answers.

Sunlight danced among the pillars on the plain. The Howler wailed. The wizard's groans echoed through the fortress.

It was closing in.

He had to capture Senjak. She was the keystone. Her head held the keys to power. She knew the Names. She knew the Truths. She contained secrets that could be hammered into weapons capable of stemming even that dark tide waiting to break out of the plain.

But first, the wizard. Before all else, Smoke. Smoke would give him Taglios and maybe Senjak.

He returned to the room where the little man battled his terror and pain. "There will be an end to this foolish resistance. Now. I have lost patience. Now I will find what you fear and feed you to it."

B lade's army moved in twenty-mile stages. He scouted heavily, used his cavalry exhaustively. Sindhu's men, who had hurried ahead to discover what had become of the Deceivers watching Dejagore, reported finding no sign of those men.

Blade took the news to Mather. "What do you think?"

Mather shook his head. "Probably killed or captured."

Swan and Mather had their own scouts out, farther south. Swan said, "Word we have is the Shadowlanders really did get whipped bad. Our guys got past their pickets and checked their camp. There's only two-thirds as many of them as there should be. Half of those are dinged up. That character Mogaba keeps hitting them with sorties, too. They never get to relax."

"Are they watching us? Do they know we're coming?"

Mather said, "You have to assume they do. Shadowspinner is a sorcerer. They don't call him a Shadowmaster for nothing. And there's the bats. Croaker thought they controlled the bats. There have been plenty of those around lately."

"Then we should be very careful. How many effectives can they field if they decide to meet us?"

"Listen to this guy, Cordy," Swan said. "He's starting to sound like a pro. Effectives. My, oh my. She's going to turn him into a real ass-kicking warlord."

Blade chuckled.

"Too many of them if you ask me," Swan continued. "If they sneak them away without Mogaba noticing they probably could put eight or ten thousand veterans in our way."

"With the Shadowmaster?"

Mather said, "I doubt he would leave. That would be an invitation to disaster."

"Then the thing to do is advance cautiously, scout thoroughly, try to know as much about them as they know about us. Right?"

Mather chuckled. "That's what the book would say. We have one factor in our favor. Their scouts don't move during daylight. And the days are long now."

Blade grunted thoughtfully.

*   *   *

Blade halted thirty miles north of Dejagore. Scouts brought word that Shadowspinner had moved troops into the hills ahead, at night, when the city's defenders could not see them go. The men who had stayed behind were making a show of preparing another assault.

"Where are they?" Blade asked. The scouts could not tell him. Somewhere along the road as it snaked through the hills. Waiting. Only four thousand, apparently, but that was enough against this mob.

"You going to mess with them?" Swan asked. "Or just hang around and keep some of them off Mogaba?"

"That would make sense," Mather suggested. "Keep some tied up while Mogaba does the fighting. If we could get a message to him . . ."

"I've tried," Blade said. "There's no way. They have the city sealed up. Sitting down there in the middle of that bowl like that . . ."

"Well?" Swan asked. "What do we do?"

Blade assembled his cavalry officers. He sent them to find the enemy. When they encountered no immediate resistance he moved his army ten miles southward and camped. Next morning, as soon as the bats went away, he formed line of battle but did nothing else. His scouts worked the hills carefully. He repeated that the next day and the day following. Late that afternoon a rider came in from the north. His news put a smile on Blade's face. He did not tell Swan or Mather immediately.

The fourth morning his battle line advanced. He entered the hills slowly, made sure his formations stayed integrated. There was no hurry. The cavalry stayed out front.

Contact came shortly before noon. Blade did not push. He let his men skirmish but avoided a general engagement. His cavalry harassed the enemy with missiles. The Shadowlanders were not inclined to attack them.

The sun dropped westward. Blade let the skirmishes grow.

The enemy commander gave the order to attack.

Blade's own officers had orders to stage a fighting withdrawal as soon as the enemy came out to play. They were to stop retreating only if the enemy stopped coming. If he did that they were to start harassing him again.

That game went on till the Shadowlanders lost all patience.

41

I halted the column, gathered Narayan and Ram and those men who passed for officers. "This is the place. On the back of the swale. We put me and the standard on the road, spread the men out to either side."

Narayan and the others looked puzzled. Nobody knew what was going on. It seemed wise to keep it that way till it was too late for anybody to worry.

I set it up, practically having to show each squad leader where I wanted him. Narayan finally figured it out. "It won't work," he decided. He had been on a negative kick since the grove. He did not believe anything was going to go right ever again.

"Why not? I doubt they know we're here. I was able to confuse their bats and shadows."

I hoped.

Once I had everybody in place I got into my armor, got Ram fixed up, led him and Narayan to where we could see what lay beyond the crest.

I saw what I expected to see, a lot of dust headed my way. "They're coming. Narayan, go tell the men that in less than an hour they'll get their chance to drink Shadowlander blood. Tell them as soon as Blade's men slip through the aisles in the formation they're to plug those up."

The dust came closer fast. I watched Narayan off to spring the surprise. I watched the nervousness spread among the men. I was especially interested in the small troops of horsemen on the wings. If they followed Jah's old example I was in for another disaster.

Blade's men were almost upon me. I took my position, set witchfires burning on my armor. Ram came up beside me, impressive in the Widowmaker armor I'd had made for him. I put fires upon him but could do nothing about giving him the crows that always attached themselves to Croaker's shoulders when he turned into Widowmaker. I doubted the Shadowlanders would notice.

Blade's men poured over the crest. There was a lot of confusion till they realized we were on their side. Willow Swan galloped up, hair flying, laughing like the demented. "Right on time, sweetheart. Right on time."

"Go get your men under control. Cavalry to the wings. Move it!"

He went.

There were Shadowlanders among the men coming now. Chaos held court. They tried to stop but their comrades behind forced them forward. They tried hard to stay away from Ram and me.

Where was Blade? Where was his cavalry?

The Shadowlanders pelted my line in no order, like hail, then turned to flee. Once they had their backs to us the outcome was not in doubt. I signalled for the cavalry to advance. I made no effort to keep my men in formation. I let them chase the enemy.

When I crested the rise I saw Blade and his cavalry. He had had them flee to the flanks, distancing the footbound Shadowlanders, then had brought them back behind our enemies, scattered so they could cut down fugitives. My own cavalry had the Shadowlanders cut off on the flanks.

Only a few got away.

It was over before darkness fell.

Swan could not get over it. "Our man Blade's done turned into a real live general. You had it figured all the way, didn't you?"

Blade nodded.

I believed him. He might actually make a commander—unless he'd had a once in a lifetime stroke of genius.

Swan chuckled. "Old Spinner ought to have the word by now. Bet he's foaming at the mouth."

"Very likely," I said. "And he might take steps. I want a strong guard posted. The night still belongs to the Shadowmasters."

"What can he do, hey?" Swan demanded.

"I don't know. I'd rather not find out the hard way."

Blade said, "Calm down, Swan. We didn't win the war."

You would have thought so from the celebrating. I told Blade, "Tell me more about this other Widowmaker and Lifetaker."

"You know as much as I do. Shadowspinner attacked and should have taken the city. But they rode out of the hills. Lifetaker kept him fighting for his life. Widowmaker rode around killing his men. They couldn't touch him. They rode away after our men drove the attackers out of the city. Mogaba tried a sortie. They didn't help. He took heavy casualties."

I checked a crow in a nearby bush, careful not to be obvious. "I see. We can't do anything about it. Let's ignore it and get on with plans for tomorrow."

"Is that wise, Mistress?" Narayan asked. "The night *does* belong to the Shadowmasters." Meaning there were shadows among us, listening, and bats whisking overhead.

"There are tools available." I could take care of the bats—and the crows—but I could not get rid of the shadows. To do anything more than confuse them was beyond my limited powers. "But does it matter? He knows we're here. He knows we'll come there. He just has to sit and wait. Or run away, if that suits him."

I had no hope Shadowspinner would elect that option. He retained the preponderance of force—if not in numbers, certainly in power. The stunt I had pulled was the limit. I would not send these men into a maelstrom of sorcery.

The victory would increase their confidence but could lead to trouble if I overvalued it. That was partly why Croaker lost his last battle. He got lucky several times and began to count on it. Luck has its way of running out.

"You have a point, Narayan. No need to ask for trouble. We'll talk about it tomorrow. Pass the word. We'll make an early start. Rest. We may have to do it again." The men had to be reminded: there were battles yet to come.

The others went, leaving Ram, Blade, and me. I looked at Blade. "Well done, Blade. Very well done."

He nodded. He knew that.

"How are your friends taking it?" Swan and Mather were off with their band of Radisha's Guards.

He shrugged. "Taking the long view."

"Uhm?"

"Taglios will be there after the Black Company goes. They've set down roots there."

"Understandable. Will they be trouble?"

Blade chuckled. "They don't even want to trouble Shadowspinner. If there was any way, they'd be running their tavern and staying out of everybody's way."

"But they take their pledge to the Radisha seriously?"

"As seriously as you take your contract."

"Then it behooves me to make sure there's no tension."

He grunted. "Shadows don't need ideas."

"True. Tomorrow, then."

He rose, went.

"Ram, let's take a ride."

Ram groaned. In about a hundred years, maybe, he would make a horseman.

We were both in armor still, uncomfortable as that was. I touched up the glamors. We rode among the men. Had to keep their minds fixed on me. I paused to thank men who had been pointed out as having done well. When the show was over I returned to my own place in the camp, indistinguishable from any other, and gave myself up to night's dreams.

I was sick again. Ram did his best to keep it from the men. I noticed Narayan whispering with Sindhu about it. I did not care at the moment. Sindhu glided away, presumably to tell Blade. Narayan came over. "Perhaps you ought to consult a physician."

"You have one handy?"

His grin was a shadow of itself. "No. There isn't one here."

Which meant some of the wounded would die needlessly, often as not victims of their own home remedies. Medical discipline had been something Croaker had started pounding into his men when they were learning to keep in step. And he'd been right.

I have dealt with a great many soldiers and armies. Infection and disease are deadlier enemies than foreign arms. Determined health discipline had been one of the strengths of the Company before Croaker's passing.

Pain. Damn me. It still hurt. I had never grieved over anybody before.

It was light enough to drive away bats and shadows. "Narayan. Are they fed?" Damn the sickness. "Let's get them moving."

"Where are we going?"

"Get Blade. I'll explain."

He got Blade. I explained. I rode out with the cavalry, leaving Blade to bring the rest. I headed east ten miles, turned into the hills. Crows followed. I was not concerned about crows. They were not reporting to the Shadowmasters.

Ten miles into the hills I halted. I could see part of the plain. "Dismount. Rest. Keep the noise down. Cold food. Ram, come with me." I moved forward. "Quiet. There may be pickets."

We did not encounter any before I could see the whole panorama.

There had been changes. When we had come before the hills had been green with farms and orchards. Now they were spotted brown, especially to the south. The canals were not delivering water as they should.

"Ram, get those two red rumel men, Abda and whatever his name is."

He went. I studied the prospect.

Shadowspinner's camps and siegeworks surrounded the city. Near the north gate the besiegers had raised an earthen ramp to the top of the wall, no mean achievement. Dejagore squatted atop a high mound, behind walls forty feet high. The ramp had been damaged badly. Men were hauling earth up to repair it.

Presumably that had been the point of attack the night whatever had happened had happened.

The besiegers looked ragged. The condition of their camps suggested low morale. Could I take advantage? Had word of yesterday's misadventure reached the line troops? Knowing that, knowing a large force could hammer them against the anvil of the city, they ought to be ripe for a rout.

I could not place Shadowspinner. Maybe he was holed up in the remnants of the permanent camp south of the city. It had its own rampart and ditch. If not, he was careful not to stand out. Maybe Mogaba had a habit of picking on him.

Ram returned with Abda and the other man. I said, "I want to find a way to get down there unseen. Spread out, try to find one. Watch for pickets. If we can get down there we can give them a nasty surprise tonight."

They nodded and slipped away, Ram with his customary worried look. He still did not believe I could take care of myself.

Sometimes *I* wondered.

I gave them a head start, then moved westward. I had a surprise for the Shadowmasters—if my limited talent was up to it.

It took longer than I hoped but it looked workable, "it" being a bat trap that would call and kill like a candle does moths. I'd been thinking about versions since we'd left Taglios. It should work on crows, too, with adjustments.

Which left only the shadows.

We had not encountered it but rumors of old, out of the Shadowlands in the days of conquest, said those shadows could be assassins as well as spies. Captains and kings had died too opportunely, with no other explanation. Maybe the deaths of two Shadowmasters had taken that weapon away. Maybe a killing took a combined effort. I hoped so but did not count on it.

I set the trap working and hurried back to where I had parted with Ram. The others were there waiting. Ram scolded me. I suffered it. I'd grown fond of him in a sisterly way. It had been a long time since anyone had been concerned about me. It felt good.

When Ram finished, Abda interjected, "We've found two routes down. Neither one is ideal. The better one might be used by the horsemen. We cleared the pickets. I sent a few men down in case there's a changing of the guard."

That could be a problem.

Blade materialized, dogged by Narayan and Sindhu. "You made good time," I told him.

He grunted, studied the city. I explained what I wanted to do. "I don't expect to accomplish much. The point is to harass Shadowspinner, demoralize his men, and let ours inside know there's an army out here."

Blade glanced at the westering sun, grunted again.

Swan and Mather joined us. I said, "Get some men moving. Abda, explain the routes. Mr. Mather, take charge of the infantry. Sindhu, you take the horsemen. Swan, Blade, Narayan, Ram, come with me. I want to talk."

Mather and Sindhu got things moving. We got out of their way. I asked Swan, "Swan, your men brought home the news about the row down here. Run through what you know."

He did. I entered questions, did not get half the information I wanted. Not that I expected to.

Swan said, "Some third party is playing his own game."

"Yes." There were crows nearby. I could not mention names. "The attackers definitely masqueraded as Lifetaker and Widowmaker?"

"Absolutely."

"Then those men down there should panic if they see them again. Get the armor, Ram."

Narayan prowled restlessly while we talked, putting in nothing, keeping one eye on the city. He said, "They're starting to move around."

"We've been discovered?"

"I don't think so. They don't act like they expect trouble."

I went and looked. After watching awhile I hazarded a guess. "The news is out. They're shook. Their officers are trying to keep them busy."

"You really going to take a whack?" Swan asked.

"A little one. Just big enough to let Mogaba know he has friends on the outside."

The day was getting on. I passed orders for the men to eat cold and keep moving. Ram showed up with our armor and animals. "Two hours of light. We ought to do something while they can see us."

Narayan said, "There's a group of four, five hundred headed out south, Mistress."

I checked. Hard to tell from so far away but they looked more like a labor battalion than armed men on the march. Curious. A similar group was forming north of the city.

Sindhu appeared. "They got the word about yesterday. They're bad rattled."

I lifted an eyebrow.

"I got close enough to hear some talk. They're making a move. Don't know what it is."

Daring, Sindhu. "You didn't hear where we could find Shadowspinner, did you?"

"No."

I sent everybody off with instructions. Ram and I donned our armor. Ram said nothing the whole time. Usually he had some small talk, thoughtless but comforting.

"You're awfully quiet."

"Thinking. All what's happened in just a couple months. Wondering."

"What?"

"If the world really is so black it's time for the Year of the Skulls."

"Oh, Ram." He was not a fast thinker but an inexorable one, now suffering a crisis of faith brought on by events in the grove but sprouting from seeds that had fallen earlier. He cared again. Kina was losing her hold.

And damn me, I let Croaker get past my defenses and turn me soft inside, too. I felt enough now that I could not just use and discard.

Maybe that soft center was there all the time. Maybe I was like an oyster. Croaker always thought so. Before we hardly knew one another he wrote about me in ways that suggested he thought there was something special inside me.

Those people down there took him. They destroyed his dreams and hamstrung mine. I did not give a damn about the Year of the Skulls or Kina. I wanted restitution.

"Ram, stop." I stepped close, placed a hand on his chest, looked him in the eye. "Don't worry. Don't tear your heart out. Believe me when I tell you I'll try to make everything work out."

He did trust me, damn him. A big damn faithful dog look came into his eyes.

The Prahbrindrah Drah took Smoke's advice. He reread the old books about the Black Company's first visit. They told a tale of death and heartbreak but reread as he might he found nothing to indict the Company returned from the north. The more he studied the more he veered from the attitude Smoke wanted him to adopt.

The Radisha joined him. "You're going to wear those things out."

"No. I don't have to read any more. Smoke is wrong."

"But . . ."

"Never mind the woman. I'd bet my life—and I am—that she has no intention of becoming the Daughter of Night. It's subtle. You have to read this stuff over and over before it sinks in, but there're signs missing that would be there no matter how hard they tried to hide them. They were exactly what they pretended."

"Oh?" the Radisha asked. "Didn't they mean to return to Khatovar?"

"Without knowing what it is. Could have been interesting seeing what would have happened if they'd made it."

"We still might find out. If anyone can pull down the Shadowmasters that woman can."

"Maybe." The prince smiled. "Peaceful as it's been, I'm tempted to ride south myself. There's no one left here to bother me."

"Don't let it go to your head."

"What?"

"People being scared of you. It won't last. Better win their respect before their fear wears off."

"Just once I'd like to go off and do something because I want to do it, not because it will strengthen the office."

That sparked an exchange halfway between argument and discussion. Smoke arrived in its midst. He stepped into the room, stopped, stared stupidly.

They stared back. The Radisha demanded, "Where the hell have you been?"

The prince silenced her with a touch. "What's happened, Smoke? You look awful."

Smoke was stunned. His thoughts oozed too slowly. This was the last thing he expected, walking right into those two. He needed time to get hold of himself.

He opened his mouth.

Longshadow flashed behind his eyes. The terror and pain closed in. He could not tell them. He could do nothing but carry out his orders. And pray.

"Where the hell have you been?" the Radisha demanded again. "Do you have any idea what's happened while you've been off fooling around?"

She was angry. Good. That would distract her some. "No."

She told him.

He was dismayed. "She murdered them? *All* of them?" It was a chance to press his point with passion but he did not have the strength or will. He just wanted to lie down and sleep all night for the first time since . . . since . . .

"All of them that counted for anything. Right now she could do anything she pleased with Taglios. If she was here."

"She isn't?" Longshadow had not kept him posted. "Where is she?"

"By now she may be in Dejagore."

Slowly, slowly, he milked the Radisha of news. A lot had happened. Perhaps Longshadow had told him none of this because he did not know himself. Which might place the situation beyond reclamation.

Who broke up Shadowspinner's attack on Dejagore?

The prince never said a word. He just sat there looking sleepy. An awful sign. The prince was most dangerous when he seemed indifferent.

He was not going to pull it off.

He did not want to. But if he failed . . . The face of the Shadowmaster burned in his brain. Terror unmanned him. He gobbled, "We have to do something. We have to control her before she devours this whole nation. . . ." The Prahbrindrah had opened his eyes. There was no sympathy in them.

"I took your advice, Smoke. I reread those old books six times. They've convinced me."

The wizard nearly collapsed with joy.

"They've convinced me you're full of shit. This Company has nothing to do with that. I'm on her side."

44

I scattered the spell that baffled shadows, though it was not yet dark. It would be dark before we finished.

The horsemen were in place. The Shadowlanders did not appear suspicious. They were up to whatever with those work parties. Both had vanished into the hills, taking a thousand men out of my way.

What temper possessed Shadowspinner? Not a good one, surely. Having four thousand men nipped off an undermanned siege force had to stick in his craw.

Blade had spread enough infantrymen around to cover the cavalry withdrawal. I told Ram, "It's time."

He nodded. He did not have much to say now.

I urged my stallion onto an outcrop from which we would be visible all over the plain. He followed. I hoped he would do nothing clumsy. Falling off your horse takes something away from high drama.

I drew my sword. It blossomed fire.

Trumpets sounded. The horsemen broke cover. The Shadar element were very nearly veterans now. Blade had them in shape. I was pleased by their performance.

Chaos broke its chains down below.

It seemed the Shadowlanders would never get together. I feared I would have another unexpected victory on my hands. It was full dark before I lowered my sword and the trumpets sounded recall. The Shadowlanders did not pursue my horsemen.

Blade showed up quickly. "What now?"

"The message has been delivered. Maybe we should back off." A gangrenous glow formed inside the walled camp beside the city. "Before that gets here." I cancelled the spells illuminating Ram and myself, dismounted, led the way out of there.

I stumbled into Sindhu, who had come from Narayan with the question Blade had asked. I told him, "I want Narayan and your friends to join me. Evacuate the cavalry. The infantry should come out behind them. We'll take tomorrow off."

I needed the rest. I felt drained all the time. All I wanted to do was lie down and sleep. I had been going on will power for so long I feared I would collapse at a critical moment.

There had been no time to filter all the infantry down the slope. Once it had become apparent that was impossible I had sent the majority back to make camp. I longed to be there now. But the night was not yet done.

The valley glowed as though a cancerous green moon was rising there. The green grew brighter. "Down!" I snapped, and hit the dirt.

A ball of ugly light crashed into the eminence from which I had observed the fighting. Earth and vegetation melted. Smoke filled the air. Fires started but burned out quickly. My companions were awed.

I was pleased. Shadowspinner had missed by two hundred yards. He did not know where I was. His bats were flying to my kill trap and his shadows were confused. Sometimes little tricks can be as useful as ones like Spinner's fireball.

"Let's move out," I said. "He'll need time to ready another shot. Take advantage of it. Ram, let's get out of the way and out of these costumes. They're too damned cumbersome."

We did that. Horsemen moved past, talking softly, wearily, in good spirits. They had made a big mess out there. They were pleased with themselves.

Narayan's friends gathered, one now, one then. By the time the infantry started out, there were eighty of them. "Mainly men of my band," he explained. "They came to Ghoja in answer to my summons. What do you plan now?"

"Down." Shadowspinner was pasting the hills with random sorceries, hurling his darts blind. From beside Narayan, with stones grinding into my belly and breasts, I murmured, "We're going to infiltrate their camp and try for the Shadowmaster."

I could not see his face. Just as well, probably. The idea did not thrill him. "But . . ."

"Never have a better chance. Longshadow knows everything that happens as soon as it happens. His resources haven't been tapped. He sees Shadowspinner in bad trouble, he'll do something." Send the Howler, probably. "We'd better get what we can while we can get it."

He did not want to try. Damn him. If he refused, his Stranglers would, too.

But he had sewn himself into a sack. I was his Daughter of Night. For his own sake he dared not argue. He grunted, whispered, "I don't like it. If it has to be done, please don't you go. The risk is too great."

"I have to. I'm the messiah, remember? It's still that time when I have to win support by demonstration."

I did not *want* to go. I just wanted to lie down and sleep. But my role demanded I play it totally.

He selected twenty-five men whose abilities he knew. The rest he dismissed. They joined the soldiers headed for camp. Lucky bastards.

"Sindhu. Take four men and scout ahead. As carefully as you can. Don't take anybody out without checking. Unless you have to." He chose the men to accompany Sindhu. We followed in a tighter crowd, with flankers out. Narayan knew his small-unit tactics.

Shadows fluttered around us, still blind to our presence. But I did not trust their blindness. Had I been Shadowspinner I would have had them pretend.

Chaos still reigned. Spinner kept pounding the hills. Maybe his shadows did not know where we were, only that we had not all departed.

Sindhu drifted back from the point. "Ground's wet ahead."

That made no sense. It had been dry before sundown. It had not rained. "Water?" I asked.

"Yes."

"Strange." But no way to see what it meant before morning. "Be careful." He went forward again. We resumed moving. Soon I was in water an inch deep. The earth beneath was not waterlogged.

The reason for part of the confusion became apparent. The Shadowlanders were trying to stay away from the hills. When they got too close to the city archers sniped at them. But the disorder was sorting itself out.

Sindhu had to eliminate several sentries.

Shadowspinner stopped hammering the hills. Narayan guessed, "His shadows were watching his sentries."

Not so. Their confusion was caused by my proximity. It would envelop the sentries. But maybe he sensed our approach some other way. I sent word to Sindhu to run for it the instant he thought we were walking into something.

I was a hundred yards from the old walled camp. Sindhu was at its shattered gate. He thought the way was clear. We might actually get our shot at Shadowspinner.

All hell broke loose.

Half a hundred fireballs jumped straight up to push back the night. Their light betrayed a hundred men stealing toward the camp. Taglian men and big black men. Some were in hand-shaking distance of my Stranglers.

I looked into the eyes of their commander, Mogaba the Nar, from thirty feet away. He had had the same idea as I'd had.

45

Longshadow glanced across a table where a bowl of mercury sat, reflecting the frightened, wavering face of his slave Smoke. The Howler floated over there. Between them they had just enough strength to communicate with the little wizard. The Howler was amused.

The slave had nothing good to report. Senjak not only was not available, she had evaded his eye well enough to have moved south perhaps as far as Stormgard. Longshadow flung a hand out above the bowl and broke the pattern. Smoke faded, chaotic colors melting.

Howler chuckled. "You should have seduced him. You're too enamored of brute force. Took more time to do it the hard way. And now he's a bent tool. And they don't trust him."

"Don't tell me how to . . ." This was not one of his powerless minions. This one was almost as strong as he. He would not endure attempts at intimidation. He had to be placated, lulled. Seduced.

"Let's check on our colleague at Stormgard."

They joined talents. Though Longshadow could reach that far without help, help did forge the connection more quickly.

It was apparent Shadowspinner was preoccupied. He responded only sporadically. The magnitude and scope of his troubles became clear only slowly.

"Damn it all!" Four thousand men lost. Chaos among the besiegers. Who knew how many more men lost tonight. Shadowspinner falling back on his last desperate device for keeping the city sealed. . . . "That's Senjak herself this time. Has to be. And she's recovered some of her skills."

"Or she's found someone to provide them."

That was Howler, always finding extra explanations, confusing issues. Damn him. It would be a pleasure killing him. Maybe it would take a century to finish him.

"Whatever. She's there. We can end the threat she poses. Have you completed the new carpet?"

"It's ready."

"I'll give you three capable men from my Guard. Bring her here. We will enjoy her for ages to come." Would Howler accept that? He was not naive.

It was a risk, sending him. He might run off with Senjak. The knowledge she possessed . . .

Forewarned is forearmed. He would send his best three men.

"Fail in this and there will be but one answer left. I shall have to loose one of the big ones off the Plain."

The Howler's concentration broke momentarily. A terrible wail tore through his lips. Then the little bundle of rags chuckled. "Consider her caught. I have a score to settle myself."

Longshadow watched the ragbag drift out, taking its odor with it. Maybe its first torment would consist of soap and water.

He sent for his best three Guards and briefed them, then tried contacting Shadowspinner again. Spinner did not respond. He was preoccupied. Or dead.

He retreated to his crystal tower. Crows perched on its top peered down. It was time he did something about them. Permanently. After he sent shadows to Dejagore.

46

Mogaba was much more surprised to see me than I was to see him. An immense displeasure marred his features, a grand measure of his surprise. He was always in control of what he showed the world.

The look persisted only a moment. He altered his course to join me. Before he reached me Ram was beside me, between him and me, and Abda had materialized to my left. Narayan was making certain no outsider caused me grief.

Up ahead Sindhu cursed the light and ordered men to move. It was hit fast or die.

"Lady," Mogaba said. "We thought you dead." He was a big man without an ounce of waste on him, muscled like a fictional hero. He was blacker than Blade and a consummate commander, one of the Nar, descendants of the original Black Company. Croaker had enlisted him in Gea-Xle during our southward journey. The Nar constituted a separate warrior class there. With a thousand Nar I could have cleaned the Shadowmasters out as fast as the men could march.

There were only fifteen or twenty left alive, I guessed. All loyal to Mogaba.

"Did you? I'm tougher than you think." His men piled into the camp with mine, trying to reach Shadowspinner before he reacted. I suspected Mogaba's men had triggered the lights. In Spinner's place I would have expected an attack from him before one from me.

"Do you have the Lance?" he asked. The question took me from the blind side. I would have thought he'd want to talk about the siege or which of us had the stronger claim to the Captaincy.

"What lance?"

He smiled. Relieved. "The standard. Murgen lost it."

He was stretching the truth somehow. I turned the conversation to business. We would not have much time. The Shadowlanders were getting ready to interrupt. "How bad off are you? I have no veterans and few trained men. I can only harass them, not break you out."

"We aren't in good shape. Their last assault nearly overcame us. Where did you get your power? Who are you riding with? Murgen saw Croaker die."

"The enemies of the Shadowmasters are my friends." Better to be cryptic than to hand him free information.

"Why don't you put an end to the Shadowmasters?"

I could not answer without lying. I lied. "My friend is no longer with me."

"Who was up there today?"

"Anyone can wear armor."

He smiled tightly, showing a thin strip of sharp teeth. "The Captaincy, then. You don't plan to let me get out of here. Do you?"

We spoke the language of the Jewel Cities, both disinclined to let our companions in on our conversation.

Men started screaming inside the encampment. I shouted, "Narayan! Come on!" The Shadowlanders west of us would be ready to move any moment. I told Mogaba, "There's no problem with the Captaincy. The progression was established. When the Captain dies the Lieutenant steps into his shoes."

"The tradition is for the Captain to be elected."

We were both right.

Mogaba shouted, "Sindawe! Let's go! It won't work." His archers and artillerymen on the wall were hard at work, laying down fire to cover his withdrawal. "We know where we stand, Lady."

"Do we? I have no enemies but those who choose to make themselves my enemies. I'm interested only in the destruction of the Shadowmasters." My men flew past me. Mogaba's flew past him. A wall of Shadowlanders hurtled toward us.

Mogaba showed me that smile, turned, headed for the city and the safety of ropes hanging down the wall.

Ram gouged me. "Move, Mistress!"

I moved.

A gang of Shadowlanders came after my band, thinking us the easier meat. In the hills some observer had initiative enough to bluff them by sounding trumpets. They slackened the chase. We vanished into the dark ravines.

We assembled. I asked Narayan, "Did we get close?"

"We would have had him if those others hadn't alerted him. Sindhu wasn't ten feet from him."

"Where is he?" Sindhu had not come back. I hated to lose him.

Narayan grinned. "He's healthy. We lost only two Stranglers. Those you don't see got caught in the confusion and fled to the city."

For once I did not mind his grin. "Quick thinking, Narayan. You think he'll find many friends there?"

"A few. Mostly I wanted him to get to your friends. Those who might not be enchanted with that Mogaba."

Mogaba was not much of a problem yet. He was in no position to trouble me. The cure for him was to let him rot. I could just pretend to look for ways to relieve the city while actually only training my men till they suffered the illusion they were soldiers. Meantime, Mogaba could wear the enemy down for me.

The flaw, of course, was that Shadowspinner had allies who might decide to help him.

Dejagore and its surroundings were not worth much anymore but the city did have symbolic value. The Shadowlands were more heavily populated down south. The peoples there would be watching. The fate of Dejagore could decide the fate of the Shadowmasters' empire. If they lost the city and we looked likely to move south again the oppressed might revolt.

All that passed through my mind while I tried to muster strength enough to cross the hills to our camp.

I could not make it. Ram had to help me.

The riders paused to consider the hill beside the road. The woman said, "She's sure gotten them busy." What had been a bald hilltop a few weeks ago now boasted a maze of stonework. Construction looked like a day and night project.

"She gets things done." Croaker wondered how Lady was getting on down south. He wondered why they had come here.

"She does. Damn her." The sorceress touched him gently, like a lover. She did that all the time now. And she looked so much like Lady. He had trouble resisting.

She smiled. She knew what he was thinking. He had his justifications lined up. She had the battle halfway won.

He ground his teeth, stared at the fortress and ignored her. She touched him again. He tried to remark on the layout of the fortress, found nothing would come out. He looked at her again, wide-eyed.

"Just a precaution, my love. You haven't surrendered your heart. But in time you'll come around. Come. Let's visit our friends." She urged her stallion forward.

Circling crows led the way. Catcher wanted to attract attention. She got it. She was a beautiful and exotic woman.

He understood when she spoke to a man as though she knew him. She meant to pass as Lady. No wonder she wanted him mute.

No one paid him any heed. As they passed through the press of sweating men and animals, dust and clatter, the stench of labor and dung, only the insects noticed him.

In this he might disappear. If her attention lapsed. If the crows became distracted. Could they pick him out of such a mob?

She led the way toward the works atop the hill, already nearing completion. She paused again and again to speak to men, usually about matters of no consequence. She was not playing the role right if she meant to usurp Lady. Lady's manner was distant and imperious unless she was striving for a specific result . . . Of course. She wanted word spread that Lady was back.

What was she up to?

His conscience told him he had to do something. But he could think of nothing.

Nobody recognized him. That did his ego no good. Only months ago all Taglios had hailed him Liberator.

Word ran ahead. As they approached the inner fortress a man came out. The Prahbrindrah Drah himself! He was here directing construction? That was not like him. He stayed holed up where the priests could not get to him. The prince said, "I didn't expect you back right away."

"We've won a small victory north of Dejagore. The Shadowmasters lost four thousand men. Blade planned the operation and carried it out. I decided to leave him in charge. I came back to recruit and train new formations. You've done well here. I take it the priests abandoned their obstructionism?"

"You convinced them." The prince looked troubled. "But you don't have any friends now. Don't leave your back unguarded." His gaze kept drifting to Croaker. He seemed puzzled. "Your man Ram seems odd today."

"Touch of dysentery. How is the recruiting going?"

"Slow. Most of the volunteers are helping here. Most men are holding off, waiting to have their minds made up for them."

"Let them know about the victory. Let them know the siege *can* be broken. Shadowspinner has no strength left. He's getting no help from Longshadow. He's on his own with an army so battered only its fear of him holds it together."

Croaker glanced up at a few clouds sliding east from the sea. Nothing remarkable about them but they did cause thoughts to click. The subtle bitch! He knew exactly what she was doing.

Lady was down there sparring with Shadowspinner, beyond the Main, which became impassable during the rainy season. A touch here, a nudge there, and that contest would go on till it was too late for Lady to get back over the river. The season was not that far away, now. Two months at the most. Lady would be trapped over there with the Shadowmasters. Catcher would have five months to take control here, without interference. Probably without anyone discovering who she was. Her crows would watch the routes north. Messengers would be intercepted.

The bitch! The black-hearted bitch!

The prince frowned at him, sensing his turmoil. But he was preoccupied with the woman. "Maybe we can do the garden again sometime."

"That would be lovely. But remember, it's my turn to put on the spread."

The prince smiled weakly. "If they'll let you. After last time."

"I didn't start it."

What was that about? Something involving Lady had happened in the gardens? Soulcatcher did not tell him everything. Only what would leave his heart raw.

He sensed someone watching, spied Smoke lurking in shadows. The wizard's face was a mask of hatred. That faded when he realized he had been spotted. He started shivering, slipped away.

Crows followed, Croaker noted. Of course. Wherever Smoke went he would be watched. Soulcatcher knew all about him.

Catcher asked, "Have my quarters been completed? It's been a long, dusty road. It'll take me two hours to get human."

"They're not finished but they should do. Shall I have someone take your horses and give you a hand with your things?"

"Yes. Of course. Kind of you." She did some trick with her eyes. The prince went shy. "There are some men I want to see." She named names unfamiliar to Croaker. "Send them to my quarters. Ram will entertain them till I'm cleaned up."

"Of course." The prince summoned his hangers-on, sent them to find the men she wanted.

At Catcher's gesture Croaker dismounted and handed his horse over. He followed her as she followed the prince. The crows did a good job scouting, he admitted. Grudgingly. She was pulling it off without a hitch.

In Lady's quarters he discovered why he could be called "Ram," why no one knew him. He encountered a mirror. He did not see himself in it. He saw a big, dirty Shadar with hair enough for a gorilla.

She had laid a glamor on him.

The men Catcher asked for were low caste, skin and bone, nervous little creatures unable to meet her eye. As he introduced himself each added words in cant that Croaker did not recognize. The honorifics were puzzling enough. Daughter of Night? What did that mean? Too much was happening and he had no way of knowing what, nor any control.

Catcher told those men, "I want you to watch the wizard Smoke. At least two of you should be within sight of him all the time. I especially want to know if he goes near the Street of the Dead Lamps. If he enters it, stop him. By whatever means necessary, though I'd rather he didn't make an early entrance into paradise."

The men all plucked at bits of colored cloth peeking from their loincloths. One said, "As you will, so shall it be, Mistress."

"Of course. Get on with it. Find him. Stick tight. He's dangerous to us."

The men hurried out, obviously eager to be away from her. "They're terrified of you," Croaker observed. His voice came back when he was alone with her.

"Naturally. They think I'm the daughter of their goddess. Why don't you get cleaned up? I can smell you from here. I'll have them bring you new clothes."

The bath and clothes were the only good things that happened that day.

48

I did not get the sleep I needed. The dreams were bad. I wandered the caverns under the earth, awash in the stench of decay. The caverns were no longer cold. The old men were rotting. They were still alive but decaying. When I passed through their line of sight I felt their appeal, their blame. I really tried. But I could get no nearer whatever my destination was supposed to be.

The thing trying to recruit me was getting impatient.

Narayan wakened me. "I'm sorry, Mistress. It's important." He looked like he had seen a ghost.

I sat up. And started vomiting. Narayan sighed. His friends moved to mask me from the men. He looked worried. He feared his investment was going to come up short. I was going to die on him.

I was not worried about that. More the opposite, that I would not die and never escape the misery. What was wrong with me? This was getting old, every morning sick—and not that great the rest of the day.

I didn't have time to be sick. I had work to do. I had worlds to conquer. "Help me up, Ram. Did I mess myself?"

"No, Mistress."

"Thank the goddess for small favors. What is it, Narayan?"

"Better you see for yourself. Come, Mistress. Please?"

Ram had brought horses. I collected myself, let him help me mount. We headed for the hills. As we left camp I saw Blade and Swan and Mather with their heads together, exercised about something. Narayan did not ride but he could lope along when he wanted.

He was right. Seeing was better than hearing. I might not have believed a verbal report.

The plain had flooded. At the north and south ends water roared out of the hills. The aqueducts had gone mad. I said, "Now we know where those work parties headed. They must have diverted both rivers. How deep is it?"

"At least ten feet already."

I tried guessing how high it could rise. The hills were deceptive. It was hard to tell. The plain was lower than the land beyond the hills but not much. The water should not get more than sixty feet deep. But that would be enough to flood the city.

Mogaba was in a fix. He had no way out—unless he built boats or rafts. Shadowspinner would not have to waste a man to keep him tied up.

"Good gods! Where did the Shadowlanders go?" I had a bad feeling I had one foot in a bear trap.

Narayan summoned a man on scout duty. He told us the Shadowlanders had pulled out in two forces, north and south, shortly after sunrise.

I consulted maps in my head, told Narayan, "We have to run. Fast. Or we'll be dead before noon. Get up here behind me. You. Soldier. Get up behind Ram and hang on. Are there other men out here?"

"A few, Mistress."

"They'll have to look out for themselves. Let's go!"

We were a sight, I'm sure, only one of us a competent rider and she so sick she had to stop twice to throw up. But we got back to camp before the hammer fell.

Blade had them ready to march. Now I knew what he'd been up to with Swan and Mather. He had heard about the water and had sensed its significance. He awaited orders.

"Send cavalry north and south to scout and harass."

"Done already. Two hundred men each direction."

"Good. You're a natural." I'd already recalled, rejected, and reexamined a trick that had been played on my armies in the north. Hurry was essential. I could see what might be dust north of us. "Move the infantry into the hills. I want every horseman to cut brush and drag it behind, headed due east. Get messengers off to the skirmishers. I want contact kept as long as possible. Draw them eastward and keep leading them as long as they'll follow."

The ruse would not work after dark—if it worked at all. Then Shadowspinner's pet shadows would tell him he'd been taken. But that would be time enough to elude him.

If he kept chasing me Mogaba's men would escape. He would not want that.

Blade wasted no time. Swan and Mather dashed around helping. Our differences would wait.

A new sense of confidence and discipline was apparent as the troops moved into the hills. They trusted me and Blade to get them through this. The horsemen headed out, raising enough dust for a horde on the march.

Blade, Swan, Mather, Narayan, and I watched from a low hill. "That will do it if he can be fooled at all," I said. "He'll see us just slipping out, get excited, try to nab us on the run."

Swan raised crossed fingers to the sky. Blade asked, "What's our next move?"

"Drift north through the hills."

"He's biting," Mather said.

Blade said, "It occurs to me that, for speed's sake, he would have left behind anyone not in top condition."

I told him, "You are learning. And you're turning nasty."

"Nasty business."

"Yes. The rest of you understand?"

Swan wanted it explained. "Spinner would leave his injured and second-line troops behind so they wouldn't slow him down. They should be up where the north road enters the hills. We can take them by surprise. Narayan, send some scouts ahead."

Narayan was pleased with me now. There was a lot of killing going on. There was promise of a real Year of the Skulls.

49

Smoke drifted into the darkness, glanced right and left, cursed softly. There they were again. Those men! He could not shake them. They knew where he was going before he went.

It was disheartening and frightening. The longer he delayed visiting his contacts the stronger Longshadow's image grew within his mind and the more terrified he became on a level so deep it was a part of his soul. Something terrible had been done to him, something that had reached into him as deeply as a man could be reached. Somehow Longshadow had hidden a fragment of himself inside him, to drive him into executing the Shadowmaster's will.

The voice within had become a shriek. If he did not shake the watchers he would not be able to avoid betraying his contacts.

He pretended not to notice the men, though they did nothing to remain anonymous. Did she know and just want to scare him away from his contacts? Maybe. Maybe it did not matter if he betrayed them.

He started walking.

His shadows followed.

He tried to elude them, relying on a superior knowledge of the city. He had haunted the shadows and alleys and hidden ways all his life. As he knew the palace better than anyone living, so he knew Taglios. He gave it his best. And when he stepped out of a shanty warren where he got lost twice himself trying to get back out, one of his stalkers was waiting, leaning against a building.

The man grinned.

Longshadow filled Smoke's mind. The Shadowmaster was angry. His patience was failing.

Smoke stamped across the street. "How the hell do you keep track of me?"

The man spat to one side, smiled again. "You can't evade the eye of Kina, wizard."

"Kina!" Another terror to pile atop his fear of Longshadow.

"You can run but you can't hide. You can twist and wiggle but you can't get off the hook. You can skulk and whisper in locked rooms but you can't keep secrets. Each breath you draw is numbered."

The fear deepened.

"And always has been."

Smoke turned to run.

"There's a way out."

"What?"

"There's a way out. Look at you. Maintain your allegiance to the Shadowmaster and you're dead if your Taglian friends find out. If they don't kill you, he will when he's done with you. But you can get out. You can come home. You can shake the terror that's like a beast starving for your soul."

Smoke was too frightened to wonder why the thug did not talk like a street creature. "How?" He would try anything to get out from under the Shadowmaster's thumb.

"Come to Kina."

"Oh. No!" He nearly shrieked. The only escape was to yield himself to a greater horror? "No!"

"Up to you, wizard. But life isn't going to get any better."

This time Smoke did run. He did not care if he was followed. Exercise reduced panic. As he neared his destination he realized that he had not seen any bats since leaving the palace. That was new. Where were the Shadowmasters' messengers?

He bustled into a tall slum tenement, hurried upstairs, pounded on a door. A voice said, "Enter."

He froze two steps inside the doorway.

The man he had been talking to leaned against the opposite wall. There were eight corpses in the room, all strangled. The man said, "The goddess doesn't want your master to know her daughter is here."

Smoke squeaked like a stomped rat. He fled. The man laughed.

The man amongst the corpses shrank. He became the imp Frogface, who chuckled, then faded away.

Smoke calmed down before he reached the palace. His mind started working. He had one bolt left. It could bite him as easily as his enemies, but . . . Engulfed by the darkness he could but flee toward the only light he saw.

He would *not* yield to Kina.

50

As dusk gathered I descended on Longshadow's stay-behinds and routed them completely. The slaughter was great. It failed being complete only because my cavalry was otherwise occupied. We had the field to ourselves before the last light left the sky.

"Old Spinner's going to know in a few minutes," Swan said. "I figure he'll have him a litter of kittens, then he'll get pissed. We ought to go somewhere where he can't catch us."

He was on the right track. Coming through the hills I had been considering going after the group left at the southern approach. Not till Swan spoke did I realize I would not be able to sneak up on that group. Night had come. Night belonged to Shadowspinner. He would know where we were and where we were headed. Unless that was away from him he would be waiting when we arrived.

Too, he might be desperate enough to appeal to Longshadow. Maybe Longshadow had help on the way already. Whatever lay between them, it would not be as great as their enmity for the rest of the world. Though premature, theirs was a squabble over the spoils of conquest.

Blade asked, "Any way we could stay here and masquerade as the Shadowmaster's men?"

"No. I don't have the skill. Our best bet is to go back north till he stops chasing us, then just keep him nervous while we decide what to do next."

Narayan had started worrying about missing his delayed Festival. Though I had passed my first test he was suspicious of my will to become the Daughter of Night. A move north would assuage him. And the men needed time away from danger, to recuperate and digest their successes.

Blade asked, "The men in the city?"

"They're safer than they were. Shadowspinner can't get at them now."

Narayan grumbled. Sindhu was in there.

I said, "Mogaba will cope. He's good at coping." Too good. We would have trouble down the road, him and me.

Nobody liked heading back north, except Narayan. But no one argued.

I had gained ground, definitely.

51

Smoke was no earthshaker as a wizard but within his limitations, which he recognized, he was competent and effective. And forewarned, he was fore-armed.

The woman knew his every move? Then she commanded some unsus-pected agency for espionage. He needed blind that only a few minutes.

He scuttled through the palace, ducking his employers, who were looking for him. He dodged into one of his shielded rooms, barred the door.

Obviously his shielding had been penetrated because that man had implied she knew everything, meaning she had been peeking here, too. She was more than she pretended. *Much* more. She *was* the Daughter of Night. And that fool the prince had been blinded by her. Hadn't they been out to the gardens again tonight?

No one could stop her but him. Maybe he could shake loose from Long-shadow later.

The Shadowmaster's face formed in his head. His legs turned to jelly. He shook his head violently, forced the apparition away, hurriedly set about check-ing his defenses.

He found a pinhole through which some wicked spirit could have oozed. Or a shadow, for that matter.

He plugged it. Then he worked a spell that pressed his limits. It would con-ceal his whereabouts till he became the object of a very determined search. Se-cure, he filled a small silver bowl from a mercury flask, working as swiftly as he dared. Before he was finished he feared that he had been too slow.

Someone tried the door. He jumped but concentrated on opening the path to Overlook. It came. It came. More quickly than he expected, it came. The Shadowmaster had been thinking of him, too.

The racket at the door became pounding and shouting. He ignored it.

The dread face appeared on the surface of the mercury, amazed. It mouthed words. There was no sound. The Shadowmaster was too far, Smoke's power too feeble. The little wizard gestured violently, Pay attention! He was startled by his own temerity. But this was a desperate hour. Desperate measures were necessary.

Smoke grabbed paper and ink and scribbled. They were trying to break down the door. Damn, the woman had reacted quickly.

He held his message up for Longshadow. The Shadowmaster read. He reread. Then Longshadow looked him in the eye and nodded. He appeared bewildered. Carefully, he mouthed words so Smoke could read his lips.

The door began to give. And something else was trying to get in now, clawing and tearing at the plugged pinhole.

The door gave a little more.

Smoke got half the message before the pinhole plug broke. Dense smoke boiled into the room. A face glared out of it. Hideous and fanged and filled with grim purpose, it came for him. He squealed, jumped up, overturned table and bowl.

The door gave way as the demon caught him. He screamed and tumbled down into an abyss of terror.

The guards took one look, cursed, dropped the ram and fled. The prince stepped inside, saw the thing ripping at Smoke. The Radisha crowded up behind him. "What the hell is that?"

"I don't know. I don't think you ought to stay to find out." He looked for a weapon, recognized the absurdity of the impulse as he grabbed a swordlike sliver split from the doorframe.

The monster looked up, startled. It stared. Apparently this situation was beyond its instructions. It hung there, motionless.

The Prahbrindrah threw the sliver like a spear.

The thing shrank away into an upper corner of the room, swiftly and dramatically, leaving behind an odor like cinnamon and mustard and wine all mixed.

"What the hell was it?" the Radisha demanded again. She was petrified. The Prahbrindrah jumped over to the wizard. Smoke's blood was everywhere, along with shreds of clothing. The thing had driven him into a corner. What was left of him had drawn itself into a tight fetal ball.

The prince dropped to his knees. "He's alive. Get some help. Fast. Or he won't be for long." He started doing what he could.

52

Longshadow let out one long scream of rage that echoed throughout Overlook. It brought toadies running, bent with fear he would take it out on them. Whatever it was. "Get out! Get out and stay . . . Wait! Get in here!"

Calm returned suddenly. He'd always had a facility for gaining control when the crisis was tight. That was when he thought his best, responded most quickly. Maybe this was a blessing in disguise.

"Bring the big sending bowl. Bring mercury. Bring that fetish that belongs to my guest and ally. I must contact him."

They scurried around in terror. That was good to see. They held him in high fear. Fear was the power. What you feared ruled you. . . . He thought of shadows and a plain of glittering stone. The rage boiled up. He rejected it, as he rejected fear. One day, when the distractions were eliminated, that plain would bend to him. He would conquer it, end the fear of it forever.

They had everything set before he was ready himself. "Now get out. Stay out till I call."

He activated the bowl and reached for his man. He touched nothing. He tried again. Again. Four times. Five. The rage was about to break through again.

The Howler responded.

"Where have you been?"

"Aloft." Scant whisper, barely perceptible. "I had to set down first. Bad news. She's tricked our friend again. Slaughtered another several thousand men."

That went past Longshadow. Shadowspinner's travails were nothing. "Is she there? At all?"

"Of course she is."

"Are you positive? Have you *seen* her? My shadows can't find her. Last night they couldn't do more than suggest she *might* be in a given general area."

"Not with my own eyes," Howler admitted. "I'm tracking her forces, though, waiting for the chance to strike. Late tonight, I think."

"I've just had a report from the wizard in Taglios. A desperate effort on his part. All our agents there have been strangled. He says she's there. With her

Shadar shadow. And she knows he's ours. Before he finished, something demonic burst in and tore him apart."

"That's impossible. She was here two days ago."

"Have you *seen* her? With your own eyes?"

"No."

"Recall. She always favored illusion and misdirection. There was evidence she was regaining her powers. Maybe much faster than she let on. Maybe she's tricked us into believing she was one place when she was another. The Taglian said our agents were killed to keep them from reporting her presence."

The Howler did not respond.

Both men thought. Longshadow finally said, "I can't fathom why she'd send an army to make us believe she was in our territories. But I know her. You know her. If it's that important to her that we believe her somewhere she isn't, then it's lethally important to us. There's something in Taglios she doesn't want us to discover. Perhaps she's on the track of the Lance. Someone carried it away from the battlefield. It hasn't been seen since."

"If I go we're liable to lose Dejagore and Spinner. His skills are impaired. His mind is as dull as a knife used to chop rock."

Longshadow cursed softly. Yes. Pray come the day when Shadowspinner was no longer needed. When there was no need for a bulwark against the north. But somebody had to bear the brunt now. "Do something. Then go." The runt could understand that. "Collect her quick. Hell will be a pleasure compared to what we'll face if she stays loose till all her powers are restored."

"Consider it done," the Howler whispered. "Consider her taken."

"I take nothing for granted where Senjak is concerned. Get her, dammit! Get her!" He slammed a fist into the mercury. That killed the connection.

He let the rage roar through him. He hurled things, broke things, till it was appeased. Then he went up into his tower and glowered his hatred at the night-hidden plain.

"Why must you torment me? Why? Turn away. Let me be." If that was not out there, ready to burst its bonds, he would be free to deal with these things himself. He would make short work of these problems if he could see to them himself. But he needs must rely on incompetents and agents with insufficient power to get the job done.

He thought of the Taglian wizard. That tool had not done the job for which it had been forged but it had served. Pity it had been destroyed so quickly.

A pity.

53

The cavalry rejoined us two days north of Dejagore, where I made camp. The general mood was positive. The men resented having been withdrawn. They did not want to believe they had just been lucky, not invincible. I wanted them to know their luck could turn. They did not believe me. Most people believe only what they want to believe.

Their confidence had infected Narayan and Blade. Those two would have turned south again without question had I ordered it. I was tempted. I considered myself lucky to be sick. It kept me thinking rationally.

They presented a plan for harassing Shadowspinner into another trap. I told them, "Spinner won't charge into traps. If we separate him from his men maybe we can trap them. But not him."

Narayan leaned close. "It wasn't luck, Mistress. It was Kina. Her spirit is loose. It is the time of foreshadowing. The Year of the Skulls approaches. She passes her hand over the eyes of her enemies. She is with us."

I wanted to tell him that the man who counts on the aid of a god deserves the help he doesn't get but I reconsidered. The Deceivers were true believers. Whatever else, however bloodthirsty and criminal their enterprises, they believed in their goddess and mission. Kina was not just a convenient fiction excusing their crimes.

After months of dreams I had trouble not believing in Kina myself. Maybe not as Narayan's kind of goddess but as a potent force that fed on death and destruction.

Blade asked, "Why not take Shadowspinner out of the picture?"

"Right. A stroke of genius, Blade. Maybe if we all wish hard enough he'll come floating belly up."

He smiled. His smile was no fawning grin like Narayan's but it was powerful because he used it so seldom. He offered me a hand up. "Take a walk with me, please."

Right on the edge there, Blade. He was not sufficiently impressed, I feared. I reminded myself to remember he probably had his own agenda and I did not have the foggiest what it might be.

We walked away from the others. Narayan and Ram and Swan all watched, each with his particular breed of jealousy.

"Well?"

"Shadowspinner is the main enemy. Kill him and his army would collapse."

"Probably."

"I have eyes and ears. My brain works. When I'm curious I ask questions. I know what Narayan is. I know what you are to him. And I think I know what they want you to become."

No great surprise, that. Probably half the army had some notion, though they might not believe Ram and Narayan deserved their legendary reputation. "So?"

"I've seen Sindhu in action. I understand Narayan is better."

"True."

"Then point him at Shadowspinner. He could have the Shadowmaster dead before he knew what hit him."

Strangling a sorcerer is a good way of disposing of him. One of Spinner's magnitude relies heavily on voice spells and, secondarily, gesture spells. Stick him with a knife or sword or missile and he can still use both voice and hands unless you kill him instantly. A Narayan could take away the voice. Assuming he could break a neck as fast as he claimed, gestures would not matter.

"Stipulated. I think. Leaving one small problem. Moving Narayan near enough to use his rumel."

"Uhm."

"Narayan, of his kind, is what I used to be of mine. The pinnacle. The acme. I've watched him. He's death incarnate. But he lacks the skills needed to get close to Shadowspinner. He just never learned how to turn invisible."

Blade chuckled. "Bet that's a trick he'd love you to teach him."

"No doubt. You've thought this through. You've seen the difficulties. You think you've seen ways around them. So tell me how we do it. I don't think it's practical but I'll listen."

"There are distinct kinds of assassins. A lone crazy who doesn't care if he gets killed himself. A cabal grasping for power, ready to turn on itself when its target is eliminated. And the professional."

I saw no point. I said so.

"To be successful we have to avoid the weaknesses of various kinds of assassins. I've watched you. Your skills aren't what they were but you sell yourself short. You could disguise a strike team sneaking up on Shadowspinner. If we create the illusion that our goals are impersonal he won't guard against personal attack. Right?"

"To a point."

"To a point. Shadowspinner shouldn't know you have problems with Mogaba. So go after ways to relieve the city. While a handful work on killing Shadowspinner."

"Tell me how."

"Narayan should do the actual killing. You will have to disguise the attack group or make it invisible. Ram goes because he must. I go because no one else is better with a weapon. Swan goes because his presence implies the involvement of the Taglian state. Mather would be better because there's a personal involvement with the Woman, but Cordy needs to hold the reins here. He's steady. He thinks. Willow is all passion, action without thought. Add however many specialists Narayan needs."

"Two arm-holders." I said it in Stranglers' cant. Blade gave me a quick glance. He was surprised I was that far into that world. We walked in silence. Then I said, "You've just talked more than I've heard since I met you."

"I talk when I have something to say."

"Do you know card games?" I had seen none south of the equator. Here the well-to-do played dominoes or board games, the impoverished games with dice or sticks you shook in a canister and tossed.

"Some. Cordy and Mather had cards but they wore out."

"Know what a wild card is?"

He nodded.

I stopped, bent my head, closed my eyes, concentrated, conjured a ferocious illusion. It took form high above, a flying lizard twice the size of an eagle. It dove.

Crows have sharp eyes. They have brains, for birds, but they are not geniuses. They panicked. The panic would make their reports of the event incomprehensible.

Blade said, "You did something." He watched the crows flee.

"The birds are spies for one of the wild cards in our game." I told him what I had found in the grove and what I thought it meant.

"Mather and Swan have mentioned this Howler and Soulcatcher. They did not speak well of them. But they didn't speak well of you, either, as you were. What's their interest here?"

I talked about them till the crows returned. Blade had no trouble grasping the intricacies of scheming in the old empire. He must have had experience.

The crows reestablished their watch. I did not disturb it. Too often would generate suspicion. Blade wore a thin, pleased smile. As we approached the others, waiting silently, watching intently, each with his concerns too evident, Blade whispered, "For the first time I'm glad Cordy and Willow dragged me out."

I glanced at him quickly. Yes. He seemed completely alive for the first time since I'd met him.

54

The Prahbrindrah Drah turned slowly before a mirror, admiring himself. "What do you think?"

The Radisha eyed his tailored dress, bright silk, and jewels. He cut a handsome figure. "When did you turn into a peacock?"

He half drew a sword he'd had forged as a symbol of the state. "Nice?"

It was as fine a weapon as could be produced by Taglian craftsmen, hilt and pommel a work of art incorporating gold, silver, rubies, and emeralds in a symbolic intertwining of the emblems of Taglian faiths. The blade was strong, sharp, practical, but its hilt was overweight and clumsy. Still, it was not a combat weapon, just a trapping of office.

"Gorgeous. And you're trying to make a fool of yourself."

"Maybe. But I'm having fun doing it. And you'd be having fun making a fool of you if Mather was here. Eh?"

The Radisha eyed him narrowly. He was not as open as he had been before Lady caught his eye. He was up to something and for the first time in their lives he was not sharing. That worried her. But she said only, "You're wasting your time. It's raining. Nobody goes to the gardens when it's raining."

"It won't last."

That was true. It was just a brief rain. They always were, this time of year. The real rains were more than a month away. But still . . . She felt he should avoid the gardens tonight, with no rational basis for her feeling.

"You're investing too much in it. Slow down. Make her work harder."

He grinned. Give the woman that. Murderess she might be but she did put a smile on his face. "Don't count me so smitten I'll give away the palace."

"I wasn't thinking that. But she's changed since she came back. It concerns me."

"I appreciate it. But I'm in control. Taglios is my first love. And hers is the Company. If she's up to anything it's trying to make sure we don't go back on our bargain."

"That could be enough." Regarding the Black Company she still hovered over the abyss between his position and Smoke's.

"How's Smoke?" he asked.

"Hasn't come to yet. They say he lacks the will to recover."

"Tell those leeches that for their sakes he'd better. I want to know what happened. I want to know what that thing was. I want to know why it wanted to kill him. Our Smoke has been up to something. It could get us destroyed."

They had discussed that again and again. There were implications in Smoke's behavior which boded evil. Till they learned the truth, they suspected, a sword hung over their heads.

"You haven't said what you think."

"I think everyone who sees you will think you look like a prince of the blood instead of a vegetable peddler someone threw ill-fitting clothing on and called a prince."

He chuckled. "You're right. In your sarcastic way. I never cared what I looked like. Wasn't anyone I wanted to impress. Time to go."

"Suppose I go along, this once?" A facetious suggestion, to see how he wriggled.

"Why not? Get ready. It ought to be amusing, seeing her response."

And instructive? The Radisha's estimate of her brother rose. He was not completely smitten. "I won't be long."

She was not. It took her longer to pass instructions to Smoke's attendants than to prepare to go out.

Croaker leaned on the lance supporting the Company standard, wearing his Shadar disguise. He was bored. He was not alert. He was depressed. He had begun to despair of escape. He was ready to say the hell with it and try walking first time a faint chance arose.

The Prahbrindrah Drah and Soulcatcher chattered and laughed beneath paper lanterns while garden staff came and went. They were oblivious to anything but one another. The surprise guest, the Radisha, was out in the cold, ignored.

Croaker had grumbled about spending so much time on the prince and not enough on preparing soldiers. Catcher had laughed, told him not to worry. She would be true to him forever. This was just politics.

He would not be able to resist her much longer. She had him on the run, desperate, on the brink of surrender. Once he did that she would have won everything.

Maybe he *should*. Maybe once she counted that final coup she would just go away, back north, where her prospects were so much finer. She talked about going north sometimes.

Being her companion was cruel. She had made of him something more than spoil. She talked about the Soulcatcher inside sometimes, when what she had chosen to be became too much to bear. In those moments, when she was human, he was most vulnerable. In those moments he wanted to comfort her. He was sure the moments were genuine, not tactical. Her approach to conquest was not subtle.

Brooding, it took him a while to notice that the Radisha was paying him more attention than a bodyguard deserved. She was not obvious but she was subjecting him to intense scrutiny. It startled him, disturbed him, then just left him curious. Why? Some flaw in his disguise? No way to tell. He'd never seen the man he was supposed to be.

He started thinking about what Lady might be doing, what relationships she might be forming. Was there yet another level to Catcher's vengeance? Did she not only want to seduce him and rape his heart but want Lady to find someone—so she could then let her know he was alive after all?

Weird people. All this for little pains. Relatively little pains. Maybe not so little to them, who in their ways were demigods. Maybe to them love was more significant than to mere mortals.

The Radisha was damned near staring at him. She frowned like someone trying to recall a face.

He had little to lose. He winked.

Her eyebrows rose, her only reaction. But she did not study him anymore. She pretended interest in her brother and the woman he thought was Lady.

Croaker resumed brooding. Lost in his own inner landscapes he did not notice the crows departing, one by one.

Though she had the greater capacity, Catcher did not show off the way Lady did. The coach was dull and quiet. Croaker, beside the driver, clutched his lance and wondered what they were talking about below. The prince and his sister had accepted a ride because the skies had begun to leak again.

The drizzle suited his mood perfectly.

The driver said, "Ho!"

Croaker glimpsed the sudden glow in an alleyway now drawing abreast. As he turned a blinding, fist-sized ball of pink fire shot out, smashed into the left-hand door of the coach. A second ripped out behind it, hit the front of the coach, flared brilliantly. The horses broke loose, leaving the vehicle. A third ball hit the coach, shattered a rear wheel. The coach heeled over almost to the point of toppling. Croaker jumped. The counter-momentum of his kickoff was just enough to stop the tipping. As the coach crashed back he hit the street on the side away from the alley.

Men charged out of that alley.

Croaker ripped open the coach door. Catcher and the Radisha were unconscious. The prince was dazed but awake. Croaker grabbed his pretty suit and yanked.

Up above, the driver cried out.

Croaker charged around the rear of the smoldering coach—smack into what looked like a floating bundle of rags. He stabbed with the lance he still clutched.

The bundle howled.

Croaker's blood stilled in his veins.

There were three men with the Howler. They turned on Croaker.

The prince stumbled around the front of the coach, dandy's sword drawn. He cut one of those men from behind.

The Howler screamed. He waved both hands wildly. Croaker stabbed him again. The whole street boomed and rocked. Croaker was flung back against the coach, thought he felt ribs give way. The boom seemed to echo endlessly up and down a deep canyon. His last clear thought was, not again. He'd just gotten over a serious injury.

People were scurrying around like panicky mice when Croaker recovered. The Radisha knelt over her brother. The more collected bystanders had dragged the attackers away. Two seemed to be dead, a third badly injured. Croaker got to his knees, pressed fingers against his ribs. Pain answered but it was not the pain of broken bones. He'd gotten through it with bruises. He pushed toward the Radisha, asked, "How bad is he?"

"Just unconscious, I think. I don't see any wounds." She did not look at him. There was shouting way up the street. Belated help was on its way.

Croaker looked into the coach.

Soulcatcher was gone.

Howler was gone.

"He took her?"

The Radisha looked up. Her eyes widened. "You! I thought there was something familiar . . ." Soulcatcher's spells had perished? He was himself now?

"Where is she?"

"That thing that attacked us . . ."

"A sorcerer called the Howler. As powerful and nasty as the Shadowmasters. Working for them now. Did he take her?"

"I think so."

"Damn!" He lowered himself gingerly, recovered the lance, used it to support himself. "You people! Get out of here! Go home. You're in the way. Wait! Did anyone see what happened?"

A few witnesses confessed. He demanded, "The thing that fled. Where did it go?"

The witnesses indicated the alley.

Using the lance as a crutch—he had a badly twisted ankle to go with the bruised ribs—he hobbled into the alleyway.

Nothing there. The Howler was gone and Catcher with him.

As he headed back he realized what the absence of Catcher's spells meant. He was free. For a while he was free.

The Prahbrindrah Drah was sitting up. The onlookers, realizing their prince had been attacked, were turning ugly, threatening the attacker who had survived. Croaker bellowed, "Back off! We need him alive. I said go home. That's an order."

Some recognized him now. A voice said, "It's the Liberator!" The title had been bestowed by public acclaim when he and the Company had undertaken to defend Taglios.

Some went. Some stayed. Those moved back.

The racket of help too late drew nearer.

The prince looked up at Croaker in amazement. Croaker offered him a hand. The prince accepted it. On his feet, he whispered, "Is the disguise part of some grand strategy?"

"Later." The prince must think he had masqueraded as Ram all along. "Can you walk? Let's get off the street before more trouble finds us."

Help arrived in the form of a half dozen palace guards. They had been summoned by someone with enough presence of mind to go for them.

The prince asked, "Someone snatched Lady?" Bemused, he muttered, "I guess that was the whole point, else we'd all be dead."

"That's my guess. Are they in for a surprise. Let's get moving." As they started walking, surrounded by the guards, Croaker asked, "Where was your pet wizard while all this was happening?"

"Why?" the Radisha demanded.

"That little shit has been on the Shadowmasters' payroll for weeks. Ask him about it."

The prince said, "I'd love to. But a demon tried to kill him and almost succeeded. He's in a coma. Won't come back."

Croaker glanced back. "Somebody ought to bring the prisoner. He might tell us something useful."

He would not. He had died while no one was looking.

Croaker was amazed at himself, taking charge the way he was. Maybe it was pressure from so many months of helplessness. Maybe it was urgency brought on by the certainty that he would not have long to grab hold of his destiny.

The prince had to be right. Lady had been the object of the attack. That meant the bad boys had lost track of her somehow and had thought Catcher was her. He smiled grimly. They would not be prepared for the tiger they had caught.

How long would Catcher toy with them before revealing herself? Long enough?

Count on nothing. Hurry.

He by damned had to grab for all he could get while the opportunity existed.

Croaker finished his story. The prince and his sister had listened agape. The Radisha recovered her poise first. She'd always had the harder edge. "Way back, Smoke cautioned us that there might be more going on than met the eye. That there might be players in the game we didn't see."

All eyes turned to the unconscious wizard. Croaker said, "Prince, you used that sticker pretty well tonight. Think you'd have trouble pricking him if he asked for it?"

"No trouble at all. After what he's done the trouble I'll have is not sticking him before we get a story out of him."

"He's not all bad. He walked into a trap trying to do what he thought was right. His problem is, he gets an idea in his head and he can't get it out if it's wrong, no matter what evidence you hit him with. He decided we were the bad guys come back for general mayhem and he just couldn't change his mind. Probably never will. If you execute him he'll die thinking he's a hero and martyr who tried to save Taglios. I think I can waken him. When I do, you stand by to stick him if he tries any tricks. Even a puny wizard is deadly when he wants."

Croaker took an hour but did tease the wizard out of life's twilight and got him to choke out his story.

Afterward, the prince asked, "What can we do? Even if he's as contrite as he says, the Shadowmasters have a hold we can't break. I don't *want* to kill him but he is a wizard. We couldn't keep him locked up."

"He can stay locked up in his mind. You'd have to force-feed him and clean him like a baby but I can put him back into the coma."

"Will he heal?"

"His body should. I can't do anything about what the devil did to his soul."
Smoke's past cowardice looked like outrageous courage now.

"Do it. We'll deal with him when there's time."

Croaker did it.

56

Shadowspinner's shadows remained blind to my whereabouts. He did not seem able to adjust. And his bats were useless. Were in fact extinct in that part of the world where my band stole through the night.

I signalled a halt a mile from where my scouts said Spinner had established his camp. We had come a long way in a short time. We needed rest.

Narayan settled beside me. He plucked at his rumel, whispered, "Mistress, I'm of a divided mind. Most of me really believes the goddess wants me to do this, that it will be the greatest thing I've ever done for her."

"But?"

"I'm scared."

"You make that sound shameful."

"I haven't been this frightened since my first time."

"This isn't your ordinary victim. The stakes are higher than you're used to."

"I know. And knowing wakens doubts of my ability, of my worthiness . . . even of my goddess." He seemed ashamed to admit that, too. "She is the greatest Deceiver of all, Mistress. It amuses her sometimes to mislead her own. And, while this is a great and necessary deed, even I, who was never a priest, notice that the omens have not been favorable."

"Oh?" I had noticed no omens, good or bad.

"The crows, Mistress. They haven't been with us tonight."

I had not noticed. I had grown that accustomed to them. I assumed they were there whether I saw them or not. He was right. There were no crows anywhere.

That meant something. Probably something important. I could not imagine their master allowing me freedom from observation for even a minute. And their absence was not my doing. And I doubted it was Shadowspinner's.

"I hadn't noticed, Narayan. That's interesting. Personally, it's the best omen I've seen in months."

He frowned at me.

"Worry not, my friend. You're Narayan, the living legend. The saint-to-be. You'll do fine." I shifted from cant to standard Taglian. "Blade. Swan. Ready?"

"Lead on, my lovely," Swan said. "I'll follow you anywhere." The more stressed he became the more flip he was.

I looked them over, Blade, Swan, Ram, Narayan, the two arm-holders. Seven of us. As Swan had observed, the obligatory number for a company on quest. A totally mixed bag. By his own standards each was a good person. By the standards of others everyone, excepting Swan, was a villain.

"Let's go, then." Before I grew too philosophical.

We did not have to talk about it. We had rehearsed farther away. There would be no chatter to alert Shadowspinner.

It was a slovenly encampment. It screamed demoralization. But for Spinner my ragbag army could have beaten those Shadowlanders. And they knew it. They were waiting for the hammer to fall.

We passed within yards of pickets who sat facing a fire and grumbling. Their language resembled Taglian. I could understand them when they were not excited.

They were demoralized, all right. They were discussing men they knew who had deserted. There seemed to be a lot of those and plenty of sentiment for following their example.

Narayan had the point. He trusted no one else to find his way. He came sliding into the hollow where we waited. In a whisper that did not carry three feet he told me, "There are prisoners in a pen to the left, there. Taglian. Several hundred."

I turned that over in my mind. How could I use them? There was potential for a diversion there. But I did not need one. "Did you talk to them?"

"No. They might have given us away."

"Yes. We'll stick to the mission."

Narayan went ahead. He found us another lurking place. I began to sense Shadowspinner's nearness. He did not radiate much energy for a power of his magnitude. Till then I had been sure only that he was in the camp. "Over there."

"The big tent?" Narayan asked.

"I think."

We moved closer. I saw that Shadowspinner felt no need for guards. Maybe he thought he was his own best guard. Maybe he did not want anyone that close while he was asleep.

We crouched in a pool of darkness, a dozen feet from the tent. One fire burned on its far side. No light came from within. I eased my blade out of its scabbard. "Blade, Swan, Ram, be ready to cover us if something goes wrong." Hell. If anything went wrong we were dead. And we all knew it.

"Mistress!" Ram protested. His voice threatened to rise.

"Stay put, Ram. And don't give me an argument." We'd had the argument already. He did not give up. I moved forward. Narayan and his arm-holders drifted with me. So did the smell of fear.

I paused two feet from the tent, drew my blade down the canvas. It cut without a whisper. An arm-holder widened the slash enough for Narayan to slip through. The other followed, I went next, then the first arm-holder.

It was dark in there. Narayan held us in place with a touch. He was a patient hunter. More so than I could have been in his place, knowing the moon was about to rise and rape away the darkness. Its foreglow had been visible as we'd approached the tent.

Narayan started moving, slowly, certainly, disturbing nothing. His arm-holders were as good as he. I could not hear their breathing.

I had to rely on extraordinary senses to keep from stumbling over things. I felt the Shadowmaster's presence but could not pin it down.

Narayan seemed to know where to go.

There had to be hangings ahead. No light from the fire outside reached us. How I wished for some light.

Light I got, unexpectedly. Just enough light to unveil the awful truth.

Shadowspinner was off to our left, seated in the lotus position, watching us through a grim beast mask. "Welcome," he said. His voice was like a snake's hiss. It was feeble. It barely carried. "I've been waiting."

So the shadows had not been fooled after all.

He guessed my thoughts. "Not the shadows, Dorotea Senjak. I know how you think. Soon I shall know all that is inside your head. You arrogant bitch! You thought you could take me with three unarmed men and a sword?"

I said nothing. There was nothing to say. Narayan started to move. I gestured slightly, a Strangler's signal. He froze. There was a chance if Shadowspinner truly believed these men unarmed.

Then I spoke. "If you think you know me, then you don't know me at all." I wanted him closer. I wanted him where Narayan could reach him. "Dark Mother, Mother Kina, listen! Thy Daughter calls. My Mother, attend me."

He did not move. He hit me with something invisible that knocked me back ten feet and tore a groan out of me.

The discipline shown by Narayan and his arm-holders astonished me. They did not rush Shadowspinner. They did not come to me and separate themselves farther from their target. They moved only slightly, so they were better balanced and disposed, their adjustment barely perceptible.

Shadowspinner rose slowly, a man in pain. He slipped a crutch beneath one arm. "Yes. A cripple. With no chance for repairs because my only ally won't lend me help he might regret when he decides I've outlived my usefulness. And I have you to thank." He extended a hand. An almost invisible rope of indigo fire snaked from his fingers to me. He made a pulling gesture. The rope dragged me forward. The pain was intense. I contained my scream, barely.

He wanted me to scream. He wanted me to waken the camp so he could show his incompetents what he had accomplished despite their inattention. He wanted to play cat and mouse.

The wall of the tent behind him exploded inward. Two blades ripped canvas and Ram came flying through. Shadowspinner turned. Ram smashed into him, sent him stumbling toward Narayan.

Narayan and his arm-holders moved like mongooses striking. Narayan had his rumel around the Shadowmaster's throat so fast my eyes insisted it was witchcraft. The arm-holders had the Shadowmaster's limbs extended before he lost momentum.

The purple rope ripped away from me. It lashed one of the arm-holders. The man's eyes grew huge. He stifled a scream and tried to hang on but lost his grip.

Shadowspinner whipped the rope at Narayan.

Narayan's eyes bugged. He lost his grip on his rumel. Shadowspinner turned on the other arm-holder.

Ram grabbed Shadowspinner from behind, by the neck and buttocks, and hoisted him overhead. Shadowspinner lashed at him. He did not seem able to feel pain. He dropped to one knee, smashed the Shadowmaster down on the other.

I heard bones break. The world would have heard an earth-shaking scream if Narayan had not been so good with a rumel. He looped Shadowspinner's neck on the fly, as Ram hurled him down. Falling with Spinner, he had a tight loop on when the cry tried to force its way out.

Ram and Narayan both hung on.

Blade stepped inside the tent, casually drove his blade through Shadowspinner's heart. "I know you people have your ways, but let's not take chances."

There is an incredible vitality in someone like Shadowspinner. Blade was right. Even stabbed several times and thoroughly strangled, back broken, Shadowspinner kept struggling. Ram, Narayan, and both arm-holders hung on. I stepped up and helped Blade cut and stab.

Swan stood outside the gap in the tent and gawked, so rattled he could do nothing but keep watch. Poor Swan. War and violence just were not his thing.

We carved Shadowspinner into a half dozen pieces before he stopped struggling. We stood around the results. All of us were covered with blood. Nobody seemed inclined to do anything but pant and wonder if we'd really succeeded. Narayan, who seldom showed any humor, broke the spell. "Am I a Strangler saint now, Mistress?"

"Three times over. You're immortal. We'd better get out of here. Everybody grab a piece."

Swan made a choked, questioning noise.

I told him, "The only way to make sure is burn him to ash and scatter the ashes. Someone like Longshadow could bring him back even now."

Swan dumped his last meal. Even so, he looked shamed, as though he thought he had contributed nothing.

I picked up Spinner's head. As I passed I winked and gave Swan's hand a squeeze. That should take his mind off his troubles.

The moon was up. It was a day short of full. Barely over the horizon, it was an orange monster. I gestured for the others to hurry, while there were still shadows to mask our going.

We were halfway to the perimeter when a terrible howl rolled down out of the night. Something wobbled across the face of the moon. Another howl tore the night. There was deadly agony in it.

Ram shoved me. "Got to run, Mistress. Got to run."

All around us Shadowlander soldiers rose to see what the racket was.

Croaker glanced at the moon as he entered the city barracks. Not four hours had passed since the attack but already all Taglios knew the Shadowmasters had struck at the Prahbrindrah Drah. The city was united in outrage.

Already the city knew that the Liberator was alive, that he had feigned death in order to lead their enemies into a fatal mistake. The military compound was swamped with men who wanted to rampage through the Shadowlands till not a blade of grass survived.

It would not last. He could do nothing with this ill-armed and untrained horde. But for their sakes he ordered them to assemble at the fortress Lady had begun, then move south in forces of five thousand. They could sort themselves out on the road.

He suspected most would change their minds before they reached Ghoja. However strong their rage they did not have the supporting resources to mount a vengeance campaign. But he knew they would not listen, so he told them what they wanted to hear and stood aside.

The Prahbrindrah Drah accompanied him. The prince was in a rage himself, but a rage channelled by realism. Croaker discharged his duties to those who wanted him to be larger than life, then found the horses that had pulled the coach. While they were being prepared he stamped around the barracks gathering equipment and supplies. Nobody questioned him. Would-be soldiers stared at him like he was a ghost.

He took a bow and black arrows from hiding. Soulcatcher had brought them out of Dejagore with his armor. "These were a gift a long time ago. Before I was anything but a physician. They've served me well. I save them for special times. Special times are here."

An hour later the two left the city. The prince wondered aloud if he had made the right choice, outarguing his sister about joining Croaker. Croaker told him, "Turn back if you want. We don't have time to examine our hearts and dither over choices. Before you go, though, tell me where Lady sent those archers."

"Which archers?"

"The ones who killed the priests. I know her. She wouldn't have kept them with her. She would've sent them somewhere out of the way."

"Vehdna-Bota. To guard the ford."

"Then we ride to Vehdna-Bota. Or I do, if you're going home."

"I'm coming with you."

58

There was no escape from the Shadowlander camp. We were trapped. And I did not know what to do.

Ram said, "Be Kina." Big, gentle, slow Ram. He thought faster than I did.

It was a task of illusion, only slightly more difficult than making witchfires run over armor. It took just a minute to transform both of us. Meantime, the Shadowlanders closed in, though not with the enthusiasm you would expect of men who had caught their enemies flatfooted.

I raised Shadowspinner's head high. They recognized it. I used an augmentation spell to make my voice carry. "The Shadowmaster is dead. I have no quarrel with you. But you can join him if you insist."

Swan had an impulse. He bellowed, "Kneel, you swine! Kneel to your mistress!"

They looked at him, a foot taller than the tallest of them, pale as snow, golden-maned. A demon in man's form? They looked at Blade, almost as exotic. They looked at me and at Shadowspinner's head.

Ram said, "Kneel to the Daughter of Night." He was so close I could feel him shaking. He was scared to death. "The Child of Kina is among you. Beg for her mercy."

Swan grabbed the nearest Shadowlander, forced him to his knees.

I still do not believe it. The bluff worked. One by one, they knelt. Narayan and his arm-holders started chanting. They chose something basic, repeated mantras, of a sort common in Gunni ceremonials and Shadar services. They differed mainly in including lines like, "Show mercy, O Kina. Bless Thy devoted child, who loves Thee," and, "Come to me, O Mother of Night, while blood is upon my tongue."

"Sing!" Swan bellowed. "Sing, you scum!" Typically Swan, he roared around, forcing the slow to kneel and the mute to cry out. His actions were not sane. Sane men do not force enemies who outnumber them a thousand to one. They should have torn us apart. The thought never occurred to them.

"We are a feeble-minded species," Blade observed in wonder. "But you'll have to keep escalating or they'll start thinking."

"Get me water. Lots of water." I held the Shadowmaster's head high and shouted for silence. "The devil is dead! The Shadowmaster is cast down. You are free. You have won the countenance of the goddess. She has blessed you though you have turned your faces away for generations, though you have denied and reviled her. But your hearts know the truth and she blesses you." I raised the intensity of my witchfire showmanship, became a fire with a face. "She has given you freedom, but no gift is free."

Blade brought a waterskin. "I need a goblet, too," I whispered. "Keep the water out of sight." I continued trying to generate a state of hysteria. That was less difficult than reason suggested it should be. The Shadowlanders were tired, terrified, hated the Shadowmasters. Narayan led another singalong. Blade brought me a goblet from Shadowspinner's tent. I prepared it. The spell was difficult but once again I achieved an unexpected success.

I knew the water in the goblet was water. It tasted like water when I took a drink. "I drink the blood of my enemy." To the Shadowlanders it looked like blood when Narayan and his arm-holders started using it to smear marks on Shadowlander foreheads. I invested those marks with the power to stick. Those men would bear the stain of blood as long as they lived.

They even put up with that. A lot of them. A lot decided to try their legs and headed for home.

After a few hundred had been marked I ordered the Shadowlander officers to join me. Several score did so, but most had chosen to stretch their legs. Their class was more committed to the Shadowmasters than were the rank and file.

I told the Shadowlander officers, "There is a price for freedom as there's a price for everything. You are mine now. You owe Kina. She asks one task of you."

They did not ask what. They wondered if they had been stupid to stay.

"Continue to beleaguer Dejagore. But don't fight the men trapped there. Take them prisoner when they try to escape, expecting only those called the Nar. They're enemies of the goddess."

That was what they had been doing anyway, I learned. The flooding had played havoc with what food stores remained in the city. Mogaba's rationing ignored the natives. Disease was rampant. The natives had revolted already. Mogaba had thrown hundreds from the wall to drown. The lake swarmed with corpses.

Such draconian measures had cost Mogaba the support of many of his soldiers. They had begun deserting. Thus the prisoners in the camp stockade.

There had been nothing but silence from that stockade. Maybe the prisoners did not know what was happening. Maybe they were scared to attract attention. I sent Blade to let them out and tell them where to find Mather.

If the Shadowlanders did not stop me I'd have to accept this absurd twist as real.

They did not raise a murmur. At dawn they marched off to take their posts in the hills.

Narayan sidled up, wearing his biggest grin. "Have you doubts yet, Mistress?"

"Doubts? About what?"

"Kina. Have we her countenance or not?"

"We have somebody's. I'll take Kina. I haven't seen anything this unlikely since my husband . . . I wouldn't believe it if I wasn't here."

"They have lived under the Shadowmasters for a generation. They've never been permitted to do anything but what they're told to do. Penalties for disobedience were terrible."

That was part of it. So was the will to defy oppression. And maybe Kina had something to do with it, too. I did not intend looking the gift horse in the mouth.

The majority of the prisoners had gone. I had had two held to interview. I told Narayan, "I'll see Sindhu and Murgen now."

They came. Sindhu remained Sindhu, wide and stolid and brief. He told me what he had seen. He told me we had friends there. They would stay in place, ready to serve their goddess. He told me Mogaba was a stubborn man who meant to hang on to the last man, who did not care that Dejagore had become a hell of disease and hunger.

Murgen told me, "Mogaba wants a place in the Annals. He's like Croaker was about throwing up times when the Company suffered worse."

Murgen was about thirty. He reminded me of Croaker. He was tall, lean, permanently sad. He had been the Company standardbearer and Croaker's understudy as Annalist. In the normal course twenty years down the road he might have become Captain. "Why did you desert?" It was not the sort of thing he would do, regardless of his opinion of his commander.

"I didn't. One-Eye and Goblin sent me to find you. They thought I could get through. They were wrong. They didn't give me enough help."

One-Eye and Goblin were minor sorcerers, old as sin, perpetually at loggerheads. Together with Murgen they were the last of the Black Company from the north, the last of those who had elected Croaker Captain and made me his Lieutenant.

We talked. He told me the men we had recruited coming south were disaffected with Mogaba. He said, "He's trying to make the Company over into crusaders. He doesn't see it as a warrior brotherhood of outcasts. He wants it to be a bunch of religious warriors."

Sindhu interjected, "They worship the goddess, Mistress. They think. But their heresies are revolting. They are worse than disbelief."

Why was he incensed? A prolonged exchange failed to illuminate me. No godless person can comprehend those minute distinctions in doctrine that provide true believers excuse for mayhem. It is hard enough to accept the fact that they really believe the nonsense of their faiths. I always wonder if they are pulling my leg with a straight face.

Those two gave me a lot to digest. I tried. But it was morning. Sleep or no sleep, it was time to be sick. I was sick.

Longshadow's insubstantial messengers warned him of Howler's return long before Howler appeared. He went to Howler's landing place to wait. He waited. And waited. And grew troubled. Had the little ragbag undertaken some treachery at the last instant?

No, shadows said. No. He was coming. He was coming.

He was slow. He was in mortal agony. Never had he endured such pain, never had he suffered so long. Pain obliterated consciousness. All that remained was will supported by immense talent. He knew only that he had to go on, that if he yielded to the pain he would tumble from the sky and end his life in the wastes.

He screamed till his throat was raw, till he could scream no more. And the poison continued spreading through his old flesh, eating him alive, raising the level of pain.

He was lost. None could save him but one who wanted him destroyed.

The blazing, crystal-topped towers of Overlook rose above the horizon.

Howler was but a few leagues away, shadows said, barely able to keep moving. He had the woman but was otherwise alone.

It began to make sense. Howler had had to fight. Senjak had been stronger than anticipated. Let Howler get her here. Let Howler manage that. Once he had the woman he would have no more need of the Howler. The woman's knowledge would be enough.

Then shadows came from somewhere far away, frolicking in with news that had him cursing before he heard the half.

Shadowspinner slain! Killed by the devotees of that mad goddess Senjak had claimed.

Was there no end to the bad news? Could not two good things happen in succession? Must a triumph always presage a disaster?

Stormgard was lost. Shadowspinner's host would evaporate like the dew. Half the Shadow empire's armed strength would disappear before sunset. Those ragged remnants of the Black Company would come out of the city. That madman who led them would pursue his insane quest.

But he had Senjak. He had a living library of every power and evil ever conceived by the mind of man. Once he broached that cask nothing on earth could deny him. He would be more powerful than even she had been, the equal of her husband at his zenith. There were things locked in her head she would never use. There had been a core of softness to her at her hardest. He was not soft. He would not discard a tool. He would rule. His empire would dwarf the Domination and the Lady's successor empire. The world would be his. There was no one in it who could stand in his way. No one could match him power for power now, with Howler crippled and under sentence of death.

A random crow fluttered by, behaving as a normal crow should, but its flight brought filth to his lips. He had forgotten, if only for a moment. There *was* one. *She* was loose out there somewhere.

The Howler's carpet came wobbling down, Howler's gurgling agony preceding it. It plunged the last dozen feet, collapsed. Longshadow cursed again. Another tool broken. The woman, unconscious, tumbled off. She lay still, snoring. Howler tumbled, too, and did not stop moving when he stopped rolling. His body jerked convulsively. A whine poured from him between attempts to scream.

A cold chill crept Longshadow's spine. Senjak could not have done this. A poisonous sorcery of tremendous potency was gnawing at the little wizard. It was so powerful he could not defeat it alone.

There was something terrible loose in the world.

He knelt. He rested his hands on Howler, forcing down his loathing. He reached inside and fought the poison and pain. It retreated a little. He pushed himself. It retreated farther.

The respite gave Howler strength to join the struggle. Together they fought it till it receded far enough for Howler to regain his reason. The little sorcerer gasped, "The Lance. They have the Lance. I did not sense it. Her bodyguard stabbed me twice."

Longshadow was too shocked to curse.

The Lance was not lost! The enemy had it! He croaked, "Do they know what they have?" They had not before. Only the mad captain in Stormgard knew what it was. If they learned the truth . . .

"I don't know," Howler squeaked. He started shaking again. "Don't let me die."

The Lance!

Take one weapon away and they found another. Fate was a fickle bitch.

Longshadow said, "I won't let you die." He had meant to until that moment. But they had the Lance. He would need every tool he could find. He shouted at his servants. "Bring him inside. Hurry. Throw her into the keystone cell. Put shadows in there with her."

He cursed again. It would be a long time before he could tap that cask of knowledge. It would be a long battle saving Howler.

The poison eating Howler was the most potent in this world because it was not of this world, if legends were true.

He glanced southward, at the plain of glittering stone, shimmering in morning's light. Someday . . .

The Lance had come out of there in ancient times. It was a toy compared to what lay there still, ready to be taken up by him who had the will to seize it.

Someday.

I invested six days arranging my own investure of Dejagore. Fewer than six thousand men remained of the three great armies Shadowspinner had gathered. Half those men were substandard for various reasons. I strung them along the shores of the lake. My own men I posted behind them. Then I sent Murgen back to the city.

He did not want to go. I did not blame him. Mogaba might execute him. But somebody had to go to the survivors and let them know they could come out. He was to tell everyone but Mogaba's loyalists.

My own people did not understand. I did not explain. They had no need to know. They needed to carry out orders.

The night after Murgen left, several dozen Taglian soldiers deserted from the city. Their reports were not pleasant. Disease was worse. Mogaba had executed hundreds more natives and a dozen of his own troops. Only the Nar were not grumbling.

Mogaba knew Murgen was back, suspected he had seen me, and was hunting him. He'd had a bitter confrontation with the Company wizards over the standardbearer.

Mutiny was in the offing—unless the desertions absorbed that energy. That would be a first. Nowhere in the Annals was there a record of a mutiny.

Narayan grew more nervous by the hour as he worried about his delayed Festival, frightened I would try to evade it. I kept reassuring him. "There's plenty of time. We have the horses. We'll go as soon as we have this set." Also, I wanted some idea what was happening south of us. I'd sent cavalry to see what effect news of Spinner's fate was having. Little information had come back yet.

The night before Narayan, Ram, and I headed north, six hundred men deserted Mogaba and swam or rafted out of Dejagore. I had them greeted as heroes, with promises of important positions in new formations.

Shadowspinner's head, with the brain removed and destroyed, greeted them at the entrance to my camp. It would be our totem in days to come, in lieu of the missing Company standard.

Six hundred in one night. Mogaba would be livid. His loyalists would make it difficult for that to happen again.

I gathered my captains, such as they were. "Blade, there's something I have to do up north. Narayan and Ram will go with me. I'd hoped to know more about the south before I left but we have to take what we get. I doubt Longshadow will do anything soon. Keep your patrols out and sit tight. I shouldn't be gone but two weeks. Three if I visit Taglios to report our success. You might reorganize now that we have some real veterans joining us. And consider integrating any Shadowlanders interested in enlisting. They could be helpful."

Blade nodded. He had few words to waste even now.

Swan looked at me with a sort of soulful longing. I winked, suggesting his time would come. I'm not sure why. I had no reason to lead him on. I did not mind him remaining attached to the Radisha. Maybe I was attracted. He was the best of the crop, in his way. But I did not want to stumble into that trap again.

The heart is a hostage, the old saw says. Better not to give it up.

Narayan was happier once we rode out. I was not thrilled but I needed his brotherhood. I had plans for them.

Shadowspinner might be dead but the struggle had just begun. Longshadow and Howler had to be faced, and all the armies they could call up. And if those failed at every confrontation in the field there was still Longshadow's fortress at Shadowcatch. Rumor had Overlook tougher than my own Tower at Charm had been and getting tougher every day.

I did not look forward to the struggle. Despite the luck I'd had, Taglios was not ready for that kind of fight.

Maybe luck had bought me time enough to raise my legions and train them, to mount leisurely expeditions, to find capable commanders, to retrain myself in the use of my lost skills.

My immediate goals had been attained. Taglios was in no immediate danger. I had my base. I was in undisputed command and unlikely to have more trouble with the priests or Mogaba. With care I could lock up the Stranglers as an adjunct to my will, an invisible arm able to dispense death anywhere someone defied me. My future looked rosy. The biggest potential nuisance was the wizard Smoke. And he could be handled.

Rosy. Positively rosy. Except for the dreams and the sickness, both of which were getting worse. Except for my beloved sister.

Will, Lady. The Will will reign triumphant. My husband had said that often, confident that nothing could resist his will.

He had believed that right up to the moment I killed him.

61

Croaker trotted his mount into the garrison encampment above Vehdna-Bota ford, which was a minor crossing of the Main used mostly by locals and open only a few months each year. He dismounted, handed his reins to a gaping soldier who had recognized the Prahbrindrah Drah.

The prince needed help dismounting. The ride had been hell for him. Croaker had shown no mercy. The ride had been little better for him.

"You really do this for a living?" the prince groaned. His sense of humor had survived.

Croaker grunted. "Sometimes you can't waste time. It's not like this all the time."

"I'd rather be a farmer."

"Walk around. Work out the stiffness."

"That will irritate the sores."

"I'll put ointment on after we talk to whoever's in charge."

The soldier now held both horses. And stared. By now others had recognized them. Word flew around like swallows dipping and darting. An officer loped out of the only permanent structure in the compound, gathering his clothing around him. His eyes bugged. He dropped onto his face before his prince.

The Prahbrindrah Drah snapped, "Get up! I'm in no mood for that."

The officer rose, murmuring honorifics.

The prince grumbled, "Forget me. I'm just following him. Talk to him."

The officer turned to Croaker. "I'm honored, Liberator. We thought you dead."

"I thought I was, too. For a while. And I need to get that way again. The prince and I are joining your company. We're not being watched now but we'll be hunted soon by a distant and wicked eye." He was sure the search had not yet begun because no crows had chased them during their ride. "When the search passes this way we want to be indistinguishable from your soldiers."

"You're in hiding?"

"More or less." Croaker explained some. He stretched the truth some, bent it some, made it clear that powerful enemies wanted to find him and that the fate of Taglios could hinge on their remaining anonymous till they joined Lady at Dejagore.

"First thing you do," he told the officer, "is make sure none of your men speak to anyone outside the camp. Our presence isn't to be discussed at all. Our enemies have spies everywhere. Most aren't human. A stray dog, a bird, a shadow could carry tales. Every man has to understand that. We can't be discussed. We'll take different names and become ordinary troopers."

"I don't quite understand, sir."

"I don't think I can explain. Take us being here as proof. I'm back, escaped from captivity, and I need to reach the main army. I can't alone, even disguised. Do you have men who know how to ride?"

"A few, possibly." Puzzled.

"These horses have to be returned to the new fortress. Hopefully before the hunt starts. They're a dead giveaway. Their riders should make no stops and should disguise themselves. We don't want them identified with this company."

Croaker had not discussed plans while travelling because someone might hear. But the prince got the drift quickly. "You're going to march this company down to Dejagore?"

"Yes. You and I will be archers in the ranks."

The prince groaned. "I have less experience walking than riding."

"And I have a tender ankle. We won't push." While Croaker talked his gaze darted, seeking the potential listener. He continued talking to the officer. Again and again he tried to drive home the need for the archers to keep quiet about their mission till they found Lady's army. One slip could kill them all. He made it sound like the Shadowmasters had all their men and demons out trying to destroy him and the prince and anyone with them.

True in theme, anyway.

The officer rounded up volunteers to return the stallions, impressed them with the need to deliver the animals rapidly, without telling anyone where Croaker and the prince had gone. He sent them off.

Croaker sighed. "I feel safer already. Get me a turban and some Shadar clothes and something to darken my hands and face. Prince, you look more Gunni."

Half an hour later they were ordinary archers except for accents. Croaker became Narayan Singh. Half the Shadar alive were Narayan Singh. The prince adopted the name Abu Lal Cadreskrah. He felt it would shield him from scrutiny because it suggested mixed Vehdna and Gunni parentage, which could only mean that his mother had been a Gunni prostitute. "No one in his right mind would think the Prahbrindrah Drah could demean himself that far."

Croaker chuckled. "Maybe so. Get some rest. Use that horse liniment. We'll pull out as soon as we get stores and transport together."

A day and a half later, grimly silent, ready for anything, the archers crossed the river. Croaker grew more fearful and excited by the hour. How would Lady react when he turned up alive?

He was scared of the answer.

Longshadow did without sleep for six days while he fought the sorcery gnawing at Howler's flesh and soul. He triumphed, but barely. Then he collapsed.

Shadowcatch was an old, old city. Forever in the looming shadow of glittering stone, it was a repository for much ancient lore, much known nowhere else, much known only to Longshadow, who had plundered its libraries and had disposed of everyone who shared any knowledge he coveted.

Among the legends of the plain, which had been old when the city had been founded, was one about the Lances of Passion. It said their heads had been forged of metal taken from the sword of a demon king devoured by Kina during the great battle between Light and Shadow. That demon king's soul was imprisoned in the steel, fragmented amongst eight lance heads. He could not be restored while Kina slept.

The shafts of the lances, too, were the object of legend. Two were supposed to have been formed from the thighbones of Kina herself, taken after she had been tricked into endless sleep. One was supposedly the penis of the Regent of Shadow, that Kina had hacked off during the great battle. The rest were supposed to be of wood from the tree in which the goddess of brotherly love, Rhavi-Lemna, had hidden her soul shortly before the Wolves of Shadow ran her down and devoured her, soon after Man was created. Kina had witnessed the concealment and had torn up the tree and had made it into arrows and lance shafts. If ever the Lords of Light did bring Rhavi-Lemna together again, out of the bellies of the hateful Wolves, she would have no soul. And they could not get that back for her while Kina lay sleeping.

Each of the outbound Free Companies of Khatovar had followed one of the Lances when they had broken into the world to bring on the Year of the Skulls. But who had sent them forth?

Longshadow could not be sure. The ghost-spirit of sleeping Kina? The Lords of Light, who would restore Rhavi-Lemna? The children of the demon king, who remained imprisoned in those lance heads while she slept? The Regent of Shadow, weary of being at a disadvantage in the lists of love?

The librarians of old recorded the return of all the Companies but one, the Black Company, which lost its own past and wandered aimlessly down the centuries, till it elected a Captain eager to seek out its roots.

Longshadow knew very little about the Lances but he did know more than anyone else alive. Howler and Catcher suspected some. No one else had a hint that the Black Company's standard was anything but an old artifact that had survived for centuries, till it vanished during the battle at Dejagore.

Only to resurface in Taglios, in the hands of a bodyguard.

Its recovery was high among Longshadow's priorities. He would send for it as soon as Howler recovered. He would devote his own time to harvesting the knowledge of his captive.

But first he slept, having conquered the Howler's wounds.

63

It took the imp Frogface five days to locate his mistress. Then he waited till the attention of Overlook's master lapsed before he made his way inside. He entered with trepidation. Longshadow was a powerful sorcerer, dreaded in the demon worlds.

His entry disturbed no one. Overlook's defenses were meant to stop shadows from the south. He found his mistress in a dark cell beneath the fortress's roots, her drugged mind in a cell of its own, deep inside her brain. He debated. He could forget her. He could help and maybe win his freedom. Freeing her was not within the specific orders she had given him.

He stretched out beside her, bit a hole in her throat, drank her blood. He cleansed it and returned it.

She wakened slowly, sensed what he was doing, let him finish. He closed the wound. She sat up in the darkness. "The Howler. Where am I?"

"Overlook."

"Why?"

"They mistook you for your sister."

She laughed bitterly. "My act was too good."

"Yes."

"Where is she?"

"Last seen near Dejagore. I hunted you for a week."

"And they couldn't see her? She's getting stronger. What about Croaker?"

"I've been hunting you."

"Find him. I want him back. I can't let him reach my sister. Do anything you have to to stop that."

"I'm forbidden to take life."

"Anything else, then, but keep them apart."

"You don't need help here?"

"I'll handle . . . You're free to roam here?"

"Pretty much. Parts are sealed behind spells only Longshadow can penetrate."

"Search the place. Tell me what everyone is doing. Then find Croaker and my sister."

The imp sighed. So much for gratitude.

She caught the sense of the sound. "Do it right and you're free. Forever."

"Right! I'm gone."

She waited for her captors to come receive their surprise. As she waited she heard the whispers of darkness carrying from the nearby plain. She caught some of what was said, began to taste the fear that plagued Longshadow.

She could not just sit there like a trapdoor spider, waiting. Longshadow and Howler were sleeping. She should go.

The very stones of Overlook had been hardened against sorcery. She melted her way out, for those stones would melt before they yielded.

The lower levels were dark. Surprising. Longshadow feared the dark. She climbed slowly, wary of ambushes, but she encountered no one. She grew nervous as she approached the light.

Nothing waited there, either. Apparently. Was the fortress deserted?

Something was wrong. She extended her senses, still detected nothing. Onward and upward. And more nothing. Where were the soldiers? There should be thousands, constantly scurrying like blood in the veins.

She spied a way out. She had to descend a stairway to reach it. She was halfway down when the attack came, a wave of little brown men carrying cruel halberds, wearing armor of wood and strange, ornate animal helmets.

She had a spell prepared, a summoning that taxed her limits. She struck a pose, loosed it. It broke a hole in the fabric of everything. Sparks of ten thousand colors flew. Something huge and ugly and hungry started through, tearing the hole wider. Steel left no mark upon its snout. Its snarls chilled the blood. It ripped itself out of the womb of elsewhere and flew after the garrison. Men screamed. It ran faster than they did.

Soulcatcher walked out into the night blanketing Overlook. "That will keep them busy." She looked north, angry. A long walk lay ahead of her.

64

The bridge I had wanted built was incomplete but we did cross on foot while soldiers brought our mounts across by the ford. My move was symbolic, meant to lend encouragement to the engineers.

Narayan was impressed and Ram was indifferent, except to say it was nice to cross the river without getting his feet wet. He did not see the implications of a bridge.

Because I was sick it took longer to reach Ghoja than I anticipated. We were pressed for time. Narayan rode the edge of panic but we reached the holy grove late the evening before the ceremonies. I was exhausted. I told Narayan, "You handle the arrangements. I can't do anything more."

He looked at me, concerned. Ram said, "You *must* see a physician, Mistress. Soon."

"I've decided to. When we're done here we head north. I can't take this much longer."

"The rains . . ."

The season would start soon. If we dallied in Taglios we would return to the Main after it started rising. Already there were scattered showers every day. "The bridge is there. We might have to leave our mounts but we can get across."

Narayan nodded curtly. "I'll talk to the priests. See that she rests, Ram. Initiation can be stressful."

That was the first I had heard it hinted that I was expected to go through the same initiation ceremony as everyone else. It irked me but I was too tired to protest. I just lay there while Ram borrowed fire and rice and prepared a meal. Several jamadars came to pay their respects. Ram warned them off. No priests came. By then I had sunk into a lassitude so deep I did not bother to ask Ram if that was significant.

I caught movement from the corner of an eye, a watcher where none should be. I turned, caught a glimpse of a face.

That was no Deceiver. I had not seen that face since before the fighting that had cost me Croaker. Frogface, they called him. An imp. What was he doing here?

I could not catch him. I was way too weak. Nothing I could do but keep him in mind. I fell asleep as soon as I'd eaten.

Drums wakened me. They were drums with deep voices, the kind men sound by pounding with fists or palms. Boom! Boom! Boom! No respite. Ram told me they would not let up till next dawn. Other drums with deeper voices joined them. I peered out of the crude lean-to Ram had built for me. One was not far away. The man pounding the drum used padded mallets with handles four feet long. There was one such drum at each of the wind's four quarters.

More drums throbbed within the temple. Ram assured me it had been cleansed and sanctified.

I did not much care. I was as sick as ever I had been. My night had been filled with the darkest dreams yet, dreams in which the whole world suffered from advanced leprosy. The smell lingered in my nostrils, worsening the sickness.

Ram had anticipated my condition. Maybe he had watched me in my sleep, predicting my sickness from how I rested. I don't know. But he put up a crude privacy screen so I would not become a public entertainment.

I was past the worst when Narayan came. "If you don't go see a physician after this I'll personally drag you to Taglios. Mistress. There's no reason not to take the time."

"I will. I will. You can count on it."

"I do. You're important to me. You're our future."

Chanting began in the temple. "Why is it different this time?"

"So much to crowd in. Ceremonial obligations and initiations. You won't have to do anything till tonight. Rest. And you'll rest again tomorrow if the ceremony wears you out."

Just lying around. Nothing to do. That was a strain itself. I could not recall a time when I'd had nothing to do but lie around. Once I got control of my nausea I tried to extend and stretch my talents.

They were coming back almost of their own accord. I was capable of more than I suspected. I was close to being a match for the wizard Smoke, now.

Good news must be balanced by bad, I suppose. My elation died when I looked up from cupped palms and found myself caught in a dream right there in broad daylight.

I could see both the horror of the worst dream and the grove around me. Neither seemed completely real. Neither was more substantial than the other.

I went from the caverns of death to a plain of death. I had gone there only rarely. I associated that plain with the battle during which Kina had devoured hordes of demons. A great black figure strode across the plain, her movements stylized, like Gunni dances. Each step shook the plain. I felt the shaking. It was as real as an earthquake.

She wore nothing. Her shape was not quite human. She had four arms and eight breasts. Each hand clutched something suggestive of death or warfare. She wore a necklace of baby skulls. From her girdle, like bunches of withered bananas, hung strings of what I first took to be severed thumbs but which, as she stamped closer, proved to be more singular and potent male appendages.

Her hairless head was shaped more like an egg than a human head. At first it impressed me as insectoid but she had a mouth like that of a carnivore. Blood dribbled down her chin. Her eyes were large and filled with fire.

The stench of old death preceded her.

That unexpected apparition shook me to the core.

And from some corner of memory Croaker stepped with his irreverent and sarcastic outlook. *Old Busybody smells ripe for her centennial bath. Might even be time for her to brush her teeth.*

The thought was so startling I looked around. Had someone spoken?

I was alone. It was just a thought in his style, loosened by the strain. When I looked forward again the apparition had faded. I shuddered.

The smell lingered. It was not imaginary. A man passing stopped, startled. He sniffed, looked odd, hurried off. I shuddered again.

Was that how it would be? Dreams awake and asleep, both?

I shuddered a third time, frightened. My will was not strong enough to resist *that*.

Several times during the day the stench came back. Mercifully, the apparition did not accompany it. I did not make myself vulnerable by opening channels of power again.

Narayan came when it was time. I had not seen him since morning. He had not seen me. He looked at me oddly. I asked, "What's the matter?"

"There's something . . . An aura? Yes. You feel like the Daughter of Night should feel." He became embarrassed. "The initiations start in an hour. I talked to the priests. No woman has ever joined us before. There are no precedents. They decided you'll have to face it the way everyone does."

"I take it that's not . . ."

"The candidates stand naked before Kina while she judges their worthiness."

"I see." To say I was not thrilled would be an understatement, though, initially, my objection was a matter of vanity. I looked like hell. Like a famine victim, withering limbs and bloating belly. We'd seldom eaten well since we had fled from Dejagore.

I gave it some thought. It presented me with little choice, really. If I refused to disrobe, I suspected, I would not leave the grove alive. And I needed the Stranglers. I had plans for them. "I'll do what has to be done."

Narayan was relieved. "You won't have to expose yourself to everyone."

"No? Just to the priests and jamadars and other candidates and whoever is helping put on the show?"

"It's been arranged. There will be six candidates, the minimum permitted. There will be one high priest, his assistant, one jamadar as chief Strangler, with orders to strike down any chanter who raises his eyes from the floor. You may pick those three men yourself if you like."

Odd. "Why so thoughtful?"

Narayan whispered, "I shouldn't tell you. Opinion is divided about whether you're the true Daughter of Night. Those who do believe expect you to have the priest, his assistant, and the chief Strangler put to death after Kina bestows her favor. They want to risk the minimum number of men."

"What about the other candidates?"

"They won't remember."

"I see."

"I'll be among the chanters as your sponsor."

"I see." I wondered what would happen to him if I failed. "I don't care who the priests and Strangler are."

He grinned. "Excellent, Mistress. You must prepare. Ram. Help me put the screen up again. Mistress, this is the robe you'll wear till you stand before the goddess." He handed me a white bundle. The robe looked like it had been used for generations without having been mended or cleaned.

I got ready.

65

The temple had changed inside. Fires burned, dull and red, around the perimeter. Their light sent shadows skulking over ugly carvings. A huge idol had materialized. It was a close representation of the thing from my vision, although equipped with an ornate headdress loaded with gold and silver and gemstones. The idol's eyes were cabochon rubies, each a nation's ransom. Its fangs were crystal.

Three heads lay under the idol's raised left foot. Priests were dragging a corpse away when my group of candidates entered. The dead man had been tortured before he had been beheaded.

Ten men lay on their faces to the right, ten more to the left. A four-foot aisle passed between groups. I recognized Narayan's back. The twenty chanted continuously, "Come O Kina unto the world and make Thy Children whole we beseech Thee Great Mother," so swiftly the words ran together. I was last in line. The chief Strangler stepped into the aisle behind me, black rumel in hand. I suspect his main function was to stop a candidate who developed cold feet, not to eliminate chanters who peeped.

Twenty feet of clear space lay between the chanters and the dais where the goddess stood. The three heads lay at eye level. Two appeared to watch our approach. The third stared at the sole of Kina's foot, clawed toes inches from its nose.

Two priests stood to my right, beside a tall stand supporting several golden vessels.

The ceremony started out basic. Each candidate reached a mark and dropped his robe, moved to another mark on a line, abased himself and murmured a ritual prayer. The prayer just petitioned Kina to accept the appellant: in the last case, me, as her daughter. But when I spoke the words a gust of wind blew through. A new presence filled the place. It was cold and hungry and carried the smell of carrion. The assistant priest jumped. This was not customary.

We candidates rose, knelt with our palms resting atop our thighs. The head priest ran through some extended rigamarole in a language neither Taglian nor Deceivers' cant. He presented us to the idol as though it were Kina herself. While he yammered, his assistant poured dark fluid from a tall spouted container into one like a gravy boat. Once he stopped chattering the head priest made holy passes over that smaller vessel, lifted it, presented it to the goddess, went to the far end of the line, placed the pouring end of the vessel to the candidate's lips and filled his mouth. The man had his eyes closed. He swallowed.

The next man took his with his eyes open. He choked. The priest showed no reaction, nor did he when two more men did the same.

My turn.

Narayan was a liar. He had prepared me but he had told me it was all illusion. This was no illusion. It was blood—with some drug added that gave it a slightly herby, bitter taste. Human blood? I do not know. Our seeing that body dragged away was no accident. We were supposed to think about it.

I got through it. I'd never endured anything like it but I'd been through terrible things before. I neither hesitated nor twitched. I told myself I was just minutes from taking control of the most terrible power in this end of the world.

That presence moved again.

It might take control of me.

The chief priest handed the vessel to his assistant, who returned it to the stand, began to chant.

The lights went out.

Absolute darkness engulfed the temple. I was startled, thinking something unusual had happened. When no one got excited I changed my mind. Must be part of the initiation.

That darkness lasted half a minute. Midway through, a scream rent the air, filled with despair and outrage.

Light returned as suddenly as it had gone.

I was stunned.

It was hard to take everything in.

There were only five candidates now. The idol had moved. Its raised foot had fallen, crushing one of the heads. Its other foot had risen. The body of the man who had been two to my left lay beneath it. His head, held by the hair, dangled from one of the idol's hands. Before the lights had gone out that hand had clutched a bunch of bones. Another hand that had clutched a sword still did so but now that blade glistened. There was blood on the idol's lips and chin and fangs. Its eyes gleamed.

How had they managed it? Was there some mechanical engine inside the idol? Had the priest and his assistant done the murder? They would have had to move fast. And I had not heard a sound but the scream.

The priests seemed startled, too.

The chief priest darted to the pile of robes, flung one my way, resumed his place, ran through one abbreviated chant, cried out, "She has come! She is among us! Praised be Kina, who has sent her Daughter to stand beside us."

I covered my nakedness.

The normal flow had been disrupted somehow. The results had the priests ecstatic and, at the same time, at a loss what to do next.

What *do* you do when old prophecies come true? I've never met a priest who honestly expected miracles in his own lifetime. For them miracles are like good wine, best when aged.

They decided to suspend normal business and go straight to the celebration. That meant candidates got initiated without standing before Kina's judgment. It meant human sacrifices forgotten. Quite unwittingly I saved the lives of twenty enemies of the Stranglers scheduled to be tortured and murdered during that night. The priests freed them to tell the world that the Deceivers were real and had found their messiah, that those who did not come to Kina soon would be devoured in the Year of the Skulls.

A fun bunch of guys, Croaker would say.

Narayan took me back to our fire, where he told Ram to drive off anyone with the temerity to bother me. He settled me with profuse apologies for not having prepared me better. He sat beside me and stared into the flames.

"It's come, eh?" I asked after a while.

He understood. "It's come. It's finally real. Now there's no doubt left."

"Uhm." I left him to his thoughts for a while before I asked, "How did they do that with the idol, Narayan?"

"What?"

"How did they make it move while it was dark?"

He shrugged, looked at me, grinned feebly, said, "I don't know. That's never happened before. I've seen at least twenty initiations. Always one of the candidates is chosen to die. But the idol never moves."

"Oh." I could think of nothing else till I asked, "Did you feel anything in there? Like something was with us?"

"Yes." He was shivering. The night was not cold. He said, "Try to sleep, Mistress. We have to get started early. I want to get you to that physician."

I lay me down, grimly reluctant to drift off into the land of nightmare, but I did not stay awake long. I was too exhausted, physically and emotionally. The last thing I saw was Narayan squatting there, staring into the flames.

Much to think on, Narayan. Much to think on, now.

There were no dreams that night. But there was sickness aplenty in the morning. I threw up till there was nothing left but bile.

The imp drifted away from the grove. The woman had not been hard to find, though that had taken longer than he had hoped. Now for the man.

Nothing. For a long, long time, not a trace.

He was not in Taglios. A frantic search produced nothing. Logic suggested he would search for his woman. He would not know her present whereabouts so he would head toward her last known location.

He was not at the ford. There was no sign he had visited Ghoja. Therefore, he had not. They would be talking about it still, as they were talking about him still in Taglios.

No Croaker. But a whole horde was headed for the ford, descending from the city. The woman had just missed meeting them headed north. A stroke of luck, that, but there was no way to keep her from learning he was alive. Not in the long run.

The prime mission was to keep them apart, anyway.

Was he amongst that mob? Couldn't be. Their talk would have pointed him out.

The imp resumed his quest. If the man had not crossed at Ghoja and was not amongst the horde, then he would cross the river elsewhere. Sneaking.

He visited Vehdna-Bota last because it seemed the least likely crossing. He expected to find nothing there. Nothing was what he found. But this was a significant nothing. A company of archers was supposed to be stationed there.

He tracked those archers and found his man.

He had to make a decision. Run to his mistress—which would take time because he would have to find her—or take steps on his own?

He chose the latter course. The rainy season was fast approaching. It might do his job for him. They could not get together if they could not cross the river.

Amidst a moonless night the growing Ghoja bridge collapsed. Most of its timberwork washed away. The engineers could not figure out what went wrong. They understood only that it was too late to rebuild this year.

Any Taglian forces not back across before the waters rose would spend half a year on the Shadowlander side.

Satisfied, the imp went looking for his mistress.

67

The archers halted in sight of the Taglian main camp. "We're safe now," Croaker told the prince. "Let's make a proper entrance."

Cavalry had found them two days earlier, forty miles north. Horsemen had visited regularly since yesterday. The archers had kept their mouths shut admirably. Willow Swan had led one patrol. He had not recognized anyone.

Croaker had had the captain borrow horses. The archers' transport consisted only of mules enough to carry what the soldiers themselves could not. Two mounts had arrived an hour ago, saddled.

The prince dressed up as a prince. Croaker donned what he called his work clothes, a warlord's outfit given him back when he had been every Taglian's hero. He had not taken it along when he had gone south the first time.

He dug out the Company standard and reassembled it. "I'm ready. Prince?"

"Whenever." The march south had been hard on the Prahbrindrah Drah but he had endured the hardships without complaint. The soldiers were pleased.

They mounted up and led the archers toward the camp. The first crows arrived during that passage. Croaker laughed at them. "'Stone the crows!' People in Beryl used to say that when the Company was there. I never did figure out what it meant but it sounds like a damned good way to do business."

The prince chuckled and agreed, then faced the greetings of soldiers from the camp who could not decide which of their visitors was more unlikely.

Croaker spied familiar faces: Blade, Swan, Mather . . . Hell! That looked like Murgen. It *was* Murgen! But nowhere did he spy the face he wanted to see.

Murgen approached in little spurts, each halving the distance between himself and his Captain. Croaker dismounted, said, "It's me. I'm real."

"I saw you die."

"You saw me hit. I was still breathing when you took off."

"Oh. Yeah. But the shape you were in . . ."

"It's a long story. We'll sit around and talk about it all night. Get drunk if there's anything drinkable." He glanced at Swan. Where Swan lighted, beer usually appeared. "Here. You left this behind when you went off to play Widowmaker." He shoved the standard at Murgen.

The younger man took it like he expected it to bite. But once he had hold of it he ran his hands up and down the shaft of the lance. "It really is! I thought it was lost for sure. Then it's really you?"

"Alive and in a mood to do some serious ass-kicking. But I've got something else on my mind right now. Where's Lady?"

Blade made a perfunctory acknowledgment of the prince's presence, said, "Lady went north with Narayan and Ram. Eight, nine days ago. Said she had business that couldn't wait."

Croaker cursed.

Swan said, "Nine days ago. That really him? Not somebody fixed up to fool us?"

Mather said, "It's him. The Prahbrindrah Drah wouldn't lend himself to any deceit."

"Ain't that my luck. Ain't that the story of my life? Just when my future is so bright I have to wear blinders."

Croaker noted a broad, stubby man behind Blade. He did not know the man but recognized personal power. This was someone important. And someone not thrilled to see the Liberator alive. He would bear watching.

"Murgen. Stop making love to that thing. Fill me in on what's been happening. I've been out of touch for weeks." Or months, if filtered truths were considered. "Can somebody take this animal? So we can all go find some shade?"

There was more confusion in the camp than might have been if Longshadow had materialized there. The return of a dead man always complicates things.

Without appearing to take particular note Croaker noticed that the short, wide man stayed close, pretending insignificance beside Blade, Swan, and Mather. He never spoke.

Murgen talked about his experiences since the disastrous battle. Blade told his tale. Swan tossed in a few dozen anecdotes of his own.

"Shadowspinner himself, eh?" Croaker asked.

Swan said, "That's the old boy's head on the pole over yonder."

"The field gets narrower."

Murgen said, "Let's hear your story while it's still news."

"You going to put it in the Annals? You been keeping them up?"

Embarrassed, the younger man nodded. "Only I had to leave them in the city when I came out."

"I understand. I look forward to reading the Book of Murgen. If it's any good you've got the job for life."

Swan said, "Lady was doing one of them things herself."

Everyone looked at him.

He wilted some. "Well, what she really did was talk about writing one. When she got the time. I don't think she ever really put anything down. She just said how she had to keep some things straight in her head so she could get them down right. The obligation of history, she called it."

"Let me think a minute," Croaker said. He picked up a stone, threw it at a crow. The bird squawked and fluttered a few feet but did not take the hint. It was Catcher's, all right. She was back in circulation, free. Or in alliance with her captors.

After a while Croaker observed, "We have a lot of catching up to do. But I suspect the critical business is to end this problem with Mogaba. How many men does he have left in there?"

"Maybe a thousand, fifteen hundred," Murgen guessed.

"One-Eye and Goblin stayed when he's become their enemy?"

"They can protect themselves," Murgen said. "They don't want to come out here. They think there's something waiting to get them. They want to sit tight till Lady gets her powers back."

"Powers back? Is she? Nobody mentioned that." But he had suspected it for a long time.

"She is," Blade said. "Not as fast as she'd like."

"Nothing happens as fast as she'd like. What are they afraid of, Murgen?"

"Shifter's apprentice. Remember her? She was there when we got rid of Shifter and Stormshadow. She took off on us. They say she's locked into the forvalaka shape but still has her own mind. And she's out to get them for killing Shifter. Especially One-Eye." One-Eye had killed the wizard Shapeshifter because Shifter had killed his brother Tom-Tom long ago. "The wheel of vengeance turning." Croaker sighed. "She's maybe out to get everybody who was involved."

"That angle hasn't come up before."

"I think they're imagining it."

"You never know with those clowns." Croaker leaned back, closed his eyes. "Tell me more about Mogaba."

Murgen had a lot to say.

Croaker observed, "I always suspected there was more to him than he showed. But human sacrifices? That's a little much."

"They didn't just sacrifice them. They ate them."

"*What?*"

"Well, their hearts and livers. Some of them. There was only four or five guys really into that with Mogaba."

Croaker glanced at the wide man. The fellow was indignant to the point of explosion. Croaker said, "I guess that explains why Gea-Xle was such a peaceful town. If the city guard *eats* criminals and rebels . . ." He chuckled. But cannibalism was not humorous. "You, sir. We haven't been introduced. You seem to have strong feelings about Mogaba."

Murgen said, "That's Sindhu. One of Lady's special friends."

"Oh?" What did that mean?

Sindhu said, "They have abandoned themselves to Shadow. The true Deceiver seldom spills blood. He opens the golden path without tempting the goddess's thirst. Only the blood of an accursed enemy should be spilled. Only an accursed enemy should be tortured."

Croaker glanced around. "Anybody know what the hell he's talking about?"

Swan said, "Your girlfriend is running with some strange characters." He chose a northern dialect. "Maybe Cordy can explain. He's spent more time trying to figure it out."

Croaker nodded. "I suppose we ought to put an end to this. Murgen. You game to go back again? Take a message to Mogaba?"

"I don't want to sound like a slacker, Captain, but not unless it's an order. He wants to kill me. Crazy as he's gotten, he might try it with you standing right there watching."

"I'll get somebody else."

"I'll do it," Swan said.

Mather jumped him. "It's not your no nevermind, Willow."

"Yes, it is. I got to find out something about myself, Cordy. I wasn't no help when we went after Shadowspinner. I froze up. I want to see if something's wrong with me. Mogaba is the guy to show me. He's about as spooky as a Shadowmaster."

"Damned poor thinking, Willow."

"I never did have any sense. I'll go, Captain. When you want to do it?"

Croaker glanced around. "Anything going on, Blade? Any reason we shouldn't walk over and take a look, send Swan?"

"No."

68

Life is full of surprises. I don't mind the little ones. They add spice. It's the big ones that get me.

I stumbled into a parade of big ones at my new fortress.

The first thing they did was arrest all three of us and shove us into a cell. Nobody bothered to explain. Nobody said anything. They seemed surprised I did not go berserk.

We sat in gloom and waited. I was afraid Smoke had won his point at last and had turned the Prahbrindrah Drah against me. Narayan said maybe I'd missed a few priests and this was all their fault.

We did not talk much. We used only sign and cant when we did. No telling who was listening.

Three hours after we went into the cell the door opened. The Radisha Drah strode in, backed by a squad of her guards. It got crowded in there. She glared at me. "Who are you?"

"What kind of question is that? Lady. Captain of the Black Company. Who should I be?"

"She even takes a deep breath, kill her." The Radisha wheeled on Ram. "You. Stand up."

Faithful Ram might not have heard. He looked to me. I nodded. Then he stood. The Radisha grabbed a torch from a guard, held it close to Ram, circled him slowly. She sniffed and sniffed. After her third circuit she relaxed. "Sit. You're who you're supposed to be. But the woman. Who is she?"

That seemed a little too tough for Ram. He had to think about it. He looked at me again. I nodded. He said, "She told you."

She looked at me. "Can you prove you're Lady?"

"Can you prove you're the Radisha Drah?"

"I have no need. No one is masquerading as me."

I got it. "That bitch! She never was short on nerve. Walked in here and took over, eh? What did she do?"

The Radisha considered some more. "We have the right one this time. Guards. You may go." They went. The Radisha said, "She didn't do much. Mostly played up to my brother. She wasn't here that long. Then somebody called the Howler knocked her out and carried her off. Thinking she was you, Croaker said."

"Ha! Serves the bitch . . . Who said?"

"Croaker. Your Captain. She brought him with her, disguised as that one." She indicated Ram.

Some sort of impenetrable membrane lay between my ears and my heart. Very carefully, before it broke, I asked, "Did Howler take him, too? Where is he?"

"He and my brother went to find you. Disguised. He said she would look for him as soon as she got free of the Howler and Longshadow."

My mind slid away from the unbelievable, dwelt on crows. Now I knew why there had been none spying till shortly before we reached the fortress. She had been in unfriendly hands. "He went to Dejagore?"

"That's my guess. My fool brother went with him."

"And I came here." I laughed, maybe crazily. That membrane was giving. "I'd appreciate it if everyone would leave. I need some time alone."

The Radisha nodded. "I understand. You two come with me."

Narayan rose but Ram did not budge. I asked, "Will you wait outside, Ram? Just for a while?"

"Yes, Mistress." He went out with the others. I'd bet he did not go five feet past the door.

Before they left Narayan started telling the Radisha I needed a physician.

The anger and frustration faded. I calmed down, thought I understood. Croaker had been struck down by a random arrow. In the confusion his corpse had disappeared. Only now I knew he had not been a corpse at all. And I thought I knew whence that arrow had come. My everloving sister. Just to get even with me for having thwarted her attempt to displace me when I'd been empress in the north.

I knew how her mind worked. I had evidence she was loose again. She would continue to keep us apart and punish me through him.

She was whole again. She had the power to do whatever she willed. She had been second only to me when I was at my peak.

I came as close to despair as I've ever come.

The Radisha invited herself in without knocking. A tiny woman in a pink sari accompanied her. The Radisha said, "This is Doctor Dahrhanahdahr. Her family are all physicians. She's my own physician. She's the best. Even her male colleagues admit she's marginally competent."

I told the woman what I had been suffering. She listened and nodded. When I was done, she told me, "You'll have to disrobe. I think I know what it is but I'll have to look."

The Radisha stepped to the cell door, used her own clothing to cover the viewport. "I'll turn my back if your modesty demands it."

"What modesty?" I stripped.

Actually, I was embarrassed. I did not want to be seen looking as bad as I did.

The physician spent a few minutes examining me. "I thought so."

"What is it?"

"You don't know?"

"If I did I would've done something about it. I don't like being sick." At least the dreams had let up since the initiation. I could sleep.

"You'll have to put up with it a while longer." Her eyes sparkled. That was a hell of an attitude for a physician. "You're pregnant."

69

Croaker posted himself where he could be clearly seen from the city. Murgen stood beside him with the standard. Swan set off in a boat the cavalry had stolen off the banks of the river north of the hills.

Murgen asked, "You think he'll come?"

"Maybe not himself. But somebody will. He'll want to make sure, one way or the other."

Murgen indicated the Shadowlander soldiers along the shoreline. "You know what that's about?"

"I can guess. Mogaba and Lady both want to be Captain. She took care of Shadowspinner but thought it might be inconvenient if she told Mogaba. As long as he's trapped in Dejagore he's no problem."

"Right."

"Stupid. Nothing like this ever happened before, Murgen. Nowhere in the Annals can you find a squabble over the succession. Most Captains come in like me, kicking and screaming."

"Most don't have a holy mission. Lady and Mogaba both do."

"Lady?"

"She's decided she'll do anything to get even with the Shadowmasters for killing you."

"That's real sane. But it sounds like her. Looks like Swan's gotten some attention. Your eyes are better than mine."

"Somebody black is getting in the boat with him. Would Mogaba make up his mind that fast?"

"He's sending somebody."

Swan's passenger was Mogaba's lieutenant Sindawe, an officer good enough to have commanded a legion. Croaker saluted. "Sindawe."

The black man returned the salute tentatively. "Is it you indeed?"

"In the flesh."

"But you're dead."

"Nope. Just a story spread by our enemies. It's a long tale. Maybe we don't have time for it all. I hear things aren't good over there."

*　　*　　*

Sindawe guided Croaker out of sight of the city, settled on a rock. "I'm caught on the horns of a dilemma."

Croaker settled facing him, winced. His ankle had taken a lot of abuse coming south. "How so?"

"My honor is sworn to Mogaba as first lord of the Nar. I must obey. But he's gone mad."

"So I gather. What happened? He was the ideal soldier even when he didn't agree with the way I ran things."

"Ambition. He's a driven man. He became first lord because he's driven." Among the Nar, chieftainship was determined by a sort of soldierly athletic contest. The all-round best man at physical skills became commander. "He joined your expedition thinking you weak, likely to perish quickly. He saw no obstacle to his replacing you, whereupon he would become one of the immortal stars of the chronicles. He's still a good soldier. But he does everything for Mogaba's sake, not that of the Company or its commission."

"Most organizations have mechanisms for handling such problems."

"The mechanism among the Nar is challenge. Combat or contest. Which is no good here. He's still the quickest, fastest, strongest amongst us. He's still the best tactician, begging your pardon."

"I never claimed to be a genius. I got to be Captain 'cause everybody voted against me. I didn't want it but I didn't not want it as badly as everybody else didn't want it. But I won't abdicate so Mogaba can rack himself up some glory."

"My conscience permits me to say no more. Even so, I feel like a traitor. He sent me because we've been like brothers since we were boys. I'm the only man left he trusts. I don't want to hurt him. But he's hurt us. He's blackened our honor and our oaths as guardians."

Sindawe's "guardians" was a Nar word for which there was no exact translation. It carried implications of an obligation to defend the weak and stand firm in the face of evil.

"I hear he's trying to stir up a religious crusade."

Sindawe seemed embarrassed. "Yes. From the beginning some have clung to the Dark Mother. I didn't realize he was one of them—though I should have guessed. His ancestors were priests."

"What's he going to do now? I can't see him getting excited about me turning up."

"I don't know. I'm afraid he'll claim you're not you. He may even believe you're a trick of the Shadowmasters. A lot of men thought they saw you killed. Even your standardbearer."

"A lot of men saw me hit. If anyone questioned Murgen closely they know I was alive when he left me."

Sindawe nodded. "I remain on the horns."

Croaker did not ask what would happen if he tried to eliminate Mogaba. The Nar would fight, Sindawe included. That was not his style, anyway. He did not eliminate a man because he was a nuisance.

"I'll come over and confront him, then. He'll either accept me or he won't. It'll be interesting seeing where the Nar stand if he chooses mutiny."

"You'll exact the penalty?"

"I won't kill him. I respect him. He's a great soldier. Maybe he can continue to be a great soldier. Maybe not. If not, he'll have to give up his part in our quest."

Sindawe smiled. "You're a wise man, Captain. I'll go tell him. And everyone else. I'll pray the gods remind him of his oaths and honor."

"Fine. Don't dawdle. Since I don't want anything to do with this I'll be over as soon as I can."

"Eh?"

"If I put off doing something unpleasant I never get around to dealing with it. Go. I'll be right behind you."

Longshadow consulted the shadows he had left in the cell with the missing woman. Then he visited the bedridden Howler. "You idiot. You grabbed the wrong woman."

Howler did not respond.

"That was Soulcatcher." *Her.* And *whole.* How had she managed that?

In a voice little more than a whisper, Howler reminded, "*You* sent me there. *You* insisted Senjak was in Taglios."

And what did that have to do with the result? "You couldn't scout the situation well enough to find out we'd been deceived?"

Contempt, poorly veiled, flashed across Howler's face. He did not argue. There was no point. Longshadow never made a mistake. Whatever dismayed him, it was always another's fault.

Longshadow pitched a tantrum. Then he went coldly calm. "Error, no error, fault, no fault, the fact is we've made an enemy. *She* won't bear it. She was just playing with her sister before. Now she won't be playing."

Howler smiled. He and Soulcatcher were not beloved of one another. He rasped out, "She's walking."

Longshadow grunted. "Yes. There is that. She's in my territories. Afoot." He paced. "She'll hide from my shadow eyes. But she'll want to watch the rest of the world. I won't look for her, then. I'll look for her spies. The crows will lead me to her. And then I shall test us both."

Howler caught the timbre of daring in Longshadow's voice. He was going to try something dangerous.

Disasters had knocked the daring out of Howler. His inclinations were toward the quiet and safe. That was why he had chosen to build his own empire in the swamps. They had been enough. And nothing anyone wanted to take away. But he had succumbed to seduction when Longshadow's emissaries had come to him. So here he was easing back from the brink of death, alive only because Longshadow still thought him useful. He was not interested in more risks. He would return to his sloughs and mangroves happily. But till he fashioned some means of flight he would have to pretend interest in Longshadow's plans. "Nothing dangerous," he whispered.

"Not at all," Longshadow lied. "Once I find out where she is the rest is easy."

71

Volunteers willing to cross the lake with Croaker were few. He accepted Swan and Sindhu, rejected Blade and Mather. "You two have plenty to do here."

Three of them in a boat. Croaker rowed. The others did not know how. Sindhu sat in the stern, Swan in the bow. Croaker did not want the wide man behind him. That might not be wise. The man had a sinister air and did not act friendly. He was biding his time while he made up his mind about something. Croaker did not want to be looking the wrong way when that happened.

Halfway across Swan asked, "It serious between you and Lady?" He chose Rosean, the language of his youth. Croaker spoke the tongue, though he had not used it for years.

"It is on my side. I can't say for her. Why?"

"I don't want to stick my hand in where I'm going to get it bit off."

"I don't bite. And I don't tell her what to do."

"Yeah. It was nice to dream about. I figure she'll forget I'm alive as soon as she hears you still are."

Croaker smiled, pleased. "Can you tell me anything about this human stump back here? I don't like his looks."

Swan talked for the rest of their passage, evolving complex circumlocutions to get around non-Rosean words Sindhu would recognize.

"Worse than I thought," Croaker said as the boat reached the city wall where part had collapsed and left a gap through which the lake poked a finger. Swan tossed the painter to a Taglian soldier who looked like he had not eaten for a week. He left the boat. Croaker followed. Sindhu followed him. Croaker noted that Swan placed himself so he could watch Sindhu. The soldier tied the boat up, beckoned. They followed him.

He led them to the top of the west wall, which was wide and unbroken. Croaker stared at the city. It was nothing like it had been. It had become a thousand drunken islands. A big island marked its heart: the citadel, where they had dispatched Stormshadow and Shapeshifter. The nearer islands sprouted spectators. He recognized faces, waved.

Ragged at first, beginning with the surviving non-Nar he had brought to Taglios, a cheer spread rapidly. The Taglian troops raised their "Liberator!" hail. Swan said, "I think they're glad to see you."

"From the looks of the place they'd cheer anybody who might get them out."

Streets had become deep canals. The survivors had adapted by building rafts. Croaker doubted anyone travelled much, though. The canals were choked with corpses. The smell of death was oppressive. Plague and a madman tormented the city and there was nowhere to dispose of bodies.

Mogaba and his Nar came marching around the curve of the wall, clad in all their finery. "Here we go," Croaker said. The cheering continued. One raft, almost awash under the weight of old comrades, began laboring toward the wall.

Mogaba halted forty feet away. He stared, his face and eyes smoldering ice. "Say me a prayer, Swan." Croaker moved to meet the man who wanted so badly to be his successor. He wondered if he would have to play this out again with Lady. Assuming he survived this round.

Mogaba moved to meet him, taking stride for stride. They stopped a yard apart. "You've done wonders with nothing," Croaker said. He rested his right hand upon Mogaba's left shoulder.

Sudden silence gripped the city. Ten thousand eyes watched, native and soldier alike, knowing how much hung on Mogaba's response to that gesture of comradery.

Croaker waited quietly. It was a time when almost anything said would be too much said. Nothing needed to be discussed or explained. Everything hinged on Mogaba's reaction. If he reciprocated, all was well. If not . . .

The men looked one another in the eye. Hot fires burned within Mogaba. Nothing showed on his face but Croaker sensed the battle within him, his ambition against a lifetime of training and the obvious will of the soldiers. Their cheers made their sentiments clear.

Mogaba's struggle went on. Twice his right hand rose, fell back. Twice he opened his mouth to speak, then bit down on ambition's tongue.

Croaker broke eye contact long enough to examine the Nar. He tried to send an appeal, Help your chieftain.

Sindawe understood. He fought his own conscience a moment, started walking. He passed the two, joined the old members of the Company forming up behind Croaker. One by one, a dozen Nar followed.

Mogaba's hand started up a third time. Men held their breaths. Then Mogaba looked at his feet. "I can't, Captain. There is a shadow within me. I can't. Kill me."

"And I can't do that. I promised your men I wouldn't harm you no matter your choice."

"Kill me, Captain. Before this thing in me turns to hatred."

"I couldn't even if I hadn't promised."

"I'll never understand you." Mogaba's hand fell. "You're strong enough to come face me when for all you knew you'd be killed. But you're not strong enough to save the trouble sparing me will cost."

"I can't snuff the light I sense in you. It may yet become the light of greatness."

"Not a light, Captain. A wind out of nowhere, born in darkness. For both our sakes I hope I'm wrong, but I fear you'll regret your mercy." Mogaba took a step backward. Croaker's arm fell. Everyone watching sighed, dismayed, though they had had little hope of rapprochement. Mogaba saluted, wheeled, marched away followed by three Nar who had not crossed over with Sindawe.

"Hey!" Swan yelled a moment later, breaking the silence. "Them bastards is stealing our boat!"

"Let them go." Croaker faced friends he had not seen for months. "From the Book of Cloete: 'In those days the Company was in service to the Syndarchs of Dai Khomena, and they were delivered . . . '" His friends all grinned and roared approval. He grinned back. "Hey! We've got work to do here. We've got a city to evacuate. Let's hit it."

From one eye he watched the boat cross the lake, from the other he kept watch on Sindhu.

It felt good to be back.

Thus was Dejagore delivered and the true Company set free.

The Howler perched atop a tall stool, out of the way while Longshadow prepared. He was impressed by the array of mystical and thaumaturgic gewgaws Longshadow had assembled during one short generation. Such had remained scarce while they had been in thrall to the Lady and nonexistent under the rule of her husband before her. They had wanted no one getting independent. Howler had very little though he was free now. He had little need to possess.

Not so Longshadow. He wanted to own at least one of everything. He wanted to own the world.

Not much of Longshadow's collection was in use now. Not much would be ever, Howler suspected. Most had been gathered mainly to keep anyone else from having it. That was the way Longshadow thought.

The room was brightly lighted, partly because it was approaching noon beyond the crystal walls, partly because Longshadow had packed a score of brilliant light sources into the room, no two of which used the same fuel. Against an ambush of shadows he left no precaution untaken.

He would not admit it but he was terrified.

Longshadow checked the altitude of the sun. "Noon coming up. Time to start."

"Why now?"

"They're least active under a noonday sun."

"Oh." Howler did not approve. Longshadow meant to catch one of the hungry big ones to train and send after Soulcatcher. Howler thought that a stupid plan. He thought it unnecessary and overly complicated. They knew where she was. It made more sense just to hit her with more soldiers than she could handle. But Longshadow wanted drama.

This was too risky. He could loose something nothing in this world could control. He did not want to be part of this but Longshadow left him no choice. Longshadow was a master of leaving one no choice.

Several hundred men climbed the old road to the plain, dragging a closed black wagon ordinarily drawn by elephants. But no animal would go near the shadowtraps, however much it was beaten. Only Longshadow's men feared him more than they feared what might befall them up there. Longshadow was the devil they knew.

Those men backed the wagon against the main shadowtrap.

Longshadow said, "Now we begin." He giggled. "And tonight, in the witching hour, your old comrade will cease to be a threat to anyone."

Howler was skeptical.

73

Soulcatcher sat in the middle of a field, disguised as a stump. Crows circled, their shadows scooting over wheat stubble. An unknown city loomed in the distance.

The imp Frogface materialized. "They're up to something."

"I've known that since they started blocking the crows. *What* they're up to is what I want to know."

The imp grinned, described what he had seen.

"Either they've forgotten to take you into account or they're counting on you feeding me incorrect information." She started moving toward the city.

"But if they wanted to feed me false information they would confuse the crows, too. Wouldn't they?"

The imp said nothing. No answer was expected.

"Why do this during the daytime?"

"Longshadow is scared to death of what might break out if he tried during the night."

"Ah. Yes. But they won't move till nightfall. They'll want their sending at full strength."

Frogface muttered something about just how much did he have to do to earn his freedom?

Soulcatcher laughed, a merry little girl's laugh. "Tonight, I think, you'll have done with me. If you can do a creditable illusion of me."

"What?"

"Let's have a look around this city first. What's its name?"

"Dhar. New Dhar, really. Old Dhar was levelled by the Shadowmasters for resisting too strongly back when they first conquered this country."

"Interesting. What do they think of the Shadowmasters?"

"Not much."

"And a new generation is at hand. This could be amusing."

When darkness fell the great public square at the heart of New Dhar was strangely empty and silent, except for the cawing and fluttering of crows. All who approached developed chills and dreads and decided to come another time.

A woman sat on the edge of a fountain, paddling her fingers through the water. Crows swarmed around her, coming and going. From the shadows at the square's edge another figure watched. This one seemed to be a gnarled old crone, folded up against a wall, her rags clutched tightly against the evening cool. Both women seemed content to stay where they were indefinitely.

They were patient, those two.

Patience was rewarded.

The shadow came at midnight, a big, dreadful thing, a terrible juggernaut of darkness that could be sensed while still miles away. Even the untalented of New Dhar felt it. Children cried. Mothers shushed them. Fathers barred their doors and looked for places to hide their babies and wives.

The shadow roared into the city and swept toward the square. Crows squawked and dipped around it. It bore straight down on the woman at the fountain, dreadful and implacable.

The woman laughed at it. And vanished as it sprang upon her.

Crows mocked.

The woman laughed from the far side of the square.

The shadow surged, struck. But the woman was not there. She laughed from behind it.

Frogface, pretending to be Soulcatcher, led the shadow around the city for an hour, took it into places where it would destroy and kill and be recognized and fire hatreds long and carefully banked. The shadow was tireless and persistent but not very bright. It just kept coming, indifferent to what effect it had on the population, waiting for its quarry to make a mistake.

The crone on the edge of the square rose slowly, hobbled to the palace of Longshadow's local governor, entered past soldiers and sentries apparently blind. She hobbled down to the strongroom where the governor stored the treasures he wrested from the peoples in his charge, opened a massive door none but the governor supposedly could open. Once inside she became not a crone but Soulcatcher in a merry mood.

She had studied the shadow carefully while Frogface led it about. That shadow had to travel all the distance between two points. Frogface did not. He could stay ahead forever as long as he remained alert.

Her studies had shown her how she might contain it.

She spent an hour preparing the vault so it would keep the shadow in, then another arranging a peck of little spells that should distract it so that, by the time someone released it, it would have forgotten why it had come to New Dhar.

She stepped outside, closed the door till it stood open only a crack, arranged an illusion that made her look like one of the governor's soldiers. Then she sent a thought spinning toward Frogface.

The imp came prancing, enjoying himself, taunting his hunter into the trap. Soulcatcher shoved the door shut behind it, sealed it up. Frogface popped into existence beside her, grinning. "That was almost fun. If I didn't have business in my own world I'd almost want to hang around another hundred years. Never a dull moment with you."

"Is that a hint?"

"You bet it is, sweetie. I'm going to miss you all, you and the Captain and all your friends. Maybe I'll come back and visit. But I got business elsewhere."

Soulcatcher giggled her little girl's giggle. "All right. Stay with me till I'm out of the city. Then you're free to go. Wow! I bet this place blows up! I wish I could see Longshadow's face when he gets the news." She laughed. "He isn't half as bright as he thinks. You have any friends over there who might want to work for me?"

"Maybe one or two with the right sense of mischief. I'll see."

They walked on, laughing like children who had pulled a prank.

Pregnant.

No doubt about it. Everything fell into place once the physician gave me that word. Everything made sense. And nonsense.

One time. One night. It never occurred to me that that could happen to me. But here I am swollen up like a gourd on toothpicks, sitting in my fortress south of Taglios, writing these Annals, watching the rains fall for the fifth month running, wishing it was possible to sleep on my stomach or side, or to be able to walk without waddling.

The Radisha has provided me with a whole crew of women. They find me amusing. I come back from trying to teach their menfolk something about soldiering and they point at me and tell me this is why women don't become generals and whatnot; it is hard to be light on your feet when you can't see them for your belly.

The baby is an active little thing, whatever it will be. Maybe it is practicing to be a long-distance runner or a professional wrestler, the way it hops around in there.

My timing seems to be good. I have gotten almost everything I have to record written. If, as the women promise me, all my fears and doubts come to nothing and I survive this, I will have five or six weeks to get into shape before the rivers go down and the new campaign season begins.

Regular messages come from Croaker at Dejagore, thrown across the river by catapult. It is quiet down there. He wishes he could be here. I wish he could be here. That would make it easier. I know the day that the Main is down enough to cross I will be on the north bank and he will be there on the south.

I am feeling very positive these days, like not even my sister can ruin things now. She knows about this. Her crows have been watching. I have let them, hoping it irks the devil out of her.

Here is Ram, back from his bath. I swear, the closer I get to my date the worse he gets. You would think it was his child.

He is scared to death that what happened to his wife and baby will happen to me and mine. I think. He has grown a little strange, almost haunted. He is terrified of something. He jumps at every little sound. He searches the corners and shadows every time he enters a room.

75

Ram was scared with good reason. He had learned something he should not have. He knew something he was not supposed to know.

Ram is dead.

Ram died fighting his Strangler brothers when they came to take my daughter.

Narayan is a dead man. He is walking around somewhere out there, maybe grinning that grin, but he will not wear it long. He will be found, if not by soldiers hunting men with indelible red stains on their palms, then by me. He has no idea how strongly my powers have returned. I will find him and he will become a sainted Strangler much earlier than he would like.

I should have been more wary. I knew he had his own agenda. I have been around treacherous men all my life. But never, ever, did it occur to me that, from the beginning, he and his ranking cronies were interested in the child developing within me instead of in me myself. He was a consummate actor.

Grinning bastard. He was a true Deceiver.

I never even chose a name before they collected their Daughter of Night.

I should have suspected when the dreams went away so suddenly. As soon as I had been through that ceremony. *I* was not the one consecrated there. *I* did not change. *I* could not be marked that easily.

Ram was only a yellow rumel man but he knew they were coming. He killed four of them. Then Narayan killed him, according to the women. Then Narayan and his band fought their way out of the fortress. All while I still lay unconscious.

Narayan will pay. I will tear his heart out and use it to choke his goddess.

They do not know what they have awakened. My strength has returned. They will pay. Longshadow, my sister, the Deceivers, Kina herself if she gets in my way.

Their Year of the Skulls is upon them.

I close the Book of Lady.

Envoi: Down There

Incessant wind sweeps the plain of stone. It murmurs across pale grey paving that sprawls from horizon to horizon. It sings around scattered pillars. It tumbles leaves and dust come from afar and stirs the long black hair of a corpse that has lain undisturbed for generations, desiccating. Playfully, the wind tosses a leaf into the corpse's silently screaming mouth, tugs it out again.

The pillars might be thought the remnants of a fallen city. They are not. They are too sparsely and randomly placed. Nor are any of them toppled or broken, though some have been etched deeply by gnawing ages of wind.

And some seem nearly new. A century old at most.

In the dawn, and at the setting of the sun, parts of those columns catch the light and gleam golden. For a few minutes each day auric characters burn forth from their faces.

For those remembered it is immortality of a sort.

In the night the winds die and silence rules the place of glittering stone.

THE SILVER SPIKE

I

This here journal is Raven's idea but I got me a feeling he won't be so proud of it if he ever gets to reading it because most of the time I'm going to tell the truth. Even if he is my best buddy.

Talk about your feet of clay. He's got them run all the way up to his noogies, and then some. But he's a right guy even if he is a homicidal, suicidal maniac half the time. Raven decides he's your friend you got a friend for life, with a knife in all three hands.

My name is Case. Philodendron Case. Thanks to my Ma. I've never even told Raven about that. That's why I joined the army. To get away from the kind of potato diggers that would stick a name like that on a kid. I had seven sisters and four brothers last time I got a head count. Every one is named after some damned flower.

A girl named Iris or Rose, what the hell, hey? But I got a brother named Violet and another brother named Petunia. What kind of people do that do their kids? Where the hell are the Butches and Spikes?

Potato diggers.

People that spend their whole lives grubbing in the dirt, sunup to sundown, to root out potatoes, cabbages, onions, parsnips, rootabagas. Turnips. I still hate turnips. I wouldn't wish them on a hog. I joined the army as soon as I could sneak off.

They tried to stop me. My father and uncles and brothers and cousins. They didn't get away with it. I'm still amazed how that one old sergeant managed to look so bad the whole clan backed down.

That's what I wanted to be when I grew up. Somebody who could just stand there and look so bad people dribbled down their legs. But I think you got to be born with it.

Raven's got it. He just looks at somebody trying to jack him around and the guy turns white.

So I joined up and went through the training and went out soldiering, sometimes with Feather and Journey, sometimes with Whisper, mostly here in the north. And I found out soldiering wasn't what I thought it would be. I found out I didn't like it a whole lot better than digging potatoes. But I was good at it, even if I kept doing something to get busted every time I made sergeant. I finally got posted to the Guards at the Barrowland. That was supposed to be a big honor but I never believed it.

That's where I met Raven. Only he went by the name of Corbie then. I didn't know he was a spy for the White Rose. 'Course, nobody did or he would have been dead. He was just this quiet old crippled guy who said he used to soldier with the Limper but had to get out after he got his leg hurt so bad. He hung out in an abandoned house he fixed up. He made his living doing things for guys that didn't want to do them for themselves. The Guards got paid good and the Barrowland was a hundred miles into the Great Forest where there wasn't nothing else to spend it on but booze. Corbie got plenty of work polishing boots and swabbing floors and currying horses. He used to come in and do the colonel's office and then play chess with him, which is where I ran into him the first time.

He smelled odd right from the start. Not White Rose odd but you knew he wasn't no runaway farm boy like me or some city kid from the slums that signed up because there wasn't nothing else to do with his life. He had some class when he wanted to show it. He was educated. He talked maybe five or six languages and he could read and I heard him talk with the old man about things that I didn't have a rooster's notion what they meant.

So I got me this idea. I'd get to be his buddy and then get him to teach me how to read and write.

It was the same old thing, see. Join the army and get off the farm and go on adventures and life would be great. Learn to read and write, I could get out of the army and go off on adventures and everything would be great.

Sure.

I don't know if everybody is that way. I'm not the kind that can ask guys about things like that. But I know me enough to know that there ain't nothing ever going to turn out to be exactly what I want and nothing is ever going to satisfy me. I'm the guy with so much ambition I'm living here in a one-room walk-up with a wino whose big talent seems to be puking his guts up after scarfing down about three gallons of the cheapest wine he can find.

So anyway I got Raven to start teaching me and we ended up buddies, even if he was weird. And that didn't do me no good when the shit storm hit and he turned out to be a spy. Lucky for me, my bosses and his bosses had to get together to gang up on the monster in the ground up there, that us Guards was getting paid so good to watch.

That's when I found out he was really Raven, the guy that used to run with the Black Company, that took the White Rose away from the Limper when she was a little kid and hid her out and raised her up till she was ready to take on her destiny.

I thought he was dead. So did everybody else, on both sides. Especially the White Rose, who had loved him, and not like a brother or father. Which is why he turned himself into a dead man and ran away. He couldn't handle what it means to have somebody in love with you. Running away was the only thing he knew how to do.

But he was some in love with her, too, and the only way he had to show it was turn himself into Corbie and go spying and hope he could find her some big weapon she could use when she came to her final confrontation with the Lady. My big boss.

So what happens? Fate sticks an oar in and stirs everything up and when we look around what do we find? The Dominator, the old monster buried in the Barrowland, the blackest evil this old world ever knew, was awake and trying to get out, and the only way to stop him was for everybody to drop their old fights and gang up. So the Lady came to the Barrowland with all her double-ugly champions, and the White Rose came with the Black Company, and things started getting interesting.

And damnfool Raven mooned around in the middle of it all thinking he could just walk over and take up with Darling like he hadn't walked out on her and let her think he was dead for a bunch of years.

The damn fool. I know more about sorcery than he'll ever know about women.

So they let the old evil come up out of the ground, then they jumped all over it. It was so big and black they couldn't kill its spirit, only its flesh, so they burned that flesh to ash and scattered the ash and imprisoned its soul in a silver spike. They drove the spike into the trunk of a sapling that was the son of some kind of god that would live forever and grow around it and keep it from ever causing any more grief. Then they all went away. Even Darling, with some guy named Silent.

There were tears in her eyes when she went. Some of that feeling for Raven was still there inside her. But she was not going to open up and let him do it to her again.

And he stood there watching her go, dumbstruck. He couldn't figure out why she would do that to him.

Damn fool.

2

It was weird that nobody else thought of it right away. But maybe that was because people were more taken with what had happened between the Lady and
the White Rose and were wondering what that would mean to the empire and
the rebellion. For a while it looked like half the world was up for grabs. Everybody who was the sort to do some grabbing was eyeballing his or her chances
and scouting around to see if they might get turned into eunuchs if they tried.

So it was up to some second-rate hustlers from Oar's north side to take first
whack at stealing the silver spike.

The news from the Barrowland was still in the shithouse rumor stage when
Tully Stahl came pounding on the door of the room where his cousin Smeds
Stahl stayed.

The room Smeds lived in had no furnishings except roaches and dirt, half a
dozen mildewed, stolen blankets, and half a gross of empty clay wine jugs that
he never got around to taking back. They made him pay deposit at the Thorn
and Crown. Smeds called the jugs his life savings. If times got really tough he
could trade eight empties for a full.

Tully said that was a dumb way to do things. Whenever Smeds got ripped
and pissed he started throwing things around. He wasted his savings.

The shards never got picked up, either, just kicked against one wall, where
they formed a dusty badland.

When Tully got on him Smeds figured he was just putting on airs because
he was flush. Tully had two married women giving him presents for helping out
around the house when the old man was gone. And he was living with a widow
he was going to clean out as soon as he found some other woman to take him
in. He thought being a success gave him the right to dish out advice.

Tully pounded on the door. Smeds ignored him. The Kinbro girls from upstairs, Marti and Sheena, eleven and twelve, were there for their "music lessons."
The three of them were naked and tumbling around on the ratty blankets. The
only instrument in sight was a skin flute.

Smeds made the girls stop bouncing and giggling. There was people who
wouldn't appreciate how he was preparing them for later life.

Pound. Pound. Pound. "Come on, Smeds. Open up. It's me. Tully."

"I'm busy."

"Open up. I got a deal I got to talk about."

Sighing, Smeds untangled himself from skinny young limbs and trudged to the door. "It's my cousin. He's all right."

The girls had been into the wine. They didn't care. They didn't cover themselves. They just sat there grinning when Smeds let Tully in.

"Some friends," Smeds explained. "You want in? They don't mind."

"Some other time. Get them out."

Smeds glared at his cousin. Getting too damned pushy. "Come on, girls. Get your clothes on. Papa has to talk business."

Tully and Smeds watched while they got into ragged clothing. It didn't occur to Smeds to dress. Sheena gave old Hank the Shank a playful slap as she went by. "See you later."

The door closed. "You're going to get your ass in a sling," Tully said.

"No more than you. You ought to meet their mother."

"She got any money?"

"No. But she blows a mean horn. Got a thing about it. She gets going she just can't quit."

"When you going to clean this pigsty?"

"Soon as the maid gets back from holiday. So what's so important you have to break in on my party?"

"You heard about what happened up in the Barrowland?"

"I heard some stories. I didn't pay no attention. What do I care? Won't make no difference to me."

"It might. You hear the part about the silver spike?"

Smeds thought. "Yeah. They stuck it in a tree. I thought that would be handy to glom on to. Then I thought some more and figured there wouldn't be enough silver in it to make it worth the trip."

"It isn't the silver, cousin. It's what's in the silver."

Smeds turned it around in his mind some. He couldn't find Tully's angle. "You better lay it out by the numbers." Smeds Stahl was not known for his keen mind.

"That big nail has the soul of the Dominator trapped in it. That means it's one bad hunk of metal. You take some big wazoo of a sorcerer, I bet he could pound it into some kind of all-time mean amulet. You know, like in stories."

Smeds frowned. "We aren't sorcerers."

Tully got impatient. "We'd be the middlemen. We go up there and dig it out of that tree and hide it out till word gets around that it's gone. Then we let it out that it's for sale. To the highest bidder."

Smeds frowned some more and put his whole brain to work. He was no genius but he had plenty of low, mean cunning and he had learned how to stay alive. "Sounds damned dangerous to me. Something we'd need help on if we wanted to come out of it in one piece."

"Right. Even the easy part, going up there and liberating the damned thing, would be more than a two-man job. The Great Forest might be a pretty rough place for guys who don't know anything about the woods. I figured we'd need two more guys, one of them who knows about the woods."

"Already we're talking a four-way split here, Tully. On how much?"

"I don't know. Give them time to bid it up, I think we'd be set for life. And I ain't talking no four-way split, neither, Smeds. Two ways. All in the family."

They looked at each other. Smeds said, "You got the plan. Tell me."

"You know Timmy Locan? Was in the army for a while?"

"About long enough to figure out how to go over the hill. Yeah. He's all right."

"He was in long enough to learn how it works. We might run into soldiers up there. Would your heart be broken if they found him in an alley with his head bashed in?"

That was an easy one. "No." His heart would be fine as long as it wasn't Smeds Stahl they found.

"How about Old Man Fish? He used to trap in the Great Forest."

"Couple of straight arrows."

"That's what we need. Honest crooks. Not some guys who might try to do us out of our share. What do you say? Want to go for it?"

"Tell me how much is in it again."

"Enough to live like princes. We going to go talk to those guys?"

Smeds shrugged. "Why not? What have I got better to do?" He looked at the ceiling.

"You better get some clothes on."

Heading down the stairs, Smeds said, "You'd better do the talking."
        "Good idea."

Heading up the street, Smeds asked, "You ever killed anybody?"
        "No. I never needed to. I don't see where I'd have any problem."

"I had to once. Cut a guy's throat. It ain't like you think. They spray blood all over the place and make weird noises. And they take a long time to croak. And they keep trying to come after you. I still get nightmares about that guy trying to take me with him."

Tully looked at him and made a face. "Then do it some other way next time."

3

Each night there was moonlight enough, a thing came down out of the northern Great Forest, quiet as a limping shadow, into the lorn and trammeled place of death called the Barrowland. That place was heavy with the fetor of corruption. A great many corpses lay rotting in shallow graves.

Limping on three legs, the thing cautiously circled the uncorrupted carcass of a dragon, settled on its haunches in the hole it was digging so patiently, night after night, with a single paw. While it worked it cast frequent glances toward the ruins of a town and military compound several hundred yards to the west.

The garrison had existed to shield the Barrowland from trespassers with evil intentions and to watch for signs that the old darkness in the ground was stirring. Those reasons no longer existed. The battle in which the digging beast had been crippled, in which the dragon had perished, in which the town and compound had been devastated, had put an end to the need for a military stewardship.

Except that it had not occurred to anyone in authority to give the surviving Guards new assignments. Some had stayed, not knowing what else to do or where else to go.

Those men were sworn enemies of the beast.

Had it been healthy, the thing would not have been concerned. It could have dealt with those men easily. Healthy, it was a match for any company of soldiers. Crippled and still suffering from a dozen unhealed wounds, it would not be able to outrun a man let alone outfight those it would have to get through before it could pursue the messenger the Guards were sure to send flying to their masters if they discovered it.

Those masters were cruel and deadly and the beast stood no chance against them even when in the best of health.

Its master could protect it no more. Its master had been hacked to pieces and the pieces burned. Its master's soul had been imprisoned in a silver spike that had been driven into his skull.

The beast was doglike in appearance but rather uncertain in size. It had a protean nature. At times it could be as small as a large dog. At other times it might be the size of a small elephant. It was most comfortable being about twice the size of a war-horse. In the great battle it had slain many of its master's enemies before overpowering sorceries had driven it from the field.

It came stealthily, again and again, despite the fear of exposure, the pain of its wounds, and its frustration. Sometimes the wall of its excavation collapsed. Sometimes rainwater would fill the hole. And always there was the inescapable vigilance of the only truly watchful guardian the victors had left.

A young tree stood among the bones, alone. It was near immortal and was far mightier than the night skulker. It was the child of a god. In time, each night, it wakened to the digger's presence. Its reaction was uniform and violent.

A blue nimbus formed among the tree's limbs. Pale lightning ripped toward the monster. It was a quiet sort of lightning, a sizzle instead of boom and crash, but it slapped the monster like an angry adult's swing at a small child.

The beast suffered no injury, only extreme pain. That it could not endure. Each time it was hit it fled, to await another night and that delay before the child of the god awakened.

The monster's work went slowly.

Darling left Raven standing there. She rode off with that guy Silent and some other guys that were all that was left of the Black Company, a mercenary outfit that really wasn't anymore. A long time ago they was on the Lady's side but something happened to piss them off and they went over to the Rebel. For a long time they was almost the whole Rebel army.

Raven watched them go into the woods. I could tell he wanted to sit down and cry like a baby, maybe as much because he couldn't understand as because she did ride off on him. But he didn't.

In most ways he was the toughest, hardest bastard I ever saw, and not always in the best ways. When I first found out he was Raven and not Corbie I like to crapped my drawers. A long time ago there was a Raven that rode with the Black Company that was the baddest of the bad. He was with them only about a year before he deserted but he made himself a big rep while he was there. And this was the same guy.

He said, "We'll give them a couple hours' head start so it don't look like we're dogging them, then we'll get out of here."

"We?"

"You want to hang around here now?"

"That would be desertion."

"They don't know if you're dead or not. They haven't counted noses yet." He shrugged. "Up to you. Come or stay."

I could tell he wanted me to come. Right then I was the only thing he had. But he wasn't going to make no special appeal. Not hard guy Raven.

I didn't have no future at the Barrowland and I sure as hell wasn't going back to ride herd on potatoes. And I didn't have anybody else in the world, either. "All right. I'm in."

He started walking into town. What was left after the fight. I tagged along. After a while, he said, "Croaker was about the closest thing to a friend I had when I was in the Company." He was still confused.

Croaker was the boss merc. He wasn't boss back when Raven was with them, but they had been through a few captains since the old days. Raven was confused because his old buddy and him had gotten in a fight after the Dominator got put down.

Probably to show off for Darling, Raven had decided he was going to round everything off and close the books by getting rid of the Lady, who lost her powers during the battle. And Croaker said no you don't and didn't back down. He put an arrow into Raven's hip just to show him he was serious.

"Is a friend somebody who just stands back and lets you do whatever you want whenever you want to do it?"

He gave me one of his puzzled looks.

"Maybe he was a whole lot more her friend than he was yours. Way I heard tell, they spent a lot of time together. They rode off into the sunset together. And you know the way those guys are about brotherhood, sticking together no matter what, the Company being their family, them against the whole world. You told me about it enough."

There was more I could have said. I could have given it to him by the numbers, how they felt about brothers who ran out on them, but he wouldn't have got it.

There wasn't nobody with more guts in a fight than Raven. He wouldn't back down from nobody or nothing. But in the emotional tight spots he was ready to pack up and run in a minute. He did it to the Company and he did it to Darling, but they could take care of themselves when he did.

I think maybe the worst stunt he ever pulled, and the one that still bugs him the most, is when he ran out on his kids.

He did that back when he enrolled in the Black Company. Maybe he had his reasons, and good ones at the time. He comes up with good excuses. But there's no getting around the fact that he left his kids when they were too young to take care of themselves. Without making any arrangements for them. He never even told anybody he had kids till he told me, sort of, when he was still being Corbie and started trying to find out what happened to them. They would be grown up now. If they survived.

He didn't find out anything.

I figured he would make finding them his quest now. He didn't have anything else going. And trudging through the forest headed south, he made noises like that was what he was planning to do.

We got as far as Oar. He went out on a drunk. And stayed on it.

I went on one, too. I went through me some bad girls. All the things a guys does when he's been out in the woods for a long time, then hits the city. Took me four days to work through that and another day to shake the hangover. Then I took a look at Raven and saw he was just getting started.

I went and found us a cheap place to stay. Then I got me a job protecting a rich man's family. That wasn't hard to do. There were all kinds of rumors about what happened in the Barrowland. The rich saw troubled times coming and wanted to get themselves covered.

Darling and her bunch were in the city somewhere, for a while. So were the bunch from the Black Company. We didn't run into any of them before they left out.

5

Smeds got sick of Tully's idea before they were four days out of Oar. Nights were cold in the forest. There was no place to hide from the rain. Whole hordes of bugs chewed on you and you couldn't get rid of them when you were sick of them like you could with lice and fleas and bedbugs. You could never get comfortable sleeping on the ground—if you could sleep at all with all the racket that went on at night. There were always sticks and stones and roots under you somewhere.

And there was that bastard Old Man Fish, hardly saying shit but always sneering at you because you didn't know a bunch of woodsy stuff. Like you needed to know that shit to stay alive on the North Side.

It was going to be a pleasure to cut his throat.

Timmy Locan wasn't much better. Little carrottop runt never shut up. All right, so he was funny most of the time. So he knew every damned joke there ever was and knew how to tell them right and half of them were the kind you wanted to remember so bad it hurt, so you could crack up your friends. But they never came out right for you even when you did remember them. . . . Damn it, even funny got old after four days.

Worse than funny, the little prick never slowed down. He bounced up in the morning like he knew it was going to be the best damned day of his life and he went after every damned day like it was. Short people weren't supposed to be joyous, they were supposed to be cocky and obnoxious. Then you could thump on them and shut them up without feeling bad about it.

Worst thing of all was, Old Man Fish said they couldn't follow the road on account of they might run into somebody who would want to know what they were up to or somebody who might remember them after they did the job. It was important that nobody knew who did it. But busting through the tangle of the woods was awful, even with Old Man Fish finding the way.

Tully hated it worse than Smeds, but he backed the old man up.

Smeds had to admit they were right. What he didn't have to admit was that the expedition was worth the slapping branches, the stabbing, tearing briars, and the for-gods'-sake spiderwebs in the face.

Or maybe the worst was the blisters on his feet. Those started practically before they got out of sight of Oar. Even though he did everything Old Man Fish told him to do, they just kept getting worse. At least they didn't get infected. That jerk Timmy kept telling cheerful little tales about guys in the army who had had blisters that had gotten infected and they'd had to have their feet or legs chopped off. Dipshit.

Fourth night in the woods he had no trouble sleeping. In fact, he was getting to that point where he could sleep whenever he stopped moving. The old man observed, "You're starting to toughen up. We'll turn you into a man yet, Smeds."

Smeds could have killed him then, but it was too much work to get out of his pack straps and go over and do it.

Maybe the pack was the worst part of it. He had to lug eighty pounds of junk on his back, and what they had eaten of the food part hadn't lightened the load a bit.

*   *   *

They reached their destination shortly after noon eight days after they departed Oar. Smeds stood just inside the edge of the forest and looked out at the Barrowland. "That's what all the fuss was about? Don't look like shit to me." He sloughed his pack, plopped down on it, leaned against a tree, and closed his eyes.

"It ain't what it used to be," Old Man Fish agreed.

"You got a name besides Old Man?"

"Fish."

"I mean a front name."

"Fish is good."

Laconic bastard.

Timmy asked, "That our tree out there?"

Tully answered, "Got to be. It's the only one there is."

Timmy said, "I love you, little tree. You're going to make me rich."

Tully said, "Fish, I think we ought to rest up some before we go after it."

Smeds cracked an eyelid and glimmed his cousin. That was as close as his cousin had come to complaining since the expedition had started. But Tully was a big-time bitcher. Smeds had wondered how long he would hold out. Tully's silence so far had helped Smeds keep going. If Tully wanted it bad enough to take what he had been, then maybe it really was as good as he talked.

The big hit? The one they had been seeking all their lives? Could it be? For that reason alone Smeds would endure.

Fish agreed with Tully. "I wouldn't start before tomorrow night. At the earliest. Maybe the night after. We have a lot of scouting to do. We'll all have to learn the ground the way we learn the geography of a lover."

Smeds frowned. Was this no-talk Fish?

"We have to find a secure place to camp and establish a secondary base for emergencies."

Smeds could not keep quiet. "What the hell is all this shit? Why don't we just go out there and chop the damned thing down and get out of here?"

"Shut up, Smeds," Tully snapped. "Where the hell have you been for the last ten days? Get the shit out of your ears and use your head for something besides keeping them from banging together."

Smeds shut up. His ears were open, suddenly, and they had caught a very sinister undertone in Tully's voice. His cousin had begun to sound like he regretted letting him in on the deal. Like maybe he was thinking Smeds was too dumb to be left to live. Right now he had on that same contemptuous look Fish wore so often.

He closed his eyes, shut out his companions, let his mind roll back over the past ten days, picking up things that he had heard without really hearing because he had been so busy feeling sorry for himself.

Of course they couldn't just strut out there and chop the damned tree down. There were soldiers watching the Barrowland. And even if there weren't any soldiers there was the tree itself, that was supposed to be big mojo. Sorcery there great enough to have survived the dark struggle that had hammered the guts out of this killing ground.

All right. It wasn't going to be easy. He would have to work for it harder than he'd ever worked for anything in his life. And he would have to be careful. He would have to keep his eyes open and his brain working. He wasn't going to give the Kimbro girls music lessons out here.

That day and night they rested. Even Old Man Fish said he needed it. Next morning Fish went to scout for a campsite. Tully said, "You got blisters up to your butt, Smeds. You stay here. Take care of them the way Fish said. You got to get in shape to move if we got to move. Timmy, come on."

"Where you going?" Smeds asked.

"Gonna try getting close to that town. See what we can find out." They went.

Fish came back an hour later.

"That was quick. Find a place?"

"Not a very good one. River's moved some since I was up here. Bank's two hundred yards over there. Not much room to run. Let me look at them feet."

Smeds stuck them out. Fish squatted, grunted, touched a couple of places. Smeds winced. "Bad?" he asked.

"Seen worse. Not often. Got some trenchfoot getting started, too. Others probably got a touch, too." He looked vacant for a moment. "My fault. I knew you was green and Tully was as organized as a henhouse. Shoulda not let him get in such a big hurry. You get in a hurry you always end up paying."

"Decided what you're going to do with your cut yet?"

"Nope. You get to my age you don't go looking that far ahead. Good chance you might not get there. One day at a time, boy. I'm going to get some stuff for a poultice."

Smeds watched the straight-backed, white-haired man fade into the forest silently. He tried to blank his mind. He did not want to be alone with his thoughts.

Fish returned with a load of weeds. "Chop these into little pieces and put them in this sack. Equal amounts of each kind." There were three kinds. "When the sack is stuffed close it up and pound on it with this stick. Roll it over once in a while. All the leaves got to get good and bruised."

"How long?"

"Give it a thousand, twelve hundred whacks. Then dump it in this pot. Put in a cup of water and stir it up."

"Then what?"

"Then do another sack. And stir the pot every couple minutes." The old man faded into the woods without saying where he was going.

Smeds was pounding his third sack when Fish returned. He sniffed. "Guess you can do a job right when you want." He settled, took the pot. "Good. That sack will be enough."

He turned Smeds's oldest shirt into bindings for his feet, packed them with soggy, mangled leaves. A cool tingle began soothing his pains.

Fish made the others treat their feet, too. He did his own.

Smeds leaned against his tree, troubled. He did not think he was hard enough or bad enough to kill the old man.

"There between sixty and eighty people still living over there," Tully said. "Mostly soldiers. But we heard them talking like a big bunch would be leaving in a couple days. Wouldn't hurt to wait them out on that. We could finish up our scouting."

Scouting the Barrowland started after sunset, by the light of a quarter moon. The village was dark and silent. It looked a good time to prowl the open ground.

Out the four went in a loose line abreast barely in sight of one another, Tully guiding on the tree. It was not much of a tree by Smeds's estimation. Right then it looked like a fat-trunked silver-bark poplar sapling about fifteen feet tall. He could not see anything remarkable there. Why the reputation?

He reached a point where the angle was right, caught a glint of moonlight off silver. It was real! And having gotten that one glance, he began to feel the throbbing dark power of it, like it was not metal at all but an icicle of pure hatred.

He shuddered, forced his gaze away.

It was real. The wealth was there to be had. If they could take it.

He hurried forward. A long, low, stony ridge barred his path. Odd that such a thing should be there, but he did not connect it with the dragon that was supposed to have devoured the infamous sorcerer Bomanz before being slain itself. Maybe if there had been more light to reveal what his hands and feet exposed as they disturbed the masking dirt . . .

He was near the top when he heard the sound. Like an animal snuffling. And another sound beneath it, like something scratching at the earth. He looked for the others. He could see no one but Tully, who was staring at the tree from ten feet away. There was something odd about the tree. The tops of its leaves glimmered with a faint bluish ghost light.

Maybe it was a trick of the rising moon.

He got up where the footing was good, stood, glanced at the tree again. Definitely something weird going on there. The whole thing was glowing.

He looked down in front of him. His heart stilled.

Something stared back at him from fifty feet away. It had a head the size of a bushel basket. Its eyes and teeth shown in the tree light. Especially its teeth. Never had he seen so many sharp teeth, or so big.

It started toward him.

His feet would not move.

He looked around wildly, saw Tully and Timmy headed away from the tree at a dead run.

He looked forward again as the monster began its leap, its jaws opening to snap at his head. He hurled himself backward. As the monster arced after him a blue bolt from the tree smacked it aside as a man's hand swats a flying insect.

Smeds landed hard, but hard did not slow him a step. He took off running and never looked back.

I saw it, too," Old Man Fish said, and that put the quietus on Tully trying to make like Smeds was imagining things. "Like he said, it was as big as a house. Like a giant three-legged dog. The tree zapped it. It ran away."

"Three-legged dog? Come on. What was it doing?"

Smeds said, "It was trying to dig something up. It was sniffing and pawing the ground just like a dog trying to dig up a bone."

"Damn it to hell! Complications. Why does there always have to be complications? That for sure means it'll take longer than I thought. But we don't got no time to waste. Sooner or later somebody else is going to get the same idea I did."

"Don't get in no hurry," Fish said. "Take your time and do it right. That is, if you want to live long enough to enjoy being rich."

Tully grunted. Nobody suggested they give it up. Not even Smeds, who had felt the monster's breath on his face.

"Toadkiller Dog," Timmy Locan said.

"Say what?" Tully snapped back.

"Toadkiller Dog. There was a monster in the fight up here called Toadkiller Dog."

"Toadkiller Dog? What the hell kind of name is that?"

"How the hell should I know? He ain't my pup."

Stupid joke, but everybody laughed anyway. They needed to.

6

Raven hardly sobered up for three weeks. One night I came back to our place, I'd had enough. I'd had to hurt a man bad that day, a nut who earned it trying to grab my boss's kids. Even so I felt bad. Somehow I worked it out that it was all Raven's fault I got in a position where I had to hurt somebody.

He was drunk on his ass. "Look at you, sucking on a wineskin like it was your mother's tit. The great and famous tough guy Raven, so bad he offed his old lady in the public gardens at Opal. So bad he went head-to-head with the Limper. Laying around feeling sorry for himself and whining like a three-year-old with a bellyache. Get up and do something with yourself, man. I'm sick of seeing you like this."

In a stumbling, slurred voice he told me to get stuffed, it wasn't any of my damned business.

"The hell it ain't! It's my damned money paying for the room here, dipshit. And I got to come home every day to the stink of old puke and spilled wine and a goddamn soil pot you ain't got time to empty yourself. When was the last time you bothered to change your clothes? When was the last time you had a bath?"

He cussed me in a cracked-voice scream.

"You're just about the most selfish, thoughtless bastard I ever seen. Won't even clean up after yourself."

I went on like that, louder and angrier. But he never really fought back, which made me think maybe he was about as disgusted with himself as I was with him. But who can go around admitting he's a hopeless, useless hunk of shit?

Finally he ran out of what little fight he had. He got up and staggered out, without any parting shot. He did not burn any bridges behind him.

A guy I worked with and I talked it over about what you do with drunks. His dad was a reformed drunk. He told me you got to stop trying to help them out. You got to stop making excuses for them and not take excuses from them. You got to put them on a spot where they can't do nothing but face the truth because they aren't going to change a bit till *they* decide to do it. *They* got to be the ones who believe they've turned into dregs and something has got to be changed.

I didn't know if I could wait around long enough for Raven to decide he was a real grown-up man and he was going to have to face reality. Darling was gone and that was that. There were kids to be found. That whole past, down in Opal, had to be hooked back out into the light and made peace with.

Actually, I was pretty sure he would come around, given time. The kind of guy he was being was the kind he held in deep contempt. That had to seep through. But it sure was frustrating, waiting him out.

He came back home four days later, sobered up and cleaned up and looking halfway like the Raven I remembered. He was all apologetic. He promised to get straight and to do better.

Sure. They do that, too.

I would believe it when I saw it.

I didn't make any big deal out of anything. I didn't preach. There wasn't no profit in that.

He hung on pretty good. He looked like he was getting somewhere. But then two days later I came home and found him so stinking he couldn't crawl.

Hell with him, I said.

They were running shorthanded, what with Timmy laid up after getting caught in a blast of the tree's blue light, but Smeds did not see where it made any difference. They were not getting anywhere. They could not go out there in the daytime without being seen from the town. After dark that monster always came and dug in its hole. They could not go out there then. And for a long time after it chased the monster, the tree remained alert, laying for more intruders. Timmy had found that out the hard way.

It looked like there was maybe an hour each morning, just before dawn, when it might be possible to get something accomplished safely.

But what? Nobody had figured that out. They sure weren't going to get a chance to chop the sucker down. Ringing it wasn't worth squat, even if you could get close enough for long enough to do it. How long for a ringed tree to die? Especially this kind?

Somebody suggested poisoning it. That sounded so good that they talked it over, recalling things they had seen used to kill weeds and stuff. Only the method demanded that they have a poison. Which meant going back to Oar to buy it. With money they did not have. And it might take as long as ringing the son of a bitch. Time was not an ally. Tully was in a panic about time already. He thought it a miracle no competition had yet shown.

"We got to do it fast."

Timmy said, "We ain't going to get it done as long as that monster keeps coming around."

"So maybe we help him find what he wants."

"You better got a mouse in your pocket when you say 'we,' cousin," Smeds said. "Because I ain't going out there to help that thing do squat."

"We burn it," Fish said.

"Huh? What?"

"The tree, fool. We burn it down."

"But we can't go out there and . . ."

Fish yanked a stick out of their woodpile. It was a yard long and two inches in diameter. He sailed it off through the woods. "Take a while, but it'll pile up. Then in with a torch or two. *Whoosh.* Up in flames. Fire burns out, we go pick up our spike."

Smeds sneered. "You forgot the soldiers."

"Nope. But you're right. Got to come up with a diversion."

Tully said, "That's the best idea yet. We'll go with it till somebody thinks up something better."

Smeds grunted. "It'll beat sitting on our asses, that's for sure." He was used to the woods now. There was no adventure left in this. Not that there had been a lot before. He was bored.

They started pitching sticks immediately. The three younger men made it a game, betting from their shares. Sticks began to accumulate.

The tree did not like the game. Sometimes it sniped back.

They thought Smeds was crazy, sneaking out every couple nights to watch the monster dig. "You got more balls than brains," Tully told him.

"Better than sitting around."

It was not that dangerous. He just had to keep down. The beast never noticed a low profile. But if you got up and showed it a silhouette, look out!

The monster's labor was slow, but it worked as though obsessed. The nights came and went, came and went.

In time it unearthed what it sought.

Smeds Stahl was watching the night it came up with a grisly trophy, a horror, a human head.

That head had been too long in too many graves, and too often injured. The monster closed its jaws on ragged remnants of hair, lifted the gruesome object. Dodging bolts from the tree, it carried the head to a backwater in the nearby river.

Smeds tagged along behind. Carefully. *Very* carefully.

The beast laved the head with care and tenderness. The tree crackled and sputtered, unable to project its power that far.

Once the head was clean, the giant hound limped back the way it had come. Smeds stole along behind, amazing himself with his daring. The beast circled the dead dragon, which more than ever appeared to be an odd feature of the terrain. It stepped over a bit of tattered leather and stone almost invisible in the soggy earth, not noticing. Smeds spotted it, though. He picked it up and pocketed it without thinking.

On the other side of the dragon the tree continued to crackle and fuss, frustrated.

When Smeds pocketed that old fetish it twitched, proclaiming to anyone properly attuned the fact that it had been disturbed.

Smeds halted in a shadow, freezing. Moonlight had fallen upon that horrible head. He saw it clearly.

Its eyes were open. A grotesque smile stretched its ruined mouth.

It was alive.

Smeds almost lost sphincter control.

Oar is the city nearest the old battleground and burying place called the Barrowland. The alarm cried by the fetish there touched two residents.

One was an old, old man living incognito because he had contrived to stage his apparent death during the struggle that had devastated the Barrowland. The alarm struck him as he sat guzzling in a workingman's tavern with new cronies who thought him an astrologer. When it hit him he knew a moment of panic. Then, tears streaming, he rushed into the street.

A questioning babble arose behind him. When his comrades came out to learn what was wrong he had vanished.

It was another of those damned days. Oar was a troubled city. There were scattered disturbances, conflict between Rebel and imperial partisans, and a lot of private crimes were getting committed under the guise of politics. My boss was talking about shutting up his city house and moving out to a place he owned near Deal. If he did that I'd have to decide whether or not to go along. I wanted to talk it over with Raven, but . . .

He was passed out when I got there.

"Over a goddamned woman you never even had," I grumbled, and kicked a tin plate across the room. The son of a bitch hadn't bothered to clean up after himself again. I thought about kicking him around the room. But I wasn't mad enough to try that yet.

Even drunk and wasted away, he was still Raven, the baddest man I'd ever met. I didn't need to get into it with him.

He woke up so sudden I jumped. He used the wall to pull himself up. He was pale and shaking and I never for a second took it for the effect of the wine. That old boy was scared shitless.

He couldn't hardly stand up without that wall to help, and he was probably seeing three of me and little blue men besides, but he gobbled out, "Case, get your stuff together."

"What?"

He was working his way along the wall toward his heap of stuff. "Something just broke out of the Barrowland. . . . Oh, god!" He went down on his knees, holding his stomach. He started puking. I handed him water to cleanse his mouth and a rag to wipe up with. He didn't argue. "Something got out. Something as dark as . . ."

Up came another load.

I asked, "You sure it wasn't just a nightmare? Or maybe the grape boogies?"

"It was real. It wasn't the wine. I don't know how I know. I know. I saw it as clear as if I was there. There was that beast everybody called Toadkiller Dog." He talked slow, trying not to slur. He slurred anyway. "Something was with it. Something greater. Something of the true darkness."

I didn't know what to say. He believed it even if I didn't. He had his mess cleaned and was starting to stuff his things into a bag. He asked, "Where did you stable the horses?"

He *was* serious. Unable to navigate and brain-pickled, but he was by-damned going to do something right now.

"Thulda's. Why? Where you going?"

"We got to get help."

"Help? We? You forgetting I got me a job here? I got responsibilities. I can't just mount up and ride off chasing lights you seen in the swamp because you got ahold of some doctored wine."

He got mad. I got mad right back. We yelled and screamed some. He threw things because he wasn't in good enough shape to run me down. I stomped his wineskin to death and watched its blood trickle across the floor.

The landlady kicked the door in. She weighed two hundred pounds and was as mean as a snake. "I told you bastards I wasn't going to put up with no more of this. . . ."

We rushed her. She was a liar and a cheat and a bully and she probably stole things from the rooms when she thought she wouldn't get caught. We threw her down the stairs and stood around laughing like a couple of kid vandals. She started screeching again down below. She wasn't hurt.

I stopped laughing. She wasn't hurt, but she might have been. And I didn't have the excuse of being drunk. "I take it you're headed out of town?"

"Yeah." The humor had fled him, too. His color was ghastly.

"How you going to get out of town? It's the middle of the night."

"Cash considerations. The magical key." He shouldered his bag. "You about ready?"

"Yeah." He knew I would come all the time.

Hey, Loo!" the gateman called into the gatehouse while Raven clinked coins. "Get your ass up. We got us another customer." He grinned apologetically. "Loo, he's got a day job plucking chickens. Got too damned many kids. You would think a guy would learn how to stop after the first dozen. Not Loo." He kept on grinning.

"You'd figure," I admitted. "This that good a job? I don't see so many guys happy with their work like you."

"Pretty boring on the night watch, mostly. Been a profitable night tonight, though."

"Others have gone before us?" Raven asked.

"Only one guy. This old man about an hour ago. In such a big damned hurry he just scattered coins all over the place."

That was what you call your basic broad hint. Raven ignored it. I made small talk till Loo turned out with the keys and opened the small port through the big gate. Raven just stared straight ahead. When Loo opened up he tossed some silver.

"Why, thank you, yer grace. Come around anytime. Any time. You got a friend down here to South Gate."

Raven didn't say anything. He just grimaced and led his horse through the gateway onto the moon-washed road.

"Thanks," I told the gatemen. "See you guys around."

"Anytime, yer grace. Anytime. I'm yer man."

Raven must have paid them off good.

The grimace was familiar, though I hadn't seen it for a while. "Your hip bothering you again?"

"It'll be all right. I've traveled with worse."

Sour bastard. He'd shaken the wine, pretty well, but the hangover was hanging over. "Taking a long time to heal."

"What the hell you expect? I'm not so young anymore. And it was one of *her* arrows Croaker got me with."

Raven didn't seem to hold no grudge. He just couldn't figure it out.

He probably didn't *want* to figure it out. His idea of Raven was that Raven was a doer, not a thinker.

Sometimes I wondered how he could feed himself so much crap.

10

The old man, worn out, stood beside his ragged mount, stared at the dusty crossroads. To the east lay Lords. Southward the road led to Roses and beyond, to other great cities. The people he had come chasing had split here. He did not know who had gone which direction, though it seemed reasonable that the White Rose had turned east toward her fastness in the Plain of Fear. The Lady should have continued southward, toward her capital, the Tower at Charm.

With that parting, the armistice between them would have ended.

"Which way?" he asked the animal. The shaggy pony did not express an opinion. The old man could not decide which woman would be best equipped to act on his news. His impulse was to keep going south, but only because by turning east he would be headed into the rising sun.

"We're too old for this, horse."

The animal made a sound that, for a moment, he took to be a response. But the pony was looking back the way they had come.

Dust cloud. Fast riders coming down. Two, looked like. After a moment the old man recognized the wild-eyed style of the man in the lead. "Here comes our answer. Let's go." He hurried along the eastbound road, turned aside into a copse, found a spot where he could watch the riders. He would take the road they ignored.

Their mission had to be the same as his. That those two men should arrive here at this moment, hurrying like hell was yapping at their heels, for any other reason, strained credulity. The one called Raven could have heard the alarm. At some time in his life he had had some small training in the art, and his spirit had spent a long time snared in the coils of the Barrowland. He was sensitive enough.

The old man's eyelids drooped. He prepared an herbal draft that would help keep him alert long enough to see what those two men would do.

II

R aven reined back to a walk. "We gave that old boy a fright."

"Probably figures we're bandits. We look it. You going to kill these horses today? Or can we string them along for a while?"

Raven grunted. "You're right, Case. No sense getting in so big a hurry we end up taking twice as long because we have to walk most of the way. Funny. That old boy reminded me of that wizard Bomanz that got eaten by the Barrowland dragon."

"All them old-timers look the same to me."

"Could be. Hold up." He studied the crossroads. I tried to spot the old man in the copse. I was sure he was watching us.

"Well?" I asked.

"They split up like they said they would."

Don't ask me how he knew. He knew. Unless he was just faking it. I've seen him do that.

"Darling went east. Croaker kept heading south."

I'd play his game. "How do you figure?"

"*She* was with him." He rubbed his hip. "*She* would be headed for the Tower."

"Oh. Yeah." Big deal. "Which way are we headed? Whichever, we got to rest soon."

"Yes. Soon. For the horses."

"Sure." I kept my face blank. Inside I was wishing I had balls enough to yell at him that he didn't have to go on being the iron man for me. He didn't have to prove anything to me but that he could stop sucking wine by the gallon and could stop feeling sorry for himself. He wanted to show me how much guts he had, let him show me he had the kind it took to go find his kids and make up with them.

He didn't have to prove anything to that old man over there in the trees, did he?

I wished he would go ahead and announce the decision I knew he was going to make. I was getting uncomfortable, knowing I was being watched. "Come on. Which way?"

He responded by spurring his mount down the south road.

What the hell was this? I even started to turn east before I realized what he'd done.

I caught up. "Why south?"

Kind of hitting it sideways, he told me, "Croaker was always an understanding kind of guy. And forgiving."

The son of a bitch was crazy.

Or maybe he'd suddenly gone sane and didn't need to whimper over Darling anymore.

The three-legged beast carried the head to the heart of the Great Forest, to the altar at the center of a ring of standing stones that had been in place for several thousand years. It could barely squeeze through the picket of ancient oaks surrounding that greatest of the holy places of the pitifully diminished forest savages.

The monster deposited the head and hobbled back into the dappled woods.

One by one the beast hunted down the shamans of the woodland tribes and compelled them to go to the head. In their terror those petty old witch doctors threw themselves upon their faces before it and worshiped it as a god. They swore oaths of fealty for fear of the jaws of the beast. Then they began tending to the head's needs.

Not once, to any, did it occur to take advantage of its powerlessness to destroy it. The fear of it was impressed too deeply into their kind. They could not imagine resistance.

And, always, there was that slavering monster to overawe them.

They went away from the holy place to collect willow withes, mystical herbs, rope grasses, leather both raw and tanned, blessed feathers, and stones known to possess magical properties. They gathered small animals appropriate

for sacrifices, and even brought in a thief who was to be killed anyway. The man
screamed and begged to be dispatched in the usual way, fearing the perpetual
bondage and torment of a soul dedicated to a god.

Most of the stuff collected was junk. Most of the shamans' magic was
mummery, but it proceeded from a deeper truth, from a fountain of genuine
power. Power that was real enough to serve the head's immediate purpose.

In that oldest and most sacred of their holy places the shamans wove and
built themselves a wicker man of willow and rope grasses and rawhide. They
burned their herbs and slaughtered their sacrifices, christening and anointing
the wicker man with blood. Their chanting invocations possessed the ring of
stone for days.

Much of the chant was nonsense, but forgotten or only partly understood
words of power lingered in its rhythms. Words enough to do.

When those old men finished the rite, they set the head on the wicker man's
neck. Its eyes blinked three times.

One wooden hand snatched a staff from a shaman. The old man fell. Tottering, the amalgam moved to a patch of bare earth. With the foot of the staff it
scratched out crude block letters.

Slowly the thing gave the old men their orders. They hurried off. In a week
they were ready to make improvements on their handiwork.

The rites this time were more bloody and bizarre. They included the sacrifice of two men snatched from the ruined town beside the Barrowland. Those
two were a long time dying.

When the rites were finished the wicker man and its corrupt burden
possessed more freedom of movement, though no one would mistake the
construct for a human body. The head could now speak in a soft, gravelly
whisper.

It ordered, "Collect your fifty best warriors."

The old men balked. They had done their part. They had no taste for adventures.

The thing they had created whispered a chant in which there were no waste
words. Three old men died screaming, devoured by worms that ate them from
within.

"Gather your fifty best warriors."

The survivors did as they were told.

When the warriors came they hoisted the wicker man onto the back of the
crippled monster. No woodland pony or ox would allow the amalgam to mount
it. He then led the band down to the wreck of the town at the Barrowland. "Kill
them all," he whispered.

As the massacre began the wicker man moved past, his ruined face fixed
southward. His eyes smoldered with a poisonous, insane hatred.

13

Timmy came flying into camp moments after the racket started. He was so scared he could hardly talk. "We got to get out of here," he choked out, in one-word gasps. "That monster is back. Something is riding it. Some savages are killing them in the village."

Old Man Fish nodded once and dumped water on the fire. "Before it remembers us. Just like we rehearsed it."

"Oh, come on," Tully snarled. "Timmy's probably seeing things. . . ."

The tree cut loose with the granddaddy of all blue bolts. It filled the forest with its glow and banged like heavenly lightning.

"Holy shit," Tully whispered. He took off like a stampeded bear.

The others were not too far behind.

Smeds was thoughtful as he trotted along, his arms filled with gear. Fish's precautions had paid off. Maybe. Like the old boy said, they weren't out nothing getting away for a while.

From behind came a flare in a rosy peach shade answered by another blast of blue. Something yowled like the lost soul of a great cat.

Tully claimed Fish thought too much. But here was Fish turning out to do more and more of the leading while Tully eased into Smeds's old place as shirker and complainer. Timmy wasn't changing, though. He was still the handy runt with the thousand stories.

Fish and Timmy were putting more into this than Tully. Smeds didn't think he could cut them. Especially not if the payoff was as big as Tully expected. No need to be bloody greedy then.

Smeds squatted beside his log, placed his stuff in the nest of branches left to hold it. Tully was on the river already, splashing away. "Sshh!" Fish said. Everybody froze, except Tully out there, splashing away.

Old Man Fish listened.

All Smeds heard was a lot of silence. Nor was there any lightning anymore.

Fish relaxed. "Nothing moving. We got time to strip."

Smeds took the old man's word but he didn't waste any time getting naked and shoving off.

Lying on his chest on a log in the middle of a river in the middle of the night, Smeds felt the first nibbles of panic. He could not see the island for which they were headed, though Fish said there was no way they could miss it from where they had left the bank. The current would carry them right to it.

That was no reassurance. He could not swim. If he missed the island he would drift maybe all the way to the sea.

A sudden barrage of blue flares illuminated the river. He was surprised to see that Fish and Timmy were nearby. And for all his furious splashing Tully was only a hundred feet ahead.

He felt an urge to say something, anything, just to draw courage from the act of communication. But he had nothing to say. And silence was imperative. No point asking for trouble.

During the coming hour he relived every moment of fear he'd ever known, every instance of misfortune and disaster. He was very ragged when he spied the darker loom of the island dead ahead.

It wasn't much of an island. It was maybe thirty feet wide and two hundred yards long, a nail paring of a mudbank that had accumulated weeds and scrub brush. None of the brush was taller than a man. Smeds thought it a pretty pathetic hideout.

At the moment it looked like paradise.

A minute later Fish whispered, "It's shallow enough to touch bottom. Walk your way around to the far side so there won't be tracks coming out over here."

Smeds slid off his log, discovered the water was no deeper than his waist. He followed Fish and Timmy, his toes squishing in the bottom muck, his calves tangling in water plants. Timmy yipped as he stepped on something that wriggled.

Smeds glanced back. Nothing. There had been no fireworks since the exchange that had shown him his companions on the river. The forest had begun to recall its night murmur.

"What took you guys so long?" Tully asked, with a touch of strain.

Smeds snapped, "We took time to pick up some stuff so we wouldn't starve to death out here. What're you going to munch, fireball?"

Smeds wondered if an occasional dose of stress wasn't good for the state of a guy's common sense. He'd dug up some useful memories during his helpless voyage.

Tully had run off on him before. When they were little, as a simple act of cruelty, and later, abandoning him to the mercies of bullies or leaving him to be beaten by a merchant when he, unwitting, had distracted the man while Tully had snatched a handful of coppers and run.

Tully bore watching.

Smeds could see the shadow of the future. Get Old Man Fish and Timmy

Locan to kype the spike. Get dumb old Smeds to croak them when they do. Then take the loot and walk. Who is Smeds going to complain to when he has the blood of two men on his hands?

That would be just like Tully. Just like him.

They stayed on the island four days, feeding the gnats, broiling in the sun, waiting. It went hardest for Tully. He mooched food enough to get by, but he could not borrow dry clothing or a blanket to keep the sun off.

Smeds had a feeling Fish drew the wait out mainly for Tully's benefit.

Fish went over to the mainland the fourth afternoon. Walking. The channel between the island and bank was never more than chest-deep. He carried his necessaries atop his head.

He did not return till after dark.

"Well?" Tully demanded, the only one of them with any store of impatience left.

"They're gone. Before they left they found our camp and savaged it. They poisoned everything and left dozens of traps. We won't go back there. Maybe we can find what we need in the village. Those folks won't be needing anything anymore."

Smeds learned the truth of Fish's report next day, after a pass near their old camp to show Tully he was wasting his time whining for his stuff. The massacre had been complete, and had not spared the dogs, the fowl, the livestock. It was a warm morning and the air was still. The wings of a million flies filled the forest with an oppressive drone. Carrion eaters squawked and barked and chittered, arguing, as though there was not a feast great enough for ten times their number.

The stench was gut-wrenching even from a quarter mile away.

Smeds stopped. "I got no business to take care of over there. I'm going to go eyeball the tree."

"I'll give you a hand," Timmy said.

Tully looked at Smeds with a snarl. Old Man Fish shrugged, said, "We'll meet you there." The stink and horror didn't seem to bother him.

14

The wicker man strode through the streets of the shattered city like an avenging god, stepping stiffly over the legions of the dead. The survivors of his forest warriors followed, awed by the vastness of the city and aghast at what sorcery had wrought. Behind them came a few hundred stunned imperial soldiers from the Oar garrison. They had recognized the invader and had responded to his call to arms—mainly because to defy him was to join those whose blood painted the cobblestones and whose spilled entrails clogged the gutters.

Fires burned in a thousand places. The people of Oar sent a great lament up into the darkness. But not near the dread thing stamping the night.

Furtive things moved in the shadows, rushing away from their places of hiding. Their fear was so great they could not remain still while the old terror passed. He ignored them. The backbone of resistance had been broken.

He ignored everything but the fires. Fire he avoided.

Bowstrings yelped. Arrows zipped into the wicker man as if into an archery butt. Chunks of willow and bits of stone flew. The wicker man reeled. But for the woodland warriors he would have toppled. Breathy rage tore through the head's tortured lips.

Then words came, soft and bitter, chilling the hearts of those near enough to hear. More arrows ripped the fabric of the night, battered the wicker man, clipped one of his ears, felled one of the savages supporting him. He finished speaking.

Screams tore the shadows fifty yards away. They were terrible screams. They brought moisture to the eyes of the soldiers who followed the wicker man.

Those soldiers stepped over the knotted, twitching, whining forms of men wearing uniforms exactly like their own, brothers in arms whose courage had been sufficient to buoy their loyalty. Some shuddered and averted their eyes. Some took mercy and ended the torment with quick spear thrusts. Some recognized old comrades among the fallen and quietly swore to even accounts when sweet opportunity presented itself.

The wicker man proved as unstoppable as a natural disaster. He passed through Oar, trailing death and destruction and accumulating followers, and came to the city's South Gate, where Loo and his sidekick vanished in a flurry of heels. The wicker man extended a hand, whispered secret words. The gate blasted to flinders and toothpicks. The wicker man stamped through and halted, staring down the darkened road.

The trail had grown confused. That of the prey was overlaid by other scents equally familiar, tantalizing, and hated. "As well," he whispered. "As well. Take them all and have done." He sniffed. "*Him!* And that accursed White Rose. And the one who thwarted me in Opal. And the wizard who set us free." Ruined lips quivered in momentary fear. Yes. Even he knew the meaning of fear. "*Her!*"

The beast called Toadkiller Dog believed that *she* had lost her powers. He wanted to believe that himself. That would be a justice beautiful beyond compare. He needed to believe it. But he dared not, not entirely, till he saw for himself. Toadkiller Dog operated from motives not his own. And she was as crafty and treacherous a being as ever any human had been.

Moreover, he had tried to disarm her himself, once, and his failure had reduced him to this.

Toadkiller Dog bulled through the gateway, shouldering soldiers aside. Gore dripped off him. For hours he had ravened through the city, feeding an ancient thirst for blood. He moved on four limbs now, though one was as artificial as the wicker man's body. He, too, peered down the road.

The forest warriors collapsed, falling asleep where they were. The wicker man was driven. He showed no inclination to baby his followers.

A tottering shaman, on his last legs, tried to speak to the wicker man, tried to make him understand that unalloyed flesh could not keep the pace he had set.

The head turned slightly. The expression that shown through the ruin was one of contempt. "Keep up or die," it whispered. It beckoned men to come lift it onto the back of the beast. It rode out, insane with a hunger for revenge.

15

The folks we was chasing never did much to cover up which way they was headed. I don't guess they thought they had any reason. Anyway, Raven knew where the guy he was chasing was headed. Some place called Khatovar, all the way down on the southern edge of the world.

I knew the guy, Croaker. Him and his Black Company boys did a job on me at the Barrowland, though they never did me too bad. I got out alive. So I had mixed feelings about them. They were a hard bunch. I didn't feel like I really wanted to catch them.

The more we rode along, the more Raven dried out and turned back into the real Raven. And I don't mean into the Corbie that I got to know when I first met him, I mean the real bad-ass so tough and hard he was death on a stick. I don't think it ever occurred to him to take a drink after he made up his mind that he had something else to do.

We had practice sessions every morning before we rode out and every evening after we set camp. Even when he was at his weakest it was all I could do to handle him. When he really started coming back he beat me at everything but throwing rocks and running footraces.

His hip never let up on him.

He wouldn't never stop over at an inn or in a village. Putting away temptation, I guess.

You ain't never going to impress me with nothing if you think you're going to tell me tall tales and you ain't never seen the Tower at Charm. There ain't nothing ought to be that big. It's got to be five hundred feet tall and as black as a buzzard's heart. I never seen nothing like it before and I don't expect I ever will again.

We never went too close. Raven said there wasn't no sense getting those people's attention. Damned straight. That was the heart of the empire, the home of the Lady and all those old evils called the Ten Who Were Taken.

I went off a few miles and kept my head down while Raven skulked around trying to find something out. I was perfectly happy to get rested up from all those hundreds of miles of riding.

He materialized out of a sunset that painted the horizon with end-of-the-world fires. He sat down across from me. "They're not in the Tower. They stopped there for a couple weeks, but then they headed south again. *She* followed them."

I got to admit I groaned. I never was a whiner in all my soldiering days, but I never got put through anything like this, either. A man ain't made for it.

"We're gaining on them, Case. Fast. If they fool around in Opal like they did here we'll have them." He gave me a fat smile. "You wanted to see the world."

"Not the whole damned thing in a week. I kind of counted on enjoying the seeing."

"We don't get them turned around and headed toward the trouble, there might not be much damned world left."

"You going to take time out to look for your kids while we're down there?" I wanted to see the sea. I wanted that since I was little. A traveling man come through and told us kids lies about the Jewel Cities and the Sea of Torments. From then on I always thought about the sea when I was digging potatoes or pulling weeds. I pretended I was a sailor, holy-stoning a deck, but I was going to be a ship's master someday.

What did I know?

More than the sea, now, I wanted to see Raven do right and get right with himself and his kids.

He gave me a funny look, then just ducked the question by not answering it.

We accumulated a fair arsenal here and there as we rode along. Just outside Opal we got a chance to show it off. Not that that done a lot of good.

This great big old hairy-ass black iron coach come roaring out of the city and straight up the road at us, them horses looking like they was breathing fire. I never saw anything like it.

Raven had. "That's the Lady's! Stop it!" He whipped out a bow and strung it.

"The Lady's coach? Stop it? Man, you're crazy! You got guano for brains." I got my bow out, too.

Raven threw up a hand in a signal for them to halt. We tried to look stand-and-deliver, your money or your life. Mean.

Them coachmen never even slowed down. It was like they never even saw us. I ended up going ass over appetite into a ditch with about a foot of muck and water in it. When I got up I saw Raven had ended up in some blackberry bushes on the other side. "Arrogant bastards!" he shouted after the coach.

"Yeah. Got no damned respect for a couple of honest highwaymen."

Raven looked at me and started laughing. I looked at him and went to laughing right back. After a minute, he said, "There wasn't anybody inside that coach." He sounded puzzled.

"When did you have time to look?"

"I think I know what's happening. Come on. We have to hurry. Catch your horse."

I caught her. She was too stupid to hold a grudge. But his kept leading him around, looking back like he was thinking, You ain't going to pull that crazy shit on me again, you son of a bitch. This game went on for a while. I finally stopped it by sneaking up on the beast from the other direction.

We blew about a half hour diddling around there.

The big black ship was about a half hour down the channel when we got to the waterfront. For a minute I thought Raven was going to chop that gelding of his into fish bait. But he just dismounted and stood there on the wharf, staring out to the sea. Whenever a local growled at us about being in the way he just gave them one of those looks that stilled the heart and quickened the feet.

He had it all back, whatever it was. Those weren't soft guys, there on that waterfront.

The black ship faded into the haze out on the water. Raven shuddered his way back to the racket and fish smells. "Guess we'll have to sell the horses and find a ship headed for Beryl."

"Hang on here, man. Enough is enough. Reasonable is reasonable. You figure on heading all the way to the end of the world? Look around here. This is Opal. Almost ever since I've known you I been hearing how you got to get back to Opal and find out about your kids. Look it! We're here! Let's do it."

The guy was my friend. But he had trouble hanging in. Before he was Raven he was Corbie, and before he was Corbie he was Raven. And sometime way back he was somebody else before he got to be Raven the first time. I don't know who, but I know he was somebody high-class and he came from Opal and he left two kids behind, twins, when he got on with Croaker and that bunch and headed north for the fighting in Forsberg.

He plain left those kids to the winds of fortune. He tortured himself because he didn't know what happened to them, because he wasn't shit as a father. Me, I figured it was high time he got that all straightened out.

He thought about it a long time. He kept looking down the coast, eastward, like the answer might be there. What I saw when I looked that way was the homes of rich people on top of cliffs, overlooking the sea. I always kind of suspected he was one of them.

"Maybe when we come back through," he said, finally. "When we're headed north again."

"Sure." Bullshit.

He heard me thinking. He sort of shrank into himself. He did not look at me.

Best ship we could get for Beryl was on some kind of fat scow leaving in two days. I got sick just looking at it.

Raven got good and polluted that night even though I never said another word about his kids. I guess he heard me thinking. Or he heard himself, which is worse.

I got up early. Raven would be nursing a hangover all day. He was one of those old farts had to tell you all about how he never got one when he was young. I went off to look around.

I did all right. I never got lost. And the city had so many different kinds in it after a couple generations being part of the empire that almost everywhere I could find somebody who spoke one of the languages that I did.

It wasn't a lot of fun rooting around in a friend's past. I didn't learn a whole lot, anyway. I couldn't find hardly anybody who remembered anything, and what they did remember mostly sounded like it was fairy tale. Good stories always get bigger. But I think I got some sense out of all the nonsense.

A long time back a character named the Limper was the governor of the province that included Opal. The Limper was one of the original Ten Who Were Taken, the undead sorcerer-devils who were the Lady's champions. They were called Taken because they had been great villains in their own right once, but they had been enslaved by a greater and darker power.

This one called the Limper was about as corrupt and rotten a governor as ever there was.

I knew the guy later. He had been up to the Barrowland for the last big battle, where he got his. All I can say is, there wasn't no one anywhere in this wide world who shed a tear when he went down. Of all the Taken he was the craziest and nastiest.

Anyway, he was the boss in Opal and him and his cronies was gutting the province, stealing the coppers off dead men's eyes. A certain Baronet Corvo, whose family had become allied with the empire when it first came into the area, went off on an assignment somewhere. While he was gone his old lady got to messing around with the Limper's gang. To the point where she helped rob the baronet's family of most of its honors and titles and all its properties. She helped frame some uncles and cousins and brothers so they could be executed and their properties confiscated.

I couldn't find out much about her. The marriage was arranged and there never was any love in it. I got the impression it was set up to end a feud that had been going on for a hundred years. It didn't work.

She cleaned out and killed off Raven's family. Then he killed her and her whole gang except for the Limper himself. Maybe he could have gotten everything back if he had wanted. The Limper never was in good with the Lady. But Raven found Darling, the White Rose, who became the Lady's mortal enemy. . . .

Not a bad job of finding out, if I do say so myself. Even if I couldn't find out

one thing about Raven's kids. I only run into two people who remembered
there was kids. They didn't know what happened to them.

Nobody cared but me, it seemed.

We sold the horses. They didn't bring enough. They was pretty ragged after the beating they took coming south. Raven had a bad hangover and
wasn't in no mood to argue. But I was getting brave in my old age.

I asked him, "What's the point in us chasing Croaker halfway across the
world? Especially when the last time you ran into him he put an arrow into you?
Say we do catch him. If he don't finish the job, if he even listens, what's he going
to do about whatever happened up north?"

I got to admit I was plenty skeptical about what he claimed maybe happened up there. Even if he did study a little black sorcery way back when.

I guess you could call it nagging. I said, "I figure you got a lot more important business right here in Opal."

He gave me an ugly look. "I don't much care what you think about that,
Case. Mind your own business."

"It is my business. It's me getting dragged halfway across the world and
maybe ending up getting killed someplace I never heard of because you got
problems inside your head."

"You aren't a slave, Case. There's no one holding a knife to your throat."

I couldn't say I owe you, man, but you wouldn't understand nothing about
that. You taught me to read and write and believe I had a little value as human
being before you went off the end. So I said, "If I drop out, who's going to clean
you up when you puke all over yourself? Who's going to drag you out after you
start a fight in some tavern and get your ass stomped?"

He'd done that last night and if I hadn't showed up when I did he maybe
would've gotten himself killed.

This guy who was riding off to save the world.

He was in a rotten mood. His head ached with the hangover. His hip hurt.
His body ached from the beating. But he could not find a way to answer me
even in that humor. He just said, "I'm going to do what I'm going to do, Case,
right or wrong. I'd like to have you along. If you can't make it, no hard feelings."

"What the hell else I got to do with my life? I got nothing to tie me down."

"Then why do you keep bitching?"

"Sometimes I like to have what I'm doing make some kind of sense."

We got on the boat, which was a grain ship crossing over in ballast to collect
a cargo, and we were off to a part of the world even Raven hadn't seen before.
And before we got to the other side we was both damned sure we shouldn't

have done it. But we did decide not to try walking back to Opal when the ship's master refused to turn her around.

Actually, the trip didn't start out all that bad. But then they had to go untie the mooring ropes.

A storm caught us halfway over. It wasn't supposed to blow at that time of year. "It never storms this season," the bosun promised us right after the wind split a sail the topmen didn't reef in time. For four more days it kept on not storming at that time of year. So we were four more days behind when we hit the dock in Beryl.

I didn't look back. Whatever I'd thought about Raven and his kids and obligations before, that wasn't interesting now. They were on the other side of the big water and I was cured of wanting to be a sailor. If Raven suddenly decided he had to go back and balance accounts I was going to tell him to go pick his nose with his elbow.

The bunch we were chasing had left a plain trail. Raven's buddy had gone through Beryl like thunder and lightning, pretending to be an imperial legate on a mystery mission.

"Croaker is in a big hurry now," Raven said. "It's going to be a long chase."

I gave him a look but I didn't say it.

We bought new horses and rounded up travel stuff. When we headed out what they called the Rubbish Gate we were seven days behind. Raven took off like he was going to catch up by tomorrow morning.

In the heart of the continent, far to the east of the Barrowland, Oar, the Tower, and Opal, beyond Lords and even that jagged desolation called the Windy Country, lies that vast, inhospitable, infertile, bizarre land called the Plain of Fear. There is sound reason for the name. It is a land terrible to men. Seldom are they welcomed there.

In the heart of the Plain of Fear there is a barren circle. At the circle's center stands a gnarly tree half as old as time. The tree is the sire of the sapling standing sentinel over the Barrowland.

The few scabrous, primitive nomads who live upon the Plain of Fear call it Old Father Tree and worship it as a god. And god that tree is, or as close as makes no difference. But it is a god whose powers are strictly circumscribed.

Old Father Tree was all a-rattle. Had he been human, he would have been in a screaming rage. After a long, long delay his son had communicated details of his lapse in the matter of the digging monster and the buried head and the wicker man's insane murder spree.

The tree's anger was not entirely inspired by the tardiness of his son. As much was directed at his own impotence and at the dread the news inspired.

An old devil had been put down forever and the world had relaxed, had turned to its smaller concerns. But evil had not missed a stride. It was back in the lists already. It was running free, unbridled, unchallenged, and looked like it could devour the world it hated.

He was a god. On the wispiest evidences he could discern the shapes of potential tomorrows. And the tomorrows he saw were wastelands of blood and terror.

The failure of his offspring could be precursor to the greater failure of his own trust.

When his hot fury had spent itself he sent his creatures, the talking stones, into the farthest, the most hidden, the most shadowed reaches of the Plain, carrying his call for an assembly of the Peoples, the parliament of the forty-odd sentient species inhabiting that most bizarre part of the world.

Old Father Tree could not move himself, nor could he project his own power beyond certain limits, but he did have the capacity to fling out legates and janissaries in his stead.

The old man could barely keep himself upright in the saddle when he reached Lords. His life had been sedentary. He had nothing but will and the black arts with which to sustain himself against the hazards of travel and his own physical limits.

His will and skill were substantial but neither was inexhaustible nor indefatigable.

He learned that he was just five days behind his quarry now. The White Rose and her party were in no hurry, and were having no trouble getting around the imperial authorities. For all his desperation he took two days off to rest. It was an investment of time he was sure would pay dividends down the road.

When he left Lords he did so with a horse and pack mule selected for stamina and durability, not for speed and beauty. The long far leg of the next stage would take him through the Windy Country, a land with a bad reputation. He did not want to linger there.

As he passed through ever smaller, meaner, and more widely separated hamlets, approaching the Windy Country, he learned that he was gaining ground rapidly—if closing the gap by four days in as many weeks could be called rapid.

He entered the uninhabited land with little optimism for a quick success. There were no regular, fixed tracks through the Windy Country, which even the empire shunned as worthless. He would have to slow down and use his talent to find the trail.

Or would he? He knew where they were headed. Why worry about where they were now? Why not forget that and just head for the place where they would leave the Windy Country? If he kept pushing he might get there before they did.

He was three-quarters of the way across the desolation, into the worst badlands, a maze of barren and wildly eroded stone. He had made his camp and had fed himself and had lain back to watch the stars come out. Usually it took him only moments to fall asleep, but tonight something kept nagging at the edge of his consciousness. It took him a while to figure out what it was.

For the first time since entering the Windy Country he was not alone within that circle of awareness open to the unconscious scrutiny of his mystic sensibilities. There was a party somewhere about a mile east of him.

And something else was moving in the night, something huge and dangerous and alien that cruised the upper airs, hunting.

He extended his probing mind eastward, cautiously.

Them! The quarry! And alert, troubled, as he was. Certain something was about to happen.

He withdrew immediately, began breaking camp. He muttered all the while, cursing the aches and infirmities that were with him always. He kept probing the night for that hunting presence.

It came and went, slowly, still searching. Good. There might be time.

Night travel was more trouble here than he expected. And there was the thing above, which seemed able to spot him at times, despite his best efforts to make himself one with the land of stone. It kept his animals in a continuous state of terror. The going was painfully slow.

Dawn threatened when he topped a knife-edge ridge and spotted his quarry's camp down the canyon on the other side. He began the descent, feeling that even his hair hurt. The animals grew more difficult by the minute.

A great shadow rolled over him, and kept on rolling. He looked up. A thing a thousand feet long was dropping toward the camp of those he sought.

The still stone echoed his shouted, "Wait!"

He anticipated the lethal prickle of steel arrowheads with every step. He anticipated the crushing, stinging embrace of windwhale tentacles. But neither dread overtook him.

A lean, dark man stepped into his path. He had eyes as hard and dark as chunks of obsidian. From somewhere nearby, behind him, another man said, "I'll be damned! It's that sorcerer Bomanz, that was supposed to have got et by the Barrowland dragon."

A serpent of fire slithered southward, devouring castles and cities and towns, growing larger even as pieces of it fell away. Only fire black and bloody red lay behind it.

Toadkiller Dog and the wicker man were the serpent's deadly fangs.

Even the wicker man had physical limits. And periods of lucidity. At Roses, after the city's punishment, in a moment of rationality, he decided that neither he nor his soldiers could survive the present pace. Indeed, losses among his followers came more often from hardship than from enemy action.

He camped below the ruined city several days, recuperating, till wholesale desertions by plunder-laden troopers informed him that his soldiers were sufficiently rested.

Five thousand men followed him in his march toward Charm.

The Tower was sealed. They recognized him in there. They did not want him inside. They named him rebel, traitor, madman, scum, and worse. They mocked him. *She* was absent, but her lackeys remained faithful and defiant and insufficiently afraid.

They set worms of power snaking over stone already adamantine with spells set during the Tower's construction: writhing maggots of pastel green, pink, blue, that scurried to any point of attack to absorb the sorcerous energy applied from without. The wizards within the Tower were not as great as their attacker, but they had the advantage of being able to work from behind defenses erected by one who had been greater than he.

The wicker man spewed his fury till exhaustion overcame him. And the best of his efforts only left scars little more than stains on the face of the Tower.

They taunted and mocked him, those fools in there, but after a few days they tired of the game. Irked by his persistence, they began throwing things back at him. Things that burned.

He got back out of range.

His troops no longer believed him when he claimed that the Lady had lost her power. If she had, why were her captains so stubborn?

It must be true that she was not in the Tower. If she was not, then she might return anytime, summoned to its aid. In that instance it would not be smart to be found in the wicker man's camp.

His army began to evaporate. Whole companies vanished. Fewer than two thousand remained when the wicker man's sorceries finally breeched the Tower gate. They went inside without enthusiasm and found their pessimism justified. Most died in the Tower's traps before their master could stamp in behind them.

He fared little better.

He plunged back outside, rolled on the ground to extinguish the flames gnawing his body. Stones rained from the battlements, threatened to crush him. But he escaped, and quickly enough to prevent the defection of his few hundred remaining men.

Toadkiller Dog did not participate. And he did not hang around after that humiliation. Cursing every step, the wicker man followed him.

The Tower's defenders used their sorcery to keep their laughter hanging around him for days.

The cities between Charm and the sea paid, and Opal doubly. The wicker man's vengeance was so thorough he had to wait in the ruins six days before an incautious sea captain put in to investigate the disaster.

The wicker man's rage fed upon his frustration. The very fates seemed to conspire to thwart his revenge. For all his frenzied and indefatigable effort he was gaining no ground—except in the realm of madness, and that he did not recognize.

In Beryl he encountered wizardry almost the equal of that he had faced at the Tower. The city's defenders put up a ferocious fight rather than bend the knee to him.

His fury, his insanity, then, cowed even Toadkiller Dog.

19

Tully sat on a log and scratched and stared in the general direction of the tree. Smeds didn't think he was seeing anything. He was feeling sorry for himself again. Or still. "Shit," he muttered. And, "The hell with it."

"What?"

"I said the hell with it. I've had it. We're going home."

"Listen to this. What happened to the fancy houses and fancy horses and fancy women and being set for life?"

"Screw it. We been out here all damned spring and half the summer and we ain't got nowhere. I'm going to be a North Side bum all my life. I just got a big head for a while and thought I could get above myself."

Smeds looked out at the tree. Timmy Locan was out there throwing sticks, a mindless exercise that never bored him. He was tempting fate today, getting closer than ever before, policing up sticks that had flown wide before and chucking them onto the pile around the tree. That was less work than gleaning the woods for deadwood. The nearby forest was stripped as clean as parkland.

Smeds thought it looked like they could set the fire any day now. In places the woodpile was fifteen feet high and you couldn't see the tree at all.

What was Tully up to? This whining and giving up fit in with his behavior since their dip in the river, but the timing was suspect. "We'll be ready to do the burn any day now. Why not wait till then?"

"Screw it. It ain't going to work and you know it. Or if you don't you're fooling yourself."

"You want to go home, go ahead. I'm going to stick it out and see what happens."

"I said *we're* going home. All of us."

Right, Smeds thought. Tully was cranking up for a little screw your buddy. "What you want to bet you come up outvoted three to one, cousin? You want to go, go. Ain't nobody going to stop you."

Tully tried a little bluster, coming on like he thought he was some kind of general.

"Stuff it, Tully. I ain't no genius, but just how dumb do you think I am?"

Tully waited a little too long to say, "Huh? What do you mean?"

"That night you went chickenshit and run off to the river on us. I got to thinking about how you done that to me before. You ain't going to pull it on me this time, Tully. You ain't taking off with the spike and leaving old Smeds standing there with his thumb up his butt."

Tully started protesting his innocence of having entertained any such thoughts. Smeds watched Timmy Locan throw sticks. He ignored Tully. After a while he watched Fish approach from the direction of the town. The old man was carrying something over his shoulder. Smeds couldn't make out what it was. He hoped it was another of those dwarf deer like the old man had got a couple weeks back. That had been some good eating.

Timmy spotted Fish. He lost interest in his sticks, wandered over.

It wasn't a deer Fish had, it was some kind of bundle that clanked when he dropped it in front of the log. He said, "Smell's gone over there. Thought I'd poke around." He opened his bundle, which he had folded from a ragged blanket. "Those guys didn't take time out to loot when they went through over there."

Smeds gaped. There were pounds and pounds of coins, some of them even gold. There were rings and bracelets and earrings and broaches and necklaces and some of them boasted jewels. He'd never seen so much wealth in one place.

Fish said, "There's probably a lot more. I just picked up what was easy to find and quit when I had as much as I could carry."

Smeds looked at Tully. "And you wanted to cut out because the whole thing was a big bust."

Tully looked at the pile, awed. Then his expression became suspicious and Smeds knew he was wondering if Fish had hidden the best stuff where he could pick it up later. Typical Tully Stahl thinking, and stupid.

If Fish had wanted to hold out he would have just hidden the stuff and not said anything. Nobody would have known the difference. Nobody was interested in that town. Nobody even wanted to think about what happened there.

"What's this?" Fish asked, glancing from Tully to Smeds.

Smeds said, "He was whining about how the whole thing was a big damned bust and he was sick of it and wanted us to go home. But look here. Even if we don't have no luck with the tree we made out like bandits. I could live pretty good for a good long time on a share of this."

Fish looked from Tully to Smeds and back again. He said, "I see." And maybe he did. That old man wasn't anybody's fool. He said, "Timmy, you got a good eye for this kind of thing. Why don't you separate that out into equal lots?"

"Sure." Timmy sat down and ran his hands through the coins, laughing. "Anybody see anything he's just got to have?"

Nobody did.

Timmy *was* good. Not even Tully found any reason to complain about his divvying.

Fish said, "There's bound to be more over there. Not to mention a lot of steel that could be cleaned up and wholesaled if we brought a wagon up and carried it back."

After they squirreled their shares, Tully and Old Man Fish headed back to town. Smeds didn't want to go anywhere near the place but figured he had to go along to keep Tully honest. Timmy wouldn't go at all. He was happy building up the woodpile.

Looting the town made for a ten-day full-time job, what with having to clean up all the weapons and some other large items of value and then bundling them protectively and hiding them for later recovery. They came up with enough money and jewelry and small whatnots to make a heavy load for each of them.

Even Tully seemed pleased and content. For the moment.

One night, though, he said, "You know what bugs me? How come nobody else in the whole damned city of Oar ever got the same idea I did? I'd have bet my balls that after this long we'd be up to our asses in guys trying to glom on to that spike."

Old Man Fish grunted. "I've been wondering why no one's come to see what happened to the garrison."

Nobody had any ideas. The questions just sort of lay there like dead fish too ripe to be ignored and too big to shove out of the way.

Fish said, "I reckon it's time we torched her and seen if she's going to do it or not. That woodpile gets any bigger Timmy ain't going to be able to throw them that high."

Smeds realized he was reluctant to take the next step. Tully didn't seem too anxious, either. But Timmy had a grin on ear to ear. He was raring to go.

Tully leaned over and told Smeds, "Little dip did some torch work back in town. Likes to see things burn."

"We got a good day for it here," Fish said. "A nice breeze to whip up the fire. A hot, sunshiny day, which is when we know it's asleep the deepest. All we have to do is look in our pants and see if we got some balls, then go do it."

They looked at each other awhile. Finally, Smeds said, "All right," and got up. He collected the bundle of brush that would be his to throw. Fish and Timmy got theirs. Tully had to go along.

They lit the bundles off down in the bottom of the hole the monster dug, then jumped out and charged the mountain of sticks from the windward side. They heaved their bundles. Tully's, thrown too far away, fell short, but that did not matter.

They ran like hell, Smeds, Timmy, and Fish in straight lines, Tully zigging and zagging. The tree did not wake up before they'd all made the cover of the woods.

The fire had reached inferno proportions by then.

Random bolts of blue lightning flailed around. They did not come for long, though.

Smeds could feel the heat from where he crouched, watching. That was one bitch of a bonfire. But he was not impressed. What he was, mainly, was sad.

The fire burned the rest of the day. At midnight Timmy went to check it out and came back to say there was still a lot of live coals under the ash and he hadn't been able to get near it.

Next morning they all went to look. Smeds was astounded. The tree still stood. Its trunk was charred and its leaves were gone, but it still stood, the silver spike glittering wickedly at eye level. And it did not protest their presence, no matter how close they got.

That was not close enough. There was a lot of heat in the ash still. They hauled water from the river and splashed down a path. Timmy Locan volunteered to take the pry bar and go pull the spike.

"I can't believe it," Tully said as Timmy leaned on the bar and the tree didn't do anything about it. "I can't goddamned believe it! We're actually going to do it!"

Timmy grunted and strained and cussed and nothing happened. "This son of a bitch ain't going to come! Oh!"

It popped loose. Timmy grabbed at it as it sailed past, grabbing it left-handed for a second.

Then he screamed and dropped it. "Oh, shit, that bastard is hot." He came running, crying, and shoved his hand into the last bucket of water. His palm was mostly red and beginning to show patches of blister already.

Fish took a shovel and scooped the spike out of the ashes. "Look out, Timmy. I'm fixing to dump it in there."

"My hand . . ."

"Ain't good to do a bad burn that way. You head back to camp. I got some salve there that'll do you a whole lot better."

Timmy pulled his hand out. Fish dumped the spike. The water hissed and bubbled. Fish said, "You carry the bucket, Smeds."

Just as Tully said, "We better make tracks. I think its starting to wake up."

It was hard to tell against that sky, but it did look like there were tiny flecks of blue out on the ends of the smallest surviving twigs.

"The spike ain't conducting heat into the heartwood anymore," Fish said. "Scat," he told the backs of a lot of pumping legs and flailing elbows.

Smeds looked back just before he plunged into the woods. Just as the tree cut loose with a wild, undirected discharge. The flash nearly blinded him. Ash flew in clouds. The pain and disappointment and . . . sorrow? . . . of the tree touched him like a gentle, sad rain. He found tears streaking his face and guilt in his heart.

Old Man Fish puffed into camp one step ahead of Tully, who was embarrassed because the old-timer had outrun him. Fish said, "We got a lot of daylight left. I suggest we get the hell on the road. Timmy, let me look at that hand."

Smeds looked over Fish's shoulder. Timmy's hand looked awful. Fish didn't like the look of it either. He stared at it, grunted, frowned, studied it, grunted again. "Salve won't be good enough. I'm going to collect up some herbs for a poultice. Thing must have been hotter than I thought."

"Hurts like hell," Timmy said, eyes still watery.

"Poultice will take care of that. Smeds. When you get that spike out of the bucket don't touch it. Dump it on that old blanket. Then wrap it up. I don't think anybody ought to touch it."

"Why the hell not?" Tully asked.

"Because it burned Timmy badder than it should have. Because it's a bad mojo thing and maybe we shouldn't ought to take any chances."

Smeds did it the way Fish said, after the old man went hunting his herbs. After he dumped the bucket he moved the spike to a dry part of the blanket with a stick. "Hey! Tully! Check this. It's still hot even after it was in that water." Passing his hand above it he could feel the heat from a foot away.

Tully tried it. He looked troubled. "You better wrap it up good and tie it tight and put it right in the middle of your pack."

"Eh?" Tully didn't want to carry it himself? Didn't want it in his control every second? That was disturbing.

"You want to come give me a hand awhile here?" Tully asked. "I can't never get this pack together by myself."

Smeds finished bundling the spike, went over, knowing from his tone Tully had something he wanted to whisper.

As they stuffed and rolled and tied, Tully murmured, "I decided not to do it on the way back. We're still going to need them awhile. We'll do it later, in the city sometime."

Smeds nodded, not saying he wasn't going to do it at all, and was going to try his damnedest to see that Fish and Timmy and he himself got fair shares of the payoff for the spike.

He had a good idea what was going on inside Tully's head. Tully wasn't going to be satisfied with the big hit they'd made already. Tully was thinking Fish and Timmy made good mules. They could haul their shares back. Once they got to town he could take them away.

Smeds had a suspicion Tully wasn't going to be satisfied with a two-way split, either.

20

Our fire burned down till it wasn't nothing but some patches of red. Once in a while a little flame would shoot up and prance around for a few seconds, then die. I stared up at the stars. Most were ones I'd known all my life, but they had moved to funny parts of the night. The constellations were all askew.

It was a good night for shooting stars. I'd spotted seven already.

"Uncomfortable?" Raven asked. He was watching the sky, too.

He startled me. He hadn't said anything since back around lunchtime. We didn't talk much anymore.

"Scared." I had lost track of time. I had no idea how far we'd come or where we were, except that it was one goddamned long ways from home and down in the south.

"And wondering what the hell you're doing here, no doubt."

"No. I think I got a handle on that. My trouble is I don't like having to sneak everywhere, like a thief. I might get treated like one."

I did not add that I did not like being in places where the only person who could understand me was him. If something happened to him . . . That was what scared me the most.

It was too awful to think about.

I said, "But it's too late to turn back."

"Some say it's never too late."

So he was thinking about his kids again, now he was plenty safe from the risk of actually having to deal with them. Also, maybe, he was having second thoughts about our ride into the unknown.

Opaque as they were to me, and maybe even to him, powerful emotions were driving him. They had Darling's name hung all over them, though he never mentioned her. One monster of a guilt was perched on his shoulders, flapping and squawking and pecking at his eyes and ears. Somehow he was going to silence that beast by catching his pal Croaker and passing the word about what happened in the Barrowland.

It didn't make no sense to me. But people never do, a whole lot.

Maybe the determination was starting to wear thin. It was one thing to take off after a guy expecting to catch him in a few weeks and a few hundred miles and something else to be on the track still after months and months and thousands of miles. People aren't built to take that without any letup. The road can blunt the most iron will.

He let the edges of it show when he said, "Croaker's been gaining on us again. He doesn't have to be as careful as we do. We have to speed it up somehow. Else we're going to chase him all the way to the edge of the world and still never catch him."

Hell. He was talking to himself, not to me. Trying to find some enthusiasm he had misplaced somewhere back up the road. There wasn't no way we were going to kick up the pace any. Not without giving up any thought of watching out for trouble from the people in the countries we were going through.

We were pushing so hard now we were killing ourselves slowly.

I glimpsed something off to the north. "There. Did you see that? That's what I was telling you about the other day. Lightning from a clear sky."

He missed it. "Maybe it's storming up there."

"Just keep an eye peeled."

We watched a series of flashes so dim their source had to be way over the horizon. Usually that kind of lightning lights up or silhouettes the tops of clouds.

"There isn't one cloud," Raven said. "And we haven't seen one for weeks. And I'd bet we won't see any as long as we're crossing this steppe." He watched another flash go. He shivered. "I don't like it, Case. I don't like it at all."

"Yeah? What's up?"

"I don't know. Not exactly. But I got that tingle again, that bad feeling I got in Oar, that set me off on this crusade."

"The thing from the Barrowland?"

He shrugged. "Maybe. But that wouldn't make sense. If it was really who I thought it was, he ought to be busy taking over the empire and making himself safe from a few loose Taken who might still be hanging around."

I'd had some time now to do some thinking about what might have moved in the Barrowland and could have had so much impact on Raven. There was only one answer that fit, though it didn't seem likely. They had burned his body and scattered the ashes. But they hadn't been able to find his head.

"If it's the Limper we really might have trouble. Nothing he ever did made a whole lot of sense. Not to us mortals. He was always crazy as a loon."

He gave me a surprised look, then a soft smile. "No sawdust between your ears, is there, kid? All right. Put those brains to work trying to figure out why even a crazy wizard would be chasing us around the world. On the thousand-to-one that really is him raising a fuss up there."

I laid back and started watching for shooting stars again. I counted six more, not really thinking about the Limper because that wasn't an idea worth taking serious. Limper didn't have no love for Raven, but he sure didn't have a grudge big enough to go chasing him, neither. Crazy or not.

"Between a rock and a hard place." It sort of just slipped out.

"What?"

"Tighten up the buckles on your ego, brother Corvus. It ain't us he's after. If it's him."

"Eh?" His eyes tightened up into a suspicious squint. That made his cold, hawkish face look more predatory than ever. I had to go use that family name.

"He's after the same thing we are. The Black Company."

"That don't make sense either, Case."

"Hell it don't. It's the only way you can get it to make any sense at all. You're just not thinking about the world the way one of the Taken would. You got a pretty screwed-up eye, but you still think people is people. Them Taken don't and never did. To them people are just tools and slaves, live junk to use and throw away. Except for the one that was so powerful she made them *her* slaves. And she's riding with your buddy Croaker, far as we know. Right?"

The idea sank in. He turned it over, looked at the sharp edges, grunting and shaking like a dog shitting peach seeds. After a while, he said, "She's lost her powers but she hasn't lost what she knew. And that was knowledge enough to conquer half a world and tame the Ten Who Were Taken. She'd be one big prize for any wizard who could lay hands on her."

"There you go." I closed my eyes and tried to sleep. It took me a while.

The old man sat quietly. When he moved at all he did so slowly and carefully. His status was ambiguous. He had chased these people across a continent, damned near killing himself, and for what?

For nothing, that's what. For nothing.

They were lunatics. They ought to be locked up for their own protection.

The woman watched him from about twenty feet to his left. She was a blue-eyed, stringy-haired blonde about five feet six inches tall, in her middle twenties. She had a square jaw, a too broad, lumpy bottom, and a goofy manner that made you wonder if anybody was home behind those watery eyes. And for all that, there was something strongly sensual there.

She was deaf and mute. She could communicate only via sign language.

She was in charge. She was Darling, the White Rose, the one who had put an end to the Lady's dark dominion.

How the hell could that be? It didn't add up.

Off to his right was a man who watched him with the warmth of a snake. He was tall, lean, dusky, hard as a stone with less sense of humor. These days he dressed in black, which had to be a statement of some sort, but who could tell what? He would not talk. He flat refused. Which is why they called him Silent.

He was a wizard himself. The tools of his trade lay scattered around him. As though he expected their unwilling guest to try something.

Silent's eyes were as black as jet, hard as diamonds, and friendly as death.

Damn it! A man made one mistake and four hundred years later they still wouldn't let him live it down.

There were three more of them around somewhere, brothers with the surname Torque who seemed to have no given names. They went by absurdities like Paddlefoot, Donkey Dick, and Brother Bear, except that Donkey Dick became Stubby when Darling was in listening distance, even though she couldn't hear.

All four men worshiped her. And it was obvious to everyone but her that the one called Silent entertained romantic ambitions.

Lunatics. Every single one.

Something behind him yelled, "Seth Chalk! What treachery are you up to now?" and exploded in giggles.

Wearily, for the thousandth time, he replied, "Call me Bomanz. I haven't used Seth Chalk since I was a boy." He did not look around.

It had been a long, long time since he had been Seth Chalk. At least a hundred fifty years. He had no exact count. It was a year since he had escaped the thrall of a sorcery that had held him in stasis most of that time. He knew the intervening years of strife and horror—the years of the rise and growth of the Lady's empire—only by repute, after the fact.

He, Bomanz or Seth Chalk, was a living artifact from before the fact. A fool who had had no business surviving it, who wanted to use these last unexpected gift years to expiate the guilt that was his for his part in the awakening and release of the ancient evil.

These idiots were not ready to believe that, no matter that he'd damned near gotten himself killed keeping that dragon off them during the big final throat cutting in the Barrowland last winter.

Damned fools. He had done all the damage he could do in one lifetime.

The three brothers came from somewhere up forward, joined the watch. So it was not one of them who had shouted. But Bomanz knew that. Two of the three could not speak any language he understood. The third managed Forsberger so brokenly it was not worth his trouble to try.

The fool who could understand a little of Bomanz's antiquated Forsberger could not sign. Of course. So any communication not heard directly by Silent or lip-read by Darling got garbled and lost.

Only the stones communicated like regular people.

He did not like talking to rocks. There was something perverse about holding converse with rocks.

The trouble with being here was that the human beings, though lunatics, were the sanest, most believable part of the furnishings.

For the first time in his life, if he wanted to build cloud castles he had to go look down.

They had press-ganged him at that camp in the Windy Country. He was on the back of one of those fabulous monsters out of the Plain of Fear, a windwhale. The beast was a thousand feet long and nearly two hundred wide. From below it looked like a cross between a man-o'-war jellyfish and the world's biggest shark. From up top where Bomanz was, the broad flat back looked like something from an opium smoker's pipe dream. Like the imaginary forests that might grow in those vast caverns said to lie miles beneath the surface of the earth.

This forest was haunted by enough weird creatures to populate anyone's fancy nightmare. A whole zoo. And all sentient.

The windwhale was going somewhere in a hurry but was not getting there fast. There had been headwinds all the way. And every so often the monster had to go down and tear up a couple hundred acres to take the edge off its hunger.

The damned thing stank like seven zoos.

A couple weird characters had singled him out for relentless harassment. One was a little rock monkey, mostly tail, no bigger than a chipmunk. It had a high, squeaky, nagging voice that made him remember his long-dead wife, though he never understood a word it said.

There was a shy centauroid creature put together backward, with the humanlike part in the rear. That part of her was disturbingly attractive. She seemed intrigued by him. He kept catching glimpses of her watching him from among the copses of uncertain organs that bewhiskered the windwhale's back.

Worst, there was a lone talking buzzard who had a smattering of Forsberger and a wiseguy mouth. Bomanz could not get away from the bird, who, if he had been human, would have hung out in taverns masquerading as the world's foremost authority, armed with an uninformed and ready opinion on every conceivable subject. His cheerful bigotry and who-cares ignorance drove the old man's temper to its limit.

Things called mantas, that looked like sable flying versions of the rays of tropical seas, symbiotes of the windwhales, with wingspans of thirty to fifty feet, were the most dramatic and numerous of his nonhuman companions. Though they looked like fish, they seemed to be mammals. They lived their whole lives on the windwhale's back. They were ill-tempered and dangerous and they bitterly resented having to share their territory with lesser life-forms. Only the will of their god contained their spite.

There were dozens more creatures equally remarkable, each more absurd than the last, but they were more shy of humans and stayed out of the way.

Discounting the mantas, the most numerous and pestiferous tribe were the talking stones.

Like most people Bomanz had heard tales of the deadly talking menhirs of the Plain of Fear. The reality seemed as gruesome as the stories. They were as shy as an avalanche and deadly pranksters. They were responsible for the Plain's deadly reputation. Near as Bomanz could tell, what everyone else considered murderous wickedness they considered practical jokery.

What could be more hilarious than a traveler who, following false directions, stumbled into a lava pit or had his mount snatched out from under him by a giant sand lion?

The stones, in the form of menhirs as much as eighteen feet tall, were the stuff of a thousand stories, hardly a one pleasant. But the seeing and hearing and having to deal with was an experience that made the stories pall—though the stones were on their best behavior now.

They were under constraint, too.

The stones had no language difficulties. Happily, many were a laconic sort. But when they did go to talking their speech was sour, acidic, caustic. The lot were verbal vandals. So how the hell come they were the ones their god had made his diplomatic corps?

It was no wonder the Plain of Fear was a wide-open madhouse. The tree god running it was a twenty-four-karat lunatic.

The stones were gray brown, mostly, without visible orifices or organs. Most were as shaggy with mosses and lichens and bugs as any normal boulder that lay around keeping its mouth shut. They intimidated the hell out of Bomanz, who liked to pretend that he was not scared of any damned thing.

There were moments when he came close to blasting them into talking gravel.

Weird damned creatures!

Every hundred miles the windwhale dropped till its belly dragged. Members of every species, including the Torque brothers, would start singing a merry "Heigh-ho!" work song and would converge on whichever menhir had made itself most obnoxious recently. Hup-hup, over the side it would go, to the accompaniment of dire threats and foul curses. Those stones that pretended to senses of humor would yodel fearfully all the way to the ground.

Damnfool crazies.

No matter how the bleeding rocks fell, they always landed upright, catlike.

The show scared the crap out of the rare peasant unlucky enough to witness it.

The stones were the Plains creatures' and tree god's communications lifeline. They spoke to one another mind to mind—though Bomanz was not about to give them credit for true sentience. No one would tell him squat, but he suspected Old Father Tree himself was running this operation—whatever this operation was—from the nether end.

One of those little things he found disconcerting was the fact that no matter how many stones went over the side, the menhir population never diminished. In fact, some of the same old stones turned up back aboard.

Goddamned insanity.

"Hey, Seth Chalk, you sour old fart, you figure out how to screw us over yet? Gawh!"

The talking buzzard had come. Bomanz replied with a gentle, tricky gesture, consisting of wrapping his hand around the bird's neck. "Just you personally, carrion breath."

Eyes watched. Nobody moved. Nobody took it seriously. The Torque brothers whooped it up. "Way to go, old man!" Paddlefoot gobbled in his outlandish lingo. "Tie his goofy neck in a knot."

"Morons!" Bomanz muttered. "I'm surrounded by morons. At the mercy of cretins." Louder. "I'm going to tie your neck in a knot and braid your toes if you don't lay off the Seth Chalk and start calling me Bomanz."

He turned loose.

The buzzard flapped off squawking, "Chalk's on a rampage! Beware! Beware! Chalk's gone berserk."

"Oh, go to hell. Marooned with lunatics."

General laughter and foolery of a sort he had not seen since his student days. But Darling and Silent neither laughed nor stopped watching him. What the hell did he have to do to make them understand that he was on their side?

"Hah!" It hit him out of the blue. An epiphany. They did not distrust him because it was he whose bumbling had wakened the old evils and loosed them to walk the earth for another dark century. He had done his part in the rectification. No. They knew what had moved his researches in the first place. His quest for tools with which to gain power. His fathomless infatuation with the Lady, which had so distracted him he had made the mistakes that had allowed her to break her bonds.

They might believe he had been broken of his hunger for power, but would they ever believe he was free of his thing for that dark woman? How could he convince them when he had yet to convince himself? She had been a deadly candle to many a man's moth and the flame did not lose its attraction by being out of sight or out of reach.

He grunted, prized himself off his butt. His legs were stiff. He had been seated a long time. Darling and Silent watched him amble past a stand of something that looked like pink ferns ten feet tall. Little eyes peeped out warily. The ferns were some sort of organ. The mantas used them for an infant creche.

He went as far as his acrophobia let him. It was the first he had looked overboard in a week.

Last time they had been over water. He had been able to see nothing but haziness and blue all the way to undefined horizons.

The air was clearer today. The view was very nearly monochromatic again, but this time brown. Just a few hints of green flecked it. Way, way ahead there was something that looked like it might be smoke from a big fire.

They had to be two miles high. There was not a cloud in the sky.

"Soon you will have your chance to prove yourself, Seth Chalk."

He glanced back. A menhir stood four feet behind him. It had not been there a moment before. They were that way, coming and going without sound or warning. This one was a little more gray and mica-flecked than most. It had a scar down its face side six inches wide and seven feet long where something had scraped through lichen and weathered surface stone. Bomanz did not understand talking-stone civilization. They had no obvious hierarchy, yet this one generally spoke for them when there was official speaking to be done.

"How so?"

"Do you not feel it, wizard?"

"I feel a lot of things, rock. What I feel most of all is grumpy about the way you all have been doing me. What am I supposed to feel?"

"The mad psychic stink of the thing that you sensed escaping the Barrowland. From Oar. It is no farther away now."

The talking stones spoke in a dead monotone, usually, yet Bomanz sensed the taint of suspicion that lay in the menhir's mind. If he could tell the old evil was stirring from as far as Oar, when it was weak, how was it that he could not sense it now, when it was so much stronger?

How was it that he, too, was alive when he was supposed to be dead?

Did he know about the resurrection of the shadow because it had been one with his own? Had they conspired together and come out of the unhallowed earth of the Barrowland together? Was he a slave of that old darkness?

"It was not that that I sensed," Bomanz said. "I heard the scream of one of the old fetish alarms being tripped when something moved that should not have. That isn't the same thing at all."

The stone stood silent for a moment. "Perhaps not. Nevertheless, we are upon the thing. In hours, or a day or two, as the winds decide, the battle will be joined. Your fate may be determined."

Bomanz snorted. "A rock with a sense for the dramatic. It's absurd. You really expect me to fight that thing?"

"Yes."

"If it's what I think it is . . ."

"It is the thing called the Limper. And the thing known as Toadkiller Dog. Both are handicapped."

Bomanz sneered and snorted. "I'd call being without a body something more than a handicap."

"It is not weak, this thing. That smoke rises from a city still burning three days after its departure. It has become the disciple of death. Killing and destruction are all it knows. The tree has decreed that it be stopped."

"Right. Why? And why us?"

"Why? Because if it continues amok its course will someday bring it to the Plain. Why us? Because there is no one else. All who had any great power were consumed in the struggle in the Barrowland except thee and we. And, most of all, we do it because the god has commanded it."

Bomanz muttered and grumbled under his breath.

"Prepare yourself, wizard. The hour comes. If you are innocent in our eyes you must be guilty in his."

Of course. There could be no ground in the middle. Not for him. He did not have the strength to hold it. Never had had, if the truth be known, though he had deluded himself in the years of his quest for knowledge about those who had been enchained by the ancients.

Did he know remorse for the horror brought on by his fumblings? Some. Not as much as he thought he should. He told himself that because of his intercession at the penultimate moment, his self-sacrifice, the outbreak of darkness had been far gentler than it could have been. Without him the night might have lasted forever.

The old man ambled away from the stone, rapt in his own thoughts. He did not notice the stone turning jerkily, keeping its scarred face toward him. The menhirs never moved while being watched by human eyes. How they knew they were being watched no one knew.

Bomanz's meander took him to the aft end of the windwhale. Small rustlings accompanied him. Chaperons. If he noticed he ignored them. They had been with him always.

He settled upon a soft, unprotesting lump of whale flesh about chair height. It made comfortable sitting. But he knew he would not be staying long. The windwhale was especially fetid here.

For the hundredth time he contemplated escape. All he had to do was jump and use a levitator spell to soften his fall. That was well within his competence. But not within the compass of his courage.

His fear of heights was not totally debilitating. Should he fall, he would retain enough self-possession to save himself. But there was no way he could bring himself to take the plunge voluntarily.

Resigned, he looked back the way he had come. Home, such as it was and had been, lay a thousand miles away. Maybe a lot farther. They were passing over lands of which he had never heard, where all who saw it marveled at the great shape in the sky and had no idea what it was.

There was no guarantee he would step into friendly lands if he did go over the side. In fact, the terrain below looked actively hostile.

Hell with it. He had gotten himself into this. He would ride it out.

"Hunh!"

He was an old man but his eyes were plenty sharp.

The high, clean air allowed him to see a long way. And up north, at the edge of discernment when he looked at them a fraction of a point off directly, were two dots at an altitude even higher than that of the windwhale. To be visible at all at that distance they had to be the size of windwhales.

Bomanz snorted.

This monster was the vanguard of a parade.

He chuckled then. There were rustles nearby, the natives disturbed by his amusement. He chuckled again and rose. This time he strolled the length of the windwhale before he alighted again, as far forward as he dared go.

The smoke was much nearer. It rose higher than the windwhale. He saw hints of the fires that fed the column, which had begun to develop a bend in its trunk down lower. Grim. Maybe the rock was right. Something had to be done.

This was the dozenth such city, though the first they had come to still in its death throes. The progress of the insanity was an arrow pointing due south, a craziness that could make sense only to the crazy himself.

The windwhale began rumbling with internal flatulences. The horizon tilted, rose. Mantas piped and squealed behind Bomanz. He got a death grip on his seat.

The monster was headed down.

Why? It was not time to drop a menhir. It was not feeding time.

Mantas hurtled past in pairs and squadrons, spade-headed darts spreading across the sky, headed toward the city and its coronet of circling carrion birds.

"There is a good wind running a mile below us, wizard." Bomanz glanced back. His scar-faced stone friend. "If it holds we will overtake the destroyer shortly after nightfall. You have only that long to prepare."

Bomanz glanced around again. The stone was gone. But he was not alone. Darling and Silent had come to stare at the stricken city. The dark man's face was impassive but Darling's was a study in empathetic agony. That touched the soft-headed, softhearted side of the old man. He faced her, said, "We will put an end to the pain, child." He spoke carefully so she could read his lips.

She looked at Silent. Silent looked at her. Their fingers flew in the speech of the deaf. Bomanz caught part of the exchange. He was not pleased.

They were discussing him and Silent's remarks were not complimentary.

Bomanz cursed and spat. That bastard had it in for him for no damned reason.

The mantas decimated the carrion birds, used the updraft from the fires to soar high, then returned to the windwhale carrying a feast for their young. They settled down to nap.

But there was no real relaxation for anyone. The windwhale had dropped till it was only half a mile high. It passed the city, scudding along at twenty miles an hour. Soon the monster had to climb back into less vigorous air so as not to catch up before nightfall.

The scar-face stone returned when Bomanz was not looking. When he did notice it, he said, "I feel it now, rock. It reeks of corruption. And I still have no idea what I could do to hurt it."

"Worry not. There is a new decree from the god. You are not to reveal yourself except in extreme circumstance. Our attack will be exploratory, experimental, and admonitory only."

"What the hell? Why? Go for the kill, I say. Hit him with everything the one time he don't know we're coming. We'll never get a better shot."

"The god has spoken."

Bomanz argued. The god won.

The windwhale began shedding altitude at dusk. Soon after nightfall Bomanz spied the campfires of an army ahead. A pair of mantas took to the air to scout. They returned, reported whatever they reported. The windwhale slanted down toward the encampment, cutting a course that would rip through its heart.

Mantas poured off the windwhale's back, scrambled around and over one another in a search for updrafts.

Bomanz felt the old terror moving closer. It was restless but did not seem alert.

The ground came up and up. Bomanz clung to his seat and awaited certain impact, now unconcerned by the insult inplicit in the fact that a dozen menhirs had moved into position around him and Darling, and her thugs were spread out, ready for trouble.

The windwhale leveled out. Campfires slid out of sight beneath it. The screaming down there was almost inaudible because of the creak and rumble and intervening bulk of the giant of the sky. Bomanz felt the shock of the old evil, caught completely unprepared. It went into a pure black rage.

Just as it began to respond mantas swooped in from every direction. They cut the heart out of the night with the glare of the lightnings they discharged from the store in their flesh. Bolts stabbed around by the hundred, keeping the old horror so busy guarding himself he had no chance to counterattack.

The windwhale dumped tons of ballast and began a slow ascent, struggling to gain altitude against the weight of plunder.

Bomanz could not see the monster's underside and was glad. Its tentacles would be grasping men and animals and anything else it considered edible. It was an intelligent beast but it did not exempt other intelligences from its food supply if they were its enemies.

Many of the Plain races ate their enemies.

Bomanz found the idea repugnant in practice, yet it had a certain moral allure. How vigorously would men prosecute their wars if they had to eat those who fell before their swords?

Interesting. But how to impose the requirement?

The mantas began returning. Near as the old man could tell, they were very pleased with themselves.

It was over. The windwhale was up and safely away and now preoccupied with its digestion. Bomanz rose. Time to turn in.

As he passed Darling, Silent, and the scarred menhir, he said, "Next time the bear is going to bite back. You should have stuck him while you had him."

The "bear" was stunned, numb, immobile within the desolation of his camp, desperately trying to grasp the sense of his sudden misfortune.

His entire existence was a headlong assault upon adversity. Having something go sour was never a surprise. But a disaster of these proportions, with its implication of vast, previously unconsidered forces in motion, had for the moment obliterated his initiative. He lacked even his usual insane volition driven by the engine of rage.

The beast Toadkiller Dog was less stricken. Its memories of the son of the tree were fresh. It had not deceived itself when it came to that sprig's connection with its sire. It had been but a matter of time till Old Father Tree showed an interest.

Toadkiller Dog had been to the Plain of Fear. He had come face-to-face with the god. His memories of the confrontation were not sweet. He had been lucky to escape.

But that had been a profitable adventure. He had seen the Plain firsthand. Now what he knew might become a useful tool. If the wicker man would listen.

Unlikely.

It was not now the half-rational thing that had been the Limper before. It had become so self-centered, so self-involved, as to be the hub of a solipsistic universe.

The beast prowled the camp, past men and the remains of men. Shock lay upon the survivors like a smothering quilt. Only a few understood what had happened. He heard mutterings about the wrath of the gods. Those men did not know how truly they spoke.

It would be hard to hold them together if that theory gained credence. Problems of conscience were endemic already.

There was a faint hiss, a crack, and a blinding flash. The beast's fur stood straight out. Little blue sparks pranced and crackled amidst it, though the bolt had missed.

Soldiers scurried around like hens in a panic.

That sniper had attained a tremendous speed, falling from several miles high. It came and went too quickly for any response. Even in daylight there would have been little chance to get it.

Flash. *Crack!* Screams. A man pranced in a shroud of will-o'-the-wisp fire.

So there it was. Having made its presence known, the windwhale was embarking on a program of terrorism and attrition that would not stop till the wicker man proved he could stop it.

Toadkiller Dog snarled at the wicker man till the glaze left his rheumy eyes and he nodded once, sharply. He began to shake so hard he creaked and squeaked. He was trying to control his rage.

To yield might prove fatal.

One of those bolts, accurately delivered, could destroy his toy body, leaving him next to powerless, his army at the mercy of the monster above. Somewhere out there, planing around the camp, were mantas watching for a chance at the quick kill missed during the surprise attack.

The shaking faded. In a controlled whisper the wicker man said, "Kill those campfires. They light us as targets." Then he began the slow, painful process of surrounding himself with spells against the mantas' bolts.

Toadkiller Dog limped around, snapping and growling to make the soldiers hurry.

Dousing the fires did not help. The mantas came in all night. Their accuracy did not decrease. Neither did it improve.

The things seemed more interested in harassment than killing. In keeping everyone awake and frightened of the moment the next blow would fall. It was a weakling's way to fight. Though no tears fell from the sky when a bolt did splatter a soldier.

The minions of the tree god were trying to panic and disperse the Limper's army. That puzzled Toadkiller Dog. They were not that tender of heart.

Men slipped away by twos and threes.

He galloped as fast as he could on three real legs and a wooden one, yelping and nipping and driving them back, and in interim moments trying to get a feel for that monster in the sky. Some of the deserters objected to his bullying. He had to kill a dozen before everybody got their minds right.

Something familiar about a few of the lesser life sparks up there.

The beast sensed the wicker man's summons. He trotted over. Spells now enfolded the wicker man in layers of protection. Pain leaked out.

Toadkiller Dog was amused. The more surely the old shadow guarded himself, the greater was his pain. To make himself absolutely safe the Limper would have to subject himself to an agony that would rob him of all reason, to the point where he might not be able to get back out from behind the layered defense.

The beast wondered if they knew that up there.

The wicker man knew the answer. "The one they call the White Rose is riding the windwhale, shaping their tactics."

Toadkiller Dog woofed in exasperation. The White Rose! Soft of heart but bitterly lethal of maneuver. It all fell into place. She had locked them into no-win positions already. Without doing her conscience an injury. The Limper could suffer protecting himself or ease the pain and get blown off his withy steed. They could watch their army evaporate through desertion or terrorize the men into staying and have them mutiny.

And, from what he recalled of the White Rose, there would be a third and subtler option, which she would push them toward. But she could not comprehend the kind of murderous obsession driving the Limper. She would leave opportunities and openings. She would give second chances when the only workable choice would be to go for the throat.

It was a night when hell was in session. No one rested. The Limper hid so deeply in his defenses he could do nothing to stay the harassment. The pace of the attacks increased as dawn neared, as though the White Rose wanted them to know she could make their day more horrible than had been their night.

The army was half-gone when the sun rose. The tree god had won the first round.

His creatures refused a second round by day. The mantas cleared the sky. The windwhale floated miles up and miles to the south. The Limper collected his ragtag horde and began marching toward his next conquest.

The time of easy killing was over. Now those who stood in the Limper's path were warned of his coming. Always that monster out of the Plain of Fear hung overheard, a sword of doom ready to fall at the slightest lapse in attention.

The White Rose made no mistakes. Whenever the Limper launched an attack the mantas came fast and hard, trying to force him to cower inside his spells of protection. He fought back, brought a few down. Increasingly, he held back in hopes the windwhale would stray too close. He looked for new weapons in the ruins of his conquests.

The White Rose made no mistakes. Not once. But the maniacal determination of the Limper kept his army moving, gaining on his quarry. Till he gained his revenge, even the enmity of the tree god was just an annoyance, the whine of a mosquito.

But after the kill . . . Oh, after the kill!

S meds said, "There's something wrong."
  "I'm beginning to get your drift," Tully said. "You think there's something wrong." Smeds had said so five times. "So does Timmy." Timmy had agreed with Smeds three or four times.

"They're right," Fish said, venturing an opinion for the first time. "There should be more industry. Carts on the road. Hunters and trappers." They were out of the Great Forest but had not yet reached cultivated country. In these parts the tide of civilization was on the ebb.

"Look there," Timmy said. He pointed, winced. His hand still hurt him.

A burnt-out cottage lay a little off the road. Smeds recalled pigs and sheep and wisecracks about the smell when they had been headed north. There was no smell now. Fish lengthened his stride, going to investigate. Smeds kept up with him.

It was grisly, though the disaster lay far enough in the past that the site was no longer as gruesome as it had been. The bones bothered Smeds the most. There were thousands, scattered, broken, gnawed, mixed.

Fish examined them in silence, moving around slowly, stirring them with the tip of his staff. After a while he stopped, leaned on his staff, stared down. Smeds moved no closer. He had a feeling he did not want to see what Fish saw.

The old man settled onto his haunches slowly, as though his own bones ached. He caught hold of something, held it up for Smeds.

A child's skull. Its top had been smashed in.

Smeds was no stranger to death, even violent death, and this was old death for someone he'd never known. It should have bothered him no more than a rumor from the past. But his stomach tightened and his heartbeat quickened. He felt a surge of anger and unfixed hatred.

"Even the babies?" he muttered. "They even murdered the babies?"

Fish grunted.

Tully and Timmy arrived. Tully looked bored. The only death that concerned him was the one awaiting him personally. Timmy looked unhappy, though. He said, "They killed the animals, too. That doesn't make sense. What were they after?"

Fish muttered, "They killed for the sake of the blood. For the pleasure of the deed, the joy in the power to destroy. For the pure meanness of it. We know too many like that already."

Smeds asked, "You think it was the same bunch that killed everybody back up there?"

"Seems likely, don't it?"

"Yeah."

Tully grumbled, "We going to hang around here all day? Or are we going to get hiking? Smeds, you decided you like it out here with the bugs and furry little things? Me, I want to get back and start enjoying life."

Smeds thought about wine and girls and the scarcity of both in the Great Forest. "You got a point, Tully. Even if five minutes ain't going to make any difference."

Fish said, "I wouldn't go living too high too sudden, boys. Might set some folks to wondering how you got it and maybe some hard guys to figuring how to get it away from you."

"Shit," Tully grumbled. "Quit your damned preaching. And maybe give me credit for a little sense."

He and Fish went off, Tully grousing and Fish listening unperturbed, with a patience Smeds found astounding. He was ready to strangle Tully himself. Once they hit the city he didn't want to see his cousin for a month. Or longer.

"How's the hand, Timmy?"

"Don't seem like it's getting any better. I don't know about burns. You? My skin's got black spots where it was the worst."

"I don't know. I saw a guy once burned so it looked like charcoal." Smeds hunched up a little, imagining the heat of the spike in his pack burning between his shoulder blades. "We get to town, you go see a doc or a wizard. Don't fool around. Hear?"

"You kidding? The way this hurts? I'd run if I didn't have to carry this damned pack."

The road was festooned with old butcheries and destructions. But the disaster had not been complete. Nearer the city there were people in the fields, and more and more as the miles passed, backs bowed with the weight of tragedies old and new.

Man is born to sorrow and despair. . . . Smeds shuddered his way out of that. *Him* wallowing in philosophical bullshit?

They crested a rise, saw the city. The wall was covered with scaffolding. Despite the late hour, men were rebuilding it. Soldiers in gray supervised. Imperials.

"Gray boys," Tully grumbled. "Here comes trouble."

"I doubt it," Fish said.

"How come?"

"There'd be more of them if they were looking for trouble. They're just making sure the repairs get done right."

Tully harrumphed and scowled and muttered to himself but did not argue. He had overlooked the obvious. Imperials were sticklers for getting things done right, obsessive about keeping military works in repair.

The only delay was occasioned by the construction, not by the soldiers. Tully was not pleased. He was sick of Fish looking smarter than him. Smeds was afraid he would start improvising, trying to do something about that. Something stupid, probably.

"Holy shit," Smeds said, soft as a prayer, half a dozen times, as they walked through the city. Buildings were being demolished, rehabilitated, or built where old structures had been razed. "They really tore the old town a new asshole."

Which left him uncomfortable. There were people he wanted to see. Were they still alive, even?

Wonderstruck, Tully said, "I never seen so many soldiers. Least not since I was a kid." They were everywhere, helping with reconstruction, supervising, policing, billeted in tents pitched where buildings had been razed. Was the whole damned city inundated with troops?

Smeds saw standards, uniforms, and unit emblems he'd never seen before. "Something going on here," he said. "We better be careful." He indicated a hanged man dangling from a roof tree three stories up.

"Martial law," Fish said. "Means the wise guys are upset. You're right, Smeds. We walk real careful till we find out what's going on and why."

They headed for the place Tully stayed first, it being closest. It was not there anymore. Tully was not distressed. "I'll just stay with you till I get set," he told Smeds.

But Smeds had not paid any rent, so they had thrown his junk into the street for scavengers—after cashing in his empties and stealing what they wanted for themselves—then had let the room to people dispossessed by the disaster.

Fish's place had gone the way of Tully's. The old man was not surprised. He said nothing. He did look a little more gaunt and haggard and slumped.

"So maybe we can all stuff in at my old lady's place," Timmy said. He was jittery. Smeds figured it was his hand. "Just for tonight. My old man, he don't like anybody I hang around with."

Timmy's parents owned the place they lived, though they were as poor as anybody else on the North Side. Smeds had heard they got it as a payoff from the gray boys for informing back in the days when there was still a lot of Rebel activity in Oar. Timmy would not say. Maybe it was true.

Who cared anymore? They'd probably been on the right side. The imperials were more honest, and better governors, if you were at a social level where who was in charge made any difference.

Smeds did not give a rat's ass who ran things as long as they left him alone. Most people felt that way.

"Timmy! Timmy Locan!"

They stopped, waited while an older woman overhauled them. As she waddled up, Timmy said, "Mrs. Cisco. How are you?"

"We thought you were dead with the rest of them, Timmy. Forty thousand people they killed that night. . . ."

"I was out of the city, Mrs. Cisco. I just got back."

"You haven't been home yet?"

People jostled them in the narrow street. It was three-quarters dark but there were so many soldiers around nobody needed to run inside to hide from the night. Smeds wondered what the bad boys were doing. Working?

"I said I just got in."

Smeds saw he did not like the woman much.

She went all sad and consoling. Even Smeds, who did not consider himself perceptive, saw she was just busting because she was going to get to be the first to pass along some bad news.

"Your dad and both your brothers . . . I'm sorry. They were trying to help fight the fires. Your mother and sister . . . Well, they were conquerors. They did what conquerors always do. Your sister, they mutilated her so bad she ended up killing herself a couple weeks ago."

Timmy shook like he was about to go into convulsions.

"That's enough, madam," Fish said. "You've buried your blade to the heart."

She sputtered, "Why, the nerve . . ."

Tully said, "Piss off, bitch. Before I kick your ass up around your ears." He used that gentle, even tone Smeds knew meant maximum danger.

So. Cousin Tully had a little canker of humanity hidden away after all. Though he would not admit it on the rack.

"I can't handle this," Timmy said. "I think I better stay dead."

Fish said, "That woman won't let you rest in peace, Timmy."

"I know. I'll do what I got to do. But not now. I know a place called the Skull and Crossbones where we can put up cheap. If it's still there."

It was there. It was a place the invaders would have ignored as too contemptible to burn. It made Smeds think of a hooker still working twenty years past her prime, pathetic and desperate.

An imperial corporal sat in a chair out front, leaning back against a wooden wall that had forgotten the meaning of paint. He held a bucket of beer in his lap. He seemed to be napping. But when they were a few steps from the door he opened his eyes, checked them over, nodded, took a drink.

"Catch his emblem?" Smeds asked Fish inside.

"Yes. Nightstalkers."

The Nightstalker Brigade was *the* crack outfit in the northern army, rigorously trained for night operations and combat under wizard's war conditions.

Smeds said, "I thought they were out east somewhere, trying to finish the Black Company." The proudest honor on the standard of the Nightstalkers was their defeat of the Black Company at Queen's Bridge. Before Queen's Bridge those mercenaries had been so glibly invincible that half the empire had been convinced the gods themselves were on their side.

"They're here now."

"What the hell is going on around here?"

"Guess we better find out. What we don't know could eat us up."

Timmy talked to the owner, whom he knew slightly. The man claimed he was full up with the dispossessed. None of those guests were evident. He hinted he might find space, though, if fate took a hand. Fishing for a bribe, Smeds figured. Which he would follow with a deep gouge.

"How much leverage on fate are we talking?" Timmy asked.

"Obol and a half. Each."

"You goddamned thief!"

"Take it or leave it."

The Nightstalker corporal stepped past Smeds and Timmy and plunked his bucket down in front of the landlord, who had gone as pale as death. "That's twice today, dogmeat. And this time I heard it myself."

The landlord gulped air, grabbed the bucket, and started to fill it.

"Don't try," the corporal said. "Offer me a bribe and you'll stay on the labor gang forever." He eyed Timmy and Smeds. "You guys pick yourself a room. On old Shit for Brains here for a night."

"I was just joshing with the guys, Corporal."

"Sure. I could tell. You had them rolling around on the floor. Bet you'll have the guy in the black mask in stitches. He loves you comedians."

Smeds asked, "What's going on around here, Corporal? We've been out of town."

"I could tell. I guess you can see your basic situation. Some bandits and deserters tore the place up. They wasn't too happy about that, down to the Tower. Since we was in the neighborhood we was one of the outfits got to come in and keep order. The brigadier, she started out life in the slums of Nihil, she figures here's a chance to get even with the kinds of assholes who made life hell when she was a kid. So you got thieves hanging from the roof trees. You got your pimps and priests and pushers, your sharpers and your fences and your whores won't learn no better working on the labor gangs eighteen hours a day so your regular citizens can get on with putting their lives back together.

"You ask me, she's too damned lenient. Gives them too many chances. Shithead here, the famous profiteer, he's done used up two of his shots now. First time he got paraded through the streets with a sign around his neck and got a week on the labor gang. This time he gets thirty lashes and two weeks. Because he's got all that shit between his ears and ain't going to learn dick about how he can't get away with it, next time they're going to drag him over to Mayfield Square and stick a spear up his butt and let him sit on it till he rots."

The corporal took a long drink from his refilled bucket, wiped his mouth on his sleeve, grinned. "Brigadier says let the punishment fit the crime." He took another long drink, looked at the landlord. "You ready to go do it, asshole?"

As he was about to follow the landlord into the street, the corporal paused. "I reckon you boys will be fair to your host, here, and treat his place right. 'Less you're looking for careers in construction." He grinned again and went.

"God damn!" Tully said.

"Yeah," Smeds agreed.

Fish said, "I have a feeling we're not going to be comfortable in this new Oar."

"Not for long," Smeds said. "But sufficient unto the day. Right now I need to get drunk, get laid, get a night's sleep somewheres besides on the ground."

"Not necessarily in that order," Tully said.

Timmy put on a strained smile. "A bath wouldn't hurt anything, either."

"Let's get doing what we got to do."

We come over this hill after what seemed like forever without seeing people and there across a valley was this walled place that covered maybe a hundred acres. The wall wasn't much. It was maybe eight or ten feet high and no thicker than the kind of stone walls cotters put around their sheepfolds.

"Looks like a religious retreat," Raven said. "No banners or soldiers or anything."

He was right. We'd seen places with the same look before, but never so big. "Looks old."

"Yes. It has a feel to it, too. Peaceful. Let's go look."

"Don't look like a place Croaker would pass up, eh?"

"No. He has a bad case of the curiosities. Let's hope he hung around long enough to let us gain some ground."

We went over and found out our guesses were right. Raven got his wish. The place was a monastery called the Temple of Traveler's Repose and was a kind of warehouse for knowledge. It had been sitting there soaking it up for a couple thousand years.

We found out the guys we were chasing had stayed long enough to teach one of the monks a little Jewel Cities dialect. In fact, they'd only left that very morning.

Raven got all excited. He wanted to head right on out and the hell with the sun was going to hit the horizon in another hour. I wanted to hit him over the head and slow him down. That monastery looked like a damned good place to take a day off and get human again.

"Look here, Case," he cajoled, "they'll be making camp by now, right? Traveling with a wagon and a coach the best they could've done is twenty-five miles. Right? We go all night we can grab off twenty of that, easy." He learned that about the wagon and coach from the priest.

"And then we die. You maybe never need a rest, but I need a rest and the horses need a rest and this looks like the perfect place to do it. Hell, look at the name."

He made exasperated noises. After all this time I still didn't understand that catching Croaker was the most important thing in the world. He was so damned tired himself his thinking was as screwy as a possum's.

He wasn't the only one running shy of a full load. That priest came down with both feet solid on Raven's side.

Raven grinned when he said, "He claims the omens are so bad they aren't letting anybody onto the grounds. They're even chasing people out."

I had enough of the lingo, learned from Raven, to have gotten part of that. Also something about "the bad storm coming down from the north." I saw I wasn't going to win this round neither, so I said the hell with it and added a few comments that would have disappointed my old potato-digging mother. I went and shared my misery with the horses. They understood me.

Raven worked a deal for some supplies and we headed out. I wondered how much farther to the edge of the world. We'd already come farther than I'd ever believed possible.

We didn't talk much. Not because I had the sulks. I'd given up on them and went fatalistic a long time ago. I think Raven was brooding about that bit I'd caught that he hadn't mentioned. A bad storm coming down from the north.

In the Jewel Cities lingo "bad" can mean a couple three different things. Including "evil."

There was barely any light left when we came to a strip of woods. "Going to have to walk this part," Raven said. "That priest said the road through is good enough, but it's going to be hard to follow in the dark."

I grunted. I wasn't thinking about the woods. My mind was on the funny-looking hills on the other side. I'd never seen anything like them. They were all steep-sided, smoothly rounded, covered with a tawny dry grass and nothing else. They looked like the humped backs of giant animals snoozing with their legs tucked up underneath them and their heads turned around behind them, out of sight.

They were very dry, those hills. The light to see them hadn't never been good, but I was sure I'd seen a few black burn scars before it got too dark to see anything.

The woods were bone-dry, too. The trees were mostly some kind of scruffy oak with small, brittle leaves that had points almost as sharp as holly leaves. They were a sort of blue-gray color instead of the deep green of oaks in the north.

A feeble excuse for a creek dribbled through the heart of the wood. We watered ourselves and the horses and took time out for a snack. I was too tired to waste energy talking, except to say, "I don't think I got what it takes for another fifteen miles. Uphill."

Half a minute later he surprised me by saying. "Don't know if I got what it takes, either. Only so far you can go on willpower."

"Hip bothering you?"

"Yes."

"Might ought to have it looked at."

"Good job for Croaker, since he done it. Let's see how much we got left."

We managed about six more miles, the last couple up the dry grass hills, before we sort of collapsed by silent agreement. Raven said, "This time we'll give it an hour before we hit it again."

He was stubborn, that bastard.

We hadn't been there five minutes before I spotted evidence of that bad storm from the north. "Raven."

He looked. He didn't have nothing to say. He just sighed and helped me watch the lightning.

There wasn't a cloud between us and the stars.

25

Toadkiller Dog, carrying the wicker man, eased over a ridge line, halted. He shivered.

For leagues now they had sensed the presence of that place over there, an aura ever increasing in intensity and its ability to irritate. If they were sons of the shadow this was a fastness of the enemy, a citadel of light. There were few such places left.

They had to be expunged when found.

"Strange magic," the wicker man whispered. "I don't like it." He glanced at the northern sky. The creatures of the tree god were up there somewhere, just beyond sight.

This was not a good place to be, sandwiched between them and that place. The wicker man said, "We'd better do it fast."

Toadkiller Dog had no desire to do it at all. He would bypass, given a choice.

He had choices, of course, but not many. He might get away with defying the wicker man once. That once had to be saved. In the meantime he responded to the ego of the wicker man, doing the insane, the stupid, sometimes the necessary, biding his time.

The army presently numbered two thousand. The men had collapsed in exhaustion the moment their commanders stopped moving. The wicker man summoned two to help him dismount.

They were rich men, every one. Their packs bulged with the finest treasure taken from cities their masters had devoured and from fallen comrades. Few had been with the army more than two months. Of the two thousand only a hundred had crossed the sea with the Limper. Those who did not desert had no cause to be optimistic about a long life.

The wicker man leaned against Toadkiller Dog. "Scum," he whispered. "All scum."

Close. Most with any spark of courage or decency deserted quickly.

The wicker man eyed the sky. A faint smile stretched the ruin of his mouth. "Do it," he said.

The soldiers groaned and grumbled as they stood to arms, but stand to they did. The wicker man stared at the temple. It abused his confidence, but he could not discern any concrete cause. "Go!" He slapped Toadkiller Dog's shoulder. "Scout it, damn you!"

He then assembled the surviving witchmen from the northern forest. They had not been much use lately, but he had a task for them now.

There wasn't a breath of warning. One moment the night was still except for the chirp of crickets and the uneasy rustle of men on the brink of an assault, the next it was alive with attacking mantas. They came from every direction, not fifty feet high, in twos and threes, and this time their lightning was not their most important weapon.

The first flights ghosted in and dropped fleshy sausage-shaped objects four feet long. Boiling, oily flame splashed everywhere. Toadkiller Dog howled in the heart of an accurately delivered barrage. Soldiers shrieked. Horses screamed and bolted. Baggage wagons caught fire.

The wicker man would have screamed in rage had he been able. But had he had the capability, he would not have had the time.

He had begun preparing a snare. And while he had concentrated on that they had caught him flat-footed.

He was enveloped in flame. He dared not think of anything else.

He suffered badly before he shielded himself with a chrysalis of protective spells. He was sprawled on the earth then, his wicker body charred and broken. His pain was terrible and his rage more so.

Bladders continued to fall. Mantas that had dumped theirs returned with their lightning. The wicker man extended his charm to include a pair of shamans. One struggled to lift the wicker man's battered frame. The other found the tag ends of the Limper's charm and began to weave it stronger.

The remnant of the wicker man waved a blackened arm.

A manta tumbled from the night, little lightning bolts popping and snapping around it.

The wicker man waved again.

Toadkiller Dog charged the temple. Most of the men followed. A quick, successful assault would mean shelter from the horror in the sky.

That horror pursued them. The air above the Limper had become too dangerous.

Fire bladders fell and blossomed orange, finishing the baggage and supplies. Safe now, the wicker man forgot the fires. He chained his anger. He returned to his interrupted task.

As Toadkiller Dog neared the monastery wall something reached out and flicked him away the way a man flicks a bug. Soldiers tumbled around him.

There would be no shelter from the devils in the sky.

Yet a few men did keep going, their progress unimpeded. Why?

The mantas came down on rippling wings. Toadkiller Dog hurled himself into the air. His jaws closed on dark flesh.

The wicker man murmured while the two shamans recovered something from the smoldering remains of a wagon. He beamed at them, oblivious to the surrounding holocaust.

The thing they brought him was an obsidian serpent, arrow-straight, ten feet long and six inches thick. The detail was astonishingly fine. Its ruby eyes blazed as they reflected the fires. The witch doctors staggered under its weight. One cursed the heat still trapped in it.

The wicker man smiled his terrible smile. He began singing a dark song in a breathless whisper.

The obsidian serpent began to change.

Life flowed through it. It twitched. Wings unfolded, long wings of darkness that cast shadows where no shadows should have been. Red eyes flared like windows suddenly opened on the hottest forges of hell. Glossy talons, like obsidian knives, slashed at the air. A terrible screech ripped from a mouth filled with sharp, dark teeth. The thing's breath glowed, faded. It began trying to break away, its gaze fixed on the nearest fire.

The wicker man nodded. The shamans released it. The thing flapped shadow wings and plunged into the fire. It wallowed like a hog in mud. The wicker man beamed approval. His lips kept forming words.

That fire faded, consumed.

The thing leaped to another. Then to another.

The wicker man indulged it for several minutes. Then the tenor of his whisper changed. It became demanding, commanding. The thing shrieked a protest. A fiery haze belched from its mouth. Still screaming, it rose into the night, following orders.

The wicker man turned his attention to the Temple of Traveler's Repose. It was time to see by what sorcery the place kept itself inviolate.

The shamans took hold and carried him toward the temple wall.

26

Bomanz's knuckles were white. They ached. He had a death grip on some windwhale organ. The monster had dropped low enough that the flash and fire and chaos down below gave him a clear perspective of just how far he was going to fall if he relaxed his grip for an instant. Silent and Darling were close by, watching. One false move and Silent would give him a kick in the butt and a chance to see if he could fly.

It was testing time. The White Rose had orders to stop the old horror here, where there might be help from its victims. This time she had woven him into her plan.

In fact, he had the feeling he *was* the plan.

She had not explained anything. Maybe she was playing woman of mystery. Or maybe she really did not trust him.

He was in charge—till he did something unacceptable and bit a boot with his butt on his way to doing a swan dive into hell.

Menhirs seldom got any feeling into their speech. But the one that materialized behind his left shoulder managed sorrow as it reported, "He's shielded himself. Neither fire nor lightning can reach him."

The surprise had seemed a wan hope, anyway, but a long shot worth trying. "And his followers?"

"Decimated again. The monster is unconquerable, though. He suffers, but pain just makes him angrier."

"He's not invincible at all. As you will see if I get close to him."

Bomanz's least favorite talking buzzard cackled wildly. "You're big-timer, eh? Ha! That thing is gonna squish you like a bug, Seth Chalk."

Bomanz turned away from the bird. His stomach flopped as he looked down again. The buzzard was determined to get his goat. He was amused by the bird's optimism. He had learned self-control in a hard school. He had been married for thirty years.

"Isn't it time you stones made your move?" He tried a disarming smile, a man with nothing on his mind but the issue at hand.

A little scheme had begun to fester in the back of his head. A way to put that snide vulture in his place.

The stone said, "Soon. What will you contribute to the farce?"

Before he could temporize the buzzard shrieked, "What the hell is that?"

Bomanz whirled. That damned bird wasn't scared of anything, but it was squeaky with fear now.

Vast dark wings spanned the night, masking the moon and stars. Fires animated wise and evil eyes. Another limned huge needle teeth. Those malignant eyes were fixed on those who rode the windwhale.

Silent made frantic warding signs that did no good.

Bomanz did not recognize the thing. It was nothing of the Domination, brought out of the Barrowland. He was an expert on those and believed he knew every rag and feather and bone that had gone into them. Neither was it something of the Lady's empire or she would have made it her own thing during her heyday. So it had to be loot from one of the cities desolated since the Limper had come out of the empire.

Whatever its provenance, it was dangerous. Bomanz began putting himself into that trance from which it was easiest for him to meet a supernatural challenge.

As he opened himself to the energies of another level of reality, fear struck.

"Get on to the next phase!" he shouted at the scarred menhir. "Now! Recall the mantas! Get everybody off this damned thing!"

Fire-edged wings beat the night. The red-eyed thing streaked toward the windwhale.

Bomanz used the strongest warding spell he knew.

The monster tortured the night with its shriek of pain. But it came on, its path deflected only slightly. The windwhale shuddered to its impact.

All across the windwhale's back talking menhirs began vanishing, leaving baby thunderclaps.

The talking buzzard cursed like a stevedore and flailed at the air. Young mantas screeched in fear. The Torque brothers rushed Bomanz, shouting questions he did not understand. They were going to throw him off.

Darling stopped them with a gesture.

Below, the windwhale's belly opened and gave birth to a boiling globule of fire. Heat rolled up its flanks. A huge shudder ran its length. Bomanz's knuckles grew whiter. He wanted to move back but his hands had a will of their own and would not turn loose.

Another explosion tore the windwhale's belly. The great sky beast dropped a short distance. Upset became panic. "We're going down!" one of the Torques shouted in his barbaric eastern gabble. "Oh, gods, we're going down!"

Darling caught Bomanz's eye and in peremptory sign language ordered, "Do something!" She was not rattled.

Before he could respond the air filled with icy water spraying from organs on the leviathan's back. Despite the departure of the menhirs the windwhale had begun to lose buoyancy. It was shedding ballast high, hoping that would dampen the fires.

The chill water helped stifle the panic.

Mantas began coming in out of the night, fluttering into the spray. The instant they came to rest their young scrambled onto their backs, followed by other Plains creatures. Once a manta had all the weight it could bear, it flopped to one of the slippery, downsloping launch slides that allowed them to hurtle into space.

Another explosion shook the windwhale. It began a slow buckle in the middle.

Darling approached Bomanz. She looked like she would put him over the side personally if he did not start doing something more than gawk and shake.

How could she stay so damned calm? They were going to die in a few minutes.

He closed his eyes and concentrated on the author of the disaster. He tried to pump himself up.

He did not know what that thing was but he would not let it intimidate him. He was the Bomanz who had slain a grandfather of dragons. He was the Bomanz who had walked into the flames, daring the wrath of the Lady in all her majesty and strength.

But his feet had rested upon solid ground those times.

Softly, surely, he murmured the calming mantras, following with the unleashing cycles that would allow him to slide free of his flesh.

In a moment he was adrift in the whale's belly, floating through the flames, watching the dark fire-eater. Only because it fed so gluttonously had the windwhale not yet been consumed by a holocaust.

He added his skills to the self-protective efforts of the windwhale and the damping of the fire-eater's feeding. The flames began to dwindle. He tried to move subtly and do his work unnoticed by the predator. That thing had only one thought. Soon the windwhale could manage the fires alone.

The fire-eater tried to breach another gas bladder. Bomanz slapped it away. It tried again, and again, and again, failing, till it flew into a frustrated fit.

While it was out of control Bomanz insinuated tendrils of sorcery. With a jeweler's touch he evicted the commands of the wicker man. He replaced them with one overwhelming imperative: destroy the wicker man. Consume him in darkness, consume him in fire, but rid the earth of his noxious presence.

Bomanz retired to his own proper flesh. Physical sight showed him the stars masked by fire-edged wings that spanned half the sky. Those wings tilted. The body they supported dropped toward the place Old Father Tree wanted defended at all costs.

Bomanz glanced at Silent and Darling. The dusky, humorless wizard smiled slightly, nodded, made a small gesture to indicate that he had witnessed a job well done.

So maybe he was finally off the shit list.

He watched the fire-eater strike.

"Damn!" It was plunging toward the compound. Limper must have broken in.

The windwhale had fallen a long way, too. It was in easy striking distance for the wicker man. The giant of the sky had buckled in the middle, become a sagging sausage. It had no more ballast to shed. Neither could it control its motion through the sky. It was at the mercy of the wind, heading south, still losing altitude.

Silent and Darling joined Bomanz. He demanded, "Why did you stay? Why didn't you get the hell off?"

Silent's fingers danced as he relayed to Darling.

"Knock it off with the waggle fingers. You can talk."

Silent gave him a hard look. He did not say anything.

The windwhale lurched. Bomanz grabbed an organ stem as he hurtled toward the monster's side and a drop still three thousand feet till it was over. A gobbet of flame rolled up, singed him. He cursed and clung for his life. The windwhale continued to reel and shudder. It began making a hollow, booming noise that might have been a cry of pain.

An overlooked spark had tangled with a slow leak from a gas bladder. The game was about over. There was nothing to be done this time.

He was going to die in a few minutes. For some reason he could not get as upset as he thought he should. Mostly he was angry. This was not the way for the great Bomanz to go out, just dragged along, without an audience and no great battle to die in. Without a legend to leave behind.

He cursed continuously, in an unintelligible mutter.

His thoughts, more agile than ever he pretended, scurried around in frantic search for a way to make sure the wicker man went with him.

There was none. He had no weapon but the fire-eater, which was a javelin thrown and now beyond his control.

The windwhale began settling more rapidly. Fire crept up the aft half of the monster. The bend in its middle grew increasingly pronounced. The sucker was going to break up. "Come on. That half is going to go." He began climbing the steepening slope of the fore half. Silent and Darling scrambled after him.

Another explosion. Silent lost his footing. Darling grabbed a treelike organ with one hand, caught him with the other. She hoisted him to his feet.

"That ain't no woman," Bomanz muttered. "Not like I ever saw."

The rear half of the windwhale began falling faster than the front half. Secondary explosions hurled comets of whale flesh into the teeth of the night. Cursing monotonously, Bomanz continued his scramble away from disaster— every second wondering why he bothered.

The fear began to come, feeding on his helplessness. His talents were of no avail. He could do nothing but run from the conquering fire till there was nowhere left to flee.

Yet another explosion ripped and wrenched the windwhale. Bomanz fell. Below, the aft half of the monster tore free and fell away, the whole enveloped in flames. The rest of the windwhale bobbed violently, trying to return to horizontal. It yawed and rolled while it bobbed. The old sorcerer hung on. And cursed.

A whimper caught his ear.

Not five feet away he saw the glowing eyes of an infant manta. When the windwhale fragment began to stabilize he crawled thither. "They forget you, little fellow? Come on out here."

The kit hissed and spat and tried to use its lightning. It could generate no more than a spark. Bomanz dragged it out into the moonlight. "You are a tiny one, aren't you? No wonder they missed you." The kit was no bigger than a half-grown cat. It could not be more than a month old.

Bomanz cradled the infant in the crook of his left arm. It ceased struggling almost immediately. It seemed content to be held.

The old wizard resumed his journey.

The windwhale had become as stable as it could. Bomanz eased nearer the side. He looked down just in time to see the other half hit ground.

Silent and Darling joined him. As always their faces were emotionless masks, one dusky, one pale. Silent stared down at the earth. Darling seemed more interested in the baby manta. Bomanz said, "Under two thousand feet now but that's still a long way to fall. And there's still *that* to concern us."

That meant the small fires still burning back where the rear half had broken away. One of those could reach another gas bladder any minute.

"We should get as far forward as we can and hope for the best." He tried to sound more hopeful than he felt.

Silent nodded.

Bomanz looked around. The monastery was burning merrily, fired by the fire-eater. So that had worked, some. But when he listened the right way he could sense a knot of rage and pain seething amidst the flames.

The Limper had survived again.

And *his* scheme had worked some, too.

27

I had a hard time believing it. Raven had given up. His hip must have hurt a lot more than he wanted to admit.

He had not moved since he had gone down, and hadn't said nothing since his body beat down his will. I think he was ashamed.

I really wished the son of a bitch would figure out that he didn't have to be a superman. I wasn't going to make him stop being my buddy because he was human.

I was as wiped out as he was but I could not lay down and die. That show up around the monastery was getting flashier all the time. In fact, some of the fireworks was headed our way. That made me too nervous to crap out, though even my toenails were tired.

Another blast. A rose of fire bloomed in the sky. A big hunk of something started falling, spinning off smaller hunks of fire.

I realized what I was seeing.

"Raven, you better get your ass up and look at this mother."

He grunted but he didn't do it.

"It's a windwhale, asshole. Out of the Plain of Fear. What do you think of that?" I saw a couple get wiped during the big bloodletting up to the Barrowland.

"So it seems."

Mr. Ambition had rolled over. His voice was cool but his face was fishbelly white, like he'd stepped around a corner and bumped noses with Old Man Death.

"So how come it's here?" Then I shut up. I'd imagined up a reason.

"Not for me, kid. Who on the Plain would know where to look for me? Who would care?"

"Then . . . ?"

"It's the battle of the Barrowland, still going on. It's the tree god head-to-head with whatever I felt breaking loose up there."

Light flashed. Fire busted out of one end of the part of the windwhale that was still up. "That thing isn't going to stay up there much longer. Should we go see if we can do something?"

He didn't say anything for at least a minute. He looked up at the humpbacked hills like he was thinking maybe he had enough left to go catch Croaker after all. He couldn't be more than five, ten miles away, could he? Then he levered himself to his feet, wincing, obviously favoring his bad hip. I didn't ask. I knew he'd claim it was just the chill air and cold ground.

He told me, "Better get the horses. I'll drag our stuff together."

Big job you took on yourself there, old buddy, since we basically just dropped in our tracks when we couldn't go anymore.

Since he didn't have much to do he mostly just stood there watching that flying disaster cross the sky. He looked like he was being asked to mount the gallows and put the noose around his own neck.

I've been thinking, Case," Raven said as we came down off the knee of the most northerly of those goofy humped hills, headed northeast, chasing that drifting windwhale fragment.

"Brooding is the word I would have picked, old buddy. And you been at it since the day they finally put the Dominator down. Looks like that explosion a while back was the last one."

The fragment was drifting on a course that would intercept ours. A few fires flickered on one end. It was turning end for end slowly but had stopped its fall.

"Maybe. But you say something definite like that, the gods will stick it to you. Let's just hope it clears the woods. Be rough landing in there."

"What were you thinking?"

"About you and me, Croaker and his gang, the Lady, Silent, Darling. About all the things we had in common but still couldn't get along."

"I didn't see all that much you had in common. Not once you got past having the same enemies."

"Neither did I for a long time. And none of them saw it, either. Else we all might have tried a little harder."

I tried to look like I gave a shit at three in the morning.

"Basically we're all lonely, unhappy people looking for our place, Case. Loners who'd really rather not be but don't know how. When we get to the door that would let us in—or out—we can't figure out how to work the latch string."

I'll be damned. That was about as open-up-and-expose-what's-inside a remark as I ever got out of him. Filled with longing and conviction. Well shave my head and call me Baldy. I been right up here beside him since a couple years ago. You don't see the changes going on in people when you're standing up close.

This wasn't the Raven I'd first met, before his ego and misadventure had gotten his soul trapped among the shadow evils of the Barrowland, before its cleansing. He had returned from the prison of the heart dramatically altered.

Hell, he wasn't even the same man who had spent all his time drunk on his ass in Oar, neither.

I had kind of mixed feelings. I'd admired and liked and gotten along pretty good with the old Raven.

Maybe I would again once he got through his transition.

I did not know what to say to him, though I was sure he wanted a response. His knack for befuddling me never changed. "So did you figure out how to work it?"

"I have an unsettling premonition, Case. I'm almost paralyzed by a dread that I'm about to find out if I've learned anything." He stared at that piece of windwhale.

I checked it, guessed it was about two miles away and five hundred feet up. The breeze was bringing it to us.

"We going to chase it back into the hills if it carries that far?"

"You tell me, Case. This was your idea." He paused to whisper to his horse. The animals were not excited about hiking around at night either. Even if they didn't have to carry anybody.

Flame mushroomed out of the windwhale. Before the roar of the explosion reached us, I said, "We're not going to have to worry about climbing any hills."

*   *   *

The windwhale came down fast, turning end for end. When it was about two hundred feet off the ground some chunks fell off and it stopped coming down so fast. I had a pretty good idea where it would hit. We hurried toward the spot.

Then what was left nosed down, sped up, and hit the ground about a mile away. It bounced back into the air, maybe a hundred feet high. It kept coming, straight at us now.

At the peak of its bounce it exploded again.

It bounced two more times before it stayed down and just slid to a stop.

Be careful," Raven said. "There might be more explosions." Fires still burned on the windwhale. Somewhere inside it was making a noise like somebody beating on the granddaddy of all bass drums.

I said, "It ain't dead yet. Look there." The end of a tentacle lay just a couple yards from me. It was jumping around like a snake with a toothache.

"Unh. Let's hobble the horses."

Excited all to hell, Raven was. Like he spent his whole life hanging around windwhales so close he could smell their bad breath. And this one had that all over.

I caught something in the firelight. "Hey! There's people up on top of that sucker."

"There had to be. Where?"

"There. Right over that black patch." I pointed. Some guys up there were hauling around on something.

Raven said, "Looks like somebody trying to get somebody else out from under something."

"Let's get up there and give them a hand." I left my horse unhobbled.

Raven grinned at me. "The exuberant folly of youth. Where does it go?"

I started climbing a blubbery, stinky cliff. He went looking for a bush to tie the horses to, that being easier than messing with hobbles. I was halfway to the top before he started after me.

The flesh of the windwhale was sort of spongy and definitely smelly, with the odor of burned flesh added. The flesh trembled with pain and failing life. Such a noble monster. I wanted to cry for it.

"Raven! Hurry up! There's three of them up here and a big fire burning back there."

Right then there was a baby explosion. It knocked me down. Gobs of fire splattered the ground. Some of the dry grass caught.

There would be trouble if that spread.

By the time Raven dragged his carcass up I had the woman across my shoulders and the old man, who was the only one on his feet, was tying her so she wouldn't slide off. Finished, the old boy whipped around and starting trying to drag a frondlike piece of windwhale off somebody else.

Panting, Raven looked at me, looked at the woman, grumbled, "It had to be, didn't it?"

I said, "Hey, this broad is solid as a rock. Or she's got a lead butt. She weighs as much as I do."

"How about you get her down?" He muttered, "I'm getting too old for this crap," and headed for the old man. "You. What the hell are you doing here?" He wasn't surprised to see the guy under the frond, though. Having Silent drop out of the sky was just the kind of trick he expected the fates to pull on him.

He was shaking as he helped the old man lift the frond. The old man started fussing over Silent. A black lump of a something glommed on to his shoulder made a sound like a kitten crying.

"Hoist him up!" the old wizard ordered. "Carry him. We don't have time for me to bring him around."

I started down then. Whatever else they said I missed. Pretty soon they started down after me.

Something whispered overhead. The lump on the wizard's shoulder mewled again. A screech tumbled down from the dark. The windwhale's mantas had come to circle their dying partner.

What happened to mantas when their windwhale died?

"Ouch!" Raven yelled. "Watch where the hell you're stepping!"

At the same time the old man said, "The arrogance of you, man! The bloody insufferable, conceited arrogance. You, without claim or right, demand— demand!—explanations of me. Of *me*! The conceit of you surpasses comprehension. I should be asking you what you're doing here, fluttering around ahead of the Limper. Are you his forerunner? His death scout? Will you get moving? Before we get crisped like bacon?"

I got my feet on the ground, watched them. Raven was thoroughly pissed. Maybe he never figured out that he wasn't a lord anymore and the world wasn't going to jump when he barked. And he never did have sense enough to be scared of the right people. People like old Bomanz, who could probably turn him into a frog if he got aggravated.

Raven didn't get to shoot off his own mouth. Another explosion almost shook him and the old man off the windwhale. A big shudder rolled through the monster. That drumbeat stopped. The beast let out with a deep groan that said everything there was to say about death and despair.

The mantas upstairs made keening sounds. Mourning sounds. I wondered how they would manage now.

The windwhale stopped shaking. The wizard yelled, "Get out of here before the whole thing blows!"

*   *   *

Raven was staggering toward the horses when it happened. The blast beggared everything we had seen before. I ducked away from a blast of hot air. It hurled Raven forward. He fell on his face. Bomanz, though closer to the explosion, rode the blast, staying upright with footwork that reminded me of my old mother dancing. He looked like he was in pain.

When the ring in my ears went I heard the sad song of the mantas, again or still.

The windwhale became its own funeral pyre.

Flying chunks started grass fires all around. The horses were upset. We were not safe yet.

Raven crawled, unable to get back up. I felt like a total Daryl Dipshit standing there doing nothing to help, but my legs just wouldn't move.

The wizard caught up, hoisted Raven. They cussed each other like a couple of drunks. I got my feet going finally and leaned into the heat. "Come on, you guys. Knock it off. Let's throw this dork on a horse and get out of here before we all get turned into pork cracklings."

I already had the woman across one saddle like a sack of rice. We had to do so much running her front side was going to be one miserable bruise.

"Move it!" I yelled. "There's a breeze coming up." I scooted back and got hold of the animals before they decided they were smarter than us and headed for the high country.

While we hoisted Silent, Raven got his first good look at Darling. She was all beat to hell. Blood leaked from her mouth, ears, and nose. Her exposed skin was all bruised or blood-caked. Silent looked about as bad, and so did the wizard, pretty much, but Raven did not care jack shit about them.

"They can be healed," Bomanz said before Raven could start fussing. "*If* we get them away from here before the grass fires get us."

That and me heading out without waiting around for him got Raven moving. He followed me, leading the horse with Darling on it. Bomanz did not wait for either of us. He headed around one end of the nearest grass fire, which the breeze was pushing toward the sleepy, humpbacked hills.

Raven went to muttering and cursing again. Bomanz was headed north, cradling the manta kit, which squeaked cheerfully at creatures that glided invisibly above our heads. Raven still wanted to catch his old crony, but I guess he decided it would not be smart to challenge the sorcerer right off, when he was in a bad mood, too.

I kept glancing back at the burning windwhale till we got too far into the woods to see it. It seemed to me there had to be some kind of lesson there, some kind of symbolism, but I couldn't unravel it.

28

Smeds walked into the Skull and Crossbones out of bright morning sunshine. When his eyes adjusted he spotted Timmy Locan in a dark corner at a tiny table for two. At first it looked like Timmy was just sitting there staring down at his bundled hand. When he got closer, though, Smeds saw Timmy's eyes were tight shut. Moisture glittered on his cheeks.

Smeds sat down across from Timmy. "You go to a doc like I said?"

"Yeah."

"Well?"

"He charged me two obols to tell me he didn't know what was wrong and he didn't know what to do about it unless I want him to cut it off. He couldn't even help with the pain."

"You need a wizard, then."

"Point me at the best one in town and turn me loose. I can afford him."

"That ain't a him, Timmy. It's two hers. Gossamer and Spidersilk. Top blades from Charm that just took over."

Timmy wasn't listening. "You hear what I said, Timmy? We got two bitches here straight from the Tower. Came in last night. Bad mojo. They're supposed to find out what happened up to the Barrowland. Tomorrow or the next day they're going to borrow a battalion of Nightstalkers and head up there. It's all over town."

Timmy still did not listen close enough to suit.

"You get it? They're going to get up there and find out that somebody messed with that tree. They're going to be out for blood, then."

Timmy ground his teeth a moment, said, "Be good advertising."

"What?"

"Fish says he don't think there's any way they can trace us as long as we just sit tight and keep our mouths shut. Meantime word gets around to all the wizards. Them that's interested will get here and start looking for the spike. Then we put it up for bids."

Smeds was less fond of that idea all the time. Too damned dangerous. But the rest of them, even Fish, were convinced that a sale could be made safely.

They didn't believe that all wizards were crazy-mean and liked to screw people and hurt them just for the fun of it.

"It's just a business deal," Tully kept saying. "We sell. They pay off and get the spike. Everybody's happy."

Dumb shit. Everybody would *not* be happy. There were a skillion wizards and only one silver spike. Every damned one of them was not only going to be trying for it for himself, they were going to be out to make sure nobody else got it first. Whoever did get it might want to cover his tracks so nobody came looking to take it away from him.

Tully kept saying bullshit whenever Smeds started worrying. Even when Smeds reminded him that that was the way wizards carried on in every story you ever heard.

"I think I know where's a guy who can work on your hand, Timmy." Smeds recalled one of his aunts talking about a wizard down on the South Side who was mostly pretty honest and decent as long as you paid him what you owed him.

The street door opened. Light spilled inside. Smeds glanced around, saw the Nightstalker corporal and a couple of his buddies. The corporal raised a friendly hand. Smeds had to reciprocate or look like a shit. Then he had to stay there talking awhile so it didn't look like he was walking out because a bunch of gray boys had walked in. He used the time to tell Timmy about the wizard his aunt knew.

"So you want to try him?"

"I'm ready to try anything."

"Let's go, then."

The wizard was a smiling, tubby, apple-cheeked little dork with thin white hair that stuck out every which way. He came on like he'd spent his whole life waiting just for them. Smeds understood why his aunt liked the man. She was so sour and ugly that a blind dog would not wait for her except to go away.

Smeds did most of the talking because he did not trust Timmy not to blurt out more than he needed to in his eagerness to get rid of his pain. "Some kind of infection that's turning his hand all black," Smeds said.

"And making it ache," Timmy said. There was a hint of a whine in his voice. Timmy Locan wasn't a whiner.

The wizard said, "Let's open her up and look at it, then." He pulled Timmy's hand down onto his worktable, went after the bandage with a thin, sharp knife. He smiled and chattered as he worked and when he laid the bandage open he said, "It does look a bit nasty, doesn't it?"

It looked a lot nasty to Smeds. He had not seen Timmy's hand unwrapped in a week. The area of blackness had tripled in size. It now covered Timmy's whole palm and had begun to creep round to the back. The blackened flesh had a puffy look.

The wizard leaned down, sniffed. "Funny. Infected flesh usually smells. Close your eyes tight, son." Timmy did and the pudgy man started poking his hand with a needle. "What do you feel when I do this?"

"Just a little pressure. Ouch!" The needle had pricked unblackened flesh.

"Strange. Very strange. I've never seen anything like it, son. Try to relax." The wizard went to a shelf and took down a baroque brass doohickey that was not much more than a one-foot empty circle supported by six eight-inch legs. This he placed astraddle Timmy's hand. He pinched powders and dribbled drops into pockets in the brass gizmo, made with some mumbo jumbo. There was a flash and a puff of noisome smoke. A shimmer like heat off pavement appeared within the confines of the circle.

The wizard stared into that.

Smeds could not see that it made any difference.

But the wizard's smile went away. The color left his cheeks. In a squeaky voice he asked, "What have you boys been into?"

"Huh? What do you mean?" Smeds asked.

"Surprised I didn't see it sooner. The mystic stench is there. But who would have thought it? The boy has had his hand on something polluted with the essence of evil. Something pregnant with the blood of darkness. A powerful amulet, perhaps. Some periapt lost in ancient times and just now resurfacing. Something very extraordinary and hitherto unknown in these parts. Have you boys been grave robbing?"

Timmy stared at his hand. Smeds met the wizard's eye but did not say anything.

"You wouldn't have been breaking any laws digging wherever you ran into whatever caused this. But you could get in deep if you don't report it to the imperial legates."

"Can you do anything for him?"

"They pay good rewards."

"Can you do anything for him?" Smeds demanded.

"No. Whatever caused this was created by someone far greater than I am. Assuming it to have been an amulet, the burn can be cured only by someone greater than the man or woman who created the amulet. And that someone would have to have the amulet itself to study before trying to effect a cure."

Shit, Smeds thought. Where were you going to find somebody big enough to undo the Dominator?

You weren't. "What else can you do? If you can't just fix him up?"

"I can remove the tainted flesh. That's all."

"What's that mean in plain language?"

"I can amputate his hand. Here. At the wrist would do it today. If that's the way you decide to go you'd better do it soon. Once the darkness works its way into the larger bones there won't be any way to tell how far or how fast it's spreading."

"What about it, Timmy?"

"It's my *hand,* man!"

"You heard what he said."

"I heard. Look, wiz, you got something that will stop the pain long enough for me to think straight?"

The pudgy man said, "I could put a blocking spell on that would help for a while, but it would hurt worse than ever when that wore off. And that's an idea you'd better get into your head. The longer you stall, the worse the pain is going to get. In another ten days you're not going to be able to stop screaming."

Smeds scowled. "Thanks for just not a whole lot. Do the painkiller thing for him and let us go talk it over."

The wizard sprinkled powders, mumbled, made mystic passes. Smeds watched Timmy relax a little, then even manage a feeble smile.

Smeds asked, "That it? Come on, Timmy. Let's hit the road."

The wizard said, "I need to wrap that again. I don't *know* that it would, but it if came in contact with someone else it *might* communicate itself. If the original evil was potent enough."

Smeds's insides knotted and curled as he tried to recall if he had ever touched Timmy's hand. He didn't think he had.

He barely waited to get Timmy outside before he asked, "Old Fish ever touch that when he was taking care of you?"

"No. Nobody did. Except that doc I had look at it. He poked it a couple times with his finger."

"Unh." Smeds did not like it. It was getting complicated. He did not like things complicated. Trying to untangle them usually made things worse.

They had to have a sitdown with Tully and Fish. He knew what Tully would want to do: drag Timmy out in the country somewhere, cut his throat, and bury him.

Tully had the soul of a snake. He had to break loose. The sooner the better. Right now probably wouldn't hurt. Except then how would he get his cut of whatever the spike went for? Shit.

"Timmy, I want you should go get drunk, have a good time, but do some serious thinking and get your mind made up. Whatever you want to do, I'll back you up, but you got to remember it affects all of us. And keep an eye on Tully. Tully ain't a guy you want to turn your back on when he's nervous."

"I'm not stupid, Smeds. Tully ain't a guy I'd turn my back on when he wasn't nervous. He ever tries anything cute he's got a nasty surprise coming."

Interesting.

Smeds figured he had some deciding to do himself. Like, with the town up to the gutters in gray boys and their bosses about to find out the spike was gone from the Barrowland, was it time to hit the road and get lost someplace they'd never think to look? Was it time to do something with the spike so it would be safer than it was in his pack back at the Skull and Crossbones? He'd already had a cute idea how to handle that. An idea that might turn into a kind of life insurance if he went ahead and did it before he told the others what he had done.

Damn, he hated it when things got complicated.

There was a hell of a row with Tully when they all got together. Tully seemed a little shorter on sense every day.

"You think you're some goddamned kind of immortal?" Smeds demanded. "You think you're untouchable? There's the goddamned grays out there, Tully. They decide to get excited, they'll take you apart one piece at a time. Then they'll give the pieces to Gossamer and Spidersilk to put back together so they can make you tell them what they want to know. And whatever you tell them then, it won't be enough. Or do you think you're some kind of hero that would hold out against the kind of people that learned to ask questions in the Tower?"

"They got to find me before they can ask me anything, Smeds."

"I think we're finally getting somewhere. That's what I've been saying for the last ten minutes."

"The hell. You've been jacking your jaw about running off to some ass-wipe place like Lords. . . ."

"You really think you could stay out of their way here? Once they knew what they were looking for?"

"How they gonna . . . ?"

"How the hell should I know? What I do know is, these ain't no half-moron bozos from the North Side. These are people from *Charm*. They eat guys like us for snacks. The best way to stay out of their way is not to be around where they're at."

"We ain't going nowhere, Smeds." Tully was turning plain stubborn.

"You want to stand around waiting for the hammer to hit you between the eyes, that's fine with me. But I ain't getting killed because you got ego problems. Selling that spike off and getting rich would be nice, but not nice enough to die for or go to the rack for. All these heavies turning up here before we even start trying to find a buyer, I'm tempted to let it go to the first bidder just to get out from under."

The argument raged on, bitterly, inconclusively, with Fish and Timmy refereeing. Smeds was as angry with himself as he was with Tully. He had a nasty suspicion he was just blowing a lot of hot air, that he would not be able to walk out on his cousin if it came to a decision. Tully was not much, but he was family.

Toadkiller Dog lay in the shade of an acacia tree, gnawing on a shinbone that had belonged to one of the wicker man's soldiers.

Only a dozen of those had survived that grisly night when they had taken the monastery. Half of those had died since. When the breeze blew from the north the stench of death was overpowering.

Only two of the witch doctors had gotten through alive. Barely. Till they recovered, he and the wicker man were in little better shape than they had been in the beginning, back in the Barrowland.

Toadkiller Dog kept one eye on the mantas gliding overhead and around the monastery, eternally probing for soft spots in the shell of magic shielding the place. Bolts ripped through any they found. Only one in a hundred did any damage, but that was enough to guarantee eventual destruction.

The wicker man's triumph over the windwhale had given a respite of two hours. Then another windwhale had appeared and had resumed the struggle. There were four of them out there now, at the points of the compass, and they were determined to avenge their fallen brother.

Toadkiller Dog rose, bones creaking and aching, and zigzagged his way between dangerous spots to the low, thin wall that surrounded the remains of the monastery. He limped badly. His wicker leg had gone in the conflagration that had come when the Limper's firedrake had turned back upon him.

He consoled himself with the knowledge that the Limper was worse off than he was. The Limper had no body at all.

But he was working on that.

How the hell had they managed that turnaround?

Toadkiller Dog rose on his hind legs, rested his paw and chin on top of the wall.

The picture was worse, as he had expected. The talking stones were so numerous they formed a circumvallation. Groves of the walking trees stood wherever the ground was moist, feasting. They had to endure eternal drought on the Plain of Fear.

How long before they moved in and began demolishing the wall with their swift-growing roots?

Squadrons of reverse centaurs galloped among the shadows of gliding mantas, practicing charges and massed javelin tosses.

That weird horde would come someday. And there would be no turning them back while the Limper had no body.

They would have come already had they known how helpless were the besieged. That was the only smart thing the Limper had done, getting himself out of sight and lying low, so those creatures out there did not know where he stood. He was counting on the White Rose to think he was trying to lure her into a trap by pretending to be powerless.

The Limper needed time. He would do anything, would sacrifice anyone, to buy that time.

Toadkiller Dog turned away and limped toward the half-demolished main structure of the monastic complex. A frightened sentry watched him pass.

They knew they were doomed, that they had become rich beyond their hopes but at the cost of selling their souls to death. They would not live to enjoy a copper's worth of their stolen fortunes.

It was too late now, even to find hope in desertion.

One man had tried. They had him out there. Sometimes they made him scream just to remind everybody they were irked enough to take no prisoners.

Toadkiller Dog squeezed through the tight halls and down steep, narrow stairs to the deep cellar the Limper had taken for his lair. Down there he was safe from the monster boulders and whatnot the windwhales dropped when the urge took them.

The Limper had set up in a room that was large and as damp and moldy as might be expected. But the light there was as bright as artificial sources could make it. The sculptors needed that light to do their work properly.

The bodiless head of the Limper sat on a shelf overlooking the work in progress. Two armed guards and one of the witch doctors watched, too. The actual work was being done by three of the dozen priests who had survived the massacre of the monastery's inmates.

They had no idea what their reward would be if they did a good job. They labored under the illusion that they would be allowed to resume the monastery's work when they finished and their guests departed.

In the southwest corner, the highest of the enclosure, there was a small spring. The monastery drew its water from this. Below the spring, kept moist by its runoff, lay a bed of some of the finest potter's clay in the world. The monks had been using it for ages. The Limper had been delighted when he had learned of the deposit.

The sculptors had the new body roughed in to the Limper's satisfaction. It would be the body he'd always wished he'd had, not the stunted, crippled thing he'd had to endure when he'd had a body of his own. With the head on it this would stand six and a half feet tall and the body itself would fit what the Limper imagined was every maiden's dream.

About a third of the detail work was done and it was very good work indeed, with all the tiny wrinkles and creases and pore holes of a real human body, but with none of the blemishes.

Only one of the three monks was doing any sculpting. The other two were keeping the clay moist, basting its surface with oil that would keep that natural dampness in.

Toadkiller Dog glanced at the clay figure only long enough to estimate how much longer their good luck would have to hold. He was not reassured. Surely those things out there would stop procrastinating in a day or two.

He retraced his route to the surface, prowled from wall to wall, eyeing potential routes of escape.

When the hammer fell he was going out of there at a gallop, straight at the talking stone and jump over. They would not expect him to bolt and leave the Limper to his fate.

He would find a more reasonable patron somewhere else. The Limper was not the only one of the old ones who had survived.

30

It was not a companionable camp where we were set up east of the monastery, where the smell of bodies wasn't as bad. I mean, I did my best and me and the Torque boys and the talking buzzard and a couple of the talking stones had us some pretty good bullshit sessions around the old campfire. But the rest of them acted like a bunch of little kids.

Raven wasn't going to talk to Darling unless she made the first move. Silent wouldn't have nothing to do with Raven on account of he thought Raven was going to try to steal his girl. A girl he never really had. Darling wasn't talking to Raven because she figured he owed her about twenty giant apologies and he had to pay off before she gave him the time of day. And she was pissed at Silent because he was being presumptuous, and maybe at herself some, too, for maybe having given him grounds for his presumptions.

Just between you and me and the pillow book, I don't think she's no blushing virgin.

But maybe that's just wishful thinking. Been so long since I been in rock-throwing range of a woman that the females of those back-assward centaurs are looking good.

The Torque boys swear by them.

Old wizard Bomanz ain't getting along with nobody. He's full up to his eyeballs with ideas about how this show ought to be run and there ain't nobody will listen to him but the talking buzzard. The buzzard's name is Virgil but the stones call him Sleazeball or Garbagemouth on account of the high intellectual content of most of his conversation.

Already I'm getting blasé about all those weird critters. They kind of rattled me at first, but we been here eight days now. If I ignore what they look like I knew stranger guys in the Guards.

What I can't figure is why we're sitting around. From what I hear there's only a few guys holed up in that monastery. With what we got we ought to be able to take the Limper even in top condition. But Darling is the high lord field marshal here. She says we wait.

She gets her orders from Old Father Tree. Must be he's happy so long as the Limper is buttoned up in a sack where he can't cause nobody no grief.

Raven said, "I misjudged her. She's not just sitting on her hands."

"Eh? What?" I wanted to go to sleep. So suddenly he wanted to talk.

"Darling isn't just sitting here. There's a dozen kinds of these Plain creatures so small you don't notice them or so much like something you're used to seeing you don't pay any attention. She's got those sneaking in and out of there all the time. She knows every breath they take. She's got somebody on every one of them all the time. The mantas and centaurs and rock dropping are all for show. If the order comes down, the real main attack will be carried out by the little creatures. They won't know what hit them in there. She's a genius. I'm proud of that girl."

When it came to sneaky petey I figured she had some pretty good teachers, hunking around with the Black Company all them years. I told him, "Why don't you go tell her she's a genius, you're proud of her, you still love her, will she forgive you for being such a butt way back when? And let me get some sleep."

He didn't go see Darling. But he did get pissed at me and left me alone.

Not that that did much good for long.

What nobody knew but maybe Silent—since Darling can't hear and she can't lip-read the stones because they got no mouths—was that she already had the go-ahead from the boss tree. She was just waiting for the right hour to give the signal.

Naturally she timed it for when I just got sound asleep.

Things were quiet in the basement where the Limper was hiding out. There was one armed guard, one shaman overseeing, one monk keeping the clay moist, and two more making a leg for Toadkiller Dog.

The earth shook. A windwhale had hit the building with an extra big stone. Everybody moved to protect the claywork.

A dozen Plain creatures exploded out of cracks and shadows. Little missiles flew. Little blades flashed. The fastest creatures climbed all over the soldier and the shaman. They let the monks escape. Once the soldier and witch doctor went down the creatures began defacing the claywork.

It was the same elsewhere. None of the Limper's men survived.

That monster Toadkiller Dog came flying out of the monastery and landed smack in the middle of a gang of centaurs. Blades flashed. Javelins flew. So did bodies. Then the monster broke loose.

Mantas swarmed overhead so thick they kept running into each other. The thunder of their lightnings made a drumroll.

The monster got to the barrier of talking menhirs and walking trees. He jumped over that, too. His fur smoldered and his flanks were pincushioned with darts. The walking trees tried to grab hold of him. His strength was too violent for them.

He kept right on coming, straight at us.

Menhirs popped into his way, stalling and tripping him. Mantas tried to cook him. Centaurs galloped with him, pelting him with javelins and dashing in to try to hamstring him. Me and Raven and the Torque boys all put three or four arrows apiece into him. He never seemed to notice. He just kept on coming, howling like all the wolves in the world at once.

"Go for its eyes!" Raven yelled. "Go for its eyes!"

Right, old buddy. Sharpshoot when I'm shaking so bad I figure if I live through this one I'm going to be cleaning the brown out of my drawers for a month.

The monster was only about forty feet away when Silent said hello by smacking it in the face with a bushel of snakes, snakes that hung on and tried to crawl into its ears and mouth and nostrils.

The snakes never slowed it down but they did take its mind off whatever it had planned for us. It just plowed through.

I went flying ass over appetite. As I sailed through the air I saw Darling step in, as cool as if she was in a kitchen slicing bread, and take a cut with a two-handed sword I wouldn't have figured a woman could lift. She was a little high. She hit ribs instead of opening the thing's belly.

I hit ground and spent the next couple minutes doing an astronomical survey of a couple hundred newly hatched constellations.

A savage rain shower soaked me and brought me out of it and to my feet, where I realized that I hadn't been rained on after all. A windwhale had passed over, dumping a little ballast to slow its fall as it came down after Toadkiller Dog.

The monster was still headed west. Right behind it was a shimmery something that looked like an elephant with a nest of tentacles for a head. Bomanz's contribution to the cause.

That was the last minute when anything made sense.

The talking stones went berserk, started popping all around. Walking trees jumped up and down. Centaurs ran in circles. Everything that could talk started yelling at everything else. The windwhales went to booming and started dropping like they meant to commit suicide by smashing into the ground. The scarred-up menhir was jabbering at Silent in a lingo I didn't get and Silent was practically doing a combination flamenco and sword dance trying to tell Darling what the rock was saying.

I stumbled over to Raven and said, "Old buddy, this looks like a good time to duck out of the party. Before the keepers come to drag them all back to the asylum."

He was watching Silent. He said, "Hush." And a minute later, "The tree god has called the whole thing off. Something's happened up north. He wants everybody to drop everything and head for home."

I looked around. Two windwhales were on the ground already. Critters were piling aboard. The only talking stone around anywhere was the one hanging out with Silent. "There goes our whaleback ride to catch your buddy Croaker."

The young tree in the Barrowland had been in a coma since the fire, intelligence damped down while its hurts healed. But there came a day when externals finally registered. There was a bustle and fuss in the Barrowland such as had not been seen since the great battle that had taken place there.

Curious, and compelled by the mandate of his father, the tree dragged himself out of his fugue, though he was far from completely healed.

The Barrowland was crawling with soldiers of the shadowed western empire. He sensed the foci of power that had to be their commanders. They were going over every inch of the surrounding ground.

Why?

Then the memories came. Not in a flood, thankfully. In snippets and dribbles. In reasonable temporal order. The thing that came to dig, the horror it uncovered. The death that had come out of the forest and fallen upon the town. The fire . . . The fire . . . The fire . . .

The soldiers went rigid with fear and awe and fled in terror as the lightning crackled among the branches of the tree. Their captains came out and gaped at the fierce blue light washing the Barrowland.

The tree concentrated its entire intellect upon its immediate forebear and finally, after so many weeks, passed the news of its great failure.

32

The twins Gossamer and Spidersilk strode toward the now quiet tree in lockstep. Both wore black leather helmets that hid them completely. Their outfits were mirror images of one another, just as their bodies were. Though their powers were an order of magnitude less deadly and ferocious than those of any of the Ten Who Were Taken, they made the world think otherwise by aping the style and dress of their predecessors.

Thus they successfully donned the mantle of what it was their ambition to become. And if they survived long enough they might hone their wickedness till they were, indeed, indistinguishable from old terrors now mostly gone from the earth.

Thus doth evil breed.

The twins halted three yards from the tree, their fear carefully concealed from their soldiers. They stopped. They stared. They circled the tree, going opposite directions. When they met where they had started they knew.

Their black hearts were heavy with fear, but also entertained a spark of wicked hope.

They summoned their lieutenants. In half an hour the troops were headed for Oar.

The hell with the Limper. There was bigger game afoot.

33

It was late afternoon. Smeds looked up from his work on the wall. He grinned. Two more hours and his sentence to the labor battalion—three days for petty vandalism and malicious mischief—would end. And the damned spike would be tucked away safe in a place no one could find. Only he would know that it lay in a pocket in the mortar under a certain merlon stone twenty-seven east of the new east-side tower overlooking the North Gate.

Smeds was smugly proud of himself for having thought of such a nifty hiding place. Who would think of that? Nobody. And if by some remote chance somebody did, who would go tearing down the whole damned wall to find it? They would pay for the information.

He grinned again.

His imperial overseer scowled but did not crack his whip. That whip had taught Smeds quickly to keep up his share of the work even while he was daydreaming.

His grin died not because the overseer disapproved but because the cloud of dust to the north, that had been approaching for several hours, had come within a mile of the wall and had disgorged two hurried black riders. They had to be Gossamer and Spidersilk.

They knew about the spike.

Man, they had come back fast. He did not like what that implied.

At least maybe now Tully would get a convincing glimpse of what these people were really like when they had their gloves off.

Time came without a bite from the whip, despite his having wandered off into reveries about a young woman he had met the day before he had let himself get caught painting an obscene slogan on a pre-imperial monument. It had cost him to get a professional letter writer to teach him to inscribe the slogan. He could not read or write his own name.

That girl was going to be waiting for him tonight, a scant fourteen years of ripening heat.

He came down out of the scaffolding thinking of a bath and fresh clothing and there was Old Man Fish waiting for him to get his release, a simple formality involving snipping a wire from around his neck. "What's up?" Smeds asked.

"I figured somebody ought to come make sure they let you go when they were supposed to. Tully couldn't be bothered. Timmy's still laid up."

Timmy had let the wizard take the hand the morning Smeds had started his sentence. "He all right? Did it work?"

"Looks like. No problem with that kind of pain. Let's go."

They walked a way, not talking much. Smeds looked around through narrowed eyes. They were tearing down three times as fast as they were rebuilding. There were clear areas that covered a dozen acres. The gray boys had been more evident since the bunch from the north had come in, but now they were everywhere. Platoons of the Nightstalkers moved around quickly and purposefully. Soldiers from other outfits seemed to be posted on every corner. Twice they were stopped and asked to state their names and business.

Unprecedented.

"What the hell is going on?" Smeds asked.

"I don't know. They were just getting started when I was coming to get you."

"Gossamer and Spidersilk got back from the Barrowland about two hours ago. I watched them from the wall. They were in a hell of a big hurry."

"Unh. So there it is." Fish glanced over, his bushy white eyebrows two ragged caterpillars arching their backs. "Did you put it into the wall?"

Smeds did not answer.

"Good. I figured that's what it had to be. You couldn't have done better. And I just forgot I even thought you might have been up to something like that."

They walked along, listening to the rumors running the streets. One refrain kept coming up. The imperials had sealed the city. Anybody who wanted could get in but they weren't going to let anyone out till they found someone or something they wanted bad. A house-to-house search had begun already and they were being as thorough as imperials always were.

"We got a problem," Smeds said.

"We have more than one."

"I told Tully till I was blue in the face."

"Maybe you should have said let's stay. Contrary as he's been, he might have decided he had to get out."

"I'll remember that. We got to have a sitdown, all four of us. We got to pound some facts into Tully's skull."

"Yes. Or just do what has to be done whether he likes it or not."

"Yeah."

They turned into the street that led past the Skull and Crossbones. The shadows made Smeds jumpy. He expected a Gossamer or Spidersilk to come bounding out of every one. He had forgotten his date entirely. "Nothing to do now but cover our asses and try to ride it out. They don't find anything they'll figure the spike went on down the road."

"Maybe."

"They have to loosen up sometime. You can't keep a city like Oar locked up very long."

"They don't find it easy, Smeds, they'll try looking hard. Maybe offer some rewards. Big ones, considering the trouble they're going to already."

"Yeah."

"I saw the doc Timmy visited. Remember? I'm pretty sure he caught whatever Timmy had. He had that same look."

Smeds stopped walking. "Shit."

"Yeah. And then there's the wizard that did his hand. Two arrows pointing straight at us and too late to dodge them by running away. We have some hard choices to make."

Smeds stood staring into the twilight indigo behind spires rising from the heart of the city. Here it was. What he had been afraid this would come to from the beginning, only it wouldn't be Fish and Timmy he'd have to stick a knife in. "I think I can do it if it has to be done. You?"

"Yes. If that's the decision."

"Let's go get a drink and look at the angles."

"You don't want to drink much. If that's the move we're going to make. That wizard will have to be done quick. He isn't stupid. It won't be long before he figures out that what the grays are looking for might be the same thing that burned Timmy's hand. And not much longer for him to realize he's the cutout between us and them. He won't be easy if he's looking for us to come."

"I'm still going to have to have one long one."

Into the Skull and Crossbones. It was the neighborhood social hour but there were tables available. The landlord did not have the sort of personality that brought in the free-spending hordes. To Smeds's relief his cousin was prominent among the missing.

Neither of them spoke till a pitcher had been delivered and Smeds had downed a long draft. He wiped his mouth on his sleeve. "Been thinking. The way I see it, we got a whatchamacallit, quorum, right here. You and me. Timmy can't do anything even if he wanted. And Tully would just argue and fuss and try to take over and make everybody do things his way. Then he'd screw it up and get us all killed."

"True."

"So what are we going to do?"

Old Man Fish smiled softly. "You telling me to decide? You want me to tell you what to do? So that way it isn't your fault, you were just doing what you were told?"

Smeds hadn't thought of it that way consciously. But there was a truth there that startled him.

"That's all right," Fish said. "You just needed to have that up where you could look at it and see if you were trying to be a weasel. How do you feel about doing it?"

That was an easy one. "I don't want to. Those guys never done nothing but try to help us when we asked. But better their asses than mine. I ain't going to let them take me down because I know I'm going to feel bad about doing what, as far as I can see, is the only thing that'll keep the grays off."

"So you just talked yourself into it."

Smeds thought about that. His stomach knotted up. "I guess so."

"That's one vote for action."

"You go the other way, we have to get Timmy or Tully to kick in a tiebreaker." Some foolish part of him harkened to a hope that he would be voted down. Another part said it would be nice to be alive to have a guilty conscience.

"I'm with you." Fish managed a weak smile. "No tie. I don't like it either. But I don't see any other way out. You think of one, let me know. I'll be plenty happy to change my mind." Fish poured himself a beer.

Smeds's stomach just kept knotting and sinking.

Toadkiller Dog slipped into the monastery as silent as death. The wind-whales were not yet below the horizon, scudding north, inexplicably abandoning their mission when it lacked only a touch of being complete. The monster was puzzled in the extreme but it did not allow that to paralyze him. He had enough distractions in the form of a thousand wounds and pains.

He slipped through the ruins and down into the subbasement, where he surprised a monk in the process of sabotaging the claywork. One snap of his jaws ended that, though it was probably too late to salvage anything.

He went over and stared at the head floating in the keg of oil. He was not a fast thinker, but steady, and he got where he wanted to go given time. The debate of the hour was whether or not there was any value in continuing an alliance with a thing so obviously mad and out of control.

The head stared back, awake and aware and completely helpless. The monster was not a subtle or reflective sort and so did not think it ironic that fate kept rendering helpless what was possibly the most powerful and most dangerous being in the world.

The head stared with great intensity, as though there was some critical message it *had* to get across. But what little unspoken communication had existed between them in the past no longer worked.

Toadkiller Dog whuffed, snapped the head up, and carried it out of the monastery. He concealed it in a place he thought would be safe, then limped away wearily.

It was start-over-from-scratch time and he had no idea, really, where to find the kinds of recruits he would need to do the tasks he needed done. He knew only where not to look. They had left nothing but desolation behind them in the north.

He did not hurry. He did not feel pressed. He would live till he ran into something powerful enough to kill him.

He thought he had all the time in the world.

There were lights in the wizard's place. "He live alone?" Fish asked.

"I don't know," Smeds said. The wizard seemed to be the wealthiest man in his neighborhood. He had real windows.

A shadow moved across a paper shade.

"Doesn't matter anyway. There's no guarantee he won't have friends in, or a client."

Smeds started. He had not thought about the chance of this becoming a massacre. He glanced up the street, the direction the patrol had gone. The gray boys were all over the place. This had to go down quick and quiet. "You able to do your part?"

"Yes. I'm working myself up the same way I did before we attacked at Charm. Big wizard, little wizard, the risks are pretty much the same."

"You were at Charm? I didn't know that."

"I was young and dumb. I don't kick it around. The grays are still fighting that one. They don't want to let anybody who went there die of old age."

"Patrol."

They faded into the shadows between two buildings, got down as low as they dared without sprawling in the garbage and dogshit. At the same moment light spilled from the wizard's doorway. A woman emerged. The clip-clop of the soldiers' boots picked up. They reached the woman as she reached the street.

"Evening, ma'am," one said. "You're out late. Consulting the wizard?"

There was not enough light to see it but Smeds knew she would be looking from one soldier to another, scared, trying to decide if she had good reason to be. She croaked, "Yes."

"May we have your name? We have to keep track of everyone who comes and goes."

"Why?"

"I don't know, ma'am. It's orders. It's the same all over town, wherever there's anybody in his line of business. Me and Luke being naturally lucky, we got this here clown on our beat that don't seem like he's going to get done all night."

"You can go loaf in a tavern or whatever it is you'd rather be doing. I was his last client tonight."

"Yes ma'am. Right after we get your name and how to find you if we need to talk to you again."

The woman sputtered but gave the soldiers what they demanded. The grays usually got what they wanted.

"Thank you, ma'am. We appreciate your cooperation. The streets being what they are at night, Luke will walk you over to make sure you get there safely."

Smeds grinned. That was one slick gray boy.

The silent partner set off with the woman. The other soldier resumed his patrol. Smeds rose. "We're lucky, he'll really stop off for a beer."

"To get any luckier than we've just been the bastard wizard would have to be in there dying of heart failure right now. You ready?"

"Yes."

"Let's get it over with. Quietly."

Smeds dashed across the street. Quietly. Fish was supposed to give him time to get around back. Then Fish, whom the wizard had not met, would knock on the front door. Smeds was supposed to get in—quietly—and come at the wizard from behind.

The tactic made no sense to Smeds but he was not the general here.

He stopped, astonished. A side window stood open to let in the cool night air. He paused to catch his breath, then peeked.

The room was the one where the wizard had seen Timmy the first time they had come. The wizard was in there, puttering around, putting things away and mumbling to himself.

This was better than any back door.

Fish's knock, when it came, was so discreet Smeds almost missed it. The wizard cocked his head, looked like he was trying to make up his mind whether or not to answer. Finally, muttering, he left the room.

Smeds hoisted himself through the window, went after the man. He did not recall the floor being creaky. He hoped his memory was playing no tricks because he was taking no precautions against floor noise. He drew his knife as he moved.

The nerves went away. It seemed almost as though he was a bystander in his own mind. He noted that he was moving much more fluidly than was usual, ready for anything in the midst of any movement.

The wizard growled, "Keep your pants on," and started fumbling with the latch as Fish knocked for the third time.

Smeds peeked carefully.

The wizard was at the door, ten feet away, back to him, just opening up.

Fish asked, "Professor Dr. Damitz?"

"Yes. What can I do—"

And that was it.

Smeds saw the wizard rise onto his toes and start to raise his hands as he moved out to get the man from behind. Then Fish was pushing into the house, supporting the wizard, kicking the door shut behind him. He saw Smeds, was surprised. He started lowering the wizard to the floor. "How did you get in so fast?"

Smeds looked at the dead man. "Open side window. How come you did it that way?" The handle of a long knife stuck out under the wizard's chin. There was not much blood.

"Blade went straight into the brain. No chance for him to do any witch stuff while he was dying."

Smeds stared at the body. Now he understood the plan. Fish had sent him around back just to get him out of the way.

"You all right? How do you feel? A little shaky?"

"I'm all right. I don't feel much of anything at all."

"Did he keep written accounts or records? Something where he might have put down something about Timmy?"

"I don't know. I never saw him do it while we were here."

"We'd better look. You start . . . You feeling something now?"

"Just feeling sorry for that woman after they find him."

"Yeah. Be rough for her for a while. Look around. Try not to mess things up too much. And don't take too long. We got to get out of here." Fish went into the room where the wizard had done his interviews.

Smeds rejoined him five minutes later, carrying a large glass jar and a couple of books.

"What the hell is that?"

"Timmy's hand. I found it in a room in the back. All kinds of weird stuff back there."

"Shit. I'm glad we took time to look." He'd picked out a few books himself. "Let's get the hell out of here and get rid of this stuff. Out the window. We pull it shut, it'll latch itself behind us. I'll go first, see if it's clear."

Smeds's hands shook as he poured the first mug of beer. But it had not been as hairy as he had thought it would be. Still, there was some reaction. More than Old Man Fish was showing.

The hand and books had been cared for. The most dangerous strand had been clipped. Only one thing left to do.

Their benefactor the Nightstalker corporal came in with his beer bucket, beamed around, went for a refill.

"Shit!" Smeds said. "I clean forgot. I had a date tonight."

Fish gave him a few seconds of a commiserating look, then said, "Drink up. Catch a nap. We've got half the job still to do."

36

It seemed like I never saw Darling do much to deserve her White Rose reputation. Maybe that was because she was so unglamorous when you saw her, just a scruffy, tangle-haired blond broad in her twenties who would have fit right in with the gang back at the potato ranch. Except that she would have looked a lot more worn out now because she would have been dropping kids for ten years.

Besides her being deaf and dumb, which is always hard for the rest of us to keep separate from stupid, I think it's hard to take her serious because she does what she does so easily, so casually. Take that attack on the monastery. Slicker than greased owl shit. And no one would have gotten hurt at all if that monster Toadkiller Dog hadn't come plopping into the middle of those centaurs when he was making a run for it. And that was their damned fault. They got too eager. If they was hanging back like they was supposed to they would have had time to get out of the way.

She sure had the respect of the tree god and all the pull with him she wanted. I think he'd indulge her in anything.

She don't put on no airs, neither.

It was strange for a while. You had Darling in one spot with Silent always close, trying to stay between her and Bomanz and her and Raven at the same time, only Raven and the wizard would not get anywhere near each other because they did not trust each other any more than Silent trusted either of them.

It was all kind of amusing. Because when you are on the back of a monster a couple of miles up in the air, sharing that back with a couple hundred critters that would have you for breakfast if you don't behave, you sure as shit ain't going to get away with nothing, no matter what you'd like to try.

The Torque boys knew that. I knew it. Darling knew it. But those other three geniuses, Bomanz, Raven, and Silent, was so busy being important plugging up the knothole at the center of the universe that that never occurred to them.

The Torques were a little nervous about me, though. I used to be Guards and they was Black Company. They thought I might be lugging a grudge.

But I was saying the White Rose don't put on no airs. Not even being the White Rose. She don't like being called anything but Darling. She did not mind when I came around trying to talk to her. Only Raven and Silent minded. I told Raven to stuff it when he objected and I guess she gave Silent the same message. He didn't do nothing but stand around looking like he was making up his mind where to start carving when I talked to her.

Mind you, these were grown men. Plenty older than me.

It was Raven's fault I could talk to her at all. He had only himself to blame. It was him insisted I learn the sign language so we could communicate in situations where we couldn't talk out loud.

Not that we talked much at first, Darling and me. Just hi-how-you-doing stuff. I wasn't very good at it. She taught me more sign as we went along.

She didn't come right out and say it, but I got the feeling she was starved for somebody to talk to besides Silent. She couldn't say it with him hovering over her like he did all the time.

When I started out the only thing I was really wanting to find out was what she really thought about Raven. I wanted to keep him from making any more of a fool of himself than he already had. Maybe she figured that. She was sharp. She never gave me a chance to work it in.

So after a couple days we were talking about what it was like being country kids growing up with a war going on all around. It was easy to understand why she had gone the way she had. Everybody knew the story so she didn't need to explain.

I told her I joined up to get away from the farm, and from where I stood back then the Rebels didn't look no cleaner than the imperials. Maybe less, because she hadn't come along to start cleaning them up yet. And the imperials got paid. Good, and on time.

She did not seem offended, so I added my secret philosophy of life: any dork who became a soldier for an idea instead of the money deserved to die for his country. You're going to put it all on the table, six up with some other guy, it damned well better be for stakes you can carry away.

That did offend her. It got scorching for a few minutes, then sort of settled down to a sustained low heat, her trying to convince me that there were abstractions worth fighting and dying for and me clinging to my position that no matter how admirable the cause there was no point getting killed for it because even only twenty years down the road nobody was going to remember you or give a rat's ass if they did.

Two days went by that way. I got a feeling that if there hadn't been so much ego getting in the way Raven and Silent would have ganged up on me for hanging around with their girlfriend.

She was easy to talk to. I let out things I never said before because I thought they had no value, considering the source. Stuff about how people and the world worked, like that.

I never realized my outlook was so cynical till I tried to tie it up and put it across in that unsubtle way you have to use with sign.

I told her I could not believe in her movement because it did not promise anything for the future except freedom from the tyranny of the past. I told her that what little philosophy I'd detected driving the movement totally ignored human nature. That if the Rebels ever did manage to topple the empire, whatever replaced it would be worse. That was the lesson of history. New regimes, to make sure they survived, were always nastier than the ones before them.

I kept after the theme of what did the Rebels offer in place of the empire? In my limited experience the people of the empire were more secure, prosperous, and industrious than they had been before its coming—except in areas where there was an active Rebel presence. I told her that for the great mass of people freedom was not an issue at all. That it was an alien concept, at least as her Rebels seemed to define it.

I told her that for a peasant—and peasants probably make up three-quarters of the population—freedom meant being able to provide for a family and market any surpluses.

When I left home the potato fields and all the rest of it were held communally. The work was long and hard and boring, but no one ever went hungry and even in the lean years there were surpluses enough to provide for a few little luxuries. In my grandfather's time, though, our fields had been just one more parcel among scores owned by one great landholder. The people who lived there were part of the furniture, like the trees and water and game, legally bound to the land. They had any number of obligations to the lord that had to be fulfilled before they could work the land. And of the product of the land they had to hand over fixed amounts to the landholder. First. If it was a bad year the lord could take everything.

But they had not had to walk in the Lady's dark shadow. So they must have been blissfully happy little farm animals.

I told her that the sons of the landholders were all backbones of the Rebel cause now, determined to liberate their enslaved homelands.

I told her I had no illusions about the Lady having any love or concern for the common people. She obliterated existing ruling classes simply to be rid of potential challenges to her own power. She had plenty of disgusting minions whose assigned domains were terrible places to be.

Finally, I argued that the empire was in no danger of falling apart, despite the fact that she had disarmed the Lady during the showdown in the Barrowland. The Lady had been obsessed with expanding her borders and the reach of her power. She had created an efficient machine to handle the domestic work of the empire. That machine had not been broken.

We had been in the air four days. Evening was coming on and ahead brown gave way to the hazy blue of the Sea of Torments. We had come a long way in a short time. When I thought about all the shit me and Raven went through to get down there to that monastery, damn! This was the only way to travel.

I left off arguing with Darling. I felt a little guilty. As that day had gone on she had argued back less and less. I think I was throwing a lot of stuff at her that she probably hadn't ever thought about. On a smaller scale I've always known people for whom a goal was everything, who never thought nothing about the consequences of the goal achieved.

Of course, I did what everybody else does. I underestimated the hell out of her.

Next day I didn't run into her till around noon. I guess I was avoiding her. But when I did see her she had bounced back.

About the same time I noticed the dark loom of land on the northern horizon and right afterward realized we were losing altitude. The windwhales were sliding into some kind of formation, a triangle above with us below. Mantas were taking to the air, gliding toward the coast.

I asked her, in sign, "Where are we? What is happening?"

She replied, also in sign, "We are approaching Opal. We are going to find Raven's children. We are going to compel him to confront his past."

That was a measure of how much the tree god valued and respected her. Though he had yanked his minions away from that monastery and had ordered them to scurry north because there was no time to lose, he would let her interrupt the journey for this because it was important to her.

I figured Raven didn't know what was coming. He'd probably need a lot of support when it hit him in. I went looking for him.

There was nothing out at the fourth hour, Smeds reflected. The soldiers were all off somewhere loafing because the bad boys all had sense enough to be home in bed. The bakers had not yet stumbled out to their doughs and ovens. The only sound in the street was that of the drizzle falling, of the water dripping from the roofs. He and Fish made no noise. Fish seemed not to be breathing.

There would be one problem with this one they had not faced with the other. He had seen them both before. On the other hand, they were making their move at this ungodly hour, reasonably expecting to catch him in his bed.

Breaking in should be easy, from what they recalled of the physician's place. The deed itself would have to be done quietly. There was, they suspected, a live-in housekeeper. They did not want to add her to their weight of conscience.

"There it is," Smeds said.

Like the wizard, the physician was prosperous enough to occupy his own freestanding combination home and place of business. The structure was barely a decade old. A few years before it had been built, that part of town had burned during an outbreak of violence between Rebel sympathizers and mercenaries in the imperial service. The middle class had come in to build homes upon the graves of tenements.

"Front door to the house and door to the office," Fish murmured. "Assume a back door. These places all have a little fenced-in garden behind them. Three windows we can see. I'm surprised vandals haven't destroyed that leaded-glass monstrosity."

The physician's office was scabbed onto the side of his home, set a little back. It had its own little porch and door, and beside the door a marvelously dramatic floor-to-ceiling leaded-glass window six feet wide.

"Go," Fish said.

Smeds dashed across and crouched in the slightly deeper shadow beneath the window on the building's right front. His thoughts about the weather were not polite. He was miserable enough without a soaking drizzle added on for frosting.

Fish came across as Smeds rose to test the window. He was not surprised to find it tightly secured. Fish went to the house door, achieved no better result. Smeds crossed behind him and checked the second front window. Solid. He slid around the corner of the house.

Fish was crouched in front of the office door, which he had pushed open about three inches. Smeds joined him, his knife sliding into his hand. "It was unlocked?"

"Yes. I don't like it."

"Maybe it's so clients can get in anytime."

Fish ran his hand up the inside of the door. "Maybe, but there's a heavy latch catch. Let's be careful."

"Careful is my middle name."

Fish pushed the door open, looked inside. "Clear." He slipped in.

Smeds followed, headed for the door connecting with the house. It was unlocked, too. It opened toward him. He pulled. It swung smoothly, sound-lessly. He heard a faint *snick* behind him as Fish closed the latch. He saw noth-ing suspicious in the room before him. He stepped inside.

Maybe it was a whisper of cloth in motion. Maybe it was a little intake of breath. Maybe it was both. Whatever, Smeds spun down and away.

A line of fire sliced across his shoulder blade.

He landed on his knees facing the office, watching a shape collide with Fish. Fish said, "Shit!" At the same moment the shape squealed. Then it threw itself sideways and floundered through the leaded-glass window a step ahead of Smeds.

Fish came to the window. "That was him."

"He was expecting us."

"Too damned smart. Figured too much out. Can't let him get away." Fish jumped through the window.

The physician was going for all he was worth, legs and arms flailing. That fat little hedgehog was no sprinter.

Smeds followed Fish. He passed the older man moments later, and gained steadily on his prey, who had gotten a sixty-yard head start. The physician glanced back once, stumbled. Smeds gained ten yards while he was getting his balance. Fear lent him renewed stamina and speed. He stayed the same distance ahead for half a minute.

The physician knew he was not going to outrun anyone. Smeds knew he knew that. Unless he was running in a blind panic he had developed a strategy, had chosen an ultimate destination. . . .

The physician zigged right, into a narrow alleyway.

Smeds slowed, approached cautiously.

Footfalls pounded away in the darkness.

He went after them. He was just as careful rounding another corner, again without need. Gods, it was dark in there! Third corner.

He stopped dead. There were no sounds of flight. He tried listening for heavy breathing but could not be sure he heard anything because his own in-truded too much.

What now?

Nothing to do but go forward.

He dropped down and advanced in a careful duck walk. His muscles protested. He was grateful for the toughening they had gotten in the Great Forest.

There! Was that breathing?

Couldn't tell for sure. The echoes of Fish's approach overrode it.

Scrape! Swish!

What must have been a foot missed his face by a fraction of an inch. He flung himself forward but the physician was already moving again. Smeds's knife ripped along his hip.

Smeds went down hard but caught hold of a heel and managed to hang on. He snaked forward, stabbing at the man's calf, his target invisible in the darkness. The man squealed like an injured rabbit.

Smeds was so startled he let go. Then he realized he was letting his man get away. He got up and charged ahead, smashed into the man.

"Please! I won't tell anyone! I swear!"

Pain slashed along Smeds's ribs on this left side.

He flailed away with his knife, hitting anything he could. The physician tried to scream and fight back and run away all at the same time. Smeds held on with one hand, kept hacking with the other. The physician pulled him out into a street.

Smeds kept hacking.

The physician collapsed.

Fish arrived. "Shit, Smeds. Shit."

"Got him."

"You sure he didn't get you, too?"

Smeds looked at himself. He was covered with blood. Some of it was his own.

Somebody yelled up the street. People had begun coming to stoops and windows.

Fish bent, slashed the physician's throat, said, "We've got to get out of here. There'll be soldiers here in a minute." He looked at the dead man's hand. "Unh. A mess. He touched you with that?"

"I don't think so."

"Come on." Fish offered him a hand. "You make it?"

"I'm all right for now."

Fish headed back into the alley.

Smeds began feeling it as soon as the excitement began to go out of him. He knew he would not be able to get away if a chase developed.

Instead of making for the Skull and Crossbones Fish headed into the West End.

"Where we going?" Smeds asked.

"Reservoir. Get you cleaned up. We take you home looking like that the gray boys are going to be around to ask what happened before you can get your boots off."

38

I don't know what I expected to see when we got to Opal. Maybe nothing changed from my last time there. I sure wasn't ready for the mess we found. I gaped incredulously as we glided over the ruins, where a few survivors scurried around like frightened mice. I went and told Darling, "Don't look to me like there's much chance we'll find the people you want."

Odds never bothered Darling.

Raven and Silent now had especially black feelings for me. I'd had the gall to tell Darling who she had to find if she wanted to force Raven to face his past. Neither of them wanted that to happen.

Both of them was so busy thinking about themselves they didn't have time to wonder what Darling really thought or felt about anything.

We crossed most of the city. Up north we spied several large, neatly arranged camps. The tents were too numerous to be all army, but they showed us that the imperials were there, responding to the destruction of the city in a quick, orderly fashion. Below, soldiers and civilians were at work leveling way for the new. Though they stopped to gawk, these people did not run away.

Darling ordered us to watch for the standard of the military commander. She figured that was the place to start since the city was obviously under martial law. I couldn't figure why she thought she'd get any cooperation, though.

I asked, "What do you feel about old Raven these days?" I was real careful to keep my hands hid from him and Silent both.

I figured she wouldn't understand what I meant. I was wrong. She signed, "Once I had a child's love for a man who saved me and nurtured me and risked everything to protect me when, long before I could believe it myself, he recognized the role I would play in the struggle with the darkness. That child was like a very little girl in some ways. She was going to marry Daddy when she grew up, and it never occurred to her that things might not turn out that way till she tried to pursue it, and to press it.

"I was never really a girl, or a woman, or a human being to Raven, Case. Even though he did awful things for me. I was a symbol, an expiation, and when I insisted on becoming a person he did the only thing he could do to keep on serving the symbol and not have to deal with a flesh-and-blood woman."

"That is kind of how I always thought it was," I signed.

"Many men admire Raven. He fears nothing concrete. He takes no crap from anyone. People who mess with him get hurt, and the hell with the consequences. But those are the only dimensions he has. They are the only dimensions he permits himself. How can I remain emotionally entangled with a man who will not allow himself emotions, however much he did for me in other ways? I appreciate him, I honor him, I may even revere him. But that is all anymore. He cannot change that with some demonstration, like a boy hanging by his knees from a branch to impress a girl."

I grinned because I had a gut feeling that's exactly what Raven had in mind.

Poor sucker. There just wasn't nothing left for him to win. But he wasn't the kind to accept that even if she told him to his face, point-blank.

I wanted to sneak in one or two about Silent, too, but I didn't get a chance. The military headquarters got spotted and the windwhale dropped down and moved up to it, anchored itself in place by dropping tentacles to grab rocks and trees. Its presence overhead was disconcerting to those in the camp.

I like that word, disconcerting. I got it from Bomanz. Such a sly way to say they were having shit hemorrhages down there.

There was a big hoorah, all kinds of whoop and holler and carrying on, when a bunch of Plain critters ganged up on the scar-faced stone and threw it over the side, almost into the lap of the command staff down there.

Them old boys were pretty shook. I wondered how much more excited they would get if they knew the White Rose her own self was right over their heads. But they wasn't going to try nothing, no matter what they knew. Who'd want to duke it out with four pissed-off windwhales, which is what they would get if they wasn't polite.

Scarstone popped back up. He talked. Silent translated for Darling. I didn't hear anything. The Torque boys had let me know I was supposed to stay back, so I stayed back. Darling made a bunch of signs that I guess the stone could see somehow. It went away. After a while it came back.

After four rounds of that it didn't go away anymore. But the windwhale stayed where it was, so I guessed a deal had been struck.

I went to try to talk it over with Raven. But he was in about as foul a mood as I ever saw, and anyway he had pegged me for some kind of traitor, so I gave it up and went off to shoot the shit with the Torques and the talking buzzard and a couple other Plain creatures that wasn't too shy.

Darling goes after something she usually gets what she wants. This time she got it just before noon next day.

A hoorah broke out downstairs. Darling sent Scarstone to check it out. It came back and reported. She got up and walked over to Raven, who watched her like she was the hangman coming. She signed at him. He got up and followed her, again with the eagerness of a man headed for the gallows.

I knew him well enough to see the signs. He was putting himself into a role. I tagged along, wondering what it would be. Most everybody else moved closer, too.

Two young people around twenty came puffing up over the side of the windwhale.

So the impossible was possible, the improbable a sure thing. Unless the army down there figured they could placate Darling with a couple of ringers.

The boy looked like Raven twenty years younger. Same dark hair and coloration, same determined face not yet hardened into grimness.

I was only a step behind when Raven got his first look at them. He cursed softly, muttered, "She looks like her mother."

It was plain they had not been told they were here for a family reunion. They were just puzzled and scared. Mostly scared. And more so as the mob closed in around them. They did not recognize Raven.

They did recognize Darling. And that scared them even more.

Everybody waited for somebody else to say something.

Raven whispered, "Do something, Case." Desperately. "I'm lost."

"Me? Hell, I don't even speak the lingo that good."

"Case, help me out. Try to get this moving. I don't know what to do."

All right. I thought of a couple of suggestions for him, but I was never a guy who kicked crippled dogs. I went to work in my feeble Jewel Cities dialect. "You have no idea why you were brought here, do you?"

They shook their heads.

"Relax. You ain't in no danger. We just want to ask about your ancestors. Especially your parents."

The boy rattled something.

"You'll have to talk slower, please."

The girl said, "He said our parents are dead. We've been on our own since we were children."

Raven winced. I figured the voice must be like that of his wife, too.

Silent translated for Darling, who really gave them the eye. Seeing they was Raven's kids, I didn't figure it was so amazing they pulled through.

"What do you know about your parents?"

The girl took on the answering chores. Maybe she thought her brother was too excitable. "Very little." She told me pretty much what I had been able to find out for myself when we were headed south. She did know that her mother had not been a nice person. "We've managed to live her down. Last year we won a judgment that took some of our father's properties from her family and re-turned them to us. We expect to win more such judgments."

That was something, anyway. The girl had conjured up no special regard for the woman who had brought her into the world.

The boy said, "I don't remember my mother at all. After our births I think she had as little to do with us as she could. I remember nurses. She probably got what she deserved."

"And your father?"

"I have vague memories of a very distant man who wasn't home much but who did visit when he was. Probably out of obligation and for appearance' sake."

"Do you have any special feeling about him now?"

"Why should we?" the girl asked. "We never really knew him, and he's been dead for fifteen years."

I faced Darling, signed, "Is there any point going on?"

She signed, "Yes. Not for their sake. For his."

I asked Raven, "You got anything to put in?"

No. He didn't. I could see him thinking maybe he was going to slide out of this after all.

It wasn't going to be that easy. Darling had me tell them that their father had not died, that he had been harried into exile by their mother's confederates. She had me hit the high spots of their years together.

They had had time to get over being scared. Now they were getting suspicious. The boy demanded, "What the hell is going on? How come these questions about our old man? He's history. We don't care. If he was to walk up right now and introduce himself I'd say so what. He'd be just another guy."

I signed to Darling, "You going to keep pushing it?" and asked Raven, in Forsberger, "You want to call his bluff?"

Negatives all around. Bunch of wimps. So Raven *was* going to slide out. I told his kids, "Your father was very important in the life of the White Rose. He was a stand-in parent to her for years and she knew how it pained him to be in exile. She stopped here because she wanted to try to give back something of what she'd had and you couldn't."

Neither Raven nor Darling liked me saying that.

I think the girl figured it out about then. She got real carefully interested in Raven. But she didn't say anything to her brother.

I got Darling to agree this was enough and our guests ought to be turned loose. She wasn't satisfied with the way things turned out. What the hell can you do with women? You can give them exactly what they ask for and they'll cuss you because that ain't what they *really* want.

Just before the girl went over the side she turned and told me, "If my father was alive today he wouldn't have to fear that he would be unwelcome in his daughter's house." Then she went.

All right. There was an open door if ever I seen one.

We took off the second the girl hit ground. Darling wanted to get far away before word she was there got to somebody who could do something about it. We lit out northeast, like we was headed for the Plain of Fear.

39

Every day more people came into Oar, and nobody left. A pigeon could not get out. Several had died trying.

Some elements of the population were growing restless. There were more fights than usual. More people ended up on the labor gangs. The searches went on and on and on. There was not a building in Oar that had not been tossed at least twice, not a citizen who had not been rousted. There were rumors of big tension in high places. Brigadier Wildbrand did not think she owed Gossamer and Spidersilk anything and resented having her Nightstalkers used as bullies for their personal benefit. They were elite troops, not political gangsters.

The nature of the people entering the city changed with time. Fewer were farmers or traders. More and more were dire characters with no obvious trade.

The news about the silver spike was spreading.

Smeds did not like it. It meant big trouble. How did Gossamer and Spidersilk expect to control all those witches and wizards, some of whom might be much more potent than they suspected? And the bullies they brought with them?

Chaos threatened.

Smeds understood the strategy. The twins meant to up the heat and pressure till the spike popped to the surface. If it came up in hands other than their own they were confident they could take it away.

Could they?

Every witch and wizard in town knew that, too. But they had come hunting anyway.

Only Tully was pleased. He thought the situation perfect for the auction he wanted to run. "We got to get the word out," he told the others, over supper.

"Keep your voice down," Fish said. "Anybody in here could be a spy. And we don't get any word out. You heard of anybody offering to buy anything?"

"No," Tully admitted. "But that's because—"

"Because most of them know they can be outbid. You notice the twins aren't offering anything. They figure they can get what they want by divine right, or something."

"Yeah, but—"

"You have no grasp of the situation, Tully. Let me offer you a challenge. . . ."

"I'm fed up with your shit, Fish."

"Indulge me in an experiment. If I'm wrong I'll shout it from the rooftops. If I'm right, you win anyway."

"Yeah? Let's hear it."

Sucked him up again, Smeds thought. His opinion of his cousin declined by the hour.

"Here's two coppers. Go find a kid somewhere away from here. One who don't know you. Pay him to go to the Toad and Rose and tell the bullies there that the wizard Nathan is looking to hire a couple men to help him sneak out of the city tomorrow morning."

"I don't get it."

Smeds said, "Gods, Tully, couldn't you just *once* do something without arguing about it first?"

Fish said, "The experiment will be more instructive if it simply unfolds, explaining itself as it goes."

"Why should I do that asshole Nathan any favors?"

Smeds stood up. "I'll do it. Otherwise we'll be here till the middle of next week."

"I want Tully to do it. I want him to see that there can be a direct connection between his saying something and what happens in the real world."

"You're putting me down again, ain'tcha?"

"Tully," Smeds said, "shut the fuck up or I'm going to brain you. Pick up the goddamned money, hit the goddamned street, find a kid, and pay him to deliver the goddamned message. Now."

Tully went. Smeds had gotten pretty intense.

"He's going to get us all killed," Timmy said as soon as he was gone.

"How's your hand coming?" Smeds asked.

"Real good. Don't try to distract me, Smeds."

"Easy, Timmy," Fish said. "I think there's a chance this trick will get through to him."

"Want to bet?"

"No."

Smeds would not have taken the bet either.

The wizard Nathan and his four men had rented rooms just up the street from the Skull and Crossbones. The grays came there shortly before dawn. They found five dead men and two rooms torn to shreds. They sealed the area, searched it again, asked a lot of questions. Fish made sure they all got a good look at the mess. He asked Tully, "You starting to catch on?"

"Who would do something like that, man? Why?"

"Nathan was a wizard. If he was going to sneak, that meant he'd found the spike and wanted to make a run for it."

"But he wasn't going to leave town."

"No. He wasn't, Tully. But you said he was."

Tully started to be Tully and argue, but he bit down on it and thought for a moment before he said, "Oh."

"Next time you say something without thinking first or checking to see who's listening, that could be us all carved up."

Smeds said, "You maybe went too far to make your point, Fish."

"Why?"

"This ain't over yet. Those soldiers didn't find anything but a mess. They're going to figure whoever made the mess got the spike."

"Yeah. And maybe everybody else will think so, too. Maybe even the guys who actually did it. The next few days ought to be interesting. And part of the ongoing lesson."

"What're you blathering now?" Tully demanded.

"That was a big gang in that place, eh? Five pro thugs and a sorcerer. No-body would try to take them alone. I figure there was at least three guys did it. Probably more. Unless they're a bunch that really trust each other they're going to have trouble. Every one of them is going to know *he* didn't get the spike, but he isn't going to be sure about the others."

Tully said, "Oh," again, and after a while, "This shit is getting scary. I never thought it would get this hairy."

"Your problem is you never thought," Timmy muttered, but Tully did not hear him.

Fish said, "It's just starting, Tully. It's going to get hairier. And if we want to come out of it with our skins on we're going to have to be very damned careful. These aren't nice or reasonable people. They aren't going to be interested in dealing till they got no other choice."

It got hairier fast, as more, and more powerful, thaumaturgic treasure hunters poured into the city. Old feuds having nothing to do with the spike flared.

The citizenry, pressed from all sides, responded by rioting on a small scale. The twins presided smugly, doing nothing to retard the escalating violence.

Smeds spent a lot of time being sorry he had let Tully get him into this in the first place. Because of the other treasure they had brought home, the living was good, but not good enough, given that he had to watch his every word every minute and spent half his time looking over his shoulder to make sure disaster was not gaining on him.

We were over the Forest of Cloud, south of Oar, east of Roses, west of Lords, hiding out from imperial eyes, too many of which had seen the windwhales cruising far from their proper range over the Plain of Fear. Darling wanted to let a little of the excitement die down before she moved on.

She would not let the tree god hurry her, though he was in a minor frenzy. I did not understand exactly what was up yet, but neither did some of the others, so we were getting an education from old Bomanz, who was suddenly Darling's number-one boy.

"Since you were all there you'll recall that in the course of the battle in the Barrowland the soul or essence, of the Dominator—the most evil being ever to walk this earth—was imprisoned in a silver spike, which was then driven into the trunk of a sapling sired by the tree god of the Plain of Fear." He really did talk that way when he had an audience.

"At the time it was believed that would effectively contain and constrain the residual evil of the man forever. The sapling was the scion of a god, invulnerable, unapproachable, and so long-lived as to be, in practical terms, immortal. As the sapling grew, its trunk would engulf the spike. In time the old evil would not persist in so much as memory.

"However. We thought wrong.

"A band of adventurers succeeded in stunning the sapling long enough to get in and prize the spike out. If we are to credit the sapling's own testimony—and we must, for the nonce, because it is the only testimony we have—none of those men had the least familiarity with the art, and were remarkable only because they came up with an idea that, logically, should have originated with someone devoted to the occult."

Damn him, he did talk like that when he had an audience. And he wouldn't stop.

"Gentlemen, the silver spike is loose in the world. It's not the Dominator. He's dead. But the undying black essence that drove him remains. And that could be used by an adept to summon, coerce, and shape powers even I cannot begin to imagine or fathom. That spike could become a conduit to the very heart of darkness, an opener of the way that would confer upon its possessor powers perhaps exceeding even those the Dominator possessed.

"Our mission, our *holy* mission, given the White Rose by Old Father Tree himself, is to recover the silver spike and deliver it for safekeeping, at whatever cost to ourselves, before someone of power seizes upon it and shapes it to his own dark purpose and is, in this turn, shaped—perhaps into a shadow so deep there would be no chance ever for the world to win free."

That bit about "at whatever cost to ourselves" got a big hand. The talking buzzard pulled his head out from under his wing, cracked an eye, went to town heckling the old wizard. That finally distracted him from his windier fancies.

"Buzzard, if you were fit to eat I'd be picking up kindling right now!" he shouted. Then he got back to business. "The tree god has reason to suspect that the spike is now in Oar. The White Rose, Silent, the Torques, and some of our smaller companions will drop into the city. With the help of the underground they will establish a secure base, then will take up the hunt. Raven, Case, and I, because of our considerable familiarity with the site, will go on to the Barrow-land to see what can be learned there."

That started a bunch of bitching. Raven didn't like being sent off someplace where Darling wasn't. I didn't think these guys had the right to draft me into their adventure. I got pretty hot.

Darling took me aside and calmed me down, then convinced me that even if I remained committed to the empire in my heart, helping her in this would not harm me. Maybe she was right when she said the evil she wanted to abort wouldn't respect allegiances or philosophies. That it would divide the world into two kinds of people, its enemies and its slaves.

That was a little heavy to get down in one or two bites but I said all right, I'm just following Raven around anyway. Might as well keep on keeping on.

So that was that. I gave in. I also started giving some thought to going back to herding potatoes as a career. No potato never talked anybody into making a fool of himself.

41

Smeds came out onto the porch of the Skull and Crossbones figuring to shoot the shit with Fish, but found the only empty chair stood between Fish and the Nightcrawler corporal. He wanted to turn around but felt like he was committed.

He plopped down. "Hey, Corp. Don't you never do nothing but sit here and drink beer?"

"Not if I can help it."

"That's the life. I oughta go sign up."

"Yeah? You wouldn't like it. Where was you at three in the morning?"

"In bed sleeping one off."

"Lucky you. Ask me where I was at three in the morning."

"Where were you at three in the morning?"

"With about two hundred others guys out Shant, where they got all those buildings tore down and nothing new put up yet. Looking for a monster. Some guy reported there was a monster out there bigger than the Civil Palace."

"Was there?"

"Not even a little one."

"Was the guy drunk?"

"Would a sober man be out there at that time of night?"

"Got something interesting coming here," Fish interjected, jutting his chin up the street.

Smeds saw three men and a woman. She was not much to look at and too old to be interesting anyway. But she looked tough. She carried weapons like a man.

As a bunch they looked as hard and tough as any Smeds had seen. But what made them stand out was the zoo they carried with them.

The woman had a live ferret draped around her neck and chipmunks peeking out of her pockets. The tall, dark, and darkly clad man who walked to her right carried an unhooded falcon on his left shoulder. The three men behind them—Smeds thought they might be brothers—carried a bunch of monkeys and one big snake.

Smeds asked, "You going to arrest them? They're lugging enough illegal hardware to start their own war."

"And give you boys a show? Eh? My mama's stupid babies never lived to make corporal." Even so, he stuck his fingers in this mouth and whistled. When those people looked he beckoned.

The tall man looked over with tight eyes for a moment, made a slight gesture at the man with the snake. That one came over. The snake looked them over like it was sizing them up for dinner. It gave Smeds the creeps.

The corporal said, "Just a friendly word of advice, pal. The city is under martial law. Ain't nobody supposed to tote a blade over eight inches long. 'Less he's wearing gray."

The snake man went back and told the tall man, who looked at the corporal hard for a moment, then nodded.

"You see that?" Smeds said. "That goddamned monkey gave us the finger."

The corporal said, "I seen that tall guy somewhere before. Down the length of a sword. Hunh! Well. Bucket's empty. Save my chair while I walk my lizard and get me a refill." He went inside.

"What you think of that bunch?" Smeds asked Fish.

"I've seen the tall one before, too. In the same circumstances as the corporal. A long time ago. No problem remembering where or when, either, since I was only ever in one battle."

That just puzzled Smeds. He asked, "You figure they're here after the dingus, too?" He could ask because by now everyone in town had a good idea what was going on.

"They're here for it, yes. They'll help make the game interesting."

"What're you yapping about, Fish?"

"Don't mind me, boy. Just an old man maundering. Ha! I thought so. Isn't there anymore, is it?"

Down the street the animals people had stopped in front of a place Timmy said used to be a butcher shop but these days was just another dump filled up with squatters. The tall man glanced back as though he had heard Fish. Then the whole bunch moved on, indifferent to stares.

The corporal came back out with his full pail and bladder empty. "I ought to give this shit up. Bothers my stomach." He took a drink. "Where were we?"

Fish said, "I was just going to ask you when they're going to unbutton the gates. Going to start getting hungry in here now the farmers won't bring anything in."

"They don't consult me on policy, Pop. But I'll tell you something. I don't think those two bitches give a rat's ass if everybody in Oar starves. They ain't going to go hungry."

Smeds was tired of listening to the corporal. "Going to get me something to drink." He went inside and had a beer drawn, wondered how long the supply would last. And how much more patience the people of Oar had. A while, for sure. Not that many were hurting yet. But if circumstances did not change a big blowup was inevitable.

Timmy Locan came in, got him a beer, stood beside Smeds awhile without saying anything, then suggested, "Let's go for a walk when we finish these."

"All right. I need the exercise."

When they were well away from the Skull and Crossbones, passing through a construction area where they were unlikely to be overheard, Smeds asked, "Well? What's up?"

"You remember that doc that looked at my hand when we first came back?"

"Yeah." More than a twinge of guilt. He and Fish had not told the others what they had done. Tully was so indifferent he had not noticed that the physician and wizard were no longer among the living. Timmy had noticed, though, and Smeds supposed he had some definite suspicions about two such coincidental and convenient murders. "What about him?"

"It looks like he got whatever it was that I had and passed it around to everybody who came to see him. And they passed it on, too. Not like the plague or probably everybody would have it by now. But there's a couple hundred people got it already. The ones that have had it the longest . . . Well, they're worse off than I was. Yesterday a woman who had it killed herself. This morning a guy whose whole arm had gone black killed four of his kids who had it before he killed himself."

"That's awful. That's really gruesome. But it isn't anything we can do anything about."

"I know that. But the thing is, see, the grays have gotten interested. They're grilling everybody with the black stuff. From the questions they're asking you can tell they think there's a connection with the spike. They're trying real hard to find out about everybody who's had it and done something about it, like me."

"I don't think you need to worry, Timmy. They can't trace it back to you."

"Yeah? Those bitches are *serious*, Smeds. What happens after they find out all the trails lead back to that doc, who turned up among the dead right after the stuff started spreading? They're going to figure he had a fatal accident on account of somebody he treated didn't want to be remembered. And they already know the only way to treat the stuff is to cut off whatever it's eating on. So pretty soon the word goes out to the grays to grab amputees. Especially guys with missing hands."

"Maybe you got a point. Maybe we better see what Fish thinks."

Fish agreed with Timmy. There was no reason to think Gossamer and Spidersilk would not go so far as to order the arrest of all amputees. They were determined.

Fish did some heavy thinking. "I reckon it's time to blow some smoke."

"What do you mean?" Smeds asked.

"This situation—the whole city sealed up like a bottle—can't go on forever. There'll be a blowup. When that comes we break loose with everybody else. Till then we buy time by getting them off on a wild-goose chase, or by taking advantage of the potential for chaos they've created."

Smeds was bewildered. He grew more so when Fish said, "Get rid of whatever you've got that's silver. Get gold or copper or jewels or whatever, but get rid of your silver. Smeds, you pass the word to Tully and don't let him give you any shit."

"What's going on?"

"Just do it."

So they did. Even Tully, who had become reasonably serious and responsive since Fish's demonstration of the deadly power of the loose word.

42

We arrived in the Barrowland by sliding down ropes with our possessions strapped on our backs. A few Plain creatures joined us. More would after we set up a safe camp. The boss menhir wanted a couple of his flint-hearted buddies there to keep an ear on us. The better to maintain quick communication, he said. Right.

The better to make sure things got done the tree god's way.

"Back where we got started," Raven said as soon as we had our feet on the ground. He'd been getting more fit to live with since Opal. He was almost back to being the old boy I'd known when I first met him.

"Back in the cold and wet," I grumped. It had been the tag end of winter when we'd left. It was sneaking up on winter again now. The leaves had fallen. We could get snow anytime. "Let's don't fool around, eh? Let's do what we got to and get out."

Raven chuckled. "How you going to keep them on the farm after they've seen the big city?"

"A little less ruckus, please," Bomanz said. "We don't yet know there aren't any imperials around."

He was halfway right. We hadn't yet seen that with our own eyes, but the Plain creatures had scouted and reported nothing bigger than a rabbit within five miles. I could trust them on that.

Bomanz had to do some wizard stuff before he was satisfied. Then he let us set up housekeeping and start a fire.

We dragged out with morning twilight and ate some god-awful cold yuck. Then we split up.

I got the town and military compound because I knew them best. Raven took the woods. Bomanz got the Barrowland itself. Near as I could tell he wasn't going to do anything but stand in the middle and take a nap.

The Plain creatures were supposed to do anything they wanted and clue us if they found anything.

I needed to do only a rough once-over to see what had happened in town. There wasn't nothing but bones left. Poking around wasn't as bad as it could have been. I did everything I could think of to find out something useful, then I went back to camp. Bomanz was just about where I'd left him, eyes still closed, but taking little tippy-toe baby steps.

At least he was moving.

Raven came back. "You done already?"

"Yep."

"Find anything?"

"A whole lot of bones. Enough to build an army of skeletons."

"Got you down, eh?"

"I knew all them guys."

"Yeah." He didn't say anything else, just waited. He can be an all-right guy when he isn't busy feeling sorry for himself.

"I figure the Limper and Toadkiller Dog did the killing. But there was some-body else there after them. Somebody went through like a mother picking a baby's nits. There ain't nothing left there that's even remotely valuable."

Raven thought about that. "Nothing at all?"

"Picked as clean as the bones."

"That might be an angle to follow up in Oar. Though they would have taken only what they could carry, and that would be the kind of thing that isn't going to make a splash. Unless they did something gaudy. Which if they had they would be in the hands of the imperials already."

Bomanz joined us. He puttered around making tea while Raven told us he'd found two campsites probably used by the guys we were after, but nothing that would help us. "If there ever was anything here the imperials got to it first."

"And if they had," Bomanz said, "they would have the spike by now."

We'd gotten reports from Oar through the stones. The news was not encouraging. It looked like a couple of imperial bigwigs were out to grab the spike and go into the empire business for themselves.

"You learn anything?" Raven asked.

Bomanz said, "Not much. There were four of them. Probably. They got away with what they did because most of the time the sapling was preoccupied with Toadkiller Dog and did not perceive them as a threat. It thought they were throwing sticks at it as a gesture of defiance."

"Sticks?" I asked.

"They threw sticks at the tree until it was almost buried. Then they set the pile on fire."

Raven muttered, "You don't have to be brilliant to be a god."

I said, "We got them now."

"What?" That Bomanz never did figure out you could be joking.

"All we got to do is look for four guys with splinters in their fingers."

Bomanz scowled. Raven chuckled. He asked, "Do we know anything about these men at all?"

Bomanz grumbled, "We don't even know they were men."

"Great."

Raven said, "Since we can't get anywhere with who, why not work on when? Can we pin down any dates? Even approximately? Then work back from them to whose movements fit?"

That sounded pretty feeble to me and I said so. "Even if Oar hadn't been attacked and half the people killed and the other half kept crazy ever since . . ."

"Forget I brought it up. Well, wizard, is it worth us hanging around here? Or should we go down to Oar and try to smoke them out?"

"Tentatively—pending reports from our allies from the Plain—I'd say we're wasting our time here."

The weirder side of the outfit didn't come up with anything either. At sundown we clambered back aboard our smelly airborne steed, planning on having breakfast in Oar.

I was looking forward to my first decent meal in months.

43

Smeds was amazed. That bastard Fish sure could stir some shit.

There was a rumor got started that this silversmith down on Sedar Row—where all the silversmiths and goldsmiths and such were located—had had a guy bring in a giant silver nail and pay him a hundred obols to turn it into a chalice and keep his mouth shut about it. Only this smith had got to celebrating his good fortune last night and had had too much to drink and had bragged to some of his cronies after swearing them to secrecy.

Today a man's life was worthless if he had anything to do with the metal-working or jewelry trades. Those who were out after the spike were getting desperate. They were stumbling over each other and causing a lot of damage in the process. Mostly to one another.

The grays were late getting into the game but when they did they did not fool around, they came with a vengeance, sweeping through the city confiscating every piece of silver they found on the assumption the spike could have been turned into anything by now. They tried giving claim chits but people were having none of that. They had been robbed by the military before.

There was resistance. There was localized rioting. People and soldiers were hurt and killed. But there were too many soldiers and even now most people were not angry enough to rebel.

"Pretty sneaky, Fish," Smeds told the old man, walking down a street where he felt safe talking. "Mean sneaky."

"It worked. That don't mean I'm proud of it."

"It worked all right. But for how long?"

"I figure three, four days. Maybe five if I feed the rumor a couple of new angles. Plus however long it takes Gossamer and Spidersilk to decide the spike isn't in any of the silver the soldiers are collecting up. So we'll be all right for maybe a week. Unless one of the freelancers stumbles onto us somehow. But in the long run we're still had. They'll get us one way or another. Unless this backward siege breaks. Let even ten people get out of this city and get away and you've opened the whole world up to the search. Because if there's a successful breakout the man who has the spike is sure to be one of the first people gone."

"He is?"

"Wouldn't you figure that if you were in the place of the twins?"

"I guess."

"Every day they send more men to guard the walls. I don't know, but I think they're maybe working against a deadline. If they are, we might use that against them."

"A deadline? How's that?"

"Those two aren't anywhere near top dogs in the empire. Sooner or later their bosses have got to get suspicious about what they're up to. Or one of them might decide to come up here and grab off the spike for himself."

"We should have left the sucker where it was and settled."

"We should have. But we didn't. We have to live and maybe die with that. And make no mistake, Smeds. We're in a fight for our lives. You, me, Timmy, Tully, we're all dead if they ever get close to us."

"If you're trying to scare the shit out of me, Fish, you're doing a damned good job."

"I'm trying to scare you because I'm petrified myself and you're the only one I think is steady enough to help me. Tully doesn't have any backbone at all and Timmy has been living in kind of a daze ever since he lost his hand."

"I got a feeling I'm not going to like whatever you're going to say. What're you thinking?"

"One of us needs to steal some white paint. Not buy it but steal it, because a seller might remember who he sold it to."

"I can handle that. I know where to get it. If the grays aren't sitting on it. What're we going to do with it?"

"Try to change the focus of this whole mess. Try to politicize it."

There he went getting mysterious again. Smeds did not understand but decided he did not have to as long as Fish knew what he was doing.

That evening was the first time Tully asked to borrow money. It was a trivial amount and he paid it back next morning, so Smeds thought nothing of it.

That night was the first night Smeds fell asleep thinking about Old Man Fish and how he seemed to have no conscience at all once you got to know him. It was like Fish had decided he was going to get through this mess and get his share from the spike even if he had to sacrifice everybody in Oar. That didn't seem like the Fish he'd always known. But the Fish he'd always known hadn't ever had anything at stake.

He could not be sure where he stood himself. He was neither a thinker nor a doer. He had spent his life drifting, doing what he had to do to get by and not much more.

He did know that he did not want to die young or even to answer questions on the imperial rack. He knew he did not want to be poor again. He had done that and having money was better. Having a lot of money, like from selling the spike, would be even better.

He could arrive at no alternative to Fish's methods of achieving salvation, so he would go on going along. But with an abiding disquietude.

44

Toadkiller Dog observed the quickening through tight eyes. He was an ancient thing and had dealt with sorcerers all his days. They were a treacherous breed. And the smell of betrayal hung thick in that monastic cellar.

He had located the necessary help more quickly than he had expected, in a country called Sweeps, a hundred miles west, where a bloody feud between families of wizards had raged unchecked for three generations. He had examined the respective families and he decided the Nacred had skills best suited to his needs. He had made contact and had struck a bargain: his help overcoming their enemies in return for theirs reconstructing his "companion."

He had told them nothing about the Limper.

The Shaded clan had ceased to exist, root and branch, sorcerers, wives, and nits that might have grown to become lice.

The twelve leading Nacred were there in the cellar, crowded around the trough of oil where the head, wedded to its new clay body, awaited a final quickening. They muttered to one another in a language he did not understand. They knew betrayal at this point would be painful and expensive.

They had seen him in action during the scouring of the Shaded. And he had been a cripple then.

He had made sure he got his own new limb first.

He growled, just a soft note of caution, an admonition to get on with it.

They did the thing that had to be done. One of the fool monks who had stayed around to restore the monastery served as the sacrifice.

Color flowed over the surface of the gray clay. It twitched and shivered almost as if it were becoming genuine flesh.

The body sat up suddenly, oil streaming off it. The Nacred sorcerers jumped back, startled. The Limper ran hands that had been clay over a body that had been clay. His smile became an ecstatic grin. "Mirror!" he said. His voice was a thunder. He looked at himself, ran fingers lovingly over a face that far exceeded the original at its best.

A bellow of rage nearly brought the ceiling down.

Toadkiller Dog caught one glimpse of what the Limper saw in the mirror.

The gorgeous new fading to reality. Truth. His face as it existed without the cosmetic overlay.

The Limper flung out of the trough, grabbed it up, hurled its contents around the cellar. The Nacreds retreated, shouted back, hastily prepared their defenses. They did not understand what was happening.

Toadkiller Dog understood. He knew the Limper's rages. This one was almost wholly contrived.

He had been looking in the wrong place when he had been watching the Nacreds for treachery. The Limper was the source of the foul smell.

He attacked. And in midleap recognized his error.

The Limper used the trough to deflect his charge, dashed to the doorway he had been blocking with his bulk. The Limper laughed, pranced up the stairs ahead of Nacred spells. Toadkiller Dog flung after him, but too late.

The stairwell collapsed.

Toadkiller Dog started digging.

"It won't be that easy, my fine pup. You thought you would use me, eh? Eh? Me! I let you think you could till you did what I needed done. Now enjoy your tomb. It's better than you deserve but I have no time to prepare you a more suitable fate." Mad laughter. Tons of earth poured in on what had collapsed already.

Toadkiller Dog dug furiously but stopped after a moment, snarled at the panic in the darkness behind him. In the ensuing silence he listened very carefully.

North! The Limper was headed north! He was crazier than ever but he had turned away from his mad quest for revenge.

There was just one answer to that puzzle. He had set vengeance aside in hopes of gathering more power.

Toadkiller Dog growled once, softly, almost amused. The shields were off the claws now.

45

If you dipped a wad of cotton in paint, then sponged semicircles around a common center you could create a passable imitation of a rose, Smeds discovered.

After the excitement of the search for Fish's phantom silversmith had died and he had failed to sell the rumor that one of the twins had taken possession already and was hiding it from her sister, the old man had decided to loose his final bolt. To take advantage of the potential for chaos. To add a new level of distraction to the mess plaguing Oar.

Which was why Smeds was out after midnight with a bucket of paint for the third night running. Fish had sent him to mark selected points with the sign of the White Rose to give the impression that there was an angry underground about to respond to imperial excesses.

Fish was after a slower but grander effect this time. He wanted the whole city to hear and begin to hope and believe. He wanted the grays to start worrying. The rest, he said, should take care of itself.

Smeds finished his three roses and headed home. Elsewhere Fish was painting roses of his own. Smeds had done two the night before and three the night before that, all in places where a partisan strike would be appreciated sincerely by the mass of citizens. Slow and easy, Fish said. Let it build.

Fish had had a stroke of luck last night. He had stumbled onto a couple of grays who had gotten themselves killed somehow and had painted white roses on their foreheads, claiming them for the movement he wanted to create out of the collective anger.

Smeds did not like this game. Too dangerous. They had people enough after them from directions enough already. He had worries enough with the spike hunters.

But that was not on his mind as he stole toward the Skull and Crossbones. He was mulling the puzzle presented by Tully. Earlier in the evening Tully had borrowed money from him for the fourth time in eight days, this time a fair sum and before he had repaid the last loan.

Smeds never approached the Skull and Crossbones in a hurry. That Nightstalker corporal would catch him sure, first time he did.

One peek and he knew he wasn't going in the front way. The corporal and his cronies occupied the porch. So it was the long way around and slide in the back.

And that was no good either. He found trouble on the way. And it almost found him.

Two men were lounging inside the mouth of the skinny, scruffy alley that passed behind the Skull and Crossbones. He would have walked into them if one had not coughed and the other had not told him to shut up.

What was this? Smeds felt no inclination to ask. He settled into a shadow to wait them out.

A half hour passed. Came the hour. Nothing happened except one man coughed and the other told him to shut up. They were bored. Smeds began to nod.

A third man arrived running. "He's coming," he said, then darted over to hide not eight feet from Smeds. Smeds was wide-awake now.

Sure enough, someone was coming, and from the sound of his steps he was a little bit drunk. He was talking to himself, too.

Smeds suffered one startled moment of recognition, then Timmy was into the ambush and the men jumped him so fast he never got a chance to yell.

Smeds almost jumped in. He half rose, half drew his knife. Then he realized that the most he could hope to do was get himself killed by the other two after he got the first one he reached.

What the hell was he going to do?

He was going to follow them. See where they took Timmy, then get Fish and . . . And listen to Fish tell him he didn't have ball one.

For sure too late to do anything here, now. He had to follow them.

He had no idea who they were but a strong suspicion as to what: bully boys for a freelance spike hunter who had decided to interview citizens who were short a hand.

Following was less trouble than he had expected. Timmy fought them all the way. That kept them from devoting much attention to their surroundings. And they did not go that far, just a quarter mile into an area of fire-gutted buildings condemned but not yet demolished, so bad the squatters had not moved in.

They took Timmy inside one of those. Smeds stood in a shadow and looked at it and wondered what he was going to do and kept hearing Fish say they were fighting for their lives now.

He'd never been much of a fighter. He'd always walked away when he could. When he could not he'd always gotten whipped. He hadn't had the desire or meanness, or whatever, even when he'd had no choice.

Which got him to remembering all the bullies who had taunted and slapped and shoved him around and puzzling the eternal *why* did they do it when he'd never done a thing to them. The old anger bubbled up, along with the nerve-tingling vengeance fantasies, the miasma of bitter hatred.

One of the men came back out of the building, urinated into the street, backed off, and just leaned against the wall. He didn't act like he was doing anything but just hanging out. He wasn't alert enough to be a sentinel.

Smeds staggered forward without the slightest damned idea what he was doing. Besides shaking so bad his toenails rattled.

He stumbled, went down on one knee onto a broken brick, could not silence a whining curse, and in the shock of pain suffered an inspiration.

He came up limping, stumbling, muttering to himself. He headed straight for the man, sort of singing, "Once there was a farmer's daughter, couldn't behave like a maiden ought-er."

The thug was alert now. But he did not move.

Smeds did a pratfall, giggled, got onto his hands and knees, pretended a bout with attempted upchucking, then got his feet under him and headed out. Straight into the wall about ten feet from the man watching him. He backed off muttering, looked at the wall like he couldn't understand where it had come from. Then he put one hand against it for support and started stumbling toward the thug. At a distance of four feet he pretended to take first notice of the man, who was watching more with amused contempt than with suspicion.

Smeds made a little "Gleep!" he hoped sounded startled and frightened and silently thanked whatever gods there might be that he hadn't been recognized. Now if the guy just stayed in character and tried to roll him in the guise of helping . . .

Smeds stumbled and went down onto hands and knees.

"Looks like you had one too many, old buddy." The thug stepped over.

Smeds made gagging sounds. Inside, he was listening to Old Man Fish. "Like taking a woman, Smeds. Slide it in. Don't stab."

The man started giving him a hand up. He did not see the blade in Smeds's palm. Smeds leaned against him and began sliding in between his ribs, into his heart.

One part of Smeds stood outside, guiding his hand. The rest was in a passion of terror and horror, oblivious to the world. Only one coherent thought splashed across that chaos. It was a lie that killing got easier each time you did it.

When he came out of the fog, consciously, he was a hundred feet away, dragging a still-twitching body.

"What the hell am I . . . ?"

Getting it out of sight, of course. Because this was just the start.

He heard a muted scream and realized that another such had opened the first rent in the fog that had possessed him.

Smeds went into the building with the caution and intense concentration of a stalking cat. He compartmented his emotion, did not let them torment him when Timmy screamed. He used the cries to move a few quick steps each time.

What the *hell* was he doing?

The screams came from a basement. Smeds started down the steps, so committed he moved as though under a compulsion. Six steps down he hunkered, then almost stood on his head to get a look around.

The base of the stair ended a few feet from a doorway without a door in it. Light and the screams came through that. Smeds eased down a couple more steps, then carefully lowered himself over the side, got underneath the stair, looked around.

It was hard to see much, but it looked like the fires had been gentle here. This part of the basement was untouched. There wasn't a whiff of old smoke.

He could make out most of what was being said in that other room. Someone was asking Timmy impatient questions. Another two men were bickering about the character Smeds had killed. One was worried that the man had run out, the other didn't give a damn.

Under the stair was not the place to be if someone decided to go looking. The light from the room would give him away. Smeds moved out carefully, got behind a pile of junk to the left of the doorway.

And there he squatted, unable to think of anything to do.

Timmy passed out or something. He wasn't yelling anymore. One man was grumbling about that while the other two went on about the man in the street. The grumbler snapped, "He *has* been gone too long. Give me some peace. Go find him. Both of you."

Two men stomped out and headed upstairs, still arguing. They were the other two who had snatched Timmy.

Smeds rose, stretched, drifted over till he could see into the room.

Timmy was tied into a chair, slumped forward, unconscious. A man bent over him, back to Smeds. Too good to be true. He slapped Timmy. "Come on! Come out of it. Don't die on me now. We're too close to the truth."

Slide it in, slide it in, Smeds told himself, gliding toward the man.

The man sensed danger, started to turn, eyes and mouth opening. . . .

Too late.

Smeds's knife pierced his heart. He made a grisly noise that wasn't quite a scream, tried to get hold of Smeds, folded up.

Maybe it was easier after all. . . . The detachment went. His heart hammered. His hands shook. His breath came in gasps. He stumbled over to Timmy, cut the ropes binding him. . . . Gods! They'd burned out one of his eyes! They'd . . .

Timmy fell over on his face.

Smeds got down and tried to bring him out of it. "Hey! Timmy! Come on. It's me. Smeds. Come on. We got to get out of here before those other guys come back."

Then it hit him. "Shit!" Timmy had croaked. "Son of a bitch! I come in here and risk my ass for nothing. . . ." Except maybe for whatever Timmy told them before he checked out.

Then he felt like a total shit, getting pissed at Timmy for dying and inconveniencing him. Then he got confused, not knowing what to do about the fact that he was in here and still had to get out and there were bodies here something probably ought to be done about.

"Hey, Abel!" somebody shouted from outside. "You better come check this out. Somebody offed Tanker."

Smeds dropped Timmy's hand, frantically jerked his knife out of the dead man—wizard?—and got himself over beside the doorframe as the someone yelled, "You hear me, Abel?" Feet *thump-thump-thumped* down the stairs. "We're maybe in deep shit here. Somebody stuck a knife in Tanker. . . . What the shit is going on here?"

The man had stopped just outside the doorway.

Smeds came around thrusting at what he guessed should be chest height. . . . and discovered that the big voice belonged to the smallest of the thugs. He turned the thrust into an uppercut, drove his blade up and in under the man's chin, not sliding it, driving it with all the force of panic into the man's brain.

He had not looked the other two in the eye at their moment of realization. Gods! That was scary. He jumped back, stumbled over Abel and Timmy, fell on his back as his victim toppled forward.

Before Smeds was all the way back on his feet someone else called some question downstairs. He dove over to reclaim his knife. The man continued to move, one leg slowly pumping. For a moment he thought of a dog trying to scratch. Crazy.

The damned knife was wedged in bone. It wouldn't come loose. He scrambled around looking for another weapon, any weapon, while the voice from the head of the stairs asked several questions more. All Smeds could come up with was the dead man's own knife, which he pulled from its sheath with a sort of superstitious dread.

He got against the wall beside the doorway again and waited. And waited. And waited.

In time the shakes went away. The nerves calmed some. He realized that his latest victim could be seen from the stairs.

He waited some more.

He had to make a move. The longer he dicked around, the more time there would be for something to go wrong.

His muscles did not want to unlock. He was completely terrified of the consequences of making any move.

But he did, finally, drag himself around far enough to peek through the doorway.

Morning light spilled down from upstairs. It showed him nothing to fear. He made his feet move. He found no trouble on the ground floor. From the doorway he could see nothing but desolation, city badlands where not a soul stirred. He wanted to run, all the way to the Skull and Crossbones.

He bore down, did what had to be done, dragging the body out of the street, to the cellar, where it was less likely to be discovered soon. Then he headed for home. But he did not run, though his legs insisted they had to stretch out and go.

46

We dropped into Oar in the middle of the night but we didn't find Darling and them till noon next day, and then only because we had Bomanz along to sniff them out. They weren't where they were supposed to be. Meantime, I ran into two guys that I knew from when me and Raven were staying in Oar, and they wanted to talk talk talk.

Nobody in town had much else to do.

"Things don't look good," Raven said as we drifted through the streets, following Bomanz's sorcerous nose. "All these people packed in here, no chance to get out, food stocks probably getting low, plague maybe getting ready to break out. The place is ripe. Would have been long gone if this was high summer and the heat was eating up everybody's tolerance. You know anything about these twins?"

He wasn't talking to me. When it comes to sorcerers and sorcery I don't know nothing about nothing except I want to stay out of the way.

"Never heard of them," Bomanz said. "That doesn't mean anything. The Lady had a whole crop coming up."

"How do you think you'd stack up against them?"

"I don't plan to find out."

I spotted a white rose painted on a door. "Look there." They looked. Other people were looking, too, and trying not to be noticed doing it.

"That damned screw-up Silent," Raven growled. "He's talked her into doing something stupid."

"Who you trying to bullshit?" I asked. "When did anybody ever talk Darling into doing something she didn't want to do?"

He grumbled some, then grumbled some more.

Bomanz's nose picked out their hideout then, and after some shibboleth stuff we got into the cellar where Darling was holding court with a gang of leftovers from Oar's Rebel heyday. They didn't look like much to me.

Raven grunted. He wasn't impressed either. He reported the high points of our visit to the Barrowland. That didn't take a minute, even using sign. Then Darling let us in on the situation in Oar, which took a lot longer than a minute.

Raven wanted to know what she was doing, painting white roses around town. She said she wasn't. In fact, she said nobody that had anything to do with the movement admitted doing it. Since none of those roses had been seen before she arrived she thought somebody recognized her in the street and was trying to get something stirred up.

She didn't have a shred of evidence. Didn't seem likely to me. Anybody that recognized her, that wasn't personally committed to the cause, should ought to go for the bounty on her, the way I figured. She would fetch a good price, and Silent not a bad sum, and even the Torque brothers were good for a chunk that could keep you in beans for a long time.

Raven figured it the way I did. But he wasn't going to argue with Darling, so he asked if there had been any progress finding the silver spike.

"None," she signed. "We have been very busy stampeding around old ground already covered by other hunters, finding nothing while we ate their dust. In the meantime our small allies have been busy spying on those other hunters that our brothers of the movement have identified for us."

Bomanz wanted names. He got them. A long string, with a half dozen noted as having enlisted with the deceased.

"You know any of those people?" Raven asked.

"No. But I've been out of touch. The curious angle is, there hasn't been any attention from the Tower. This thing is pulling in every hedge wizard and tea-leaf reader with a smidge of ambition. These twins are pretty plainly up to exactly what you'd expect from their kind, faced with an opportunity like this. News like this gets around faster than the clap. It's got to have reached the Tower. Why isn't some real heavyweight up here to sit on those two?"

I suggested, "Because they don't have windwhales to carry them around and all their flying carpets got skragged back when."

"They have other resources."

There wasn't no point worrying about it since we weren't going to come up with an answer.

Raven wanted to know how the other guys were trying to find the spike. He figured maybe the problem was that the hunters were attacking it from the wrong direction.

Darling signed, "Spidersilk and Gossamer have made repeated direct searches. They also provoke and watch the other hunters, who have been concentrating on finding the men who stole the spike and brought it to Oar."

I asked, "How do we know the damned thing is even here?"

Bomanz said, "You can sense it. Like a bad smell."

"But you can't tell where it is?"

"Only very vaguely. Right now I'd guess it's somewhere north of us. But I can't narrow that directionality to below about a hundred thirty degrees of arc." He raised his arms to show what he meant. "It's the nature of the thing to maximize the evil around it. If it could be sniffed out easily there would be little chance for the play of chaos. It isn't sentient but it responds to and feeds back the dark emotions and ambitions around it. One way to find the men who brought it out of the Barrowland might be to look for people who were out of town during the proper time period and who have shown changed patterns of behavior. Generally, aggravated tendencies toward indulging weaknesses they've had all along."

Darling got that from Silent. She signed back, "That method has been tried. Without success. The Limper's raid killed so many and left people so mixed around that the necessary information cannot be gathered."

"There's got to be a way," Raven carped.

One of the local guys said, "Gossamer and Spidersilk already thought of it. Get so many bad guys in that the thieves have to panic and do something to give themselves away. Sooner or later."

"Dumb," Raven said. He sneered. "All they'd have to do is snip a few loose ends, if there were any, and sit tight."

"That's what they're doing. We think." The guy went off about some really gruesome disease called the black hand that had been traced to a physician that got himself knifed an eyeblink after the twins closed the city. There was still some debate, but a lot thought the black hand maybe got started when somebody accidentally touched the spike barehand, then passed it on when he went to the physician for help. The physician passed it around to his clients and they passed it around some more, till the soldiers rounded them up so they couldn't.

Darling signed, "The twins cleave to this theory. The physician's murder was witnessed. Two men were involved. They have not been identified or even well described."

The local man went on about theories and about how none of the people with the black hand had had anything to do with grabbing the spike. The twins made sure of that right away. So there was some guy running around who maybe had been fixed up by the doc and that was an angle a lot of hunters were working.

"Maybe," I said. "But what if maybe his buddies was smart enough to put him six feet under?"

Seemed like nobody had thought about that. Nice people tend to think everybody is nice.

"What about them roses?" I asked. "If it ain't your people painting them, who is? And why?"

"A diversion, obviously," Raven said. "If we could catch whoever is doing it we might get a break."

The local talker said, "Go teach your grandma to suck eggs, fella. We've got everybody we have on the street, calming people down and asking questions. Tonight everybody is going to be watching likely places to put more up. We see somebody, he'll be over here answering questions before he can blink."

I sat myself down out of the way, fixing to take a nap. "Want to bet they don't walk into it?"

Does clay tire? Does the earth? No. The clay man loped northward, hour after hour and mile after mile, day and night, pausing seldom and then only to freshen the coat of grease, spell-supported, that retained moisture and kept the clay supple.

The miles passed away. The hulks of raped cities fell behind. Suns rose and set. He crossed the southern frontier of the northern empire. It was early in the day.

He had not gone far when he realized he was being paced by imperial cavalry. He slowed. They slowed. He stopped. They drifted into cover and waited.

They had been waiting for him. His return had been expected.

How? By whom? For how long? What lay ahead, specially prepared for him?

He resumed his run, but more slowly, his senses keyed.

The cavalry worked in relays, no party riding more than five miles before being relieved. If he turned toward them they retreated. When he held to the road they closed in slowly, as though carefully daring his might. He suspected they wanted him to pursue them. He refused. He followed the road. In time he increased his pace.

A subtle mind opposed him.

After a while the indrift of the riders sharpened, like a charge starting to take shape. . . .

His attention ensnared thus, he nearly missed the slight discoloration, the minuscule sag, in the road ahead. But catch it he did. Pit trap. He hurled himself forward in a prodigious leap.

Missiles filled the air. Several slammed into him, batting him around, and he knew he had been taken. Arrows from saddle bows were whistling around him before he regained his equilibrium. The cavalry to his left had grown a little too daring. He faced them, about to welcome them with death.

A five-hundred-pound stone ripped across his right shoulder so close it brushed away the protective grease. He jumped, whirled. If that had caught him square . . . He sensed no presence on which to spend his wrath. He whirled again. The cavalry were galloping away, already beyond retribution.

He removed the shafts from his body, surveyed the area. There was no pit. Just the appearance of one with a trigger board much better hidden under the dust where his foot must fall if he was going to jump over. Even the stone had been hurled by an engine triggered remotely and fortune had placed him a step out of the line of fire.

That was the first trap. The next was a bridge over a small, sluggish river. Barrels of naphtha had been rigged beneath it, fixed to break open and catch fire when he stepped upon the bridge decking.

This time the diversionary troops waited atop a ridge beyond the river. Light engines hurled missiles at him as he used his power to jam the mechanism meant to breach the barrels and start the fire.

A five-pound rock hit him in the chest, flung him backward. He sprang up angrily and sprinted toward his tormentors.

Held only by a feeble peg, the center section of the bridge collapsed under his weight. The falling timbers smashed the naphtha barrels. A swarm of fire missiles was in the air before he hit water.

They had made a fool of him twice.

They would not live to try a third time.

He came boiling out of the water, up the bank below the burning bridge, into the face of renewed missile fire, bellowing. . . .

He tripped something. A vast net flew up, toward, and over him. Its cables were as strong as steel but of a sticky, flexible substance like spider silk. The more he struggled, the more tangled he became. And something kept drawing the net tighter and dragging him back toward the water. He would have great difficulty with the verbal parts of his sorcery beneath the river.

The knowledge of the possibility that he might be vanquished by lesser beings stabbed through him like a blade of ice. He was up against something he could not overcome by brute force.

The blow of fear—the existence of which he could not confess even to himself—stilled his rage, made him take time to think, to act appropriately.

He tried a couple of sorceries. The second effected a break in the net just before he was pulled beneath the surface.

He came out of the river carefully, with concentration, and so avoided a trap armed with a blade that could have sliced him in two. Safe for the moment, he took stock. Minor, all the damage done him. But a dozen such encounters could accumulate into something crippling.

Was that the strategy? Wear him down? Likely, though each phase of each trap had been vicious enough.

He proceeded much more carefully, his emotions, his madness, under tight rein. Vengeance could await achievement of the more important triumph in the north. Once he had taken that keystone of power he could requite the world a thousand times for its cruelties and indignities.

There were more traps. Some were deadly and cunning. He did not escape unscathed, alert as he was. His enemies did not rely upon sorcery. They preferred mechanisms and psychological ploys, which for him were more difficult to handle.

Not once did he see anyone other than the cavalrymen who dogged him. He found the gates of the great port city Beryl standing open and its streets empty. Nothing stirred but leaves and bits of trash, tossed by winds from the sea. The hearthstones were cold and even the rats had gone away. Not a pigeon or sparrow swooped through the air.

The murmur of the wind seemed like the cold whisper of the grave. In that desolation even he could feel alone and lonely in spirit.

There were no ships in the harbor, no boats on the waterfront. Not so much as a punt. The haze-distorted shape of a single black quinquirireme hovered beyond the harbor light, well out to sea. There was a statement here. He would not be allowed to cross the sea. He was sure that whichever way he chose to walk along the coast he would find the shores naked of boats.

He considered swimming. But that black ship would be waiting for that. He was so massive that all his energy would have to go to staying afloat. He would be vulnerable.

Moreover, salt water would leak through his protective spells and gnaw at the grease, and then at the clay. . . .

So there was little choice. He must do what they wanted him to do and go around. He pictured the map, chose what seemed to be the shorter way. He began running to the east.

The horsemen paced him the rest of that day. When dawn came they were gone. After a few hours he became confident enough to increase his pace. Curse them. He would do what they wanted and slaughter them anyway.

The miles passed away as they had before he had entered the empire.

As he ran he pondered the hidden purpose behind his having been turned onto this extended course. He could not prize loose the sense of it.

48

Smeds found Old Man Fish as soon as he had gotten himself some rest. Fish listened intently and watched him through narrowed eyes as he told his tale. "Didn't think you'd have what it takes, Smeds."

"Me neither. I was scared shitless the whole time."

"But you thought, and you did what you had to do. That's good. Think you'd know the man who got away if you saw him again?"

"I don't know. It was dark and I never got a real good look at him."

"We'll worry about him later. Thing we got to do now is get rid of those bodies. Where's Tully?"

"Who knows? Probably sleeping. Why not just leave them where they are? It ain't like they're out where somebody's going to trip over them."

"Because somebody besides you and me knows where they are and he might tell somebody else who might go take a look and maybe recognize Timmy Locan as a guy who used to hang around with you and me and Tully. Get it?"

"Got it." Also, maybe Fish wanted a look just to make sure Timmy had gone out the way Smeds said he had. Smeds was related to Tully Stahl and Fish already had a habit of not taking on faith anything *that* Stahl said.

"So get Tully and let's move."

Smeds went inside the Skull and Crossbones, nodding to the Nightstalkers corporal as he passed. The owner, who didn't have much use for them, scowled at him across the common room. Smeds had to pass close by him. The man asked, "You boys going to pay for your room? You're two days late."

"Tully was supposed to take care of it. It's his turn."

"Surprise, friend. Tully didn't. And he's running a pretty steep beer tab, too. Another day or two, I'll mention it to your buddy the corporal." He grinned wickedly. Nothing he'd like better than to send them to the labor companies.

Smeds held his eye till he flinched, then tossed him a coin. "There's for the rent. I'll tell Tully to cover his tab."

Tully was not asleep. He'd maybe heard some of that. He was pretending. Smeds said, "Come on. We've got work to do." When Tully didn't move, he added, "I'm going to count to five, then I'm going to kick your ribs in."

Tully sat up. "Shit, Smeds. You get more like that asshole Fish every day. What's so damned important you got to get me out of bed?"

"In the street." Meaning he couldn't say there, where somebody might hear. "On our way out you might pay the landlord what you owe him. He's getting edgy. Talking about mentioning you to that corporal."

Tully shuddered. "Shit. That asshole. How about you cover it for me for now, Smeds? I'll get it back to you soon as I can sneak off and tap my stash."

Smeds eyed him. "All right. We'll be waiting outside. Don't fool around." He went out, tossed a heavy coin at the landlord as he passed, said, "Don't give him no more credit," and joined Fish outside. "Back when we hit town I figured my share of the cash take should keep me pretty good for four or five years. How about you?"

"Easy. I'm an old man. My needs are simple. What's up?"

"Tully. You think even a dipshit like him could have blown his whole share already?"

"Tell me about it."

"Tully's been hitting me up for loans. The first couple times he paid me back, but not the last three times. I just now found out he didn't bother to pay the rent and he's running a big beer tab."

"Yeah?" Fish looked downright nasty for a second. "I have something to do.

When he comes out you and him head out to the place. I'll catch up before you get there." He stalked off.

Tully stomped out a minute later. "All right. I'm here. What's so goddamned important? Where's Fish and Timmy?"

"Fish had something to do." Smeds thought he knew what. "He'll catch up. Timmy's dead. We're going to bury him."

Tully looked at him blankly, not watching where he walked. "You're shitting me."

"No, I'm not." Smeds told it in driblets, when no one could overhear. There were a lot of people in the street, moving restlessly, aimlessly. There was tension in the air. Smeds figured the grays wouldn't be able to keep the lid on much longer. A little more patience, a little more care, and they would have weathered the siege.

Wherever they went, wherever there were no grays, people whispered about the white roses, fed the rumor that the White Rose herself had come to Oar and was just awaiting the right portents to start the insurrection.

The grays had spies everywhere, Smeds knew. Spidersilk and Gossamer would have heard of the whispers within an hour of their first muttering. They would have to act, absurd as the rumors might be. Else someone would see something as a sign and would raise the torch of rebellion.

There was another whisper, more sinister, running beneath the foolish hope of an adventure by the White Rose. This one was harder to catch because the rumormongers were much more cautious in retailing it.

The twins, this fable insisted, had begun to feel pressed for time. They were getting set for mass executions in which they would slaughter the men of Oar till someone bought his life by surrendering the silver spike.

There was no mystery at all now about what was happening to Oar. Everyone knew about the silver spike. The knowledge seemed to signal the opening measure of a long, dark opera of dread.

Tully fussed and worried about the impending massacre till they neared the fire-gutted section where the bodies lay. Then he shifted the focus of his whine. "I ain't going in there, Smeds. They're dead, let them lay."

"The hell you're not. This whole mess came jumping out of your pointy head. You're going to hang in and help the rest of us do whatever it takes to get through it alive. Or I'll break your head personally."

Tully sneered. "Shit."

"Maybe not. But you goddamned well better believe I'll give it my best shot. Move."

Tully moved, startled by his intensity.

Fish caught up a minute later. He exchanged glances with Smeds, said, "There isn't anybody behind us. Slow down while I scout ahead." He went. Two minutes later he signaled all clear and Smeds slipped into the killing place.

The smell of death was in the air already, though not yet strong. Fish growled outside. Tully responded with a snarl but clumped inside. Smeds eased down the cellar stairs and was surprised to find the death room still illuminated by the stubs of some of the candles that had been burning before.

Nothing had changed except that the corpses had stiffened and relaxed again and a roaring swarm of flies had gathered, working their eyes, nostrils, mouths, and wounds.

Tully said, "Oh, shit!" and dumped whatever was in his stomach.

"I've seen worse," Fish said from the doorway. "And there's just a bare chance this scene here could get worse. Sit down in the chair, Tully."

"What?"

"Sit down. Before we get to work we have to have a talk about who got into the money Timmy kept in his bedroll."

Tully started, went pale, tried bluster. "What the shit you trying to pull, Fish?"

Smeds said, "Sit your ass down, Tully. Then tell us how come you got to be stealing from Timmy and mooching from me when you just made the biggest hit of your life."

"What the hell are you . . . ?"

Fish popped him in the brisket, pushed him into the chair. "This here is serious business, Tully. Real serious. Maybe you don't realize. Maybe you haven't been paying attention to what's going on. Look around. Come on. That's the boy. See this? This was our pal Timmy Locan. Just a sweet happy kid you conned into thinking he could get rich. These other guys did this to him. And they were gentle as virgins compared to some of the people who are after us. Look at them, Tully. Then tell us how you've been dicking up, being too damned stupid to be scared, too damned dumb to sit tight and wait the storm out."

Malevolent rage filled Tully's eyes. He looked like he was thinking about getting stubborn where stubborn was pointless.

Smeds said, "You're a screw-up, cousin. You had one damned good idea in your whole damned life and as soon as we get to work on it you got to go and try to mess it up for all of us. Come on. What did you do? Are we all in a hole?"

A flicker of cunning, quickly hidden. "I just made a couple bad bets is all."

"A *couple*? And you lost so much you had to go stealing from Timmy?"

Tully put on his stubborn face. Fish slapped it for him. "Gambling. You dip-shit. Probably with somebody who knew you from before and knew you didn't have a pot to piss in. Tell us about it."

The words came tumbling out and they did not disappoint Smeds's suspicions in the least. Tully told an idiot's tale of bad bets made and redoubled bets laid then doubled again and lost again till, suddenly, here was Tully Stahl not only broke but behind a stack of markers that added up to a bundle and the boys holding them were not the sort to laugh it off if he reneged. So he'd had no choice. Anyway, he would have paid Timmy back out of his share as soon as they'd sold the spike, so . . .

Fish cut him off before he started justifying his idiot behavior. Smeds knew it was coming. And knew if Tully went at it he would turn the whole thing around so it was all their fault. He asked, "How much you still owe, Tully?"

That hint of cunning again. Tully knew they were going to bail him out.

"The truth," Fish snapped. "We're going to cover you, yeah. But one of us is going to be there to see you pay off. And then you're not getting a copper more. And you're going to pay back every bit, with interest."

"You can't treat me like this."

"You don't want to get treated like an asshole, don't act like an asshole."

Smeds said, "You act like a spoiled brat. . . ."

Fish continued, "You'll get treated a lot worse if you screw up again. Come on. Let's get to work."

Tully shrank from the menace in Fish's voice. He turned to Smeds in appeal. Smeds told him, "I'm not getting killed because you can't understand why you have to act responsible. Grab Timmy's legs and help me carry him upstairs. And think about the condition he's in next time you get a wild hair and go to thinking about doing something. Like anything."

Tully looked down at Timmy. "I can't."

"Yes you can. Just think about what if somebody else was to find him and figure out who he was and who he hung around with. Grab hold."

They moved the bodies upstairs, then waited for nightfall. Fish knew a place not far away that would be perfect, some low ground that turned marshy when it rained and bred diseases. The imperial engineers were using it for a landfill. One day the bodies would lie fifty feet below new streets.

They took Timmy out first, of course. He represented the greatest peril. The man who had been questioning Timmy went next, then the thugs, with the little one going last. Tully and Smeds did the carrying while Fish floated around watching for the grays or an accidental witness.

It went beautifully. Till the last one.

"Somebody coming," Fish breathed. "Move it. I'll distract them if they spot us."

49

Toadkiller Dog was amused by his companions in misfortune, so eager to spend themselves in the digging yet so loath to do what had to be done to ensure their strength. After four days of increasing hunger he killed the weakest. He fed, and left the remains to the others. It did not take them long to overcome their reservations and revulsion. And that quickened their determination. None wanted to be next on the menu.

But the digging took another eight days.

Only the monster himself came up out of the earth. But that would have been the case had the digging taken only an hour.

He escaped the darkness of underground into the darkness of night. The trail was not hard to find. It had not rained since the hour of the Limper's perfidy. Ha! Headed north again!

He began to trot. As he loosened up he stretched himself more and more, till he fell into a lupine lope that left a dozen leagues behind him every hour. He did not break stride till he had crossed the bounds of the empire and had come to the place where the Limper had encountered a major obstacle. He stopped. He prowled and sniffed till he understood what had happened.

The Limper had not been welcomed back with tears of joy.

He caught something on the breeze, cast about, spied a distant black rider armed with a flaming spear. The rider flung that blazing dart northward.

Puzzled, Toadkiller Dog resumed his journey.

He came to another place where the Limper had had difficulties. Again he saw a black rider with a fiery spear who hurled his dart to the north.

One more repetition and the monster understood that he was being encouraged to overtake the Limper, that he would be guided to the inevitable confrontation, and that the Limper was being stalled all along his northward journey.

What could he do when he caught up? He was no match for that son of the shadow.

A black rider sat outside the gate of Beryl. He threw a blazing spear to the east. Toadkiller Dog turned. He found the trail quickly.

So. The old doom had been forced to take the long road, around the sea. He loped on, gaining two miles for each three he ran. He swam the River Bigotes and the Hyclades and streaked across the seventy silvery miles of lifeless, mirror-flat salt desert called the Rani Poor. He raced between the countless burial mounds of Barbara to reach the forgotten highways of Laba Larada. He circled the haunted ruins of Khun, passed the pyramids of Katch, which still stood sentinel over the Canyons of the Undead. Warily, he circled the remnants of the temple city of Marsha the Devastator, where the air still shimmered with the cries of sacrifices whose hearts had been torn out on the altars of an aloof and disdainful goddess.

The trail grew warmer by the hour.

He came into the province of Karsus, past outposts of the empire where auxiliaries recruited from the Orain tribes guarded the frontier against the depredations of their own kind more ferociously and faithfully than did the imperial legions. A black rider armed with a spear of fire watched him race across the Plain of Dano-Patha, where a hundred armies had contested the right of passage north or south or east and where some legends said the Last Battle of Time would be fought between Light and Darkness.

The Mountains of Sinjian lay beyond, and in their savage defiles he found evidence that the Limper was again being tormented and delayed, again with vicious traps narrowly escaped.

The spoor was heavy and hot and had the taint of newly opened graves.

He came out onto a prominence overlooking the Straits of Angine, where the fresh waters flowed down from the Kiril Lakes to meld with the salty waters of the Sea of Torments. His vantage was not far from that narrowest part of the strait that seafarers called Hell's Gate and overland travelers had dubbed Heaven's Bridge.

Hell was in session down there.

The Limper was on the south shore and wanted to cross over. But on the north shore someone demurred.

Toadkiller Dog settled on his belly, rested his chin on his forepaws, and watched. This was not the place to reveal himself. Maybe at the Tower, if the Limper turned west and sought a vengeance there.

As though they sensed his arrival, those who held the north shore closed up shop and hauled out. The Limper hurled glamorous violences after them. The distance was too great to do them any harm.

The Limper went across immediately. He encountered traps immediately. Toadkiller Dog decided he would hazard a more difficult crossing. After dark.

There was no need to hurry now. He had the quarry in sight. He could bide his time.

He might range ahead and lie in wait. Or he might stalk the enemies of his enemy in order to discover the nature of their game.

50

We got a break. Raven came rolling in where I was reading a book I borrowed from the guy who owned the place where we was staying. "We got a break. Come on, Case."

I put the book aside, got up. "What's happening?"

"I'll tell you on the way." He stuck his head in the next room, yelled and invoked Darling till one of the Torques joined us. We hit the street. He started talking. "One of those little characters from the Plain hit paydirt. He overheard a man telling his cronies about an incident that almost has to involve the men who stole the spike."

I told him, "Slow down. You're getting the soldiers interested." And he was. He was that eager to get at this first assignment from Darling. "What did the guy say?"

"He and two others were hired to snatch a man and then help question him. Which they did. But someone came along and broke it up. This fellow was the only one who got away. We're going to round him up and let him walk us through his adventure."

Right.

It might be the best lead we'd get but it didn't look that great to me. "This guy is shooting his mouth off about what happened to him we're going to have to get in line to talk to him."

"We heard first. Almost direct. We're ahead of the pack. But that's why I'm in a hurry."

I noticed he was hardly limping. "Your hip finally starting to do right?"

"All this sitting around. Nothing else to do but get healthy."

"Speaking of which. I went out for a beer this afternoon. I heard talk there's cholera down near South Gate."

We walked in silence a while. Then the Torque—I still didn't know any of their real front names—said, "That'll tear it, won't it? Get a cholera outbreak going and the pot will boil over, sure."

Raven grunted.

Maybe this wasn't just our best break but our only one. Maybe we had to make it count.

We went into a place with the dumb name Barnacles. Raven looked around. "There's our man. Right where he's supposed to be." His voice had got hard as jasper. He had changed while we walked, turned into a critter like the Raven that had ridden with the Black Company.

Our man was alone. He was drunk. Fortune was smiling today. Raven told us, "You guys have a beer and keep an eye out. I'll talk to him."

We did, and he did. I don't know what he said but I never got a chance to get even with Torque by having him buy the second round. Raven got up. So did our man. In a minute we were all in the street. It was almost dark out now. Our new friend was not full of small talk. He did not seem pleased to be with us.

Raven told us, "Smiley here figured getting fifty obols for showing us around was a lot better than the alternative."

Smiley took us to an alley. "This is where we grabbed the guy."

Raven had asked questions while we walked. "And you didn't know anything about the guy? Like where he was coming from or where he was headed?"

"I told you. This Abel set it up and gave it to Shorts. Shorts just hired me and Tanker to back him up when he grabbed this guy with only one hand that was supposed to come through here. Maybe Shorts knew what was going on. I didn't."

"Convenient."

"Yeah. The more I think about it the more I figure the only reason they had me and Tanker hang around after we got the guy down to the cellar was they planned on us never leaving if they got what they wanted."

"You're probably right. That's the way those kind work."

"And you guys don't?"

"Not when we get cooperation. Show us that cellar."

I was glum. Our big strike looked like it was turning into a pocket of fool's gold. The guys who could give us answers had checked out.

Raven thought we might get something out of a look at the bodies. I was willing to bet all we would get was gagged. "Shit, this is desolate," I said as we was getting close. "How much farther?"

"About a block . . ."

"Hold it!" Raven said. "Quiet!"

I listened. I didn't hear nothing. But my eyes were good at night. By looking slightly to the side of them I could make out some guys. Three of them carrying a fourth. They were headed somewhere in a big hurry.

I told Raven. He asked, "You know this area?"

"Only vaguely."

"Try to get ahead of them. They won't be able to move too fast if they're carrying a body. We'll run them down from behind."

Smiley said, "I'll do a fade now."

Raven replied, "You'll come with us and tell us if you recognize any faces."

Smiley started cursing.

I took off. I figured it was a waste of time but I'd give it a shot. Five minutes and I'd be lost and they'd be long gone.

I went about three hundred yards and found myself on open ground. It looked like the area where we had landed, seen from a different direction. I couldn't see anyone in the open. Figuring they'd been to my left when I started and I'd paralleled them, I moved to my left, along the face of the ruins still standing.

Nothing. Nothing. Nothing. Just like I expected. Where were the others? I worried. I thought about yelling but decided not to. I didn't want to look silly.

I thought I was paying attention but I guess I wasn't.

Somebody stepped out of nowhere and kicked me in the noogies. A perfect shot. The pain exploded through me. I bent over and puked and didn't care about anything else in the world.

He hit me in the back of the head. I went down, rooted up a little pavement with my chin. Somebody got onto me and forced me to lay out flat, facedown. He was not gentle. I wiggled a couple fingers by way of fighting back. He was not impressed.

He twisted one arm up behind me till I thought it was going to break, then whispered in my ear, "I don't want you tromping around in my life, boy. You hear?"

I did not answer.

He twisted my arm a little more. I let out a yell, proving I was getting my wind back faster than I thought.

"You hear me, boy?"

"Yeah."

"Next time I even see you or one of your buddies they're going to be picking up pieces all over Oar. You understand?"

"Yeah."

"You tell that slit she don't mind her own business she's going to be up to her twat in grays. You listening?"

"Yeah."

"Good." He hit me on the head again. I don't know why—maybe because my skull is as thick as my old man used to tell me it was—he didn't put me all the way out. I lay there powerless but aware as he drew a knife across my left cheek. Then he got up and went away and my only companions were pain, nausea, and humiliation.

After a while I got my feet under me and stumbled off to find Raven. I hadn't been whipped up on so bad since I was a kid. The slash burned like hell but wasn't as bad as I'd feared.

I actually found them pretty easy, considering. Only took me about fifteen minutes. There was a little light now from a big fire burning down south. Later I found out they were getting rid of the bodies of the first hundred people to die from the cholera. The twins must have anticipated epidemics. They'd had the engineers save all the scrap lumber from the demolished buildings.

I stumbled over Raven is how I found him.

He was out cold. He had a slash just like mine.

The Torque was about ten feet away and just starting to twitch and make noises. He had been cut, too.

So had Smiley. Twice. The second cut was about four inches below the first, ran from ear to ear, and was the last wound he'd ever suffer.

They'd done a number on us, all right.

Raven hadn't gotten him a swift kick but a good whack on the head. He was still rocky as we reported. His hands shook badly as he tried to sign to Darling: "One man, I think. Took us by surprise." He was embarrassed.

I don't think I ever saw him embarrassed like that before. But he never got took like that before, either.

I was embarrassed when my turn came because I had to report every word the man had said. I was afraid I was going to have to explain a couple of them.

She surprised me for the hundredth time by not being as ignorant as I expected.

Silent touched his cheek, signed, "Queen's Bridge."

Darling nodded.

I had to ask.

Silent signed, "When we fought the Nightstalkers at Queen's Bridge they took eighteen prisoners. They marked them all on the left cheek and turned them loose."

"What the hell? Could the soldiers themselves have the spike? Is that why they haven't had any luck finding it? Is the brigadier playing some game of her own?" I did it in sign. You get into the habit when you're around Darling long.

She looked at me weird for a few seconds, then signed, "We have to get out of here now. Soldiers—not Nightstalkers—are going to come any minute."

I saw it then.

Somebody was a mad genius, a wizard at thinking on his feet. In the minutes he'd had us at his mercy he'd put together a plan that could hurl Oar into a whirlpool of chaos and violence.

He had spared us only to spark a greater bloodletting.

The twins' soldiers would grab us, with the marks on us, and eliminate the White Rose menace. Word would get out. A significant portion of the population would start raising hell. Meantime, the twins would take our testimony on the rack and find cause to suspect the Nightstalkers and their commander. There was no love lost there now and there was no way the Nightstalkers were going to let their brigadier be arrested or even relieved of her command.

The Nightstalkers were outnumbered by the other gray regiments but they were the better, tougher soldiers and they would win in any confrontation, unless the twins themselves intervened directly.

Bloody-minded genius. Who could keep his or her mind on the silver spike with all that shit going on?

While I was thinking, Darling was flinging orders left and right. She sent all the little Plain creatures out to scout around and see who was in the neighborhood and to watch for soldiers. She sent the Torque brothers off to warn our Rebel friends. Bomanz and Silent she sent to the area where we got bushwhacked to see if they, with their talents, could pick up anything.

She looked from me to Raven and back again, deciding who should be their guide.

She picked Raven.

Before they could all work up a good scowl for me—I think Silent was pleased that he would not be leaving her alone with Raven—one of the Plain creatures zipped in to report the area clear except for an antiquated wino passed out on the wooden sidewalk half a block away.

Darling signed, "Let us go now."

We all went.

The wave of raids and arrests started less than an hour later.

51

Smeds looked at Tully across the little table. His cousin was drinking with a grim determination but he was still stone-cold sober. Those bodies. Gruesome. Those men chasing them through the night. Those fires in the south, where they were burning the bodies of cholera victims. Now there were bands of soldiers tramping through the streets, about some nocturnal business that had set the rumors flying. It was not a time to inspire confidence in one's security.

The soldiers—some of them—were troubled, too. Moments before, several Nightstalkers had come in to consult the resident corporal. Now the whole bunch was headed out. They looked like they expected bad trouble.

"It's starting to come apart," Smeds said. He felt breathless.

Shivering, Tully nodded. "If I knew what we was going to go through I would've said screw the spike."

"The big hit, man. I guess when you think about it it wasn't never that easy for nobody that ever made it."

"Yeah. What I did, I never thought it through. Or I would've figured the world would go crazy. I would've figured there'd be just a whole mob of them who'd kill anybody and do anything to get ahold of it. What the hell is wrong with this beer? It's got a kick like a mouse."

"Better enjoy it." Fish appeared out of nowhere. He had a haggard, harried look. He joined them. "It might be the last beer in town." He slumped, wrung out. "I've done what I can. All we can do is wait. And hope."

Smeds asked, "What's going on out there? With the soldiers."

"They're rounding up Rebels. They're going to execute a big bunch in the morning. That ought to set off the explosion that will break the city wide open."

"What if it don't?" Tully asked.

"Then we're screwed. Sooner or later they'll get us. Process of elimination." Fish stole a sip of Smeds's beer. "Cheer up. They're between us and the cholera. Maybe it'll get them before they get us."

"Shit!"

"We ought to get some sleep."

"You kidding?"

"We ought to try. We ought, at least, to get out of sight. Out of sight, out of mind, as they say."

Smeds fell asleep in about two minutes.

He was not sure what wakened him. The sun was up. So were Tully and Fish. Up and out of there. Something made him start shivering. He went to the common room. It was empty.

It hit him as he crossed to the door.

The silence.

The morning was as still as the grave. But for his footsteps he would have feared he was deaf. The door groaned as he opened it.

Everyone stood in the street, looking toward the center of Oar, waiting for something.

The wait was short.

Smeds felt it in the earth before it reached his ears, a monster vibration pursued by an avalanche of rage, a roar almost like a blow.

Fish told him, "They started the executions. I was afraid they would chicken out."

The roar grew louder, rolled closer, as an entire city, in a moment, decided that it had had enough of tyranny and oppression.

The wave came into the street outside the Skull and Crossbones. The people reeled with it.

Then mothers began herding children inside. Men began moving toward city center, in a rage for death, few of them armed because the repeated searches by the grays had turned up most of the privately held weapons. They had confiscated everything but the personal knife.

Smeds decided he must be getting old and cynical. He hadn't the slightest urge to get involved.

Neither did Fish. Tully twitched for a moment, then stood fast.

Many of the men in the street did the same. The rage was like the cholera. Not everyone had it yet. But both would claim many more before they subsided.

Fish got Smeds and Tully inside the Skull and Crossbones and sat them down. "We don't move. We let the rumors come to us. If they turn favorable enough we'll head for the wall whenever it looks like we've got a chance to get out. Smeds, go put yourself a pack together. Stuff you'll need to travel."

Tully whispered, "What about the spike?"

"It can take care of itself."

"Where the hell is it, anyway?"

"Smeds, go pack. I don't know, Tully. I don't want to know. All I care is, Smeds found a place so good nobody else has found it."

Smeds felt Tully's angry stare as he moved away.

The first flurry of rumors spoke more eloquently of human savagery than it did of human nobility.

Despite knowing the mob was in an ugly mood, the regiment handling the executions had been caught off balance by the violence of the outburst following the first execution. They were swamped by the responding fury. Eight hundred died before panicky reinforcements, in no good order, arrived. Several thousand civilians and several hundred more soldiers died before it broke up. The fleeing citizens took a fair supply of arms with them.

Small-to-medium-sized riots bubbled up all over Oar, anywhere the grays appeared weak.

A mob tried to storm the Civil Palace. They were driven off but they left several fires burning, the worst of which raged out of control for hours.

A huge mob attacked the regiment that had moved in to beef up protection of the South Gate. Many captured weapons surfaced there. The mob overwhelmed the regiment but failed to flush the gate guards and failed to take the top of the wall. Archers posted there soon dispersed them.

Fish did not let Tully or Smeds go out once.

Come nightfall the situation grew both more chaotic and more sinister. The hard-pressed soldiers began to lose discipline, to indulge in indiscriminate slaughter. Youths got out and set fires, vandalized, looted. Individuals pursued private feuds. And the world's densest population of wizards decided to become involved. Decided to gang up and eliminate their toughest competitor.

They rallied a mob and went after Gossamer and Spidersilk. This time the attackers broke through. They exterminated the bodyguard force. One of the twins was injured, maybe killed. The entire center of the city seemed to be afire. And total madness spread with the news. It got so it seemed everyone in the city was trying to murder someone else.

The crowd of wizards turned on one another.

Chaos had not trespassed much in the neighborhood of the Skull and Crossbones earlier. But now it came creeping in with a crash and a clash and a scream.

Smeds said, "We got to get out of here."

Fish surprised him by agreeing. "You're right. Before it gets impossible. Let's grab our stuff."

Tully was too worn out to do anything but go along.

The other hangers-on watched them dully as they slipped out. Half an hour later, without serious misadventure, they had established themselves in the dark murk of a partly collapsed basement barely a hundred yards from the place where Timmy Locan had died.

The madness had no hunger for that part of Oar already gnawed to the bone by the Limper's passage.

B omanz was bad worried. "There's no limit to the insanity out there. If they keep on they'll continue till there's only one man left standing."

Raven cracked, "Let's make sure that's us."

We had hidden ourselves in the bell tower of an old temple less than a bow shot from the Civil Palace. If I wanted I could peek out and watch the place burn. We didn't let anybody know where we were going to hide out. So far, thanks to the old wizard, nobody had tripped over us.

"You think it's the spike's fault?" I asked.

"Its influence. And the more evil done around it, the thicker the miasma of madness will get."

So why weren't we busting our knuckles on somebody?

Darling was upset about what was happening. Far as I could tell, she was the only one. The rest of us was just scared of it, just wanted to stay out of the way till it burned itself out.

She would have done something if she could.

I asked, "So what we going to do? Sit?" I was thinking how the craziness must have ruined the quarantine on the cholera area.

"You got a better idea?" Raven asked.

"No."

Them that had gone out looking the other night hadn't found nothing. Only good thing turned out to be I got to spend a couple hours talking to Darling without Silent and Raven giving me the evil eye.

"But I feel like the buzzard who got so tired of waiting for something to die he went to thinking about killing something."

Bomanz said, "We need to decide what to do if there's a breakout. You can bet if there is the people who know about the spike will be the first ones gone."

"Everyone will know if it starts moving, won't they?"

"They wouldn't move it. Why should they? It's safe. Or somebody would have found it. They'll just be worried about staying alive till they can sell it."

"What makes you think they want to sell?" I asked.

"If they could use it they would have."

Made sense. That's the way bandits would work. "So why haven't they tried to hawk it?"

"Because all these assholes here think they can take it away from them and outrun each other."

I decided to take a nap. Talk was getting us nowhere. We weren't doing nothing but yak and wait on the Plain critters to drop by with reports. When the spirit moved them. They don't think like us. Some got no sense of time at all.

Which is maybe why Donkey Torque sounded so damned surprised after he took a look outside. "You guys better take a gander here."

We crowded around him.

We had us a whole new angle on all our troubles. Everybody did.

A new gang had come to town.

A black coach had just rolled into the square in front of the Civil Palace. Four black horses pulled it. Six black riders on six black horses surrounded it. An infantry battalion followed. Surprise. Those boys were all duded up in black.

"Where the hell did they come from?" I muttered.

Raven said, "You got your wish, wizard."

"Eh?"

"The Tower has taken an interest."

I felt a hand on my shoulder. Darling. I scrunched over so she could get up beside me and see. She left her hand where it was. You can guess how many friends that made me.

Someone got out of the coach. No black for this clown. "A popinjay," Bomanz said.

And me, "I always wondered what that meant."

The peacock looked around at the bodies, at the remains of the palace, said something to one of his outriders. The horseman rode up the steps and into the unburned part of the building. A minute later people started tumbling out. The other riders herded them together facing the clown.

Gossamer and Spidersilk came out. A rider chivied them toward his boss. "Called on the carpet," Bomanz said. "Be interesting to hear that."

There wasn't no doubt who was senior to who down there. The twins did everything but get down on their bellies. A back and forth went on for maybe ten minutes. Then the twins started sending their people scurrying off.

"What now?" Raven muttered.

Next thing the peacock did was set up housekeeping in the only undamaged building in the neighborhood. The temple. Downstairs.

We was stuck.

People started coming to see the new nabob. Brigadier Wildbrand was one of the first. The Nightstalkers had not been involved in any of the fighting so far.

The chaos died away for a few hours while the madmen of Oar digested the news about the new boy in town. Then it blazed up, white-hot.

But it died out, spent, before sundown.

We got the word well after dark, knew why it had gotten quiet.

The Limper was headed for Oar, bent on grabbing the silver spike.

Oar was not going to let him have it. According to Exile, the new man from the Tower.

"Shit," I muttered. "That Limper has more lives than a cat."

"I knew we should have made sure of him," Raven growled. He glared at Darling. Her fault. She had been so sure she had seen no need to argue with the tree god.

Exile had orders to hold Oar and destroy the Limper. Our spies said he meant to do that if it cost every life in the city.

Shit. The Tower *would* have to send some guy who took his job serious.

Smeds woke first. Before he had his wits in hand he knew there was something wrong.

Tully was gone.

Maybe he had to go take a leak.

Smeds scrambled out into the unexpected brightness of morning. No sign of Tully. But the nearby street, unused in recent times, was choked with traffic. Every vehicle carried corpses.

Smeds gaped. Then he ducked back down into the ruined cellar and found Fish, shook him till he growled, "What the hell is the matter?"

"Tully's gone. And you got to see what's outside to believe it."

"That idiot." Fish was wide-awake now. "All right. Get your shit. We got to move just so he don't know where to find us."

"Hunh?"

"I've run out of trust for Cousin Tully, Smeds. I want to know where he is, not the other way around. A man who can lose a fortune the way he did? That's stupid to the point of being suicidal. A man who gets over a fit of common sense as fast as he did and goes sneaking off with this city the way it is? I'm pretty close to the end of my patience. Every stunt he pulls puts us all at risk. If he's screwed up . . . I don't know."

"Go look outside."

Fish went. "Damn!" He came back. "We have to find out what's happening."

"That's obvious. They're using that landfill to dump bodies from the riots."

"You missed the point. Who thought that up and got all those people to work on it? When we crawled in here they were trying to rip each other's throats out."

They soon discovered that the chaos had not so much died as gone into momentary remission. And not universally. There were hot spots, most surrounding wizards reluctant to embrace a new order that had come in overnight.

The twins from Charm were out and somebody called Exile was in. And Oar was supposed to be girding for another visit from the Limper.

"Things are getting crazy," Smeds said as they approached the Skull and Crossbones.

"There's an understatement if ever I heard one."

Their landlord seemed disappointed that they hadn't been killed in the riots. No. He hadn't seen Tully since he'd wanted breakfast and had stormed out because he couldn't get credit. Wasn't anything to fix, anyway.

"You got nothing?" Smeds asked.

"I got a dried-out third of a loaf I'm gonna soak in water and have for supper. You want to dig around in the cellar you might find a couple of rats. I'll roast them up for you."

Smeds believed him. "Tully didn't happen to say where he was headed, did he?"

"No. He turned right when he left out."

"Thanks," Fish said. He started toward the street.

The landlord asked, "You heard about the re-ward?"

"What reward?" Smeds asked.

"For that silver spike thing all the commotion's supposed to be about. The new guy says he'll give a hundred thousand obols, no questions asked, no tricks, no risks. Just take it in and get the money."

"Damn-O!" Fish said. "A guy could live pretty good, couldn't he? Wish to hell I had it."

Smeds grumbled, "You was to ask me, there ain't no such thing. All them witches and wizards would have found it if there was. Come on, Fish. I got to find that shithead cousin of mine."

Outside, Fish asked, "You think he'd try something?"

"Yeah, if he heard. He'd figure we deserve to get screwed on account of we been treating him so bad. Only he don't know where it's at. So he'll have to make up his mind if he can sell me to the torturers."

"I think he can. Without remorse. There isn't really anyone in this world who really matters except Tully Stahl. He probably started out just figuring to use us, then get rid of us one by one. Only things didn't go as simple as he thought they would."

"You're maybe right," Smeds admitted. "Guess we got to assume he's going to sell us out, don't we?"

"We'd be fools to give him the benefit of the doubt. You know his habits and hangouts. Look for him. I'll find out where Exile holes up and wait for him to show up there."

"What if he's already . . . ?"

"Then we're screwed. Aren't we?"

"Yeah. Hey. What about *we* sell this guy the spike? A hundred thousand ain't bad. I can't even count that high."

"It's good. But if the situation is what they say—the Limper coming back—they'll go way higher. Let's let it ride a couple days."

Smeds did not argue but thought they ought to get what they could while they could get it. "I'll catch up if I can't find him."

Fish grunted and walked off.

Smeds began his rounds. He crossed Tully's trail several times. The spike was all the talk everywhere he went. Tully had to know about the reward. He wasn't running to Exile. That was a good sign. Except . . .

Except that a dozen independents had let out that they would go higher than Exile. A witch named Teebank had offered a hundred fifty thousand.

Smeds believed none of them except Exile. He had seen them when the hunt had been a race between thieves. They wouldn't change. They would talk mountains of obols but the payoff, when it came, would be death.

But Tully had that knack for deceiving himself. He might decide they were legitimately offering. Or he might fool himself into thinking he could outwit them. He had an inflated opinion of his own guile.

Smeds soon concluded that the pattern of Tully's movements indicated he was looking for someone.

Likely one of those fabulous purses.

He had no regard left for his cousin.

The evidence suggested Tully was gaining no ground on his quarry. Smeds was, though. He wondered if Tully was getting nervous, knowing they would be after him as soon as they knew he was gone.

Probably.

Smeds caught up but the situation was not suited to the confrontation he had been rehearsing for hours.

He was moving along a street unnaturally quiet even for after the riots, getting nervous about that, when Tully came flying out a doorway a hundred feet ahead and across the way. He hadn't yet gotten stable on his hands and knees when soldiers in black surrounded him. They bound his hands behind him, put a choke cord on him, and led him off toward the center of town.

There were six of those soldiers. Smeds stared numbly, seeing the end of his days. What the hell could he do? Get Fish? But what could Fish do? No two men were going to ambush six soldiers in broad daylight.

He tripped along behind. With each step he became more certain what had to be done, became more sick at heart. No matter that Tully had been ready to write him off.

He ducked into an alley and ran, the energy starting to burn in his veins. He went faster than necessary, trying to leech the growing fear in frenzied physical activity.

His pack hammered against his back. Like half the men in Oar he was carrying his home on his back. He had to get rid of it somehow. Somewhere safe. Most of his take from the Barrowland was in it.

He came on a pile of rubble in deep shadow. No one was around. He buried the pack hastily, hurried on to the point where he wanted to intercept Tully and the soldiers.

They were not in sight. His heart sank. Had they decided to go some longer way?

No. There they were. He'd just gotten way ahead.

He crossed the street to a dark alley mouth. He would run back the way he had come, to his pack, through some useful shadows, on a route barren of witnesses.

The wait stretched interminably. He had time to get scared again. To talk himself into freezing up, almost.

Then they were there, a pair of soldiers out front, a pair behind, one leading

Tully by the choke cord and one behind to poke him if he slowed down. Smeds's knife slipped into his hand. It was the knife he'd taken off that man in that cellar.

He flung himself forward, running hard. They barely had time to turn and see him coming. Tully's eyes got huge as he saw the knife come to his throat.

Smeds hit the choke cord and smashed through and in a moment was back in shadows clutching a knife that dripped family blood. Soldiers shouted. Feet pounded after him.

There was very little physical or emotional reaction. His mind turned to the pursuit. Two men, he decided. Very determined bastards, too. He wasn't gaining on them.

He did not want to deal with them but it looked like they might give him no choice.

He knew the place. It was only a few yards from where he had hidden his pack, where the alley was darkest. He would use the trick the physician had tried. If they went on by he would sneak away behind them.

He was amazed at himself. Smeds Stahl, scared, could still think.

He slipped into a crack in a brick wall that, probably, was a legacy of the Limper's visit. It had been improved upon by someone who had used it to get into the building, a thief or squatters. He could slide through and get away, but something that was not concern for his pack stayed him.

He picked up a broken board and waited.

They did not continue their headlong rush once his footsteps stopped. They exchanged breathless words in an unfamiliar language. Smeds grew tense. If they stuck together . . .

He still had the out through the building.

One soldier put on a burst that took him a hundred feet past Smeds. He called to the other. They began moving toward one another.

The one who had not run was much closer.

He did not notice the gap in the wall till Smeds popped out behind his knife. He made one strange noise, surprise that turned to pain.

Smeds tried to pull the knife free as the man fell and the other soldier yelled. It would not come. Goddamn it! Again!

Feet pounded toward him.

He grabbed his board and swung it just as the other soldier arrived. The impact slammed the man against the wall. Smeds hit him again. And again and again, feeling bones crunch, till the broken thing stopped whimpering.

He stood there panting, unaware that he was grinning, till he heard more men coming. He darted toward where his pack lay, realized he did not have time to dig it out, darted back, and tried the knife again. It would not come.

Still. Then he was out of time before he could appropriate a weapon from one of the dead men. He slithered through the crack into the darkness inside the building.

Moments later there was an outraged roar from the alleyway.

S meds kept his head down as he stepped into the street. There was little foot traffic. No one paid him any mind. He set off at a brisk pace, but not one so fast it would attract attention.

What now?

He didn't dare go find Fish. Some damned soldier might recognize him.

But Fish would hear about Tully. Fish would understand. Best thing would be to go back to the Skull and Crossbones and wait. Fish was sure to check there.

As his heartbeat slowed toward normal he became aware of the hollow in his stomach. He had not eaten since yesterday. The Skull and Crossbones was dry. Where could he find something? With stores getting low, nobody might be willing to sell. . . .

I t was a meal. Of sorts. A bowl of bad soup and a chunk of stale bread, and the fat old geek who ran the filthy place hadn't tried to rob him.

He was nearly done when a kid blew in, yelled, "Run, mister! Press gang!" and sailed out the back.

"What the hell?"

"Press gang," the greasy fat man said. "Round here the grays been grabbing all the young men they can find—"

Two grays stamped in. One grinned and said, "Here's a likely-looking patriot."

Smeds sneered and went back to work on his meal. He did not feel troubled.

A wooden truncheon tapped him on the shoulder. "Come along, then."

"You better hope there's no splinters in that thing. You touch me again I'm going to shove it up your ass."

"Oh, a tough one, Cord. We like them tough, don't we? What's your name, boy?"

Smeds sighed, hearing the voices of all the bullies who'd ever baited him. He turned, looked the soldier in the eye, said, "Death."

Maybe the man saw seven murders in his eyes. He backed off a step. Smeds decided the one who kept his mouth shut was probably more dangerous.

He felt no fear at all. In fact, he felt invulnerable, invincible.

He rose slowly, flipped his bread into the talker's face, kicked him in the groin. A bully had done that to him once. He shoved his chair at the other man's legs and while he was dealing with that shoved his soup into the man's face. Then he grabbed the truncheon away from the first and went to work.

He might have killed them both if half a dozen more soldiers had not showed up to help.

They didn't beat Smeds much more than they had to to get him under control. They seemed to think the whole thing was a good joke on the man with the big mouth.

They dragged Smeds outside and added him to a group of cowed youngsters about thirty strong. Several of the youngsters got told off to carry the men Smeds had injured.

So Smeds Stahl became one of the gray boys. Sort of.

The little critters was in and out so much I was sure the people downstairs was going to find us out any minute. Bomanz and Silent was having trouble enough keeping curiosity types away without attracting the attention of the new big boy.

Raven was loving every minute of it. "What the hell are you grinning about?" I demanded.

"Those guys with the spike. They got balls down to their ankles."

"Hunh!" He *would* appreciate their brass.

"Come on, Case. Look. One of them decides to cut a deal for himself and winds up getting grabbed by Exile's boys for his trouble. So what do his buddies do? Big rescue attempt, against the odds? Hell, no. Before they get the guy halfway here one man just casually trots through the escort and practically lops the guy's head off. He does it so quick they can't get two descriptions that agree no matter how many witnesses they ask. And when the soldiers get riled and go after the killer, he offs two of them and leaves the rest standing around with their thumbs in their ears."

"Just your kind of fun-loving boy, eh?"

"They have style, Case. I appreciate style. It's a sort of bringing of artistry to even the most mundane—or gruesome—things that have to be done. Bet you something. If the man who made that hit had had five more minutes he would have been wearing a Nightstalker uniform, just to mess with people's minds. It's not the deed. It's how it was done."

Here was a shade of the Raven of old. Maybe the shell was ready to break. "You think these guys are just having a good time, sticking their tongues out at the world, yelling 'Catch us if you can'?"

"No. You don't understand. They're probably hiding out somewhere not fit for a pig. They're probably hungry, filthy, scared, sure they're not going to get out of it alive. But they're not letting it break them. They're going right on clawing at the faces of the wolves and vampires trying to feed on them. You see?"

I agreed mostly because I didn't and if I admitted that we'd end up spending the whole day getting me lessons in never surrender, even if the ground you're holding springs from stupid or wrong.

Agreeing worked. He moved over and got into a discussion with Silent and Darling. All business, I assume, since no sparks flew.

I got into a conversation with Bomanz, who was trying to work his way through some moral catch trap where the spike was concerned. He had some questions that nobody had answers for. I wasn't sure there *were* any answers. That spike was like a drop of black dye plunked into a pool of already murky water, spreading. It had poisoned Oar already. We had resisted it because we knew about it and could think it away consciously. But what would happen if our bunch got lucky and glommed on to it?

Scary.

And what the hell were we going to *do* with the damned thing if we did get it? I never heard none of those clowns talk about that. It was all keep the other guys from grabbing it and doing dirty.

It sure as hell hadn't been safe where they left it before.

I didn't have no ideas. Not that looked like they would work. There wasn't no place in the world you could put it that somebody else couldn't get it back from except maybe if you dropped it in the deepest part of the ocean. And that probably wouldn't do the job neither.

Some damned fish would probably gulp it down before it sank ten feet, then the fish would beach itself or get hooked by some goddamned fisherman with a hidden talent for sorcery and a secret lust for conquest.

That's the nature of evil talismans.

My best notions were to get a bunch of sorcerers together who could elevate it to the outer realm and stick in on a passing comet or to have a bunch break a little hole through to another plane, pop the spike through, and plug the hole.

Both ways was just cheaters that put the problem off on somebody else. The people of the future when the comet came back or the people of the other plane.

I had been picking up bits of the sign exchanges between Raven, Darling, and Silent, without paying much attention, just like you can't help catching snatches of a nearby conversation when it don't really interest you. Raven was getting antsy. He was finger grumbling about all this sitting around waiting for something to happen instead of getting out and making it happen.

He was on his way back all right. That was the old Raven. You got a problem you kill somebody or at least beat the shit out of them.

I was almost tempted to yell, "Hey!" when I caught him voluteering me and him to go look around the landscape where the morning's excitement had taken place. I choked it. Why let the boys downstairs know we were here when Darling could tell him to go soak his head?

Treacherous witch.

She thought it was a great idea. We should drag Bomanz along, just in case a wizard might turn up handy.

Silent grinned all the way around his face. The prick saw himself talking his talk and making his pitch every second we were gone.

I decided I was going for the head recruiter's job if I was going to get stuck as a Rebel for life. The movement could use a few more women. And a few soldiers who weren't screwballs, too.

With a little illusion help from Bomanz we just went downstairs and strutted out the front door, walking like we belonged there. Like Raven said, if we didn't belong we wouldn't't've been in there in the first place. Would we?

Balls and style. That's my buddy Raven.

They had carted the body off with all the others but we had no trouble finding the place. There was blood all over and a crowd of kids still hanging around telling each other all about it.

Raven only gave the stains a glance. Bomanz had no use for that scene either. He wasn't looking for dead men.

We strolled down the alley the killer had used to make his escape. I was surprised they didn't have soldiers watching, though I couldn't imagine who they'd think they'd be laying for, either. It just seemed like something some officer would think was a dandy thing to do. If what officers use their heads for is to think.

The place where the two soldiers got killed was a little harder to find because of all the dark. That alley was a creepy place. It felt like it never got light in there. Like a place where people didn't belong at all. A place already claimed by other things, impatient with our intrusion.

Weird thoughts. I shivered.

Maybe the shades of the murdered soldiers were hanging around.

Then Bomanz conjured up a ball of light and hung it out overhead. "That's better," he said. "It got spooky for a minute, there."

He was good for something after all.

"Yeah," Raven said. They started poking around. There wasn't a whole lot to see. I went over to a rubble pile to sit and wait them out. A fat rat sauntered past without so much as a nod to intimidation by a superior species. I chucked a hunk of broken brick at him.

He stopped and eyeballed me over his shoulder, red eyes glowing. Arrogant little sucker. I grabbed another hunk of brick and this time put some arm behind it.

He charged me.

Rabid! I thought, and tried to scramble up the pile while grabbing a broken board to beat him off. The pile collapsed. I went sliding down, kicking and cussing. The rat zagged out, to be seen no more. He took him a good brag to hand his buddies.

Raven got a big chuckle out of the whole thing. "Hail, O Mighty Hunter, Terror of Ratkind."

"Stuff it." I rolled me over and saw about a square foot of raggedy-ass canvas peeking out of the rubble pile. I had me a stroke of cunning. I stood up, dusted me off, and sat back down. They went back to their sniffing around. I dug the thing out, decided it was somebody's backpack, then decided it might be why our villain had made a stand here when all he really needed to do was duck through that hole and leave the soldiers sucking dust.

"What have you got there?" Raven yelled when he noticed. Bomanz didn't say nothing but his beady little eyes lit right up.

They caught on quick. Raven wanted to open the pack right there. Bomanz told him, "This isn't the place. Anybody could come along."

Raven thought about sneaking into the building the killer had used to make his getaway. Great idea, only somebody had boarded up the hole from inside. "Guess we might as well take it back to the temple," he said.

The soldiers were waiting for us at the end of the alley. There were a dozen of them and they were ready for trouble. We would've walked right into them if we hadn't had a tame wizard along to sniff them out.

We backed off to talk. Bomanz supposed all the exits from the maze of alleys would be covered by now. Pretty soon they would come in after us. He could get us out right now but that would take so much flash and show it would get Exile all twisted out of shape.

"Over the rooftops, then," Raven said. Like it was obvious and easy.

"Great idea. But I'm an old man. Sneaking up on five hundred. A wizard, not a monkey."

"Give him the pack, Case. He can cover his own butt and get it home to Mama. We'll play tag with the soldiers."

"Say what? Oh. Yeah. Sure. You're the guy with style. You play tag with them." But I took the pack off. Bomanz wiggled into it. It was too big for him.

Softly, he told me, "Don't take silly chances. She'll want you to come back."

Chills up the spine, and some more thoughts about what kind of a crazy man was I, being here in the first place. Potato farming never looked so good.

I don't know if Raven heard. He didn't give no sign. We went off and found a way up to the roofs, which was a crazy country of steep pitches, flats, chimneys, slate, copper, tile, thatch, and shingle. Like no two builders ever used the same materials. We stumbled and clunked around and did our damnedest to fall off and break a head or a leg, but something always got in the way.

I might have been better off if I'd busted my bean.

For a while it didn't look like hunking around on the roofs was going to do no good. Whenever we took a peek to see if it was safe, there was some soldiers hanging out. But just when I asked Raven, "How do you like pigeon? 'Cause it looks like we're going to spend the rest of our lives up here," some kind of hoorah broke out back about where we left the old wizard and every soldier in sight headed that way.

I said, "That silly sack probably did something subtle like turn somebody into a toad."

"Must you always be negative, Case?" Raven was having him a good time.

"Me? Negative? The gods forfend! I've never had a negative thought in my life. Where did you get a notion like that?"

"It's clear. Drop on down there."

On down there was a two-story fall to a rough cobblestone landing. "You're shitting me."

"No."

"Then you go first so I can land on you."

"You *are* in a contrary mood, aren't you? Go on."

"No, thank you. I'll just go find me a place where I can climb down."

Maybe I crowded it a little. He gave me a nasty look and said, "All right. You do what you have to do. But I'm not going to hang around waiting for you to catch up." He rolled over the edge of the roof, hung down, kicked out, let go.

I know he done it just to give me some shit. And he got what he asked for, showing off. He sprained an ankle. When he slowed down cussing and fussing enough, I told him, "You hang on right there. I'll be there in a minute."

I wasn't, of course.

I cut across a couple roofs and found a way to climb down into the street parallel to the one where I left Raven. I hitched up my pants and headed around the corner into the nearest cross street—and ran smack into a whole gang of gray boys.

Their sergeant laughed. "God *damn*! Here's one so eager he came running."

I guess I didn't react too well. I just stood there gawking for about five seconds too long. When my feet finally decided it was time to get moving it was too late. There was five of them around me. They had nightsticks and mean grins. They meant business. The sergeant told me, "Fall in with the rest of the recruits, soldier."

I eyeballed about ten numb-looking guys in a bunch, most of them looking the worse for wear. "What is this bullshit?"

He chuckled. "You just enlisted. Second Battalion, Second Regiment, Oar Home Defense Forces."

"Like hell."

"You want to argue about it?"

I looked at his buddies. They were ready. And I wasn't going to get no help from the other "recruits." "Not right now. We'll talk it over later, one-on-one." I gave him my best imitation of Raven's I'm-going-to-make-a-necklace-out-of-your-toes look. He got the idea.

He wanted to try some bluster but he just said, "Fall in. And don't give us no shit. We ain't no more excited about this than you are."

So that was how I got me back into the army.

55

Raven waited awhile, then, troubled, hobbled around looking for Case. He didn't find a trace. Case might have stepped off the edge of the earth.

He could spend hours in a futile search that would keep him at risk himself or he could go home and have Silent and Bomanz hunt the easy way.

The pain in his ankle had awakened the old pain in his hip, so that he was stove up in both legs and moved with the spryness of an eighty-year-old arthritic. It was no time for heroics.

He had no trouble entering the temple, reaching the tower, and getting up-stairs. Except from his own body. Someone up top had been watching. Silent covered his progress with a curtain of gentle, selective blindness.

Bomanz got after him before he got through the door. "Where's Case? What happened?"

"I don't know. He disappeared. How about you do something for this ankle while I tell it?" He settled with his back against a wall, leg outthrust. He told what there was to tell.

Bomanz poked, prodded, and twisted. Raven winced. The wizard said, "Not much I can do but kill the pain. Silent? You know more about healing than I do."

Silent paused in his translation for Darling, moved in on the ankle without enthusiasm. Bomanz puttered around, muttering, "Got to come up with some-thing of his he had long enough to make his own." Grumble, grumble, paw through Case's few possessions, come up with his journal. "This ought to do it." He shuffled into a corner and went to mumbling and twitching.

Silent did not do much more for Raven's ankle than Bomanz had. The pain was gone but it still did not want to work right when Raven put his weight on it. He wasn't going to win any footraces for a few days.

Everyone waited tensely for Bomanz. No one expressed the common fear, that Case had been caught by Exile's soldiers.

Bomanz finally looked up. "I need the city map."

Silent got it from Darling. Bomanz fussed over it a minute before saying, "He's somewhere in this area."

Raven said, "That's that open area where the windwhale dropped us."

"Yes."

"What the hell is he doing out there?"

"How should I know? Somebody maybe better go out there and find out. Aw, hell! Me and my big mouth." Darling had pointed at him, clicked her tongue, and winked. He was elected.

Raven closed his eyes, relaxed for a few minutes, letting the tension and aches fade. Then he asked, "What was in the pack?"

One of the Torques said, "More money than I ever heard of one guy lugging around. It's in the corner, you want to look it over."

"Don't know if I have that much ambition." But he levered himself up. "Nothing there that was useful?"

"I tell you, I can't remember me a time when found money wasn't useful to me."

That did not sound promising. Raven went through the pack, was disap-pointed. He looked at Darling. She signed, "Anything?"

He shook his head, but signed, "It does prove that the assassin, and therefore the murdered man, were linked with the theft of the spike. This stuff came from the Barrowland. Some of these kinds of coins haven't been in circulation anywhere else for centuries. But Bomanz told you that already."

She nodded.

"And he could not use anything here to get an idea where the man is, the way he did with Case?"

She shook her head. She got up and started pacing, pausing occasionally to look outside. After a while, she caught Silent's attention, signed, "Slip down and eavesdrop on Exile. Carefully. I do not want him getting too far ahead of us."

Bomanz did not return till after midnight. "Where have you been?" Raven grumped. "You had us worried we were going to lose you, too."

"It's not that easy to get around out there. They have patrols everywhere, trying to keep another blowup from happening. The fighting is sporadic tonight. Exile had Gossamer and Spidersilk doing donkey work, rounding up wizards and whatnot who came here to grab the spike. That's where all the excitement is tonight. Excitement for the future is going to be provided by the cholera. It's showing up everywhere now."

Everyone glared at him. "What about Case?" Raven snapped. "Get to the point, old man."

Bomanz smiled. But there was no humor there. "He's gone back into the army."

"What?"

Darling flashed some signs at Raven. Raven said, "She's right. Quit dicking around and tell it."

"They've put up a camp in that open area. With a fence around it. And they're grabbing every man between fifteen and thirty-five they can lay hands on. They're shoving them in there and calling them the Oar Home Defense Forces Brigade. They may give them a little training so they can use them to do most of the dying if there's an attack, but I think the main reason they're there is Exile wants the most dangerous part of the population locked up where it can't cause any more trouble for the grays."

Darling signed, "How do we get him out?"

"I don't know if we can. He may have to get himself out." He stopped them before they jumped all over him. "I tried. I went to the gate and gave the guards a long sob story about how they had my only grandson and means of support. While they were still being polite they told me there wasn't nobody going to get out of there, and anyway they didn't remember taking in anybody by the name Philodendron Case. I think they would have."

Raven said, "He's technically a deserter even if he's the only man from the Guards still around. He wouldn't have given them his real name."

"I realized that while I was talking. So I gave it up before they got too angry. They were pretty reasonable considering they'd had people after them all day."

Everyone looked to Darling. She signed, "We will leave him there for now. He is safer there than we are here. We have the means if there is a desperate need to communicate with him. We have other matters to concern us. I suggest we give them some attention. Time is running out on us. And everyone else."

Old Man Fish had grown first troubled, then frightened when Smeds didn't show. Smeds had cared for the problem posed by Tully Stahl alive, but how about the problem of Tully Stahl dead? The grays had the body. If they identified it how long would it be before they discovered who Tully had run with?

Not long enough. Smeds had bought some time but the sands in the glass kept on running and the bodies kept falling.

That was the trouble with this thing. They kept beating the inevitable back, but always the margin was a little narrower afterward. And the cost of holding it at bay escalated and the price of failure became more dreadful while the pay-off never looked any better.

He felt no remorse over Tully Stahl. Tully had begged for it. The wonder was that he had lasted so long. But Timmy Locan bothered him a lot. Of the four of them Timmy had been the least deserving of an unpleasant end.

He was about to give up on Smeds and go back to hiding in the ruins when he heard how the grays were conscripting all the citizens of military age they could grab.

Intuition told him what had happened. Smeds was in the army now.

Which was, probably, the safest place he could be. If he'd had sense enough to give them a false name.

The boy had sense.

Old Fish headed for the ruins, to tuck himself away from the eyes of the hunters, and on the way had him an inspiration. Why not hide in plain sight himself? They would argue a little because of his age, but they would take him. And it would be a damned good hedge against the coming privations of the siege. Soldiers, even militiamen, would get fed better than guys hiding in collapsed cellars. And the witch people running Oar should protect their soldiers from the cholera more diligently than they would the general population.

He headed for the camp the grays had set up on the razed ground.

It went about as he expected. They let him in after a little argument and a quick check for signs he was carrying cholera. He gave his name as Forto Reibas, which was a joke on himself and the grays alike. It was the name he had been given at birth but no one had used it for two generations.

For all the black riders had harassed the Limper into a frothing rage repeatedly with their tricks and traps and stalls, they had used sorcery very little. He did not understand their game. It troubled him, though he did not admit that even to himself. He was confident his own brute strength would carry him, was confident there was no one else in this world any longer who could match him strength for strength.

They knew that. That was what troubled him. They stood no chance against him, yet they harassed and guided him in a way that suggested they had every confidence in the efficacy of what they were doing. Which meant a big and terrible pitfall somewhere ahead.

They had used so little sorcery that he had stopped watching for it. His own style was smashing hammer blows. Subtlety was the last thing he expected from anyone else.

It was not till he came upon the same disfigured tree for the fourth time that he woke to the realization that he had seen it before, that, in fact, his tireless run had been guided into a circle about fifty miles around and he had been chasing himself for hundreds of miles.

Another damned stall!

He controlled his rage and found his way off the endless track. Then he paused to take stock of himself and his surroundings.

He was a little north of the Tower. He felt it down there, somehow mocking, daring, almost calling him to come try its defenses again. An affront, it was.

It seemed likely there was nothing his enemies would like more than to have him waste time beating his head against that adamantine fortress. So he put temptation aside. He would deal with the Tower after he had taken possession of the silver spike and had shaped it into the talisman that would give him mastery of the world.

He headed north, toward Oar.

His step was sprightly. He chuckled as he ran. Soon, now. Soon. The world would pay its debts.

Toadkiller Dog loped nearer the Tower, uncertain why he tempted fate so. He sensed the Limper running in circles north of him and was amused. These new lords of the empire were not as terrible as the old, but they were smart. Maybe smarter than any of the old ones except the Lady herself and her sister. He was satisfied that the power had passed into competent hands.

Something he had heard some wise man say. About the three stages of empire, the three generations. First came the conquerers, unstoppable in war. Then came the administrators, who bound it all together into one apparently unshakable, immortal edifice. Then came the wasters, who knew no responsibility and squandered the capital of their inheritance upon whims and vices. And fell to other conquerers.

This empire was making the transition from the age of the conquerer to that of the administrator. Only one of the old ones was left, the Limper. The heirs of empire were out to crowd him off history's stage. Conquerers were too rowdy and unpredictable to keep around if you wanted a well-ordered empire.

He would do well to consider his own place in this nonchaotic future.

He trotted to what he considered a safe distance from the Tower gate, sat, waited.

Someone came out almost immediately. A someone whose vision of the future had room for a timeless old terror like Toadkiller Dog.

They formed an alliance.

Smeds groaned as he pushed his blanket aside and rolled over. He had bruises on his bruises and aches in every muscle and joint. Sleeping on the ground did not help.

This was the third time he had wakened in this tent he shared with forty men. He was not looking forward to another day in the militia.

"You all right, Ken?" a tentmate asked. He was using the name Kenton Anitya.

"Stiff and sore. Guess I'll get a chance to work out the kinks before the day is over."

"Why keep fighting them? You can't win."

Someone looked outside. "Hey! It snowed. Got about an inch out there."

Jeers and sarcastic remarks about their good fortune.

Smeds said, "Since I was a kid people been kicking me around. I ain't gonna take it no more. I'm gonna kick back and keep on kicking till they decide it's easier to leave me alone." He'd had four fights with the grays running their training platoon already.

Another neighbor said, "You're getting to them. But your tactics aren't so great. Got to use your head a little, too."

That was Cy Green. Already he was pretty much the leader inside the tent. Everybody figured Green wasn't his real name. He didn't wear it very good. Everybody figured he'd been in the army before. He handled the military crap like he was born to it and he always let you know how you could make it easier on yourself—if you wanted to know. The guys liked him and mostly took his advice.

Smeds was reserving judgment. The guy was too much at home for him. He might be a spy. Or maybe a deserter who got swept up by the gray recruiters. Smeds had a notion that at least here in Oar, a deserter with a long military background probably had served with the Guards at the Barrowland.

"I'm open to suggestions, Cy. But I ain't going to back down."

"Look at what's going on, Ken. Originally they worked on you because they wanted to show us what could happen if we weren't good boys. You provoked so easy they kept coming back."

"Over and over. And probably again today. And I won't back down then, either."

"Calm down. You're right. It's gone past what's reasonable. But every time you see red you go for Corporal Royal."

"Only because I can't get to the sergeant."

"But the sergeant and corporal are halfway decent guys just trying to do a job that they don't think there's any point or hope to. Your real problem is Caddy. Caddy waits till they're a hair short of having you under control, then he jumps in and kicks the shit out of you."

Several of the men agreed. One said, "Caddy's got his bluff in on the rest of them."

Green said, "And he's covered as long as he don't kill you."

Smeds didn't really want to talk about it. But they were probably right about Caddy. "So?"

"Go after Caddy if you have to go for somebody. He's the root of the meanness. He's the one going to hurt you. Make him pay. And try to put a leash on that temper. You got to blow up, do it when you're right, not just 'cause you don't like how things are going. Don't none of us want to be here. We keep our heads, maybe we'll all get out of this."

Smeds wanted to throw a fit right then but he held back, mainly because he'd be doing it in the face of common sense, which would cost him the respect he had won.

He was real worried about Smeds Stahl. Smeds Stahl was getting inclined to let himself get carried away. He *did* need to keep a better grip. Or he'd end up doing himself in the way Tully did.

He wondered if it was the influence of the spike.

His determination to do right got a big boost at morning roll.

Fortune was all smiles. The tent next on the left started earlier and he overheard the corporal over there bellow, "Locan, Timmy," so he was ready for the trick when Corporal Royal tried it. He just kind of glanced around dumbly like everybody else, and did not respond at all when Royal tried, "Stahl, Smeds."

They were getting closer. They knew the names now.

He got another shock an hour later. They were stomping around in the mud, doing close order drill. His platoon passed another headed the other way and there in the outside file was Old Man Fish.

Fish winked and skipped to get in step.

Exile watching had become a permanent assignment for Silent. And now it looked like it was paying off. He was excited when he slipped in.

He signed, "They have come up with the names of three men who were regular companions of the murdered man. Timmy Locan. Smeds Stahl. Old Man Fish."

"Fish?" Raven asked aloud.

Silent signed, "Yes. The description was vague but he could be the man who whipped you three."

"*Old Man* Fish?"

Silent smiled wickedly, but signed, "They have been traced to a place known as the Skull and Crossbones, which is abandoned now, except for squatters. But the Nightstalkers had a corporal billeted there till the night the riots started. They are looking for him. They think he can identify the men. Exile feels very close. He is mobilizing all his resources. Also, the Limper is expected tomorrow."

Darling was excited. She looked like she had stumbled onto an unexpected answer. She clapped her hands, demanding attention. "You will prevent them from bringing that soldier to Exile. I want him. Deliver him to Lamber Gartsen's stable."

She had worked hard, using her Plain allies, to take stock of what little remained of the Rebel cause. Gartsen was it.

"Likewise, identify and collect the owner of the Skull and Crossbones. And anyone else who made an extended stay during the appropriate period. Be careful. They have made no great effort to catch us but they know we are here. They will be alert for their opportunities. Outfit yourselves as Exile's guards. Let us go."

They tried to argue. Arguing with Darling was like arguing with the wind. Faced with no other choice, they went with her, to guard her.

They departed the temple one by one, unnoticed in the press. Darling gathered them two blocks away, took reports from Plain creatures she had sent ahead, signed, "Exile's guards are billeted in the Treasury Annex. There are twelve there now, off duty. Silent, you and Bomanz will neutralize them."

No if you can or give it a try. Just do it.

The men were rattled. They were not prepared for a head-to-head with a city very much in imperial hands.

They did not argue this time, though.

Silent knew a spell for putting people to sleep but it was verbally based. Pruned up in disgust, he gave it to Bomanz. The wizards went away. Darling gave them a five-minute start.

Silent awaited them at the annex door. He signed, "They are asleep."

Darling countered, "I want them under so deep they will not awaken for days. Then hidden where they are not likely to be found."

Silent scowled but nodded.

Shortly afterward, as they donned a guise acceptable on the streets of Oar, Bomanz said, "Let's keep it neat here. The longer it takes them to figure it out, the longer we've got to take advantage of their costumes."

Raven grunted. Silent nodded. One of the Torques asked, "What are these brooch things with the garnet faces? Allegiance badges?"

Silent examined one, set it down quickly, made signs at Bomanz. The old wizard looked at the brooch. "Allegiance badges, yes, but also a way for Exile to track his people. We'd better do something with them. Like have that idiot buzzard fly them out into the country."

Darling signed impatiently.

"All right, all right," Bomanz grumbled. "I'm hurrying as fast as I can."

Another half hour passed before they left the Annex. Darling, Raven, and Bomanz rode, guised as black riders. The rest went as foot soldiers. Wherever they went people got out of their way.

Once they cleared the city's center Darling and the injured Torque split off for the Gartsen stable. There was a talking stone there. Darling wanted to get in touch with Old Father Tree. The rest went off to see what they could do about keeping the imperials from getting their hands on anyone who could identify the men who had stolen the silver spike.

61

After I figured out I was probably safer in the militia than hanging around Darling I settled down and made myself to home. It was kind of comfortable back in the old rut. Didn't have to do no thinking or worrying.

But I guess I spent too much time running loose. It got old fast. First time I felt like going out for a beer and couldn't I knew I was getting out and staying there.

That idea got a boost when the sergeant had us our first weapons practice. We stood around in the mud while the breeze gnawed on us. Half the guys weren't dressed for it. But that wasn't what got me. That was what the sergeant told us.

"Listen up, you men. We just got word trouble gets here tomorrow. All the learning you're going to get you're going to get today. You want a half-ass chance of getting through alive, pay attention. The only weapon we got to give you is the spear. So that's all we're going to work with." He indicated soldiers who had their arms wrapped around bundles of spears. The spearheads were inside wooden covers so nobody would get stabbed or cut. "These two new guys are experts. They was loaned to us by the Nightstalkers. They're going to run us through the drills. You don't do what they tell you, you get your butt kicked same as if you don't do what I tell you." He gestured at one of the Nightstalkers.

They all learn their piece at the same place, I think.

The Nightstalker stripped the cover off the head of a spear. "This is a spear." He was going to blind us with illuminating information. But I'd played with these toys lots. Those others guys hadn't. Maybe some of them needed to be told. You got to crawl before you walk and walk before you run. Except my littlest brother Radish. The way I remember, he hit the ground running.

"This edge is sharp enough to shave with. This point will go through armor if you put some muscle behind it. The spear is a very versatile weapon. You can stab with it, jab with it, cut with it, slash with it. You can use it to hold your tent up or use it for a fishing pole. But one thing you can't *never* do with it is throw it. It ain't a javelin. You throw it and you don't have shit anymore. You're meat for the first guy that wants you."

So. Rule One.

And so forth. While we froze our butts off.

Came to the part where they start sparring, going through the basic moves. The Nightstalkers called for seven guys to pair off with our regular instructors. I was proud. The recruits had listened to me. Nobody volunteered.

The Nightstalkers grabbed seven guys and started them through the moves. The sergeant took four pairs and his buddy took three.

Just like I figured, when they got moving faster the soldier named Caddy made him a chance to "accidentally" hurt the guy he was sparring with.

The Nightstalker broke it up. "Seven more. Come on."

This one hothead named Ken something was all set to go after Caddy and get his head busted good. I told a couple guys, "Hang on to him. Cool him down. And don't let him pair off with Caddy."

I went up and took the spear from the guy Caddy had decked. His nose was bloody.

Clumsy as Caddy had looked, I figured I could stumble around and get in a "lucky" whack that would slow him down for the rest of the guys that would have to face him. I was rusty but I used to be pretty good with the standard infantry spear. Always was about my best weapon.

The body will betray. I went into a stance without thinking. Caddy looked puzzled. I figured he was mean because everything puzzled him.

The Nightstalker came and moved my hands and feet and butt around into what he considered a more acceptable stance. When he had everybody set he started us through the moves. It got hard to stay looking inept as they came faster. The muscles and bones remembered and wanted to do things right.

Caddy decided to break my nose. When he went for it I stumbled out of the way and accidentally whacked him in the shin. He barked. Somebody in ranks said, "Yeah!" Somebody else laughed.

That did it for Caddy. He came after me.

I stumbled around and tried to make like a scared kid trying to defend himself. Had we been playing for keeps I could have killed him over and over.

Then he gave me an opening a blind man couldn't miss. I tore up his left ear, tripped him, sent him sliding through the mud. I backed off, trying to look scared and unable to believe what I'd done.

"That's enough!" our sergeant snapped. "Give me the spear and get back in ranks, Green. Caddy! Go get cleaned up. Get that ear fixed."

I surrendered the spear and moved. The guys were all working hard not to grin.

"Green!" It was the Nightstalker sergeant. "Come here."

I went back. I stood at attention. He looked me in the eye, hard. Then he touched the cut on my cheek. He backed off, took a spear from one of the grays, removed the headguard, threw it aside. "Give him a spear."

It got real quiet. Everybody wondered what the hell, except my sergeant. I thought I knew. Queen's Bridge. But it didn't make no sense. It was over a long time ago. My sergeant tried to argue. The Nightstalker just growled, "Give him a spear."

I gave him my best imitation Raven look and tried not to shake too much as I took the guard off the spear somebody handed me. I didn't throw the guard away. That bastard was serious. I wasn't going to play around and I wasn't going to give up a trick.

He did some fancy moves to loosen up.

My mouth felt awfully dry.

When he turned on me I shifted to a left-handed stance, which guys always have trouble with for a couple of minutes. I kept the guard in my right hand.

He tested me with a thrust toward my eyes. I brushed it away, gently, just manipulating the spear with my left hand. I shot my right forward, cracked his knuckles with the guard. Cold as it was, that had to hurt like hell. In the second the pain distracted him I brought my spear around, still one-handed, in a wild roundhouse edge cut at his throat. He threw himself backward to avoid it. I grabbed my spear with my right hand and went into a clumsily balanced right-handed stance, the butt of my spear forward. I flung myself and the butt of the spear straight ahead and got him under the ribs, taking the wind out of him.

After that it was just a couple of easy moves to disarm him and put him on his back in the mud with the tip of my spear at his throat. The whole thing didn't take ten, twelve seconds.

"You're wrong," I told him. "I wasn't there. But if you was right you should've remembered that the Nightstalkers are only second best, one-on-one."

I lifted the spear, stepped back, put the guard on, handed the weapon to Corporal Royal, headed for my place in ranks. I prayed a lot as I did. Nobody would look me in the eye. The guys were all scared shitless.

The Nightstalker took his time getting up. He was as pale as I've ever seen a guy get without doing a lot of bleeding, which he knew he could have done. He waved off any help. He recovered spear and guard and made a point of cleaning the weapon while forty-seven guys waited for something to happen.

He looked around, said, "You learn something every day. If you're smart. Let's have the next six men up here."

Everybody sighed. Me included. The shit storm was on hold for a while.

I noticed that hothead Ken looking at my cheek like he never noticed the mark there before. Maybe the cold made it show up more.

62

With a little sorcery and a little luck Bomanz learned that the men Exile had sent for the valuable corporal had just gone to Nightstalker headquarters and told them to produce him.

"Nothing like getting somebody else to do your work for you," Raven said.

"Sounds like a fine idea to me," Bomanz said. "Why don't we find a place and wait for them to bring him to us?"

As easily done as said. There was just one decent, straightforward route running from the Nightstalkers' headquarters to the heart of Oar.

Finally coming," Bomanz said. "Silent. Lay down that haze now. Don't make it so thick they smell trouble."

Silent walked a ways away, just kind of stood there. People passing looked at him and stayed as far away as they could. Soon there was a stronger than normal smell of woodsmoke. The air grew hazy.

"This is them," Bomanz said of a tight little group approaching.

As the group came abreast the haze suddenly thickened. Bomanz struck at the escort of four men, flattened them, called his favorite buzzard in to dispose of their allegiance badges.

The four had been escorting a man and a woman. Silent looked at the female and started signing so fast only Raven could follow him. "Brigadier Wildbrand," he said. "We have to take her, too. You don't refuse a gift from the gods."

Despite their apparel they got into the Gartsen stable without attracting attention. Wizards were handy sometimes. Raven asked the man who met them, Gartsen, "Where is she?"

"Loft."

Raven stepped around a small menhir, climbed, made signs one-handed.

Neither the corporal nor Wildbrand had said a word yet. They had no real idea what their situation was. Till Darling came to look them over. Wildbrand recognized her. The Brigadier said, "Oh, shit. It's true."

Bomanz said, "Tell Darling we're ready to go get the rest of them."

Silent's hands were fluttering. He ignored the old wizard. He asked Darling, "Did you talk to the tree?"

She answered his signs, "Yes. He is troubled. He suggests we remove Case from that camp. Something happened there, involving Case, that he has heard of from his creatures. We will shackle these two and leave them with Gartsen."

Silent started arguing. She donned the clothing of one of Exile's guards. Sometimes she used her handicap for all it was worth. As when she did not want to argue.

Silent and Raven were livid. Neither one believed the tree had mentioned Case at all.

S meds kicked his copper's worth into the discussion. "I ain't hungry and I ain't sick and that's worth something even if I got to be sore and tired all the time." It had been a hard day.

Somebody said, "Yeah. Bet it's hell out there now."

Another said, "What I'm wondering, suppose we whip the Limper? Then back to the same old horseshit till they find their silver whatsit?"

The group grew quiet. That was the first anyone had mentioned the future. Nobody wanted to think about that.

Smeds glanced at Green. Crowded as the tent was, there was a clear space around Green. Nobody understood what had happened this afternoon but they did know there was going to be some shit come down about it. Nobody wanted to be too close to Green when it hit.

Somebody said, "The Limper comes and the shit gets to flying, they're going to be too damned busy to watch me. I see the chance, I'm gone. Even if I have to stick Caddy or somebody."

The sergeant ripped open the entry flap. "Fall out and fall in!"

What now? Smeds wondered. More drills? Hadn't they done enough for one day? Hell! He was too tired to get pissed off.

At least they hadn't been singled out. Every tent was spilling men. As soon as they formed up, the sergeant marched them over to stand with their backs to the stockade. Grays ran around with lamps and torches.

Smeds caught a glimpse of Fish in the back rank of the platoon two to his left. The old man had done something to darken his hair.

The sergeant called them to attention.

Three dark riders came from the direction of the gate. A man in black walked beside each. They advanced slowly, studying each platoon. A review. Exile's men down to give the raggedy-ass militia the once-over . . .

Smeds's stomach sank. They acted more like they were looking for somebody.

But they passed Fish's platoon without pausing. Maybe it would be all right after all.

The black riders passed the next platoon and started across the face of Smeds's outfit. . . .

The lead rider halted. One arm thrust out, pointing. Fingers danced. The footman beside the rider pushed in among the men.

Smeds nearly messed himself.

The dark soldier grabbed Green.

Smeds sighed. Green! Of course! The shit had to come down, didn't it?

He was so turned inward he missed the arm pointing again, did not notice the two footmen coming till they were almost to him.

His blood turned to ice.

They took hold and dragged him out of ranks.

The riders headed for the gate. Smeds trudged along behind Green, a horseman on his left and a foot soldier on his right. After the first overwhelming shock he began to take control. He'd gotten out of a couple tight places already. He just had to stay calm and alert and move fast when his moment came.

A minute after they were in among buildings, masked from watchers in the camp, Green burst out laughing. "You guys got more balls than brains!" He punched one of the riders in the thigh. "Thanks."

"Don't thank me. I figured you belonged in there. This was Darling's idea."

"Yeah?" Green laughed again. "I'll remember that when your turn in the barrel comes. Why'd you grab my buddy Ken?"

"She says he's one of the men who stole the spike."

Green looked at him. "No shit?"

Smeds clamped down hard. Panic would not get him out of this one.

64

Fish understood what was happening the moment he glimpsed Exile's soldiers pulling Smeds out of formation. He didn't really think, he just reacted. Everybody was intent on what the blacks were doing.

He took a few steps back, turned, hoisted himself over the low stockade. A few of his neighbors in the platoon noticed but did not holler. Better, none got the bright idea of joining him.

He dropped to the ground, ran, softly cursing his body for having aged well past the point where this made any sense for him. He was all aches and stiffness from the day's drills and he doubted if he'd ever loosen up.

But by damn he wasn't going to give in, to those imperial vampires or to the weakness of his flesh.

He reached the uncleared ruins facing the stockade gate minutes before the riders came out. He crouched in darkness, waiting, and took stock.

He had two knives. Because he had come in as a volunteer the grays had not searched and disarmed him the way they had the conscripts. But two knives weren't going to be much use against that gang.

Craft was the answer. Like hunting and trapping and surviving in the Great Forest. Craft and stealth and surprise.

There were possibilities he rejected, like doing Smeds the way Smeds had done Tully. Smeds did not deserve that. It would do no good now because they knew who they were looking for anyway. Besides, Smeds was the only one who knew where the damned spike was hidden.

He watched the silhouettes of the blacks come out. Before they left the cleared area he was sure there was some game running. They weren't headed toward Exile's setup in the goddess's temple uptown. Unless they were planning on going the long way.

What now?

Since he had expected them to streak straight to Exile he was set near their most direct route. He would have to move fast if he wasn't going to lose them.

He flitted through the ruins like a filthy ghost, making less noise than most haunts. He was very good at sneaking. One worry, not quite facetious, was that his quarry would smell him. For days before volunteering he had been too pressed to clean up and the days in the stockade had just been time to ripen.

In the Great Forest, to survive where the savages prowled, you paid attention to how you smelled.

He caught up quickly, was watching from twenty yards away when a couple of them started congratulating each other.

The key word trumpeted: Darling.

He was thunderstruck.

He hadn't really expected the White Rose bunch to be scared off by his threats but he hadn't figured them for so bold they'd take uniforms from Exile's people so they could ride into the training camp to spring one of their own, either.

This changed a few things. This made time less critical. This meant the odds were not nearly as bad. There couldn't be many of them left after the purges that had begun last week. Maybe, once they went to ground, he could pick them off. The big worry would be how aggressively they would press Smeds.

He followed them so closely he might have been an extra shadow, and so carefully none of them got that chill-on-the-neck sense of being watched. And, wonder of wonders, they led him to a place he knew.

He'd only been in and out of the Gartsen stable a few times, back during his flirtation with the Rebel cause. But knowing anything about the lie of the land was better than going in blind.

He had one scare shortly before the Rebels reached their hideout.

A big bird dropped out of nowhere and landed on the shoulder of one of the horsemen. The rider cursed and swatted at it. It laughed and started talking about how Exile was in a tizzy because he couldn't find some of his guards.

Fish recalled that the White Rose called the Plain of Fear home and talking creatures supposedly infested the place.

His luck was with him still. He had to consider the bird's advent a good omen.

Not so the man it had selected as its perch. He wanted the bird gone. The bird did not want to go. "I'm riding from here," it said. "I can't see diddle-shit in the dark."

Fish recalled the zoo they had been carrying the day he had seen them outside the Skull and Crossbones. There would be that to consider, too.

After they went into the stableyard Fish circled the place once, carefully. He did not spot any sentries but that didn't mean they weren't there, hidden from the cold.

It was getting chillier faster. And if that overcast was what he thought, it would snow before morning. A snow cover would make getting around unnoticed a real pain in the ass.

He faded into the shadows and went looking for a crawl-in entrance that used to be around back, where a lean-to junk shed had had the fence as its rear wall.

It was there, still, after all those years, and looked like it hadn't been used since the olden days. He opened it very carefully. It did not make half the noise he feared but what it did make sent chills scampering along his spine. He went in smoothly as a stalking snake.

Something cat size, that was not, started awake. He reacted first, his hand closing around its throat.

There was another thing, like a mouse or chipmunk, that he stomped as he was stealing toward the main stable, where a ladder nailed outside led to the hayloft. It died without a sound. He went up the ladder like a syrupy shadow.

The loft doors were secured only by a latch inside. He slipped a knife between, lifted it, eased inside. He dropped the latch into place.

There was a little light from below. There were voices down there, too.

And not ten feet from him were a man and woman, bound and gagged. The woman was looking his way but not at him. He eased closer. . . .

By the gods! These people had their brass! That was Brigadier Wildbrand herself. And that corporal from the Skull and Crossbones. It fell into place. The imperials and these people knew the names but not the faces. That corporal would be about the best witness available.

Down below, somebody started yelling at Smeds. Smeds didn't say anything back. Somebody else said keep it down or the neighbors would think there was cholera here.

Fish eased forward some more. "Corporal," he breathed, staying behind a bale. The soldier jumped, then grunted. Wildbrand looked for the source of the whisper. He might have been a ghost for all the luck she had. "You want to get out of here?"

Another grunt, affirmative.

"They're going to ask you to look at a man and tell them who he is. Tell them his name is Ken something. You stick to that, when they bring you back up here you're out of this. You don't stick to it, it's good-bye, Brigadier."

The man glanced at his commander. She nodded, do it.

Fish wormed his way into loose straw, out of the way, to wait. He had it all scoped out now.

65

Raven and Bomanz ragged my old tentmate Ken and each other. He sat in a chair—the only one we had—and didn't say nothing. He was totally pissed off, but in a way so stubborn I don't think they could have got a squeak out of him with a hot poker. He just looked at them like he figured on cutting their throats in about one minute. He even refused a meal.

I didn't. I stood around stuffing food in my face and wondering what the hell was going on since nobody bothered explaining anything to me.

Darling stomped, got everybody's attention, signed, "Get the soldier."

Now what?

Raven and Silent went climbing into the hayloft. In a minute they came back with a Nightstalker who was gagged and, from the way he chafed his wrists, had been tied. They brought him over. He glanced indifferently at Ken. Ken didn't react at all.

Silent took the gag off. Raven asked, "Do you know the man in the chair?"

"Yeah," the Nightstalker croaked. He worked some spit back into his throat. "Yeah. Name's Ken something. He used to come around the place I was billeted sometimes, drink a few beers with us."

Silent and Raven looked at each other and had a frowning contest. Raven asked, "You sure his name isn't Smeds Stahl?"

"Nah . . ."

Silent corked him one upside the head and knocked him down. Raven asked, "You sure? This man here and the woman over there were at Queen's Bridge. They still have grudges."

The Nightstalker looked up at him and said, "Man, I'll call him Tommy Tucker, King Thrushbeard, or Smeds Stahl if that's going to make you happy. But that ain't going to turn him into Smeds Stahl."

"He fits the description."

The soldier looked at Ken. "Maybe. A little. But Smeds Stahl has got to be at least ten years older than this guy."

Raven said, "Shit!" I don't think I ever heard him use the word before.

It was not the right time but I couldn't help it. "There we was, headed into the last turn in the inside lane, leading by a neck as we headed toward the stretch. And the damned horse pulled up lame."

They appreciated it. For a second I thought Silent might actually say something. Probably something I didn't want to hear.

Darling stomped, asked what was going on. She read lips some but could not keep up with all that.

Raven and Silent signed like hell. She made a gesture she hadn't taught me, probably cussing, then told them to put the Nightstalker back in the loft. Raven and Silent dragged him off like it was his fault things didn't work out the way they wanted. Darling signed at anybody who would pay attention that it was all her fault for jumping to conclusions about some guys she saw on a porch one day. I didn't know what the hell she was going on about. When Silent and Raven came back we had us a big woe-is-me session. Bomanz's buzzard pal damned near got strangled by everybody.

A banging up in the loft broke that up. Everybody went charging up to see what the racket was.

The loft doors, where they hoisted the hay bales up and brought them inside, were banging in the wind. The Nightstalker and Brigadier Wildbrand, that they hadn't told me about before, were gone. Silent and Raven looked at the discarded ropes and gags and got into it over whose fault it was the Nightstalker didn't get tied up tight enough.

I dropped back down and told Darling. She had me yell at them to knock off the crap and get out there and catch them. They came, still bickering. She started giving orders aimed at stopping the Nightstalkers before they could get back to their own. "Paddlefoot stays here. He is in no shape." The Torque was crapped out in one of the horse stalls and had been since I'd come in. "Case. You stay and keep track of our guest."

That went over big. Raven and Silent gave me their famous deadly looks, like maybe I'd arranged the whole damned thing just so I could get her alone. Hell. After three days in that camp I didn't feel like doing anything anyway.

We were in a spot. From what Darling signed I gathered we was out of places to run. We couldn't even go back to the temple because Wildbrand and the corporal probably heard them talk about how we hid out right in Exile's pocket.

Even that buzzard got out to do some aerial scouting. I was glad. He hadn't started in on me yet but I was up to my ears with him nagging Bomanz. The old boy was all right.

I never saw Darling rattled before. She paced and stomped and made incomplete gestures and signed at me without ever finishing a thought. She wasn't afraid, just worried about what would become of the rest of us and the movement if the guys didn't catch the Nightstalkers in time.

I don't know what I thought we might get up to but at the time it seemed a good idea to tie old Ken up. Then I stood behind his chair, conversing with Darling, like I suddenly needed something to hide behind.

I don't know how much later it was, probably only a couple minutes, when I saw somebody move behind Darling and thought it was Paddlefoot Torque finally waking up. I went to work on me for being too damned chickenshit to have grabbed an opportunity when it was there. . . .

That wasn't Torque! That was somebody else. . . .

The second I realized that, before I could give her any warning, the guy laid a knife across her throat. "Turn him loose," he told me. And when I just stood there gawking he drew a little blood. "Do it!"

I started fumbling with knots.

Torque did decide to wake up then.

I don't think the poor silly sack ever knew what was going on. He stumbled out, rubbing his eyes and mumbling. The guy holding Darling turned around and stuck him with a knife he had in his left hand, came back and got Darling in the side with the same knife as she was turning toward him, and in almost the same motion threw the knife with which he had threatened her.

It hit me in the hip. I felt it go deep and hit bone. Then the grungy stable floor opened its arms and jumped up to meet me. The guy yanked his knife out of Darling and bounced over to cut our guest loose. Then he got set to cut my throat.

"Hey!" our guest yelled. "Knock it off! They weren't going to croak me."

"This is the second time they shoved their faces in our business. They want to clean us out. I warned them last time. . . ."

"Let's just find my pack and get the hell out before the rest of them come back."

I could have kissed him if I could have done anything at all. I wasn't too spry right then.

The other one looked down at me. "You tell the bitch this was her last free chance. Next time, *skitch*!" He flashed his bloody knife past his throat. Then Ken found the pack I'd found in that alley. He put it on and they went away.

When the stable door closed behind them I ground my teeth and yanked the damned knife out of me. I didn't bleed to death on the spot, so I knew it didn't get any big veins. I crawled over to Darling. She was pale and she was hurting but she wanted me to check on Torque first.

He was still alive but I didn't think there was a whole lot that could be done to keep him that way. I told Darling. She signed we had to do something.

Of course we did. But I didn't know the hell what.

Raven busted in. "We caught them! We're safe for . . . What the hell happened, Case?"

By then they were all inside, recaptured prisoners included. I told it. While I was, one of our little spies came in from the temple to report that Exile had ordered an all-out search for Brigadier Wildbrand and persons unknown masquerading as his guards.

Bomanz and Silent did what they could for us casualties, then everybody that could hit the street again. It was starting to snow out there.

"Some fun, eh?" I asked the Nightstalkers. They didn't see the humor.

Frankly, neither did I.

What the shit are we going to do?" Smeds growled at Fish when they stopped running to catch their breaths. "There ain't no safe places left."

Fish said, "I don't know. I used up all my ideas just getting you out."

"They know our names, Fish. And that bunch knows our faces."

"You're the one wouldn't let me take them out. You end up paying for that, don't whine at me."

"There's been enough killing and hurting. All I want is out." He tried to get his pack settled more comfortably. "I don't even give a damn about selling the spike anymore. I just want to wake up from the nightmare."

Snowflakes had begun to swirl around them. Fish grumbled about leaving tracks, then asked, "You know of anywhere to lay up even for a little while? Twelve hours would do. Twenty-four would be better. The Limper would be here and there wouldn't be any more ducking and slinking because the soldiers would be busy."

The only thing Smeds could think of was a drainage system that had been built when he was a kid, to carry water away from the neighborhood when it rained. Before the system there'd always been little local floods when it stormed. Some of the ditching was covered over. They had played and hidden out in there. But he hadn't paid any attention in ten years. Public works which did not serve the rich and powerful had a way of dying of neglect.

It was no place he wanted to spend any time. It would be cold and damp and infested with rats and, these days, probably, human vermin. But he could think of nowhere else to get out of sight, even for an hour.

"When I was a kid we used to—"

"Don't tell me. If I don't know I can't tell anybody. Just tell me where's a good place for you to see me without me or anybody watching me seeing you."

Smeds thought about it and mentioned a place he did know was there because his labor battalion had passed that way every morning and evening when he was doing time. He described it, asked, "What are we up to?"

"I'm going to see if Exile will talk deal."

"Oh, shit, man! He'll take you apart."

"He might," Fish admitted. "But we know somebody's going to do that real soon anyway. He's the only one who's offered any serious deal."

"I think if I had my druthers I'd rather the Rebels got the damned thing. The imperials are nasty enough without it."

Fish grunted. "Maybe. But they don't want to pay for it. They want you to do it for love. I'm a whore too old and set in her ways not to want to get paid for my trouble."

Smeds said, "I guess for guys like us it don't matter who's running things anyway. Whoever it is they're going to try to stick it to us."

The heavens had cut loose now, dumping snow so heavily it had become their ally.

Fish started explaining what he wanted Smeds to do.

The gang came smashing in out of the blizzard. Raven snarled, "We lost them."

Stubby Torque said, "You can't see your hand in front of your face out there."

"You tracked Raker down in a snowstorm in Roses, didn't you?" I asked Raven.

"Different circumstances." He was double-pissed now because of what he thought he saw when he busted through the door. As if we could have done anything about it carved up the way we were.

Darling shut them up. She made it clear she'd had her mind on business because she told them what we were going to do if those guys told the gray boys where to find us again. She felt almost sorry for those two.

She overdid the empathy sometimes. I don't have any for guys who stick knives in me.

The excitement started a few hours later when a couple of our little spies from the temple came charging in to tell us how a guy who sounded like the one who stabbed me had dropped in on Exile to see if he could cut a deal. As a good-faith gesture he'd told Exile where he could find us and Brigadier Wildbrand. He'd also told Exile his headquarters was so riddled with spies he couldn't sneeze without some Plain creature reporting it.

That meant big excitement over there. A bunch of our little allies didn't get the word in time to get out. Gossamer and Spidersilk led the exterminator squads. Meantime, they were throwing together a gang to come after us. They figured we'd hear they were coming but counted on us getting caught being on the move in a city alert for us.

I thought they were a little optimistic there, considering Bomanz and Silent had done a good job keeping us from being noticed before. But Exile probably wouldn't know we had those kinds of resources. Not about Bomanz, at least. I figured his big panic would come when he started wondering what resources Darling could call up out of the Plain.

She did have something cooked up with the tree god. What I didn't know. It wouldn't be anything small.

Nothing like being nailed down on the bull's-eye of history in the making without a fool's notion of what was going on. Nothing personal, Case, old buddy, but they can't make you tell what you don't know.

Darling told Silent and the Torques to get the horses out so they could not be recaptured. They were going to hide them on an empty lot nearby. Yeah? What would they do about tracks? Something wizardly, I guess.

Horses were part of her plans. Whatever they were. I had caught part of an argument with Silent where she told him she wanted to steal a bunch more.

One heroic little rock monkey hung in the temple till the last moment, near getting himself fried by the twins so he could find out as much as possible about Exile's deal for the spike.

There was a deal. The monkey said Exile was going to play it straight and keep his end of the bargain if the guys with the spike kept theirs. The monkey said the guy dealing for them had no idea where the spike was nor any idea where the guy who did know was hiding.

Made sense to me. And to Exile, I guess. He didn't waste no time jacking the guy around, just asked the go-between how they wanted to make the exchange.

We'd had the guy who knew! I'd lived in the same damned tent with him for days! I wanted to kick some Nightstalkers around for lying to us.

Raven got the wind up, too. "How the hell are we supposed to con people into fighting the empire if the bastards go honest on us? Whoever heard of a wizard dealing straight?"

Bomanz gave him some dirty looks but never got no chance to argue because right then we got word that Exile's boys were closing in.

When they busted in all they saw was Brigadier Wildbrand and her buddy sitting on the floor by our runt menhir. The rest of us were still there but Bomanz had disguised us as heaps of manure and whatnot while we gave the Nightstalkers the idea we were sneaking out.

The talking stone boomed out, "Hi, guys! You're too late again. You're always going to be too late. Why don't you wake up and come on over to the winning side? The White Rose don't hold no grudges."

The raiders were all Exile's personal guards, unlikely recruits, but the stone kept nagging them.

They spread out. Some rushed into the loft where nobody was hiding. Some went to work to get the Nightstalkers loose. And some went to work trying to figure how to silence that bigmouth stone.

The menhir vanished. And just when their eyes stopped popping, here it came back. "You boys better get your hearts and heads right fast. It's almost dawn now and before sunset tomorrow the White Rose is going to cure this berg of the imperial disease." Away it went again.

That crack rattled them some.

Here it came, spewing more mockery. They got so pissed they stopped doing a thorough job of searching.

There was some noise outside. Three of them charged out into the blizzard. There was a flash, a scream. A guy staggered inside. "They're all dead out there. They took the horses."

That damned Silent was showing off for Darling. She would be pissed at him for wasting them when he didn't have to. I didn't blame him, though. He'd been keeping a lot bottled up. These guys were some he could make pay.

A bunch more went charging off to avenge their buddies. The talking stone whooped and laughed and carried on.

They never caught Silent, of course. But he got some more of them. They finally took Brigadier Wildbrand and got out of there while there were some of them left to get.

A little later Silent brought ten horses in. Him and the Torques were real pleased with themselves. I think maybe Darling was the only one who wasn't pleased with them.

The snowfall had ended. The sky had cleared. The world had grown almost intolerably bright by the time the Limper topped the rise that gave him his first glimpse of his destination. The silence troubled him some. There should have been birds out if nothing else. And why was there so much smoke drifting downwind from Oar, more than could be explained by all the city's hearth and heating fires?

No matter. No matter at all. He could feel that piece of haunted silver calling him as though he had been born to wield it and it had been wrought for him and him alone. His destiny lay there, ahead, and all the mousy scrabbling around by those who would deny him would not prevent him taking that power that was rightfully his.

He strode forward, walking now, no longer rushed, confident yet still ill at ease with the silence and a lingering suspicion that all the horizons were masks being worn by his enemies.

69

Toadkiller Dog was only one of a varied pack of monsters running on the Limper's trail. But he was out in front, their leader, the only one of the crowd not carrying some dread lord or lady out of the Tower. He was the scout, the champion, and before this day was through he hoped to be entered in the annals of history as the destroyer of the last of the Ten Who Were Taken, as the closer of the door on the olden times.

He topped a low ridgeline, saw Oar for the first time. He saw, from disturbances in the snow, that the Limper had paused there, too. There he was now, a remote speck tramping a lonely track across the pristine snowscape.

He dropped down onto his belly to lower his profile, listened to the silence. He watched the smoke drift from the city, noted that everything that had stood outside the walls last time had been cleared away, leaving nothing but a flat white surround. Uneasily for a moment, he surveyed the horizons, feeling almost as if distant groves were the massed helmets and spears of legions waiting in tight array.

His companions crowded up behind him. They waited till the speck that was the Limper vanished against the dark loom of the city's walls. Then they all moved forward, marching toward doom or destiny in a gradually widening line abreast.

70

Smeds sat in the icy shadows shivering, unable to stop. His stomach felt hollow. It ached. He was scared. He hoped it was the cold and hunger but was afraid it was the first bite of cholera.

The air was filled with smoke and the stench of bodies being burned. Death had reaped a rich harvest during the night. Few who were not soldiers had eaten well in days. Disease made easy headway in bodies already weakened.

He watched the bridge up the ditch and wondered if Fish would ever come, and what he would do if Fish didn't. Then he sat there and gradually convinced himself that he was the last of the four of them, possessed of the greatest treasure in the world and so poor he was forced to live in a sewer like a rat.

He scavenged through his pack for the dozenth time, looking for some scrap of food that might have gotten into it somehow. Again he found nothing but the gold and silver he had brought out of the Barrowland. A fortune, and he would have given it all for a good meal, a warm bed, and confidence that the great terrors of the world had forgotten his name.

He started. Daydreaming, he had not noticed the two men come onto the bridge. One looked like Fish. He made the signal he was supposed to make before he walked away from the other, who stayed where he was.

Smeds shoved his pack into a gap in the culvert wall, where some of the building stone had fallen away and high water had washed out some of the earth behind. Then he ran toward the light at the nether end, a hundred yards away.

Midway he stumbled over a corpse that the rats had been at for a while. He had become so inured to horror that he just went on, giving it hardly a thought.

He rushed out the other end, floundered through drifted snow, and hurried around to where he was supposed to meet Fish, masked from the man on the bridge by a hump of earth six feet high. Fish was carrying a sizable blue canvas bag. "Is it safe?" Smeds croaked.

"Looks like they'll play square. This is the first third, along with some food and clothes and blankets and stuff I thought you could use."

Smeds's mouth watered. But he asked, "What now?"

"You go out on the bridge, get the second third, tell him where to find the spike. I watch from cover. He messes with you, I hunt him down and kill him. Go on. Let's get it done."

Smeds looked at the old man a moment, shrugged, went off to meet the man on the bridge. He was calmer than he had expected to be. Maybe he was getting used to the pressure. He was still pleased with himself for not having bent for a moment while the Rebels had him.

The man on the bridge leaned on the rail, staring at nothing. He glanced at Smeds incuriously as he approached. Another blue bag leaned against his leg. Smeds sidled up and planted his forearms on the rail on the other side of the bag.

The man was younger than Smeds had expected and of a race he'd never before seen. Easy to see why he had taken the name Exile.

"Smeds Stahl?"

"Yes. How come you're playing this square?"

"I've found honesty and fair play productive over the long term. The second third is in the bag. Do you have something for me?"

"In the city wall. One hundred eighty-two paces east of the North Gate, below the twenty-sixth archer's embrasure, in the mortar behind the block recessed to take the support brace of a timber hording."

"Understood. Thank you. Good day."

Smeds hoisted the bag and got the hell out of there.

"Go all right?" Fish asked.

"Yeah. Now what?"

"Now I join up with him to go see if you told the truth. If you did he gives me the final third. If not he kills me and comes looking for you."

"Shit. Why not head out now? What we got ought to be enough."

"He's played straight. I figure it would be smart to play it that way with him. We aren't going to get out of Oar for a while. Be nice to know there was somebody who wasn't out to get us. You go back wherever you was hiding. I'll come back to the bridge."

"Right."

Smeds was just about to drop back into the ditch when alarm horns began blowing all over the city.

The Limper had come.

71

Raven got him a wild hair. He'd go snag the spike and that would be a big foot in the door with Darling. The guy's head was getting a little bent. He didn't tell nobody but Brother Bear Torque, who he conned into going along with him.

He started out lucky. They hit no gray patrols. As they got into the heart of the city, here came Exile and an older guy just like they had timed it for Raven's benefit. They followed the two.

Exile and his companion ended up leaning on the rail of a footbridge over a big drainage ditch. Raven and Torque watched from a distance. The area around the ditch was clear. They couldn't get as close as Raven wanted.

"What the hell are they doing?" Torque asked.

"Waiting, looks like."

The older man resumed moving, went on, and vanished among tenements beyond the ditch. Five minutes later another man came out to the bridge, talked to Exile a little, walked away with a bag.

"That tears it," Torque said. "Time to bend over and kiss our asses goodbye."

"He hasn't got hold of it yet," Raven growled. "We stick and see what turns up. Look here." The older man was coming out to rejoin Exile.

They just stood there.

"Look!" Raven pointed.

The covert from which they watched was about ten feet higher than the bridge. Just enough of an elevation to reveal the head and shoulders of a man crossing the snow north of the bridge, behind a mound that would mask him from the men on the bridge. He carried two blue bags.

Alarm horns tore the guts out of the quiet.

The men on the bridge took off.

Torque said, "We better get back. . . ."

"Wait!" There was a nasty gleam in Raven's eyes. "Exile will be busy with the Limper. We get that man to tell us where the spike is, maybe we can get to it first."

72

Smeds had gotten back to his starting point. He put the two bags into hiding with his pack, except for a couple of army blankets, a heavy coat, a knife, food, and a bottle of brandy. He stuffed, warmed his veins, listened to the horns. They were going berserk up there.

A noise from down the culvert shocked him. He listened closely, figured it had come from about where the corpse lay, and had been made by something a lot bigger than a rat.

He rose carefully, filled his coat pockets with food, laid his blankets in atop the treasure—and froze.

A man stood silhouetted in the nearer end of the culvert. One of those Rebels. Fish had been right. The bastards just wouldn't let up.

The man was coming in.

Smeds lifted himself into the hole with his plunder. It was a tight fit and a pathetic attempt at concealment but he was counting on the man's vision needing a long while to adjust from the brightness outside.

Absolutely.

The man was still moving tentatively when he came abreast of Smeds. Smeds reached out and cut his throat.

The man made an injured-rabbit noise and started thrashing around. Smeds climbed down and walked to the mouth of the culvert. He paid no attention to the noise made by someone stumbling toward him from behind. He looked out into the glare, his eyes smarting. He moved out carefully, ready for anything. And found himself alone.

The ditch bank was almost vertical there, faced with stone, twelve feet high, spotted with ice. A lot of snow had blown into the ditch. Smeds floundered through it.

An angry bellow from inside the culvert gave him added incentive to make sure of his hand- and toeholds as he climbed.

He heard the man come out as he rolled over the lip of the ditch. He got to his feet and waited.

An angry face rose above the brink. Smeds kicked as hard as he could, caught the man square in the center of the forehead. He pitched backward. Smeds stepped to the edge, looked down at the figure almost buried in the snow. He caressed the knife in his coat pocket, thought better of going down there because two women and several children had paused near the footbridge, watching. "I hope you freeze to death, you son of a bitch." He kicked loose snow down, turned, and walked away.

He felt better than he had in a week and right then did not much give a damn *what* the future held.

Darling was foaming at the mouth when the alarm horns brayed. She had discovered Raven and Bear missing and was as thoroughly pissed off as I could imagine her getting. Whatever she had in mind, whatever she was making us get dressed up for, she had counted on having more bodies backing her.

Right then she had me and Silent and Bomanz and Stubby Torque. Paddle-foot Torque had died a half hour earlier. She stomped her feet and signed, "I do not need him. I survived without him before. Get moving. Get those horses ready." She pulled a knee-length shirt of mail over her head, followed that with a white tabard. As she buckled on a very unfeminine sword she snarled and grimaced so nobody argued.

Bomanz helped us both mount up. Stubby Torque handed her a lance he'd jury-rigged from junk from around the stable. She had her banner tied to it, furled. If her wound bothered her she didn't show it.

Silent finally got his balance enough to try arguing with the whirlwind. The whirlwind almost rode him down and there was nothing for him to do but jump onto his own animal and try to keep up.

Darling paused once, in the street outside. She looked at the sky, seemed pleased with what she saw. When I looked up all I saw was a gliding hawk, very high, or an eagle, higher still.

She took off. She hadn't bothered to tell any of us what she was going to do, probably because she figured we would have tied her up to stop her.

She was right.

We kept busy now keeping up and sorting ourselves out so the two wizards were closest to her, able to guard her with their skills.

She headed in the direction the alarms said the threat lay. The madwoman.

The imperials had several minutes' jump on us but we made most of that up. As we moved into that part of the city near the southeast wall we overtook hundreds of hurrying soldiers. Silent or Bomanz conjured an ugly sound and set it running ahead of us, to scare everybody out of our way. We burst out into the cleared space behind the wall. Darling headed straight for a long ramp that had been put up so heavy engines could be dragged to the ramparts. She headed up it, making soldiers jump to get out of her way.

I told myself it had been an exciting past year and now it was time to die.

Soldiers scampered away as we hit the rampart. I glimpsed Limper walking toward Oar, all by his lonesome.

Darling made her mount rear and scream. She unfurled her vermilion banner with the white rose embroidered in silk.

Utter silence. The imperials gawked, petrified. Even the Limper stopped his implacable advance and stared.

Then the shriek of the eagle—it *was* an eagle!—ripped the air. The raptor came screaming down. Before it lighted on Darling's shoulder, with what had to be bone-rattling impact, she pointed out at the land beyond the walls.

All heads turned. Three, five, six, seven, eight! The windwhales rose into the sky. Squadrons, troops, battalions of centaurs came cantering out of hiding, the drum of their hooves a continuous thunder despite the muting effect of the snow. Whole sections of woods started moving toward the city. Mantas began to slip off the backs of the windwhales, scouting for updrafts. More glided over the city from behind us, just to let the world know the place was surrounded.

Darling rose in her stirrups and surveyed her surroundings, searching for someone who did not agree that this was the day of the White Rose.

The snowfields erupted and talking stones began appearing, assuming posts along predetermined lines, forming the skeleton of a wall that would close the Limper in.

Damn me! The tree god must have started on the buildup clear back when we first hit Oar.

Darling settled into her saddle. She was pleased with herself. Everybody watched her for a cue, even the Limper.

Bomanz faced north, a resolute sentinel, never letting events behind him distract him from his watch for trouble. Silent remained as fixed on the wall to the south while Torque and I tried to keep a lookout everywhere at once. Bomanz said, "Case, tell her Exile is coming."

I backed my horse till Darling could see my hands without having to surrender her attention for the Limper and her continuing dispositions. She nodded. I told her I had spotted Gossamer and Spidersilk sneaking around north and south of us, respectively. She nodded again, unperturbed.

Exile approached us at a normal walk, careful not to give offense before he understood the full scope of his predicament. I was surprised that he looked so young despite the fact that I had seen the Lady, who was at least four hundred and looked a well preserved twenty. I noticed the old guy who stuck me and Darling drifting along in Exile's shadow.

Exile came up and looked the situation over. He showed no special response except to look at Gossamer and Spidersilk as if warning them to behave themselves.

He came to us. "Most impressive." He did not look impressed. "You quite took me by surprise. I am Exile. Who are you, and who speaks for you?" Just a stranger chance met, making casual introductions.

Bomanz and Silent were busy. Torque still didn't have the lingo so good. That left old Case. I was elected. "I'll do the talking." I indicated Darling. "The White Rose."

"So I see."

I didn't figure on naming anybody else, but Bomanz decided I should. He said, "Bomanz. The Wakener."

Exile showed a little surprise at that. Bomanz had a reputation. He was also supposed to be dead.

I indicated Silent. "Silent. Formerly of the Black Company. I'm Philodendron." I didn't name Torque. Seemed a good idea to leave something to nag on Exile's imagination.

"I suppose you're here for the same reason everyone else is?" He kept one eye on the Limper, I noticed. Right then the Limper was eyeballing the situation and counting up his options.

I signed at Darling. She signed back. I told Exile, "The silver spike. The tree god will not allow it to fall into the hands of anyone who wants its power. Whatever the cost."

"So I see," said Exile. It did look like the Plain had belched up all of every one of its weirdnesses. I wondered who was at home keeping the shop spooky. "That thing out there might have something to say about that to all of us."

Darling signed some more. I said, "We will destroy it if you can't. The tree has concluded that it has tormented itself and the world long enough. It will be destroyed."

Exile started to say something but never got the chance. I reckon Limper heard us well enough to get pissed because everybody wanted to put him into the past tense.

He had something all ready to go. But as he was about to cut loose, Spider-silk beat him to the punch, hit him from the side and knocked him ass over appetite. His spell went screaming straight up, making a sound like the biggest bullroarer in the universe. Gossamer hit him from the other side. A missile storm pounded away at him. Glowing red balls arced in from the fields to the south and for the first time I noticed a group of black riders down there, all mounted on the nastiest-looking critters I've ever seen. I thought I recognized our old buddy Toadkiller Dog. When the red balls came down they hit the ground like a giant stomping, leaving steaming black holes pounded into the snow and the earth beneath.

Exile just stood there with his hands in his pockets, watching.

None of my bunch did anything either.

The Nightstalkers came marching into the cleared area behind the wall, all spit and polish, neatly in step, their band playing. They began taking over positions as though this was nothing more than a changing of the guard. Brigadier Wildbrand, all squeaky-clean, came marching up to report to Exile.

The uproar died down. Nobody had done much damage to the Limper. He hadn't done any either.

Wildbrand glanced at us. I winked. That startled her, so I tried another trick, pixie that I am. "What you doing after work, sweetie?"

She snubbed me. Not good enough for her, I guess. Just as well. She was too old for me.

A shadow fell on us all as she and Exile talked tactics. A granddaddy windwhale had moved into position overhead, not all that high up. I was impressed.

Exile and Wildbrand checked it out. He seemed the more perturbed. They went back to tactics. I glanced at the world outside. Limper was getting set to try something. The black riders had dismounted. Their steeds had disappeared. Toadkiller Dog was among the missing, too. The riders were walking closer. I noticed that talking stones, walking trees, and centaurs had gotten in behind them.

Limper charged the wall, a dark cloud forming around him. Everything cut loose again. And didn't bother him at all. He jumped up and kicked the wall—and knocked a hole in it fifty feet wide. Exile joined the party, somehow pouring on an endless, torrential shower of fire.

Limper hadn't much liked fire last time we saw him. He didn't mind it now, except he had trouble seeing straight. He wanted to knock down the wall where we were. He hit it two more times, once to either side of us, then backed off to think about what to do next. Exile gave up with the flames. They hadn't done much.

The Nightstalkers were busy repairing the gaps already.

I knew what I'd do next if I was the Limper. I'd prance through one of those breaches and start taking out my top enemies.

Being almost as smart as me, he figured it that way himself.

The snow was pretty torn up out there now but he strayed onto some virgin stuff while he was making up his mind which breach to charge. About fifty slimy green tentacles shot up out of it, glommed on to him, and started trying to pull him apart. The snow all around erupted. A whole pride of monsters piled on Limper. Toadkiller Dog got his head in his jaws and tried to bite it off. Something else shoved a hoof in his mouth so he couldn't do no hollering. The people who had ridden those monsters ran toward the excitement.

Exile and the twins paid no attention. They faced the city now, making concerted, complex come-hither gestures. What looked like a flock of birds rose from deep in the city and headed our way. Close up I saw it wasn't birds at all but lots of chunks of wood.

The flock settled outside the wall, neatly building a monumental pyre. Did they think they were going to roast Limper? They'd tried fire already.

No.

A giant pot followed the wood, sloshing, settled amidst the pyre. A big lid followed. It just hung around in the air, waiting.

The black riders got in on the fun down below. Everybody and everything was trying to cut the Limper up or tear him apart. I asked Torque, "You got an onion we can toss in?"

Brigadier Wildbrand said, "That's the spirit." She winked when I looked at her.

The spirit? I didn't have no spirit left. This wasn't even my fight, when I thought about it. And my hip was hurting so bad I expected to fall off everything in a minute.

The Limper bit the hoof off the thing that had one in his mouth, spit it out, let out a howl like the world's death scream. Bodies and pieces of body flew. Only Toadkiller Dog hung on. He and the Limper rolled around, growling and screaming while the others tried to get back into it.

Exile assessed the damage. He looked at me. "He's too strong for us. It wasn't a great hope, anyway. Will you contribute?"

I signed to Darling, "He wants help."

She nodded, fixed on the action. For a moment I thought she wasn't going to answer. Then she made a complicated series of hand gestures. The eagle plunged off her shoulder, went flapping off and up.

I saw what Exile meant about Limper being too strong. One of the monsters was doing the foot-in-mouth trick to keep his sorceries silent. Toadkiller Dog was on his back, hanging on with all four limbs, his jaws still locked on the Limper's head, which he had almost completely turned around. But the others could not keep his limbs pinned. He used those to devastating effect.

The shadow of the windwhale grew more and more deep. It was coming down. Already I could smell it.

It dropped tentacles into the fray, grabbed Limper without any care to avoid getting anyone or anything else. Toadkiller Dog was in that mess, a couple other monsters, and a couple of human beings too squished to scream. A windwhale has the strength to snap five-hundred-year-old royal oaks. The Limper did not. The windwhale tore the whole mess into bitty pieces and dumped it into the giant pot.

Something to be said for brute strength sometimes.

The pot lid slammed down. Clasps clanked. The pyre roared to life.

I wondered how the Limper would get out of this one. He'd survived the worst so many times before.

I looked at Exile. "What about the silver spike?"

He was not happy.

"You couldn't take the Limper, you can't take us."

He checked the windwhales, the talking stones, the walking trees, the centaurs and mantas, said, "You have a point. On the other hand, why surrender a tool you can use to knock the empire down? I have good soldiers here. The chances of battle look no worse than those of not fighting."

I couldn't answer that. I took it to Darling. Everyone in sight was watching, waiting for a clue to their next move.

Tension was not down a bit because the Limper was out of the game.

I signed. Darling had me hold the standard so she would have both hands free to answer. I felt funny doing that, like I was making a commitment to a cause I still did not truly support. She signed at me for a long time.

I told Exile, "The spike will not be used at all, by anyone, whatever the cost. A place has been prepared by the tree god, in the abyss between universes, where only a power greater and more evil can retrieve it." Which meant, I guess, that anybody bad enough to get the damned thing back would be bad enough not to need it in the first place.

Exile looked around, shrugged, said, "That's good enough for me. We planned to isolate it, too, but our method would have been less certain."

A flash and crash trampled his last word.

Bomanz had stirred himself. Up the way, Gossamer took a couple drunken steps and walked right off the rampart. The old wizard said, "She disagreed with the decision."

Exile stared at Spidersilk, frozen in midmotion. She relaxed slowly, lowered her gaze, after a minute went to check on her sister.

I checked Bomanz. The old boy looked real pleased with himself.

Speaking of old men. Where the hell was that guy who'd been following Exile around?

Gone. And I never noticed him go.

That old bastard was half-spook.

Raven came to slowly, shaky and disoriented. Memory of a flashing boot and savage impact. Realization that he had a ferocious headache. That his hip had begun to ache. That he was so cold he had begun to feel warm in his extremities.

A moment of panic. He tried to thrash around, found his limbs only vaguely cooperative. Worse panic before the onset of reason.

He wriggled his way out of the snow, got to his feet carefully. He felt himself over, scraped frozen blood off his face. The bastard had got him good. Almost had to admire those guys, the way they were hanging in there against the whole world.

Painfully, he dragged himself out of the ditch, stood on wobbly legs looking around, the old hip wound gnawing. Things had changed. There were monsters in the sky and witch fires flaring in the distance.

The Limper had come. Darling would be in the middle of it. And he wasn't there.

She would think he had run out again.

Raven reached the center of excitement in time to witness Gossamer's fall. Everyone seemed to relax after the incident. The Limper must not be a threat right now.

The crowd came down off the wall. Soldiers brought horses for Exile and Brigadier Wildbrand. A platoon of Nightstalkers fell in around them and they started moving north. Raven wondered what the hell was happening. It looked like Darling and Exile had cut a deal.

He could not catch them now, wobbly as he was.

The twins had their heads together. They threw dark looks after the departing company. They radiated a stench of wickedness about to break loose.

Better stick with them.

When the monsters began sliding across the sky Smeds suffered an attack of caution. Able to think of nowhere else to run, he headed back to the ditch.

The guy he had kicked was still there, twitching once in a while. He backed off and watched, waiting to see what the guy would do. After a while the guy woke up, dragged himself out, and tottered off. Good. Now he had a place to wait for Fish. He went over and around and entered the culvert from the northern end, passed through, and sat down to wait.

Fish showed up a forever later, standing over there on the footbridge. . . . He didn't have the other blue bag. Damn. Smeds whistled just loud enough to carry to Fish, waved cautiously.

"What happened?" he asked when Fish arrived. "Where's the other bag?"

Fish explained.

Smeds told his story.

Fish said, "We need to get out of here, then. Let's get the stuff. We might be able to get out one of the breaches if there's any more excitement. With the spike up for grabs we can count on that."

They got the blue bags, which they rubbed up with dirt, and Smeds's pack, and headed for the area where the wall had been breached. The city was a place of ghosts. The living cowered behind locked doors and barred windows, praying their gods would keep them safe from the terrors without and the cholera within.

The occasional cry of a cholera victim made Smeds think more of haunts bedamned than of the living in pain.

76

Exile wouldn't say where the spike was hid. He didn't act like he wanted to pull something, just like he wanted to be in on the whole thing. Like he wanted a look at the cause for all the fuss. Can't say I blame him. I saw it back when it was just a big nail. I wanted to see how it had changed.

He led us up toward Oar's North Gate, got up on the wall, and started marching back and forth. We stuck tight. Outside, the friendly troops had begun a shift to the north. Exile took inspiration, told Brigadier Wildbrand to seal off the area inside the wall. We'd had enough trouble over that hunk of metal already. He asked for masons and heavy lifting equipment to be brought, too.

The damned spike was in the wall! No wonder nobody ever found it.

Wildbrand sent messages. Nightstalkers moved in. I was concerned. I would've been more concerned if the sky wasn't filled with monsters.

It took two hours to assemble machinery and workmen, and another for them to get set up to start pulling the wall apart. Nobody could stay tense all that time.

Sometime during the wait Bomanz asked Exile, "What arrangements did you make to keep your fire fueled? Rendering the Limper was a good idea but you'll have to pressure-cook him for days. The fire seems to be failing."

Exile looked down south. Bomanz was right. Exile frowned, muttered, grumbled at Brigadier Wildbrand. Next time I looked some of my scabrous old buddies from the militia were running firewood to the pot. And not doing a very good job.

Once everything was set and the spike's hiding place was sealed off inside the city and out, Exile asked Darling if she was ready to see it brought to light. She told him to get on with it.

There was a new kind of tension around, like everyone's temper was short and we were all waiting for somebody to do something inexcusable so we could let off steam by kicking his butt.

Guys started banging away with sledges and wedges and pry bars and ten minutes later the first stone rose out of its setting.

The day got on into late afternoon before the workmen exposed the layer of mortar supposed to contain the spike. For a moment everyone forgot enmities and allegiances and crowded up to stare at the blackened half of the spike that lay exposed. Darling told Silent to go get it.

He borrowed a mason's hammer, put on heavy leather gloves, took along a lined leather sack and somebody's old shirt to wrap and pack it in. He wasn't going to take any chances with the damned thing.

Darling readied a small wooden chest.

About the time Silent chopped the spike loose I glanced toward that giant pot. So I missed the beginning of the excitement around me but not its start at the pot, where the men feeding the fire suddenly scattered, like a school of minnows when a large hungry fish appears.

The top blew off the pot.

Something made of pieces of all the things that had gone into the pot, with way too many limbs and those in all the wrong places, crawled over the pot's lip, fell into the fire.

Someone screamed behind me. I whirled.

One slight Nightstalker had knocked Brigadier Wildbrand off the back of the wall. Another had stuck a knife into Exile. The first was hurtling toward Bomanz.

Gossamer and Spidersilk!

Bomanz went over backward, flailing the air, and plunged headfirst into the snow that had drifted against the wall.

Only Darling retained any presence of mind. She let go the White Rose banner, yanked out her sword, gave Bomanz's attacker a hearty chop, and followed him over the edge.

The one after Exile screeched.

That screech plain demolished everybody. We all just collapsed.

She jumped down and started hacking and slashing at Silent. She took the spike away, climbed back up, raised it overhead, and howled triumphantly.

Raven appeared out of nowhere, stuck her in the brisket, tried to knock the spike away, failed on his first try but got it his second. It tumbled down into the snow outside. Raven and whichever twin followed it a moment later, Raven grinding his knife into her belly while she screamed and tried to strangle him.

And outside the wall the thing from the pot humped and waddled and dragged itself toward us, oblivious to the resistance of the Plain creatures.

77

"Time to go," Fish told Smeds.

They stepped out of hiding and strode toward the nearest breach like they were on a mission from the gods. Men wild-eyed with panic paid them no heed. They scrambled over rubble, dropped down outside, and started moving southward.

Smeds expected disaster every step. Not till they crossed the first low ridge and Oar disappeared did he begin to feel at all positive. "We did it! Goddamn! We really got out!"

"It could still go to hell on us," Fish cautioned. Then he grinned. "But I'll tell you, the future looks brighter than it has for months."

78

Impressions swirled as Raven toppled from the wall with the screaming sorceress: ground turning and rushing upward, a windwhale making its booming protest as its attempt to grab the thing from the pot was rebuffed.

Impact! He felt his blade reach her spine, going between vertebrae. He felt his right leg twist beneath her and snap. They screamed at one another as their faces smashed together.

He got the better of it. He retained consciousness and even a fragment of will. He dragged himself away, a few feet, started trying to guess the damage to his leg. Didn't feel like a compound fracture. Hurt bad enough, though.

Bodies lay all around him. Only Bomanz seemed to be breathing.

Packing snow around the leg helped numb it a little.

People were yelling above. He saw Case jumping around, waving, pointing. He looked.

The thing from the pot was coming. It wasn't a hundred yards away. And nothing seemed able to stop it. Mantas pounded it with their lightnings. It didn't pay them any attention. It had only one thought: the silver spike.

Case was trying to get him to get the spike and get it up top before the thing got hold of it.

Bomanz rolled over, got to his hands and knees, shook his head, looked around dumbly, spotted the thing, turned almost as pale as the snow. He croaked, "I'll try to hold it off. Find the spike. Get it up to Darling."

He staggered to his feet, tottered toward the thing.

Raven supposed it really could not be called the Limper anymore, though the Taken's insanity, ambition, and rage drove it.

He looked for some sign of the spike. The pain in his leg was the worst he had felt since Croaker had got him with the Lady's arrow.

79

Raven finally seemed to get it through his skull what we wanted. I'd already volunteered to go down. Darling wouldn't let me. Now I signed, "Looks like his leg is broke."

She nodded.

Bomanz hit the thing from the pot with a grandpa power spell. It stopped the thing in its tracks. It went down on its belly, lay there glowing biliously, making a nasty whining noise.

A couple of Nightstalkers brought Brigadier Wildbrand back up. She had a

busted arm and some busted ribs and looked like death on a stick, but she was
ready to fight. I told her, "I think you're the top imperial left."

She looked at the mess, said, "Yes," but seemed fresh out of ideas.

A talking stone dropped out of the sky, hit the rampart. It was my old buddy
with the scar. He wanted orders from the White Rose. The White Rose didn't
have any orders.

Raven scrabbled around in the snow. The thing from the pot started moving again. Centaurs raced around it, throwing javelins. Bomanz's spell had soft-
ened its protection. Most of the javelins got through. The thing looked like a
porcupine. But it didn't seem to notice or care about the missiles.

Talk about your single-minded obsessions!

Bomanz popped it again.

Stopped it in its tracks again, too. It smoldered. The javelins burned. But it
was not out of the game, it was just stalled. Bomanz looked up, shrugged. What
more could he do?

Raven kept digging in the snow, dragging his broken leg. He didn't bother
looking around to see what was gaining on him. He'd find it in time or he
wouldn't.

I told Wildbrand, "Long as we're standing around not doing anything, why
don't we get some ropes down there so we can hoist my buddies up?" Silent was
on his feet now but looked like he was only maybe ten percent in this world. In
fact, he looked like a lunatic, foaming at the mouth.

Wildbrand looked at me like I had brain fever if I thought she was going to
lift a finger to save any Rebel. I reminded her, "We got a whole gang of hungry
windwhales up there." Scar flashed away to cue the nearest. It started dropping.
Scar reappeared, chuckling.

Wildbrand gave me a classic dirty look, put some of her boys to work on
one of the cranes that had been used to pull the wall apart.

I yelled at Silent, "Get ready to come up!" He ignored me. He was getting
ready to give the Limper thing some kind of surprise.

Old man Bomanz yelled, cut loose with his best shot, and tried to dive out
of the way all at the same time. None of it did him any good.

The thing smashed into him, flowed over him. He screamed once, more in
outrage than pain or terror, then tried to fight.

Silent looked up at Darling, smiling through tears. He sort of bowed with
just his head . . . and jumped.

Goddamned madman!

He hit the thing's back. Flesh splashed like water and burned like naphtha,
though the flame was green. The thing started rolling over and over and over,
leaving pieces of itself behind.

Raven kept on looking for the spike.

Darling started hammering stone with her fist, shedding silent tears. I was afraid she'd break something she was so violent. . . . She stopped, whirled, signed, "Have the windwhale take it now. It will never be weaker."

I didn't have to tell Scar. He read sign. He flashed away. By the time he got back the windwhale was pulling the thing apart again.

I asked Wildbrand, "You think you can keep the pot boiling this time, if we put the pieces back in?"

She got a face like a fishwife looking for a fight. "You do your part, I'll take care of mine. How do you plan to get the lid back on?"

That was easy. "Scar, have one of the big guys put the top back on the pot. Maybe carry a few hundred tons of firewood, too."

Wildbrand gave me the look, checked her temper, said "Maybe you aren't stupid," and had her men help her down to the street.

Down south, where the breaches were, there was mass confusion. People were heading out, a flood the grays could not stem if they were bothering to try.

The thing tumbled into the pot. The lid went on with a big, final clang.

R aven screamed.
He had found the silver spike. Or it had found him.

By the time I looked at her Darling was hammering the wall again, both fists bloody.

He had gotten hold of the thing with his naked hand.

He got to his feet. On a broken leg! He held the spike up toward us. I yelled.

He looked at me. I did not know him. A terrible change had come over him. He laughed horribly. "It's mine!"

His eyes were the Dominator's eyes. Eyes of insanity and power, that I had seen in the Barrowland the day the Lady had brought her husband down. They were the eyes of the Limper, ready to be entertained by the agony of a world that had given him nothing but pain. They were the eyes of everyone who ever nursed a grudge and suddenly found it within their power to do whatever they wanted, without fear of reprisal.

"Mine!" He laughed.

I looked at Darling, as sour with despair as ever I'd been.

She turned off the water, started signing. She was as pale as a sheet of paper. I shook my head. "I can't do that."

"We have to." Tears streaked her face. She didn't want to do it, either. But it had to be done or the hell we'd put ourselves through would have been time and pain utterly wasted.

Raven had studied sorcery long ago. Just enough to blot his soul, a taint the spike could rip into and use as a channel for its evil.

"Do it!" she signed.

Damn her! He was my best friend. Damn that rock Scar. He could have given the order anytime, but he waited and made us do it so we couldn't lay off the blame on his precious tree god.

"Kill him," I said. "Before it possesses him completely."

Near as I could tell Scar didn't do a damned thing.

But down there a centaur's arm shot forward. A javelin flashed. The shaft smashed in through one of Raven's temples and out the other.

This time he would not be back from the dead. This time he wasn't faking.

I sat down and turned inside myself, wondering if I hadn't dragged my feet so much while we were headed south would we have caught up with Croaker and so maybe never have gotten into this spot. This monster was going to be riding my shoulders for the rest of my life.

Darling did her own version of going into a pout.

Only Torque kept his mind on the job. He got the wooden chest from Darling, shinnied down the crane rope, got the spike away from Raven. He climbed back up, set the box down by Darling, came over to me and said, "Tell her I'm out of it, Case. Tell her I just couldn't take it no more." He walked away, maybe going looking for the brother who had left with Raven and hadn't come back.

I didn't much blame him for going.

80

Smeds laid the last stone on the old man's cairn. The tears were gone. The anger was quiet. It was not right that Fish should have fallen to cholera after taking the worst that could be thrown by the world's nastiest villains. But there was no justice in this existence.

If there was, Timmy Locan would be here, not Smeds Stahl.

Smeds went on, into the city Roses. A year later he was a respected member of the community, owner of a struggling brewery. He lived well but without ostentation that would excite unwanted curiosity. He never told his story to a soul.

Epilogue

No matter how many times I walked around it, the hole into the tree god's "abyss" still looked like a piece of black silk suspended a yard above the ground. It refused to have more than two dimensions.

Darling brought the little chest containing the silver spike, threw it through. It took both of us to do the coffin that contained all that had been left in the big pot when, after a week of cooking, it had been allowed to boil dry. The black circle vanished as though a stage magician had sucked the cloth up his sleeve.

We went and got clean for what seemed like the first time in years, then Darling showed me around the rabbit warren that had been home for the Black Company and Rebel movement for so many years. Fascinating. And repellent. That people should put themselves through such hell . . . I wished them better times than mine, wherever they were.

Somehow we ended up doing what men and women seem unable to avoid. Afterward, she dressed in the clothing of a peasant woman, without a hint of mail or a single hidden blade.

"What goes?" I asked.

She signed, "The White Rose is dead. There is no place for her anymore. No need."

I didn't argue. I never was on that side.

For want of anything better to do we got Old Father Tree to give us a ride to where we could check out the progress of the potato industry.

It hadn't changed a whole lot, except the people I knew had got older.

The grandkids wouldn't believe a word of our stories but they'd fight anybody who didn't agree that we told the most exciting lies in the world.